The Mammoth Book of
COMIC FANTASY

Also available

The Mammoth Book of True Crime
The Mammoth Book of True Crime 2
The Mammoth Book of Modern War Stories
The Mammoth Book of the Western
The Mammoth Book of Short Horror Novels
The Mammoth Book of Puzzles
The Mammoth Book of Historical Whodunnits
The Mammoth Book of Erotica
The Mammoth Book of Mindbending Puzzles
The Mammoth Book of Historical Detectives
The Mammoth Book of Victorian & Edwardian
Ghost Stories
The Mammoth Book of Symbols
The Mammoth Book of Great Lives
The Mammoth Book of Pulp Fiction
The Mammoth Book of the West
The Mammoth Book of International Erotica
The Mammoth Book of Oddities
The Mammoth Book of IQ Puzzles
The Mammoth Book of Love & Sensuality
The Mammoth Book of Chess
The Mammoth Book of Fortune Telling
The Mammoth Puzzle Carnival
The Mammoth Book of Dracula
The Mammoth Book of Gay Short Stories
The Mammoth Book of Fairy Tales
The Mammoth Book of Ancient Wisdom
The Mammoth Book of New Sherlock Holmes Adventures
The Mammoth Book of Gay Erotica
The Mammoth Book of the Third Reich at War
The Mammoth Book of Best New Horror

The Mammoth Book of

COMIC FANTASY

Edited by

Mike Ashley

ROBINSON
London

Robinson Publishing Ltd
7 Kensington Church Court
London W8 4SP

First published in the UK by Robinson Publishing 1998

A copy of the British Library Cataloguing in
Publication Data is available from the British Library.

ISBN 1–85487–530–2

Printed and bound in the EC

10 9 8 7 6 5 4 3 2

CONTENTS

A QUIVER OF SPOOKS

COPYRIGHT AND ACKNOWLEDGEMENTS

"The Warlock's Daughter" © 1937 by Anthony Armstrong. First published in *The Strand Magazine*, January 1938. Unable to trace the author's estate.

"Fall'n Into the Sear" © 1998 by James Bibby. First printing, original to this anthology. Printed by permission of the author and the author's agent, Peake Associates.

"Press Ann" © 1991 by Terry Bisson. First published in *Isaac Asimov's Science Fiction Magazine*, August 1991. Reprinted by permission of the author and the author's agent.

"The Fifty-First Dragon" © 1921 by Heywood Broun. First published in *Seeing Things at Night* (New York: Harcourt, Brace, 1921). Copyright expired in 1977.

"Ruella in Love" © 1993 by Molly Brown. First published in *Interzone*, October 1993. Reprinted by permission of the author.

INTRODUCTION:
Still Crazy After All These Years

Mike Ashley

INTRODUCTION THE FIRST – FOR THOSE WHO DON'T READ INTRODUCTIONS

INTRODUCTION THE SECOND – FOR THOSE EXPECTING A SILLY INTRODUCTION

No, I'm sorry. You've got the rest of the book to laugh at. You're not laughing at my introduction as well. This is the one chance I get to say something, and I mean to say something sensible.

INTRODUCTION THE THIRD – FOR THOSE EXPECTING A PROPER INTRODUCTION

"Beauty," they say, "is in the eye of the beholder." That's probably true about humour as well. Well, not in the eye, maybe in the ear . . . or is it the brain . . . ? Well, no matter, what one person finds funny, another may not.

So, I can't guarantee that every story in this book will make you laugh, but I'd be very surprised if most of them don't. I've cast my net far and wide (or should that be deep?) to bring together many of the best writers in the world of comic fantasy. There are the ones you're bound to know – Terry Pratchett, Tom Holt, Robert Rankin, Terry Jones, Alan Dean Foster. And maybe the ones you're just getting to know – James Bibby, Esther Friesner, Neil Gaiman, Craig Shaw Gardner. Then there are the ones you don't want to know – um, no, we'll leave them out of it.

There are certainly some you ought to know. I've been reading fantasy fiction for over thirty years, and there are many delightful stories tucked away in old books and magazines by writers who are not as well known as they should be. Some, like Anthony Armstrong, Avram Davidson, Jack Sharkey and Randall Garrett, are, alas, no longer with us, but we can still have the pleasure of reminding ourselves just what great writers they were. Others, like Harry Turtledove, John Morressy, Richard Lupoff, Harvey Jacobs and Ron Goulart, are, thankfully, still with us, and still producing excellent stories – and they should be better known, too.

I've coaxed a few writers to this book that you might not immediately associate with humorous fantasy. Amy Myers, for instance, the renowned writer of Victorian/Edwardian mystery novels, has an irrepressible sense of humour which jumped at the opportunity to express itself. Louise Cooper is best known for her sinister occult fantasies, and doesn't get much chance to trip the light fantastic. Terry Bisson is the award-winning author of several off-beat stories, some of which are darkly comic.

I hope I've included something for everyone. About half the stories are set entirely in fantasy lands and half set in an almost recognizable here and now (or there and then in some cases), so I've alternated the settings more or less with each story.

If you like your stories in the style of Terry Pratchett, then you also want to try the stories by Avram Davidson, Craig Shaw Gardner, Esther Friesner, John Morressy, James Bibby and Molly Brown. If you like your humour a little on the dark side, then check out the stories by Lawrence Schimel, Jane Yolen,

Al Sarrantonio and Harvey Jacobs. If you go for the off-beat story, then try the ones by Terry Bisson, Anne Gay, Tom Holt, Harvey Jacobs, R.A. Lafferty and, for that matter, Edward Lear. If you're into spoofs, then check out Anthony Armstrong, Louise Cooper, David Langford and Peter Cannon. Or, if you just like to laugh at the world about you, then try Neil Gaiman, Robert Rankin, F. Gwynplaine MacIntyre or Al Sarrantonio.

I hope most of the stories will make you laugh out loud. Others will make you smile. All, I'm sure, will entertain.

Okay, even a proper introduction has to end, and I'm sure you're all the better for reading it. Now you can join the others in the rest of the book. They won't be that far ahead of you.

Mike Ashley

PEREGRINE: ALFLANDIA

Avram Davidson

Avram Davidson (1923–93) was one of the great treasures of fantasy and science fiction. He was critically acclaimed, winning all kinds of awards, and for forty years produced his own style of idiosyncratic stories which earned him a vociferous cult following. There is a profusion of material I could have drawn upon. I was originally tempted to use one of his bizarre stories featuring Doctor Eszterhazy, set in an alternate world just prior to World War I. A number of these will be found in The Enquiries of Doctor Eszterhazy *(1975). In the end, though, I found myself irrestistibly drawn to this opening sequence from* Peregrine: Secundus *(1981), which Davidson wrote originally as a separate story. This was a sequel to* Peregrine: Primus *(1971), set in the last days of the Roman Empire. It might be history, but not as we know it.*

The King of the Alves was taking his evening rest and leisure after a typical hard day's work ferreting in the woods behind the donjeon-keep, which – in Alfland – was a goodish distance from the Big House. It was usual, of course, for the donjeon-keep to be kept as part and parcel of the Big House, but the Queen of Alfland had objected to the smell.

"It's them drains, me dear," her lord had pointed out to her more than once when she made these objections. "The High King isn't due to make a Visitation this way for another half-a-luster, as well you know. And also as well you know what'd likely happen to me if I was to infringe upon the High Royal Monopoly and do my own plumbing on them drains, a mere pettiking like me."

"I'd drains him, if I was a man," said the Queen of Alfland.

"*And* the prices as he charges, too! 'Tisn't as if he was contented with three peppercorns and a stewed owl in a silver tassy, like his father before him; ah! *there* was a High King for you! Well, well, I see it can't be helped, having wedded a mouse instead of a proper man; well, then *move* the wretched donjeon-keep, it doesn't pay for itself no-how, and if it wasn't as our position requires we have one, blessed if I'd put up with it."

So the donjeon-keep had been laboriously taken down and laboriously removed and laboriously set up again just this side of the woods; and there, of a very late afternoon, the King of the Alves sat on a hummock with his guest, the King of Bertland. Several long grey ears protruded from a sack at their feet, and now and then a red-eyed ferret poked his snouzel out of a royal pocket and was gently poked back in. The Master of the Buckhounds sat a short ways aways, a teen-age boy who was picking the remnants of a scab off one leg and meditatively crunching the pieces between his teeth. He was Alfland's son and heir; there were of course not really any buckhounds.

"Well, Alf, you hasn't done too bad today," the royal guest observed after a while.

"No, I hasn't, Bert, and that's a fact. Stew for the morrow, and one day at a time is all any man dare look for to attend to and haccomplish, way *I* look at it." The day was getting set to depart in a sort of silver-gilt haze, throstles were singing *twit-twit-thrush*, and swallows were flitting back and forth pretending they were bats. The Master of the Buckhounds arose.

"Hey, Da, is they any bread and cheese more?" he asked.

"No, they isn't, Buck. Happen thee'll get they dinner soon enough."

The Master of the Buckhounds said that he was going to see could he find some berries or a musk-room and sauntered off into the thicket. His sire nudged the guest. "Gone to play with himself, I'll be bound," said he.

"Why don't 'ee marry 'im off?" asked the King of Bertland, promptly. "There's our Rose, has her hope chest all filled and still as chaste as the day the wise woman slapped her newborn bottom, ten year ago last Saturnalia, eh?"

The King of the Alves grunted moodily. "Hasn't I sudggestered this to his dam?" he asked, rhetorically. " 'Here's Bert come for to marry off his datter,' says I, 'for thee doesn't think there's such a shortage o' rabbiting in Bertland he have to come here for it, whatever the formalities of it may be. And Princess Rose be of full age and can give thee a hand in the kitching,' says I. But, no, says she. For why? Buck haven't gone on no quest nor haven't served no squire time at the High King's court and ten-year-old is too old-fashioned young and he be but a boy hisself and she don't need no hand in the kitching and if I doesn't like the way me victuals be served, well, I can go and eat beans with the thralls, says she.

"—Well, do she natter that Buck have pimples, twill serve she right, say I. Best be getten back. Ar, these damp edgerows will give me the rheum in me ips, so we sit ere more, eh?"

He hefted his sack of hares and they started back. The King of Bertland gestured to the donjeon-keep, where a thin smoke indicated the warder was cooking his evening gruel. "As yer ransomed off King Baldwin's heir as got tooken in the humane man-trap last winter what time e sought to unt the tusky boar?"

The walls of Alftown came into sight, with the same *three breeches and a rent* which characterized the walls of every castle and capital town as insisted on by Wilfredoric Conqueror, the late great-uncle of the last High King but one. Since that time, Alfish (or Alvish, as some had it) royalty had been a-dwelling in a Big House, which was contained behind a stout stockade: this, too, was customary.

"What, didn't I notify you about that, Bert?" the Alf-king

asked, with a slightly elaborate air of surprise. "Ah, many's the good joke and jest we've had about that in the fambly, '*Da has tooken King Baldy's hair, harharharhar!*' Yus, the old man finally paid up, three mimworms and a dragon's egg. '*Mustn't call him King Baldy now he's got his heir back, horhorhorhor!*' Ah, what's life wiffart larfter? Or, looking hat it another way, wiffart *h*honor: we was meaning to surprise you, Bert, afore you left, by putten them mimworms and that dragon's hegg hinto a suitable container wif a nice red ribbon and say, 'Ere you be, King o' Bertland, hand be pleased to haccept this as your winnings for that time we played forfeits last time we played it.' Surprise yer, yer see. But now yer've spoiled that helement of it; ah, well, must take the bitter wiv the sweet."

That night after dinner the three mimworms and the dragon's egg were lifted out from the royal hidey-hole and displayed for the last time at Alf High-Table before being taken off to their new home. Princess Pearl and Princess Ruby gave over their broidered-work, and young Buck (he was officially Prince Rufus but was never so-called) stopped feeding scruffles to his bird and dog – a rather mangy-looking mongrel with clipped claws – and Queen Clara came back out of the kitchen.

"Well, this is my last chance, I expect," said Princess Pearl, a stout good-humored young girl, with rather large feet. "Da, give us they ring."

"Ar, this time, our Pearl, happen thee'll have luck," her sire said, indulgently; and he took off his finger the Great Sigil-Stone Signet-Ring of the Realm, which he occasionally affixed to dog licenses and the minutes of the local wardmotes, and handed it to her. Whilest the elders chuckled indulgently and her brother snorted and her baby sister looked on with considerable envy, the elder princess began to make the first mystic sign – and then, breaking off, said, "Well, now, and since it *is* the last chance, do thee do it for me, our Ruby, as I've ad no luck a-doin it for meself so far—"

Princess Ruby clapped her hands. "Oh, *may* I do it, oh, please, please, our Pearl? Oh, you are *good* to me! Ta ever so!" and she began the ancient game with her cheeks glowing with delight and expectation:

Mimworm dim, mimworm bright,
Make the wish I wish tonight:
By dragon egg and royal king,
Send now for spouse the son of a king!

The childish voice and gruff chuckles were suddenly all drowned out by screams, shouts, cries of astonishment, and young Buck's anguished wail; for where his bird had been, safely jessed, there suddenly appeared a young man as naked as the day of his birth.

Fortunately the table had already been cleared, and, nakedness not ever having been as fashionable in East Brythonia (the largest island in the Black Sea) as it had been in parts farther south and west, the young man was soon rendered as decent as the second-best tablecloth could make him.

"Our Pearl's husband! Our Pearl's husband! See, I *did* do it right, *look*! Our Mum and our Da, *look*!" and Princess Ruby clapped her hands together. King Alf and King Bert sat staring and muttering . . . perhaps charms, or countercharms . . . Buck, with tears in his eyes, demanded his bird back, but without much in his tone to indicate that he held high hopes . . . Princess Pearl had turned and remained a bright, bright red . . . and Queen Clara stood with her hands on her hips and her lips pressed together and a face – as her younger daughter put it later: "O Lor! Wasn't Mum's face a study!"

Study or no, Queen Clara said now, "Well, and pleased to meet this young man, I'm sure, but it seems to me there's more to this than meets the heye. Our Pearl is still young for all she's growed hup into a fine young 'oman, and I don't know as I'm all that keen on her marrying someone as we knows nuffink abahrt, hexcept that he use ter be a bird; look at that there Ellen of Troy whose dad was a swan, Leda was er mum's name; what sort of ome life d'you think she could of ad, no better than they should be the two of them, mother and daughter – what! Alfland! Yer as some'at to say, as yer!" she turned fiercely on her king, who had indeed been mumbling something about live and let live, and it takes all kinds, and seems a gormly young man; "Ah, and if another Trojan War is ter start, needn't think to take Buck halong and—"

But she had gone too far.

"Nah then, nah then, Queen Clara," said her king. "Seems to me yer've gotten things fair muddled, that 'ere Trojing War come abaht acause the lady herself ad more nor one usband, an' our Pearl asn't – leastways not as *I* knows of. First yer didn't want Buck to get married, nah yer wants our Pearl ter stay at ome. I dessay, when it come our Ruby's time, yer'll ave some'at to say bout that, too. Jer want me line, the royal line-age o' the Kings of Alfland, as as come down from King Deucalion's days, ter die aht haltergether?" And to this the queen had no word to utter, or, at least, none she thought it prudent to; so her husband turned to the young man clad in the second-best tablecloth (the best, of course, always being saved for the lustral Visitations of the High King himself) – and rather well did he look in it, too – and said, "Sir, we bids yer welcome to this ere Igh Table, which it's mine, King Earwig of Alfland is me style and title, not but what I mightn't ave another, nottersay other *ones*, if so be I ad me entitles and me right. Ah, ad not the King o' the Norf, Arald Ardnose, slain Earl Oscaric the Ostrogoth at Slowstings, thus allowing Juke Wilfred of Southmandy to hobtain more than a mere foot'old, as yer might call it, this ud be a united kingdom today instead of a mere patch'ork quilt of petty kingdomses. Give us an account of yerself, young man, as yer hobliged to do hanyway according to the lore."

And at once proceeded to spoil the effect of this strict summons by saying to his royal guest, "Pour us a drain o' malt and one for his young sprig, wonthcher, Bert," and handed the mug to the young sprig with his own hands and the words, "Ere's what made the deacon dance, so send it down the red road, brother, and settle the dust."

They watched the ale go rippling down the newcomer's throat, watched him smack his lips. Red glows danced upon the fire-pit hearth, now and then illuminating the path of the black smoke all the way up to the pitchy rafters where generations of other smokes had left their soots and stains. And then, just as they were wondering whether the young man had a tongue or whether he peradventure spoke another than the one in which he had been addressed, he opened his comely red lips and spoke.

"Your Royal Grace and Highnesses," he said, "and Prince and Princesses, greetings."

"Greetings," they all said, in unison, including, to her own pleased surprise, Queen Clara, who even removed her hands from under the apron embroidered with the golden crowns, where she had been clasping them tightly, and sat down, saying that the young man spoke real well and was easily seen to have been well brought hup, whatsoever e ad been a bird: but there, we can't always elp what do befall us in this vale of tears.

"To give an account of myself," the young man went on, after no more than a slight pause, "would be well lengthy, if complete. Perhaps it might suffice for now for me to say that as I was on the road running north and east out of Chiringirium in the Middle, or Central, Roman Empire, I was by means of a spell cast by a benevolent sorcerer, transformed into a falcon in order that I might be saved from a much worse fate; that wilst in the form of that same bird I was taken in a snare and manned by one trained in that art, by him sold or exchanged for three whippets and a brace of woodcock to a trader out of Tartary by way of the Crimea; and by *him* disposed of to a wandering merchant, who in turn made me over to this young prince here for two silver pennies and a great piece of gammon. I must say that this is very good ale," he said, enthusiastically. "The Romans don't make good ale, you know, it's all wine with them. My old dadda used to tell me, 'Perry, my boy, clean barrels and good malt make clean good ale . . .' "

And, as he recalled the very tone of his father's voice and the very smell of his favorite old cloak, and realized that he would never see him more, a single tear rolled unbidden from the young man's eye and down the down of his cheek and was lost in the tangle of his soft young beard, though not lost to the observation of all present. Buck snuffled, Ruby climbed up in the young man's lap and placed her slender arms round his neck, Queen Clara blew her nose into her gold-embroidered apron, King Bert cleared his throat, and King Alf-Earwig brushed his own eyes with his sleeve.

"Your da told yer that, eh?" he said, after a moment. "Well, he told yer right and true— What, call him dadda, do 'ee? Why, yer must be one a them Lower Europeans, then, for I've eard it's

their way o' speech. What's is name, then – and what's yours, for
that matter?"

Princess Pearl, speaking for the first time since giving the ring
to her small sister, said, "Why, Da, haven't he told us that? His
name is Perry." And then she blushed an even brighter red
than ever.

"Ah, he have, our Pearl. I'll be forgetting my own name next.
Changed into a falcon-bird and then changed back again, eh?
Mind them mimworms and that 'ere dragon hegg, Bert; keep
em safe locked hup, for where there be magic there be mischief—
But what's yer guvnor's name, young Perry?"

Young Perry had had time to think. Princess Pearl was to all
appearances an honest young woman and no doubt skilled in
the art of spindle and distaff and broider-sticking, as befitted
the daughter of a petty king; and as befitted one, she was passing
eager and ready for marriage to the son of another such. But Perry
had no present mind to be that son. Elliptically he answered with
another question. "Have you heard of Sapodilla?"

Brows were knit, heads were scratched. Elliptics is a game
at which more than one can play. "That be where you're from,
then?" replied King Alf.

The answer, such as it was, was reassuring. He felt he might
safely reveal a bit more without revealing too much more. "My
full name, then, is Peregrine the son of Paladrine, and I *am*
from Sapodilla and it *is* in Lower Europe. And my father sent
me to find my older brother, Austin, who looks like me, but
blond."— This was stretching the truth but little. Eagerness
rising in him at the thought, he asked, "Have any of you seen
such a man?"

King Bert took the answer upon himself. "Mayhap such a
bird is what ee should better be a-hasking for, *horhorhor!*" he
said. And then an enormous yawn lifted his equally enormous
mustache.

Someone poked Perry in the side with a sharp stick. He did not
exactly open his eyes and sit up, there on the heap of sheepskin
and blanketure nigh the still hot heap of coals in the great hall;
for somehow he knew that he was sleeping. This is often the
prelude to awakening, but neither did he awake. He continued

to lie there and to sleep, though aware of the poke and faintly wondering about it. And then it came again, and a bit more peremptory, and so he turned his mind's eye to it, and before his mind's eye he saw the form and figure of a man with a rather sharp face, and this one said to him, "Now, attend, and don't slumber off again, or I'll fetch you back, and perhaps a trifle less pleasantly; you are new to this island, and none come here new without my knowing it, and yet I did *not* know it. Attend, therefore, and explain."

And Peregrine heard himself saying, in a voice rather like the buzzing of bees (and he complimented himself, in his dream, for speaking thus, for it seemed to him at that time and in that state that this was the appropriate way for him to be speaking). "Well, and well do I now know that I have passed through either the Gate of Horn or the Gate of Ivory, but which one I know not, do you see?"

"None of that, now, that is not my concern: explain, explain, explain; what do you here and how came you here, to this place, called 'the largest island in the Black Sea', though not truly an island . . . and, for that matter, perhaps not even truly in the Black Sea . . . Explain. Last summons."

Perry sensed that no more prevarications were in order. "I came here, then, sir, in the form of an hawk or falcon, to which state I was reduced by white witchery; and by white witchery was I restored to own my natural manhood after arriving."

The sharp eyes scanned him. The sharp mouth pursed itself in more than mere words. "Well explained, and honestly. So. I have more to do, and many cares, and I think you need not be one of them. For now I shall leave you, but know that from time to time I shall check and attend to your presence and your movements and your doings. *Sleep!*"

Again the stick touched him, but now it was more like a caress, and the rough, stiff fleece and harsh blankets felt as smooth to his naked skin as silks and downs.

He awoke again, and properly this time, to see the grey dawnlight touched with pink. A thrall was blowing lustily upon the ember with a hollowed tube of wood and laying fresh fagots of wood upon it. An even lustier rumble of snores came from the adjacent heap of covers, whence protruded a pair of hairy feet belonging, presumably, to the King of Bertland. And crouching by his own side was Buck.

Who said, "Hi."

"Hi," said Perry, sitting up.

"You used to be a peregrine falcon and now you're a peregrine man?" the younger boy asked.

"Yes. But don't forget that I was a peregrine man before becoming a falcon. And let me thank you for the care and affection which you gave me when I was your hawk, Buck. I will try to replace myself . . . or replace the bird you've lost, but as I don't know just when I can or how, even, best I make no promise."

At this point the day got officially underway at Alfland Big House, and there entered the king himself, followed by the Lord High Great Steward, aged eight (who, having ignominiously failed his apprenticeship as kitchenboy by forgetting to turn the spit and allowing a pair of pullets to burn, had been demoted), carrying hot water and towels; the soft-soap, in a battered silver basin, being born by King Alf. He also bore an ostrich feather which had seen better days, and with this he ceremoniously tickled the feet of King Bert, whose snores ceased abruptly. The hot water and towels were set on a bench and the burnished tray set up in a convenient niche to serve as mirror. King Bert grunted greetings, took his sickle-shaped razor out of his ditty bag, and, seizing one wing of his mustache and pulling the adjacent skin out, began to shave.

"Buck," said King of the Alves, "yer mum wants yer. Nar then, young Perry," he said, "what I wants ter know is this: Haccording to the charm as our Ruby's been and done unto yer, yer supposed to be the son of a king. Sometimes magic gets muddled, has we all knows, take for hinstance that time the Conqueror e says to iz wizard, 'Conjur me up the ghost of Caesar,' not specifying *which* Caesar e meant but hassuming e'd ave great Caesar's ghost hand no hother, which e adn't; the resultant confusion we needn't go hinter. *How*ever, '*Bring now for spouse the son of a king*,' says the charm, doesn't say *which* king, do it, but meantersay: His you hor hisn't you, a fair question, lad, give us a fair hanswer."

This Peregrine felt the man was entitled to, but he was by

no means delighted with the implications. "In a manner of speaking, Sir King," he said, wiggling slightly – and then, reflecting that the truth is more often the best than not, he added, "I am my father's youngest bastard son, and he has three heirs male of his body lawfully begotten."

King Alf digested this. It could almost be seen going down. "Well, then, we can homit *Prince* Peregrine, can we. Mmmm. Which means, *Queen* Pearl, we needn't look forrert to that, neither. Er dowery ud be smaller, there's a saving, right there. Nor she needn't move far away, Lower Europe, meantersay, might's well be Numidia for all the chance us'd ever get to visit. As a one or two by-blows meself. Fust one, wasn't never sure was it by me or was it by a peddler as'd been by awking plaice; lad turned fifteen, stole a fishing smack one night and run wif it: I crossed is name horf the Royal Genealogical Chart hand ad a scribe write *Denounciated hand Renounciated* hafter it. Tother un was the spit and image of me Huncle Percy, long afore deceased; but this lad went to the bad just like tother one, hexcept e become a physician specializing in the infirmities of women, as yer might say, ope yer own da as ad better luck . . ."

His voice ended in a mumble, then plucked up again. "Now, no doubt yer da has enobled you, give yer some such title as it might be, say, Count of Cumtwaddle and Lord of the Three Creeks in the peerage of Sapodilla, hey?" he inquired, hopefully.

Peregrine sighed, shook his sleek head, informed the host-king that what his father had given him was his blessing, a month's rations, three mules, a suit of the best second-rate armor, and a few other similar items; plus the ritual warning, established by law, that it would be Death for him to return either armed or at the head of an armed multitude.

King Alf grunted. "Well," he said, tone halfway between disappointment and approbation, "spose that's one way to preserve the loreful succession, makes sense, too bad, well, well," he shook his head. The gesture seemed to indicate bafflement rather than a negative decision. Another grunt announced a fresh idea . . . or two.

"Well, be that as it may, Queen Clara sends her good wishes and says please to excuse as she needs back the tablecloth. Now, we can't ave yer traipsing round in yer bare minimum, for folk ud larf hat us ha-keeping hup them hold-fashioned Grecian himfluences. So." He displayed an armful of garments. "One o' these is what's left o' what I've grew out of, but maybe it be still too large. And tother is for Buck ter grow into, maybe it be still too small. Only way to find out is to dive and try."

Perry thanked him, dived and tried. The pair of trews, woven in a tessellated pattern according to the old Celtish style, and intended for Buck to grow into, fit him well enough; but the tunic was a bit tight across the chest and shoulders; the tunic which Buck's father had grown out of, though an outsize round the waste, had exactly Perry's sleeve length. The same lucky fit obtained with the sandals, formerly the property of King Baldy's heir. "And here," said the royal host, setting down a casket inlaid in ivory, "is the gear box, and you may poke around for clasps, buckles, fibulae, and such; please elp yerself. No urry, hexcept that betwixt dawn and noon we as a rightchual ceremony to hattend; like ter ave yer wiff us."

The clepsydra at Alfland Big House had been for some time out of order, the king insisting with vigor that fixing it would constitute making plumbing repairs and thus an infringement on the High Royal Monopoly, the queen – for her part – insisting with equal vigor that the king was trying to cover up his ignorance of how to make the repairs. Be that as it may, the great water-clock remained unfixed, only now and then emitting a gurgle, a trickle, and a groan, rather like an elderly gentleman with kidney trouble. Be that as *that* may, at an hour approximately between dawn and noon, Peregrine, alerted by a minor clamor in the courtyard, made his way thither.

He saw gathered there the entire royal family and household, including thralls; the guest king, who had delayed his departure in order to witness the ritual ceremony; a number of citizens, whose abrupt discontinuance of conversation, and interested examination of Peregrine as he approached, gave him reason to believe they had been talking about him; and three archers, three slingers, and three spearmen: these last nine constituting the Army of the Realm (cavalry had been strictly forbidden by Wilfred the Conqueror).

"Ah, Peregrine the son of Paladrine the Sovereign of Sapodilla in Lower Europe," the King of the Alves announced, slightly pompously. And at once said, in his usual gruffly affable manner, "Come on over, Perry, and leave me hexplain to yer the nature of this hoccasion. See," he gestured, "that there is Thuh Treasure. Likewise, the Treasury."

"What, that single sack?" is the sentence which Perry had in mind to say, but, tactfully, did not.

King Alf continued, portentously, "Now, this is the third day hafter the full moon of the month of Hecatombaeon haccording to thuh hold Religion," he coughed delicately into his fist, "meantersay we're hall good Harians ere, and so naturally we've tried to git this fixed hup proper and right haccording to the New Faith, that is," another cough, "the True Faith. And ave wrote the bishops. Fergit ow many times we've wrote the bishops. First hoff, they hanswers, '*If any presbyter shall presume to ordain another presbyter, let him be anathema.*' Well, well, seems like sound enough doctrine and no skin hoff my, berumph! Caff caff. But what's it got to do wif dragons? Second time what they replied, '*Satan is the father of lies and the old dragon from the beginning; therefore let no presbyter presume to ordain another presbyter, and if he do presume, let him be anathema.*'" He cast an eye up and around the sky, for all the world like an augur about to take the auspices, then dropped his glance earthwise, and went on. "Next time we put the question, what's it as the bishops said, why they said, '*The waters of life may flow even through the jaws of a dead dog, but if any presbyter presume to ordain another presbyter—*'"

The gathering murmured, "–'*let him be anathema.*'"

King Alf then went on, briskly, to inform his younger guest that from time immemorial, on or about the hour midway between dawn and high noon on the third day after the full moon of the month of Hecatombaeon, a dragon was wont to descend upon the Land of the Alves for the purpose and with the intention of carrying off the treasure. "*Dragon?*" asked Perry, uneasily, "Then why is the treasure out in the open? And for that matter, why are *we* all out in the open?" The gathering chuckled.

"Why, bless yer, my boy," the king said, grinning broadly, "doesn't believe them old tales about dragons a-living on the

flesh of young virgin females, does yer? Which you be'n't in
any event, leastways I know you be'n't no female, a horhorhor!—
No no, see, all them dragons in this zone and climate o' the
world is pie-skiverous, see? Mayhap and peradventure there be
carnivoreal dragons in the realms of the Boreal Pole; then agin,
mayhap not. No skin hoff my— *Ow*ever. Yus. Well, once a year
we aves this ceremonial rightchual. The dragon, which e's named
Smarasderagd (meaning, Lover of Hemeraulds, in th' original
Greek), the dragon comes and tries to carry orf the treasure.
One story says, originally twas a golden fleece. Nowadays, has
we no longer lives in thuh world of mye-thology, the treasure
is the Treasury. All the taxes as as been collected under the
terms of my vasselage and doomwit to the High King, and
which I am bound to transmit to im – minus seven percent to
cover handling expenses – dog licenses, plowhorse fee, ox-forge
usage, chimbley tax, jus primus noctae commutations in fee
simple, and all the rest of it; here he comes now, see im skim,
thuh hold bugger!"

The crowd cheered, craned their necks, as did Peregrine; sure
enough, there was a speck in the sky which rapidly increased
in size. Peregrine asked, somewhat perplexed, "And does
the dragon Smarasderagd transmit the treasury to the High
King, or—"

King Alf roared, "What! Fancy such a notion! No no, lad.
Old Smarry, e makes feint to nobble the brass, yer see, and we
drives im orf, dontcher see. *I* as to do it hin order to maintain
my fief, for, '*Watch and ward agayn Dragons and Gryphons*,' it
be written in small print on the bottom of the paytent. And Old
Smarry, *e* as to do it hin order to maintain *is* rights to hall the
trash fish as gits caught in the nets, weirs, seines, wheels, traps
and trots hereabouts.— As for gryphons, I don't believe in them
things an nor I shan't, neither, hunless the bishops resolve as I
must, hin Council Hassembled.— *Ere* e come!"

The spearmen began a rhythmical clashing of their shields.

"Ho serpentine and squamous gurt dragon Smarasderagd,"
the Alf-king began to chant, "be pleased to spare our
treasure . . ."

With a sibilant sound and a strong smell of what Perry assumed
was trash fish, the dragon spread his wings into a silent glide

and replied, "I shan't, I shan't, so there and so there and so there . . ."

"Ho serpentine and squamous gurt dragon Smarasderagd – ullo, Smarry, ow's yer micturating membranes? – be pleased to spare . . ."

"I shan't, I shan't, I shan't – hello, Earwig, mustn't grumble, mustn't grumble – so there and so there and so there . . ."

Clash, clash, clash! went the spearmen. Peregrine observed that their spears had dummy heads.

"Then we'll drive yer away with many wounds and assailments – what's the news, Smarry, is there any news? – assailments and torments . . ."

Swish, swishl, swish, swishl, Smarasderagd flapped his wings and circled low. "—That's for me to know and you to find out— My hide is impervious to your weapons, insquamous issue of Deucalion—" He dug his talons into the sack of treasure, and, on the instant, the spearmen hurled their spears and the slingers whirled their slings and the archers let loose their arrows. And seeing the arrows – which, being made of reeds, and unfletched – bounce harmlessly off Smarasderagd's tough integuments and observing the sling stones to be mere pea gravel, fit for affrighting pigeons, to say nothing of the mock-spears rattling as they ricocheted, Peregrine realized that the resistance was indeed a mere ritually ceremonial one. The dragon in sooth seemed to enjoy it very much, issuing steamy hisses much like giggles as he dug his talons into the sack of treasure and lifted it a space off the ground, while his bright glazey eyes flickered around from face to face and his huge wings beat the air.

Grinning, King Alf said, "Ere, ave a care now the way yer've got that sack eld, Smarry, or ye'll spill it. Don't want us to be a-picken of the Royal Hairlooms, ter say nuffink of the tax drachmae, up from this ere muck, do yer?"

"Perish the thought, Earwig," said Smarasderagd, shifting its grip, and flying higher.

The king's grin slipped a trifle. "Don't play the perishing fool, then," he said. "Settle it back down, smartly and gently."

"I shan't, I shan't, I shan't!"

"What, ave yer gotten dotty in yer old age? Set it back down at once directly, does yer ear?"

"Screw you, screw you, screw you!" And the dragon climbed a bit higher, whilst the king and his subjects looked at each other and at the dragon with a mixture of vexation and perplexity. "I'm not putting it down, I'm taking it with me, a-shish-shish-shish," Smarasderagd snickered steamily.

"But that's again the rules!" wailed the king.

"It *is* against the rules, isn't it?" the dragon agreed, brightly. "At least, it *was*. But. You know. I've reviewed the entire matter very carefully, and what does it all add up to?— To this? you get the treasure and I get the trash fish. So – as you *see*, Earwig – *I've changed the rules!*" He flew a bit higher. "*You* keep the trash fish! *I'll* keep the treasure!"

Buck, who was evidently much quicker than Peregrine had perhaps credited him for, gave a leap and a lunge for the bag of treasure; not only did he miss, but Smarasderagd, with a tittering hiss, climbed higher. Queen Clara, till now silent, tradition having provided no place for her in this pageant save that of spectator, wailed, "Do suthing, Alfland! E mustn't get to keep the treasure!"

"I shall, I shall, I shall!" sang out the dragon, and in a slow and majestic manner began to rise.

"Ere, now, Smarry," the king implored. "What! Cher going to destroy thur hamicable relations which as ithertofore hobtained atween hus for the sake o' this little bit o' treasure which is such in name honely?"

The dragon shrugged – a most interesting sight. "Well, you know how it is," he said. "Here a little, there a little, it all adds up." The king's cry of rage and outrage was almost drowned out by the noise of great rushing as the great wings beat and dragon and treasure alike went up – up – and away. It seemed to Peregrine that, between the sound of the king's wrath and the sound of the beating of the vast ribbed and membranous pinions, he could distinctly hear the dragon utter the words, "Ephtland – Alfland – which will be the next land—?"

Needless to say that it was not possible for him then to obtain of this impression either confirmation or refutation.

Having dismissed the Grand Army of Alfland (all nine members of it) and – in broken tones – informed the citizenry that they had his leave to go, King Earwig sat upon an overturned barrel in the middle of his courtyard and, alternately putting his head in his hands and taking it out again, groaned.

"Oh, the hairlooms as come down from King Deucalion's days! Oh, the tax moneys! (Buck, my boy, never trust no reptyle!) Oh . . . What will folk say of me?"

Queen Clara, her normal russet faded to a mere pale pink, had another question to ask, and she asked it. "What will the High King say?"

King Alf-Earwig groaned again. Then he said that he could tell her what the High King would say. " 'Malfeasance, misfeasance, disfeasance, and nonfeasance h'of hoffice: horf wif is ead hon heach count!' – is what e'll say . . ."

The silence, broken only by the snuffing of Princess Pearl, was terminated by her mother. "Ah, and speaking of counts," said she, "what about my brother-in-law, Count Witenagamote?"

The king's head gave a half flop, and feeling it as though for reassurance, he muttered, "Ah, and I spose our only opes is ter seek refuge of im, for e lives hin a different jurisdiction, e does, and holds not of the High King; holds of the emperor, is what, the vassal of Caesar imself."

A touch of nature was supplied at this point by the cock of the yard, who not only ran a slightly frazzled hen to earth but began to tread her. Buck barely glanced, so serious was the other situation. Peregrine asked, automatically, "Which Caesar?"

He asked it of Alf's back, for the king had gotten up from the barrel and started pacing at length – a lengthy pace which was now leading him into the house by the back way. "Which Caesar?"

"Why, bless you," said the king, blankly, "of Caesar Haugustus, natcherly. What a question. Has though there were more nor one of im."

Peregrine, who knew very well that there was not only more than one but that the number of those using the title of *Caesar*, including heirs, co-heirs, sovereigns of the East and the West and the Center, claimants, pretenders, provincial governors and rather powerful lord mayors and mayors of the palace, ambitious army commanders – Peregrine, who knew it would be difficult at any given moment to calculate how many Caesars there were, also looked blank, but said nothing. He was clearly very far from Rome. From any Rome at all.

"Well, well, go we must as we must," muttered the king. "As we must go we must go. Meanwhile, o' course," he stopped suddenly, "can't be letting the Kingdom go wifourt authority; you, there," he beckoned to the kitchenboy. "How old are you?"

The lad considered, meanwhile wiping his snotty nose on his apron. "Six, last Mass of the Holy Martyrs of Macedonia, an it please Your Worship," he piped.

His Worship did some visible arithmetic. "Ah, that's good," he declared, after a moment. "Then ye'll not be seven for some munce after the High Kingly Inquisition gits ere to check hup . . . as they will, they will.— Below the hage of reason, they can't do a thing to yer, my boy, beside six smacks hand one to go on; so kneel. Hand let's ear yer name."

The boy knelt, rather slowly and carefully placing both palms on his buttocks, and slowly said, "Vercingetorix Rory Claudius Ulfilas John" – a name, which, if perhaps longer than he himself was, gave recognition to most of the cultures which had at one time or another entered East Brythonia within at least recorded history.

King Alf tapped him on each shoulder with the royal dirk without bothering to wipe off the fish scales (Queen Clara had been cleaning a carp for supper). "Harise, *Sir* Vercingetorix Rory Claudius Ulfilas John," he directed. "—Not all the way hup, aven't finished yet, down we go again. Heh-hem," he rolled his bulging and bloodshot blue eyes thoughtfully. "Sir Vercingetorix Rory Claudius Ulfilas John, we nominates and denominates yer as Regent *pro tem* of the Kingdoms and Demesnes of the Lands of the Alfs *in partibus infidelidum*, to have and to hold from this day forward until relieved by Is Royal Highness the High King – and don't eat all the raisins in the larder, or he'll have yer hide off yer bottom, hage of reason or no hage of reason. —And now," he looked about. "Ah, Bert. Yer've been so quiet, clean forgot yer was present. Ye'll witness this hact."

The King of Bertland, simultaneously stiff, uneasy, unhappy, said, "That I will, Alf."

Alf nodded. "*Hand* now," he said, "let's pack and hit the pike, then."

Peregrine had been considering. Amusing though it might be to tarry and observe how things go in Alfland under the regency of Sir Vercingetorix Rory Claudius Ulfilas John (aged six and some), still, he did not really consider it. And fond though he already was, though to be sure not precisely deeply fond – their acquaintance had been too brief – of the Alvish Royal House; yet he did not really feel that his destiny required him to share their exile; could he, even, feel he might depend upon the hospitality of Count Witenagamote? It might, in fact, be just the right moment to take his leave . . . before there was chance for anything more to develop in the way of taking for granted that he and Princess Pearl—

He was not very keen on dragons. Smarasderagd was a good deal larger than the last and only previous dragon he had ever seen. Piscivorous the former might or might not be; now that he no longer had all the trash fish to dine upon, who could say? Peregrine did not feel curious enough to wish to put it to the test. Dragons might lapse. King Alf's prolegomenal discourse, just before Smarasderagd had appeared, seemed to take for granted that the dragon was not a treasure-amassing dragon; yet all men in Lower Europe had taken it for granted that all dragons were by nature and definition just that. Peregrine remembered his first dragon, rather small it had been, and so – at first glance – had been the treasure it had been guarding. Yet a further investigation (after the dragon had been put to flight by the sprig of dragonbane from the geezle-sack of Appledore, the combination sorcerer, astrologer, court philosopher and *a cappella* bard of Sapodilla . . . and Peregrine's boyhood tutor as well . . .) – a further, even if accidental, investigation of the contents of the small dragon's cave had resulted in Peregrine's – literally – stumbling upon something of infinitely more value and weal than the bracelet of base metal inscribed *Caius loves Marianne* and the three oboli and one drachma (all stamped *Sennacherib XXXII, Great King, King of Kings, King of Lower Upper Southeast Central Assyria* – and all of a very devaluated currency) – he had tripped over a rotting leather case which contained what was believed by the one or two who, having seen it, were also competent to comment on it to be the mysterious and long-lost crown of the Ephts.

And what *had* Smarasderagd said, as though to himself, and evidently overheard only by Peregrine over the noise of the shoutings and the beatings of leathern wings? – it was . . . was it not? . . . "Ephtland, Alfland, which will be the next land?"

Peregrine said aloud, "It would be a good thing, in pursuing after him, were we to have with us a sprig or even a leaf of dragonbane."

King Alf's head snapped back up, his swollen small eyes surveyed his younger guest from head to buskin-covered toe. " 'Pursue after im,' the lad says.— Ah, me boy, you're the true son of a king, lawfully hillegitimate though yer be, hand proper fit for dragon unting, too, for, ah, wasn't yer brought back to human form by means h'of dragon's hegg?"

Buck's face turned red with pleasure and his teeth shone in his mouth. "That's it, Da!" he exclaimed. "We'll hunt him down, the gurt squamous beasty-thief! And not go running off like—"

Again, though, his mother "had summat to say". And said it. Did Alf think that she and her daughters were going to traipse, like common camp followers, in the train of the Grand Army, whilst he and it went coursing a dragon? ("*Hand* a mad, crack-brain scheme that be, too!") Did Alf, on the other hand, intend that she and her precious daughters should attempt to make their own way to the court of Count Witenagamote, regardless of all perils and dangers along the way, and *unprotected*?

Her husband's reply commenced with a grunt. Then he turned a second time to his older guest, who had been standing first upon one leg and then upon the other. "Bert," he said, "Hi commends me wife and me datters hunto yer mercy, care, and custody, hentreating that ye keeps 'em safe huntil arriving safe at sanctuary, the court of Count Wit. Does yer haccept this charge?"

"*Hac*-cepted!" said the King of Bertland. "Ave no fear."

Queen Clara's mouth opened, closed. Before it could open again, the two pettikings were already drawing maps in the

sawdust of the kitchen floor with a pair of roasting spits. "Now,
Alf, one spot on rowt as yer mussn't homit, is *ere*—" he made
a squiggle. "'Whussat?' why, that's Place Where The Dragons
Dance—"

"Right chew are!" exclaimed King Alf. "For e'll be a-prancin
is trihumph there for sure (Buck, my boy, never trust no
reptyle)."

"Likewise," King Bert warmed to the matter, "don't forgit
e'll ave to be returning *ither*," he made another scrawl, "to
is aerie-nest at Ormesthorpe, for e've a clutch o' new-laid
heggs—"

Peregrine, puzzled, repeated, with altered accent, "He's got
a clutch of – *what*?"

"Come, come, young man," said King Bert, a trifle testily,
"Hi asn't the time ter be givin yer lessons hin nat'ral istory: suffice
ter say that hall pie-skiverous dragons his hambisextuous, the
darty beasts!"

Something flashed in Peregrine's mind, and he laid his
hand upon King Bert's shoulder. "It seems destined that I
be a party to this quest for the Treasury carried off by gurt
dragon Smarasderagd," he said, slowly. "And . . . as King Alf
has pointed out, it was a dragon's egg that helped restore me to
human form . . . a dragon's egg which, I have been informed, is
now in your own and rightful custody: now therefore, O King of
Bertland, I, Peregrine, youngest son of the left hand of Paladrine
King of Sapodilla, do solemnly entreat of you your kindness and
favor in lending me the aforesaid dragon's egg for the duration
of the aforesaid quest; how about it?"

Sundry expressions rippled over King Bert's craggy face.
He was evidently pleased by the ceremonial manner of the
request. He was evidently not so pleased about the nature of
it. He swallowed. "What? . . . Wants the mimworms, too, does
yer? . . . Mmmm."

"No, no. Just the egg, and purely for purposes of matching
it with any other eggs as I might be finding; a pretty fool I'd
look, wouldn't I, were I to waste time standing watch and
ward over some nest or other merely because it had eggs in
it? – and then have them turn out to be, say, a bustard's . . .
or a crocodile's . . ."

This argument was so persuasive to the other king that he even, as he unwrapped the object from its wad of scarlet-dyed tow, bethought himself of other reasons – " 'Like cleaves hunto like,' has Aristottle says, may it bring yer hall good luck, ar, be sure as it will" – and rewrapping it, placed it in his very own privy pouch. He then had Peregrine remove his own tunic, slung pouch and contents so that it hung under the left (or shield) arm. "There. Cover hup, now, lad," he said.

Matters suddenly began to move more rapidly after that, as though it had suddenly occurred to everyone that they didn't have forever. Provisions were hastily packed, arms quickly and grimly sorted and selected. The Grand Army of the Alves was also remustered, and four of its nine members found fit for active duty in the field. Of these, however, one – a young spearman – was exempted because of his being in the first month of his first marriage; and a second, an archer, proved to have a painful felon or whitlow on his arrow thumb. This left one other archer, a short bowman whose slight stature and swart complexion declared more than a drop or two of autochthonous blood, and a very slightly feeble-minded staff slinger, said to be quite capable of doubling as spearman in close-in fighting. ("Moreover e's the wust poacher in the kingdom and so should damn well be able to spot dragon spoor – d'ye hear, ye clod?" "Har har! – Yus, Mighty Monarch.")

The procession was obliged to pause momentarily in the open space before the cathedral church (indeed, the only church), where the apostolic vicar had suddenly become very visible. As usual, he had absented himself from the dragon ceremony on the ground of dragons being essentially pagan creatures which had not received the approbation of any church council; he was uncertain if he should pronounce a ritual gloat at the dragon's having been the cause of the king's discomfiture, or if he should give the king the church's blessing for being about to go and hunt the heathen thing; and he had summoned his catechumens, doorkeepers, deacons, subdeacons, acolytes and excorcists to help him in whichever task he hoped right now to be moved by the Spirit to decide.

A small boy who had climbed the immemorial elm abaft

the cathedral church to get a good view, suddenly skinnied down and came running. Peregrine's was the first face he encountered and recognized as being noteworthy; so, "Eh, Meyster!" he exclaimed. "There come three men on great horses towards th' Eastern Gate, and one on 'em bears a pennon with a mailed fist—"

King Alf whirled around. "*Kyrie eleison!*" he exclaimed. "'Tis Lord Grumpit, the High King's brutal brother-in-law and *ex officio* Guardian of the Gunny Sacks (Treasury Division) – what brings him here so untimely? – he'll slay me, he'll flay me—"

Peregrine said, "Take the Western Gate. See you soonly," – and gave the king's mount a hearty slap on the rump. The clatter of its hooves still in his ears, he strode up to the ecclesiast on the church steps, the vicar regarding him so sternly that one might almost have thought he was able to discern that the waters of baptism had never yet been sprinkled, poured, or ladled upon Peregrine's still-pagan skin.

"Your Apostolic Grace," Peregrine asked, in urgent tones, "it is surely not true – *is* it? – that one presbyter may ordain another presbyter?"

The hierarch beat the butt of his crosier on the church step with such vehemence that the catechumens, doorkeepers, deacons, subdeacons, acolytes and excorcists came a-running.

"It *is* false!" he cried, in a stentorian voice. "Cursed be who declares the contrary! Where is he, the heretic dog?"

Peregrine gestured. "Coming through the Eastern Gate even now," he said. "And one of them bears the pennon of a mailed fist, alleged to be the very sign and symbol of presbytocentrism!"

The apostolic vicar placed two fingers in his mouth, gave a piercing whistle, hoisted his crosier with the other, beckoned those in minor orders – and in none – "All hands fall to to repel heretics!" he bellowed. He had long formerly been chaplain with the Imperial Fleet. The throng, swelling on all sides, poured after him towards the Eastern Gate.

Peregrine mounted the wiry Brythonic pony which had been assigned him, smote its flanks, whooped in its ears, and passed out through the Western Gate with deliberate speed. The dragon egg nestled safe beneath his arm.

PIZZA TO GO

Tom Holt

Tom Holt (b. 1961) has produced a stream of humorous and anarchic fantasy since he turned to the field with Expecting Someone Taller *in 1987. There was some evidence of his wit in his continuations of E.F. Benson's* Mapp and Lucia *books,* Lucia in Wartime *(1985) and* Lucia Triumphant *(1986), but it is for books like* Who's Afraid of Beowulf? *(1988),* Flying Dutch *(1991),* Ye Gods! *(1992),* Grailblazers *(1994),* Faust Among Equals *(1994),* Odds and Gods *(1995),* Paint Your Dragon *(1996),* My Hero *(1996) and* Open Sesame *(1997) that he has become best known. Here's a brand-new story written especially for this collection.*

"I see," said Jesus Christ. "You forgot to tell them to bring sandwiches."

The green valley was full of people, as far as the eye could see: men and women of all ages sitting or reclining on the grass, children chasing and hiding and splashing in the shallow water of the little stream that ran down from the rocky crest above. There were *thousands* of them.

"It's Peter's fault," said Barnabas pre-emptively. "I asked him what we were going to do about catering, and he said no worries, he had a mate who could give us a really special price—"

"I never said that," Peter replied. "I said *if* we were going to organize caterers, then I *might* be able to get us a good deal, *provided*—"

Five thousand eager new converts, filled with the grace of God and not much else, hummed in the valley like a hive of bees. A nice walk in the desert, a jolly good show with lots of parables, followed by a slap-up feed and home in plenty of time for *Gladiators*; who could ask for a better way to spend a bank holiday Monday?

"We're going to get lynched," John groaned. "There'll be little bits of us scattered about all the way to Caesarea."

"Don't be silly," said the Messiah. "Leave this to me. Honestly, if it wasn't for me, I don't know what you'd do."

From his sleeve he took a mobile phone and a small piece of card, on which was written:

PIZZA TO GO
We deliver
Any time
*Any*where.

The kitchen is an inferno. Can't take the heat? Stay out. Even if you can survive in temperatures well in excess of 60°C, don't go in there unless you know exactly what you're supposed to be doing, and can do it faster and more efficiently than the most sophisticated machine. The penalty for getting under Zelda's feet is getting spoken to by Zelda. Being eaten alive by termites would be infinitely preferable.

Because this is Zelda's kitchen, possibly the most extraordinary place in spacetime. From this small prefabricated industrial unit perched in the cleft of an anomalous singularity in the heart of the interface between the weirdest outposts of science and the credible end of magic, there flows a never-ending stream of wide, flat styrofoam trays, whisked away by the delivery guys through fissures and wormholes to every part of everywhere and everywhen. Because Zelda's kitchen exists simultaneously in every moment of time, from the theoretical Beginning to the presumably inevitable End, all the countless billions of pizzas and dips and side-salads and portions of garlic bread ever sold by Pizza to Go, the greatest and most successful delivery service in the universe, have to be cooked and prepared *at the same time*. A certain degree of efficiency is, therefore, essential.

When asked how she copes, Zelda shrugs. "It's a family business," she says. "We manage."

There's Rocco and Tony, who make the bases; Freddy and Mike, who do the toppings; Carlo, who minds the ovens; Rosa and Vito, who chop the vegetables and deal with the side-orders; Frankie, Ennio and young Gino, who do the deliveries; and then there's Zelda, who takes the orders, writes out the tickets and does everything. In the far corner sits Poppa Joe, grunting and mumbling in his sleep, very occasionally waking up and being allowed to slice pepperoni or fetch a new jar of olives. As soon as the rush is over, they're going to take a break and sort out the physics of it all. But the rush is never over, because it hasn't even started yet. And never will.

"We're nearly out of mozzarella," Mike warned, not looking up from what he was doing. Nobody took any notice. There wasn't time to run out of mozzarella, and so they never would.

"Three Margeritas and a Seafood," Zelda shouted, her hand over the mouthpiece, "and two garlic breads. Frankie, you still here? You shouldn't be here. Get going."

"I been and came back," Freddie replied calmly. "What's next?"

Zelda pointed to a stack of trays. "That lot for the seventeenth century," she said, "and one for 1862; you can do it on your way back. Carlo, where's that Double Pepperoni, hold the onion? There's customers waiting."

Carlo, a bald, black-bearded giant with sweat pouring down his face, nodded and muttered "Inna minute." The searing heat of the controlled fusion reactor, shielded by 70 ft of pure zephronite crystal, had long since roasted his skin into pink leather, but he didn't have time to worry about things like that, not when customers were waiting.

The mathematics were quite simple, when you thought about it. When you don't have time, there is no time. When there is no time, you have all the time in the world. Or, as Zelda puts it, if you want something done, ask a busy woman.

"Hello, Pizza to Go?" Zelda stuffed a finger in her other ear, the receiver cradled in the slot it had long ago worn between her shoulder and her jaw, while she wrote the ticket. "Two Neptunos extra sweetcorn and a salad, and where's that for? Okay, I got it, that'll be with you in twenty minutes." She covered the mouthpiece, relayed the order and put the ticket on the spike. "Gino," she called out, "instead of just standing there, do something. Address is on the ticket."

Gino had just got back from delivering six Quattro Stagioni to a bunker in the middle of the decisive battle of World War VI; he was glowing bright blue and whenever he touched anything, it crackled. That was okay; you got used to stuff like that when you delivered. He glanced at the ticket, nodded and grabbed the pile of trays.

"On my way," he said.

"I don't know where they could have got to," said Lady Macbeth apologetically. "The woman who gave me their card said they were very reliable."

Typical, she thought. Unexpected guests, nothing in the larder, the obvious thing to do was to send out for pizza. Now she had twenty-six ravenous thanes sitting round her table looking as if they were ready to eat the wall-hangings. She caught her husband's eye and gave him a savage look. Serve him right for bringing people home without telling her.

Out of the corner of her eye, she caught sight of a slight movement. She was about to look round and investigate when her husband suddenly jumped up, knocking his chair over. He was pointing at an empty place at the table, and his eyes were as round as cartwheels.

"Which of you has done this?" he croaked. "Thou canst not say I did it: never shake your gory locks at me." He stepped back and trod on the cat's tail.

Everybody was staring; not at the empty place, but at King Macbeth, who was starting to froth at the mouth a bit, and at the cat, which was half-way up the arras and going like a train. If they'd looked to where he was pointing, some of them might just have made out a pale blue shimmer, in the shape of a human figure holding a stack of trays.

"Excuse me?" Gino repeated. "Six tuna and anchovy and a meat feast?" Nobody was paying any attention, the host was having hysterics and a footman with a jug of water had just walked straight through him. He recognised the symptoms. Not *again*!

It happened, sometimes. When the batteries in the interface frequency modulator started running down, or a bit of dirt got on the points of the symbionic condenser, there were these awkward moments when he wasn't 100 per cent there. Either people couldn't see him at all, or they saw something which wasn't actually him; it had given rise to all kinds of problems, including a widespread belief in ghosts and a surprising number of successful religions, and it was bad for business. Carlo had promised to take a look at the equipment as soon as the rush was over.

"Hello?" he said. "Can anybody hear me? Six tuna and anchovy and a meat feast?"

There had been that awful time when King Belshazzar had ordered a jumbo Four Cheeses and dips for 108. Gino never had worked out what had gone wrong there; as far as he could tell, the words 'Service Not Included' had come out as '*Mene Mene Tekel Upharsin*', and there'd been some kind of minor war . . . Zelda was going to call them up and explain as soon as she had a spare moment. Gino pulled a face. He hoped this wasn't going to turn out to be one of *those* deliveries.

"Approach thou like the rugged Russian bear," the man was shrieking, "the armed rhinoceros or the Hyrcan tiger—" The guests were at the carefully-looking-the-other-way stage, and his wife had deliberately annihilated two napkins and a small floral ornament. And the pizzas were going cold. He put them down on the table with the ticket on top of the boxes, muttered something about coming back later for the money, and stepped back into the anomaly.

★   ★   ★

"Yeah, sure," Zelda muttered, when he got back. "I'll tell Carlo, soon as the rush is over. Meanwhile, there's pizzas waiting. You think they deliver themselves?"

With a sigh, Gino picked up the stack of trays and glanced down at the ticket. He groaned.

"Not them again," he said unhappily. "Hey, Zelda, why can't someone else go this time?"

Zelda looked up from her table. "Get outa here," she said. "You should be grateful you got a job at all."

"Okay, everyone," said Lucrezia Borgia cheerfully, "pizza's here." She took the pile of trays, handed over a handful of gold coins and gave Gino an unpleasant grin. "I'll just heat them through and then it's pizza time," she called back over her shoulder. From behind her came happy, hungry noises; Lucrezia's parties were always popular. For some reason.

"Excuse me," Gino said.

Lucrezia looked at him. "Sorry," she said, "wasn't that the right money? Just a moment, I'll get my purse."

Gino took a deep breath. "It's not that," he said cautiously. "Money's exactly right, thank you. It's just . . ."

"Hm?"

"Miz Borgia," Gino said, "please, I'm sorry if I'm talking out of turn here, but these pizzas—"

"Yes?"

"You do like our pizzas, don't you?"

Lucrezia frowned. "They're very good," she said. "Why do you ask?"

"And you know we can do you any extra toppings, whatever you want? All you gotta do is ask."

"I'll bear that in mind. And now if you'll excuse me—"

"Only," Gino said, "I get the impression you, um, add things to them. Extra, er, toppings and stuff. There's no need, really."

"Oh yes there is," Lucrezia said, with a smile.

"Really," Gino said desperately, hopping from foot to foot, "you shouldn't have to bother, a busy lady like yourself. Next time, if you just let us know—"

"It's fine, really," Lucrezia replied. "Many thanks. Goodbye."

She closed the door. Gino raised his hand to knock again, but let his knuckles relax. Not his place to go interfering, after all. It wasn't as if they were doing proper sit-down catering.

He climbed back into the anomaly, pulled out the choke and pressed the starter. It wouldn't go. That was another thing Carlo was going to have a look at as soon as the rush was over, and at times it was a damn nuisance. Once it had flatly refused to work at all, and he'd been left hanging around for thirty-six years until he'd made another delivery in the neighbourhood and had been able to hitch a ride back with himself.

Sometimes it helped if you kicked it. He kicked it. It didn't help.

Bugger.

He sat down and wondered what to do. If the worst came to the worst, it wouldn't be long before Lucrezia placed another order; but Renaissance Italy wasn't the sort of place he wanted to hang about in for too long if he could possibly help it. He could ask Lucrezia if he could borrow her phone; no, that wouldn't work, because she didn't have one. Only a few very special customers had fully operational anachronisms; the rest patched their orders through by leaving messages sealed in bottles or buried in lead cylinders, which were subsequently dug up by archaeologists and phoned in from the twentieth century or later; the pizzas could then be delivered retrospectively in the usual way. Stupidly, Gino had come out without a bottle or a lead cylinder; and somehow he didn't fancy knocking on the door of the Borgia residence and asking if he could borrow a spade and bury something in their back garden. There was no telling what you might dig up if you tried that.

He was considering scratching something on a nearby statue when someone coughed meaningfully behind him, trying to attract his attention. That was odd; apart from when he was making the actual delivery he wasn't supposed to be visible.

"Hello?" he said.

"Hello," replied the stranger. "You're Gino, aren't you?"

The stranger was a short, fat man with grey hair and a cigar sticking rather incongruously out of his Renaissance face. Gino wasn't sure what to make of that; still, none of his business.

"That's right," he said. "Sorry, do I know you?"

The man smiled. "Not yet," he replied. "But I have a feeling you will. You're the pizza delivery boy, right?"

Gino nodded. He wasn't sure he liked what appeared to be going on. He didn't know exactly how it worked (it was one of the things Zelda always did; she'd promised to explain it to him as soon as the rush was over), but there was a system whereby nobody was supposed to take any notice of the delivery guys. As far as the customers were concerned, they were just a collection of arms and legs who stood behind the pizza boxes when the door opened. If this man knew who he was, something had gone wrong. Still, he couldn't say that without being rude.

"That's right," he said. "But if you want to place an order, you've got to call in. I just do the deliveries."

The man shook his head. "It's okay," he said. "I already ate. There's something else I wanted to talk to you about. You got a minute?"

Gino bit his lip. "Actually," he replied, "we're really busy right now." He thought of something. "Maybe I could get back to you once the rush is over," he suggested.

"I don't think so," the man replied. "You aren't going anywhere or anywhen, because the anomaly's busted. Am I right?"

"Yes. Hey, how do you know about that?"

The man fished in his pocket and produced a brilliant node of blinding orange light. "Because I busted it," he said, and put the light away again. "*Now*, let's talk."

"Hey," Zelda called out, "anybody seen Gino? He's been gone a long time."

Keeping track of the deliveries was one of Zelda's principal nightmares. Because, on paper at least, everything in the kitchen was happening at the same time, Frankie and Ennio and young Gino really ought to be making all the deliveries simultaneously, which should mean they were (a) always here, just about to go out or just coming back; (b) never here, because they were out delivering; and (c) never anywhere else, because nobody can be in two places at once. Sometimes it could get quite awkward, and it was then that she missed Nicky, who used to

be the fourth delivery boy until he left to set up on his own as
Father Christmas.

Not, of course, that he'd left *yet*. Or, indeed, that he'd ever
worked there at all. That was something else she was going to
have to do once she had a moment's peace; make up Nicky's
back wages. At a rough guess, she owed him something between
an infinite sum of money and nothing at all.

"Gino's out on a call," Frankie said as he dashed past, a
quivering tower of boxes balanced in his arms. "Here, I'll take
his order if you like."

"Okay." Zelda pointed, and Frankie scooped up twelve
further trays. "But you can't do it all. If he's got held up in
traffic or something, someone else'll have to make his calls
instead." She looked round, but there was no way she could
spare anybody right now. Maybe later, when it wasn't quite so
busy, but . . .

Unless—

"Hey, Poppa," she yelled, drowning out the scream of the
antimatter blender. "You wanna make a few calls for me? I
don't like to ask, but you can see how we're fixed."

Poppa Joe opened one eye. "Sure, Zelda," he muttered.
"Anything you say."

Carlo looked up from the tray of pizzas he was watching. "Just
a minute, Zelda, you can't go sending Poppa out on calls. He
ain't up to that sort of thing no more."

Poppa glared at him out of his one good eye. "You shut your
face, Carlo," he grumbled. "I was delivering pizzas before you
were even born."

"Poppa, *I* was delivering pizzas before I was ever born, that
don't mean to say you can go wandering off at your . . ."

Wisely, he left the sentence unfinished. Most of the time,
Poppa Joe sat in his chair, no trouble to anybody; but he
was still the owner of the business, and their father. He
wasn't so old he couldn't still give them a smack round the
ear, even if, in Carlo's case, he'd have to stand on a chair
to reach.

"Thanks, Poppa," Zelda said. "The address is on the ticket.
Mind how you go."

"It's quite simple," the man said. "All I want is a lift. Not far out of your way," he added. "After all, what is?"

Gino shook his head. "I'm sorry," he said, "but we're not allowed. If Zelda found out—"

The man nodded. "Your sister Zelda. Formidable woman. But how's she going to find out ever? And if you don't, how are you going to get home without a main anomaly drive?"

Gino fidgeted nervously. Things like this didn't happen to Frankie or Ennio, only to him. Just because he was the youngest. It wasn't fair.

"All right," he said. "Where do you want to go?"

The man smiled. "That's better," he said. "Actually, it's more a case of when. You wait there, I'll be right back."

The man's name was Edwin Potter, and he was an art dealer. Thanks to a chance discovery he'd made in his youth, he was the richest and most successful art dealer ever. In fact, if it hadn't been for Edwin Potter, there probably wouldn't be any art at all. That didn't necessarily make him a nice man.

Edwin Potter had a small but functional single-seater anomaly of his own, which he used to transport paintings by struggling young artists from the fifteenth century forward in time to where he could sell them for the sort of money that avarice only dreams of if it's been breathing in glue fumes. If he wanted to, he could even sell the same painting over and over again (which is why there are several versions of the same Leonardos and Michelangelos, all fervently claimed as genuine by their owners, who have the receipts to prove it). True, there was only room in the anomaly for himself and one medium-sized canvas balanced awkwardly on his knees; but at approximately 9 million per cent pure profit per trip, he was prepared to rough it. Accordingly, he was rich; so rich, in fact, he could have anything he wanted.

Almost anything.

Almost anything *so far*.

And now, he reflected as he walked back towards the Borgia house, he was in a position to complete the set. How nice.

"Oh dear," Lucrezia said, looking around the table. "It must have been something they ate."

Bianca di Fiesole stared dumbly at the corpses, unable to move for sheer horror. All her family, the entire ruling house of the Duchy of Arezzo, was slumped over the odd-looking boxes and the half-eaten slices of pizza. All, it seemed, except her. And, of course, Lucrezia.

"Probably just as well you and I had the Hawaiian Surprise," Lucrezia added cheerfully. "I think I'll write and complain. Now then, let's give you a moment for your dinner to go down, and then we can have the wedding."

"Wedding?" Bianca croaked. It seemed such an incongruous thing to say. Presumably cousin Lucrezia had meant funeral.

"That's right, dear. Oh, didn't I mention it? I've arranged a wedding for you. Very nice man, you'll like him." She leaned over and pulled up a corpse by its hair. "Oh drat," she added, "I forgot we'd need a priest." She slapped the corpse's face. "Cardinal Ordelafo? Are you still with us? Oh dear," she sighed, letting the head fall forward into a slice of tuna and anchovy, "some people have no consideration for others. Never mind, you'll just have to get married when you get there."

"Where?" Bianca demanded, as the shock thawed into fear. "Cousin Lucrezia . . ."

"It's all right, dear," Lucrezia Borgia replied, "you'll like it when you get there. Or should that be then? Anyway, you'll like it."

Bianca stood up, her mouth open to speak; but Lucrezia popped an apple into it, then hit her over the head with a candlestick. Crude; but she didn't have time for pre-wedding jitters.

As if on cue, Edwin Potter strolled in, paused to admire a vinegar-stained Giotto canvas—

"Where'd you get that?"

"What? Oh, *that*. Last night's chips came in it. Why?"

—and helped Lucrezia Borgia to lug his unconscious bride out of the door and into the anomaly.

"It's quite simple," Potter explained, as he wired the main drive back in. "I fancied her the first time I saw her, when I was in these times on business. So I thought, why not? These things are so much easier to arrange now than they will be in my time; you just find the senior relative and haggle over money for a bit." He frowned. "Actually, Bianca's father refused to be reasonable, he wanted far too much. So I suggested to my old friend Lucrezia that we might find it easier to sort out if we discussed it over dinner at her place."

"Oh," Gino said.

"Quite. It worked out rather well for both of us, because Lucrezia's now the heir to the Duchy of Arezzo, and she's also Bianca's only surviving relative." He smiled pleasantly. "I think she wanted Arezzo to make up the set, like in Monopoly. There," he added, dropping his screwdriver back in his top pocket, "I think that ought to work now. New York 1997, please, as near to Fifth Avenue as you can make it."

Gino pulled out the choke and put the anomaly in gear. "But what about when she wakes up," he objected. "Won't she—?"

Potter shook his head. "That's the beauty of it," he said. "Now you and I are used to whizzing about through time so it doesn't affect us; we're hardened to it. She isn't. Do you remember your first trip?"

Gino thought for a moment. "No," he admitted.

"Of course you don't. The first time you go through, it wipes your memory clean. I nearly found that out the hard way myself. So, when Bianca arrives in my time, she won't remember anything at all. Which is where I patiently explain that she's had a bang on the head and lost her memory. Then I tell her that we've been married for three years, her father used to run a shoe factory in Queens until her whole family died in a fire last year, and that we're extremely happy together and very much in love. Neat, yes?"

"That's awful," Gino said.

"So glad you think so. It means we'll have to skip the actual wedding, which is a pity. I was going to ask your lot to do the catering. Well, come on, I haven't got all day."

"No," Gino said, "I'm not going to do it. It's kidnapping and brainwashing and what's that you're pressing into the back of my neck?"

"The course of true love never did run smooth," Potter replied. "Now get this thing moving before I slit your throat."

Poppa Joe, who in some respects was eighty-seven, was also as young as he felt. He'd started out in the catering business as a pizza delivery boy, and now here he was again, delivering pizzas. He grinned as he closed his fist and tapped it against the door. Right now, he felt like he was fourteen again. The smell, the warmth soaking through the tray onto his skin; it surely took him back—

—And forwards, too, of course. Sometimes it got confusing that way. A lifetime in the business, millions of deliveries all over space and time; there were the inevitable disconcerting moments when his skinny, spotty fourteen-year-old self dashed up the stairs of a block of flats and passed a wheezing, knock-kneed old wreck coming down, and the old man looked at him sadly and said, "Save your energy, son, they weren't in." Sometimes, the frustrations of his physical age tempted him to cheat. It would be so easy for him to be twenty-one again (and again, and again . . .); except that, when he looked back, what had he ever done with his youth except deliver pizzas?

If I had my time over again . . .

The door opened.

"Two Seafood Deluxe and a Napolitana," he said, with an echo of the old cheerfulness, "that'll be $10.65 – Gino, what the hell do you think you're *doing*?"

Gino's face fell. Oh well, he said to himself, it seemed like a good idea at the time; to offer to help Potter carry the unconscious Bianca up the stairs, then quickly phone through an order and hope that Frankie or Ennio would turn up and help him right the terrible wrong he'd been forced to participate in. Even if *he'd* turned up, he'd have been better than nothing; two of him would have stood a chance against Potter and his knife, or at least they could have made a fight of it. But Poppa Joe—

"It's okay," he muttered. "Leave the pizzas, let's go home."

But Poppa Joe stood his ground. "Not so fast, kid," he said. "There's something the matter. What's up? You tell Poppa."

Gino shrugged and explained, and Poppa Joe listened. When he'd finished, he saw that the old man was actually grinning.

"Bianca di Fiesole," he muttered under his breath. "Well, if that don't just beat all. You know, I was just thinking about her the other day."

"Other day?"

Poppa Joe waved his hand impatiently. "You know what I mean," he said. "Kid, you know what? This is going to be good. You wait there, don't even move."

"Poppa Joe? Where are you going?"

"Just stay there, that's all. And look after your momma."

"My *what?*"

—Back to a time, in the late fifteenth century, when a princess in Arezzo had opened a door to a pizza delivery boy, and their eyes had met across the centuries . . .

Not that he'd done anything about it, not then; she was a princess and he delivered pizzas, and in fifteenth-century Italy that was an end to it. Still gazing dumbly at the girl of his dreams, drowning in the sudden and unexpected love he saw reflected in her eyes, he thrust the trays into her hands, stepped back and—

Bumped into an old man, who pushed him aside and said, "Get outa the way, kid. You leave this to me. Hey, Bianca, wait up."

The vision of loveliness hesitated for a moment. "Me?" she said.

"Yes, you. Now you be quiet and do what you're told, 'cos I'm old enough to be your grandfather and I know about things. You see that kid there? You gonna marry him, okay?"

"Marry him?" Bianca repeated, stunned. "What . . . ?"

"Marry him," the old man said categorically. "Elope. Now. 'Cos if you don't, you gonna get kidnapped through time and space and all your family gonna get murdered by the Borgias. And," he added thoughtfully, "a whole lot of other things ain't gonna happen, which'd be a real shame, believe me." He stopped, as if aware that he was rambling. "Now you tell me something. Do you love me? I mean, him."

The girl hesitated, then nodded firmly.

"You want to run away with him and get married and have kids, maybe start a good, sound family business, possibly in catering?"

Bianca looked bewildered, then nodded again.

"Good," the old man said. "So grab your coat and get outa here." He reached back and grabbed the young boy's collar. "The two of us."

Gino blinked, and looked at the door.

A moment ago, he could have sworn it was open and he was standing inside it. Now he was outside, holding a stack of trays.

The door opened; but it wasn't Potter who answered. It was an elderly black woman with a nice smile, who said thank you and gave him the right money. He shrugged and walked down the stairs to the anomaly.

Something about looking after his momma?

Which was crazy; Momma wasn't here, she was back in the kitchen where she'd always been, answering the phone, ruling the place with a rod of iron—

—Because this is Bianca's kitchen, possibly the most extraordinary place in spacetime. From this small prefabricated industrial unit – well, indeed, skip all that. We may have been here before.

There's Rocco and Tony, who make the bases; Freddy and Mike, who do the toppings; Carlo, who minds the ovens; Rosa and Vito and Zelda, who chop the vegetables and deal with the side-orders; Frankie, Ennio and, of course, young Gino, who do the deliveries; and there's Momma Bianca, who takes the orders, writes out the tickets and does everything. Occasionally her eldest daughter Zelda suggests it might help if she were to take a turn answering the phone occasionally, so as to give Momma a break at her age. And Bianca says yeah, that'd be good. As soon as the rush is over.

When people ask her how she copes, Momma Bianca grins. "It's a family business," she says. "We manage."

And in the far corner sits Poppa Joe, grunting and mumbling in his sleep, remembering the way things were and how they might have been.

A MALADY OF MAGICKS

Craig Shaw Gardner

Craig Shaw Gardner (b. 1949) first appeared in the magazines in 1978, and one of his earliest stories was "A Malady of Magicks". This introduced his well-meaning sorceror's apprentice, Wuntvor, and his master Ebenezum, who suffers from an allergy to magic. Other stories followed, which were later reworked as Gardner's first novel, A Malady of Magicks *(1986), but the original story has not been reprinted in this form. Other books in the first Ebenezum sequence are* A Multitude of Monsters *(1986) and* A Night in the Netherhells *(1987), plus the continuing Wuntvor trilogy* A Difficulty with Dwarves *(1987),* An Excess of Enchantments *(1988) and* A Disagreement with Death *(1989). Gardner's other humorous fantasies include the Cineverse sequence –* Slaves of the Volcano God *(1989),* Bride of the Slime Monster *(1990) and* Revenge of the Fluffy Bunnies *(1990) – set in a series of alternate worlds where the very worst of B-movie sets exist as a reality, and his Arabian Nights series –* The Other Sinbad *(1991),* A Bad Day for Ali Baba *and* Scheherazade's Night Out *(1992).*

I

"A good magician always watches his feet. It also does no harm to be constantly aware of the nearest exit."
—from *The Teachings of Ebenezum* Vol. 3

May I state now, once and for all, that I did not see the bucket.

My master, the wizard Ebenezum, was expounding at great length to a potential client concerning his abilities to sniff out sorcery wherever it might occur. He was also carefully avoiding any mention of the affliction that allowed him to do this so well.

I was crossing the room with a full load of firewood. The last of it, I might add, which we could ill afford to burn, save that, in those days and that place, the best way to attract a client was to pretend that you didn't need one. Thus the roaring fire on a day only moderately cool. And Ebenezum, who filled the room with grand gestures while speaking smoothly from beneath his great grey beard. Like any magician worth his runes, he could easily talk a customer into enchantment before any magicks were expended. Such an expert was he in fact, that I got caught up in the conversation and did not watch my feet.

Curse that bucket anyways! Down I went, spilling firewood across the table between the wizard and his client, neatly breaking his spell.

Ebenezum turned on me with eyes full of cosmic anger, another trick he was all too good at.

"See!" the client shrieked in a high voice. "I am cursed! It follows me wherever I go!" He hugged short arms around his pudgy body.

The wizard turned back to him, anger replaced by a smile so warm it would melt the ice on Midwinter Eve. "You don't know my apprentice," he said softly. "Cursed, no. Clumsy, yes."

Pudgy's hands came back to the table. "B-but . . ."

"The only curse here is when I signed a seven-year contract for his services." The magician smiled broadly. "I assure you, no magic is involved."

"If you say so." The client managed to smile. I picked

myself off the bench and smiled back. Just joy and happiness all around.

"I feel I can trust you," the client continued. "Will you look at my barn?"

"Certainly." The magician managed to cough gently without losing his smile.

The client, who had obviously dealt with artists long enough to know what such coughs meant, reached within the blue silk sash that circled his ample waist and pulled out a small purse. It thunked most satisfyingly when he dropped it on the table.

The client shrugged. "My crops have been good . . ." He frowned. " 'Till late."

"They shall be good again. When shall we—"

"As soon as possible. Perhaps tomorrow, at dawn?"

The wizard's face did not betray the slightest agony at the mention of so early an hour, a fact which conclusively proved our dire straights.

"Dawn then, good Samus," he said. They bowed, and the gentleman farmer took his leave.

"Put out that fire," were the wizard's first words to me. He scratched his neck below the beard. "Interesting. Your fall shortened our negotiations considerably – yet favorably. Mayhaps there is a way we can even get your clumsiness to work for you. We'll make a wizard of you yet!" He clapped me on the shoulder. "I have to check my scrolls. Clean up in here. We start work all too early on the morrow."

II

> "Illusions can be created in multitudinous forms, and vary in effectiveness to the degree your customer wishes to be fooled."
>
> —from *The Teachings of Ebenezum*, Vol. 12

"If my calculations be right," Ebenzum said with a tug at his beard, "the farm should be over the next rise."

I silently thanked all the gods, few though they were, who looked kindly on sorceror's assistants. Ebenezum had loaded such a variety of magical paraphernalia into the pack on my back that I was near to doubled over with the weight. Only my stout oak staff kept my head from reaching my feet, and even that sturdy wood seemed to bend considerably every time I leaned against it.

Ebenezum studied my discomfort for a moment, then raised his hand in the way he does when on the verge of a great pronouncement.

"Remember, Wunt," he said. "The total sorceror must develop both mind *and* body." He waved me to follow him with an ease of motion made possible by the fact that he carried nothing at all.

We reached the top of the hill. There was the farm, laid out before us in the full colors of dawn. The light hurt my eyes.

"Come, come, good Wunt!" Ebenezum called as he started down the hill. "Granted that the hour is ungodly. Still, this is a small job at best, finished before the end of morning." He tugged his beard again. "What could it be? Some crops trampled, a few animals loose from their pens? A minor elemental, at worst!"

The beard-fingers came free to wave in the air. "There is, of course, the matter of the dead sow. In my opinion, however, that turn of events was as much the sow's fault as the elemental's. In all, an easy day's work!"

Despite my back, I must admit that it cheered me to see Ebenezum once again embarking on a professional errand. A few mystic passes, a quick spell, and the sprite would be on its way. Even Ebenezum should be able to manage that before his malady overtook him. And that meant money in the coffers, not to mention an opportunity to reconfirm a reputation.

There were certain malicious types in the local mystical community who claimed that Ebenezum's wizardry was done. Just jealous of his great power, they were. Certainly, the outcome of Ebenezum's recent battle with that major demon of the third Netherhell had had its unfortunate side. The demon had, of course, been removed. Quite possibly destroyed. But the highly charged struggle had had its effect on the wizard as well. He had emerged from his trance to discover that he had developed an aversion to all things sorcerous. In fact, any great concentration of magicks would cause Ebenezum to go into an uncontrollable fit of sneezing.

A misfortune of this type might have totally defeated a lesser mage, but not Ebenezum. He had immediately set to discovering strategies in which he might use his malady to advantage.

All thoughts of magicians and misfortunes fled from my morning-dulled head, however, when I saw the girl.

I was to discover, when we were at last introduced, that she was farmer Samus' daughter, Alea. But what need had I for names? The vision of her alone was enough to keep me for the rest of my waking moments. Her skin was the color of young peaches plucked fresh from the tree and highlighted by the colors of dawn. Her hair took the color of sunlight breaking through the clouds after a spring rain. The rest of her? How could I possibly describe the rest of her?

"Wunt!" Ebenezum called over his shoulder. "Are you coming, or have you decided to grow roots?"

I hoisted my pack more firmly on my shoulders and hurried after him, never taking my eyes from the girl. Perhaps I might talk to her. And then, of course, there were touching, and kissing, and other activities of a similar nature.

"Ho!" Ebenezum called. I dragged my eyes away from perfection to discover he wasn't calling me at all. Rather, he was hailing a small knot of men involved in animated discourse slightly up the road.

The group turned to look at us. There were four of them. From their drab garb, I guessed three of them to be farmers. Probably hired hands or sharecroppers for the richer Samus. Two of these were virtually identical in appearance. Short and broad, their shoulder width close to their height, they both wore caps, earth colored like the rest of their garments, pulled close to their eyes. One of them picked at his teeth with a dirty fingernail. The other absently twirled a finger about in his ear. Beside this, they were mirror images.

The third hand was thinner, taller and younger than the other two; close to my age and height. Of course, he did not carry himself with one-tenth my stature, but what can you expect of farmers? Besides this, his eyes were much too small, brown bugs darting about in his face. Altogether not a fit companion for the young lady in the nearby field.

Now that I had suitably disposed of the first three, I turned my attention to the last member of the group. He was dressed differently, even flamboyantly, his coat a riot of red and blue, his pantaloons a yellow-green. And the conical black cap that rose at an angle above his head of curly red hair carried a seal. The seal of the magician's guild. I turned to Ebenezum.

He waved an arm clad in the much more respectable royal blue, inlaid with threads of gold, in the other's direction. "A merchant mage," he said, his voice heavy with distaste. "Sometimes you just can't avoid them."

The gaudily clad pretender to the sorcerous arts bowed low as we approached. "Greetings, fellow practitioners!" he called behind a smile that cut across the lower third of his face. "I am Glauer, master magician."

Although the merchant stood a good two inches taller than my master, Ebenezum still managed to stare down at him. "Ebenezum," he said, his tone quiet and clear in its authority, "and Wuntvor, his apprentice."

"Ebenezum," Glauer whispered, and his eyes shifted away for a minute, stunned by the presence of so great a mage. But his gaze snapped back just as quickly, his eyes filled with a cunning that brought new meaning to his merchant smile. Glauer had heard the rumors.

"I have been talking to these good citizens," the merchant continued, his voice, if possible, even bolder and more brash than before. "They tell me that their employer is having a bit of trouble with the spirits. 'Tis probably far too small a matter for one of your eminence, but I thought I might offer my humble assistance."

"Magician Glauer," Ebenezum intoned in a voice so powerful that it caused the farmhands to take a few steps back from the merchant. "These are my people. They are my trust. No task is too large, nor too small, where the people of this village are concerned!"

Glauer stepped closer, his voice and expression both subdued. "I meant no disrespect, sir. We in the profession must do everything we can to help one another. I have heard of your recent misfortunes, and would like to offer my not insubstantial services. Very discreetly, of course. And for the merest portion of the fee you will receive from the grateful farmer. Come now!" He touched my master's deep blue sleeve. "Surely you could use my services?"

"Services?" Ebenezum shook away the other man's hand, his voice full of wizardly rage. "I can think of nothing of yours we can use. We have no need at the moment for pots or pans!"

He turned towards the others. "Now, can someone tell us where we might find Master Samus?"

The thin hand pointed. "He'll be in the main house, beyond the barn there."

Ebenezum nodded and strode briskly towards the main house, leaving me hard pressed to keep up. Behind us I could hear the twin laughter of teeth and the ear, and I imagined the merchant still scowled in our direction. The other man seemed not to have reacted one way or the other to the incident. Rather, the last time I glimpsed him, he had stared thoughtfully off towards the horizon.

We rounded the barn enclosure and spied the great stone house, closer to a mansion than a cottage, with a bit of a fortress thrown in for good measure. The place looked as if it had been built to withstand any discretion of man or nature. It occurred to me that there was only one power that the formidable structure was not proof against: magic.

Shutters banged open on an upper story, and Samus' balding head appeared between two elaborately carved gargoyles. "Good! Good!" he cried. "I'll be down immediately!"

"You must be the magicians," a voice said behind us. A voice, which at the very least combined the sweetest notes ever sung by nightbirds with the fluid music of a forest stream. I turned to see the young woman of the field. The pack I had been removing from my back slipped and threatened to fall. Whether it was my quick move or the moisture that had suddenly appeared on my palms where I gripped the straps, I do not know, but what was apparent was the imminent breakage of many arcane and irreplaceable pieces of sorcerous equipment on the stone steps on which we stood. I tried to juggle the load back to balance, but it was beyond me. The pack fell. If not for the quick moves of Ebenezum, who worked with the speed known only to magicians and others familiar with sleight-of-hand, the box would have met stone and sure destruction.

I turned and smiled at the girl. Her look of alarm over recent events turned to a smile in return. Behind me, Ebenezum said something that I did not quite catch, save that the tone was rather harsh in the presence of one as perfect as the loveliness approaching.

"Rather a close call," she said softly. Her lips made each word a beautiful experience.

I waved aside her concerns. "'Tis nothing. Are we not magicians? A wave of our hands, and the box would fall up!" A good choice of words, that. Her eyes grew wide with wonder.

I became aware of other voices. One was that of Samus. "This is Alea, my only daughter."

"Most pleased," said my master, and I lost the blue of her eyes for a minute as she acknowledged the mage. Fortunately, they returned to me almost immediately, and my world was whole again.

Someone was calling my name. Repeatedly.

"Wunt!" It was Ebenezum. I nodded vaguely in his direction. "Master Samus is taking me on an inspection of his lands, so that I might see the affected areas for myself. If you could manage it, I would like you to set up our equipment just inside the barn."

"The barn?" I said, unable to take my eyes away from Alea. "Very good."

"Yes, the barn! This very minute!"

That broke the spell for a second. I glanced at my master (avoiding the eyes) and grabbed my pack and staff.

"Would you like me to show you the way?" Alea said. Her hand brushed against mine, cool and light.

I smiled and nodded and we walked the twenty paces to the livestock enclosure.

A graceful finger pointed to one of the pens. "That's where the hog was killed. We found him dead one dawn, wedged between two fence slats." I nodded, savoring every word. Each of her inflections was like a minstrel song.

We walked in silence for a minute. "How do you find farm life?" I said, mostly to hear her voice again.

The corners of Alea's mouth turned down, bringing a charming wistfulness to her face. "Mosttimes, dull," she said. "Life is slow out here; full of chores and the same old faces. It is not one tenth so interesting, I am sure, as your exciting life in the village."

I shrugged. "I suppose so. Still, you have the open air and the friendship of the others working on the farm, don't you?"

"Ah, Wuntvor, there are some things that the air cannot give you. As to the others, all Father ever thinks of is money. Two of our hands. Frinak and Franik, they're brothers, you know, they're nice, but – frankly – they're rather simple. And as to the other hand . . ." She sighed.

"The other hand?" I prompted, hoping that my interest in the matter was not too obvious.

"Tollar? He's sweet, I guess, in a way. A little coarse, of course. He's very taken with me, you know. He even asked for my hand in marriage. Of course, that would never do. As Father is continually reminding me, Tollar is far below my station."

She touched my elbow. "If we turn here, we can enter the back door of the barn." She led me around a corner of the weathered wooden structure. She held my arm firmly now. "There's a hay loft that I think you'll be particularly interested in."

I was looking at her, and so did not see the foot until it struck me on the forehead. I stumbled against her but managed to keep from falling. She hugged me suddenly and strong, an action I found delightfully surprising until I saw the reason for it. The foot that hit me belonged to Tollar, the third hand, or at least what was left of him. His body hung from the rafters, strangely dark and bloated.

"Perhaps," I whispered, "we should go out and find my master."

Alea agreed that that was a very good idea. Neither of us particularly cared to pass beneath the corpse again, so that we decided to walk as quickly as possible through the barn's all-too-dark interior. Holding each other as tightly as movement would allow, we began our flight through the shadowed recesses to the small square of light at the other end.

Then came the banging in the loft, so loud that we would have heard it even if we hadn't lost the power to speak (and possibly to breathe). We ran.

Out into the sunlight. Both of us, shouting at the top of our voices. Out to the approaching Samus and Ebenezum, both clearly astonished at our behavior.

"Is there something wrong?" Ebenezum inquired.

"Magic!" Alea said.

Ebenezum pulled at his beard. "If so, it will be the first I've seen today. Come. Show us this sorcery."

We led them back to the barn. As we walked, I told the wizard about the strangely altered farm hand.

"But you say there's been no sorcery?" I asked.

"Nary a twitch." Ebenezum rubbed his nose.

"But Farmer Samus—"

The mage cut me off with a wave of his palm. "There is more here than is apparent to the eye."

We turned the corner of the barn. The doorway was empty. The body was gone.

"Obviously," Ebenezum added.

"What are you trying to do, daughter?" Samus exploded.

"But Tollar!" Alea said. "And the noise—"

Ebenezum raised his hand for silence. There were still noises inside the barn.

"What does this mean?" Samus asked.

The mage's hand went even farther up in the air. He sneezed.

Two figures could be seen in silhouette as they escaped through the far door of the barn.

"Sorcery!" Ebenezum cried.

"Those two, running?" the farmer asked.

"No, closer! Much closer." The wizard's sleeve flew to his nose. He lowered it after a moment. "That's better. Near this door. A recent spell, but minor at best." He turned to me. "Describe what happened again."

I retold the story carefully, point by point: the foot; Alea and then me seeing the body with the odd distortions.

Alea began to sob. "Poor Tollar. What did he do to deserve

this? He might have been beneath my station, but he was sweet."

I put my hand on her shoulder to comfort her. Samus glared at me rather pointedly. I took my hand away.

Samus looked at my master. "But what about the body?"

Ebenezum sniffed, "Oh, I expect we'll see it again, sooner or later."

Alea's tears broke out anew.

"I believe the best course would be to explore our surroundings," Ebenezum continued, already walking out of the barn, "and interview everyone we meet."

Especially anyone traveling in pairs, I silently added. I retrieved my staff. I might have need of it.

We met the two other hands at the edge of the pens. They were herding a small flock of sheep into one of the enclosures.

"Franik!"

One hand looked up. "Yes, Master Samus?"

"Have you seen anyone pass here?"

The hand's broad brow wrinkled. He took his finger from his ear to scratch at his receding hairline. "Anyone? Since when, master?"

"Any strangers, then?"

"Strangers?"

"Two of them!" Samus was getting a bit red in the face.

"Let's see. Not that I can recall. Wait a minute. Frinak?"

"Yes, brother?"

"Did you see anyone?"

"Any strangers? Not that I can recall. Leastways, not today. As I remember, someone new passed by a week ago Tuesday. Would that be any help? Don't get many new faces around here."

This was getting us nowhere. There was obviously only one pair of men unaccounted for anywhere around the farm. I decided to take a more direct approach.

I stepped forward, pointing my staff at the two villeins.

"What were you two doing in the barn?"

That startled them. "In the barn?" one of them said (I think it was Franik). "We do all sorts of things in the barn."

"That's true. We bail hay."

"Feed the stock."

" 'Course we shovel manure." They both made a face – the same one. "That job always takes too long. Be surprised how much manure just one horse or cow can come up with. Some of them not even full grown, either."

"No!" I said, frantic to end this line of conversation. "Not what do you do when you're in the barn. *When* were you in the barn?"

"Oh, all sorts of times. Days, nights. Can't tell, exactly."

I rapped my staff on the poached earth. "No! When were you in there *last*?" My brow was getting moist from the mental exertion. Were they going to thwart me in front of my master? In front of Alea?

Even worse, could they really be innocent?

My questioning was cut short by a clatter on the road. I looked past the hands. Whatever made the noise was hidden by a copse of trees.

"Aha!" Ebenezum cried. "I thought he'd show himself eventually! Quick, Wunt! Through those trees!" I followed him at a good trot into the woods.

The trees soon thinned to bushes, and the shrubbery boarded a road. A wagon was leaving a hiding place of overgrown greenery, making for the mud path that passed for a country highway.

"Quick, Wunt! They mustn't get away!"

I sprinted ahead as the wagon turned onto the lane. It was brightly painted in red and yellow, drawn by a single horse whose harness was decorated with multi-colored plumes. Large letters on the side proclaimed "The Great Glauer, Magician-at-Large."

I put on extra speed and darted in front of the horse. "Stop!" I cried and raised my staff. "If you value your safety!"

The staff almost dropped from my hands. There, on the wagon seat, was Glauer, reins in hand. But next to him sat the unexpected. Tollar. Alive.

Well, we had faced worse things than reanimated corpses. Or so I told myself at the moment. I reaffirmed my grip on the staff, ready to thwack anyone who made a move against me.

"Oh, Fesnard Encundum!" Glauer said in a peeved tone. He made a series of three mystic passes.

A spell of entanglement! I tried to fight it off, but the magic was already at work in my system. My arms wrapped around my body, reaching with intertwined fingers for the legs which in turn sought my chin. Soon, I would be caught in a hopeless knot!

Ebenezum stepped in front of the carriage. "Stop, knave!" he cried. "You'll not find me so easy to deal with!"

Was there going to be a magician's duel? I watched helplessly from my prison of arms and legs.

"Wait!" It was Tollar speaking. "Everything can be explained!"

Ebenezum stopped himself mid-gesture and wiped his nose, his hands ready to conjure should there be any treachery.

"This is my fault entirely," Tollar said. "It's all for Alea. I couldn't live without her. Oh, she's friendly enough. I'll grant that. But she wouldn't marry me. Her father insists that I am beneath her station!"

He hit the wooden seat beside him with his fist. "Beneath her station! I couldn't bear it! I decided to take matters into my own hands. I'd arrange for certain small disasters to occur. When Samus was convinced that he was cursed, I would bring Glauer in. And circumstances would present themselves so that Glauer could remove the curse only with my help. I would be a hero. Perhaps enough of a hero to marry Alea.

"The plan was a good one. Samus is notoriously tight. Even with a curse, I figured he would not pay for a magician with a stature greater than Glauer's!" The last remark warranted a vitriolic look from the merchant.

"But," Tollar continued, "as fortune would have it. Samus heard that Ebenezum's rates had declined. To get a sorceror of his reputation for little more than Glauer was a bargain even Samus couldn't pass. It was hopeless – unless we moved quickly and put our plan into effect before Ebenezum could interfere.

"The barn was the best place; in the midst of the farm, yet our actions would be hidden. What better place to come up with a quick supernatural explanation, not to mention a magical cure?

"And all would have gone well, if you hadn't stumbled on me before we were ready."

Tollar's bloated body returned to my mind's eye. "But your—"

"Simple hallucination spell," Ebenezum muttered.

"Well, I had to think fast!" Glauer barked. "You can't expect a masterpiece every time!"

"Master—" Ebenezum growled, but stopped to let Tollar finish his tale.

"Once you'd spotted us, the game was over. I decided we should leave as quietly as possible. However, we failed even there."

"Little wonder," Ebenezum said, glaring at the other magician.

"That does it!" Glauer screamed. "I'll not suffer humiliation at the hands of a mage who has lived off his reputation for the past twenty years!"

"What?" Ebenezum quickly returned his hands to gesture position.

"I have resources far beyond your imagination, mage!" Glauer shouted. "My plan was brilliant, dazzling in scope!" He pulled a large bottle, mottled blue and green, from behind the seat of the cart. "Would you expect a minor magician to control such as this?"

Ebenezum's hands dropped to his sides. "Netherhells, man! You know not what you hold!"

Glauer smiled at that. "Quite the contrary. I know its power, and its risk."

Tollar and I looked from one magician to the other. Tollar said it first: "What is it?"

Glauer held it aloft, the better for all to see. "Bottled demon."

"Put it down, man!" Ebenezum urged. "If it gets loose it might devour us all."

Glauer's smile got broader still. "What? The great magician is afraid? What will people say, when Glauer defeats a demon the great Ebenezum was afraid to face?"

With that, he pulled the cork from the bottle.

And a demon materialized in our midst. Short, squat, the color of dirty brick. He appeared to be a bit musclebound, although it just may have been that he had four arms where most of us have two.

"Good afternoon," the creature said in a voice of cultured gravel. "Dinner time."

"He must be contained!" Ebenezum cried, clutching his nose.

"Contained?" Glauer waved the bottle. "I thought that was part of the enchantment. The fellow who sold me this bottle assured me . . ."

"Tasty, tasty morsels," the demon said, allowing its head to circle completely around and survey each of us in turn. It stopped when it saw me. "Entangled. How nice. A quick bite."

It stepped towards me.

Glauer continued to make a series of gestures towards the creature, none of which seemed to have any effect at all. Tollar mentioned something about it being high time he sought his fortune in the west and sprinted into the fields. Ebenezum waved his hand towards me just before he sneezed. I was free! I grabbed my staff and jumped to my feet.

"Come now, lad," the demon said. "Let's not be difficult. Just one swallow. You'll like it in my stomach. They tell me it's quite colorful." It took another step forward.

I hit the top of its head as hard as I could with my staff.

"Upstart!" The creature's eyes filled with demonic anger. "It would have been so easy. A simple swallow! Now, I'll be forced to chew!"

It lunged for me. My feet, seeking to get as far and fast as possible, tripped. I fell. The creature's claws swept the air above me. I managed to rap its head with my staff again. The demon screamed in a rage beyond the human as Ebenezum shook his head briskly and managed a quick breath. He mumbled a few quick words before the sneezing started again. The demon was pulled away from me by invisible forces.

"Magicians!" The demon spun to face the other two; Ebenezum caught in a sneezing fit, Glauer lost in his ineffectual gestures.

"You!" It pointed at Glauer, who, after all, was the only one currently involved in anything vaguely sorcerous. "I'll teach you to come between me and my dinner!"

"Stop, demon!" Glauer shrieked. He waved interlocked fingers at the creature as he stamped his right foot in a peculiar rhythm. It appeared to do as little good as anything he had done before.

The demon's tail flicked with irritation. "Must we be so tiresome?" It surveyed the merchant mage, a forked tongue passing over crooked fangs. "Yes, you'll do quite nicely."

"Hold!" Glauer said, changing his gestures. "I am not the great magician here!"

"Really?" the demon said as it strolled towards its snack. "And who is? Perhaps," it gestured towards Ebenezum, "that pitiful human lost in a sneezing fit?"

Glauer gave up his gestures altogether. The demon was upon him. "Wait!" he cried. His voice was getting higher by the word. "My resources are virtually without limit. Perhaps I have something to offer you."

"Most assuredly." The demon reached for him. " 'Tis called a full stomach."

"But . . ."

"Alas, magician. We all have our bad days." It swallowed Glauer with rather more noise than was necessary.

The creature wiped its fangs with the back of a clawed hand, then turned to face Ebenezum and me. "Who's next?"

Ebenezum took a deep breath. A dozen words flew from his mouth, his hands dancing around them.

The demon began to fade. It looked down at its disappearing form. "Oh, drat!" it said. "And me without a decent meal in eight hundred years! Ah, well." It waved in our direction. "Perhaps we shall meet again, my tasty tidbits. Ta ta – for now."

Its words hung in the now empty air, only a faint sulfur smell left behind. Ebenezum had a final sneezing fit, then was able to breathe again.

Alea ran towards us out of the woods, followed by Samus walking at a more leisurely pace. She rushed straight to me, saying how worried she had been and how brave I was. After so arduous a day, I decided that I could stand there for a moment and absorb the praise.

"What happened?" Samus asked as he approached Ebenezum.

The wizard shrugged his sleeves out to a more respectful position before looking the gentleman farmer in the eye. "Alas," he said. "Poor Glauer. He let the bottle get the better of him."

III

"There is nothing so rewarding as a day's work well done, save perhaps for a full stomach with a warm fire, a purse full of gold, or a three day vacation in the pleasure gardens of Vushta."

—from *The Teachings of Ebenezum*, Vol. 23

Ebenezum had gone into the great house with Samus to explain what had happened on the farm, as well as to demand a larger fee (it *had* been a demon, after all!). So it was that I found myself alone with Alea again. I must admit, had it not been for her presence, I would have long since quit this dismal countryside.

I walked with her in silence around the farm, caught in her fragile web of beauty. She took my hand at last and led me to the door of the barn, the place where we had first come together – unpleasant though the initial circumstances might have been. Now, with all sorcery fled, the enclosure was a different place, filled with quiet dark and the soft smell of hay. I looked into Alea's face, the lines even more graceful in shadow.

"Alea," I said, my voice stuck in my throat. "Do you think that – the two of us . . ."

She laughed; the wind through a mountain stream. "Dear Wuntvor! I'm afraid that's impossible. Father would never allow it. You are far beneath my station."

My world fell away from me. Agony stabbed my chest. My eyes searched the straw-strewn floor for answers.

Alea pulled my hand. I blindly followed. She spoke brightly. I forced myself to make sense of the words.

"—and I want to show you the hay loft. It's very comfortable. And very private."

She turned to me, her eyes catching mine. "Father conducts my formal affairs. He pays no attention to my recreation."

She smiled a tiny smile and led me to a ladder in the hay-strewn dark.

I began to see some advantages to the farming life.

GOLDEN APPLES OF THE SUN

Gardner Dozois, Jack Dann and Michael Swanwick

I can't think of many occasions when three authors have collaborated on a single short story, and three such distinguished writers at that. Gardner Dozois (b. 1947) is the esteemed editor of Asimov's Science Fiction Magazine *and has been writing science fiction and fantasy since 1966. His few novels are either fast-paced adventures, as in* Nightmare Blue *(1975), or explore emotional relationships, as in* Strangers *(1978), and it is only in his short stories that his humour breaks to the surface. Jack Dann (b. 1945) has been writing since 1970, mostly science fiction such as the intensely charged* The Man Who Melted *(1984). Michael Swanwick (b. 1950) began writing in 1980 and is also best known for his science fiction, especially the award-winning* Stations of the Tide *(1991), but he also produced the challenging fantasy* The Iron Dragon's Daughter *(1993). Quite how the three produced this seamless story is a miracle in itself.*

Few of the folk in Faërie would have anything to do with the computer salesman. He worked himself up and down one narrow, twisting street after another, until his feet throbbed and his arms ached from lugging the sample cases, and it seemed like days had passed rather than hours, and *still* he had not made a single sale. Barry Levingston considered himself a first-class salesman, one of the *best*, and he wasn't used to this kind of failure. It discouraged and frustrated him, and as the afternoon wore endlessly on – there was something funny about the way time passed here in Faërie; the hazy, bronze-colored Fairyland sun had hardly moved at all across the smoky amber sky since he'd arrived, although it should certainly be evening by *now* – he could feel himself beginning to lose that easy confidence and unshakable self-esteem that are the successful salesman's most essential stock-in-trade. He tried to tell himself that it wasn't really *his* fault. He was working under severe restrictions, after all. The product was new and unfamiliar to this particular market, and he was going "cold sell". There had been no telephone solicitation programs to develop leads, no ad campaigns, not so much as a demographic study of the market potential. Still, his total lack of success was depressing.

The village that he'd been trudging through all day was built on and around three steep, hive-like hills, with one street rising from the roofs of the street below. The houses were piled chockablock atop each other, like clusters of grapes, making it almost impossible to even find – much less *get* to – many of the upper-story doorways. Sometimes the eaves grew out over the street, turning them into long, dark tunnels. And sometimes the streets ran up sloping housesides and across rooftops, only to come to a sudden and frightening *stop* at a sheer drop of five or six stories, the street beginning again as abruptly on the far side of the gap. From the highest streets and stairs you could see a vista of the surrounding countryside: a hazy golden-brown expanse of orchards and forests and fields, and, on the far horizon, blue with distance, the jagged, snow-capped peaks of a mighty mountain range – except that the mountains didn't always seem to be in the same *direction* from one moment to the next; sometimes they were to the west, then to the north, or east, or south; sometimes they seemed much closer or farther away; sometimes they weren't there at *all*.

Barry found all this unsettling. In fact, he found the whole *place* unsettling. Why go *on* with this, then? he asked himself. He certainly wasn't making any headway. Maybe it was because he overtowered most of the fairyfolk – maybe they were sensitive about being so *short*, and so tall people annoyed them. Maybe they just didn't like humans; humans *smelled* bad to them, or something. Whatever it was, he hadn't gotten more than three words of his spiel out of his mouth all day. Some of them had even slammed doors in his face – something he had almost forgotten *could* happen to a salesman.

Throw in the towel, then, he thought. But . . . no, he *couldn't* give up. Not yet. Barry sighed, and massaged his stomach, feeling the acid twinges in his gut that he knew presaged a savage attack of indigestion later on. This was virgin territory, a literally untouched route. Gold waiting to be mined. And the Fairy Queen had given this territory to *him* . . .

Doggedly, he plodded up to the next house, which looked something like a gigantic acorn, complete with a thatched cap and a crazily twisted chimney for the stem. He knocked on a round wooden door.

A plump, freckled fairy woman answered. She was about the size of an earthly two-year-old, but a transparent gown seemingly woven of spidersilk made it plain that she was no child. She hovered a few inches above the doorsill on rapidly beating hummingbird wings.

"Aye?" she said sweetly, smiling at him, and Barry immediately felt his old confidence return. But he didn't permit himself to become excited. That was the quickest way to lose a sale.

"Hello," he said smoothly. "I'm from Newtech Computer Systems, and we've been authorized by Queen Titania, the Fairy Queen *herself*, to offer a *free* installation of our new home computer system—"

"That wot I not of," the fairy said.

"Don't you even know what a computer *is*?" Barry asked, dismayed, breaking off his spiel.

"Aye, I fear me, 'tis even so,' she replied, frowning prettily. "In sooth, I know not. Belike you'll tell me of't, fair sir."

Barry began talking feverishly, meanwhile unsnapping his sample case and letting it fall open to display the computer within. "—balance your household accounts," he babbled. "Lets you organize your recipes, keep in touch with the stock market. You can generate full-color graphics, charts, graphs . . ."

The fairy frowned again, less sympathetically. She reached her hand toward the computer, but didn't quite touch it. "Has the smell of metal on't," she murmured. "Most chill and adamant." She shook her head. "Nay, sirrah, 'twill not serve. 'Tis a thing mechanical, a clockwork, meet for carillons and orreries. Those of us born within the Ring need not your engines philosophic, nor need we toil and swink as mortals do at such petty tasks an you have named. Then wherefore should I buy, who neither strive nor moil?"

"But you can play *games* on it!" Barry said desperately, knowing that he was losing her. "You can play Donkey Kong! You can play *PacMan*! *Everybody* likes to play PacMan—"

She smiled slowly at him sidelong. "I'd liefer more delightsome games," she said.

Before he could think of anything to say, a long, long, *long* green-gray arm came slithering out across the floor from the hidden interior of the house. The arm ended in a knobby hand equipped with six grotesquely long, tapering fingers, now spreading wide as the hand reached out toward the fairy . . .

Barry opened his mouth to shout a warning, but before he could, the long arm had wrapped bonelessly around her ankle, not once but *four* times around, and the hand with its scrabbling spider fingers had closed over her thigh. The arm yanked back, and she tumbled forward in the air, laughing. "Ah, loveling, can you not wait?" she said with mock severity. The arm tugged at her. She giggled. "Certes, me-seems you cannot!"

As the arm pulled her, still floating, back into the house, the fairy woman seized the door to slam it shut. Her face was flushed and preoccupied now, but she still found a moment to smile at Barry. "Farewell, sweet mortal!" she cried, and winked. "Next time, mayhap?"

The door shut. There was a muffled burst of giggling within. Then silence.

The salesman glumly shook his head. This was a goddamn tank town, was what it was, he thought. Here there were no knickknacks and bric-à-brac lining the windows, no cast-iron flamingoes and eave-climbing plaster kitty cats, no mailboxes with fake Olde English calligraphy on them – but in spite of that it was still a tank town. Just another goddamn middle-class neighborhood with money a little tight and the people running scared. Place like this, you couldn't even *give* the stuff away, much less make a sale. He stepped back out into the street. A fairy knight was coming down the road toward him, dressed in green jade armor cunningly shaped like leaves, and riding an enormous frog. Well, why not? Barry thought. He wasn't having a lot of luck door-to-door.

"Excuse me, sir!" Barry cried, stepping into the knight's way. "May I have a moment of your—"

The knight glared at him, and pulled back suddenly on his reins. The enormous frog reared up, and leaped straight into the air. Gigantic, leathery, batlike wings spread, caught the thermals, carried mount and rider away.

Barry sighed and trudged doggedly up the cobblestone road toward the next house. No matter what happened, he wasn't going to quit until he'd finished the street. That was a compulsion of his . . . and the reason he was one of the top cold-sell agents in the company. He remembered a night when he'd spent five hours knocking on doors without a single sale, or even so much as a kind *word*, and then suddenly he'd sold $30,000 worth of merchandise in an hour . . . suddenly he'd been golden, and they couldn't say no to him. Maybe that would happen today, too. Maybe the next house would be the beginning of a run of good luck . . .

The next house was shaped like a gigantic ogre's face, its dark wood forming a yawning mouth and heavy-lidded eyes. The face was made up of a host of smaller faces, and each of *those* contained other, even smaller faces. He looked away dizzily, then resolutely climbed to a glowering, thick-nosed door and knocked right between the eyes – eyes which, he noted uneasily, seemed to be studying him with interest.

A fairy woman opened the door – below where he was standing. Belatedly, he realized that he had been knocking on a dormer; the top of the door was a foot below him.

This fairy woman had stubby, ugly wings. She was lumpy and gnarled, and her skin was the texture of old bark. Her hair stood straight out on end all around her head, in a puffy nimbus, like the Bride of Frankenstein. She stared imperiously up at him, somehow managing to seem to be staring *down* her nose at him at the same time. It was quite a nose, too. It was longer than his hand, and sharply pointed.

"A great ugly lump of a mortal, an I mistake not!" she snapped. Her eyes were flinty and hard. "What's toward?"

"I'm from Newtech Computer Systems," Barry said, biting back his resentment at her initial slur, "and I'm selling home computers, by special commission of the Queen—"

"Go to!" she snarled. "Seek you to cozen me? I wot *not* what abnormal beast that be, but I have no need of mortal kine, nor aught else from your loathly world! Get you gone!" She slammed the door under his feet. Which somehow was every bit as bad as slamming it in his face.

"Sonofa*bitch*!" Barry raged, making an obscene gesture at the door, losing his temper at last. "You goddamn flying fat pig!"

He didn't realize that the fairy woman could hear him until a round crystal window above his head flew open, and she poked her head out of it, nose first, buzzing like a jarful of hornets. "Wittold!" she shrieked. "Caitiff rogue!"

"Screw off, lady," Barry snarled. It had been a long, hard day, and he could feel the last shreds of self-control slipping away. "Get back in your goddamn hive, you goddamn pinocchio-nosed mosquito!"

The fairy woman spluttered incoherently with rage, then became dangerously silent. "So!" she said in cold passion. "*Noses*, is't? Would villify *my* nose, knave, whilst your *own* be uncommon squat and vile? A tweak or two will remedy *that*, I trow, and exchange the better for the worse!"

So saying, she came buzzing out of her house like an outraged wasp, streaking straight at the salesman.

Barry flinched back, but she seized hold of his nose with both hands and tweaked it savagely. Barry yelped in pain. She shrieked out a high-pitched syllable in some unknown language and began flying backward, her wings beating furiously, *tugging* at his nose.

He felt the pressure in his ears change with a sudden *pop*, and then, horrifyingly, he felt his face begin to *move* in a strangely fluid way, flowing like water, swelling out and out and *out* in front of him.

The fairy woman released his nose and darted away, cackling ling gleefully.

Dismayed, Barry clapped his hands to his face. He hadn't realized that these little buggers could *all* cast spells – he'd thought that kind of magic stuff was reserved for the Queen and her court. Like cavorting in hot tubs with naked starlets and handfuls of cocaine, out in Hollywood – a prerogative reserved only for the elite. But when his hands reached his nose, they almost couldn't close around it. It was too large. His nose was now nearly two feet long, as big around as a Polish sausage, and covered with bumpy warts.

He screamed in rage. "Goddammit, lady, come back here and *fix* this!"

The fairy woman was perching half-in and half-out of the round window, lazily swinging one leg. She smiled mockingly at him. "There!" she said, with malicious satisfaction. "Art *much* improved, methinks! Nay, thank me not!" And, laughing joyously, she tumbled back into the house and slammed the crystal window closed behind her.

"Lady!" Barry shouted. Scrambling down the heavy wooden lips, he pounded wildly on the door. "Hey, look, a joke's a joke, but I've got *work* to do! *Lady!* Look, lady, I'm *sorry*," he whined. "I'm sorry I swore at you, honest! Just come out here and *fix* this and I won't bother you anymore. Lady, *please*!" He heaved his shoulder experimentally against the door, but it was as solid as rock.

An eyelid-shaped shutter snapped open above him. He looked up eagerly, but it wasn't the lady; it was a fat fairy man with snail's horns growing out of his forehead. The horns were quivering with rage, and the fairy man's face was mottled red. "Pox take you, boy, and your cursed brabble!" the fairy man shouted. "When I am foredone with weariness, must I be roused from honest slumber by your hurble-burble?" Barry winced; evidentally he had struck the Faërie equivalent of a night-shift worker. The fairy man shook a fist at him. "Out upon you, miscreant! By the Oak of Mughna, I demand SILENCE!" The window snapped shut again.

Barry looked nervously up at the eyelid-window, but somehow he *had* to get the lady to come out and fix this goddamn *nose*. "Lady?" he whispered. "*Please*, lady?" No answer. This wasn't working at all. He'd have to change tactics, and take his chances, with Snailface in the next apartment. "LADY!" he yelled. "OPEN UP! I'M GOING TO STAND HERE AND SHOUT AT THE TOP OF MY LUNGS UNTIL YOU COME OUT! YOU WANT THAT? DO YOU?"

The eyelid flew open. "This passes bearing!" Snailface raged. "Now Cernunnos shrivel me, an I chasten not this boisterous doltard!"

"Listen, mister, I'm *sorry*," Barry said uneasily, "I don't mean to wake you up, honest, but I've *got* to get that lady to come out, or my ass'll really be grass!"

"Your *Arse*, say you?" the snail-horned man snarled. "Marry, since you would have it so, why, by Lugh, I'll do it, straight!" He made a curious gesture, roared out a word that seemed to be all consonants, and then slammed the shutter closed.

Again, there was a *popping* noise in Barry's ears, and a change of pressure that he could feel throughout his sinuses. *Another* spell had been cast on him.

Sure enough, there was a strange, prickly sensation at the base of his spine. "Oh, no!" he whispered. He didn't really want to look – but at last he forced himself to. He groaned. He had sprouted a long green tail. It looked and smelled suspiciously like grass.

"Ha! Ha!" Barry muttered savagely to himself. "Very funny! *Great* sense of humor these little winged people've got!"

In a sudden spasm of rage, he began to rip out handfuls of grass, trying to *tear* the loathsome thing from his body. The grass ripped out easily, and he felt no pain, but it grew back many times faster than he could tear it free – so that by the time he decided that he was getting nowhere, the tail trailed out six or seven feet behind him.

What was he going to do *now*?

He stared up at the glowering house for a long, silent moment, but he couldn't think of any plan of action that wouldn't just get him in *more* trouble with *someone*.

Gloomily, he gathered up his sample cases, and trudged off down the street, his nose banging into his upper lip at every step, his tail dragging forlornly behind him in the dust. Be damned if this wasn't even worse than cold-selling in *Newark*. He wouldn't have believed it. But *there* he had only been mugged and had his car's tires slashed. *Here* he had been hideously disfigured, maybe for life, and he wasn't even making any *sales*.

He came to an intricately carved stone fountain, and sat wearily down on its lip. Nixies and water nymphs laughed and cavorted within the leaping waters of the fountain, swimming just as easily up the spout as down. They cupped their pretty little green breasts and called invitingly to him, and then mischievously spouted water at his tail when he didn't answer, but Barry was in no mood for them, and resolutely ignored their blandishments. After a while they went back to their games and left him alone.

Barry sighed, and tried to put his head in his hands, but his enormous new nose kept getting in the way. His stomach was churning. He reached into his pocket and worried out a metal-foil packet of antacid tablets. He tore the packet open, and then found – to his disgust – that he had to lift his sagging nose out of the way with one hand in order to reach his mouth. While he chewed on the chalky-tasting pills, he stared glumly at the twin leatherette bags that held his demonstrator models. He was beaten. Finished. Destroyed. *Ruined*. Down and out in Faërie, at the ultimate rock bottom of his career. What a bummer! What a *fiasco*!

And he had had such high hopes for this expedition, too . . .

Barry never really understood why Titania, the Fairy Queen, spent so much of her time hanging out in a sleazy little roadside bar on the outskirts of a jerkwater South Jersey town – perhaps *that* was the kind of place that seemed exotic to *her*. Perhaps she liked the rotgut hootch, or the greasy hamburgers – just as likely to be "venison-burgers", really, depending on whether somebody's uncle or backwoods cousin had been out jacking deer with a flashlight and a 30.30 lately – or the footstomping honkey-tonk music on the jukebox. Perhaps she just had an odd sense of humor. Who knew? *Not* Barry.

Nor did Barry ever really understand what *he* was doing there – it wasn't really his sort of place, but he'd been on the road with a long way to go to the next town, and a sudden whim had made him stop in for a drink. *Nor* did he understand why, having stopped in in the first place, he had then gone *along* with the gag when the beat-up old barfly on his left had leaned over to him, breathing out poisonous fumes, and confided, "*I'm* really the Queen of the Fairies, you know." Ordinarily, he would have laughed, or ignored her, or said something like, "And *I'm* the Queen of the May, sleazeball." But he had done none of these things. Instead, he had nodded gravely and courteously, and asked her if he could have the honor of lighting the cigarette that was wobbling about in loopy circles in her shaking hand.

Why did he do this? Certainly it hadn't been from even the *remotest* desire to get into the Queen's grease-stained pants – in her earthly incarnation, the Queen was a grimy, gray-haired, broken-down rummy, with a horse's face, a dragon's breath, cloudy agate eyes, and a bright-red rumblossom nose. No, there had been no ulterior motives. But he had been in an odd mood, restless, bored, and stale. So he had played up to her, on a spur-of-the-moment whim, going along with the gag, buying her drinks and lighting cigarettes for her, and listening to her endless stream of half-coherent talk, all the while solemnly calling her "Your Majesty" and "Highness", getting a kind of role-playing let's pretend kick out of it that he hadn't known since he was a kid and he and his sister used to play "grown-up dress-up" with the trunk of castoff clothes in the attic.

So that when midnight came, and all the other patrons of the bar froze into freeze-frame rigidity, paralyzed in the middle of drinking or shouting or scratching or shoving, and Titania manifested herself in the radiant glory of her *true* form, nobody could have been more surprised than *Barry*.

"My God!" he'd cried. "You really *are*—"

"The Queen of the Fairies," Titania said smugly. "You bet

your buns, sweetie. I *told* you so, didn't I?" She smiled radiantly, and then gave a ladylike hiccup. The Queen in her new form was so dazzlingly beautiful as to almost hurt the eye, but there was still a trace of rotgut whiskey on her breath. "And because *you've* been a most true and courteous knight to one from whom you thought to see no earthly gain, I'm going to grant you a *wish*. How about *that*, kiddo?" She beamed at him, then hiccuped again; whatever catabolic effect her transformation had had on her blood-alcohol level, she was obviously still slightly tipsy.

Barry was flabbergasted. "I can't believe it," he muttered. "I come into a bar, on *im*pulse, just by *chance*, and the very first person I sit down next to turns out to be—"

Titania shrugged. "That's the way it goes, sweetheart. It's the Hidden Hand of Oberon, what you mortals call 'synchronicity'. Who knows what'll eventually come of this meeting – tragedy or comedy, events of little moment or of world-shaking weight and worth? Maybe even *Oberon* doesn't know, the silly old fart. Now, about that *wish*—"

Barry thought about it. What *did* he want? Well, he was a *salesman*, wasn't he? New worlds to conquer . . .

Even Titania had been startled. She looked at him in surprise and then said, "Honey, I've been dealing with mortals for a lot of years now, but nobody ever asked for *that* before . . ."

Now he sat on cold stone in the heart of the Faërie town, and groaned, and cursed himself bitterly. If only he hadn't been so ambitious! If only he'd asked for something *safe*, like a swimming pool or a Ferrari . . .

Afterward, Barry was never sure how long he sat there on the lip of the fountain in a daze of despair – perhaps literally for weeks; it *felt* that long. Slowly, the smoky bronze disk of the Fairyland sun sank beneath the horizon, and it became night, a warm and velvety night whose very darkness seemed somehow luminous. The nixies had long since departed, leaving him alone in the little square with the night and the splashing waters of the fountain. The strange stars of Faërie swam into the sky, witchfire crystals so thick against the velvet blackness of the night that they looked like phosphorescent plankton sparkling in some midnight tropic sea. Barry watched the night sky for a long time, but he could find none of the familiar constellations he knew, and he shivered to think how far away from home he must be. The stars *moved* much more rapidly here than they did in the sky of Earth, crawling perceptibly across the black bowl of the night even as you watched, swinging in stately procession across the sky, wheeling and reforming with a kind of solemn awful grandeur, eddying and whirling, swirling into strange patterns and shapes and forms, spiral pinwheels of light. Pastel lanterns appeared among the houses on the hillsides as the night deepened, seeming to reflect the wheeling, blazing stars above.

At last, urged by some restless tropism, he got slowly to his feet, instinctively picked up his sample cases, and set off aimlessly through the mysterious night streets of the Faërie town. Where was he going? Who knew? Did it matter anymore? He kept walking. Once or twice he heard faint, far snatches of fairy music – wild, sad, yearning melodies that pierced him like a knife, leaving him shaken and melancholy and strangely elated all at once – and saw lines of pastel lights bobbing away down the hillsides, but he stayed away from those streets, and did his best not to listen; he had been warned about the bewitching nature of fairy music, and had no desire to spend the next hundred or so years dancing in helpless enchantment within a fairy ring. Away from the street and squares filled with dancing pastel lights and ghostly will-o'-the-'wisps – which he avoided – the town seemed dark and silent. Occasionally, winged shapes swooped and flittered overhead, silhouetted against the huge mellow silver moon of Faërie, sometimes seeming to fly behind it for several wingbeats before flashing into sight again. Once he met a fellow pedestrian, a monstrous one-legged creature with an underslung jaw full of snaggle teeth and one baleful eye in the middle of its forehead that blazed like a warning beacon, and stood unnoticed in the shadows, shivering, until the fearsome apparition had hopped by. Not paying any attention to where he was going, Barry wandered blindly downhill. He couldn't think at all – it was as if his brain had turned to ash. His feet stumbled over the cobblestones, and only by bone-deep instinct did he keep hold of the sample cases. The street ended in a long curving set of wooden stairs. Mechanically, dazedly, he followed them down. At the bottom of the stairs, a narrow path led under the footing of one of the gossamer bridges that looped like slender gray cobwebs between the fairy hills. It was cool and dark here, and almost peaceful . . .

"AAAARRRRGGHHHHH!"

Something *enormous* leaped out from the gloom, and enveloped him in a single, scaly green hand. The fingers were a good three feet long each, and their grip was as cold and hard as iron. The hand lifted him easily into the air, while he squirmed and kicked futilely.

Barry stared up into the creature's face. "Yop!" he said. A double row of yellowing fangs lined a frog-mouth large enough to swallow him up in one gulp. The blazing eyes bulged ferociously, and the nose was a flat smear. The head was topped off by a fringe of hair like red worms, and a curving pair of ram's horns.

"Pay *up* for the use a my bridge," the creature roared, "or by Oberon's dirty socks, I'll crunch you whole!"

It never ends, Barry thought. Aloud, he demanded in frustration. "What bridge?"

"A wise guy!" the monster sneered. "*That* bridge, whadda ya *think*?" He gestured upward scornfully. "The bridge *over* us, dummy! The Bridge a Morrig the Fearsome! *My* bridge. I got a royal commission says I gotta right ta collect toll from *every* creature that sets foot on it, and you better believe that means *you*, buddy. I got you dead to rights. So cough up!" He shook Barry until the salesman's teeth rattled. "Or *else!*"

"But I *haven't* set foot on it!" Barry wailed. "I just walked *under* it!"

"Oh," the monster said. He looked blank for a moment, scratching his knobby head with his free hand, and then his face sagged. "Oh," he said again, disappointedly. "Yeah. I guess you're right. Crap." Morrig the Fearsome sighed, a vast noisome displacement of air. Then he released the salesman. "Jeez, buddy, I'm sorry," Morrig said, crestfallen. "I shouldn't't'a'oughta have jerked ya around like that. I guess I got overanxious or sumpthin. Jeez, mac, you know how it is. Tryin' to make a buck. The old grind. It gets me down."

Morrig sat down, discouraged, and wrapped his immensely long and muscular arms around his knobby green knees. He brooded for a moment, then jerked his thumb up at the bridge. "That bridge's my only source a income, see?" He sighed gloomily. "When I come down from Utgard and set up this scam, I think I'm gonna get *rich*. Got the royal commission, all nice an' legal, everybody gotta *pay* me, right? Gonna clean *up*, right?" He shook his head glumly. "*Wrong*. I ain't making a lousy *dime*. All the locals got *wings*. Don't use the bridge at *all*." He spat noisily. "They're cheap little snots, these fairyfolk are."

"*Amen*, brother," Barry said, with feeling. "I know *just* what you mean."

"Hey!" Morrig said, brightening. "You care for a snort? I got a jug a hootch right here."

"Well, actually . . ." Barry said reluctantly. But the troll had already reached into the gloom with one long, triple-jointed arm, and pulled out a stone crock. He pried off the top and took a long swig. Several gallons of liquid gurgled down his throat. "Ahhhh!" He wiped his thin lips. "That hits the spot, all right." He thrust the crock into Barry's lap. "Have a belt."

When Barry hesitated, the troll rumbled, "Ah, go ahead, pal. Good for what ails ya. You got troubles too, aintcha, just like me – I can tell. It's the lot a the workin' man, brother. Drink up. Put hair on your *chest* even if you ain't got no dough in your *pocket*." While Barry drank, Morrig studied him cannily. "You're a mortal, aintcha, bud?"

Barry half-lowered the jug and nodded uneasily.

Morrig made an expansive gesture. "Don't worry, pal. *I* don't care. I figure all a us workin' folks gotta stick *together*, regardless a racè or creed, or the bastards'll grind us *all* down. Right?" He leered, showing his huge, snaggly, yellowing fangs in what Barry assumed was supposed to be a reassuring grin. "But, say, buddy, if you're a mortal, how come you got a funny nose like that, and a tail?"

Voice shrill with outrage, Barry told his story, pausing only to hit the stone jug.

"Yeah, buddy," Morrig said sympathetically. "They really worked you over, didn't they?" He sneered angrily. "Them bums! Just *like* them little snots to gang up on a guy who's just tryin' ta make an honest buck. Whadda *they* care about the problems a the workin' man? Buncha booshwa snobs! Screw 'em all!"

They passed the seemingly bottomless stone jug back and forth again. "Too bad *I* can't do none a that magic stuff," Morrig said sadly, "or I'd fix ya right up. What a shame." Wordlessly, they passed the jug again. Barry sighed. Morrig sighed too. They sat in gloomy silence for a couple of minutes, and then Morrig roused himself and said, "*What* kinda scam is it you're tryin' ta run? I ain't never heard a it before. Lemme see the merchandise."

"What's the point—?"

"C'mon," Morrig said impatiently. "I wantcha ta show me the goods. Maybe *I* can figure out a way ta move the stuff."

Listlessly, Barry snapped open a case. Morrig leaned forward to study the console with interest. "Kinda pretty," the troll said; he sniffed at it. "Don't smell too bad, either. Maybe make a nice planter, or sumpthin."

"*Planter?*" Barry cried; he could hear his voice cracking in outrage. "I'll have you know this is a piece of high technology! Precision machinery!"

Morrig shrugged. "Okay, bub, make it march."

"Ah," Barry said. "I need someplace to plug it in . . ."

Morrig picked up the plug and inserted it in his ear. The computer's CRT screen lit up. "Okay," Morrig said. "Gimme the pitch. What's it do?"

"Well," Barry said slowly, "let's suppose that you had a bond portfolio worth $2,147 invested at 8¾ percent compounded daily, over eighteen months, and you wanted to calculate—"

"Two thousand four hundred forty three dollars and sixty-eight and seven-tenths cents," said the troll.

"Hah?"

"That's what it works out to, pal. Two hundred ninety-six dollars and change in compound interest."

With a sinking sensation, Barry punched through the figures and let the system work. Alphanumerics flickered on the CRT: $296.687.

"Can *everybody* in Faërie do that kind of mental calculation?" Barry asked.

"Yeah," the troll said. "But so what? No big deal. Who *cares* about crap like that anyway?" He stared incredulously at Barry. "Is that *all* that thing does?"

There was a heavy silence.

"Maybe you oughta reconsider that idea about the planters . . ." Morrig said.

Barry stood up again, a trifle unsteady from all the hootch he'd taken aboard. "Well, that's *really* it, then," he said. "I might just as well chuck my samples in the river – I'll never sell in *this* territory. Nobody needs my product."

Morrig shrugged. "What do *you* care how they use 'em? You oughta *sell* 'em first, and then let the *customers* find a use for 'em afterward. That's logic."

Fairy logic, perhaps, Barry thought. "But how can you *sell* something without first convincing the customer that it's useful?"

"Here." Morrig tossed off a final drink, gave a bone-rattling belch, and then lurched ponderously to his feet, scooping up both sample cases in one hand. "Lemme show you. Ya just gotta be *forceful*."

The troll started off at a brisk pace, Barry practically having to run to keep up with his enormous strides. They climbed back up the curving wooden steps, and then Morrig somehow retraced Barry's wandering route through the streets of Faërie town, leading them unerringly back to the home of the short-tempered, pinocchio-nosed fairy who had cast the first spell on Barry – the Hag of Blackwater, according to Morrig.

Morrig pounded thunderously on the Hag's door, making the whole house shake. The Hag snatched the door open angrily, snarling, "What's to – GACK!" as Morrig suddenly grabbed her up in one enormous hand, yanked her out of the house, and lifted her up to face level.

"Good evenin', ma'am," Morrig said pleasantly.

"A murrain on you, lummox!" she shrieked. "Curst vile rogue! Release me at once! At *once*, you foul scoundrel! I'll – BLURK." Her voice was cut off abruptly as Morrig tightened his grip, squeezing the breath out of her. Her face turned blood-red, and her eyes bulged from her head until Barry was afraid that she was going to pop like an overripe grape.

"Now, *now*, lady," Morrig said in a gently chiding tone.

"Let's keep the party polite, okay? You know your magic's too weak to use on *me*. And you shouldn't'a'oughta use no hard language. We're just two workin' stiffs tryin' ta make a honest buck, see? You give us the bad mouth, and, say, it just might make me *sore*." Morrig began shaking her, up and down, back and forth, his fist moving with blinding speed, shaking her in his enormous hand as if she were a pair of dice he was about to shoot in a crap game. "AND YOU WOULDN'T WANT TA MAKE ME SORE, NOW, WOULD YOU, LADY?" Morrig bellowed. "WOULD YOU?"

The Hag was being shaken so hard that all you could see of her was a blur of motion. "Givors!" she said in a faint little voice. "Givors, I pray you!"

Morrig stopped shaking her. She lay gasping and disheveled in his grasp, her eyes unfocused. "There!" Morrig said jovially, beaming down at her. "That's better, ain't it? Now I'm just gonna start all over again." He paused for a second, and then said brightly, "'Evenin', ma'am! I'm sellin'... uh..." He scratched his head, looking baffled, then brightened. "... compukers!" He held up a sample case to show her; she stared dazedly at it. "Now I could go on and on about how swell these compukers are, but I can see you're *already* anxious ta buy, so there ain't no need ta waste yer valuable time like that. Ain't that right?" When she didn't answer, he frowned and gave her a little shake. "Ain't that *right?*"

"A-aye," she gibbered. "Aye!"

Morrig set her down, keeping only a light grip on her shoulder, and Barry broke out the sales forms. While she was scribbling frantically in the indicated blanks, Morrig rumbled, "And, say, now that we're all gettin' along so good, how's about takin' your spell offa my friend's nose, just as a gesture a good will? You'll do that little thing for me, *won'tcha?*"

With ill-grace, the Hag obliged. There was a *pop*, and Barry exulted as he felt his nose shrink down to its original size. *Part* of the way home, anyway! He collected the sales forms and returned the receipts. "You can let go of her now," he told Morrig.

Sullenly, the Hag stalked back into her house, slamming the door behind her. The door vanished, leaving only an expanse of blank wood. With a freight-train rumble, the whole house sank into the ground and disappeared from sight. Grass sprang up on the spot where the house had been, and started growing furiously.

Morrig chuckled. Before they could move on, another fairy woman darted out from an adjacent door. "What bought the Hag of Blackwater, so precious that straight she hastens to hide herself away with it from prying eyes?" the other fairy asked. "Must indeed be something wondrous rare, to make her cloister herself with such dispatch, like a mouse to its hole, and then pull the very hole in after her! Aye, she knew I'd be watching, I doubt not, the selfish old bitch! Ever has she been jealous of my Art. Fain am I to know what the Hag would keep from my sight. Let *me* see your wares."

It was *then* that Barry had his master-stroke. "I'm sorry," he said in his snidest voice, "but I'm afraid that I can't show it to *you*. We're selling these computers by *exclusive* license of the Queen, and of course we can't sell them to just *anyone*. I'm afraid that we certainly couldn't sell *you* one, so—"

"What!" the fairy spluttered. "*No one* is better connected at Court than I! You *must* let me buy! And you do *not*, the Queen's majesty shall hear of this!"

"Well," said Barry doubtfully, "I don't know . . ."

Barry and Morrig made a great team. They were soon surrounded by a swarm of customers. The demand became so great that they had no trouble talking Snailface into taking his spell off Barry as part of the price of purchase. In fact, Snailface became so enthusiastic about computers, that he bought *six* of them. Morrig had been right. Who cared what they used them for, so long as they *bought* them? That was *their* problem, wasn't it?

In the end, they only quit because they had run out of sales forms.

Morrig had a new profession, and Barry returned to Earth a happy man.

Soon Barry had (with a little help from Morrig, who was still hard at work, back in Faërie) broken all previous company sales records, many times over. Barry had convinced the company that the floodtide of new orders was really coming from heretofore untouched backwoods regions of West Virginia, North Carolina, and Tennessee, and everyone agreed that it was simply *amazing* how many hillbillies out there in the Ozarks had suddenly decided that they wanted home-computer systems. Business was booming. So, when, months later, the company opened a new branch office with great pomp and ceremony, Barry was there, in a place of honor.

The sales staff stood respectfully watching as the company president himself sat down to try out one of the gleaming new terminals. The president had started the company out of his basement when home computers were new, and he was only a college dropout from Silicon Valley, and he was still proud of his programming skills.

But as the president punched figures into the keyboard, long, curling, purple moose antlers began to sprout from the top of his head.

The sales staff stood frozen in silent horror. Barry gasped; then, recovering swiftly, he reached over the president's shoulder to hit the cancel key. The purple moose horns disappeared.

The Old Man looked up, puzzled. "Is anything wrong?"

"Only a glitch, sir," Barry said smoothly. But his hand was trembling.

He was afraid that there were going to be more such glitches.

The way sales were booming – a *lot* more.

Evidently, the fairyfolk had finally figured out what computers were *really* for. And Barry suddenly seemed to hear, far back in his head, the silvery peals of malicious elven laughter.

It was a *two*-way system, afterall . . .

DEATH SWATCH

Esther Friesner

Esther Friesner (b. 1951) is rapidly becoming the Queen of Comic Fantasy. Although she has produced much excellent serious fantasy, it is for her humorous work that she is best known. These include the Demons *sequence,* Here Be Demons *(1988),* Demon Blues *(1989) and* Hooray for Hellywood *(1990), and the* Gnome *sequence,* Gnome Man's Land *(1991),* Harpy High *(1991) and* Unicorn U *(1992), plus some wonderful one-off books such as* Druid's Blood *(1988) and* Yesterday We Saw Mermaids *(1991). She has also edited the audacious anthology* Chicks in Chainmail *(1995) and its follow-up* Did You Say Chicks? *(1996). She has produced scores of clever short stories since her first sale in 1982, all too few of which have been collected in book form, although you'll find a good selection in* It's Been Fun *(1991).*

Jorc the orc shifted his warty bulk from paw to paw and lugubriously announced, "I don't like it," to his companion on guard duty. "I don't like bein' held r'sponsible fer what's behind this door. Gives me the willies, it does."

"Two questions," the troll replied through his tusks. "One: What's not to like? And two: If you think the Grim Lord cares whether us poor menial slaves like his doings or not, you're crazy, even for an orc."

Jorc blinked slowly, his thick eyelids making an audible *thunk* every time they met. "Tha's not a question. I know. I can tell. Hasn't got one o' them twizzly rune-thingies at the end o't to tell you that yer voice's gotta go *up*. What makes it sound more interrogative-like."

"Ahhh," the troll said, his face showing as much innocence as possible, given its aesthetic limitations. "So it's things that make your voice go *up* that makes it a question?" And to be honest, his own voice did lift a bit at the end of that sentence, giving a creditable imitation of a rusty door hinge.

Jorc nodded vigorously and leaned back against the jamb of the monstrous door that he and the troll had been set to guard. It was a post of honor, being as it was the sturdiest portal in the Grim Lord's castle, the gateway to the tower rooms where His Awfulness lodged only those "guests" of the highest rank or the most amusing pain thresholds.

None of which had much bearing on the matter presently under discussion between these two minions.

"'Sright," Jorc said. "If it makes yer voice go up, then s'a question-rune."

"Oh," said the troll, and he took his mace and bashed Jorc squarely between the legs.

"*eee!*" Jorc trilled, folding over double.

"Well, I'll be," the troll said, regarding his mace with a false expression of maiden startlement. "And all this time I've been toting a question-rune into battle and I never knew it! If that doesn't beat all!"

"That does not beat all," came a deep voice from the shadows of the stairwell. "I do."

A figure stepped out of the stairwell, into the light cast by the twin torches flanking the great portal. The troll saw and trembled, then fell to his knees. Jorc the orc was already on his knees, but one look at this dread caller knocked him all the way down onto his belly. Both guards groveled in terror.

"My-my lord!" the troll gasped.

"Is this how you ward my prisoner?" the Grim Lord thundered. "Nutting one another?"

"N-now my lord, strictly speaking I did not 'nut' Jorc. In the first place, the term 'nutting' refers to a severe blow to the head, and in the second place, orcs do not have—"

A bolt of pure red power arced from the Grim Lord's fingertips and barbecued the troll where he stood. Even his sturdy mace was reduced to a pitiful puddle of slag. The Grim Lord casually blew the smoke from his nails. "Mmm. A shame. Now I'll never know what it is that orcs do not have. Unless you can tell me?" He bent the gaze of his awful Eye upon the still-writhing Jorc.

"Job security!" Jorc blurted, and scuttled down the stairwell and out of the castle without so much as a note of resignation left behind on his captain's desk.

The Grim Lord sighed. "I lose more Level G-7 personnel that way." A sphere of Faroverthereseeing materialized in his hand. "Captain Slugwallow! Dispatch two fresh guards to the Tower Ruthless. I am going to visit the princess. They had better be on post by the time I leave her apartments. Do I make myself clear?"

The face of a much-harried orc appeared in the sphere. The whims of optics distorted his features in the crystal so that he looked like a cross between a true orc and a hamster with fully-stuffed cheek pouches. *Then again*, the Grim Lord mused, *considering the barrack-room gossip about Captain Slugwallow's mother and her sexual inclinations* . . .

"Aye, Dread One," Captain Slugwallow said wearily. "It shall be as you command."

"It always is," the Grim Lord replied affably (for a magical megalomaniac). "By the way, give your mother my regards." He tossed the sphere into the stairwell and smiled to hear it smash. "Plenty more where that came from," he told the shadows. Turning, he regarded the heavy portal. It was secured by a large oaken bar, a crisscross of iron chains, and a combination lock threaded through a hasp in the upper right-hand corner. The Grim Lord merely gave it a pointed glance with his Eye and the whole thing turned to raspberry gelatin.

As he stepped through the swiftly melting mess, the Grim Lord yanked a pixie out of his tunic pocket and squeezed it until the sprite's eyes bugged out of their sockets. "Memo to Captain Slugwallow:" he said. "Send the royal carpenter up here along with those guards." Then he lobbed the pixie over his shoulder and went on his way.

Beyond the now-liquefied portal stood the twisty narrow stairway that scaled the dark heights of the Tower Ruthless. Even though this was the highest point in all Dire Garde, the Grim Lord's fortress, it was still as dank and moldy as the lowest dungeon. Not so much as the glimmer of a candle flame broke the pitchy blackness of this dismal aerie. Even the scuttling vermin seemed to go about their filthy lives with constant squeals and chitterings of misery. The Grim Lord set his lipless mouth in a grimace of satisfaction. Could he build 'em or could he build 'em?

At the top of the stair stood another door. This one was not locked or barred. Why bother? Anyone who could breach the lower portal clearly knew his business. Setting a second barricade in his path would accomplish nothing and merely serve to irk him. Even the Grim Lord, who could number his living enemies on the fingers of one tomato, knew better than to irk a worthy opponent. On principle, anyway.

The Grim Lord paused at the second portal and harked. No sound reached him from the other side. "Perhaps she is asleep," he murmured, and for an instant his mind – normally preoccupied with a thousand plans of conquest, world domination, and the enslavement and torture of anyone whose face he didn't like – strayed to gentler images. In his imagination he saw the wide, silk-hung bed which he had provided for his captive. Upon it slept the princess, a maiden of transcendent beauty, even for an elf of the blood royal. He sighed wistfully as he imagined her milk-white eyelids closed in blissful dreams, her diaphanous wings chastely folded over the scented curves of her lithe yet voluptuous body, her full, ripe bosom glimpsed beneath the golden veil of her hair, her slender legs inexorably drawing the beholder's eye up, up, up to rest at last upon the exquisitely tempting sight of her—

"Yipe!" cried the Grim Lord as the door spontaneously burst into flames. His musings upon the princess's many charms had caused him to inadvertently confuse the controls governing his mind's eye with his mind's Eye and the inevitable had happened. A mystic gesture turned on the castle sprinkler system, dousing the blaze. He stepped over the smoldering timbers and into the princess's chamber.

"Knock, knock," he said sheepishly.

She was not asleep. She was fully awake and dressed. (*Dang!* thought the Grim Lord.) Attended by her two handmaidens, the Princess Minuriel stood before the sole window of her tower prison, all her regal dignity upon her. She wore the gown in which she had been captured by the Grim Lord's minions, although since her imprisonment he had sent her a hundred lavish robes, each more dazzling than the last. The princess scornfully cut them up and used them for unmentionable purposes, in spite of the fact that all those sequins had to hurt.

Elves! the Grim Lord thought bitterly. *Proud creatures! If I had it my way, I'd scour them from the face of this world. Except the cute ones.* He stared at the princess, and for all his dark powers he could not conceal how he hungered for her.

"What do you want?" the princess demanded.

"The same thing I always want," the Grim Lord replied. "Your consent to be my bride."

"That you shall never have while I live, while yet there is justice in the world, hope in my heart, or breath in my body," she shot back.. "So buzz off."

The Grim Lord's mouth turned up at the corners, an uncanny expression that made him look like a soup tureen (if soup tureens could smile with an air of hovering menace). "I do not think so," he said. "My lady, the time for trifling has passed. You know, do you not, the reason why I ordered your capture, abduction, and imprisonment?"

Princess Minuriel's huge blue eyes opened even wider. "You mean it's not just because you're a squidhead?"

The Grim Lord's chuckle was deep, false, and patronizing. "I am afraid not. Although I am flattered that you noticed." He tucked a stray tentacle back into place behind his left ear. "No, my lady; charming though the, ah, charms of your body are, there is more than mere raw physical lust behind my actions."

"According to what they say about you in the elfin court, mere raw physical lust is *never* behind your actions." The princess gave him a nasty, knowing grin. "If you release me, I'll use my magic to whip you up a batch of Uncle Oriel's Quick Fix Elixir, guaranteed to put a little lift in your driftwood."

The Grim Lord's smile blinked away. Small thunderheads gathered themselves over his brow. "I do not have that problem!" he snapped. "As you will be the first to know after you give your consent to our marriage!"

"Which I will never do," Minuriel returned haughtily. "Nor is there any way for you to force your loathsome attentions upon me. Truly it is written that an elf maiden of royal blood, so long as she keep herself virgin and pure, may never be possessed in body or spirit by a pig like you unless she gives her express consent. Fat chance."

"Then you leave me no alternative. I tire of the waiting game. Behold!" The Grim Lord snapped his fingers and a fresh sphere of Faroverthereseeing materialized. This was the larger model, a crystal taller than the Grim Lord himself. It took up most of the floor space in the princess's tower cell and almost nudged one of her handmaidens out the window.

Princess Minuriel and her attendants gazed into the vision that swam out of the crystal's depths. All three of them gasped. There, before their eyes, they saw the full complement of the Grim Lord's forces massed on the borders of the elfin homeland. Ravening orcs, repulsive trolls, host upon host of the living dead, ghastly wraiths, and really ugly dogs stood poised and ready for the invasion. But this was not the deepest horror.

"*Picnic baskets!*" the princess whispered.

"Yes!" The Grim Lord was never famous for being able to suppress that nasty habit of gloating. "Packed full with all manner of noxious edibles, for my loyal forces' delectation: Limburger cheese! Garlic bagels! Lutefisk! Poi! Kim chee! Sauerkraut! Quiescently frozen artificial chocolate flavored extruded dessert product! *And there's more where that came from!*" He clapped his hands together over his head and the panorama of the dark hordes, on pleasure bent, vanished from the sphere. It was replaced by a vision of the forest elves falling like autumn leaves before the onslaught of having to watch sentient beings happily devouring foodstuffs that looked and smelled like landfill.

How can they put stuff like that in their mouths? *Eeeeeeewwwww!*
The dying cries of hapless elves echoed mercilessly within
Princess Minuriel's brain as she watched her people perish.
And of course there was the matter of litter.

"Enough!" The elfin princess threw out her hands, her own
considerable magic shattering the sphere into a billion pieces.
Her wings drooped and she bowed her head. "No more. I cannot
stand by and allow my subjects to suffer so. I will give my consent
to wed you, Grim Lord. And well I know that you do not seek to
possess me for my beauty alone, nor for the sake of true love,
and positively not because you lust for my fair young body, I
don't care what you say, you *do* have that problem. No, I know
that the real reason you would have my hand in marriage is
so that you might conquer my father's lands through his only
child. You stink."

"Not as much as lutefisk," the Grim Lord said, that old
contented-soup-tureen look back on his face. "You are as wise
as you are beautiful, my lady. I will give orders that the wedding
preparations begin at once." He turned on his heel and strode
from the room.

"Ow! Owowowowowowowow!" The Grim Lord hopped from
foot to foot, pulling slivers of the shattered Faroverthereseeing
sphere from his soles. With a single poisonous glance of his Eye,
he caused the rest of the shards to melt and fuse into a glassy
carpet. Then he departed, very much on his dignity. The elfin
maidens heard him clump down the tower stairs and slam the
brand-new door at the bottom shut behind him.

"Well, *someone's* in a pissy mood," said Shikagoel, the
princess's right-hand handmaiden. She sneered at the now-
empty doorway through which the Grim Lord had so recently
passed.

"He'll get over it," said her companion, Shiksael, as she fussed
over her mistress's wings. "Just as soon as he remembers that
he's going to get his own way with our lady."

"No, he's not," said Minuriel. Her mouth was set in
a taut, determined line that might have given even His
Abominability pause.

"But, my lady, you gave your consent!"

"So I did. And by the same enchantment that seals the

marriage bond between a highborn elfin virgin and her chosen mate, now it is his turn to give *me* something."

Shiksael was puzzled. "I heard he couldn't."

Shikagoel gave her a sharp poke with her elbow. "Not *that*. Her Highness speaks of the Gift."

"Gift?" Shiksael's usually vacant face lit up at the mention of this Word of Power.

"It is the requirement of all who would wed a daughter of the elfin royal house to grant the bride one Gift, of her own asking, before the wedding may take place," Minuriel intoned. "Unless this condition be fulfilled, the maiden is freed of her promise and must be returned to her father's house, lest a great evil befall."

"Oh, like *that's* going to scare the Grim Lord." Shikagoel snorted. "He lives with evil. He lives *for* evil. Evil is just so much diaper rash to him."

"This is a really, really, *really* great evil," Minuriel reproved her skeptical attendant. "And he knows it." A scary little half-smile touched her lips. "That's why he'll do anything to fulfill my request for a Gift . . . and that is why my Gift shall spell his doom."

"Ooh! Ooh! I get it now!" Shiksael jumped up and down, clapping her hands together excitedly. "You're going to ask him for something impossible, right?"

Shikagoel sighed. "*Not* the decimal equivalent of pi. It's been done to death."

"No," the princess replied. "By the laws governing all magic, I am forbidden to demand the impossible for my Gift. But not—" there was that nerve-scraping smile again, "—the unpleasant."

The great hall of the Grim Lord's castle was being decked out in finery suitable for the celebration of His Atrocity's nuptials. Gray garlands of swamp-blooming bug-in-the-coleslaw dripped from the rafters, nosegays of smuksmuk flowers were set out on the banquet tables, and orange crepe paper had been strewn about with a hand that understood the meaning of "lavish" but hadn't a clue to the implications of "tacky".

A raised platform had been set up directly beneath the minstrels' gallery, mercilessly out of sight of that selfsame gallery's decor. (The Grim Lord had ordered that the stone balcony be adorned with the severed heads of minstrels who refused to believe that their dread patron's *Absolutely No Polkas!* rule meant them.) It was draped with costly black silks and carpets of the finest weave. Pearls and diamonds had been scattered hither and yon to sparkle at the feet of bride and groom. The attar of rare blossoms drenched the fabrics underfoot, filling the air with their heady fragrance, although not heady enough to overcome the lingering aroma of yogurt. A bower constructed entirely of wrought silver and gold rose from the center of the platform, crowned by a single sapphire whose worth in lives and souls could not be calculated by mortal men. A honeycomb paper wedding bell dangled from the center of the pavilion.

Minuriel's expression was unreadable as her handmaidens led her into the great hall and her eyes first lit upon her future husband's decorating efforts.

"This is going to serve him right," she gritted.

The Grim Lord stood awaiting her upon the platform. He offered her a hand to help her climb the stairs, which were made entirely of the prone bodies of troll cadets who had proved themselves unable to master the making of hospital corners on their cots. There was a brief pause when one of the cadets tried to sneak a peek up the elf-maiden's wedding gown and needed to be beheaded and replaced. At last the princess stood upon the dais, facing the Grim Lord in the shadow of the paper wedding bell.

Due to religious differences, the ceremony could be performed by neither a Singer of the Light (bride's side, Orthodox) nor a Howling Priest of Slaughter (Groom's side, Reformed). As a compromise, the Grim Lord's minions trundled a heavy pulpit onto the platform, set upon it the Great Book of Intonations for All Occasions, and placed on the open pages the Grim Lord's pet chipmunk, Skully. Being the Grim Lord's pet chipmunk had transformed the simple forest creature into a green, slavering, one-eyed killing machine, as many a foolhardy servant had learned who crossed paths with the mad rodent in the castle's endless corridors. And yet, being a chipmunk, Skully still managed to retain that quality which the elves prized above all others:

"Oooooooh! He's sooooo cuuuuuuute!" cried Shiksael. She tried to pet the beast. It snapped off one of her fingers.

"Bad Skully!" said the Grim Lord severely. "No eating the attendants until after the wedding."

The chipmunk stuffed the severed digit into his cheek pouch and tried to look remorseful.

"And now," the Grim Lord announced to the massed congregation – his own warriors to an orc, the bride's family not having been notified of the impending ceremony – "Skully will scamper back and forth over the text, chittering after the fashion of his kind. When he pauses, the fair Princess Minuriel will give her spoken consent before you all to be my submissive, obedient, totally subservient spouse and I will say more or less the same thing, excluding adjectives."

"I don't understand this," Shikagoel whispered in her mistress's ear. "How can a chipmunk perform the holy ceremony of marriage?"

"In my father's court, when the Singers of the Light offer up their paeans in the High Tongue of the Somewhat Misplaced Elves, do you understand what they're saying?"

"Not a word. I don't speak High Tongue."

"Do you understand fluent Mutant Chipmunk?"

"Not a chitter."

"Then by the rule of mutual ignorance – very big in most marriage ceremonies – the Grim Lord's pet is just as qualified to unite us as any cleric in the land."

"Do you mind?" The Grim Lord glowered at the elfin maidens. "We are trying to conduct a wedding here. There'll be lots of time for gossiping with your girlfriends on the honeymoon."

"So I suspected," Minuriel muttered. Aloud, in a voice that carried to the farthest reaches of the great hall, she cried, "Halt! Grim Lord, I charge thee, stay thy chipmunk!"

"What's this?" The Grim Lord frowned. "Are you trying to back out of our agreement? Do so and you shall be condemned by the highest bonds of magic that rule our realms! I understand it hurts."

"I am backing out of nothing, my lord," the princess returned smoothly. "But by those same bonds of magic, whose power not even you dare to challenge, I call to mind the fact that we cannot be wed until you have satisfied the one condition of a royal elfmaid's marriage."

"I had the blood test," the Grim Lord snarled.

"Not that. I mean . . . the Gift!"

There came a slowly swelling murmur of expository affirmation from the assembled throng below the dais:

"Ah, yes, the Gift!"

"The Gift, of course, the Gift!"

"Well, naturally, the *Gift*."

"How could we have forgotten about the Gift?"

"Does this mean we've got to return the steak knives? Me an' t'other orcs in Company C chipped in an'—"

"Shut up, bonehead, we're talking about the *Gift*."

"Oh. I gets yer," said the young orc, who didn't.

"*The Gift*," the Grim Lord hissed – no easy task when uttering words devoid of sibilants. "You speak the truth, my lady, for which I thank you. Verily it is written in volumes as old as time and monstrously overdue at the library that unless all conditions governing the marriage of royal elf-maidens are met, grievous are then the ills which shall befall he who did not heed them. Name what it is you would have! I swear by all the dark and awesome powers at my command, it shall be done!" He thrust his mail-sheathed fists heavenward and an earthshaking peal of thunder shook the castle to its very foundations. Orcs trembled and trolls fled. Wraiths paled to mere specters of their former selves, and the Grim Lord's mortal servants left the hall to change their underwear.

And when the last reverberations of that unholy thunderclap had faded from the hall, the Princess Minuriel spoke:

"I want to redecorate."

"*What?*"

Acting as if she had just heard the most eloquent of blessings (as opposed to the monosyllable of blankest confusion) Minuriel flung her arms around the Grim Lord's neck and exclaimed, "Oh, *thank* you, darling! You won't regret this. And it'll be no trouble to you, absolutely no trouble at all. All I need from you is your cooperation; I'll handle everything else. Just wait, you'll be *so* pleased with the results, you won't know *what* to think!"

With a light laugh on her lips, she danced a few steps away from her intended spouse and began to wave her slim hands sinuously before her face, weaving invisible patterns on the air. At the same time, she recited an eldritch elfin chant of great power and antiquity.

In the front ranks, one wraith nudged another in the intangible short ribs and inquired, "What means this 'Eeny meeny chili beenee'?"

The second wraith shrugged misty shoulders. "Elves. Go figure."

As Minuriel's chant rose in intensity, a lozenge of dappled golden light took shape between her and the Grim Lord. It grew until it was man-high, then the watery curtains of brilliance parted and a tall, masterful, mighty-limbed, keen-eyed specimen stepped forth. His chin was cleft, his shoulders monumental, his hair a froth of gold, his eyes of a blue lambence to dim the great sapphire of the wedding bower with shame. He wore naught save a loincloth, a cape, and sandals laced to the knee. They were very attractive knees. Needless to add, his thews were of steel, and his very presence seemed to proclaim that he possessed the brilliance of mind to know what *thews* meant without having to go look it up in the dictionary.

His cool gaze swept the room, coming at last to rest upon the Grim Lord who, despite himself, felt distinctly uneasy under that silent evaluation. One perfectly arched eyebrow raised in inquiry. The stranger spoke:

"You are the owner of these premises?" His voice caused Shiksael to collapse in an ecstatic faint (or maybe it was just the loss of blood from where Skully had bitten off her finger) and sent Shikagoel staggering under an assault of suddenly unleashed elfin hormones.

The Grim Lord moistened the edges of his mouth. "Uh, why, yes. Yes, I am."

"Then take *this*!" cried the stranger. His hand dropped to his belt. A slender shape flashed straight for the Grim Lord's heart. Instinctively the Grim Lord launched the spell for shattering dagger blades, but to no avail. He reeled backward as the object struck him full in the chest.

"That's my standard contract," the stranger said, still holding one end of the scroll. "Go on, read it; you'll find it entirely reasonable."

Wordlessly, trying to beat back all outward signs of the heebie-jeebies, the Grim Lord accepted the scroll. As he unrolled it, the stranger turned his back to him and contemplated the great hall. "You didn't summon me a moment too soon," he pronounced. "This is all wrong, wrong, *wrong*. Whatever were you thinking of? I mean, did you decorate in the dark? Black. Oh, dear, why does it always have to be black? It's sooooo depressing." The stranger strolled across the dais, making frequent tsk-tsk sounds. From time to time he would give the trolls in the front row a sideways glance that sent them into a self-conscious frenzy, running their paws through their greasy thatches and sucking telltale bits of bone marrow out from under their yellowed fingernails.

The Grim Lord made a heroic effort and wrenched back his self-possession. "It's supposed to be depressing," he boomed. "It's a stronghold of evil. *The* stronghold of evil!"

"*Do* tell." The stranger pivoted on tiptoe to confront his employer. "And where is it carved in stone that evil has got to be done in black? I mean, evil is supposed to be an attitude, not a color scheme. Why can't evil be, oh, *que voulez-vous* . . . green? I don't know about you, but when it comes to evil incarnate, creamed spinach gets my vote."

"*Who in the nineteen netherworlds are you, you lizard-hipped blatherer?*" the Grim Lord bellowed. "And what's all this prattle of evil and spinach and voting?"

The stranger took a single, small step backward and waggled a reproving finger at him. "Temper, temper," he said. "It's all there in the contract. I am Selvagio Napp of the Borders, whom the dwarf-folk call Dado and the eleven races name Velour. I'm from the Interior Decorators' Guild, and I'm here to help you."

"I'll help you to your death, you threadbare remnant of a—" The Grim Lord's stream of invective was abruptly dammed by a gentle tap on his shoulder.

"You promised," Princess Minuriel reminded him.

The Grim Lord put his head down on his desk and screamed.

"Beg pardon, m'lud?" his living-dead manservant inquired. "I didn't quite hear that. All this racket, donchaknow."

He was right: the sound of saws, drills, and hammers reverberating through the castle made a ruckus over which not even the Grim Lord's loudest shriek might be heard. There was also the slop-slip-slap of an army of glue- and paintbrush-wielding dwarves to add to the cacophony.

The Grim Lord raised his head slowly from the desktop. "I think I shall go mad," he told the world.

"Very good, m'lud," said the zombie. "Will you be wanting to change your shirt first?"

From somewhere in the castle's innumerable suites of rooms came the sound of Selvagio bullying trolls. "No, no, *no*! *Much* too dark, *much* too gloomy! I tell you, that dungeon simply screams for pastels!"

And the hapless troll's meek reply came creeping to the Grim Lord's ear: "Surr, 'tis a dungeon. O' *course* it screams."

The Grim Lord's hand reached out to seize a statuette that stood upon his desktop. It was not a very attractive object – no doubt Selvagio would banish it to the nethermost recesses of the castle basement once he got a look at it. It might pass for the bust of a man, although such a lantern-jawed, pop-eyed, unnaturally elongated physiognomy made this a difficult call. No matter. The Grim Lord crushed it in his fist as readily as though it had been the very acme of artistic beauty. "Barkwell, bar the door," he gritted.

"Yes, m'lud," said the zombie, doing so with his own gray-green arm. "Will there be anything else, m'lud?"

"Yes, Barkwell. Stand brave. Maintain your post. *No pasaran.* That— that *creature* has been prowling my castle for months, mucking up an interior scheme it took me aeons to perfect. When the folk of these realms speak of my stronghold, they speak in tones of awe and mortal terror. The mere mention of Dire Garde is enough to make strong men faint and send lovely women into a tizzy. But now—!" He shuddered. "Now *he* is afoot. He has thrown away all the nice, thick, blocky uncomfortable furniture which I accumulated by unbending force of will and attending many, many garage sales. Cushions, Barkwell! There are now *comfy cushions* within the precincts of Dire Garde! Is there no end to the fellow's degeneracies?"

"No, m'lud," said Barkwell from his post at the door. "It would appear not."

"Have you seen what he has done with the barracks?" the Dark Lord demanded in piteous tones. "Floral wallpaper. Pleated blinds. *Ferns*, Barkwell!"

"Yes, m'lud. Ferns, as you say."

The Dark Lord let his head sink to the desktop once more, where he cradled it in his arms. His words emerged badly muffled, but still audible: "You know, Barkwell, I used to be a happy fellow. And do you know why I was happy?" Barkwell allowed that he was unaware of the cause. "I had orcs. It's a point that's been proven time and time again: unhappiness is practically an impossibility if a fellow's got enough orcs on hand. When it comes to following orders for pillage and rapine, nothing beats an orc, that's what I always say." He looked up, and his Eye held a suspicious moisture. "Barkwell, do you know why I am no longer a happy fellow?"

"No, m'lud. That is not my place to say."

"Guess."

"Very well, m'lud, in that case I should venture to surmise that your present unhappiness stems from the fact that you no longer have orcs."

"Gone!" the Grim Lord wailed. "Expelled from my sanctuary, evicted under my very Eye! And do you know why? *Because he said they didn't go with the drapes in the great hall!*"

Barkwell knit his rotting brow. "Begging your ludship's pardon for the liberty of an unsolicited observation, but there are no drapes in the great hall."

"There are now." The Grim Lord's fingers dug trenches an inch deep in the desktop. "Pink ones. He says the color's something called Shire Sunset, but I know pink when I see it and those drapes are damn well *pink*!"

"Aye, m'lud," Barkwell agreed. "Pink, as you say." The zombie sighed loudly, launching a squadron of maggots into free fall from his ashy lips. As one of the Grim Lord's living-dead servants, there were many things he wanted very badly to remark which were Not His Place To Say. Given the choice this very moment of bringing up just one of those *verboten* topics – with instant, *permanent* death to follow, naturally – he knew precisely which one he'd choose: "Goddamit, m'lud, if you can't stand the way that crepe-kisser's screwing up your castle, why don't you just drop the silly bugger off the Tower Ruthless and be done with it?"

There was a moment of silence as Barkwell realized that he had inadvertently spoken his thoughts aloud. "Oh, poop," he commented. With another sigh he disengaged his arm from the door and said, "My apologies, m'lud. I forgot myself. I'll just be toddling down to the Executioner's office to have myself burned at the stake. Might I bring you a nice cup of tea before I perish utterly?"

"Sit down," the Grim Lord directed, motioning the zombie into a hardbacked chair near the desk. Barkwell sat. "I don't blame you for this uncharacteristic outburst, Barkwell," the Grim Lord said. "None of us can be held responsible for our actions while our dear, familiar little world of torture and mayhem and elvish harassment is being set on ear by that— that—"

"Teacup twiddler?" Barkwell suggested.

"Oooooh, that's a good one!" The Grim Lord gave his servant a thumbs-up. Four times. All at once. "Now Barkwell, you've been a good and loyal servant. You posed a fair question and you're entitled to a straight answer without fear of reprisal or incineration. The reason I don't just boot Selvagio into the moat – and don't think the image doesn't taunt me damply in my dreams – is that I can't."

"Can't, m'lud?" It was not a word frequently heard from the Grim Lord, unless one counted the number of times he'd said: *No, honestly, I just* can't *eat another bite of stewed halfling!*

"Not if I ever want to make the Princess Minuriel my own. And her father's kingdom with her. If I evict her chosen champion – I mean, interior decorator – then not only do I forfeit all claim to the maiden's hand, but by the bonds of magic that invest this realm, I will be cast down from my position of power and reduced to the status of a— a— *a common archetype of evil*!" The strain was too much. The Grim Lord broke down in tears. Those corrosive drops shed by his Eye had the expected effect on the desk, which disintegrated into chunks of acid-washed wood.

The Grim Lord staunched his tears and regarded their handiwork. "Damn. And I really liked that desk," he said.

"Very true, m'lud," said Barkwell. "However, perhaps it is better thus. You have no guarantee that Selvagio would have liked it, nor that he would have allowed you to keep it."

"*Allowed* me to keep it?" The Grim Lord's words crackled through the air, leaving little puffs of ozone in their wake. "*Allowed*, say you? This is my private study! This is my refuge from the demands of absolute sorcerous omnipotence! This, Barkwell, is my *thinking corner*! I like it the way it is. Dust bunnies are our friends. Would the rascal dare to take liberties with even this, my most personal space?"

"Begging your pardon, m'lud, but you seemed to be under that impression not too long ago. When you instructed me to bar the door against him, m'lud," Barkwell elucidated.

"Oh, *that*." The Grim Lord waved away the zombie's words with a nervous laugh. "I just didn't want to be bothered by any of my underlings bursting in upon me with yet another complaint against that awful man. Since I'm not in a position to do anything to stop him, I'd only have to kill all the complainers. I've lost enough of my fighting force as it is."

"Ah, yes." Barkwell nodded. "Orcs. Drapes. Quite so."

"Do you think I *enjoy* feeling this helpless, Barkwell?" the Grim Lord implored. "It's not something I'm accustomed to, believe me. I tell you, lord-to-lich, that if someone can come up with a way for me to be rid of this meddlesome beast, I will— I will— well, I'll do my level best to keep from killing him in an offhanded manner in future."

"An offer both magnanimous and tempting, m'lud," said Barkwell. "Who could ask for anything more?" The zombie lapsed into a profound and significant silence.

"What are you thinking, Barkwell?" the Grim Lord asked.

"I, m'lud?" Barkwell returned innocently. "Thinking is not part of my job description."

"You are too thinking!" The Grim Lord smashed his fist onto his desktop. He had forgotten that he no longer had a desktop, overbalanced himself and sprawled at the zombie's feet. "Don't toy with me, Barkwell. I am a desperate locus of unfathomable evil."

"I admit, m'lud, that I did have an idea. However, I do not think you are going to like it."

"At this point, I'm ready to like *anything*. Except those goddamn pink drapes."

"In that case, m'lud, I do have a suggestion: dump her."

"What?"

"The princess, m'lud. Disentangle yourself from any alliances, domestic or otherwise, with the lady in question. Concede the match and allow her to return unharmed to the bosom of her family. Give her the royal kiss-off and get the hell out now."

"*What?*" This time the Grim Lord said it more vehemently, with a lot of veinage showing in his Eye.

Barkwell shrugged. "There comes a time in every man's life when he must examine his priorities and ask himself whether the game is worth the candle. In this case, our artistic guest will very likely adorn the niches of the Tower Ruthless with hand-dipped, patchouli-scented beeswax candles set in candelabra shaped like unicorns. He may even use *bobeches*."

"What?" Now the word was used in its purely information-seeking sense. The Grim Lord got to his feet and dusted himself off.

"Those little collars you put around the bases of candles so you don't get wax drips on the floor," Barkwell provided.

The Grim Lord shivered at the horror of it. "You're right, Barkwell. It will be hard for me to admit defeat, but better surrender and save what's left of my sanity than put up with one more day of Selvagio."

"Yoo hoo!" came a familiar voice from the far side of the study door. "I just wanted to let you know that I haven't forgotten you! I'll be coming in tomorrow to give you the high concept for a completely new vision of your study. I've found some corduroy swatches that—"

"Not a moment too soon, m'lud," Barkwell murmured.

"Corduroy . . ." The Grim Lord mouthed the word as charily as if it were a live lizard. More charily; he liked keeping live lizards in his mouth. "Is the fiend a living cornucopia of cruelties and perversions?"

"Let us fervently hope we need never learn the answer to that, m'lud," said Barkwell. Ever the considerate servant, he provided his master with a set of earplugs while on the far side of the door Selvagio continued to rhapsodize over the many uses of terra-cotta and chintz.

"Would it help if I said I'm sorry?" the Princess Minuriel asked. She was mounted on a fine steed, ready to depart Dire Garde. Her handmaidens had already passed beneath the portcullis and awaited her on the road.

"It would help if you said you're taking him with you," the Grim Lord replied. He held the bridle of her horse in a death grip. Despite all he had done to her, the expression of panic and desperation now on his face called up pity in the elf-maiden's heart-of-hearts.

"But I can't," she replied. "My father banned him from the elfin lands—"

"Your father is one smart elf."

"—and besides, you signed the contract. You can't get rid of him until he's finished the job; otherwise he'll file a grievance and the Guild of Interior Decorators will investigate."

"What do I care if—"

"Sixty-eight more Selvagios?"

The Grim Lord began to weep. This time he was able to keep his Eye out of it, so the tears that fell did not melt anything save Minuriel's heart. To her surprise, she found herself leaning over in the saddle to stroke the Grim Lord's hair – which was a very nice shade of brown if you could manage to catch sight of it between the tentacles.

"There, there," she said. "I feel just awful about this, especially since you've been so nice about letting me out of my marriage agreement with you."

"I thought you'd take him away with you!" the Grim Lord wailed. "That's the only reason I let you go free!"

"Nevertheless—" The princess didn't like to be corrected when she was riding the crest of an altruistic moment. "I feel a certain obligation to you. I must rescue you from this plight. I feel responsible. *Noblesse oblige.*"

"Is that anything like *bobeches*?" the Grim Lord asked suspiciously.

The elf-maiden dismounted. "Wait here," she instructed the

Grim Lord. "I'm going to ask Selvagio to let you out of your contract as a personal favor to me."

The Grim Lord held her horse's bridle with one hand while with the other he pressed her fingertips to his mouth. "Oh, thank you, thank you!" he enthused between grateful smooches. "I know he'll listen to you! How could anyone resist granting you anything your heart might desire?"

Despite having no lips, he was a surprisingly capable kisser. (It is a little known fact that the predominating elvish erogenous zone resides in the fingers. This accounts for the preponderance of pickpockets in the population, as well as why most elves don rubber gloves before shaking hands with orcs.) The princess felt an unwonted flush rising to her cheeks at his attentions. Almost reluctantly she disengaged her hand. "Please, there— there's no need to thank me," she stammered. Flustered, she fled into the castle.

She emerged a short time later, much changed. No longer did she blush or flutter. She was in full command of herself. She was every inch the royal virgin elf-maiden. She was nursing a slow-burning rage the size of a yak.

"That miserable little *grub*!" she bellowed, stamping her foot. One of the forecourt paving stones cracked right up the middle. The Grim Lord jumped at the sound and dropped the bridle; Minuriel's mount bolted.

"Oh! Uh . . . oops. Sorry. I'll have my men fetch you another one in just a—"

"Forget the frammin' horse!" the princess swore. "I don't *want* a horse. I want *blood*!"

"Er . . . You do?" The Grim Lord teetered between shock and hospitality. "What— what vintage?"

"*His* blood," Minuriel specified. "The thin, worthless, probably pastel blood of Selvagio Napp!"

"He— he turned you down? He refused to cancel my contract?"

"Worse!" She began to pace up and down before the Grim Lord, working herself up into a royal snit. "Just because it was my magic that summoned him to Dire Garde, he presented *me* with a bill for his travel expenses. The gall!"

"But if your magic brought him here, he *had* no travel expenses." The Grim Lord was well and truly ferhoodled.

"Well, he did have to send for his clothing and a few personal toiletry articles," Minuriel admitted. "But you'd think a real businessman would write off things like that."

The Grim Lord gazed shyly at the elfin maid. "I'd – I'd be honored to pay the bill for you," he said.

"Would you?"

The Grim Lord nodded.

"No strings attached?"

He shook his head.

Princess Minuriel looked at him – really *looked* at him – for the first time. "Why— why Your Infernality, in a certain light you're— you're— why, you're *cute*!"

"*Shhhhhh!*" The Grim Lord hushed her desperately. "You already ruined my home. Are you trying to ruin my reputation, too?"

Minuriel smiled and patted his cheek. "It'll be our little secret . . . Grimmy."

At this tender moment, Shiksael came trotting back into the castle forecourt. "What's the holdup, Your Highness?" she demanded. "Shikagoel and I thought you maybe stopped to powder your nose and fell in."

"Ah, the elegance of high elfin court training," Minuriel muttered. More audibly she said, "Come on back in and bring Shikagoel with you. We're not leaving."

"What? Why not?"

"You'll see," she said meaningfully.

The scene in the great hall was almost identical to the first time the Grim Lord attempted to espouse the Princess Minuriel. True, the severed heads on the minstrels' gallery had been replaced by plaster cherubs, the black draperies on the dais were now saffron, apricot, and gold, a thick layer of aquamarine stucco coated the walls, the drapes were unarguably pink, and someone had tied a white lace bow around Skully's neck. Other than that, everything was the same.

Her eyes luminous with devotion, the princess Minuriel spoke the wedding vows of her people: "I, Minuriel, highborn elfin virgin, which nobody can deny, do pledge to thee my heart, my hand, and my dowry, freely and of my own will, so may these witnesses attest!"

The Grim Lord then gave the proper response according to his own beliefs, namely: "Her: *Mine*!" But to do him credit, he had the good grace to look embarrassed. The massed troops cheered.

"*What* is going on here?" Selvagio came tromping into the great hall, bolts of baize and seersucker trailing behind him. "You can't marry him!" He dropped the cloth and produced his copy of the contract. "It says right here that the wedding may not take place until such time as I have been paid for my services."

Coolly Minuriel regarded the obstreperous decorator. "And how much do you expect to be paid, pray?"

Selvagio named a sum that made trolls quail and wraiths give up the ghost. Even the Grim Lord went a little chalky around the gills. The decorator was unmoved by this display. He folded his arms across his chest and said, "I don't know what all the fuss is about. Did you think monogrammed towels for a castle that has fifty-eight bathrooms were going to come cheap? Have you seen the price of terry cloth on the open market lately? I have honored my part of the contract. I expect to be paid. And furthermore, there's the matter of my travel expenses—"

"Well, it says here—" Minuriel whipped a copy of the contract from the bosom of her wedding gown, "—that you don't get paid until you've finished the job!"

"But I have!" Selvagio objected. "I've only just finished his study." He pointed at the Grim Lord.

"*My study!*" His Atrocity echoed. "Why didn't Barkwell stop you?"

"Barkwell?" Selvagio's brows knit in perplexity.

"My zombie manservant."

"Ohhhhh." The decorator was enlightened. "I mistook him for a stubborn mildew stain. A little lemon-scented cleanser, a little elbow grease, a half dozen bunny-shaped air fresheners, and he was gone."

The Grim Lord groaned. "He was my best servant! Do you know how hard it is to dig up good help nowadays?"

"I thought he was rather outspoken for mildew," Selvagio admitted. Then he shrugged. "I'll deduct the cost of the air fresheners from your final bill, but that's the best I can do."

"You'll have to do better than that," said the princess. "Or this contract is null and void. You agreed to redecorate every interior on the premises."

"But I have!" Selvagio asserted.

Minuriel's lips curved up ever so slightly at the corners. "Not quite. There is one you missed."

By now the decorator was growing irate. "I suppose you're talking about a secret chamber or some such tired old gimmick. Well, you don't get out of paying me that easily. The contract specifies that you've got to show me any interior I might have missed."

"Would you like me to show it to you now?" Minuriel asked sweetly.

"*Yes, I would!*" The veins on Selvagio's neck stood out in an alarming manner when he shouted like that.

"All right. If you insist." The elfin princess raised her hands and gestured in a style familiar to mystics and hooch-dancers everywhere. There was a thrumming, a flash of green, and the air between herself and the decorator gelled into a conveniently compact indoor-sized dragon. It tilted its head quizzically at the quaking Selvagio and, without any fuss worth mentioning, devoured him.

The princess produced a memo pad and well-chewed pencil stub. With a fine flourish she ticked an item off a list known but to herself. "That's the last interior," she announced cheerfully. "I'd say Selvagio's redecorating it just fine. Of course, as for his bill—"

The dragon gave a short, polite little cough and hawked up the former decorator's paperwork, along with half a bolt of seersucker. Ignoring the fabric, Minuriel picked up the partially digested bill and duly marked it VOID. This done, she noticed the groundswell of terror currently pervading the congregation, all of whom were regarding the dragon askance. "Oh, calm down," she directed. "He's just my dowry."

"Your dowry?" the Grim Lord echoed. "A dragon's your dowry?"

"It's an elf thing. Royal virgins receive the power to command dragons as soon as we're married; it's sort of like practice for handling husbands. Or do you think I'd have stood for being locked away in that tacky old tower of yours for so long if I could've summoned up something like *him* anytime I wanted?" The lady shrugged. "Besides, I already have a blender."

The Grim Lord regarded his bride with renewed respect. "Why, darling, in a certain light you're— you're— why, you're completely merciless!"

Minuriel blushed becomingly. "This old personality trait? I've had it for years!"

Tenderly he took her into his arms, and to the cheers of his subjects and the insane chittering of Skully, they embraced.

Jorc the orc peered around the great hall doorway. "I got fired off me paper route. Any chance o' me gettin' m'old job ba—?" He paused, awestruck by the spectacle he now beheld. "D'I miss anythin'?" he asked, hesitantly creeping to the head of the assemblage.

The dragon, who had digested Selvagio's sense of style along with the rest of the decorator, ate him. He didn't match the drapes.

PRESS ANN

Terry Bisson

Like Avram Davidson, Terry Bisson (b. 1942) is one of those treasures of fantasy and science fiction who produces highly original stories that defy categorization. Novels like Talking Man *(1986) and* Fire on the Mountain *(1988), as well as the ingenious stories in* Bears Discover Fire *(1993), show a rare talent that is always testing the boundaries of fantasy. Even the following story, which is one of his most straightforward, is far from simple.*

WELCOME TO CASH-IN-A-FLASH
1342 LOCATIONS
TO SERVE YOU CITYWIDE
PLEASE INSERT YOUR CASH-IN-A-FLASH CARD

THANK YOU
NOW ENTER YOUR CASH-IN-A-FLASH NUMBER

THANK YOU
PLEASE SELECT DESIRED SERVICE—

DEPOSIT
WITHDRAWAL
BALANCE
WEATHER

"Weather?"

"What's the problem, Em?"

"Since when do these things give the weather?"

"Maybe it's some new thing. Just get the cash, it's 6:22 and we're going to be late."

THANK YOU
WITHDRAWAL FROM—
   SAVINGS
   CHECKING
   CREDIT LINE
   OTHER

CHECKING

THANK YOU
PLEASE ENTER DESIRED AMOUNT—
   $20
   $60
   $100
   $200

$60

$60 FOR A MOVIE?

"Bruce, come over here and look at this."

"Emily, it's 6:26. The movie starts at 6.41."

"How does the cash machine know we're going to the movie?"

"What are you talking about? Are you mad because you have to get the money, Em? Can I help it if a machine ate my card?"

$60

$60 FOR A MOVIE?

"It just did it again."
   "Did what?"
   "Bruce, come over here and look at this."
   "$60 for a movie?"
   "I'm getting money for dinner, too. It is my birthday after all, even if I have to plan the entire party. Not to mention get the money to pay for it."
   "I can't believe this. You're mad at me because a machine ate my card."
   "Forget it. The point is, how does the cash machine know we're going to a movie?"
   "Emily, it's 6:29. Just press *Enter* and let's go."
   "Okay, okay."

WHO IS THE GUY WITH THE WATCH?
   BOYFRIEND
   HUSBAND
   RELATIVE
   OTHER

"Bruce!"
   "Emily, it's 6:30. Just get the money and let's go."
   "Now it's asking me about you."
   "6:31!"
   "Okay!"

   OTHER

"Excuse me, do you two mind if I . . ."
   "Look, pal, there's a problem with this machine. There's another cash machine right down the street if you're in such a goddamn hurry."
   "Bruce! Why be rude?"
   "Forget it, he's gone."

HAPPY BIRTHDAY EMILY
WOULD YOU LIKE—
   DEPOSIT

WITHDRAWAL
BALANCE
WEATHER

"How does it know it's my birthday?"

"Jesus, Em, it's probably coded in your card or something.
It is now 6:34 and in exactly seven minutes . . . what the hell
is this? *Weather*?"

"That's what I've been trying to tell you."

"You're not going to press it!"

"Why not?"

WEATHER

THANK YOU
SELECT DESIRED CONDITIONS—
    COOL AND CLOUDY
    FAIR AND MILD
    LIGHT SNOW
    LIGHT RAIN

"Em, will you quit playing around!"

LIGHT RAIN

"Rain? On your birthday?"

"Just a light rain. I just want to see if it works. We're going
to the movie anyway."

"Not if we don't get out of here."

PERFECT MOVIE WEATHER
WOULD YOU LIKE—
    DEPOSIT
    WITHDRAWAL
    BALANCE
    POPCORN

"Em, this machine is seriously fucked up."

"I know. I wonder if you get butter."

"It's 6:36. Just press *Withdrawal* and let's get the hell out of here. We have five minutes until the movie starts."

WITHDRAWAL

THANK YOU
WITHDRAWAL FROM—
   SAVINGS
   CHECKING
   CREDIT LINE
   OTHER

"Excuse me. Are you two going to see *Gilded Palace of Sin*?"

"Shit. Look who's back."

"I was just at the theater and the newspaper had the time listed wrong. According to the box office, the movie starts at 6:45. So you have nine minutes."

"I thought you were at the other machine."

"There's a line and I didn't want to stand outside in the rain."

"Rain? Bruce, look!"

"It's just a light rain. But I'm wearing my good suit."

OTHER

"Emily it's 6:37 and you're pressing *Other*?"

"Don't you want to see what else this machine can do?"

"No!"

THANK YOU
CHOOSE OTHER ACCOUNT—
   ANDREW
   ANN
   BRUCE

"Who the hell are Andrew and Ann? And how the hell did my name get in there?"

"You told me the machine ate your card."

"That was – another machine."

"Excuse me. Ann is my fiancée. Well, was. Sort of. I thought."

"Are you butting in again?"

"Wait! You must be . . ."

"Andrew. Andrew P. Claiborne III. You must be Emily. And he must be . . ."

"He's Bruce. Don't mind him if he's a little uncouth."

"Uncouth!"

BRUCE

"Hey, that's my account, Emily. You don't have any right to press *Bruce*!"

"Why not? You say you wanted to pay for dinner and the movie, but the machine ate your card. So let's go for it."

GO FOR IT, EMILY
PLEASE ENTER DESIRED AMOUNT—
   $20
   $60
   $100
   $200

$60

SORRY. INSUFFICIENT FUNDS. WANT TO TRY FOR $20?

$20

SORRY. INSUFFICIENT FUNDS.
WOULD YOU LIKE A BALANCE CHECK?

"No!"

YES

BRUCE'S BALANCE: $11.78
SURPRISED?

"Surprised? I'm furious! Some birthday celebration! You didn't even have enough to pay for a movie, much less dinner! And you lied!"

"Excuse me, it's your birthday? It's my birthday too!"

"You stay out of this, Andrew or whatever the fuck your name is."

"Don't be vulgar, Bruce. He has an absolutely perfect right to wish me a happy birthday."

"He's not wishing you a happy birthday, he's butting into my life."

"Allow me to wish you a very happy birthday, Emily."

"And to you, Andrew, the very same."

"Plus he's an asshole!"

NO NAME CALLING PLEASE
WOULD YOU LIKE ANOTHER BALANCE CHECK?
  BRUCE
  EMILY
  ANDREW
  ANN

"Ann is your girlfriend?"

"Was. She just stood me up for the last time."

"How terrible! On your birthday! Andrew, I know exactly how you feel."

"As a matter of fact, you're both a couple of assholes!"

NO NAME CALLING PLEASE
EMILY AND ANDREW,
PLEASE ALLOW ME TO TREAT YOU
TO A BIRTHDAY DINNER AND A FILM

"A hundred dollars! Andrew, look!"

"It says it's treating us. Take it, Emily."

"You can call me Em."

"I can't fucking believe this!"

"We'd better hurry. Excuse me, Bruce, old pal, do you have the time?"

"6:42. Asshole."

"If we run, we can catch the 6:45. Then, how about Sneaky Pete's?"

"I love Tex-Mex!"

PLEASE REMOVE YOUR CARD
DON'T FORGET TO TRY
THE BLACKENED FAJITAS

"You're all three assholes! I can't fucking believe this. She left with him!"

WELCOME TO CASH-IN-A-FLASH
1342 LOCATIONS
TO SERVE YOU CITYWIDE
PLEASE DON'T KICK THE MACHINE

"Go to hell!"

PLEASE INSERT YOUR CASH-IN-A-FLASH CARD

"Fuck you."

GO AHEAD, BRUCE
WHAT HAVE YOU GOT TO LOSE?

THANK YOU
IT WASN'T 'EATEN' AFTER ALL, WAS IT?

"You know it wasn't. Asshole."

NO NAME CALLING PLEASE
WOULD YOU LIKE—
    SYMPATHY
    REVENGE
    WEATHER
    ANN

"Excuse me."

"Jesus, lady, quit banging on the door. I know it's raining.

Tough shit. I'm not going to let you in. This is a cash machine, not a homeless shelter. You're supposed to have a card or something. What?"

"I said, shut up and press *Ann*."

TROLL BRIDGE

Terry Pratchett

*Terry Pratchett (b. 1948) certainly didn't invent comic fantasy –
many of the writers included in this anthology were at it long before
he was – but the success of his brilliant Discworld novels, starting
with* The Colour of Magic *in 1983, certainly created the publishing
niche for comic fantasy that didn't previously exist. Pratchett has been
writing for most of his life – his first story, "The Hades Business",
was sold when he was scarcely fifteen – but he didn't start to write
regularly until after his third novel,* Strata *(1981). That's when
the Discworld novels began to flow. Since then he's been so busy
producing them and the occasional non-Discworld book, that he's
had little time for short stories. In fact, Pratchett says he doesn't
feel comfortable working in the limitations of the short story, but you
wouldn't think that from the following, which is loosely connected to
the Discworld series.*

The air blew off the mountains, filling the air with fine ice
crystals.

It was too cold to snow. In weather like this wolves came

down into villages, trees in the heart of the forest exploded
when they froze.

In weather like this right-thinking people were indoors, in
front of the fire, telling stories about heroes.

It was an old horse. It was an old rider. The horse looked like
a shrink-wrapped toast rack; the man looked as though the only
reason he wasn't falling off was because he couldn't muster the
energy. Despite the bitterly cold wind, he was wearing nothing
but a tiny leather kilt and a dirty bandage on one knee.

He took the soggy remnant of a cigarette out of his mouth
and stubbed it out on his hand.

"Right," he said, "let's do it."

"That's all very well for you to say," said the horse. "But
what if you have one of your dizzy spells? And your back is
playing up. How shall I feel, being eaten because your back's
played you up at the wrong moment?"

"It'll never happen," said the man. He lowered himself on to
the chilly stones, and blew on his fingers. Then, from the horse's
pack, he took a sword with an edge like a badly maintained saw
and gave a few half-hearted thrusts at the air.

"Still got the old knackaroony," he said. He winced, and
leaned against a tree.

"I'll swear this bloody sword gets heavier every day."

"You ought to pack it in, you know," said the horse. "Call
it a day. This sort of thing at your time of life. It's not right."

The man rolled his eyes.

"Blast that damn distress auction. This is what comes
of buying something that belonged to a wizard," he said,
to the cold world in general. "I looked at your teeth, I
looked at your hooves, it never occurred to me to *listen*."

"Who did you think was bidding against you?" said the
horse.

Cohen the Barbarian stayed leaning against the tree. He was
not sure that he could pull himself upright again.

"You must have plenty of treasure stashed away," said the
horse. "We could go Rimwards. How about it? Nice and
warm. Get a nice warm place by a beach somewhere, what
do you say?"

"No treasure," said Cohen. "Spent it all. Drank it all. Gave it all away. Lost it."

"You should have saved some for your old age."

"Never thought I'd *have* an old age."

"One day you're going to die," said the horse. "It might be today."

"I know. Why do you think I've come here?"

The horse turned and looked down towards the gorge. The road here was pitted and cracked. Young trees were pushing up between the stones. The forest crowded in on either side. In a few years, no one would know there'd even been a road here. By the look of it, no one knew now.

"You've come here to *die*?"

"No. But there's something I've always been meaning to do. Ever since I was a lad."

"Yeah?"

Cohen tried easing himself upright again. Tendons twanged their red-hot messages down his legs.

"My dad," he squeaked. He got control again. "My dad," he said, "said to me—" He fought for breath.

"Son," said the horse, helpfully.

"What?"

"Son," said the horse. "No father ever calls his boy 'son' unless he's about to impart wisdom. Well-known fact."

"It's *my* reminiscence."

"Sorry."

"He said . . . Son . . . yes, OK . . . Son, when you can face down a troll in single combat, then you can do anything."

The horse blinked at him. Then it turned and looked down, again, through the tree-jostled road to the gloom of the gorge. There was a stone bridge down there.

A horrible feeling stole over it.

Its hooves jiggled nervously on the ruined road.

"Rimwards," it said. "Nice and warm."

"No."

"What's the good of killing a troll? What've you got when you've killed a troll?"

"A dead troll. That's the point. Anyway, I don't have to kill it. Just defeat it. One on one. *Mano a* . . . troll. And if I didn't try my father would turn in his mound."

"You told *me* he drove you out of the tribe when you were eleven."

"Best day's work he ever did. Taught me to stand on other people's feet. Come over here, will you?"

The horse sidled over. Cohen got a grip on the saddle and heaved himself fully upright.

"And you're going to fight a troll today," said the horse.

Cohen fumbled in the saddlebag and pulled out his tobacco pouch. The wind whipped at the shreds as he rolled another skinny cigarette in the cup of his hands.

"Yeah," he said.

"And you've come all the way out here to do it."

"Got to," said Cohen. "When did you last see a bridge with a troll under it? There were hundreds of 'em when I was a lad. Now there's more trolls in the cities than there are in the mountains. Fat as butter, most of 'em. What did we fight all those wars for? Now . . . cross that bridge."

It was a lonely bridge across a shallow, white, and treacherous river in a deep valley. The sort of place where you got—

A grey shape vaulted over the parapet and landed splay-footed in front of the horse. It waved a club.

"All *right*," it growled.

'Oh—" the horse began.

The troll blinked. Even the cold and cloudy winter skies seriously reduced the conductivity of a troll's silicon brain, and it had taken it this long to realize that the saddle was unoccupied.

It blinked again, because it could suddenly feel a knife point resting on the back of its neck.

"Hello," said a voice by its ear.

The troll swallowed. But very carefully.

"Look," it said desperately, "it's tradition, OK? A bridge like this, people ort to *expect* a troll . . . 'Ere," it added, as another thought crawled past, " 'ow come I never 'eard you creepin' up on me?"

"Because I'm *good* at it," said the old man.

"That's right," said the horse. "He's crept up on more people than you've had frightened dinners."

The troll risked a sideways glance.

"Bloody hell," it whispered. "You think you're Cohen the Barbarian, do you?"

"What do *you* think?" said Cohen the Barbarian.

"Listen," said the horse, "if he hadn't wrapped sacks round his knees you could have told by the clicking."

It took the troll some time to work this out.

"Oh, *wow*," it breathed. "On *my* bridge! Wow!"

"What?" said Cohen.

The troll ducked out of his grip and waved its hands frantically. 'It's all right! It's all right!" it shouted, as Cohen advanced. "You've got me! You've got me! I'm not arguing! I just want to call the family up, all right? Otherwise no one'll ever believe me. *Cohen the Barbarian*! On *my* bridge!"

Its huge stony chest swelled further. "My bloody brother-in-law's always swanking about his huge bloody wooden bridge, that's all my wife ever talks about. Hah! I'd like to see the look on his face . . . oh, no! What can you think of me?"

"Good question," said Cohen.

The troll dropped its club and seized one of Cohen's hands.

"Mica's the name," it said. "You don't know what an honour this is!"

He leaned over the parapet. "Beryl! Get up here! Bring the kids!"

He turned back to Cohen, his face glowing with happiness and pride.

"Beryl's always sayin' we ought to move out, get something better, but I tell her, this bridge has been in our family for generations, there's always been a troll under Death Bridge. It's tradition."

A huge female troll carrying two babies shuffled up the bank, followed by a tail of smaller trolls. They lined up behind their father, watching Cohen owlishly.

"This is Beryl," said the troll. His wife glowered at Cohen. "And this—" he propelled forward a scowling smaller edition of himself, clutching a junior version of his club – "is my lad Scree.

A real chip off the old block. Going to take on the bridge when I'm gone, ain't you, Scree. Look, lad, this is Cohen the Barbarian! What d'you think o' that, eh? On *our* bridge! We don't just have rich fat soft ole merchants like your uncle Pyrites gets," said the troll, still talking to his son but smirking past him to his wife, "we 'ave proper heroes like they used to in the old days."

The troll's wife looked Cohen up and down.

"Rich, is he?" she said.

"Rich has got nothing to do with it," said the troll.

"Are you going to kill our dad?" said Scree suspiciously.

"*Corse* he is," said Mica severely. "It's his job. An' then I'll get famed in song an' story. This is Cohen the Barbarian, right, not some bugger from the village with a pitchfork. 'E's a famous hero come all this way to see us, so just you show 'im some respect.

"Sorry about that, sir," he said to Cohen. "Kids today. You know how it is."

The horse started to snigger.

"Now look—" Cohen began.

"I remember my dad tellin' me about you when I was a pebble," said Mica. "'E bestrides the world like a clossus, he said."

There was silence. Cohen wondered what a clossus was, and felt Beryl's stony gaze fixed upon him.

"He's just a little old man," she said. "He don't look very heroic to me. If he's so good, why ain't he *rich*?"

"Now you listen to me—" Mica began.

"This is what we've been waiting for, is it?" said his wife. "Sitting under a leaky bridge the whole time? Waiting for people that never come? Waiting for little old bandy-legged old men? I should have listened to my mother! You want me to let our son sit under a bridge waiting for some little old man to kill him? That's what being a troll is all about? Well, it ain't happening!"

"Now you just—"

"Hah! Pyrites doesn't get little old men! He gets big fat merchants! He's *someone*. You should have gone in with him when you had the chance!"

"I'd rather eat worms!"

"Worms? Hah? Since when could we afford to eat worms?"

"Can we have a word?" said Cohen.

He strolled towards the far end of the bridge, swinging his sword from one hand. The troll padded after him.

Cohen fumbled for his tobacco pouch. He looked up at the troll, and held out the bag.

"Smoke?" he said.

"That stuff can kill you," said the troll.

"Yes. But not today."

"Don't you hang about talking to your no-good friends!" bellowed Beryl, from her end of the bridge. "Today's your day for going down to the sawmill! You know Chert said he couldn't go on holding the job open if you weren't taking it seriously!"

Mica gave Cohen a sorrowful little smirk.

"She's very supportive," he said.

"I'm not climbing all the way down to the river to pull you out again!" Beryl roared. "You tell him about the billy goats, Mr Big Troll!"

"Billy goats?" said Cohen.

"I don't know *anything* about billy goats," said Mica. "She's always going on about billy goats. I have no knowledge whatsoever about billy goats." He winced.

They watched Beryl usher the young trolls down the bank and into the darkness under the bridge.

"The thing is," said Cohen, when they were alone, "I wasn't intending to kill you."

The troll's face fell.

"You weren't?"

"Just throw you over the bridge and steal whatever treasure you've got."

"You were?"

Cohen patted him on the back. "Besides," he said, "I like to see people with . . . good memories. That's what the land needs. Good memories."

The troll stood to attention.

"I try to do my best, sir," it said. "My lad wants to go off to work in the city. I've tole him, there's bin a troll under this bridge for nigh on five hundred years—"

"So if you just hand over the treasure," said Cohen, "I'll be getting along."

The troll's face creased in sudden panic.

"Treasure? Haven't got any," it said.

"Oh, come *on*," said Cohen. "Well-set-up bridge like this?"

"Yeah, but no one uses this road any more," said Mica. "You're the first one along in months, and that's a fact. Beryl says I ought to have gone in with her brother when they built that new road over his bridge, but," he raised his voice, "I said, there's been trolls under this bridge—"

"Yeah," said Cohen.

"The trouble is, the stones keep on falling out," said the troll. "And you'd never believe what those masons charge. Bloody dwarfs. You can't trust 'em." He leaned towards Cohen. "To tell you the truth, I'm having to work three days a week down at my brother-in-law's lumber mill just to make ends meet."

"I thought your brother-in-law had a bridge?" said Cohen.

"One of 'em has. But my wife's got brothers like dogs have fleas," said the troll. He looked gloomily into the torrent. "One of 'em's a lumber merchant down in Sour Water, one of 'em runs the bridge, and the big fat one is a merchant over on Bitter Pike. Call that a proper job for a troll?"

"One of them's in the bridge business, though," said Cohen.

"Bridge business? Sitting in a box all day charging people a silver piece to walk across? Half the time he ain't even there! He just pays some dwarf to take the money. And he calls himself a troll! You can't tell him from a human till you're right up close!"

Cohen nodded understandingly.

"D'you know," said the troll, "I have to go over and have dinner with them every week? All three of 'em? And listen to 'em go on about moving with the times . . ."

He turned a big, sad face to Cohen.

"What's wrong with being a troll under a bridge?" he said. "I was brought up to be a troll under a bridge. I want young Scree to be a troll under a bridge after I'm gone. What's wrong with that? You've got to have trolls under bridges. Otherwise, what's it all about? What's it all *for*?"

They leaned morosely on the parapet, looking down into the white water.

"You know," said Cohen slowly, "I can remember when a man could ride all the way from here to the Blade Mountains and never see another living thing." He fingered his sword. "At least, not for very long."

He threw the butt of his cigarette into the water. "It's all farms now. All little farms, run by little people. And *fences* everywhere. Everywhere you look, farms and fences and little people."

"She's right, of course," said the troll, continuing some interior conversation. "There's no future in just jumping out from under a bridge."

"I mean," said Cohen, "I've nothing against farms. Or farmers. You've got to have them. It's just that they used to be a long way off, around the edges. Now *this* is the edge."

"Pushed back all the time," said the troll. "Changing all the time. Like my brother-in-law Chert. A lumber mill! A *troll* running a lumber mill! And you should see the mess he's making of Cutshade Forest!"

Cohen looked up, surprised.

"What, the one with the giant spiders in it?"

"Spiders? There ain't no spiders now. Just stumps."

"Stumps? *Stumps?* I used to like that forest. It was . . . well, it was darksome. You don't get proper darksome any more. You really knew what terror was, in a forest like that."

"You want darksome? He's replanting with spruce," said Mica.

"Spruce!"

"It's not his idea. He wouldn't know one tree from another. That's all down to Clay. He put him up to it."

Cohen felt dizzy. "Who's Clay?"

"I said I'd got *three* brothers-in-law, right? He's the merchant. So he said replanting would make the land easier to sell."

There was a long pause while Cohen digested this.

Then he said, "You can't sell Cutshade Forest. It doesn't belong to anyone."

"Yeah. He says that's why you can sell it."

Cohen brought his fist down on the parapet. A piece of stone detached itself and tumbled down into the gorge.

"Sorry," he said.

"That's all right. Bits fall off all the time, like I said."

Cohen turned. "What's happening? I remember all the big old wars. Don't you? You must have fought."

"I carried a club, yeah."

"It was supposed to be for a bright new future and law and stuff. That's what people said."

"Well, I fought because a big troll with a whip told me to," said Mica, cautiously. "But I know what you mean."

"I mean it wasn't for farms and spruce trees. Was it?"

Mica hung his head. "And here's me with this apology for a bridge. I feel really bad about it," he said, "you coming all this way and everything—"

"And there was some king or other," said Cohen, vaguely, looking at the water. "And I think there were some wizards. But there was a king. I'm pretty certain there was a king. Never met him. You know?" He grinned at the troll. "I can't remember his name. Don't think they ever told me his name."

About half an hour later Cohen's horse emerged from the gloomy woods on to a bleak, windswept moorland. It plodded on for a while before saying, "All right . . . how much did you give him?"

"Twelve gold pieces," said Cohen.

"Why'd you give him twelve gold pieces?"

"I didn't have more than twelve."

"You must be mad."

"When I was just starting out in the barbarian hero business," said Cohen, "every bridge had a troll under it. And you couldn't go through a forest like we've just gone through without a dozen goblins trying to chop your head off." He sighed. "I wonder what happened to 'em all?"

"You," said the horse.

"Well, yes. But I always thought there'd be some more. I always thought there'd be some more edges."

"How old are you?" said the horse.

"Dunno."

"Old enough to know better, then."

"Yeah. Right." Cohen lit another cigarette and coughed until his eyes watered.

"Going soft in the head!"

"Yeah."

"Giving your last dollar to a troll!"

"Yeah." Cohen wheezed a stream of smoke at the sunset.

"Why?"

Cohen stared at the sky. The red glow was as cold as the slopes of hell. An icy wind blew across the steppes, whipping at what remained of his hair.

"For the sake of the way things should be," he said.

"Hah!"

"For the sake of things that were."

"Hah!"

Cohen looked down.

He grinned.

"And for three addresses. One day I'm going to die," he said, "but not, I think, today."

The air blew off the mountains, filling the air with fine ice crystals. It was too cold to snow. In weather like this wolves came down into villages, trees in the heart of the forest exploded when they froze. Except there were fewer and fewer wolves these days, and less and less forest.

In weather like this right-thinking people were indoors, in front of the fire.

Telling stories about heroes.

THE TOLL BRIDGE

Harvey Jacobs

I couldn't resist putting this story after the previous one, because of the titles, and because the two stories, whilst very different on the surface, are remarkably similar deep down. Harvey Jacobs (b. 1930) is a much underrated author of fables, utilizing his Jewish background much like Bernard Malamud and Isaac Bashevis Singer. Only Jacobs usually goes for broke. Some of his irreverent stories will be found in The Egg of the Glak *(1969). You might also check out his novel* Beautiful Soup *(1996).*

Dr Maxfield Shnibitz was no slave to a single discipline. He described his work as eclectic. He refused to be classified as a Freudian, Jungian, or Reichian – or any *ian*. He once told a seminar on *Directions in Psychiatry: The New Age*: "The modern analyst must be a bridge between the secular and spiritual worlds, albeit a toll bridge." Dr Shnibitz – a stocky man with a large, round head bald at the top; a bush of a mustache; sideburns that flared; and a compassionate face – then leaned intimately toward his audience and said, "And while the tolls may be generous, they take a toll." Dealing with the anguished, the off-center, even the mildly troubled was exhausting, and Dr Shnibitz did not feel overpaid.

His reward was not all monetary, of course. Occasionally he helped a patient achieve a "breakthrough", and he played midwife to the birth of a restructured soul. He had been catalyst for amazing change, and those patients who were fortunate enough to shed burdens of fuzzy guilt for a fresh, positive outlook were obviously grateful. Sometimes they gave him presents.

Such was the case with a man who came in a basket case and climbed successfully from his basket after years of turmoil. During his final session he handed Dr Shnibitz an amulet on a gold chain. "I actually bought this thing from a psychic in Albania," the cured man said. "That's a measure of how bad off I was. She told me it was a power symbol that once belonged to a werewolf or some damn thing that went broke and pawned it. That was before the country went Commie. She's probably the minister of culture now." Dr Shnibitz accepted the gift without commenting on the symbolic overtones. The redeemed patient was handing his doctor something he himself had redeemed, an amulet that linked him to magic, the uncontrolled, a kingdom of shadows, the dark forces of madness, no longer a threat. He was handing his bit of ersatz power to the man powerful enough to overcome those demons. Dr Shnibitz just smiled from his ample face and shook hands with his departing patient. It was the first time they had ever touched physically, and it satisfied the psychiatrist that the hand he gripped was dry, the handshake firm and confident.

The amulet was put in a desk drawer. That night, after finishing with his caseload, Dr Shnibitz was filled with a strange curiosity about the object. He took it out of the drawer and laid it on his desk. It was shaped like a pyramid and made from some amalgam of stone, metal, and bone. His fingers brushed over it; there was a porous quality, slightly gritty, like stroking a dry sponge. God knows what it was made of or when or why. A friend of Dr Shnibitz brought back an amulet from Africa formed of rag and wood chips that turned out to be home to a devilish larva. Worms infested the poor man's apartment. They had to be bombed by exterminators using chemicals that made the place smell like a toxic dump. The amulet on Dr Shnibitz's desk did not seem like it would harbor anything organic. It felt cold, lifeless. He decided it was no hive or nest.

Besides, the patient had worn it for years. Curiously, it was never mentioned during their hundreds of sessions. Had it been, the timetable of discovery and recovery might have been quickened. Treasured objects often mirror the most secret images. They can be valuable shortcuts to the core of infection. Perhaps that is why they are so defended. Dr Shnibitz was hurt that his patient had never spoken of the amulet, and he laughed alone in his office to find himself reacting like a child. It was, as they say, "water under the bridge".

More interesting was the fact that the patient had actually purchased such a talisman. The man ran a successful business, was married, had children. For all his problem he was a creature of this scientific century. Yet he paid American dollars for something he knew to be worthless. Maybe that was the motivation, a shared sense of worthlessness. Or was it simple, old-fashioned desperation? What had Nixon's daughter said to the press? "Never underestimate the power of fear." Well, the patient was no longer a patient, no longer troubled, a closed file.

Dr Shnibitz wished he could say the same about himself. In recent months he had felt a growing dissatisfaction with his own life. He found himself angry at patients who complained of things that were no more than the ordinary viruses of life. He was bored by transparent dreams and frustrated ambitions that were never worthy of achieving. Dr Shnibitz suspected his own burnout. He needed a vacation, a change, but he could think of no place he wanted to go, nothing he wanted to see.

Stroking the amulet, his mind wandered to exotic places on the globe – Marrakesh, Tahiti, the isles of Greece, Kyoto – and rejected them one by one. No, it was not a vacation he needed. It was some kind of challenge. He knew that the patient who would replace the patient who left would come trembling with doubt, armed against ghosts that would prove to be made from curds of milk from some denying tit; that he would have to listen to hours and hours of the same old crap, the moaning and groaning, the evasions and denials, and, finally, with luck, confrontation and rejoicing. Another triumph, another little gift, and on and on and on. The truth about people is that they are often duller than dishwater . . . dishwater is a complex swirl about to confront the ultimate drain. Most neurotics confront nothing more than their own borders. Perspective sets them free. They leave satisfied with their limitations. They find strength in the acceptance of weakness. And often they grow arrogant with their new identity as blades of grass, not towering trees, on the human landscape. With that knowledge they go on to intimidate other neurotics, and so on and on and on.

Dr Shnibitz let out a long, loud sigh. He remembered the case of a secretary who was terrified when she thought of all the papers she would type over a lifetime. She saw them as an Everest of papers. She had been saved with the insight that she would type up pages one at a time. That was enough to liberate her from nightmares. Actually, it should have caused worse nightmares for the poor woman. But she became a more efficient secretary, eventually an office manager, then a vice president, and she still sent a card every Christmas. She also referred patients. *Sic transit.*

A challenge, enormous challenge, combat. Maybe that would open arteries clogged with predictability and send a rush of blood to the large eggplant brain under Dr Shnibitz's bald pate. The doctor found himself tapping at his skull. He also found himself sucking the amulet like a lollipop. Sometime during his meditations he had unconsciously put the trinket into his mouth. It was his first unconscious gesture in years. He marveled while he tongued the weird thing, the gold chain dangling from his lips like dribble, and he thought, "Maybe it is time for the travel folders."

There was a loud noise in Dr Shnibitz's reception room. He jumped. His own secretary had left early to make a theater curtain. There were no arrivals scheduled. The building had experienced several burglaries despite a good security system, and Dr Shnibitz realized that he might become a statistic. The evening news might carry pictures of his dead body.

There was somebody out there, no question. He could hear sounds of an intruder, even hard breathing. Some of his colleagues carried guns, had cans of Mace, warned him to be prepared. Theirs was a hazardous profession at best. But Dr Shnibitz was a peaceable man who called himself a "black-belt conversationalist". His conceit was that he could negotiate himself out of any danger. At that moment he wasn't so sure. Suppose the thief were drugged beyond the spell of spoken word? Bang, it would be over. He would cease to exist as a man and become a scholarship, a memory, a collection of papers stored in a university library. He plucked the amulet from his mouth. How would the police interpret that? It would send them after some voodoo cult in Brooklyn.

To remain silent was the wrong tack. Better to announce his presence. That would be enough to frighten most petty criminals. And whoever it was would find his way into the consulting room anyhow. Dr Shnibitz said in a strong voice, "Yes, who is it? Who are you and what do you want?"

The response was a guttural gurgle mingled with a growl. It was not a person out there, no felon; it was an animal, a beast, a predator. Dr Shnibitz felt an old fear, the kind he once knew in the pitch dark of his parents' beach house on Cape Cod when the ocean seemed to lick at the windows. Well, he had learned to cope with that kind of terror. He took deep, slow breaths, moving quietly toward the thick office door. He flipped the lock, heard the bolt set. Whatever was out there would not have an easy time getting in. Dr Shnibitz ran for his telephone. There was not time to dial.

The consultation room door disintegrated. It splintered and fell apart. Holding the phone, paralyzed with sheer amazement, Dr Shnibitz saw what was standing there looking in at him. It was only a shape at first, like a fogbank, like steam spitting from a sewer grate. Then it crystallized. Dr Shnibitz put down the telephone.

A man watched. The shape became a man. A man with horns. No, a man wearing a helmet that sprouted horns. A man with a bull's head. No, the face was human, mustached, bearded with a prow for a nose and enormous blue eyes. And the neck, thick as a thigh, a pedestal. The body, a chunk, a rock, covered in furs – black fur, brown fur, white fur. Braceleted arms, poles with gold rings, hanging apelike from the trunk. Bare legs dangling, stubby legs heavy and muscled, the feet protected by boots made from russet leather skins. The man grunted at Dr Shnibitz but made no move.

Instinctively, Dr Shnibitz positioned himself behind his formidable desk. He sat in his chair, keeping control, aware that he fused with the desk, became a centaur with a mahogany frame. He knew the effect of that combination on even the most disturbed patients. It calmed them to be in such a presence.

"You have no appointment," Dr Shnibitz said. "Leave now. Call my secretary, Ms Rosen, in the morning. She'll give you a proper time."

The visitor came forward and paused at the Eames Chair where new patients sat outlining their misery. Great hands fondled the chair, then grabbed it up off its base and cracked it in two. The hands lifted the metal base and twisted it. The metal bent and finally fractured.

"Impressive," said Dr Shnibitz. "But hardly sensible. You're going to be billed for damages. I suggest you restrain yourself. We both know you're strong. Now tell me what you want here?"

"I am Attila."

"The Hun?"

"Of course the Hun."

"Your fixation is that you are Attila the Hun?"

"No fixation. It's who I am. The damned, accursed, blood-thirsty son-of-a-bitch Teuton who terrorized the civilized world and ate babies for dessert."

"Very well. I am Dr Maxfield Shnibitz."

"Jesus, I know that much."

"Then we have the basis for communication."

"Possibly. But don't be smug. Don't give me shit about calling for an appointment. If you rub me the wrong way, I will strangle you with your own intestines."

"You feel aggressive?"

"I always feel aggressive. I am aggressive. You called me to come and kill you. The only reason I hesitate is curiosity. And I am in no hurry to return to Hell."

"I called you to come and kill me?"

"You sucked the amulet, wishing for death."

"I did not suck the amulet. I did insert it into my mouth

in a purely unconscious gesture. But I was not wishing for death."

"You certainly were. I don't know your exact thoughts – something about boredom and challenge – but it added up to a definite death wish."

"Yes, I can see how you might have interpreted it that way. I do see that. You come from Hell?"

"I did. And you want to know what kind of place it is. Terrible. At first I enjoyed it. They had clever tortures, interesting agonies. But after centuries, repetition replaces surprise, and that is the worse torture."

"You feel tortured?"

"I am tortured. By professionals. Corporate professionals. With amoebic imagination. When I am called back by the amulet, I welcome the change. But I can't stay too long. They sulk. That is beyond endurance. So I will kill you now in the most amusing way possible. Would you like to be skinned alive? Broiled? What? Give me some guidance."

"Attila, if I may – and you call me Maxfield; forget the 'Doctor' – if I did wish for death in my deepest unconscious, then that was a regressive, immature response to the curious mix of triumph and frustration at turning a patient loose. I do become involved with my patients. I don't want to die just yet, but thank you for making a prompt house call."

"I came for nothing? For nothing?"

Attila began to wring his hands. Dr Shnibitz saw the neck bulge, the face turn purple.

"You want to break something?"

"I think I do. Yes. No. No, I don't want to break anything. I came to grant your wish, not dismantle your office."

"And you handle frustration in a most predictable way. Smash, burn, loot, rape, crow. That's what you want; admit it."

"I admit it. Big news. Patients pay you for such insight?"

"Snide remarks now. More anger. Perhaps your trip was not a total loss."

"I came to kill. Now you tell me you want to live. I came to do you a favor. You spurn my gesture. That's what I call a total loss. I haven't heard bones crunch in God knows how long."

"God? You said *God knows how long.*"

"I know what I said."

"Strange coming from Attila the Hun. Talk of God. Tell me, do you think about God very often?"

"Absolutely not. It was only an expression."

"Do you regret renouncing your place in Heaven? I assume there must be a Heaven if you say you live in Hell."

"Certainly there is a Heaven. I never thought much about it. My renunciation was made in the equivalent of kindergarten. I chose a lifestyle. That mandated a death-style."

"You must question the choice from time to time."

"Not really. Sometimes. But negative thinking is a waste of time and energy."

"Negative thinking? Don't you mean positive thinking?"

"Did I say negative? I meant positive."

"You must ask yourself if Heaven is better."

"You've never seen my rap sheet. In one lifetime I accomplished more than a thousand Mafias, a dozen Hitlers, fifty Vlad Tepises. My own Dobermans were afraid of me. I shed more blood than the American Medical Association. Heaven is a place I will never visit. If I were to come within a million leagues of Heaven, angels would throw up on me. No, Maxfield, I don't think much about Heaven as a viable alternative. Let me kill you. You go to Heaven. See for yourself. I'll crush your skull between your own feet. Nice headlines. Prime-time coverage. I'll rip off your ears."

"Just suppose, Attila, that you were to renounce your past life and ask forgiveness."

"Some are beyond redemption, as the phrase goes."

"Suppose, just suppose, that you could prove that your antisocial behavior was no fault of your own."

"That would make some difference. If I were a victim, well, they can appreciate that. It makes them feel guilty, as if they were conspirators, as if they failed. But in my case, a clear choice was made. I loved evil from my first breath. I bit my mother's nipples just for the Hell of it. No, Maxfield, I couldn't mount any kind of defense. I could never earn Gray Time."

"Gray Time?"

"The chance to live again. Make up for past indignities. If

you can get them to grant an appeal, it is possible to earn a certain period of Gray Time."

"Return to life?"

"Naturally. Do good deeds. Tell ugly women they are beautiful. Cross cripples. Sympathize with the blind. Comfort the losers. Like that. Don't you watch television? They do that plot to death."

"Fascinating. Why not sit down on the couch and tell me about it. Better, lie down. Relax."

"I don't have all night. Suppose I peel back your lips and leave your skull exposed. Or unravel your navel. Or split your buttocks. You could have an interesting and provocative demise. You'd be the first topic of conversation tomorrow morning. They might even remember until evening. What do you say?"

"We'll decide about that later. Make yourself comfortable."

Attila bellowed a sigh. Dr Shnibitz remembered his own recent sigh. He looked down at the amulet, still damp, draped over his appointment calendar. Talk about a challenge. To tempt the humanity in Attila the Hun. To give Gray Time to the deathmonger maniacs swear by. It would be a feather in any psychoanalyst's cap. Freud himself would give a testicle for the chance.

Dr Shnibitz watched his guest test the Naugahyde couch. Attila sat, suddenly reclined. Without thinking, Dr Shnibitz slipped a paper doily under Attila's enormous head.

"What for?"

"Disposable."

"Ah."

"So you nipped at your mother's nipple just to see her reaction?"

"Yes, I did. Nice woman. Deserved better."

"And were you punished?"

"Harsh words, the usual. My father was the enforcer. When they first put me on the pot, he would make me sit for hours."

"You had a difficult toilet training?"

"Not difficult. Firm. Father was a disciplinarian. A nasty old bastard. Drank. Fermented goat's milk."

"And when he got drunk . . . ?"

"Behaved like a slob."

"And you attacked a source of milk . . . your mother's breasts . . ."

"Are you suggesting that I was actually attacking my father?"

"You said that, not I."

"Hmmm. Funny about that. When I ordered all nonvirgins in Gaul to be eviscerated on the shortest day of the year, I had a dream about bosoms that looked like fountains. In fact, I ordered fountains that looked like bosoms. For my castle in the mountains. The snowcapped mountains . . ."

"You ordered nonvirgins eviscerated on the shortest day of the year?"

"You're not suggesting that my first act of political violence was rooted in concern about the size of my phallus?"

"You said it. *Rooted*. Your words. Fountain bosoms . . . snowcapped mountains . . ."

"Mom?"

"Possibly."

"But why would I associate my mother with concerns about the length of . . ."

"Why? Why indeed? It's just possible that . . ."

Attila jackknifed, stood, slammed his fist into the wall. Dr Shnibitz had seen all that before.

"I've got to get back. If you want to go on living, fine. That's your problem,. But I'm expected for skewering."

"Wait just a minute. How can I best put this? Don't be so hard on yourself. Boys will be boys. Mothers are often the objects of desire, possessiveness. It isn't uncommon for a male child to feel inferior comparing his penis to his father's."

"Inferior? I never felt inferior. Didn't I build the tallest obelisk outside Egypt just outside my wading pool?"

"You built an obelisk outside your wading pool?"

"Well, yes, I did. To commemorate the sack of Rome. Or was it Constantinople?"

"An obelisk . . . a wading pool . . ."

"Now tell me I sacked whatever it was I sacked just for an excuse to build an obelisk to prove I had an impressive organ to a wading pool. Come on, Maxfield."

"What were you doing with a wading pool?"

"I enjoyed wading. It was a nice round pool surrounded by pines."

"Wading? Or *waiting*. A nice round, wet pool surrounded by pines?"

"Oh, now, cut it out. Not Mom. If I accept all that, you could say every single act of vicious abandon I ever perpetrated was nothing but a charade to conceal a hidden desire to . . ."

"You said it. I didn't."

"You know how to make a fellow feel cheap."

Attila began to cry. He rose from the couch and stared into a mirror on the far wall. That mirror had seen many such broken faces. Dr Shnibitz came and put his arm around the sulking hulk.

"If you were a victim of an innocent childhood obsession, surely you don't deserve eternal damnation."

"Grounds for an appeal? Me?"

"Why not?"

"Maxfield, do you begin to realize what you've done for me?"

"All in a day's work. Sit and rest. Have yourself a glass of water. There's plenty in the pitcher on my desk."

"I feel wasted. Empty. Naked. Reborn."

While Attila sipped ice water, Dr Shnibitz, elated, went to the outer office. He found a key in his pocket and opened a closet marked PRIVATE. The closet had not been opened in years. It had a musty smell. Dr Shnibitz undressed to his underwear. From the closet he took a fur coat that had once belonged to his wife. It was repossessed during a nasty divorce settlement.

He put on the coat, then a helmet crowned with the antlers of an eight-point buck, the gift of a saved bank president. A pair of sandals replaced his shoes, though he kept on his long socks because of a chill in the air. At the back of the closet, near a set of golf clubs, he found a sword and shield. He had bought them at the auction of an old woman's estate for no special reason beyond irony. Ready, he came back into his consulting room and stood with his legs wide apart. The sniveling mass on his couch sipped water and moaned while he beat his chest with a limp fist.

"Stand up and fight," Dr Shnibitz yelled, waving the sword over his head. Attila looked up at him with watery eyes. The Hun only shrugged.

"Do battle, barbarian," said Dr Shnibitz.

The Hun's eyes were blank.

"I demand you defend yourself."

Dr Shnibitz leapt across the oriental rug and sank home his sword just under the thick neck. He felt very good, elated, ready to take on a multitude of neurotics. He made a mental note to send his former patient a brief thank-you note.

ALASKA

John Morressy

John Morressy (b. 1930), a US professor of English, has been writing since 1966, turning to science fiction in 1971, and then to fantasy. He has written a long series of short stories featuring the wizard Kedrigern and his motley associates. The stories began with "A Hedge Against Alchemy" in The Magazine of Fantasy and Science Fiction *in 1981, and they now fill five books –* A Voice for Princess *(1986),* The Questing of Kedrigern *(1987),* Kedrigern in Wanderland *(1988),* Kedrigern and the Charming Couple *(1990) and* A Remembrance for Kedrigern *(1990). The following is one of the longer stories.*

A light touch on his shoulder woke Kedrigern from a dreamless nap. He opened his eyes and immediately, with a little cry of annoyance, shut them tightly against the glare of the afternoon sun.

"Yah, yah," said a subdued voice beside him.

Shielding his eyes with one hand, he sat up. He could see, over the arm of his chair, the bald, warty head and tiny eyes of his house-troll. Those eyes were now rounded, and the little creature was quivering with excitement.

"What is it, Spot?" the wizard asked.

"Yah," said the house-troll urgently. It extended an oversized hand toward the road and repeated, "Yah."

Still shielding his eyes, Kedrigern looked in the direction Spot had indicated. He saw nothing. Knowing that Spot's eyes, though no bigger than cherry pits, were keen as a hawk's, he fumbled in his tunic and drew out the silver medallion of his guild. Raising it to his eye, he sighted through the Aperture of True Vision. The cause of Spot's concern became clear.

At the foot of the long hill, where the road emerged from the dense wood, were two mounted figures. First came a larger man on a white stallion, and behind him a youth on a pony. Trailing the youth were a well-laden pack mule and a great gray war-horse. It was a knight and his squire and equipage, and the whole train was heading for Kedrigern's little cottage. He let the medallion fall, rubbed his eye, and groaned in frustration.

"Is your eye all right?" Princess inquired, fluttering from the house to come down lightly at his side.

"Yes. Yes, my dear, I'm all right."

She looked down on him solicitously. "You rubbed your eye, and you sounded as if you were in pain."

"My eye is fine. That's not why I groaned."

"Well, *something* must be wrong. Spot is all anxious and jumpy, and you sound upset. What's the matter?"

"We're having visitors," he said with profound loathing.

"Visitors? Company?!" Princess cried joyously. She rose, with a soft hum of her little wings, clapping her hands and laughing for delight.

"Yes, visitors. A great unruly mob of drunken brawlers trampling over everything, shouting and swearing and smashing things . . . I'll probably have to spell the lot of them if we're to have any peace and quiet. And of course they'll demand our best food and wine, and stabling for their horses," said the wizard, climbing to his feet, gesturing wildly, his face reddening. "And I suppose they'll expect to be entertained, too, and . . . and . . ." He grew inarticulate with outrage.

"Are you finished?" Princess asked coolly.

"For the time being."

"How many knights are there?"

Looking away, he muttered, "One. And his squire. And three horses. And a mule."

"That really isn't a mob."

"You don't know knights and squires, my dear."

"Of course I know knights and squires! I'm a princess! Didn't I grow up surrounded by knights and squires?" she retorted.

"I suppose so. You keep saying you don't remember."

"I may not remember all the details, but I recall the general atmosphere of my father's court very clearly. It was not riotous, whatever you may have read, or heard. Knights are chivalrous and courteous and brave, and they're usually charming company. They recite romances and sing ballads, and most of them can play the lute."

"Badly," he muttered sourly.

Princess gave him a cool glance. "Quite well, actually."

"Maybe. But *all* of them can play the sword, and the mace, and the battle-ax, and the lance, and they do so at every opportunity. Guest or no guest, knight or squire or serf, anyone who starts brandishing weapons in this house will be turned into something nasty forthwith."

"No danger of that. Knights know how to behave," said Princess with utter certainty.

"Oh, do they? Do they really? Do you mean that Round Table gang? They're the best of the lot, and just look at them, always squabbling among themselves, brothers fighting brothers, uncles hunting down their nephews, fathers bashing sons. And half the time they don't know which is which, the way they carry on with women – when they're not carrying them off."

"I take it you're finished now," Princess said. Her tone suggested that to be finished was the wiser course. Kedrigern nodded, and she went on, "Then you'd better change into something a little more dignified." Noticing his irate look, she quickly said, "No, no, I mean change your clothing. Put on the dark green tunic. And brush off your boots."

"Oh. All right, my dear. Should I do anything else?"

"Leave everything to Spot. Hurry now, so you'll be here to

greet our guests when they arrive," said Princess, shooing him inside with urgent gestures.

Guests indeed, he thought bitterly as he walked into the cool, shaded interior of the cottage. *Intruders* is the word called for; *interlopers* is better; *invaders* is better still. No decency, no consideration, no respect. Hardly better than barbarians, bursting in on a man's calm and privacy, bringing the noise and squalor of the world with them like a nasty smell that will linger in the house for weeks after they've gone.

Kedrigern disliked the world beyond Silent Thunder Mountain, and most of the things and people in it. He preferred to venture from his cottage only when it was essential for the well-being of an old client or when the reward offered for his services was sufficient to compensate for the inevitable horrors of travel: i.e., exorbitant. His wife, on the other hand, loved to travel, to visit, to entertain and be entertained, to move in company, to see new places and meet new people and, when that was not possible, to revisit old friends and familiar scenes. Conceding the obvious fact that princesses are raised differently from wizards, Kedrigern had learned to compromise. But however much he altered his behavior, his outlook remained unchanged: travel was nothing more than going out of one's way – literally – to be uncomfortable, and he hated it. He did not much like travelers, either, particularly when their destination was his cottage. They all wanted him to go somewhere he did not wish to be and do something he preferred to avoid.

This knight, he was certain, would be like all the rest: off on a quest, looking for someone or something to bash, hack, and pummel for the sake of honor and glory or the favor of some fair lady. It's little they have to do, any of them, Kedrigern thought sourly, or they wouldn't have time for such foolishness. Why can't they play chess, or read aloud to one another, or plant gardens? Them and their blasted chivalry. It was all such humbug.

Kedrigern emerged dressed in a clean, plainly cut tunic of dark green homespun stuff, his old brown trousers tucked into comfortable, well-worn boots that had been freshly dusted off. Princess and Spot were nowhere to be seen; he assumed that they were busy withindoors. He went to the front gate to await the arrival of the knight and squire, who were now in plain view, approaching at an unhurried pace.

When they were close enough for facial features and expressions to be distinguished, and Kedrigern could see that the knight was young, with dust-coated blond hair and dark eyes and a rudimentary mustache, he raised a hand in salutation. The knight reined in about ten feet from the gate, and his squire drew up just behind him, on his right.

"Good day to you, cottager," said the knight.

"And to you, sir knight," Kedrigern replied. Polite youngster, he thought, but none too bright. Couldn't tell a wizard from a cottager. Probably been hit on the head in the tiltyard too many times for his own good.

"Tell me, my good man, is this Silent Thunder Mountain?"

"It is indeed, sir knight."

"Ah, then my direction holds. And is it—"

The knight stopped in mid-question, sprang from the saddle, and bowed low. Kedrigern turned and saw Princess approaching. She had folded her wings flat and thrown a gray cloak over her shoulders. Her dark hair shone, and her simple golden coronet gleamed in the sun.

"Turll of the Bronze Shield, at your service, my lady," said the knight. He gestured to his squire, who held up a large bronze shield to verify his master's title.

"Welcome, Sir Turll. My name is Princess. This is my husband, Kedrigern," she said.

Turll gave a start, looked at Kedrigern, then at Princess, grinned, and turned to his squire, who returned the grin and clapped his hands enthusiastically. "Kedrigern, the great wizard who purged the evil from the Desolation of the Loser Kings? And Princess, who turned the wicked Grodz into a toad?"

"The very same," said Princess with a smile.

"Then I am the most fortunate of men! I had hoped to find you, but I was told you were on a great quest."

"We got back early," Kedrigern said unhappily.

Turll's face fell. "But Master Kedrigern must think me a fool – I mistook you for a cottager. Can you forgive me?"

Before the wizard could frame a dignified and kindly response, Princess said, "Don't give it another thought, Turll. People are always mistaking my husband for a cottager, or a scribe, or a merchant, and it's his own fault. He refuses to dress in a manner befitting his profession. He won't even grow a long silken beard. So there's no need to apologize."

"You're forgiven, Turll," Kedrigern quickly added.

"Now, you must stop to take some refreshment, and tell us all the news. Have your squire take the horses to the stable, and I'll have Spot bring out a snack."

"My lady is too kind," said Turll with a bow and a flourish.

"She certainly is," Kedrigern muttered under his breath, adding aloud, "Am I to understand that you've been seeking us, Turll?"

"I have, Master Kedrigern. I am a knight as yet untested, on a quest perilous."

"And you need help professional?"

"I do. I must learn the ways of gnomes if I am to have any hope of succeeding in my quest."

Kedrigern brightened. "All you want is information, then? You don't want me going off into some accursed wilderness with you?"

"I would not dream of imposing on the time of such a renowned and busy wizard – especially since the fortunes of my family have declined in the past few generations, under the curse of Cashalane."

"Cashalane? That miserable old witch?"

"Yes, Master Kedrigern, it was she who—" Turll stopped short as his squire went into a series of vigorous gesticulations, like a man throwing a fit. "Please excuse me," said the knight, responding with lively gestures of his own. Kedrigern and Princess exchanged a quick glance of bewilderment, but said nothing. The dumb show went on, with animation on both sides, for several minutes. At last, Turll folded his arms; the squire nodded, and, saluting, he led the animals to the stable.

"Forgive the interruption, I beg you. My squire, Jeniby, does not speak," said Turll.

"The poor lad," Princess murmured. "Is it because of the family curse?"

"Oh no, my lady. Well, not directly. It was entirely his own idea. He has vowed to speak no word until I have rescued the fair Floramella, mistress of my heart."

"What loyalty! What devotion!" said Princess, her eyes shining.

"I rather wish he'd consulted me first. It's very loyal and all that, but it can be extremely inconvenient when one is in a hurry . . . all that waving, you know."

The distant flapping of feet and an echoing "Yah" announced the approach of Spot with refreshments. To forestall unpleasantness, Kedrigern asked, "You haven't taken any vow to attack trolls, have you, Turll?"

"No, Master Kedrigern. My quarrel is with gnomes."

"Good. We have a troll to help out around the house, you see. Handy little chap. We call it 'Spot'. Ah, here it comes," said the wizard, as the knee-high house-troll came caroming out the front door and skidded to a halt before them, holding aloft a tray on which rested a tall pitcher of ale and four mugs. Not a drop spilled.

"Well done, Spot. You can leave everything here. I'll pour," said Kedrigern.

"I'm glad you warned me, Master Kedrigern. I would have considered Spot a gnome."

"Oh, dear me, no. Trolls and gnomes have nothing in common except a predilection for subterranean residence. No resemblance at all. Gnomes look like wizened little men and women. Trolls look like . . . well, Spot is one of the better-looking trolls I've encountered. And one of the smallest. Of course, Spot is still very young. In another century or so, it will start growing."

"Keddie, you're talking shop," Princess admonished him. "Perhaps Turll would simply like to relax in peace."

"Oh no, my lady, quite the contrary," Turll assured her. "I must learn gnome-lore, the more the better. It is my only hope."

"You mentioned your interest in gnomes earlier, and then you spoke of rescuing a fair lady. Is there some connection?" Kedrigern asked.

"There is, good master. My Floramella, the fairest of princesses – of unmarried princesses – has been carried off by a gnome."

"Carried off?" Princess repeated incredulously. "Gnomes are strong for their size, but . . ."

"This was a big gnome, my lady. A very big gnome. A *giant* gnome."

Kedrigern reached out to seize Turll's wrist in a firm grip. "Are you quite sure of that?" he snapped.

"Her entire family witnessed the dastardly act. It occurred at the local spring festival, just as Floramella entered, dressed all in green, a vision of loveliness. There can be no doubt."

"Then this is a very serious business, my boy," said the wizard. His expression was grave.

"Aren't you exaggerating the danger, Keddie? The worst thing a gnome can do to a princess is bore her to tears," Princess objected.

"Ordinarily, that's true, my dear. Gnomes are among the most boring little people in creation. But we're dealing here with a giant gnome, and when a gnome gets big, he's gone bad. It's something every gnome family fears . . . a rare occurrence, but invariably tragic in its consequences."

"Tragic? Oh, my fair Floramella!" cried Turll. He staggered, flung up his hands, and fell in a swoon.

"Poor lovesick boy," Princess said.

"When Jeniby is finished in the stable, we'll have him lug the poor lovesick boy inside. Meanwhile, I'll do some research into—" A shrill, wordless cry of terror interrupted the wizard, and Jeniby burst from the stable, pale and wild-eyed, waving his arms wildly. Kedrigern snapped his fingers in chagrin. "I forgot to tell him about our horses."

"It's all right," Princess reassured him. "I'm sure his vow permits an occasional scream."

When he regained his senses, Turll was persuaded to stay for dinner and spend the night at the cottage. Princess listened patiently and sympathetically to his ardent protestations of undying love and eternal devotion to Floramella, paled appropriately at his promises of bloody revenge should a single flaxen hair of her fair head be disturbed, and then settled back comfortably to hear an update of the news of the neighboring kingdoms, principalities, dukedoms, palatinates, provinces, territories, domains, and dominions. Since Turll had to check most of his facts with Jeniby, his narration was lengthy, with frequent chiromantic interludes, and went on well past the accustomed dinner hour, until Kedrigern finally rejoined the company. Under the wizard's arm was a thick book bound in green. He was solemn of countenance, pensive of mien, and empty of stomach, and his message was that there would be no further talk until after dinner.

Spot, who was a capable chef when carefully supervised, served up a splendid meal this night: a thick soup, a civet of hare, starling pie, a stew, finely minced venison, lampreys in galantine, and roast capons, with frumenty, fruit, and nuts for dessert. The food was enhanced by wines from the vineyards of a satisfied client, Vosconu the Openhanded. Turll was lavish in his praise, and Jeniby expressed his satisfaction as best he could by gestures, overeating, and exaggerated moans of delight.

When dinner was over, they rose from the table with many a satisfied sigh and took their places before the fire. Kedrigern opened the green book, checked several passages he had marked off, and cleared his throat.

"The phenomenon of a gnome going bad is uncommon, but the symptoms have been noted and recorded. First comes melancholy, and withdrawal from community affairs. Second is molting: hair and beard disappear completely, though the bushy eyebrows remain. At this point the afflicted gnome is moved out-of-doors, because the third step is rapid growth. The little fellow bursts right out of his clothing," he began.

"But Master Kedrigern, all who saw the creature stated that he was clad in the garb of a typical gnome!" Turll interjected.

"As, no doubt, he was," said the wizard patiently. "Gnomes are a prudish lot. The thought of one of their number crashing about in the woodland stark naked greatly distresses them. So every gnome community keeps an oversized suit of clothing on hand, just in case. In the interest of decency."

"I see."

"Good. To continue, then: in step four, the gnome, now twice human size or more, develops an irresistible craving for beautiful young princesses. He will wade any moat, batter down any gate, scale any wall, to attain his objective. Once having captured a beautiful young princess, he carries her off to a secluded place, where he—"

"Stop! I can't bear to hear more! One more word and I swoon!" Turll cried, burying his face in his hands.

"Must you go on?" Princess said anxiously.

"I must. He takes her to a secluded place, where he puts her down and then runs off to look for another princess."

Turll looked up, astonished. "He runs off?"

"He does. As I said, gnomes are prudes. And the ones who get to this stage are disoriented as well. They want to carry off beautiful princesses, but they don't know what to do once they've got them. They may carry off half a dozen before they're stopped."

"But then she's safe – my Floramella is safe!"

"Well . . . her virtue is safe, and that's a comfort. But she stands a good chance of dying from starvation, thirst, exposure, misadventure, savaging by wild beasts, or sheer terror. How long is it since she was taken?"

"Five days."

"If I were you, Turll, I'd be off first thing in the morning. There's no time to lose."

"Whither shall I seek her, Master Kedrigern? The giant gnome came in this direction, but I have no idea where he might have left poor Floramella."

"There's a small community of gnomes a day's ride from here. They might know something. I'll draw you a map, so—"

"We will accompany you on your quest, Turll," Princess broke in.

With a look of dismay, the wizard said, "But my dear—"

"We must!" she repeated, stamping her dainty foot and looking with blazing eyes at each of the men in turn. "Turll is as interested in spitting that overgrown gnome on his lance as he is in finding Floramella, and he'll be trying to do both, and he probably won't manage to do either. Think of the poor child, alone in the dark woods, jellied with fear, racked with hunger, drenched to the skin . . . her feet bruised, her hands numbed . . . her hopes dwindling with each passing hour!"

"Floramella was never a light eater, my lady. And she was wearing her warmest cloak," Turll said.

"And think of her feelings!" Princess went on, ignoring the interruption. "To be carried off and then abandoned like a sack of dirty laundry while your abductor goes charging after another woman! It's humiliating, that's what it is. And you're not even mildly disturbed by the fact. Men are all alike."

"My dear, you're being unfair. It wasn't a man who carried her off. It was a gnome," Kedrigern pointed out, his voice wounded.

"Little men are all alike, too."

Jeniby burst into a flurry of urgent gestures. Turll observed him, nodded, and said, "Jeniby reminds us that the weather has been mild this past week. There is yet hope."

"Not the way you're handling it. *Any* of you," Princess snapped, turning to dart a challenging glance at Kedrigern. "*You* want to draw a little map and then go off to your workroom and forget the whole thing. And *you*" – addressing Turll – "when your fair lady is carried off by a gnome, go running to a wizard for information instead of staying on the gnome's track, relentlessly, day and night, neither eating nor sleeping until Floramella is safe in your arms – *if* she cares to be, which I seriously doubt after the way you've botched everything so far." Turning to Jeniby, she snapped, "And *you* can stop waving your arms and try to do something useful."

"My lady, we are your slaves. Only command us," Turll said, flinging himself to one knee before her, arms wide in supplication.

"Now, just a minute," Kedrigern began. He got no further.

"We leave at dawn. You three will seek the gnome settlement. I will fly overhead and search the woods for—"

"Fly?" Turll blurted in bewilderment.

"Yes, fly. What do you think wings are for, to churn butter?"

"Wings?" Turll's voice was faint.

With a sigh of sheer exasperation, Princess rose, flung aside her light surcoat with a sweeping gesture, and unfurled her compact opalescent wings. As Turll and Jeniby looked on in awe, she rose with a soft hum, circled the room, and came lightly to rest on the corner of the mantel.

"You can fly," Turll said, almost inaudibly.

"I certainly can. And now I'm flying off to pack for our quest. Remember – we leave at dawn," said Princess, rising from the mantel and soaring from the room.

"I was a bit abrupt last night, wasn't I?" said Princess as they made their way down the mountain next morning.

"Perhaps just a bit," Kedrigern said.

"I couldn't help myself. There we all were, full and warm and comfortable and safe, and that poor child Floramella huddled in the cold and dark, slowly wasting away from hunger and thirst. Nobody was *doing* anything!"

"Something will be done," said the wizard, pausing to cover a yawn. "The gnomes will help us. They want to avoid scandal."

"Yes, but *you* would have left it up to Turll. He probably couldn't have found the gnomes, even with a map and clear directions; and if he did manage to stumble upon them, he wouldn't have understood what they told him, or would have forgotten it, if they talked to him at all – which, given Turll, seems unlikely. He's the sort to burst upon them, threatening and making demands, and have them all disappear. And then he'd swoon."

"It's possible," Kedrigern conceded lukewarmly.

"It's just about certain. And if he does find this big gnome, he's going to need your help. Turll's handsome, and devoted, and probably brave enough, but . . ."

"But?"

"Well, he impresses me as a man who's done too much jousting without a properly padded helmet. I think he could get lost inside his own armor. And that squire of his is no help."

Kedrigern did not reply at once. Finally he said, "I must confess I agree, my dear."

"So you admit I did the right thing."

"Much as I dislike traveling – especially at this hour – and distasteful as I find it to go off on a quest . . . yes, you did the right thing. Floramella wouldn't have had a chance if we'd left things in Turll's hands. A pity someone isn't paying for our services, though."

"Don't be mercenary."

"I'm being professional."

"Turll can pay you when this is all over and he's settled down. Handsome, bold knights always manage to make a decent living. The main thing now is to find Floramella. Once the mist has dissipated, I'll see if I can spot any sign of her."

Princess went up in midmorning. It was a glorious day for flying, and she spent the remainder of the morning and all of the afternoon aloft, except for short breaks to rest her wings. Though she crisscrossed the woods methodically, and at different altitudes, she found no trace of the unfortunate Floramella.

Turll and Jeniby kept a respectful distance from Princess and Kedrigern, chiefly out of awe at the mounts they were riding. Princess's horse was a dainty little creature, entirely transparent. Once the morning's condensation had evaporated from its sides, it was all but invisible, except for its silver saddle, deep blue caparison, and the glints of light that flashed from its hide when the sun struck at the proper angle.

Kedrigern's horse was terrifying to behold. It stood eighteen hands high and gleamed like polished ebony. Its eyes were lozenges of fire, and a spiral silver horn jutted from its forehead. Silver hooves the size of kettles trod leaf-light on the dank trail. Except for an occasional snort of flame from its nostrils, the great beast moved in utter silence. The creature was, in fact, gentle and good-natured, but Kedrigern saw no point in broadcasting this to all. It certainly looked like the proper steed of a great and powerful wizard; the less people knew about it, the more formidable would be their speculations, and that was all to the good.

Late in the afternoon, at the end of her longest flight, Princess came to earth. She glanced at her husband sadly and lighted on her saddle without a word. After a time, Kedrigern rode to her side.

"Would you like me to massage your wings, my dear? They must be sore," he said.

She shook her head and sighed.

"You can give them a good rest. We'll make camp soon. The gnome settlement is close by," he said.

She nodded disconsolately and sighed once again. Kedrigern

could tell that she preferred to be alone with her thoughts. He rode ahead until he found a grassy knoll near a rushing stream, and here he dismounted to await the others.

Jeniby pitched the tents and cared for the horses – very gingerly, in the case of Kedrigern's – while Turll and the wizard gathered wood. Before the sun had set, a cheery fire was burning, and the odor of grilled fish was in the air. Kedrigern announced the evening's agenda: a brief rest, and then a visit to the gnomes.

"Do you have a plan for stealing up on them unseen?" Turll asked eagerly.

"One does not steal up on a gnome. Particularly not on a night when the moon is almost full. Princess and I will approach them openly and announce ourselves as we go."

"What about us?"

"You and Jeniby will stay here and do nothing to alarm anyone in any way. Is that understood?"

It was understood, and events proceeded as Kedrigern had directed. At moonrise he and Princess donned their cloaks and set out on foot for the gnomes' settlement. When they had gone a few hundred paces, Kedrigern removed the silver medallion from around his neck and held it before him, dangling by its chain from one finger, slowly turning in the moonlight.

"This will let them know we're coming," he explained. "It gives off a signal."

"I don't hear anything," said Princess.

"You're not a gnome."

They proceeded several hundred paces farther along the moonlit forest path without a word spoken, then the wizard said, "It would help, I think, if you removed your cloak and let them see your wings."

"Why? I'm not a gnome," Princess replied crossly.

"Please, my dear."

"Keddie, it's chilly. They'll stiffen up."

"Just for a few minutes. To win their confidence."

Muttering, she unfastened her cloak and flung it to him. In the bright moonlight her wings looked like pearl. They gleamed as she slowly fluttered them. A few paces on, in a clearing, Kedrigern laid a hand on her arm. They halted. Small voices came faintly from the base of a tree, and then were still. A single piping voice almost at their feet said, "A wizard, a good fairy, and a full moon are always welcome arrivals."

Kedrigern replaced the medallion around his neck and wrapped Princess's cloak about her shoulders. Hunkering down, he softly said, "However tall the tree, its leaves must fall to the ground."

From all around them came a low murmur of approbation. The voice at their feet said, "He who eats salt is soon thirsty."

"But a drowning man does not beg for water," the wizard responded.

This time the encircling voices were more distinct in their expressions of approval, such as, "Well said," and "Hear, hear," and "Good thinking." When they subsided, there was a profound pause, and then the single voice nearby said, "The oak gives more shade than the acorn."

Kedrigern stood erect, nodded, and murmured his approval. At an urgent wink from him, Princess clapped her hands and said, "Oh, how very true!" Kedrigern stood with folded arms, silent, motionless, for a full minute before saying, "Even the king's horse has only four legs."

This was received more enthusiastically than his earlier pronouncements. There were even a few cheers from the unseen audience. Kedrigern acknowledged them by a gracious wave of his hand. It was some time before complete silence was restored.

"He who does not know one thing, knows another," the tiny interlocutor solemnly declared.

Kedrigern and Princess both applauded, and nodded with manifest agreement. The wizard cleared his throat, placed his hands on his hips, and said, "It is better to know something about nothing than to know nothing about everything."

A moment of absolute stunned silence followed, and then the clearing erupted with little shouts and cheers and wildly supportive cries. Here and there, pinpoints of light appeared, and brightened, and Princess and Kedrigern could see, illuminated by glowworm lanterns, a score or so of little men in hooded garments.

One of them mounted a flat stone and signaled for silence.

To the visitors, he said, "Welcome. Your command of gnomic sayings attests to your wisdom and goodness, and you give off emanations of benign wizardry. What do you seek?"

"A gnome has gone bad and carried off a beautiful princess," said Kedrigern. Cries of anger and dismay arose from the little people, and in the fuss, two of the lanterns fell to the ground. The wizard went on, "Help me to find him, and save the princess, and I will use my power to seek a cure for him."

There was much excited murmuring, some running back and forth, and a clustering into talkative groups. Princess looked at Kedrigern in inquiry, but he was gazing resolutely ahead, unmoved by the uproar at ground level. It subsided in time, and the gnomes' spokesman gave his response.

"You have been misinformed, wizard. Gnomes do not go bad."

"As we both know well, gnomes sometimes *do* go bad; and a bad gnome is a big gnome. The one I speak of is already twice human size," said Kedrigern coolly.

After a lengthy pause and some whispered exchanges, the gnome said, "You have obviously mistaken a giant for a spoiled gnome. Giants are all bad to begin with. Gnomes are pleasant, helpful, and law-abiding."

"This giant had lost his hair and beard—"

"Shaven," the gnome interrupted.

"And wore the traditional gnome's hood and breeches—"

"Stolen."

"And carried off a beautiful princess from the bosom of her family."

The gnome hesitated for an instant, then said lamely, "Giants are notoriously impulsive in their courtship."

"This won't do. You can't cover it up. There's a bad gnome running around loose, a princess is lost somewhere in the woods, and a bold knight is pursuing them both. If you don't cooperate, there may be violence and bloodshed. Quite a bit of it."

"It's all a mistake. Gnomes are nonviolent. You must—" the gnome began, but another little voice, this one slightly cracked, cried out, "Speak truth to the wizard! Tell all, and there may be hope for my boy!"

As Kedrigern and Princess watched, a stooped and venerable

gnome made his slow and painful way, with the aid of a tiny stick, to the flat stone. Shouldering the speaker aside, he tapped his stick sharply against the stone to bring the assembly to order. Kedrigern dropped to one knee, and Princess came to his side and seated herself on the grass, so they might hear the old gnome clearly.

"The unfortunate creature you seek is my youngest son, Alaska," he wheezed. "I blame myself for his tragic plight."

"It's not your fault. It can happen to any gnome," the wizard assured him.

"I should have acted sooner. When he began to mope, I blamed the weather. When he molted, I told myself it was his diet. Only when he began to grow did I accept the truth, and by then it was too late." He stretched out a tiny hand in appeal. "Alaska's a good boy, wizard. He's not himself anymore."

"I understand."

"You'll cure him, won't you?"

"I'll try. There's no known cure. I'm a wizard, not a magician."

The aged gnome shrugged. "It's better than nothing. All right, here are the facts. One week ago this very night, Alaska shot up to more than human size. We took out the great suit, and scarcely had we made him decent, when he gave an awful cry and rushed off."

"What did he say?"

"Something about a princess. I didn't catch the exact words."

"Did anyone try to follow him?"

"No. It was almost sunrise. The big ones can take sunlight pretty well, but we find it painful. But he came back this way two nights ago."

"Was he carrying a princess?" Princess asked excitedly.

"I can't really say. Alaska had *something* in his hands. It was green, as I recall. But he was moving pretty fast, and my eyesight isn't what it used to be. I'll be 410 next Nargeldarf, you know."

"Congratulations. I'm only 170 myself."

"You're only 168. Don't exaggerate," Princess whispered disapprovingly.

"Just rounding off," was the wizard's whispered reply. Addressing the gnome, he asked, "Which direction did he go?"

"Off to the northeast. Somebody once told him there was a castle up that way."

"I see. Good," said Kedrigern with evident satisfaction. "Well, thank you very much. You've been most helpful." He rose and dusted off his knee.

"You'll help Alaska now, won't you?" said the aged gnome hopefully.

"I'll do all I can to get him back to you, safe and small," Kedrigern assured him. Helping Princess to her feet, he said, "Let us take our leave of these good folk, my dear."

"They won't even notice I'm gone. They don't pay much attention to a princess," Princess said sotto voce.

"Don't take it personally, my dear. Gnomes don't pay very close attention to anything. And these particular gnomes have a lot on their minds just now."

"I can't help it. Nobody's worried about poor Floramella, or the other princesses this big gnome may have carried off by now."

"Turll is concerned."

"Yes, but it's not a consuming, single-minded concern. Turll is as much interested in doing a bold deed as he is in rescuing Floramella."

Kedrigern did not respond until they were well out of the gnomes' hearing, and then he said, "Turll may have his chance to do both, my dear. Alaska will be coming back this way, and he will probably be carrying Floramella. We'll head northeast and meet him."

Princess stopped, tugged at Kedrigern's sleeve, and looked into his face. He halted at her side. In the moonlight she could see his confident smile.

"What makes you so sure of all this?" she demanded.

"First of all, there is no castle in the northeast. There is a *chasm*, and it's impassable, so Alaska will have to return this way."

"Why did someone tell Alaska that he would find a castle up that way?"

"You've seen for yourself that gnomes are very inattentive.

Someone must have mentioned the chasm, and Alaska thought he had said *castle*, and when he wanted to seek a beautiful princess, he naturally thought of looking in a castle. It makes perfect sense."

Princess frowned thoughtfully. "And how can you be so sure he'll be carrying Floramella?"

"Well, his father said that Alaska was carrying something green, and we know that Floramella was wearing green when she was abducted. And since there are no other beautiful princess in the vicinity except yourself, he has probably hung on to Floramella."

"Oh, that poor girl!"

"Aside from the inevitable shaking up, Floramella's not too badly off. Gnomes aren't cruel, and they're very possessive. The only danger is that Alaska will put her down in some remote place and forget about her."

"Then we must find her tomorrow. We must!"

"It will all be up to you, my dear. You must fly as you've never flown before. I'll give your wings a good massage before we turn in."

Princess gave a brave little nod and set her jaw. Hand in hand, they returned to the campsite.

Next morning at dawn they set out in a northeasterly direction. Princess went aloft while the mist was still clearing ahead of a stiff breeze, and despite buffeting winds, she stayed up with only the shortest breaks until they stopped in a grassy clearing by a pond for a light midday collation. She finished her bread and cheese quickly, took a sip of water, and flexed her wings.

"Surely you're not going up again without a rest," said Kedrigern, laying a hand on her forearm.

"I must. That poor child is out there somewhere, waiting for help."

"You'll exhaust yourself. You'll strain your wings."

"Once I've spotted Alaska, my part of the work is done. I'll rest then," Princess said. She waved a brisk farewell, took three light steps forward, and soared up and over the treetops.

"My lady Princess is plucky," said Turll, and Jeniby

seconded his words with vigorous gestures signifying courage and determination.

"Her back will be stiff for six months," Kedrigern muttered with a resigned sigh as he watched her diminish and finally vanish into the bright sky. He cut himself a fresh slab of cheese, tore off a chunk of bread, and settled back against a tree trunk.

Turll was silent, but visibly fidgety. When Kedrigern had finished lunch and was flicking the larger crumbs from his tunic, the young knight blurted, "Master Kedrigern, is there really hope for Floramella? Will we find the wicked gnome, that I might wreak a just vengeance on him?"

"We'll find them, Turll. There's nowhere else for Alaska to go. He has to come back this way."

"Then shall I confront him. If I overcome, and rescue my Floramella, do you think it will count as a feat?"

Kedrigern studied Turll's eager countenance for some sign of derangement. Finding none, he replied cautiously, "I should say there's a good chance it might."

Shaking his head and gesturing in frustration, Turll said, "I have failed to make myself clear, good master. I was referring to the terms of the curse of Cashalane."

"Oh, that. Yes, of course. You mentioned it the other day," Kedrigern said, relieved.

"The curse was placed upon my grandfather, Turll of the Golden Helmet, for words he uttered in a moment of anger. It passed on to my father, Turll of the Silver Spur, and thence to me, Turll of the Bronze Shield."

"It's certainly affected the family fortunes. Another generation or two, and you'll be down to Turll of the Big Wooden Club."

"Such is my fear. The curse of Cashalane is a devilish curse. It requires a Turll to accomplish a feat, but does not specify what that feat is."

"The uncertainty must be difficult to deal with."

"It is the worst part. My grandfather did many a great feat, especially in taming giants, but all to no avail. Father also did great things. His specialty was monsters. He slew them, tamed them, restored them to human form, tricked them into self-destruction – one great feat after another, but not, alas, the right feat to free us from the curse. And if I should fail, it may be as you say . . . the decline and eventual collapse of the house of Turll."

Kedrigern shook his head in sympathy. Both men were silent for a time, and then the wizard asked, "Is Floramella aware of the family curse?"

Turll brightened; became, in fact, flushed with joy. "Yes, angelic creature that she is, she knows, and she is willing to be my wife in spite of it!"

"That's very sweet of her."

Turll nodded in eager agreement. Then his face fell, and he shook his fists at the heavens and cried in a mournful voice, "Oh, the injustice! The unfairness! One fair princess willing to marry a wretch like me, and *she's* the one to be carried off! So many beautiful princesses lie sleeping for a hundred years, or enchanted in some inconvenient way, and under awful spells – nobody would miss *them* but that stupid gnome had to find my Floramella!"

"Look at the positive side, my boy: this may be your chance to do the proper feat."

"That's true. And even if it isn't, there's the honor of the reward."

"Reward?" Kedrigern's interest quickened.

"Floramella's father, Llunn of Lavish, has promised a rich reward to the one who saves his daughter. I could not accept it, of course."

"I could," said Kedrigern, springing lightly to his feet. "To horse! We're wasting time."

Scarcely had he vaulted into the saddle of his great black steed, when Princess dove to his side, where she hovered, breathless, for a moment, pointing up the path. By the time she could gasp, "Alaska! Coming this way!" the sound of thudding footsteps and cracking branches was already unmistakable. Turll snatched up his helmet and ran to his horse, Jeniby close behind him, bearing lance and shield. Haste made them clumsy, and Kedrigern rode before them, to intercept the fast-approaching Alaska.

"No, wizard! Let it be my hand that saves the fair Floramella, else my feat may not be accomplished!" Turll shouted.

"All right. I'll just get his attention and make sure he stops."

As the gnome burst into the clearing, bearing a limp girl in one arm, Kedrigern's horse reared, tossed its mane, and snorted twin jets of bright flame. Alaska stopped in his tracks, fascinated by the sight. When the horse settled, Kedrigern sat with folded arms, boldly staring down the oversized gnome, who peered out from under his bushy white brows in befuddled astonishment, making low, unintelligent noises.

"He's all yours, Turll," said the wizard as the knight rode to his side.

"Hear me, gnome!" Turll cried in a mighty voice. "Release that fair maid and prepare to meet thy fate!"

Alaska gave a deep, angry growl and shook his fist in a menacing gesture. Turll countered by brandishing his lance and giving his battle cry, "A Turll and a bold feat!" The gnome growled again, louder, and put Floramella down gently. He stepped before her and thumped his chest.

Turll charged. Since only about ten paces separated him and the gnome, he could not work up much speed. As he closed, Alaska reached out and grabbed the lance, lifting Turll clear out of the saddle. Eye to eye they glared at one another, then Alaska shook the knight loose.

Turll climbed to his feet and drew his sword. Alaska swung at him with the lance, narrowly missing, and Turll countered with a jab to the great toe. The gnome gave a howl of pain and slammed the lance down on the spot Turll had just vacated, and received another jab in the same toe. Howling with mingled pain and rage, he hopped up and down on his good foot, waving his fists wildly.

His hopping motion made him a difficult target. Worse yet, it presented a serious threat to Floramella, who lay unmoving perilously close to where his large foot came down. A third blow by Turll, to the same toe, made the gnome hop even higher, and this time he landed no more than a finger's breadth from the helpless maiden.

Then, as Alaska gathered himself for another hop, out of the sky came Princess, swift as a stooping hawk, and snatched Floramella by her silken girdle. As she rose, Alaska flailed out wildly, and one long fingernail caught in the hem of Princess's skirt.

Gamely, she struggled upward. The frenzied humming was audible below as she slowly rose, bearing the weight of Floramella and Alaska on her delicate wings. She hovered; she wavered; she began to sink. "Keddie! Help!" she cried.

Kedrigern raised his hand and sent a blast of magic at the thrashing gnome. A silent burst of blinding light and a great wind shook the trees; Princess shot upward, then steadied herself and began a smooth descent; a large hooded garment and a pair of oversized breeches fluttered lazily to the ground: Alaska was nowhere to be seen.

"Gnome! Alaska! Reveal thyself, miscreant!" Turll cried, waving his sword and dashing back and forth in the clearing.

"I'm afraid I've done for him. You'd better see to Floramella," Kedrigern said.

"But my feat! I have not accomplished a feat!"

"Alaska's defeated and Floramella's been rescued. Your feat is done, Turll, if that's what it was in the first place."

"*You* defeated Alaska, with your magic."

Kedrigern waved off the remark. "I only shook him loose from my wife. It's you who attacked him."

"And my lady Princess rescued Floramella."

Gently depositing the unconscious maid on the soft greensward, Princess touched down and said, "You made him put her down, Turll. I couldn't let her be squashed flat, could I? We beautiful princesses have to stick together."

"But I should have done *more*! All along, I had the feeling that this was the real thing, the one bold deed, the very feat of all feats that would free my family from the curse of—"

A shrill, piercing cackle of nasty laughter came from overhead, freezing Turll into silence. They looked up as one. High above them, slowly circling the clearing, rode a crone all in tattered black, riding a broomstick.

"Cashalane," whispered Kedrigern with loathing.

"You had your chance, sonny, and you wasted it, and Cashalane has come to gloat," the witch cried, cackling once again. "This could have been the feat that freed the house of Turll, but you missed it. Too late now."

"See? I told you!" Turll said angrily, throwing down his sword and helmet and kicking at the turf.

"Cashalane, what do you mean?" wizard called to her. "The gnome is defeated, the maiden rescued. A noble feat has been done. Free the lad of your curse."

"Kedrigern? Is that you? Keep out of this, wizard! It's *my* curse!"

"Turll is my client. You're not being fair."

"Fair? Me, fair? I'm a wicked witch – I can be as unfair and nasty as I please!" Cashalane gave another bone-chilling laugh.

"No, you can't. There are rules, Cashalane. You put a curse on this lad's family, and you never told anyone how it could be lifted. 'Go do a feat' is not precise enough."

"It's precise enough for me. Besides, his feat was easy. Any fool could have figured it out, even a Turll. All he had to do was put three arrows – a gold, a silver, and a bronze – into the rump of a fleeing giant gnome. He had to be blindfolded at the time, wearing one white glove and one green stocking, and he had to hum 'The Ballad of the Four Fat Friars' backward. That's all there was to it."

"That's not a feat; that's a stunt," said Kedrigern scornfully.

"In my book, it's feat, and now it's too late for a Turll to do it. There won't be another giant gnome in these parts for three generations. By then, the house of Turll will be reduced to beggars and swineherds." She cackled once again, triumphantly.

Princess tugged at Kedrigern's cloak. "You'll be standing here arguing all afternoon, and I'm exhausted. I'm going over under the trees and rest."

"You've certainly earned it, my dear. I'm only sorry things didn't work out better," Kedrigern said, squeezing her hand fondly. Then, to Cashalane, he said, "That's a perfectly reasonable procedure, but you should have made it clear to the accursed."

"I wanted them to use their imagination," the witch called down.

"Why do you hate my family so, witch?" Turll asked.

"Your grandfather called me a vile, disgusting, repulsive, ugly, withered old crone."

"Perhaps he meant it as a compliment," Kedrigern suggested.

"It was the *way* he said it – as if I had something to be ashamed of."

"Well, this young man's done nothing to you, Cashalane. He's been very polite, all things considered. So why don't you just lift the curse?" said the wizard.

Slowly and silently, deep in thought, Cashalane flew in a great circle around the perimeter of the clearing. Twice she circled the little group, and on her third swing, just as she came over the pond, she howled, "No! I won't! Let the house of Turll be cursed forever! That'll teach them!"

At the first word, Princess shot up from the cover of the trees, unseen by the crone. She snatched the broom from under Cashalane's bony bottom, and the witch, as she uttered her final defiance, went plummeting toward the water. Kedrigern pointed, and the broom homed in on his gesture and skidded to a stop before him. He placed a foot upon the handle to secure it, and turned to greet Princess as she came down at his side, unsteady on her feet from sheer exhaustion.

"Well done, my lady!" Turll cried jubilantly.

Jeniby, free of his vow, burbled, "Yes, my lady, well done! Marvelously done! Boldly and bravely done! A most courageous act, a deed of daring, a masterstroke! Never have I seen—" until Turll silenced him.

"A clever move, my dear," said Kedrigern, putting his arm around her shoulders.

"I wasn't sure I could bring it off," she said wearily. "My wings are killing me. But it was the only chance."

"Let's see if you've persuaded Cashalane to change her mind," Kedrigern said. He took up the broom, which wriggled in his grasp. "You behave yourself, or you'll be a pile of toothpicks and kindling," he snapped. The broom was still at once, its bristles sagging in terror.

Cashalane hung from a branch, the pointed toes of her cracked and dusty shoes almost touching the surface of the pond. "Get me out of this, Kedrigern," she said in a low, nervous voice.

"That's the deepest spot right there, Turll," Kedrigern said languidly, pointing with the broom to the water beneath

Cashalane's feet. "Drop something in there, and it would sink without a trace."

"Good," said Turll.

"I can't hold on much longer. Help me, Kedrigern!"

"Lift the curse."

Cashalane paused, agonized by the choice, and at last cried, "I lift the curse! Turll and his descendants are free of my curse, and need not do a feat, now or ever!"

"And you will seek no other vengeance on them, or us, or anyone at all, ever, and there will be no tricks about this. Swear by the heads of Hecate and the wens of Sycorax."

"I swear! I swear!"

"Go get her," said Kedrigern, tossing the broom in the witch's direction. It glided swiftly over the water until it came to rest beneath her, then it rose and settled snugly under her skinny rump. When her perch was secure, she loosed her handgrip.

"All right for you, Kedrigern," she said. "And for your flying lady, too. You'll regret this, I'll—"

"Remember what you swore, Cashalane," said Kedrigern in a cold and ominous voice. "Have you forgotten what became of Wozbog when she violated that very same oath? Would you like me to remind you?"

Cashalane's face contorted. She clenched her fists and grew very pale. After a moment she calmed herself. Her bony hands dropped to her lap. "I'll be good," she whispered hoarsely, and flew off without another word or a backward glance.

Kedrigern let out a long sigh of relief. "Well, that wraps it up, Turll. You can bring Floramella home, announce the wedding, and have Llunn the Lavish deliver the reward to me. You know the directions."

Jeniby spoke up at once. "May I be the messenger? Not only am I familiar with the roads, I am loyal and trustworthy as well, and those are rare qualities in these parlous times when an enemy lurks behind every smile, travel is fraught with perils, and even the bravest knight must look with uncertainty at—"

"You may be the messenger," Turll broke in. "Leave at once. And now I must see to my fair Floramella."

"It's about time," Princess muttered.

As Turll cradled Floramella in his arms, dabbed her brow

with a moist cloth, and lifted his water bottle to her lips, Kedrigern and Princess walked to the heap of clothing that lay in the middle of the clearing. Kedrigern lifted one roomy sleeve and felt the material between his fingers.

"That looks like good stuff," Princess said.

"Gnomes are skilled weavers. We should take this home. You could make two cloaks for each of us out of the tunic alone."

"I might as well. Alaska won't be needing it anymore."

"No," said the wizard gloomily.

"I almost feel sorry for the poor creature. He didn't really hurt anyone, and if it hadn't been for him, Turll would still be cursed."

"I know," said Kedrigern, almost inaudibly.

"Did you really have to annihilate him?"

By this time, Kedrigern was feeling terrible about the whole thing. He recalled his promise to Alaska's aging father, and his heart sank at the thought of explaining his impulsive action to the old gnome. He lowered his eyes, gazing vacantly and despondently on the expanse of empty breeches.

Something in the left leg stirred, was still, then stirred again. It was about the size of a small cat. Kedrigern turned to Princess with a confident smile.

"What makes you so sure I annihilated him? Didn't you hear me promise his father I'd find a cure for the lad?" he said.

"You promised to try. But surely . . ."

A tiny groan came from the left leg of the breeches. Kedrigern knelt, reached in, and drew out a little man, stark naked. The gnome covered his eyes against the bright sunlight, scrunched up to preserve his modesty, and groaned, "Where am I? What hit me?"

"Just a bit of magic, that's all. I'll put you inside my tunic until we can find something for you to wear, and then we'll take you home."

"He had a pouch at his belt. It should be just about the right size for him now," said Princess, scanning the ground. "There it is. I'll cut holes in it for his little arms and legs."

"I seem to remember . . . being big. Was I big?" Alaska asked from inside Kedrigern's tunic.

"Yes. Very big."

"Was I bad?"

"You might have been worse. Now you'd better rest. You've had a busy time of it. We'll take you home tonight."

Floramella was unharmed, but too weak to travel. Turll pitched a tent for her in a sunny corner of the clearing, near the pond, and there she rested. Princess and Kedrigern remained to serve as chaperones. Floramella accepted Alaska's apology graciously, as did Turll, who saluted him as a valiant adversary and helped bandage his injured toe. All was harmony.

That night, Kedrigern was awakened from a sound sleep. The warning spell he had laid around their little encampment had gone off, but very mildly. Whoever was approaching was small, and probably friendly. Nevertheless, an intruder was an intruder, and not to be ignored. The wizard dragged himself from his blanket and groped for his boots. Princess stirred and mumbled.

"No cause for alarm, my dear," said Kedrigern, yawning.

"Ngff. Larm," she said in a muffled, sleepy voice.

"I'm just going to look outside."

He left the tent. Outside, wide awake, looking preposterous in his makeshift attire, Alaska was waiting. "They've come to fetch me," said the gnome. He pointed to the forest, where tiny points of light moved along close to the ground.

At Alaska's suggestion, they withdrew to a nearby tree, a huge old oak with a small mound near its base, the kind of site favored by little men. They were soon joined by Alaska's kin. There were subdued greetings, expression of joy, some laughter, and then a familiar voice called, "Wizard!"

"Yes?" Kedrigern replied.

"You cured my boy. He's as healthy as ever, and not a mark on him, except for his toe."

"I use only the best magic."

"You have done what no one, gnome or wizard, has ever done before. You must be rewarded."

A praiseworthy attitude, Kedrigern thought. The sort of attitude to be encouraged. But not abused. He was likely to receive a staggering reward from Llunn the Lavish, and there was no need to be greedy. Especially since Alaska's cure had been a matter of sheer luck. "What I'd really like most is the big suit of clothes Alaska was wearing during his . . . his affliction," he said.

Embarrassed silence followed his words. After a very long pause, the aged gnome said, "The great suit is a tradition in every gnome settlement, the work of many hands over many years. It will take us long to replace it. But if this is the reward you wish—"

"No, no. I couldn't think of taking it from you," said Kedrigern, waving the old gnome to silence. "I didn't realize its significance."

"All the same, you must have a reward."

Kedrigern pondered for a moment, then said brightly, "I have it! The gnomon on my sundial is bent, so I'm always ahead of time, or behind time, and never exactly *on* time. I know you make the best ones, so just give me a new gnomon and we'll call it even."

"Is this all you ask of us?"

"It's all I really need at the moment."

"Then you shall have it before the sun rises."

"Oh, there's no need to rush. I don't really have to . . ." But his protests were vain. The little lights vanished, and all was still. Kedrigern waited for a time, but heard only the accustomed noises of the night. Eventually he became uncomfortably chilly, and returned to the tent. Princess did not move or make a sound.

Sometime later the warning spell went off again. Kedrigern groaned, stirred himself, and peeked from the tent. The sky was pale with false dawn, but he could see nothing and no one. The silence was profound. He listened for a time, even inspected the clearing through the Aperture of True Vision in his medallion. All was in order; the world was at peace. He gratefully returned to Princess's side.

Next morning, when he took up his boot, a slender bundle fell out. It was the length of his forearm, and was wrapped in soft cloth and bound with thread as fine as gossamer. It was heavy and solid. He took it outside the tent and undid it carefully, and when he pulled back the last fold of wrapping, he blinked at the sudden blaze of light as the morning sun infused a multifaceted diamond the size of his thumbnail, set into a golden gnomon engraved with words and signs of power. He gave a long, muted whistle of astonished gratitude, but he had no proper words to say, even to himself. He whistled again.

"Keddie? Have you got a lantern out there? It's awfully bright," came Princess's sleepy voice from within the tent.

"It's a gnomon. From the gnomes. For our sundial."

"From the little men?"

"There's nothing little about them, my dear. Come have a look."

THE CAT WITH TWO TAILS

Terry Jones

What Spike Milligan and the Goons achieved for radio, the Monty Python brigade achieved for television. It was also a special boon for comic fantasy as most of the Python team, especially Terry Jones (b. 1942) and Terry Gilliam (b. 1940), have a fascination for fantasy, both visually and in the written word. In the case of Terry Jones this has manifested itself in such books as The Saga of Erik the Viking *(1983) and the not unrelated film* Erik the Viking *(1989), the television series* Ripping Yarns *(1976) with Michael Palin, and the children's books* Fairy Tales *(1980),* Nicobobinus *(1985),* The Curse of the Vampire Socks *(1988) and* Fantastic Stories *(1992), from which the following story is taken.*

In the olden days all cats had two tails – one for the daytime and one for the night. During the day they kept their long, thick daytime tail curled around themselves and slept tight and snug. But when it grew dark – ah! then each cat would go to a secret place and there it would reach in its paw and pull out a bundle wrapped in mouse-fur. Then it would wait until it was sure . . . absolutely sure . . . that nobody and nothing . . . absolutely nothing . . . was looking. (For cats, you must know, are crafty as only cats can be.) And then it would unwrap the bundle of mouse-fur, and there, inside, would be its own – its very own – night-time tail.

Its night-time tail was an ordinary length and an ordinary thickness, but it would twitch as it lay there in the bundle of mouse-fur. And although it was only an ordinary length and an ordinary thickness, it was nevertheless a very remarkable tail indeed.

Can you guess why? Well . . . I'll tell you . . . It shone – as bright as day. And every cat would *off!* with its daytime tail in the twinkling of an eye, and *on!* with its shining night-time tail. And they'd hold their tails above their heads, and light the night as bright as day, and all the mice would tremble in the darkest corners of their holes.

When the cats stepped out, the badgers and the foxes would stop whatever they were doing to watch and clap. But every family of mice huddled together deeper in their holes, and their whiskers shook.

When the cats stepped out, the weasels and the stoats would stand on each others' shoulders to get a better view, but the mouse babies crept closer into their mothers' arms.

Now one day, a certain mouse said: "I've had enough!"

And his wife replied: "You're always right, of course, my dear. But enough of what? We haven't had anything to eat for days."

"That's right!" said the mouse. "We've had nothing to eat because those cats sleep outside our holes all day, wrapped up in their long, thick daytime tails. And at night, just when you'd think it would be safe to tiptoe out and steal a piece of cheese . . ."

"Just *one* piece of cheese!" twittered all his children.

"Those cats put on their night-time tails, and light the night as bright as day!"

"You never spoke a truer word, my dear," said his wife. "Those cats are crafty as only cats can be . . ."

"*That's* why I've had enough!" exclaimed the mouse, and he

banged his paw on the nest. And his children felt very frightened
– as they always did whenever their father got cross.

"So, since nobody else seems to be doing anything, I,
Frederick Ferdinand Fury-Paws The Forty-Fourth, intend to
do something about it!"

"Oh, do be careful!" twittered his wife, who was always
alarmed when her husband used his full name. "Don't do
anything rash, my dear! Don't let your strength and size lead
you to do things you might regret!"

But before you could say "cheesefeathers!" that mouse had
scuttled off to the Father Of All Things, and made his
complaint.

The Father Of All Things listened with his head on one side.
And then he listened with his head on the other side.

Then he turned to the Mother Of All Cats, who was pretending
to be asleep nearby, and said: "Well, Mother Of All Cats? It
doesn't seem fair that you should have two tails when every
other creature has only one."

"Oh, I don't know," replied the Mother Of All Cats. "Some
creatures have two legs, some creatures have four legs, some
creatures have six legs and some – like the ungrateful centipede
– have a hundred! So why shouldn't us cats have two tails?"

"Because," said the mouse, "it's unfair to us mice. You can
see us by day *and* by night! We don't stand a chance."

And so they argued all day long, until the Father Of All
Things said: "Enough! All creatures have only one head. And
as it is with the head, so it should be with the tail."

At this all the mice cheered. But the Mother Of All Cats
twitched her crafty whiskers and smiled and said: "Very true.
Therefore let us cats have only one tail in future – but do you
agree to let us choose which sort of tail?"

The Father Of All Things turned to the mouse and asked:
"Do you agree to this?"

And the mouse replied: "Yes! Yes! But only the one tail!"

So the Father Of All Things said: "Very well, you may
choose."

"Then," said the Mother Of All Cats, giving her tail a crafty
flick, "please take note that we cats choose the sort of tail that
is thick and long to keep us warm (like our daytime tails) *and*

shining bright to light the night (just like our night-time tails)
– both at the same time."

"That reply was crafty as only a cat's can be," said the Father
Of All Things.

And all the other mice turned on Frederick Ferdinand
Fury-Paws The Forty-Fourth and said: "There! Now see what
your meddling's done! It'll be twice as bad as it was before!"

The mouse bent his whiskers to the floor and cried out: "Oh,
please, Father Of All Things, don't allow the cats to have tails that
are like their daytime tails *and* like their night-time tails both at
the same time, or, I fear, we mice will all be destroyed!"

But the Father Of All Things replied: "I cannot go back on
my word." And he turned to the Mother Of All Cats, who was
sitting sleek and crafty as only cats can be, and he said:

"Mother Of All Cats, do you promise to be satisfied if I give
you a tail that is like your daytime tail and like your night-time
tail – both at the same time?"

And the Mother Of All Cats smiled a crafty smile, and said:
"I agree."

And all the cats and stoats and weasels cheered, and the
baby mice crept even further into their mothers' arms and their
fathers wrung their paws in despair.

"Then, from this day forth," said the Father Of All Things,
"let all cats' tails be like their night-time tails – ordinary in
size, neither thick nor long. And let them be also like their
daytime tails – not shining bright to light the night – but just
ordinary tails."

And no sooner had the Father Of All Things said this, than
there was a crack and a whizz, and all the cats' tails turned into
ordinary tails, very much like they are today.

When they saw that, all the mice cheered, and the cats blew
on their whiskers and slunk off into the forest.

But now I have to tell you a terrible thing, which goes to show
that cats really are as crafty as only cats can be.

That very night – the mouse said to his wife: "My dear,
now it is dark, let us go for a promenade, for – thanks
to my efforts – it is now perfectly safe to walk abroad at
eventide, since cats no longer have tails that are shining

bright to light the night, and they will not be able to see us."

And his wife said: "As always, my dear, you know best."

And so they put on their best summer coats and frocks, and they stepped out of their hole and at once were pounced upon by the cat. For cats, of course, have all got special night-time eyes, and have always been able to see as perfectly well by night as they can by day – with or without their shining tails.

They really are as crafty as only cats can be . . .

THE WARLOCK'S DAUGHTER

Anthony Armstrong

We start this fairy-tale sequence with one by the too-soon-forgotten Anthony Armstrong, or to call him by his real name, George Willis (1897–1976). He was a regular contributor to Punch *and similar magazines, and was at his peak in the 1920s and 1930s, when his output was comparable to P. G. Wodehouse. He wrote a number of clever parodies of fairy tales which were published as* The Prince Who Hiccupped *(1932) and* The Pack of Pieces *(1942), required reading for anyone who thinks that comic fantasy first appeared last week.*

Once upon a very long time ago there was rather a pleasant young man called Erroll, who lived with his father in a wood. This was because his father was a woodcutter by profession, and found it handier than living, say, on the seashore.

Well, one day the old woodcutter unfortunately got on the

wrong side of a tree he was felling and left Erroll fatherless, and – since he had rather stupidly neglected to teach him the art of woodcutting – without a job as well. So the young man gathered up all his possessions in a bundle and set out into the world to seek his fortune, which was about the best thing he could have done, for in those days a humble woodcutter's son generally fell on his feet.

Towards nightfall some evenings later he came up to a large castle and wondered if there'd be a chance of getting a job there, as under-scullion or something. So he asked a passing farmer if he could tell him who was the owner.

The farmer replied morosely that he did hear tell a warlock or some such lived in the place; at any rate, that there castle had appeared suddenly during the night a week ago. Looking at it more closely, Erroll could well believe this, for it seemed to have been set down very carelessly on an angle of four fields with one side in each, and, moreover, had a small river running right through it. The farmer, he soon learnt, was very bitter about the whole incident; because it seemed he owned two of the fields, and the pesky thing hadn't done his root crop no good. In those days countrymen had worse things than mere weather and poor fat-stock prices to contend against.

Erroll thanked him and was hurrying past the castle – he preferred to keep clear of magic if possible – when he was hailed cheerily from a window and told to come on in and spend the night.

The young man paused doubtfully. Warlocks were warlocks, and you never knew what they'd be up to next. Often it was something quite distressing, such as getting your head set backwards on your shoulders, which the warlock, however, seemed to think funny. On the other hand, this particular warlock sounded friendly enough.

"It's getting dark," he yelled again, "and it looks like rain! You must stop over. I insist."

Erroll went. One didn't cross warlocks who insisted.

His fears were groundless. This warlock was a pleasant old man and apparently delighted to see him, though he waved aside any suggestion of taking Erroll into his employ.

"Nearly all my servants are fairies," he pointed out. "Got a gnome as under-scullion, a wizard chef, and so on. Brought 'em all with me from fairyland. No, you be my guest for to-night. Only too glad to have company. The people round here don't seem to like me. Come to that, they don't anywhere. I keep moving house, but I can't find a really friendly neighbourhood. Had the old shack over in Latavia the other day and the local farmers tried to burn it. Never mind that now though. I'm glad you've turned up. Shall we take a stoup before supper?"

Well, what with one thing and another, Erroll spent a very cheery evening, and they even played cards without the slightest suspicion of his host materializing magical aces at a moment favourable to himself – which in his position he might quite reasonably have been expected to do. In fact, the warlock's only drawback was a tendency to harp on the subject of his unpopularity in every neighbourhood he visited, and when Erroll, pointing out that the question of land tenure had something to do with it, tactfully suggested that he might have big parties now and then and invite all the people round, by way of showing his friendly disposition, the warlock seemed to think it a grand idea.

"Only drawback though," he said, when referring to it again next morning as Erroll was on the point of departure, "is that I ought to wait till my daughter is home to act as hostess . . . That reminds me," he broke off, "if you see her on your travels you might tell her where I am."

"Your daughter? But how shall I know her?"

"Oh, she's very pretty, dark hair, grey eyes, name of Joy – her mother's idea, poor soul," he added hastily. "She— er— went out for a walk a fortnight ago and hasn't come back yet."

Erroll was frankly puzzled. "Doesn't she *know* where you are? Aren't you afraid something's happened to her?"

"Oh, she can look after herself all right. It's just that she's lost. You see," he went on in rather an embarrassed manner, "I suppose it's in a way my fault. I forgot she was out and went and moved the castle over a mountain range because it started to rain. And then I found it was snowing there, so I moved on, and— er— to cut a long story short, forgot where I'd been at first. So when she, as it were, got back home, home wasn't there."

"I should think she'd be pretty angry by now."

"That's what I'm afraid of," admitted the other frankly; "she takes after her poor mother. Of course I take out the big touring carpet every morning and fly around, but I haven't come across her yet. Trouble is, she may have changed herself into something for fun – girls won't be girls these days. So do tell her where I am, if you come across her, there's a good chap."

"Certainly," said Erroll, and set off. He had just reached the gate when he was called back.

"Just remembered. I may have to move about a bit – don't like the look of these peasants – so you'd better take one of our travelling rugs with you." Seeing Erroll's puzzled look, he went on, "Air travel, you know. It's just a little runabout. I'd let you have the big saloon carpet, but the great thing about this one is it always flies straight home – *wherever* home is."

He handed the young man a little green rug, said a friendly good-bye, and Erroll at last set off. At lunch time he halted and, because it was a little damp, he sat on the rug. Five minutes later he was in the castle again, the rug apparently having a concealed self-starter somewhere.

"Should have warned you," said the warlock, who was just sitting down to a chop. "Never mind, now you're here you'd better stop to lunch." He waved a wand over the dish and another chop appeared beside the first.

After lunch Erroll set off again. At supper he halted, but took care not to sit on the rug. That outward journey on foot was becoming a little monotonous.

Some days later he came to a little stream and was just starting to wade across when a voice said:

"Here! Steady on, please! Mind me!"

Erroll looked round, and soon saw a green lizard sunning itself. "I beg your pardon," he said and made it a sweeping bow. The lizard merely ran away. Rather mystified, for generally at this point disguised fairies assumed their own shape and wanted something done for them – and you had to be pretty polite as well, or you got something you didn't like done for *you* – Erroll was starting across the stream again when the same voice repeated:

"I said, 'Mind me!'"

"Where are you?" asked Erroll.

"I'm the stream, and that's my face you've got your foot on."

Erroll removed it.

"Are you really the stream, or just *being* a stream?" In those days a little point like that often made a lot of difference: one could ignore a mere stream to a certain extent.

"No, I'm being one for the moment. It's cool and one can talk to oneself and so on. I was rather enjoying it till you came along in that clumsy fashion. Treading on a girl's face!" the stream concluded rather huffily.

This struck Erroll as unreasonable. "Look here. I don't know who you are," he said, "but if you go around like that you must expect things to happen to you. Why, I might have— might have spat into you to see which way you were flowing, or something. Be reasonable!"

There was a silence.

Then, "Sorry!" said the voice in a subdued manner. "Silly of me."

"That's all right," acknowledged Erroll kindly.

"You know, you look rather nice."

"You look— er— cool and inviting at the moment," responded Erroll gallantly. "And I love your voice. But what are you *really* like?"

"Well, my name's Joy, and I'm . . ."

"But *how* lucky!" cried Erroll. "I've just been with your father, and he's sent you this rug."

"What? Our homing rug?" The voice gave quite a squeak of relief.

"Yes. He wants you to go home on it."

"I will. *And* I'll tell him off, too. Stupid old thing! Can't turn my back on home for a moment and home's gone. But what can I do for you in return? I'm terribly grateful. I was really getting a little scared."

"Well, I'm off to seek my fortune. Perhaps you . . ."

"In those clothes?"

"All I've got," replied Erroll ruefully. "I'm only a woodcutter's son."

"I'll tell you what I'll do then for a start. Go on on your journey, and when you wake next morning you'll find yourself travelling with everything even a Prince could want."

"I say! That's charming of you."

"Not at all. Just a simple little spell. Learnt it a year ago. And if ever you're in a real difficulty, take this jewel . . ."

"What jewel?"

"Right in front of you."

Peering into the water Erroll saw at the bottom of the stream a glittering red gem on a gold chain.

"Am I to take it now?"

"Certainly."

"Then— er— excuse me!" He reached down his hand and fumbled for the jewel.

"Hurry up! You're tickling!"

"Terribly sorry!" stammered Erroll, rather embarrassed, as he at last secured the jewel and hung it round his neck.

"When you turn the jewel round three times I shall appear— and, well, see what I can do to help you."

"I say – it's awfully decent. How can I ever thank you?"

"Don't! I'm doing it to thank *you*. And because I rather like you," the voice added softly.

"I like you, too – that is, if I could see you. *Can't* you change back for a bit?"

"Not till you're out of sight." The stream gurgled with laughter. "You see, I've got no clothes on. They're behind that bush. Now, leave my rug on the bank, there's a nice boy, and set off."

Gallantly Erroll raised a handful of water to his lips and kissed it, then with a cheery farewell continued on his travels, wondering a good deal what the unknown Joy was really like. By now, he imagined, since he was safely out of sight, she must just have changed into her real shape and be making for her clothes. An idea struck him and he began to turn the jewel. After all, he reflected, as he finished turning, he could always say that he just wanted to see if it really worked . . .

Next moment he was spluttering under a shower of water and a gay laugh was sounding in his ears.

"I *thought* so!" came Joy's mocking young voice from the midst of it, "so I waited. I said, only use when you're in a *real difficulty*. Now get along do, and don't be so naughty again!"

Erroll laughed and resumed his journey. He was keeping an eager eye open for real difficulties.

He awoke next morning in considerable surprise. For a moment he couldn't think what had happened. Then as he fingered his rich clothes and saw the gay silk tent in which he lay, he remembered.

He went out and found a squire waiting with his horse, also two pack-mules laden with luxuries, and half a dozen respectful servants. Evidently he had become, as Joy had promised, practically a Prince overnight. He mounted and rode on, feeling more and more like a Prince as he went. Three days later he came in sight of a magnificent castle.

"That is the King of Cabbodia's Castle," announced his squire, who seemed to know everything. "His daughter is the Princess Serena, and every Prince in the neighbourhood is at the moment competing for her hand. I have already sent ahead entering your name for the contest."

"Oh, have you," said Erroll. "I'm not a Prince."

"*They* won't know that."

"But I mightn't like her."

"Wait till you see her. She's as beautiful as the day is long," replied the squire, putting his fingers to his lips and blowing a kiss into the air.

At that very moment the King of Cabbodia was hurriedly finishing his breakfast, with one eye on the sundial just outside the window. He was already late for an important Grand Council. He gulped down the last bit of toast, wiped his mouth, and only pausing to pick up a crown from the crown-rack in the hall, strode into the Second Best Throne Room, where his Counsellors were assembled.

"Morning, all!" said the King, seating himself on the Second Best Throne, not liking it much, and sending a young Counsellor for another cushion. "I'm not really *late*, you know. The Dining Room sundial is slow again. Now to business. Court Chamberlain!"

The Court Chamberlain shuffled apprehensively forward. He was an aged man who, judging from an occasional champing of the jaws and several crumbs in his long white beard, had also only just finished breakfast.

"About the competition! Everything arranged? By the way, there's a new Prince entered. Ear-oil, or some such name."

"Erroll, Your Majesty. He arrives to-night."

"Good! That makes fourteen. Have you drawn the lots yet, for who has first go?"

"Well, Your Majesty, there's a difficulty . . ." The old man paused and swallowed twice, apparently from nervousness, though it may have been because he had just found some hitherto overlooked bit of breakfast. "I'm— er— afraid," he went on in increasing confusion, "that the fierce Aurochs which the Princes had to fight in order to decide . . ." He paused again, this time agitatedly to comb crumbs out of his beard.

"Come on," said the King. "What's happened to our Aurochs . . . There's still a bit of toast, by the way, down in the left-hand corner. Or else it's haddock. No, further over! There! Now leave your beard alone and get on with it."

"I'm afraid he's *died*," the old man blurted out.

"Died?"

"Yes, he ate some varlet that disagreed with him."

"Tut, tut!" said the King. "Poor old Towser! Now we *are* in a hole. What are they to do instead?"

"If I might suggest, Your Majesty," put in a shrewd-looking Counsellor, "why not change the competition and make it one to find water in that patch of desert just outside the town. We've always wanted a well there, so it would serve a double purpose . . ."

"Good idea!" cried the King. "And we'll give them each one night to do it in."

"Only *one* night, Your Majesty?" interposed the Court Chamberlain.

"Why not? One of them might quite well strike it right away. Besides – *do* leave your beard alone, please; it looks all right from the outside, but heaven knows what'll come to light if you keep stirring it up like that – besides, we must make it a *little* difficult for them, otherwise it reflects on Princess Serena."

"Still, we musn't risk them *all* failing," pointed out another Counsellor. "I mean, then we mightn't get our well at all."

"In that case we'll ask the Court Magician to provide one. It'll be child's play to him. Come to think of it, he might have done it before. That sort of thing is *his* job. However . . ." He rose from his throne. "That's settled then. We'll announce it to the Princes to-morrow. I'm sorry about Towser, but perhaps *they* won't be. So long, all! I mean— the Grand Council is now terminated."

He bustled from the room. The Counsellors all bowed. The Court Chamberlain ran to earth the final crumb of toast that had been annoying him. The shrewd-looking Counsellor hurried off to buy a cheap option on the bit of desert land in question.

The following day the terms of the Well-Finding Contest were formally announced, and for the next three nights three Princes tried and failed. Erroll, who had drawn fourth place, had spent the interval in getting to know the Princess Serena, who, as his squire had said, was as beautiful as the day was long – and the fellow obviously hadn't meant any December day either. Erroll decided he liked her very much, and that he would win her if humanly possible. But when his turn came that night and he found himself outside the town moodily surveying the desert, he realized he was up against a real difficulty.

At once he thought of his jewel and turned it three times.

Next moment a lovely young girl stood smiling before him.

"I wondered when I was going to get a call," she said.

"Are you really Joy?" he asked incredulously.

"Yes. Don't you recognize my voice? And look! Here's the green travelling rug. It's just brought me."

She stepped off it as she spoke and came nearer to him. "Well how do you like me?"

"I— I think you're lovely," stammered Erroll. He wanted to say a lot more on the subject, but all he could get out was: "So you got home all right?"

"Naturally," smiled Joy. "But Father had moved again. Still, it's a much nicer neighbourhood, near a delightful spring, and he's decided to have parties and try and get to know people."

"Talking of springs," said Erroll thoughtfully, "my difficulty is . . ." He stopped. He had suddenly realized he didn't now want to find that well as much as he had a short while before. "That is . . . let's talk, shall we?"

"First, what's your difficulty?"

"Nothing at all. Matter of fact, I was just looking at the jewel and turned it by mistake."

"Liar! You've got to tell me – if you want me to stay and talk to you."

So Erroll naturally had to tell her.

"Oh, that!" cried Joy. "That's easy." She clapped her hands and suddenly a stream of water was gushing out at their feet.

"Here, I say!" cried Erroll in dismay. "You've done it now. I shall have to marry the Princess Serena."

"Don't you want to?"

"I should be marrying her under false pretences."

"Meaning you're not really a Prince – and haven't found the water yourself?"

"No. Meaning I want to marry someone else, now I've seen her."

Joy looked a little embarrassed. "I— I don't quite follow."

"Yes, you do." He moved towards her.

She retreated to the travelling rug. "But suppose I . . ."

She stopped speaking, largely because Erroll, who could not be accused of being backward, was kissing her rather thoroughly.

"What will Father say?" Joy managed to get out at last.

Next minute they knew, for by then they were both standing on the travelling rug, and once again Erroll had inadvertently trodden on the self-starter.

What the warlock said, however, cannot really be repeated here, for it was very impolite. On the other hand, the rug *had* taken them on to his best corn as he sat in front of the fire having a nightcap. Moreover, he had upset his wine.

"You do flip about, Joy!" he grumbled, wiping himself down. "Why, Erroll's here, too! What's he doing?"

"Can't you see? Kissing me. He's going to be your son-in-law."

"Bless my whiskers! Congratulations! We must celebrate this." He clapped his hands and a fairy major-domo appeared.

"Tell you what! This is a chance for that idea of yours."

He turned to the fairy. "Let there be a big party to-morrow," he commanded, "and invite everyone in the neighbourhood. Particularly the— er— as it were, ground landlord of the castle at the moment . . ."

The celebratory party next day was, as one may imagine with a warlock as host, done in slap-up style, starting off with a big banquet with vintage nectar, honey-dew cup, and a new dish specially created for the occasion by the wizard Head Chef and named in Joy's honour, *Filets de Joie d' Ambrosia*. Many of the elderly people present, while considering that the name sounded a little vulgar, took two helpings and said it was better than anything they'd ever tasted before. As a matter of fact, the Head Chef hadn't really taken very much trouble over creating the dish. Being a wizard, he had simply waved his wand over the range and said, "Let there be a dish better than anything anyone has ever tasted before," and there the darn thing was – almost before he could add that he was catering for three hundred.

About halfway through the subsequent dance the warlock, who had been doing himself well, called for silence.

"I want all you nice people," he announced, "to drink a lil toast. The health, gemmen, of the yappy cung hupple."

"And yours, too, zur," cried all the peasants and farmers, after they had done so, at which the warlock beamed very happily. It seemed he had achieved popularity at last. He took a large drink himself and invited them all to another party the following week, took another, and made it a weekly fixture. Then he drank the happy pair's health again and, having cried loudly, "On with the dance. Let Joy be unconfined," sat down in considerable embarrassment, muttering to himself that it was just a figure of speech, and that nothing was further from his thoughts.

And as for Princess Serena? Well, Erroll was considered to have let her down very badly by disappearing after he had legally won her hand; and she rather cleverly sent all the other Princes off on a quest to find him and avenge her honour. Then while they were safely out of the way she married a handsome young knight at her father's court, whom she'd had her eye on all the time.

But Erroll and Joy lived happy ever after.

THE GLASS SLIP-UP

Louise Cooper

Louise Cooper (b. 1952) doesn't write many short stories. She is probably best known for her long-running Indigo sequence of fantasy novels which began with Nemesis *(1988), although she had her first novel,* The Book of Paradox *(1973), published when she was twenty. Here she turns her hand to exploring what happened after Cinderella married the Prince.*

When his wife started telling Baron Grog the one about the three nuns and the deaf centaur, Charming shut his eyes and prayed that the ground would open up and swallow him. The prayer was not answered – they never were – so after a few seconds he opened his eyes again and with a sickly smile started a one-sided, trivial and utterly desperate conversation with the Dowager Duchess to his right at the banqueting table.

". . . unseasonably warm for the time of year, I think, Duchess. The crops are all ripening early, and—"

"—So the centaur says, 'Eh? What?' and the second nun –

she's red as a beetroot by now, right? – shouts at the top of her voice—"

". . . all the palace gardeners are predicting an absolute glut, more than any year in their experience, and most of them have been in our service for—"

"—Then the nun shrieks, 'BALLS – I SAID, BALLS!' And the centaur turns to the third nun and says—"

". . . And the *roses*! Father says he hasn't seen such a display since—"

"*AHAHAHAHAHAHA!*" The noise, which had the volume, if not the melody or anything dimly resembling it, of a full symphonic crescendo, ripped through the hall. The joke was finished, and Charming's wife was laughing. Those closest to her at the table, including Baron Grog, made great efforts to pull their faces into expressions of hilarity (protocol was protocol, after all), but it was clearly costing them. From the head of the table the king, Charming's father, drew his brows together and gave his son a Look, and Charming could only offer silent thanks that his mother had pleaded a diplomatic headache and excused herself before the feast began.

Rell was reaching for the port, which she vastly preferred to wine and insisted on having to hand during every meal, to the horror of the palace's senior steward. She filled her glass, drained it, smacked her lips and filled it again before taking another hearty swig.

"Cor, that's better. Makes you thirsty, laughing, eh?" Her head came up and she waved coquettishly towards her husband. "All right, Charm?"

Across the table Araminta, the younger and uglier of Rell's stepsisters, gave a snigger that she quickly disguised as a genteel cough. Two seats up, her elder sister, Arabella, raised her plucked and pencilled eyebrows, then met Charming's gaze with an unequivocal message, tempered by a meaningful warning glance in the direction of her own husband. But for once Charming felt no stir of excitement. Even the prospect of Arabella's particular brand of consolation couldn't move him tonight. He felt too downhearted. It was all becoming just *too* much.

The banquet ended at last, and guests began to mingle less

formally in the great hall and adjoining anterooms. No one saw Charming slip away into the gardens, but a little while later his stepmother-in-law, who needed a breath of fresh air, found him glooming among the rhododendrons on the palace's west side.

The second Lady Hardup was, to use Charming's own words, quite a good egg. She had tried at the start to warn Charming obliquely about Rell, though Charming had then been too besotted to pay any heed. An error he regretted now, of course. As Lady H had once gently pointed out, she and her natural daughters weren't monsters out of some childish fairy tale. There had been a *reason* why they kept Rell at home in the kitchen. She was, quite simply, an embarrassment. It was Charming's sheer bad luck that she had happened to behave herself at that first ball and, later, during the glass slipper business when the royal party had come knocking unsuspectingly at their door. Beyond that, though, Lady H had never once said "told you so". She had tried, indeed, to help him. And, under the weight of parental and social disapproval that now dogged his every step, Charming sometimes suspected that she was the only real friend he had.

She fell into step beside him and, after a few paces of sympathetic silence, said, "She told me that joke once; about four years ago. We were in the garden at the time. Countess Aniseed was paying a courtesy call . . ."

Charming nodded. Countess Aniseed, he recalled, was very religious. For a few moments there was a silence of mutual understanding. Then Lady Hardup spoke again.

"I blame that wretched pumpkin woman, of course. She was new to the district, and in my opinion she was simply looking for a way to ingratiate herself with a wealthy patron." She paused. "You haven't found her yet, I presume?"

Charming shook his head. "She seems to have vanished without trace. We haven't found a single clue."

"Hmm. That's always the problem with witches. They have methods that aren't available to the rest of us." Lady H scowled. "White mice, indeed . . . at least the cat put paid to *them*."

"A little late, unfortunately," said Charming.

"Quite." She sighed. "Well, we can but hope that she'll turn up eventually. Thanks be that there are no children on the way to complicate matters." Then her expression changed and she looked worriedly at him. "Um . . . I *presume* that situation hasn't changed?"

Charming thought back to his wedding night, and what Rell had suggested when they were alone in the royal bedchamber. All that *cream* . . . the kidskin gloves and feather boa had been brand new; and wanting to use the antique damask curtains really had been the last straw. It was off-putting in the extreme, and had stayed that way.

"No," he said aloud. "It hasn't changed."

"Well, that's a small mercy." Lady H had noted his embarrassment and drew her own, reasonably accurate, conclusions. She patted his arm gently. "Have patience. We'll find an answer. And in the meantime, you have the sympathy of us all." She paused, then smiled meaningfully. "Especially Arabella."

Charming's entire face turned scarlet, but before he could start to stammer out a denial she added, "Don't worry, my dear; Arabella's husband hasn't the smallest suspicion. But she and I have *always* been close."

Charming gulped. "Yes, I . . . I see. Ah . . . thank you for . . . um . . ."

"My discretion? Not at all; not at all. I only wish that the glass slipper had fitted Bella in the first place. If it had, we should all have avoided a great deal of trouble."

Charming was saved from replying as light footsteps clicked along the terrace behind them. They both looked, and saw a sumptuously dressed slim figure with piled-up golden hair approaching.

"Ah." Lady Hardup's eyebrows lifted, just an iota. "Someone is searching for you, I think. With your permission, I shall take my leave."

She didn't wait for permission to be given, but turned and glided away towards the steps at the terrace's opposite end. As her shape faded into the gloom, the newcomer reached the balustrade and leaned over.

"Oho, so *there* you are!" Gold satin and purple velvet gleamed in the light spilling from the great hall, and the figure skimmed down the nearer steps to join Charming. "What's the matter, petal; feeling a bit under the weather? Never mind; here's Uncle Dandini to kiss it all better!"

Charming evaded the attempt at an embrace, and Dandini shrugged, stepping back and patting a strand of his coiffe into place. Then his brown, cow-like eyes flicked to the vanishing form of Lady Hardup. "The Gorgon been bothering you, has she? What was it this time; complaining about that joke?"

"She's heard it before. And she's not a gorgon. Far from it, in fact. She's very sympathetic."

'Well, I suppose she can afford to be, since it's only through your connections that she found a husband for that *appalling* daughter of hers. But I'm not here to have a nice bitch about her, more's the pity." Dandini's painted mouth widened into a conspiratorial smile and, leaning forward, he whispered in Charming's ear, "I've got some *news*."

Despite the overpowering scent assailing his nostrils, Charming's interest quickened. "News?" he repeated eagerly. "About—"

"About *that*, yes."

"You've found her? You've found the pumpkin woman?"

Dandini's triumphant smirk gave him the answer without any need for words, and for one utterly reckless moment Charming could have kissed him. Then sanity came back, and instead he clasped Dandini's hand and pumped it up and down.

"Wonderful!" he said. "*Wonderful!* Dandini, you're a miracle worker!"

Dandini freed his fingers. "My, aren't you strong!" He shook his hand. "Much more of that and I'd have been quite useless! But honestly, petal, it wasn't that difficult. In fact, it was Buttons who gave me the ideal – all right, I know you don't approve, but he's *nearly* twenty-one now, and he's a *very* clever boy. Well, Buttons and I went fishing the other day – we've got this little lodge down by the river, you know the one. Didn't catch a *thing* all day, except nearly our deaths when it started to rain, but that's another story . . . Oh, listen to me, digress-digress; it's a *deplorable* habit. Anyway, Buttons said that the reason why we didn't catch any fish was because the bait wasn't up to the mark. Very choosy creatures, fish, he said; they'll only rise for something they really want, and if you haven't got it, you might as well pack up and go home. So *I* thought what about applying the same principle to the pumpkin woman?"

"Bait?" Charming was beginning to lose track.

"Precisely. Now, we know she's got a big thing about being Rell's fairy godmother, don't we? Bit of a complex, if you like; fancies herself in the part. So I thought what little bait can we dangle that a fairy godmother couldn't resist? And the answer was obvious."

"Was it?"

"Of *course*! So I dangled it. 'Wealthy and influential patron with own coat of arms seeks Fairy Godmother for newborn baby son. Usual perks, plus generous bonus, to the right candidate. Apply in the first instance to Duke Emerald—'"

"Duke Emerald?" Charming interrupted.

"Me, dear." Dandini put a hand to his own heart. "Just my little joke. They've always been my favourite gems because they go so well with my eyes. So anyway, Duke Emerald's got a little Dukeling, so he simply *has* to have a fairy godmother for it, doesn't he? It's the ultimate fashion accessory." He beamed. "All it took was one teeny-weeny little advert in *Ideal Gnome*, and up she popped. Easy as saying boo to a footman."

With a conjuror's flourish he produced a small business card from the ermine-trimmed sleeve of his coat and slapped it into Charming's hand. The card was circular, shining faintly with stale fairy-dust, and had a stylized pumpkin drawn on one side.

"Dead give-away, isn't it?" Dandini said. "And *quite* crass. Read it, petal, do."

Charming turned the card over. In an ink whose colour could best be described as fainting mauve, it announced:

Gifts, Wishes and Spells by
ROSA RUGOSA
Fairy Godmother to the Gentry
Fully Trained & Experienced, At Home and Overseas:
All Tastes Catered For and Religions Respected
The Hemlocks, Murkwood (3rd Clearing)
Also Fresh Fruit & Veg In Season – Pumpkins a Speciality

"*Rosa Rugosa*, indeed!" Dandini said disdainfully, leaning over Charming's shoulder. "If that's her real name, I'll marry Araminta."

"But it is her," said Charming softly.

"Oh, I think we can rely on that, dear heart. There was a covering letter as well, but if you read that you'll probably be ill – it's got enough syrup in it to stun an entire hive of bees."

Charming was still staring at the card. In a voice of faintly dangerous relish he asked, "Where's Murkwood?"

"Oh, we don't need to send that far to find her. She's got another job as well, much nearer to here. Receptionist at the Ogre's Castle Country Hotel and Conference Centre; it's part of that new Leisure Experience, you know, where old Grimboots used to hang out until that macho foreigner chopped his head off for him. He's on the Experience's board of directors now; the foreigner I mean of course. I saw him just the other week. Quite the tycoon now, but he still can't drum up the manners to pass the time of day with me . . . anyway, that's all by the by, isn't it? What do you want me to do about the pumpkin woman?"

Charming was still studying the card, and a smile was spreading slowly across his face. He wondered briefly what reward Dandini would most like for his success, then thought that it might be better not to speculate on such a question. And then, he thought of Rell . . .

"We-ell," he said, "There's no need to hurry, of course. Matters like this must be handled with tact and diplomacy, after all. Bring her here to the palace, Dandini. Say . . . tomorrow morning? At dawn?"

The sun was just showing its face when Rosa Rugosa, sandwiched between two burly guards who owed Dandini a special favour or two, was frogmarched unceremoniously into one of the palace's largest, bleakest and most echoey rooms. She was protesting loudly and fluently, but when she saw Charming, seated in full regalia on his father's second-best throne (which she didn't know was only second-best), the protests died, spluttering, into a single, dismayed word.

". . . Ah . . ."

"Ah, indeed, Miss Rugosa." Charming stood up, and at a signal the guards departed, shutting the door with a portentous and well-rehearsed *boom* behind them. Rosa Rugosa looked desperately over her shoulder. Dandini, who had stayed, smiled sweetly at her, folded his arms and leaned back against the door.

"Come forward, please," Charming said ominously. "Stand in front of me."

Her face turned white, pink, white again, then she swallowed and tiptoed a few paces towards the throne, where Charming could see her more clearly. Fundamentally, he thought, the receptionist of the Ogre's Castle Country Hotel and Conference Centre ("All Rooms *En Suite*, Your Comfort is Our *Raison d'Etre*") was not classic fairy godmother material. Her hair had been painstakingly permed into *the* fashionable style of the season, her nails were painted (more subtly, admittedly, than Dandini's), and she gave the impression that chic was her middle name. However, she had made some effort to look the required part, for her tailored business suit was made of gossamer (though *very* understated), there was a small, tasteful tiara on her head, and one hand held a silver wand with a discreetly elegant diamond gleaming at its tip. The effect was impressive – or at least would have been if she had not suddenly started to tremble violently at the knees.

Charming smiled, not pleasantly, pointed to a strategically placed chair, and said, "Sit down."

She collapsed rather than sat. The chair had been set to put her at a psychological disadvantage: it was at just the right level below the throne, and was positioned so that she was obliged to sit at an awkward angle and crane her neck in order to see Charming's face. As he resumed his own place on the throne she scrambled her courage together and made an attempt at a smile.

"Your Highness . . ." There was a simper in her voice, disguising quivering desperation. "I am *charmed* to meet you, naturally, but I really don't understand—"

"Ah," Charming said. "You recognize me, then?"

"Well—" She laughed coquettishly. "How could I not? Moving, as I do, among the *cream* of society; in my work, you see, the Ogre's Castle encourages only the most exclusive—"

"I can't say I've ever been there. But I congratulate you on your choice of a hiding place. Most ingenious. Who would think to look for a genuine fairy godmother behind the reception desk of a country hotel and conference centre?"

"Your Comfort is Our *Raison D'*—" From habit she started to repeat the slogan before she could stop herself, but the unctuous words fizzled out as she saw his expression. She coughed genteelly. "Please excuse me, Your Highness. Dust, you know. I've always had a *teeny* tendency to be allergic . . . You were saying, um, something about . . ."

"Hiding."

"Oh, yes." Smile. "I'm afraid you've lost me."

"Oh, no," Charming corrected her. "I've *found* you. And now that I have, I want answers to some questions. Beginning with this one. Why did you do it?"

She blinked, affecting surprise. "Do, ah, what, exactly?"

Dandini made an extraordinary noise that might or might not have been a suppressed snigger, and Rosa did her best to look affronted. "Your Highness, I assure you that I really do not know what you mean!"

"You knew about her, didn't you?" Charming continued, ignoring the protestation. "That was why you didn't come to the wedding, even though we sent you an invitation. You knew what she was really like – and you knew that I'd soon find out, too!"

Rosa made one last attempt to dissemble. "Ah – when you say, *she*, Your Highness—"

"You probably knew her as Cinderella. These days, she prefers to be called Rell."

"Rell?" Rosa's face looked as if she had just bitten into a lemon. "I'm sorry, Your Highness, but I really can't recall ever counting a person with such a name among *my* acquaintances."

"Then let me refresh your memory, dear Miss Rugosa." Charming tilted his head on one side in a fair imitation of her earlier coquetry. "Pumpkins? White mice?" Playfully, he raised his right foot and tapped it. "And the teeny-weeny matter of a glass slipper . . . ?"

Rosa's jaw dropped. She wanted to say something, Charming could see she could. But the right words would not come, and all she could manage, at last, was, "Oh, dear . . ."

Charming said, quite pleasantly, "Dandini, will you be so kind as to lock the door?" He held out a hand towards the dismayed fairy godmother. "Your wand, madam, if you please. And then we have some talking to do!"

It didn't take long to break Rosa Rugosa down. Once the first admission, that she did actually know Rell, was made, the rest followed fairly easily. There were one or two minor hiccups: the first an attempt to explain everything soothingly away, and the second a brief show of reproachful virtue that bordered on defiance. But then Dandini slipped away for a few minutes, to return dressed entirely in black leather, with several short lengths of chain (borrowed from the chief dungeon-master) draped significantly across the ensemble. He looked dangerous – though not, perhaps, in the way he intended – and as he stood twirling a set of manacles, and Charming let the word *pain* drop casually into the discussion, Rosa caved in.

"Oh, dear." It was becoming her favourite phrase, and she dabbed at her eyes, although without a scented handkerchief the gesture wasn't as effective as it might have been. "I should have known that this would happen. I really should have *known*."

Charming was inclined to agree, but at the same time he wasn't about to let her remorse influence him. "In that case," he asked icily, "why did you do it?"

"Well, you see . . . oh, this is *so* difficult . . ." Rosa sniffed loudly, then suddenly flicked him an uneasy look. "I hope she hasn't gone so far as to tell you that joke about the three nuns and—"

"The centaur. Yes. She told it last night. At a banquet."

"Oh *dear*. So tasteless . . . I did try to *warn* her that she would have to mend her ways and learn to be . . . well . . ."

"Civilized," Charming supplied.

She managed a pained smile. "May we put it a little more genteelly and say, 'cultured'?"

"No," said Charming, "we may not. She is *uncivilized*, Miss Rugosa, and she will never be anything else. I know it, and you know it, and it cannot be tolerated in the royal household any longer!"

Rosa sniffed again, crestfallen. "But the power of youthful love—" she began.

"Is no match for the power of middle-aged monarchy. In other words, my father, who intends to disown me unless something is *done*."

"Oh. Oh, well. Naturally, in that case . . ."

"Quite. So, Miss Rugosa, I want a solution. And you will provide it."

Rosa nibbled her lower lip. "When you say 'a solution', Your Highness, I trust you don't mean . . ." She raised her eyes to his and drew a finger across her own throat.

"Of course not!" Charming paused, then added, "At least, not for Rell."

She blanched. "But you— ah— still wish to— now, how can I best put this . . . You still wish to make her your *un*-wife."

Charming smiled. "We understand each other at last. It was your spells that got me into all this trouble, so I think it's the merest justice that your spells should also get me out of it."

"Um. Yes, I see . . . It— ah— won't be easy."

"I didn't imagine it would."

"Divorce is out of the question, I presume . . . ? Yes. Yes, I quite appreciate the . . . um . . . And banishment? That too I suppose would be . . . ? Yes, of course. In that case, Your Highness, there is only one solution. We must do a little tinkering with Time itself."

Dandini swallowed a yawn, suddenly looking interested, and Charming leaned forward on the throne. "Explain."

"Oh, dear . . ." Rosa waved her hands with vague helplessness. "It is *not* an easy spell, and so terribly draining . . . But if you insist . . ."

"I do."

"Then we must plunge boldly into the pages of history, Your Highness, and, as it were, rewrite them. In other words, go back to the very day when you went in search of your lost beloved with only a glass slipper to help you in your quest." Her eyes had misted sentimentally. Abruptly, she collected herself and frowned. "Only this time, we must make sure that events do not *quite* follow the same pattern as they did before . . ."

Charming said, "I hope she knows what she's doing."

"Oh, I wouldn't worry, petal." Dandini glanced at himself in a handy mirror and adjusted the angle of his chains a fraction. "After all, her bona fides are sound enough. She fooled you."

Charming scowled. "She fooled all of us." He returned his gaze to the far side of the room, where Rosa, enveloped in a fog of fairy-dust, was gesturing and muttering over something that lay on a purple velvet cushion on a small table. It had taken some nerve to creep into Rell's room and remove the glass slipper from its customary place next to the port bottle beside her bed. Rell liked to drink her "bedtime bevvy", as she called it, out of the shoe, and it was the worse for wear as a result, with several chips out of the rim and a crack down the length of the heel. But Charming had achieved it without waking her (not that anything short of a full-scale invasion could wake Rell before 11 a.m.), and delivered it to Rosa, who now was ensconced in an ante-room behind his own suite. There had then followed some ten minutes of chanting and the striking of dramatic poses ("To create the right ambience, Your Highness. We artistes are very sensitive to ambience") before, finally, she got down to work. She had produced the fairy-dust from her handbag, together with a few other ingredients whose provenance Charming didn't especially want to question, and the handbag itself (classic Magicci: patent dragon-skin and a clasp in the shape of a stylized M) now sat in the middle of the floor. Charming knew perfectly well that Dandini had had a quick rummage inside it while Rosa was occupied, and he was not surprised when Dandini leaned towards him and whispered,

"She's got a letter in there. A very interesting letter."

"Oh?"

"Mmm. It's from the management of the Ogre's Castle. They're making her redundant."

"Are they, now? I wonder why."

"Reading between the lines – and *strictly* 'twixt you, me and the guard-house cat, of course – I think she's an embarrassment to them." Dandini indicated Rosa, who seemed to be getting completely carried away by this time. "I mean, can you imagine the impression she creates at the reception desk? Pretentious isn't the word, and the Ogre's is *very* up-market: the kind of people who stay there can spot a parvenu at fifty paces. No, our Miss Rugosa wouldn't suit at all, once they saw that she wasn't really in their league. And if you ask me, that's why she answered my little advert."

"You mean, she knew what she was letting herself in for?"

"Of course she did. She's been lying low ever since the wedding, hasn't she? So why suddenly come into the open now? She needs the work, dear. She hasn't got any choice. Rather sad really, isn't it?"

"Yes . . ." Charming was basically soft-hearted, and suddenly began to see Rosa in a different light. "Yes, it is. Well, if she can solve my problem, I'll reward her. In fact, I'll offer her a job at the palace. There's sure to be *something* she can do."

Before Dandini could comment, Rosa Rugosa gave a loud sniff. They both looked, and were in time to see her emerging from the rainbow dust cloud and walking, a little unsteadily, towards them. She was carrying the glass slipper on its cushion, and to Charming's surprise it looked as good as new. A faint aura glowed around it, then the aura died and Rosa let out her breath in a thankful sigh.

"There," she said. "All done. And, though I say it myself, quite, quite perfect. *Très bien*, in fact."

Dandini raised his eyebrows, but Charming ignored him. "And you're absolutely sure that it won't fit Rell's foot?" he asked.

"*Certainement!*" Rosa declared huffily. "I am, as I told you, Your Highness, an artiste!" She sniffed again. "Now, if I may just have a *few* teeny moments to make myself presentable, I suggest that we all put our minds to the next part of the spell."

"Of course," Charming said. "There's a dressing-room next door. Please feel free."

"Thank you. So kind." She presented the slipper to Dandini, who took it with a straight-faced bow, and headed for the door Charming had indicated. "I shall return *tout de suite*."

"Do you know," Dandini stage-whispered as she walked away, "she refers to herself as *moi*?"

"You're joking."

"I only wish I wasn't, petal. She did it twice while you were on your errand." He put a finger in his own mouth and pantomimed being sick. "Fancy a little wager? I'll bet my peridot ring against your topaz that she works '*n'est-ce pas*' into the conversation within two minutes of her return."

"Make it one minute and I'll take the bet," said Charming.

"Oh, you always drive a hard bargain! All right then, one minute. I still think I'll win."

"Now, Your Highness, you must stand *exactly* here, on this *very* spot." Rosa pointed with her wand to one of the flagstones outside Baron Hardup's front door. The stone, along with two others, had been marked with a chalk arrow, and according to Rosa the choice would minimize the disorientation Charming would feel when Time came back. Charming was already feeling disorientated enough, largely because of a blackbird that hung fixed and motionless in mid-air only a few inches from his nose. The bird had been flying unsuspectingly past at the very moment when the three of them materialized and Time jolted to a halt, and now it was frozen in an endless moment, with its wings outspread and its lunch, in the form of a particularly fat and succulent worm, gripped in its beak.

"Right, everyone!" Rosa clapped her hands. "Places, please! We all know what to do, *n'est-ce pas*?"

Dandini, who now sported a topaz ring in addition to six others, smirked at Charming as he shuffled to his appointed spot. Rosa, too, had taken up her position, and she raised her wand. "All ready?" she trilled. "Good! Then *one*, and *two*, and *THREE!*"

There was a noise like the buzzing of a bee the size of a carthorse, and Charming felt as if – it was the only way he could describe it to himself – his brain was being licked out of his skull by a gargantuan tongue. He seemed to swoop backwards, then upwards, then over and over in a series of dizzying somersaults, and as he tumbled helplessly the events of the past few months reversed at high speed through his mind. The banquet, other banquets before it, the fury of his father, the wedding night, the marriage ceremony, the unutterably giddy feeling of being totally and helplessly and passionately in love – it was all rushing and racing backwards, and as it went he found himself forgetting what had come before . . . or rather, later. Miss Rugosa had warned him about that. It had to happen, she had said, or the spell wouldn't work; the rules of magic couldn't allow him to have two separate sets of memories at once. That was the biggest danger: that, unable to recall what *had* actually happened, he would go and make the same mistake all over again. That was why she had altered the slipper. This time, it wouldn't fit Rell.

Then the one question that Charming had overlooked hit him like a punch on the jaw from a troll's fist.

If the slipper didn't fit Rell . . . who *would* it fit?

Panic nearly throttled him and he opened his mouth to yell, "STOP, WAIT, I THINK I MIGHT HAVE CHANGED MY MIND!" But even as he did so, there came a crack and a bang like stage thunder. One more stomach-churning somersault, and Charming opened his eyes to find himself sitting on the ground with his legs stuck out before him and his jaw hanging down as if he was trying to catch flies. Time came back with a crunch; the blackbird uttered an agitated squawk and zipped away into the trees. And Charming was convinced that there was something he ought to remember . . .

"Get up, dear heart, do," said Dandini, standing solicitously beside him. "I know how tired you must be, but I promise, this *is* the last house we'll do today." He smiled sympathetically. "We'll find her, don't you fret."

For some inexplicable reason Charming felt a stab of terror at those words, but he put it down to weariness and depression. He was *so* much in love. And the only clue he had to lead him back to the beautiful girl who had taken his heart was a glass slipper . . .

"Come on," said Dandini. He consulted a list. "There are three daughters in this household, I gather. That's three chances, isn't it?"

He walked elegantly to the door and knocked. The knock was answered by a fresh-faced boy with a great many polished buttons on his uniform. Charming saw the way Dandini's eyes lit up, but he didn't comment, only followed him over the threshold. The third member of their party – a woman in a tailored gossamer suit – walked briskly after him on her pencil heels, and Charming wondered briefly who she was. He couldn't recall bringing anyone else along, and though her face was vaguely familiar he couldn't put a name to it. But there was no time to wonder about that, for Baron and Lady Hardup were welcoming them into the parlour, the boy with the buttons was bowing low while exchanging challengingly significant looks with Dandini, and two girls were rising from a chaise-longue and simpering towards them . . .

Charming's heart sank into his deerskin boots. If these two weren't quite the ugliest females in the kingdom, they were certainly up among the prizes. The elder was half a head taller than he was, thin as the proverbial rake, with dyed black hair and the most enormous nose he had ever seen in his worst nightmares. While the younger, who came no higher than his chest even with her brassy hair piled up like a hayrick on top of her head, was a perfect enough replica of a boisterous bacon pig to delight the eye of any farmer.

Charming said, "Er . . ." He looked for help to Dandini, but Dandini and the buttons-boy were whispering and giggling together by the door. Then the woman in the gossamer suit stepped forward.

"*Dear* Baron and Baroness!" With a mannered fluttering of her fingers that made Charming wonder fleetingly if she might have been a receptionist in her time, she oozed between Charming and the two girls, who were both eyeing him as ferrets might eye a rabbit. "Such lovely girls! *Charmante; très, très charmante!* I'm sure that we have found the right house at last!"

Charming opened his mouth to say that they had done no such thing, but she jabbed his ankle with one of her lethal heels and he was so astounded that it silenced him.

Lady Hardup, more than a little bemused, started to proffer tea, but Rosa waved the idea away. "So kind, dear Baroness, but we are here for a purpose, *n'est-ce pas?* Young ladies, young ladies; sit down, do! We cannot try the slipper unless we are seated, can we? Not if we wish to retain our grace and elegance!"

Charming hissed, "*Dandini!*" but to no avail; in fact, Dandini and the boy had disappeared altogether by this time. Feeling as if he was being carried along by a horrible nightmare over which he had no control, he watched as the two girls plonked themselves back on the chaise, and the pretentious, *dreadful* woman (who *was* she? He still couldn't remember!) produced the glass slipper. She handed it to him, kicking him again when he seemed reluctant to take it, and he steeled himself to do what he must.

Kneel down, proffer the cushion, look up at the elder daughter. (*Smile, damn it; it won't kill you!*) A foot appeared from under a froth of petticoats and thrust itself at the glass slipper. Charming could have yelled aloud with relief as, with six inches of heel still hanging over at the back, Arabella's big toe jammed against the shoe's tip.

"Oh *dear*!" said Rosa, dripping regret like honeydew from an aphid-infested tree. "How *very* sad . . . But perhaps your sister . . . ?"

Araminta all but rolled Arabella off the seat in her haste to take her turn. Her foot was short enough, certainly, but its width was another matter, and after three minutes of grunting and straining and sweating she was forced to admit defeat.

"*Such* a pity!" Rosa sympathized. "But there; so many beautiful girls in the kingdom, and all but one must be disappointed! Well, we have taken up enough of your valuable time, dear Baron and Baroness – we shall take our leave, and bid you all *à bientôt*!"

She grasped Charming's arm and started to pull him upright. But Charming abruptly remembered something Dandini had said.

"Just a moment." He shook Rosa's hand off irritably. "Will you kindly stop *pawing* me, madam!" And, turning to Baron Hardup, said, "According to my list, Baron, you have three daughters. Where is the third?"

Lady Hardup's face turned very red, and the baron humphed and ha-harrhed as though in embarrassment. "I think there – ah – must be some mistake, Your Highness. We've only the two girls; Bella and Minta; yes, just the two, you know."

"And who should know better than their own father?" said Rosa, taking hold of Charming's arm again and pulling even harder. "Come, Your dear Highness, we mustn't waste—"

"Be quiet!" Charming snapped. "Answer me truthfully, Baron. Is there a third girl in this house?"

Rosa was saying, "Well *really*, how *unchivalrous*," but no one took any notice of her. Baron Hardup had begun to perspire.

Then, from the door, a new voice said clearly, "Yes, Your Highness. There is Cinderella."

The boy had reappeared. His hair was tousled and most of his buttons had come undone, but there was a look of heroic truth in his eyes.

"They are ashamed of her, Your Highness," he said, "and so they keep her in the kitchen, hidden from sight. But I have told her of your visit. And she is here, now, to try on the glass slipper!"

Rosa said a hair-singeing word, and Baron Hardup spluttered something about a week's wages in lieu of notice. But Buttons paid no heed. He stepped aside – and there, framed on the threshold, was the loveliest girl that Charming had ever seen. The rags she wore could not disguise the slender grace of her figure. The smuts of the kitchen that marred her face and her long, golden hair could not hide the beauty that shone from her like a summer sunrise. She stood trembling, gazing at Charming with huge blue eyes.

And Charming fell head over heels in love.

"My lady!" He dropped to one knee, sweeping his hat from his head and returning her gaze with rapt adoration. "Will you honour me by trying on the glass slipper?"

She didn't speak. She only came forward, slowly, hesitantly, and sat down in the chair he indicated with a courtly gesture. The room was utterly silent as Charming cupped her foot in one hand, resisted with difficulty the urge to cover it in kisses, and slipped the glass shoe over her slender toes.

Or tried to. But the glass slipper did not fit.

Charming stared at it in disbelief. Then he looked up at the girl, his beloved, his darling, the sole and only joy of his heart. She in her turn looked back at him. Her exquisite lips parted . . .

And Rell said, in a voice that could have cut sheet metal, "Oh, *buggering* hell!"

*   *   *

Quite how they got out of the house Charming didn't know, but he suspected that it was the woman in the tailored suit who had somehow dragged Dandini away from his preoccupations, made vague farewell noises in the Hardup family's general direction and hastened them away down the drive. Now, looking hot and cross against the background of some towering rhododendron bushes, she waited until Charming stopped sobbing enough to listen, then said, "Your Highness, the slipper simply didn't fit, and that's all there is to it! Anyway she can't *possibly* be the same girl you met at the ball! Oh, she's pretty, one can't deny that, but her *personality* . . . uff!" She shuddered fastidiously, while Dandini nodded agreement and looked wistfully back at the house.

With a vast effort Charming forced himself to come to his senses. She – whoever she was, and he *still* couldn't remember – was right. For all her beauty, the girl back there in the house was not a possible choice for a royal bride. If his father met her, he would have an apoplexy. And when she had started to tell that joke about the deaf centaur . . .

He sighed a sigh in which all the cares of the world seemed to be gathered and coagulated, and replied, "How can I argue with you? It's true."

"*Vraiment*." She tapped his arm with a wand, which he hadn't noticed before. "There, now. All better? Would you like my hankie?"

"No, thank you." He could smell the hankie from here, and he didn't like Otto of Roses. He sniffed. "But . . . the slipper must fit *someone*. And if I don't find her soon, I think I shall die!"

"Well, now, as to that . . ." Rosa's voice was suddenly full of import. "I think – just *think*, mind you – that I might have the answer to your little problem!"

His head came up sharply. "You might?"

"*Mais oui!* Dandini, my sweet – might I trouble you for the slipper? Just for a *teeny* moment?"

Dandini handed it to her, looking down his nose, and she took it with a little flourish. "*Well* now," she said again. "Let's see, shall we?"

The smile she gave Charming then was the practised smile of a trained receptionist, but with just the slightest hint of fairy godmother. It was only cheating a *weeny* bit, after all; and needs must, et cetera. She *needed* a job, and there wasn't the demand for godmothering these days; certainly not enough to pay the bills, even with the pumpkin-growing as a sideline. And, when one thought about it, she was doing Charming and the royal household a positive favour. Thanks to her magic, Charming might have forgotten about it, but *she* knew perfectly well what had happened the first time around. That *dreadful* girl . . . if she hadn't made her natural mother a deathbed promise, Rosa reflected, she would *never* have got involved in the first place. But then, Rell's mother had always had ideas above her station. And the cloud she caused had a silver lining after all.

She took off her pencil-heeled shoes. Dandini realized belatedly what was about to happen, but Rosa silenced him with a look that promised an extremely nasty piece of magic if he dared utter a word. She lowered the glass slipper. She placed her foot delicately inside it.

It fitted as though it had been made for her. Which, albeit belatedly, it had.

Charming stared at Rosa Rugosa in speechless astonishment. "It fits . . ." he said in a weak, disbelieving and faintly horrified voice.

"Yes!" Rosa wished that the board of directors at the Ogre's Castle Country Hotel and Conference Centre could be here to see the moment of her triumph. *Redundant*, indeed . . . They had sacked her, *she* knew, because they were jealous. Obviously they had recognized a talent greater than their own, and they feared it. Another year and she would have been on the board herself, no doubt of it, and *then* they would have seen some improvements! Still, she had a *far* more challenging project ahead of her now. Princess Rosa. In time, *Queen* Rosa. Everyone would love her. With her sure and cultured sense of taste, how could they not?

Charming was still staring at her. "Then the girl at the ball . . . it was . . ."

Rosa fluttered her eyelashes. It was only a little white lie, was it not? *Petite*, a mere *soupçon*. She smiled at her bridegroom-to-be, and, with affected genteelness, touched one hand to her heart.

"Yes, my dearest," she said, in a low, tremulous voice. "It was . . . *moi*."

THE DISTRESSING DAMSEL

David Langford

When I was researching the stories for this book I was surprised at how often I encountered the Frog Prince motif, sometimes in serious stories, but usually in satires and spoofs. Some of them were amusing but relied heavily on the basic idea and a clever punch-line. The following story was one of the few that took the idea further. David Langford (b. 1953), whose first story, "Heatwave", appeared in 1975, enjoys spoofs. He caused something of a stir with An Account of a Meeting with Denizens of Another World, 1871 *(1979), a purported account of a Victorian close encounter recorded by William Robert Loosley, which ufologists zealously leaped on as further proof. He has written a humorous science-fiction novel,* The Leaky Establishment *(1984), drawing on his own experiences as a physicist, and compiled* The Unseen University Challenge *(1996), based on Terry Pratchett's Discworld. He has won many Hugo Awards for his writings in science-fiction fan magazines and for his own news and gossip magazine,* Ansible. *Some of his fan writings have been collected as* The Dragonhiker's Guide to Battlefield Covenant at Dune's Edge: Odyssey Two *(1988) and* The Silence of the Langford *(1996) – need I say more?*

Once upon a time, in a far-off land, there lived a princess who developed an unfortunate social problem.

The kingdom of Altrund extended over more square leagues of fertile land than the Court Mathematician could compute. So its King would occasionally boast, delaying as long as possible the admission that his Court Mathematician (a retarded youth of fourteen) had never yet fathomed the intricacies of numbers after VIII.

The Mathematician, who also bore the titles of Palace Swineherd and Master of the Buckhound, was the only child of the peasant classes – both members of which seemed discouraged by their first experiment in being ancestors. King Fardel periodically worried that his peasant classes might at any moment die out altogether; and likewise the kingdom's upper middle class, consisting of a decrepit imbiber called Grommet (Grand Vizier, Chancellor of the Palace Exchequer, Wizard Pro-Tem, Steward of the Royal Cellars, Scullion, Seeker of the King's Treasury, et cetera). Even the King's own dynasty showed every sign of decay. Twenty years ago he had looked forward to the sedate begetting of three sons, two of whom would do tremendously well in the world while the youngest would somehow contrive to outdo them both and be extraordinary virtuous in addition. Alas, Queen Kate was a woman of sadly independent mind and womb, and had called a halt to the dynasty after the inconvenience of producing the Princess Fiona. Fardel could only resign himself to the passive role of devising tests, ready to assess the worthiness of the princes who (in threes) must inevitably arrive to seek the hand of his daughter. The King's first thought had been to avoid the formalities of quests and dragons by, quite simply, asking each suitor how old he was: the virtues of the youngest prince in any representative trio were well known. Later it occurred to Fardel that this was *too* well known, and that all but the youngest would undoubtedly lie about their age.

His next experiment had been to station a hideous dwarf on the one road into the valley of Altrund. Only the most morally sound princes would have a kind word for this creature, and thus virtue would be revealed. It failed, however, to be revealed in the dwarf, who took to supplementing his weekly pittance by severely beating and robbing passers-by – including, the King was sure, at least one incognito prince. The dwarf had had to be discharged, just as Fiona came to marriageable age with enough princess-like beauty to make the King study his plump Queen with wonder and suspicion. After considering and rejecting a version of the ancient shell game which involved caskets of gold, of silver, and of lead, King Fardel sighed and arranged for the construction of a traditional golden road.

Fiona was walking along it now, brooding as usual on her horrid obligation to marry a prince of peculiar virtue. The theory of the golden road was that crasser and more worldly princes would give too much thought to the road's market value, and would discreetly ride along the grassy verge to the left or right; only a prince preoccupied with Fiona's beauty would unconsciously ride down the middle of the road, to victory. How anyone who had not yet reached King Fardel's dilapidated palace could have known so much about Fiona's beauty was not explained by the theory. The princess had never had the heart to point this out, nor to add that, personally, she would incline towards a prince who could be trusted to wipe his boots at the door rather than walk in preoccupied with beauty. Meanwhile the surface of the golden road, never very thick at the best of times, had suffered the depredations of brigands, jackdaws, itinerant tax collectors, and (Fiona was sure, though the King refused to believe it) at least one incognito prince. Tiny gleams of gold could still be seen amid the trampled earth and grass, though only in brilliant sunshine like today's; fewer such gleams were visible in the King's treasury, and Fardel was rumoured to be having second thoughts about crassness and worldliness.

Fiona walked down the middle of the formerly golden road and dreamed again of her own ambition, which did not involve princes. She rather wanted to be a witch.

"A plague of frogs," she crooned happily. "A plague of boils. A plague of toads. That would show them. Princes!"

There was almost no magic in Altrund, apart from the heavily mortgaged magic mirror which was the palace's last valuable asset . . . but a wisp or two of enchantment had been left behind, like forgotten tools, by the obliging Graduate Sorcerer who had polished up the golden road; and perhaps one of these wisps twined itself into Fiona's girlish daydreams of epidemic frogs, boils and toads. Certainly, without her noticing it, her aimless walk swerved off the road, through a clump of trees, through a stand of nettles (which despite her long skirt she did emphatically notice) and finally, at a slight run, to a malodorous pond she had not seen before.

"Be careful!" said a croaking voice from almost underfoot.

Princess Fiona recoiled slightly, and stared down at a singularly obnoxious and wart-encrusted toad on the damp grass at the pond's rim. It stared back at her for some moments, breathing heavily. "Stamping on toads," it complained at last, "is not in accordance with Royal protocol."

"A fig for Royal protocol," said Fiona airily, though uncertain of precisely what a fig might be.

"Well, you might as well get on with it," said the toad.

"Pardon?"

"Oh dear me, I can see your education has been neglected. Did they never tell you about certain, *erk*, traditions of enchantment?"

Something was indeed beginning to dawn on the princess, who drew still further away. "Ah," she said, "The Acting Royal Governess is a dear old fellow called Grommet, but I don't think he knows very much except about vintages. Suppose I go and ask him, though—" She took another cautious step backwards.

"Stop!" said the toad. "And let me tell you a tale."

Alarmingly, the princess found herself rooted to the ground.

The toad said, complacently, "I have strange power of speech; even though I can only usually stop one of three."

"I rather think this is lese-majesty," said Fiona, still struggling to lift her feet.

The toad fixed her with its glittering, golden eyes. "Once upon a time I fell foul of a wicked wizard in the College of Sorcery, who laid upon me the curse which you see, and in addition caused me to be magically flung to the most God-forsaken land in all the world."

"Where was that?" asked Fiona, curious.

The toad gave a croaking cough. "Let me put this tactfully. Where did you find me?"

"Oh," said the princess.

"But the incantation of binding did include a customary reversion clause. *Erk.* A matter of, as one might say, osculatory contact."

"No," said Fiona.

"A momentary and fleeting matter. None of your exotic requirements like being taken into a princess's bed all night. Merely the kiss of a good person whose moral worth stands in a certain relation to one's own."

"No."

"Think of it like this. Obviously you are a princess of high breeding—"

"At least you can tell," said Fiona, flattered.

"The tiara *is* rather a giveaway."

"It's pewter. We're a very poor kingdom; my father has only fivescore subjects even when you count the sheep."

"All the better," said the toad. "In poverty there is tremendous moral worth. And as I was saying – since you are a princess I'll wager five to one that your father has planned all sorts of grotesque and ridiculous ways of testing the princes who come seeking your hand."

She sighed, and nodded.

"Precisely! But are *you* worthy? Should *you* not be tested according to the ancient customs of the world? Have *you* given a crust of bread to a dwarf recently?"

Princess Fiona opened her mouth and closed it again. She looked critically at the toad. "Look. If I take your curse off you, can we simply leave it at that? I'm going to the College of Sorcery myself – if my parents will ever let me – and I'll learn to make my own living. Getting involved with princes can wait, thank you very much."

"I shall make no further claims on you," said the toad in the sincerest of croaks. And then, as she still hesitated: "You could always shut your eyes."

Looking the toad severely in the eye, the princess knelt, bent forward, and bestowed an exceedingly chaste kiss somewhere in the general region of its head. For an instant a cloud seemed to pass over the Sun, and there was that unmistakable tingle which comes with enchantment or champagne.

She leant back, still kneeling. Sure enough, where an ugly, warty toad had squatted, there was now a sleek and handsome frog.

"*I* see," the princess said after a moment.

"Ahh, it's good to be back to normal," said the frog. "Thank you, your majesty. I feel as fit as a . . . prince." At this point it appeared to notice something. "Oh. Conservation law. Well, I must be going. *Awwk.*"

The last agonized croak was because Fiona had noticed the same something, and had seized the wriggling frog in a firm grip. Her previously pale and lily-white hands were now covered in warts that crowded together like cobblestones.

"You knew this was going to happen!" she shrieked.

"Well, it was just a bare possibility," said the frog.

Fiona squeezed it vengefully, and with distaste repeated the kiss. Nothing happened.

"Now that is interesting," said the frog. "I suppose we are no longer equal in moral worthiness, as is necessary for such curses to be transferred."

Distracted, the princess dropped the slimy creature. "*Equal?* You're not telling me a princess is morally the same as a toad?"

"Ah. You are very virtuous, for a princess; and I was very virtuous, for a toad. As a frog I'm far more despicable, since I'm gloating terribly over having shifted my curse to a poor innocent creature like yourself.—Excuse me," it added, dodging the princess's foot as it came down. "I must go and see a man about a frog." With a splash, it was gone.

Princess Fiona stared into the murky water; the ripples died and her own reflection took shape. It seemed an appropriate time to shut her eyes, but she forced them to stay open: her fingers could feel the swarming warts on her face, and she might as well learn just how unprincesslike her complexion had become. In the water, though, it looked the same as ever. Apparently magical warts had no reflections; possibly they did not even cast shadows, though this would be slightly more difficult to test.

The sun was lower in the sky. The princess's vague thoughts of throwing herself with a despairing cry into the pool, or of becoming a hermit never again to be seen by mortal man, were dispelled by the more practical considerations of duckweed and dinner.

She walked more and more slowly, though, as the palace came into view – a quarter-mile frontage of crumbling marble and alabaster. It seemed uncountable ages old, though in fact the former King of Altrund had caused it to be erected in a single night by means of a substandard wishing ring. Alas, the accumulated cost of servants and repairs was somewhat further beyond the dreams of avarice than the wealth King Sivvens had requested with this second wish; while the wasted third wish, said to have involved the former Queen and a sausage, was among the family's best-kept secrets.

Taking a short cut through the disused portions of the palace, Fiona passed in succession through the Great Hall, the Great Ballroom with its litter of shrivelled pumpkins, the Great Dungeon, and the cobwebbed Great Cupboard before nearing the inhabited rooms. There she paused, hearing voices beyond the half-open door of the Great Sitting-Room.

". . . exceedingly sorry about this wine," her father the King was saying. "We have far finer vintages, but the Steward of the Royal Cellars keeps, ah, misplacing them. But, to business! Naturally you come seeking the hand of my daughter, the beauteous flower of a most wealthy and kingly line. – I must apologize that so much of the palace is being redecorated just now," he added inventively.

There was a uneasy triple murmur.

"Well, my good princes, what dowry would you bring to be worthy of such a bride?"

The first prince's voice was loud: "I am a crafty conqueror whose blood-dripping sword will hack a ruinous path of carnage through battlefields steeped in gore. And my consort will be no mere Queen but the Empress of an all-destroying Emperor!"

"Creditable," said the King.

The voice of the second prince inclined towards oiliness. "Emperors may hold the world by the throat, but a merchant prince can put a noose of purse-strings about the throats of Emperors. Already I possess an immense fortune, and ultimately my Queen will share wealth beyond the dreams of avarice."

"*Very* creditable," said the King. On the tip of his tongue, Fiona thought, was the urgent question: "How *far* beyond the dreams of avarice?"

The third voice was thin and reedy and set her teeth on edge. "When tyrants, moneylenders, and even the stones about their unhallowed graves have fallen all to dust, my name shall linger on. To my Queen I bring no more than an unquenchable love and immortality in verse and song. I am a poet," he explained.

Outside, Fiona made a hideous face and was sobered by the thought of how much more than hideous it must be. Inside, there was an embarrassed little pause.

"More wine, perhaps?" said the King at last.

"Thanks," said the three princes together: "I don't mind if I do."

After a tentative query about the suitors' ages (which shed a sad light on the tendency of palace records to become lost, burnt or consumed by rats), the King suggested that some simple test of worthiness for the Princess Fiona's hand would be appropriate.

"None of those meaningless, old-fashioned tests," he said with great fervour. "It is nonsense to have a beautiful princess's fate decided by whether or not one speaks kind words to a dwarf—"

("Yes indeed," said the first prince grimly.)

"Or by the ability to slay huge and ferocious dragons—"

("Hear, hear," said the second prince.)

"Or by impractical talents like the soothing of savage beasts with verse and song—"

("Oh, I say," said the third prince.)

"No. We are practical men, you and I. Let us straightaway agree that he who at the end of three days returns with the most colossally valuable dowry shall win the hand of the Princess Fiona."

"*Colossal?*" the merchant prince said in a pained voice.

Feeling it was nearly time to put a stop to this, Fiona peered around the half-open door. Without showing herself, she could

see all four men reflected in the magic mirror on the far wall –
a tall slab of pure, enchanted silver which magically attracted
dust and smears (or so Fiona felt, one of her household duties
being to keep it polished).

The King sat on a portable throne with his back to the
mirror: facing him across the table were the three princes, and
Fiona squinted to study them. The first was short and looked
bad-tempered; for some reason he kept one hand tucked into
his tunic. The second was sufficiently stout that he had to sit
some way back from the table. The third, the poet, was tall
and might have been almost handsome; but at the time of his
christening, someone had neglected to invite whichever fairy is
responsible for bestowing chins.

"Happiness," the King was saying, "is all very well, but it
can't buy money."

The merchant prince glanced at his companions, as though
estimating the strength of the bidding. "A moderate amount,"
he began – and his moist eyes met Fiona's in the mirror. "Oh.
Perhaps even a reasonably substantial amount," he went on,
and licked his lips.

Before Fiona could move, the wary gaze of the soldier also
found her. He, too, licked his lips. He, too, studied his rivals;
absent-mindedly he dropped a hand to the pommel of his sword.
Meanwhile the poet also had seen Fiona's reflected glory, and
was mumbling what appeared to be an impromptu villanelle.

With a certain inner glee, Princess Fiona strode into the room
and let her suitors see her, warts and all. Betrothal to any of these
three, she considered, would undoubtedly be a fate worse than
. . . well, warts.

"Father," she said sweetly, "I seem to have this curse."

King Fardel turned, gaped, closed his eyes and moaned
softly.

"Only making a preliminary tactical survey, of course—" said
the first prince.

"Cannot be expected to enter into a binding commitment at
this stage of negotiation," said the second.

"Tomorrow to fresh woods and pastures new," muttered
the poet.

The princess helped herself to a glass of the wine – which

was indeed only a locally produced Falernian type – and told a discreetly edited version of her adventure. "And so," she concluded, "only the kiss of a man of proper moral worth can lift this dreadful enchantment from me!"

"Meaningless, old-fashioned tests," said the King through his teeth. With a visible effort he steeled himself to the necessities of tradition. "Very well. Whosoever shall with a kiss lift the curse from my fair daughter, him shall she wed, and we'll have a quiet chat about marriage settlements afterwards."

Inwardly Fiona was praying a twofold prayer: firstly, that one of these unlikely princes would somehow prove equal to her in moral worth, and secondly, that the King would not countenance her betrothal to a prince invisible beneath layers of warts.

After heartening himself with several long looks at the princess's unspoilt reflection, the first suitor stepped forward. He hesitated, though, on the very brink. "You could always shut your eyes," she said. He snorted, and Fiona bent down to receive a kiss of military efficiency. Nothing happened. The prince made a strategic withdrawal to the previously prepared position of his chair.

When the second prince had screwed his determination to the sticking-place, Fiona found that she had to lean forward over his firkin of a stomach before their lips were close enough for an economical and businesslike kiss. Again, nothing happened.

"I am, after all, the youngest," the third prince murmured; and Fiona turned up her face for a final kiss which was not so much poetic as chinless. The only result was that the poet-prince turned green as a frog and lurched backwards, gabbling something about aesthetic values. Fiona found this disheartening.

With a resigned expression, the King rose and clapped his hands to draw attention. "Whosoever shall in three days return with a healing spell, charm, cantrip, physic, unguent, balm, lotion, potion, philtre, talisman, relic, totem, fetish, icon, incantation, rune, amulet, panacea—" At this point his breath failed him and he collapsed into uncontrollable coughing. But the suitors had gathered the general drift; they bowed to the King and (with averted gaze) to Fiona, and departed as one prince.

"Oh . . . *rats*," said Princess Fiona.

". . . theurgy, thaumaturgy, sorcery, wizardry, necromancy, invocation, conjuration . . ." continued the afflicted King, rallying slightly. His voice died away as he noticed an absence of princes. There followed a stern lecture on the perfidy of faithless daughters who abandoned themselves to the embraces of strange frogs on the very day when three superlatively eligible suitors presented themselves, or at any rate two, or perhaps just one, but all the same . . . Still muttering, he left to consult the Court Physician, yet another post ineptly filled by the man Grommet.

Fiona pulled up a footstool and sat staring into the magic mirror. "Mirror, mirror," she said briskly. There was a soft chime, and the silver clouded over.

"Good afternoon," said the mirror. "What seems to be the trouble?"

Fiona regarded the mirror suspiciously. "You may have noticed this wart," she said, touching one at random.

"That is not a problem. That is a solution."

"That's not exactly an answer," said Fiona.

"You did not exactly ask a question," the mirror said smugly. "But consider. You have always wished to be a witch. Now you look the part, if not more so. You have always wished half-heartedly to run away and enrol at the College of Sorcery. Now, with one of three eminently unlovable princes likely to cure your complexion and claim your hand in two days, twenty-three hours and thirty-seven minutes, you have an excellent reason for running away. What more could you ask?"

"I was thinking more in terms of being a beautiful sorceress full of sinister glamour," said the princess. "*Not* a warty crone. Now is there a way I can lift the curse myself in the next day or two?"

"Indeed . . . there . . . is," said the mirror with what sounded like reluctance.

"What is it?"

"Unfortunately . . . I cannot actually tell you, for reasons you would find absolutely inarguable if only I could tell you them." The fog in the mirror began to clear again. "Your three minutes are nearly up."

"If you can't tell me that cure, suggest another," Fiona said furiously.

"You might try throwing a party for all the peasantry," said the silvery voice, diminuendo. "There is this party game called Postman's Knock . . ."

Then the voice and the fog were gone, and the omniscient magic mirror (which, as it happened, could be consulted only once in any three days) was again no more than a mirror.

Resisting her urge to give the silver a vicious kick, Princess Fiona left the room and climbed the eight flights and three spirals of stairs to the Great Boudoir. There she found Queen Kate placidly sewing hair shirts for the peasantry, who generally used these royal gifts to repair the roof of their hovel.

"Oh dear," said the Queen when Fiona had told her tale. "You're such a trial to me, sometimes I think you must have been changed for a goblin when you were a baby, that's all I can say, well you brought it on yourself, going out without your warm shawl . . ."

Fiona was used to being called a changeling in the course of any and every scolding, though in fact the local goblins were notoriously choosy. Several times, and with good reason, the peasantry had abandoned their ill-favoured son Dribble (Court Mathematician) outside known goblin caves, and each time he had been politely returned.

"Well," said her mother, coming to the point as she occasionally did: "I can see I still have to clear up your messes after you, just like when you were a baby, let me see, I know I put it somewhere, yes, here it is . . ." She pulled a dusty and unsavoury looking object from a cluttered drawer. "There you are, you just put this in your hair like a good girl, something my stepmother gave me once, a poisoned comb . . ."

Fiona hastily retreated a pace or two.

". . . just you put it in your hair and there you are, you stay asleep like the dead for ten years or a hundred or whatever, until Prince Right comes along and takes the comb out of your hair and kisses you and all the rest of it, nothing like outliving your troubles, that's what my mother always used to say . . ."

But Fiona was already on her way to ask the advice of Grommet. She found him in the Great Pantry, testing the quality of the King's best wine with his usual conscientiousness. When he had recoiled from her appearance and listened to her story, he recalled his position as Chief Palace Torturer and made a slurred suggestion.

"Down in, um, down in one of the Great Torture Chambers, um, can't remember exactly which one, there's a, mmm, very nice iron mask. Very nice indeed. Good, um, workmanship. You might like to wear it . . . ?"

"Thank you," said Fiona coldly.

The next day, heart hardened by the bedtime discovery that her affliction was by no means confined to hands and face, she set about a systematic programme of being kissed by the entire reluctant population of Altrund – even the all too aptly named lad Dribble. Every one of them, it seemed, was either despicably lacking in moral worth or unfairly endowed with it. In the afternoon, after a lack of success with several sheep, she waylaid a wandering friar. The friar denounced her both before and afterwards as a sinful temptation sent by the devil; Fiona considered this to be undue flattery.

On the second day she gathered, compounded, infused, and drank no fewer than sixty-four traditional herbal remedies, whose taste varied across a wide spectrum from unpleasant to unheard-of. An omen presented itself when the word NARCISSUS was found written in frogspawn across the palace forecourt, but no decoction of this plant's flowers, leaves, stem, or root had the slightest visible effect. The day's only success was scored by a mysterious and forgotten elixir found in the Great Medicine Cabinet: the dose remaining in the phial sufficed to remove one medium-sized wart from the back of the princess's left hand. This was hailed as a great stride forward by almost everyone, except Fiona.

On the morning of the third day, a more than usually appalling dwarf arrived at the palace. He boasted a squint, a bulbous nose, a club foot, a humped back, a cauliflower ear, and all the other impedimenta so fashionable among dwarves. Moreover, his complexion bore a startling resemblance to Fiona's.

"I'll riddle ye a riddle, my maiden fair," he said to the princess, leaping and capering with repulsive agility. "I'll riddle your warts away with riddling words, that I will, and ye must riddle my name. If ye riddle it not aright, then ye must be mine forever. Will ye riddle me this riddle, fair princess?"

At this difficult juncture the King came into the Great Reception Room to inspect the visitor. "Why, Rumpelstiltskin, old chap," he cried.

"Bah," said the dwarf, and left in considerable dudgeon.

The afternoon wore on; the sun sank in the sky; and the Court Mathematician, stationed in the topmost tower of the palace, presently came running down to announce the sighting of four princes in the distance. When sent aloft to count again, he corrected this estimate to two. Sure enough, three princes came riding up to the Great Door and took their turns to blow the Great Horn which had hung there since the rusting of the Great Knocker.

Fiona's spirits sank lower as once again the King and princes sat about the table. Would it be worst to endure a husband steeped in gore, like the first prince; or one glistening with greasiness, like the second; or one who like the third was simply wet?

Unwrapping his burden, the soldier prince slammed an iron bowl down on the table. Something slimy and dark red bubbled within, and a fearful, mephitic stench expanded to fill the room. "I bring as my gift the hot blood from a dragon's heart, slain by my own staunch sword this very morn! Let the princess sup deep ere it cools, and all her ills shall be healed."

"Let the bowl be covered lest it cool too soon," the King suggested, with all the dignity possible to a man firmly clutching his nose.

The second prince unveiled an exquisite golden chalice studded with costly gems. Little blue flames flickered over it; there was a yet more choking and paralyzing reek. "Let not the fair princess's lips be sullied with horrid gore," said this prince, already speaking with the air of a favourite son. "Here is fiery brimstone and quicksilver torn at *colossal* expense from the heart of the Smoking Mountain! Let its cleansing fire now burn this affliction from the maiden's skin."

"Excellent," the King said manfully through paroxysms of coughing. "Now it merely remains—"

"Excuse me," said the third prince, producing a thick roll of parchment.

"Oh yes," said the King. "Sorry."

"Let not these crude and crass remedies defile the sweet princess either within or without. I bring the Master Cantrip of Purification, prepared by myself from the most authentic sources. Let the princess but listen to its nineteen thousand stanzas – of a wondrous poetry withal, fit to charm the very soul from the body – and doubtless the bane which lies upon her shall melt away and be gone like the snows of, ah, last winter."

For some reason Fiona found this prospect the most depressing of the three.

At the table there was a hot altercation as to whether the dragonblood or brimstone should be tested first; even the poet agreed half-heartedly that his nineteen thousand stanzas should be allowed to come as a climax rather than be squandered too early in the proceedings. Fiona herself was stationed by the mirror so that her wartless and undeniably attractive reflection could maintain the princes' enthusiasm at a decent level. Admiring her profile out of the corner of one eye, she was struck by a sudden thought.

Thanks more to the resources of the Great Library than those of the Acting Royal Governess, the Princess Fiona had had an excellent classical education.

"Very well," the King was saying. "Let blind Chance make the choice between you: let the Fates guide my unseeing finger." He stood, clapped the fingers of his left hand over both eyes, and waved the other hand in mystic arabesques. It came to rest pointing unerringly and confidently at the second, or merchant, prince. "So be it!" said the King when he had made a great show of peeling the fingers from his eyes. "Now, as to the method of application—"

The stench of brimstone was alarmingly strong. But the princess had discovered that when one is about to be forcibly cured of warts in mere minutes, it concentrates the mind wonderfully. She reached the end of her train of thought, nodded, murmured "Narcissus" under her breath – and leant to touch lips with her own morally identical image in the mirror.

For an instant shadows flitted in the room, and Fiona felt an unmistakable tingle. Rapidly the mirror filled with fog; she had never before seen warty fog.

"Oh *fie*," said a silvery but exasperated voice. "You guessed."

When the fog cleared Fiona saw that her image was thoroughly encrusted with warts; so, interestingly, were the images of the King, the princes, the walls, and the furniture. Rubbing her once again lily-white hands with satisfaction, she stood and moved towards the table.

"Father," she said sweetly, "I have some good news for you."

King Fardel turned, gaped, closed his eyes, and moaned faintly. The princes appeared momentarily speechless.

"Alackaday," she cried, "the royal word of my father the King must prevent my marrying any of you good and noble princes. Only the curer of my affliction may seek my hand. Oh woe!" Fiona was beginning to enjoy herself.

"I do not remember those particular words," said the merchant.

"You left before he'd finished," she reminded him.

"All's well that ends well," said the King tediously, "and no doubt some simple quest on the sound cash basis I originally suggested—"

"Oh woe!" said Fiona, injecting as much agony into her tones as she could. "The royal word of my father the King may not be lightly set aside. It is my doom to travel now to the College of Sorcery, there to learn which mighty enchanter has lifted my curse from afar – and thus earned my hand in marriage."

"Now wait a minute," the first prince said.

"But perhaps wiser counsels may be found over good food and good wine," said the princess in softer tones. "I shall summon the Master of the Revels, the Palace Butler, the Steward of the Royal Cellars, the Court Jester, the Chef to the King's Court, the Royal—"

"All right," said the King, brightening somewhat. "He's in the Great Pantry, I believe. Wiser counsels, yes, over food and drink and merriment . . ." Again he studied the second prince and seemed to be inwardly calculating.

"And I could still read you my lovely cantrip," the third

prince was saying wistfully as Fiona slipped out of the room.

She sent Grommet to the men with quantities of wine; she retreated to her room, changed clothes, and picked up a bundle of necessities she had had packed for some little while; she made her stealthy way to the normally disued Great Stables. There was no difficulty at all in choosing between the three steeds there. The huge fiery stallion which constantly rolled its eyes and foamed at the mouth looked more inclined to devour princesses than carry them; the asthmatic and broken-backed donkey reminded her too much of its owner. Bowing at last to the King's whim, she saddled the stout gelding with the richly bejewelled harness and set off. There was an inn not far outside the valley, the Prancing Prince; Fiona thought she could reach it before dark.

Near the pond she reined in and dismounted.

"Thanks for the hint," she called. "About Narcissus."

A croak answered her. "Don't mention it; a mere afterthought. *Noblesse oblige*."

"I have a proposition for you," said Fiona. "I'm off to the College of Sorcery to enrol as a student witch, and I'll be needing a familiar. Talking cats are ten a penny, but a talking frog, now . . ."

"Pint of fresh milk every day and it's a bargain."

And so the princess and the frog rode out of the tale together, and lived happily ever after.

A Pair of Lovecraftians

TENDER IS THE NIGHT-GAUNT

Peter Cannon

Cults are there to be spoofed, and what better cult is there than the work of the American weird-fiction writer, H.P. Lovecraft? (Answers in a plain brown envelope, please.) The first of our Lovecraftians is Peter Cannon (b. 1951), an American writer resident in England. He has written extensively about Lovecraft and his work, so knows what he's talking about. Several of his stories are reworks of Lovecraft in the style of P.G. Wodehouse, and three were collected as Scream for Jeeves *(1994). He has since written several more, but for this anthology he turned his hand to emulating F. Scott Fitzgerald. You don't have to have read either Lovecraft or Fitzgerald to enjoy the following story, but I'm sure it would help your sanity if you did.*

"Already with thee! tender is the night
Gaunt, faceless flutterer, in cold damp flight."
– "Ode to a night-Gaunt"

I

Three times Rosemary Hoyt dreamed of Dick Diver at the large, proud, rose-coloured hotel on the French Riviera, about half-way between Marseilles and the Italian border, and three times was she picked up on suspicion of unlawful loitering while still she paused on the pleasant shore below it. All reddish and rugose he blazed in her memory, with his soft, dull brown eyes and his somewhat probosidian nose. There was never any doubt where to find its nearest rival – at the circus or the zoo. His voice, with some faint Irish melody running through a fanfare of supernal trumpets and a clash of immortal cymbals, wowed the world-weary. Mystery hung over erudite Richard Diver (AM Yale, MD Johns Hopkins, degree in neuropathology Zurich) like poor children around a Christmas tree; and as Rosemary stood sunburned and shivering on the beach at sunset there swept up to her the poignancy and suspense of an almost-empty bank account, the pain of lost virginity, and the maddening need to locate the Ladies'.

At length, sick with longing for that marvellous psychiatrist, nor able sleeping or waking to drive him from her mind, she asked the concierge at Gausse's Hôtel des Étrangers whether or not he had checked out.

"I am afraid so, Mademoiselle. He and Madame left nearly a month ago."

"For Paris?"

"No, Mademoiselle, for dreamland."

"Where's that?"

"I am not sure, Mademoiselle. Maybe I forget."

While she could ill afford it, Rosemary fished a 500 franc note out of her purse.

"Merci, Mademoiselle. Now I remember. You must descend the 700 steps to the Gate of Deeper Slumber."

"Is that near here?"

"About 5 miles away, on the road to Cannes."

II

As she stood in the green-litten vegetable garden, feeling lousy from the moon-wine at lunch, Nicole contemplated the less-than-marvellous guest list; then she went on through a cabbage patch to a little menagerie where cats and zoogs were making a medley of spitting and caterwauling noises. From there she descended to a balustraded parapet and looked down 700 feet to the River Skai. Through a telescope she could see Dick waterskiing in his transparent black lace drawers lined with flesh-coloured cloth, a curious garment which had provoked complaints from silly milksops in Provençal.

So they had left Provençal and rented a villa above hilly Ulthar, where according to an ancient and significant law no man may kill a cat but a cat may kill a zoog even in the off season. The villa and its grounds, made out of a row of little green cottages and neatly fenced farms, encompassed a circular tower of ivied stone, once the modest Synagogue of the Reformed Ones. It afforded a splendid view of the quaint town itself, with its old peaked-roofed bars, overhanging upper-storey casinos and numberless brothels, and narrow cobbled streets slippery with zoog blood.

Presently Dick tumbled over the balustraded parapet, slippery with sweat from the well-nigh vertical climb from the river below.

"Nicole," he gasped, "I forgot to tell you that I invited King Kuranes, the Lord of Ooth-Nargai and the Sky around Serennian."

"Okey-dokey."

"I'm going to invite some ghouls too. I want to give a really hideous, noxious, detestable party. I mean it. I want to give a party where there's baying at the moon and grave-robbing and babies snatched from cradles and replaced with changelings. You wait and see."

"I'll tell governess to lock the nursery door."

At seven o'clock that evening he came out to greet his first guests: the patriarch Atal, who had been up the forbidden peak Hatheg-Kla in the stony desert and had come down again alive but was still in therapy; and the perfumed and powdered priests Nasht and Kaman-Thah, whose cavern-temple with its flaming-pink decor was the most popular dive in the Six Kingdoms.

"This had better be good, Richard dear," said Nasht.

"Yes, Saturday's our biggest night at the club," added Kaman-Thah.

"You boys make yourselves at home," said Dick. "You'll find gourds of moon-wine on the ivory dais in the circular tower."

"Moon-wine?" said Atal, mumbling in his beard. "Don't know about moon-wine. Had my share and more already today. How about a cup of water?"

To resume Rosemary's point of view it should be said that, by the time she reached the villa after getting lost in Ulthar, the guests were gathered on benches around a long diorite picnic table on the high terrace. Stout black men of Parg in maids' uniforms were serving the meat course. Dick smiled from his golden throne at the table's head then pointed his nose decisively at Rosemary, saying with a lightness seeming to reveal a grandfatherly interest. "I'm going to save your virtue – I'm shall seat you between Atal, who's 301 and Old Kranon, the burgomaster." Nith, the lean notary, Shang, the blacksmith, Thul, the cutter of stone, and Zath, the coroner, all looked disappointed. Rosemary noticed she was the only woman present.

"Thank you, Dick. I know you're a gentleman of the old school," she said. "Not like those pushy zoogs. While I was walking through the enchanted wood one of them nipped loathsomely at my— Well, talk about fresh!"

"As I was saying earlier," said Atal, sipping his Oukranos river water, "I was trying to discourage this young fella from his quest, you see. I told him I was under a lot of pressure and didn't have time to answer all his questions even if I wanted to. Then he did a terrible thing. He plied me with moon-wine until I spilled the beans, hinting that the stone face carved on Mount Ngranek may be a likeness which Earth's gods wrought of their own features in the days when they danced the Black Bottom. In disguise the younger among the Great Ones often espouse the comely peasant maidens, you see—"

"Espouse?" said Kaman-Thah. "*Please*, Atal. When did the gods ever *espouse* those sluts?"

"Don't use such language!" cried the venerable patriarch.

"Those gods can come off their mountain and *espouse* me all they want," said Nasht.

"You laugh now," muttered Atal into his cup, slopping water down his wispy white beard, "but it could mean big trouble for everyone in dreamland if this young fella – Randall Porter I think he said his name was – gets to Kadath in the cold waste and finds the Other Gods. As deities go they're all right, I suppose, but you have to remember that their soul and messenger is the crawling chaos Nyarlathotep."

"Tell me, has anyone heard the latest about poor Menes?" asked Dick. The ease with which he changed the subject, Rosemary thought, was astonishing.

"It is said that he has been appointed honorary president of this new quarantine programme for cats who want to enter Ooth-Nargai," said Old Kranon.

"King Kuranes himself insisted," said Nith, the lean notary. "Cats can be detained even if they fly through the Sky around Serannian."

"I suspected it. It's an outrage," said Shang, the blacksmith.

"It's a scam to line the vets' pockets," said Thul, the cutter of stone.

"Six months is absurd," said Zath, the coroner.

"Are zoogs exempt?" enquired Dick, waving his nose politely around the table.

Rosemary admired how he showed an interest in what each of his guests had to say about this controversial if ultimately boring topic. In turn, she talked shop with Old Kranon, or rather she listened while he talked shop, explaining that Menes had never really recovered from the traumatic loss of his favourite kitten as a boy. Her mind soon wandered elsewhere, as did her gaze, which strayed towards her other dinner partner, aged Atal, who was now dozing face-down in his untasted plate of meat.

"Where *is* Her Royal Highness anyway, Richard?" asked Nasht. "I thought you said she was invited."

Where was Nicole for that matter? wondered Rosemary. At that point Kaman-Thah, who had excused himself earlier, rushed back to the terrace and announced: "Hey, girls, you aren't going to believe what I just saw in the bathroom!"

III

Before Kaman-Thah could savour the impact of this show-stopper, he was upstaged by the entrance of two more guests. The entire company rose as one, with the exception of Rosemary, who lagged a second behind – but as she did so she realized who one of the new arrivals must be.

"Awfully sorry, dear boy," said King Kuranes to Dick, motioning for everybody to resume their seats. "I would've been here sooner, but on the road to Ulthar I met this American chappie, an old friend I used often to visit in waking days. Trust you don't mind my bringing him along. Allow me to introduce Mr Randolph Carter, of Boston."

"I sure appreciate your letting me join your party, Dr Diver," said the newcomer, pumping his host's rough and ruddy hand. "According to Ole Kuranie here, to be included in your world for a while is a remarkable experience."

"I certainly look back in awe, dear boy, at that carnival of affection you gave when you and your wife first came to dreamland," said the Lord of Ooth-Nargai.

"The happiness of my friends is my preoccupation," said Dick. "One has only to recognize the proud uniqueness of their destinies."

"Speaking of which, Doc," said Randolph Carter, squatting on the armrest of the golden throne, "I was wondering if you could help me realize my unique personal destiny."

"So long as you subscribe to my extraordinary virtuosity completely."

While he could have taken the vacant silver throne at the foot of the table, King Kuranes elected instead to squeeze in between Rosemary and Atal. This disturbance provoked the aged patriarch to lift his head from his plate and gape at the rising moon. Since Rosemary had no hope of getting Dick to herself that evening, she was content to settle for the attention of royalty.

Intermittently she caught the gist of the general conversation, concerning whether or not Carter should seek Kadath in the cold waste, wherever that was, for her new dinner companion insisted on hearing in detail her initial impressions of dreamland. At last she succeeded in asking him what he, as an old friend, would advise Carter to do.

"My dear, I've been out beyond the stars in the ultimate void," said the king, "and I'm the only one ever to return sane from such a voyage – though I admit at times I suffer from post-cosmic stress syndrome. I told Randy earlier he ought to go back to Boston and forget this silly dream-quest, but you know how it is with you enterprising Yanks. For the sake of an aesthetic thrill you'll blithely risk all your marbles."

"I'm just a simple American girl, but the inhabitants of dreamland do seem to have more than their fair share of mental problems."

"Yes, there's a desperate need for qualified physicians to treat all the cases. That's why we're so lucky Dick has agreed to join our staff."

Kuranes went on to explain that he was director of the Dylath-Leen clinic, which he visited whenever he wasn't reigning in the rose-crystal Palace of the Seventy Delights at Celephaïs or in the turreted cloud-castle of sky-floating Serannian. In his spare time he liked to escape to his grey Gothic manor-house, near an ersatz Cornish fishing village and a Norman abbey he had reared to remind him of England. His latest fancy was to set up his own judiciary to enforce English law.

"Can't have all those disease-ridden cats infecting your green and pleasant land, can we?" teased Rosemary.

In the meantime, Kaman-Thah, evidently blotto after another gourd of moon-wine, kept hinting to Shang, the blacksmith, and Thul, the cutter of stone, that the nasty thing he had seen in the bathroom concerned their absent hostess.

"I say, old man," said King Kuranes, "please don't talk that way about Mrs Diver."

"I wasn't talking to you, Your Highness."

"You weren't? My apologies."

"You bully!" screeched the priest.

"Steady, old man."

"You're stronger muscularly than I am, you brute!"

The Lord of Ooth-Nargai turned to Nasht and calmly recommended that he take his partner home – or better yet to their cavern-temple where such behaviour was more acceptable.

Kaman-Thah declared in shrill tones that he was not about to leave for any man while the night was young, and did his lordship wish to step out on the balustraded parapet to discuss it further. This performance had the incidental effect of rousing Atal from his stupor. After rubbing the dried gravy from his eyes, the sage peered at Randolph Carter – and suddenly it was as if some fool had accidently set off a cheap alarm clock.

"Don't go!" he shrieked. "It's not allowed, I tell you! Don't go, unless you want to end up like Barzai the Wise, who was drawn screaming into the sky for merely climbing the known peak of Hatheg-Kla. With unknown Kadath, if ever found, matters would be worse, much worse, I tell you. We're all doomed!"

While Dick had drunk about a zoogshead worth of moon-wine himself, he still had the presence of mind to signal to the black men of Parg to remove the party-poopers with the meat course. Aged Atal was going quietly enough, and Kaman-Thah appeared to be actually enjoying the manhandling, when a flock of ghouls, all naked and rubbery, vaulted onto the terrace. The subsequent cavalry charge scattered the pair and their ebony escorts like nine pins. At last, thought Rosemary, they were about to have some real fun.

IV

Dick led the survivors of the previous night's party through a trench towards the rugged grey headlands. He was full of excitement that he was eager to communicate, although the ghoul who was once the Boston artist Richard Upton Pickman – dressed for the occasion in beret and paint-spattered smock – had seen battle service and he had not.

"These rocky headlands here cost one-quarter of the ghoul army two weeks ago," he said to Rosemary. She looked out obediently at the blasted landscape, littered with broken javelins and hellish flutes. The ghoul that was Pickman and his entourage of dog-like lopers stopped gibbering in respect for their fallen comrades.

"See that cliff?" continued Dick. "As the night-gaunt flies you could soar there in two minutes. The frightful detachments of moon-beasts and almost-humans spent half the day lumbering up to the top. It took the ghouls half an hour to annihilate those toad-like lunar blasphemies and their sardonic, wide-mouthed allies on the western headland. On the east cliff, however, where the leader of the moon-beasts was present, the ghouls didn't fare so well."

Pickman, who still remembered a little English, grunted a few monosyllables in protest.

"Okay, okay," said Dick. "I'm getting to that part. After the western battle was over, the surviving ghouls hastened across to the aid of their hard-pressed fellows and forced the invaders back along the narrow ridge of the east headland, thus turning the tide. In the end it was a total victory for the good guys."

The erstwhile Pickman meeped with approval, while one ghoul attempted to pinch Rosemary and several others eyed her full figure speculatively.

"Any chance I can see a battle while I'm here in dreamland?" she asked, slapping away a mould-caked paw.

"Why, the gugs and ghasts haven't quit in the vaults of Zin, dear girl," said King Kuranes. "And in the vale of Pnath—"

"That's different," said Dick. "Gugs hunt ghasts underground – it's too dark for tourists. This moon-beast and almost-human business won't happen again soon, not for another few months anyway, but when it does you can be sure—"

"Maybe next time the gugs and ghasts will fight the moon-beasts and almost-humans above ground," said Rosemary.

"No, the gugs and ghasts would never be any good in the open air. Ghasts cannot live in real light and gugs tend to drowse on sentry duty."

They dropped behind the others. Suddenly a shower of broken javelins and hellish flutes came down on them and they ran into the next transverse, where they found Nasht and Kaman-Thah collecting battlefield souvenirs.

"Oops, my mistake," said Kaman-Thah, on the verge of hefting another load of debris over the top. "I thought you were the Lord of Ooth-Nargai." The high priest had challenged Kuranes to a duel – leather handbags at twenty paces – and was still smarting from the king's refusal to take him seriously. Rosemary burst out laughing.

"That Kaman-Thah, what a kidder," Dick said when they came out of the trench and faced a partly consumed refuse heap left by the ghoul army two weeks before.

"I fell in love with you the first time I saw you," she said quietly.

"My dear, I cannot tell you how much I appreciate you."

"I know you don't love me – I don't expect it."

"At my age a wholesome replacement process begins to operate, and love attains calm, cool depths based on tender association beside which the erotic infatuation of youth takes on a certain shade of cheapness or degradation. Mature tranquillized love—"

"Take me!"

"Take you where?"

Embarrassment moved him to confess that his mother had described him as "hideous" as a boy and unfit for the draft as a young man, even though her nose was nearly as prehensile as his own. To compensate he had married Nicole, who suffered from an insufficiency complex. The reason she had missed the party was because she was having a nervous breakdown in the bathroom. This time Nicole would have to cure herself. He was hoping a long trip would do the trick. Then rather bashfully he said: "What I am coming to is this – Nicole and I are going with Randolph Carter to try to find Kadath in the cold waste. I wonder if you'd like to go with us."

"Oh, *would* I!"

V

In the event their journey included a few unexpected detours. First, Dick and Randolph Carter got drunk on moon-wine with a wide-mouthed merchant in Dylath-Leen, and the next thing they knew they were all shanghaied to the dark side of the moon in one of the reeking galleys of the moon-beasts. Luckily, friendly cats flew to their rescue. Back in Dylath-Leen, they caught a boat to the port of Baharna on the isle of Oriab. There the whole party hiked up the hidden side of Ngranek, only to be seized by night-gaunts. Soon they were dodging gugs and ghasts in the vale of Pnath, and only narrowly escaped with the help of a few ghouls through the tower of Koth. Sensing that Dick was playing the hero in order to impress Rosemary, Nicole seized the helm of their galleon as they cruised into the harbour at Celephaïs, their next destination, and crashed into a wharf.

By this time everyone was ready for a rest at King Kuranes' rose-crystal Palace of the Seventy Delights, where the Lord of Ooth-Nargai proved an especially courteous host. Dick, though, after one too many gourds of moon-wine at a local tavern, felt the king was being a bit too attentive to Rosemary and picked a fight that ended up involving a waiter, a cab driver and a bhole. Kuranes considered himself a benevolent monarch, but disturbing the peace was a very serious matter. He had lately constructed a quarantine station for cats in his grey Gothic manor-house's dungeon, as yet unoccupied, and there Dick and the enormous viscous bhole were placed in a cell to dry out until their case could come to trial. In the circumstances the king deemed it best as well to suspend Dick from his position at the Dylath-Leen clinic.

Meanwhile, Nicole, eager to show she was well on the road to recovery, agreed to accompany Carter on the last leg of his journey. Rosemary elected to stay behind in Celephaïs and assist the king with his various projects to expand "little England". In truth, she was coming to appreciate that Kuranes was quite the catch, being not only rich and nobly born but single and available. Never mind that he was dead in the waking world; she was happy to remain indefinitely in dreamland, where her lord and master would protect her from the unwanted advances of its less attractive entities.

To speed along this story further, it should be said that Nicole and Randolph Carter – after several more adventures, each more sanity-threatening than the last – did finally reach their goal: the dazzling neon-litten castle atop unknown Kadath. They had to wait only a minute or two before they were let past the velvet rope.

Inside, they followed the maddening beat of vile drums and the ecstatic blasts of tenor saxophones into a cocktail lounge, where a combo was performing an up-tempo version of "Yes, We Have

No Bananas", to which were dancing slowly, awkwardly and with frequent stepping on toes the gauche and ultra *nouveau* Other Gods.

"Not exactly the scene you were expecting, is it?" said Nicole.

"Gosh, no," said Randolph Carter, making no effort to hide his disappointment. "Atal didn't prepare me for this. Maybe we came on the wrong night."

Then the band took a break and the leader strode across the dance floor: a tall, slim figure in evening clothes with the mature face of an Egyptian gigolo. Close up to Randolph Carter and Nicole strode that dapper figure, who was not quite light enough to travel in a Pullman south of Mason-Dixon. He spoke, and in his suave tones there vibrated the syncopated rhythms of the jazz age.

"Nicole Diver," said the band leader, "you have had a long and tiresome voyage. First, you have had to put up with that drunken and philandering husband of yours. What a waste of talent! Second, you have had since your husband's unfortunate run-in with the law only this proper and provincial New Englander for company. What a waste of beauty! You deserve better."

"Hey, what about me?" interrupted Carter. "What about my quest?"

"You could have saved yourself a lot of trouble if you had just stayed in Boston – which is where I suggest you return a.s.a.p. As we speak a shantak is waiting to fly you express to Dylath-Leen. I have it from the highest authority that by the time you get there a certain American psychiatrist will have received his sentence – transportation to the waking world. You can do everyone a big favour and see him safely home to New England."

"I don't mean to sound rude," said Randolph Carter, "but who the heck are you to give me orders? Nyarlathotep?"

"No, I am Nodens," the elegant figure replied, "and that is my group, Nodens and the Night-gaunts. The Crawling Chaos and the Bubbling Blasphemers won't start their gig at the castle for another three weeks."

Before Randolph Carter could respond to this surprising news, a pair of bouncers showed him outside to the waiting shantak. Nodens gave the band the nod to resume playing.

"Shall we dance?" he said to Nicole.

"Do you like what you see?" she murmured. "You know I was once white-Saxon-blonde."

"Baby, you are more beautiful now that your hair has darkened. When you were a kid it must have been like King Kuranes' turreted cloud-castle of sky-floating Serannian and more beautiful than you."

VI

Nicole kept in touch with Dick after her commitment ceremony to Nodens; there were handwritten letters dozens of pages long on political and socio-economic matters, and about the children, who were now taking figure drawing from the ghoul who had once been Richard Upton Pickman.

In the last letter she had from him he told her that he was practising in Arkham, Mass., and she got the impression that he had settled down with one of his aunts to keep house for him. She looked up Arkham in an atlas and couldn't find it. Perhaps, she liked to think, he was waiting to get going aesthetically again, like Napoleon on St Helena – or was it Elba? His latest picture postcard was postmarked from Dunwich, Mass., which is some distance inland from Arkham and ridiculously old, older by far than any of the communities within 30 miles of it; in any case he is almost certainly in that section of New England, in one imaginary town or another. And vast infinities away, past the Gate of Deeper Slumber and the enchanted wood, Nicole and Nodens danced cheek to cheek at the exclusive neon-litten castle atop unknown Kadath.

SHOGGOTH'S OLD PECULIAR

Neil Gaiman

Our second Lovecraftian is a British writer now resident in the States (there's something about these Lovecraftians who can't stay in the country they were born in). Neil Gaiman (b. 1960) is probably best known for his Sandman series of comic-book novels, starting with The Doll's House *(1990), although he had earlier achieved some notoriety with his reinterpretation of biblical stories in* Outrageous Tales of the Old Testament *(1987). His television series,* Neverwhere *(1996) introduced him to a wider audience, although he is also well known for* Good Omens *(1990), a collaboration with Terry Pratchett. The following story, which was specially written for this anthology, owes something not only to H.P. Lovecraft but also to Peter Cook and Dudley Moore.*

Benjamin Lassiter was coming to the unavoidable conclusion that the woman who had written the *Walking Tour of the British Coastline* book he was carrying in his backpack had never been on a walking tour of any kind, and would probably not recognize the British coastline if it were to dance through her bedroom at the head of a marching band, singing "I'm the British coastline" in a loud and cheerful voice while accompanying itself on the kazoo.

He had been following her advice for five days now, and had little to show for it, except blisters and a backache. "All British seaside resorts contain a number of bed-and-breakfast establishments, who will be only too delighted to put you up in the 'off-season' ", was one such piece of advice. Ben had crossed it out and written, in the margin beside it, "All British seaside resorts contain a handful of bed-and-breakfast establishments, the owners of which take off to Spain or Provence or somewhere on the last day of September, locking the doors behind them as they go."

He had added a number of other marginal notes, too. Such as "Do not, repeat, not, under any circumstances, order fried eggs again in any roadside café", "What is it with the fish and chips thing?" and "No they are not". The last was written beside a paragraph which claimed that, if there was one thing that the inhabitants of scenic villages on the British coastline were pleased to see, it was a young American tourist on a walking tour.

For five hellish days Ben had walked from village to village, had drunk sweet tea and instant coffee in cafeterias and cafés, and had stared out at grey rocky vistas and at the slate-coloured sea, shivered under his two thick sweaters, got wet, and failed to see any of the sights that were promised.

Sitting in the bus-shelter in which he had unrolled his sleeping bag one night he had begun to translate key descriptive words: "charming" he decided, meant nondescript; "scenic" meant ugly but with a nice view if the rain ever lets up; "delightful" probably meant we've never been here and don't know anyone who has. He had also come to the conclusion that the more exotic the name of the village, the duller it was.

Thus it was that Ben Lassiter came, on the fifth day, some-where north of Bootle, to the village of Innsmouth, which was rated neither charming, scenic nor delightful in his guidebook. There were no descriptions of the rusting pier, nor the mounds of rotting lobster-pots upon the pebbly beach.

On the seafront were three bed-and-breakfasts next to each other: Sea View, Mon Repose and Shub Niggurath, each with a neon "Vacancies" sign turned off in the window of the front parlour, each with a "Closed for the Season" notice thumbtacked to the front door.

There were no cafés open on the seafront. The lone fish and chip shop displayed a "Closed" sign. Ben waited outside for it to open, as the grey afternoon light faded into dusk. Finally, a small, slightly frog-faced woman came down the road and unlocked the door of the shop. Ben asked her when they would be open for business, and she looked at him, puzzled, and said, "It's Monday, dear. We're never open on Monday." Then she went into the fish and chip shop and locked the door behind her, leaving Ben cold and hungry on her doorstep.

Ben had been raised in a dry town in northern Texas: the only water was in backyard swimming pools, and the only way to travel was in an air-conditioned pick-up truck. So the idea of walking, by the sea, in a country where they spoke English of a sort, had appealed to him. Ben's home town was doubly dry: it prided itself on having banned alcohol thirty years before the rest of America leapt onto the Prohibition bandwagon, and on never having got off again; thus all Ben knew of pubs was that they were sinful places, like bars, only with cuter names. The author of *A Walking Tour of the British Coastline* had, however, suggested that pubs were good places to go to find local colour and local information, that one should always "*stand one's round*", and that some of them sold food.

The Innsmouth Pub was called The Book of Dead Names and the sign over the door informed Ben that the proprietor was one A. Al-Hazred, licensed to sell wines and spirits. Ben wondered if this meant that they would serve Indian food, which he had eaten on his arrival in Bootle, and rather enjoyed. He paused at the signs directing him to the public bar or the saloon bar, wondering if British public bars were private like their public schools, and eventually, because it sounded more like something you would find in a western, went into the saloon bar.

The saloon bar was almost empty. It smelled like last week's spilled beer and the day-before-yesterday's cigarette smoke. Behind the bar was a plump woman with bottle-blonde hair.

Sitting in one corner were a couple of gentlemen wearing long grey raincoats and scarves. They were playing dominoes and sipping dark brown, foam-topped beerish drinks from dimpled glass tankards.

Ben walked over to the bar. "Do you sell food here?"

The barmaid scratched the side of her nose for a moment, then admitted, grudgingly, that she could probably do him a ploughman's.

Ben had no idea what this meant, and found himself, for the hundredth time, wishing that the *Walking Tour of the British Coastline* had an American-English phrasebook in the back. "Is that food?" he asked.

She nodded.

"Okay. I'll have one of those."

"And to drink?"

"Coke, please."

"We haven't got any Coke."

"Pepsi, then."

"No Pepsi."

"Well, what do you have? Sprite? Seven-up? Gatorade?"

She looked blanker than previously. Then she said, "I think there's a bottle or two of Cherryade in the back."

"That'll be fine."

"It'll be five pounds and twenty pence, and I'll bring you over your ploughman's when it's ready."

Ben decided, as he sat at a small and slightly sticky wooden table, drinking something fizzy that both looked and tasted a bright, chemical red, that a ploughman's was probably a steak of some kind. He reached this conclusion, coloured, he knew, by wishful thinking, from imagining rustic, possibly even bucolic, ploughmen leading their plump oxen through fresh-ploughed fields at sunset, and because he could, by then, with equanimity and only a little help from others, have eaten an entire ox.

"Here you go. Ploughman's," said the barmaid putting a plate down in front of him.

That a ploughman's turned out to be a rectangular slab of sharp-tasting cheese, a lettuce leaf, an undersized tomato with a thumbprint in it, a mound of something wet and brown that tasted like sour jam, and a small, hard, stale roll came as a sad disappointment to Ben, who had already decided that the British treated food as some kind of punishment. He chewed the cheese and the lettuce leaf, and cursed every ploughman in England for choosing to dine upon such swill.

The gentlemen in grey raincoats, who had been sitting in the corner, finished their game of dominoes, picked up their drinks, and came and sat beside Ben. "What you drinkin'?" one of them asked, curiously.

"It's called Cherryade," he told them. "It tastes like something from a chemical factory."

"Interesting you should say that," said the shorter of the two. "Interesting you should say that. Because I had a friend worked in a chemical factory and he *never drank cherryade*." He paused dramatically, and then took a sip of his brown drink. Ben waited for him to go on, but that appeared to be that: the conversation had stopped.

In an effort to appear polite, Ben asked, in his turn, "So, what are *you* guys drinking?"

The taller of the two strangers, who had been looking lugubrious, brightened up. "Why, that's exceedingly kind of you. Pint of Shoggoth's Old Peculiar for me, please."

"And for me too," said his friend. "I could murder a Shoggoth's. 'Ere, I bet that would make a good advertising slogan. 'I could murder a Shoggoth's.' I should write to them and suggest it. I bet they'd be very glad of me suggestin' it."

Ben went over to the barmaid, planning to ask her for two pints of Shoggoth's Old Peculiar and a glass of water for himself, only to find she had already poured three pints of the dark beer. Well, he thought, might as well be hung for a sheep as a lamb, and he was certain it couldn't be worse than the cherryade. He took a sip. The beer had the kind of flavour which, he suspected, advertisers would describe as "full-bodied", although if pressed they would have to admit that the body in question had been that of a goat.

He paid the barmaid, and manoeuvred his way back to his new friends.

"So. What you doin' in Innsmouth?" asked the taller of the two. "I suppose you're one of our American cousins, come to see the most famous of English villages."

"They named the one in America after this one, you know," said the smaller one.

"Is there an Innsmouth in the States?" asked Ben.

"I should say so," said the smaller man. "He wrote about it all the time. Him whose name we don't mention."

"I'm sorry?" said Ben.

The little man looked over his shoulder, then he hissed, very loudly, "H.P. Lovecraft!"

"I told you not to mention that name," said his friend, and he took a sip of the dark brown beer. "H.P. Lovecraft. H.P. bloody Lovecraft. H. bloody P. bloody Love bloody craft." He stopped to take a breath. "What did *he* know, eh? I mean what did he bloody know?"

Ben sipped his beer. The name was vaguely familar; he remembered it from rummaging through the pile of old-style vinyl LPs in the back of his father's garage. "Weren't they a rock group?"

"Wasn't talkin' about any rock group. I mean the writer."

Ben shrugged. "I've never heard of him," he admitted. "I really mostly only read Westerns. And technical manuals."

The little man nudged his neighbour. "Here. Wilf. You hear that? He's never heard of him."

"Well. There's no harm in that. *I* used to read that Zane Grey," said the taller.

"Yes. Well. That's nothing to be proud of. This bloke – what you say your name was?"

"Ben. Ben Lassiter. And you are . . . ?"

The little man smiled; he looked awfully like a frog, thought Ben. "I'm Seth," he said. "And my friend here is called Wilf."

"Charmed," said Wilf.

"Hi," said Ben.

"Frankly," said the little man, "I agree with you."

"You do?" said Ben, perplexed.

The little man nodded. "Yer. H.P. Lovecraft. I don't know what the fuss is about. He couldn't bloody write." He slurped his stout, then licked the foam from his lips with a long and flexible tongue. "I mean, for starters, you look at them words he used. *Eldritch*. You know what Eldritch means?"

Ben shook his head. He seemed to be discussing literature with two strangers in an English pub while drinking beer. He wondered for a moment if he had become someone else, while he wasn't looking. The beer tasted less bad the further down the glass he went, and was beginning to erase the lingering aftertaste of the cherryade.

"*Eldritch*. Means weird. Peculiar. Bloody odd. That's what it means. I looked it up. In a dictionary. And *gibbous*?"

Ben shook his head again.

"Gibbous means the moon was nearly full. And what about that one he was always calling us, eh? Thing. Wossname. Starts with a b. Tip of me tongue . . ."

"Bastards?" suggested Wilf.

"Nah. Thing. You know. *Batrachian*. That's it. Means looked like frogs."

"Hang on," said Wilf. "I thought they was, like, a kind of camel."

Seth shook his head vigorously. "S'definitely frogs. Not camels. Frogs."

Wilf slurped his Shoggoth's. Ben sipped his, carefully, without pleasure.

"So?" said Ben.

"They've got two humps," interjected Wilf, the tall one.

"Frogs?" asked Ben.

"Nah. Batrachians. Whereas your average dromederary camel, he's only got one. It's for the long journey through the desert. That's what they eat."

"Frogs?" asked Ben.

"Camel humps." Wilf fixed Ben with one bulging yellow eye. "You listen to me, matey-me-lad. After you've been out in some trackless desert for three or four weeks, a plate of roasted camel hump starts looking particularly tasty."

Seth looked scornful. "You've never eaten a camel hump."

"I might have done," said Wilf.

"Yes, but you haven't. You've never even been in a desert."

"Well, let's say, just supposing I'd been on a pilgrimage to the Tomb of Nyarlathotep . . ."

"The black king of the ancients who shall come in the

night from the east and you shall not know him, you mean?"

"Of course that's who I mean."

"Just checking."

"Stupid question, if you ask me."

"You could of meant someone else with the same name."

"Well, it's not exactly a common name, is it? Nyarlathotep. There's not exactly going to be two of them, are there? 'Hullo, my name's Nyarlathotep, what a coincidence meeting you here, funny them bein' two of us.' I don't exactly think so. Anyway, so I'm trudging through them trackless wastes, thinking to myself, I could murder a camel hump . . ."

"But you haven't, have you? You've never been out of Innsmouth harbour."

"Well . . . No."

"There." Seth looked at Ben triumphantly. Then he leaned over, and whispered into Ben's ear, "He gets like this when he gets a few drinks into him, I'm afraid."

"I heard that," said Wilf.

"Good," said Seth. "Anyway. H.P. Lovecraft. He'd write one of his bloody sentences. Ahem. 'The gibbous moon hung low over the eldritch and batrachian inhabitants of squamous Dulwich.' What does he mean, eh? *What does he mean?* I'll tell you what he bloody means. What he bloody means is that the moon was nearly full, and everybody what lived in Dulwich was bloody peculiar frogs. That's what he means."

"What about the other thing you said," asked WIlf.

"What?"

"Squamous. Wossat mean, then?"

Seth shrugged. "Haven't a clue," he admitted. "But he used it an awful lot."

There was another pause.

"I'm a student," said Ben. "Gonna be a metallurgist." Somehow he had managed to finish the whole of his first pint of Shoggoth's Old Peculiar, which was, he realized, pleasantly shocked, his first alcoholic beverage. "What do you guys do?"

"We," said Wilf, "are acolytes."

"Of Great Cthulhu," said Seth, proudly.

"Yeah?" said Ben. "And what exactly does that involve?"

"My shout," said Wilf. "Hang on." Wilf went over to the barmaid, and came back with three more pints. "Well," he said, "what it involves is, technically speaking, not a lot right now. The acolytin' is not really what you might call laborious employment in the middle of its busy season. That is, of course, because of his bein' asleep. Well, not exactly *asleep*. More like, if you want to put a finer point on it, *dead*."

" 'In his house at sunken R'lyeh dead Cthulhu lies dreaming,' " interjected Seth. "Or, as the poet has it, 'That is not dead what can eternal lie—' "

" 'But in Strange Aeons—' " chanted Wilf.

"—and by *strange* he means *bloody peculiar*—"

"Exactly. We are not talking your normal Aeons here at all."

" '—*But in Strange Aeons even Death can die.*' "

Ben was mildly surprised to find that he seemed to be drinking another full-bodied pint of Shoggoth's Old Peculiar. Somehow the taste of rank goat was less offensive on the second pint. He was also delighted to notice that he was no longer hungry, that his blistered feet had stopped hurting and that his companions were charming, intelligent men whose names he was having difficulty in keeping apart. He did not have enough experience with alcohol to know that this was one of the symptoms of being on your second pint of Shoggoth's Old Peculiar.

"So right now," said Seth, or possibly Wilf, "the business is a bit light. Mostly consisting of waiting."

"And praying," said Wilf, if he wasn't Seth.

"And praying. But pretty soon now, that's all going to change."

"Yeah?" asked Ben. "How's that?"

"Well," confided the taller one. "Any day now, Great Cthulhu (currently impermanently deceased), who is our boss, will wake up in his undersea living-sort-of-quarters."

"And then," said the shorter one, "he will stretch and yawn and get dressed—"

"Probably go to the toilet, I wouldn't be at all surprised."

"Maybe read the papers."

"—And having done all that, he will come out of the

ocean depths and consume the world utterly."

Ben found this unspeakably funny. "Like a ploughman's," he choked.

"Exactly. Exactly. Well put, the young American gentleman. Great Cthulhu will gobble the world up like a ploughman's lunch, leaving but only the lump of Branston pickle on the side of the plate."

"That's the brown stuff?" asked Ben, still giggling. They assured him that it was, and he went up to the bar and brought them back another three pints of Shoggoth's Old Peculiar.

He could not remember much of the conversation that followed. He remembered finishing his pint, and his new friends inviting him on a walking tour of the village, pointing out the various sights to him: "That's where we rent our videos, and that big building next door is the Nameless Temple of Unspeakable Gods and on Saturday mornings there's a jumble sale in the crypt . . ."

He explained to them his theory of the walking tour book, and told them, emotionally, that Innsmouth was both *scenic* and *charming*. He told them that they were the best friends he had ever had, and that Innsmouth was *delightful*.

The moon was nearly full, and in the pale moonlight both of his new friends did look remarkably like huge frogs. Or possibly camels.

The three of them walked to the end of the rusted pier, and Seth and/or Wilf pointed out to Ben the ruins of Sunken R'lyeh in the bay, visible in the moonlight, beneath the sea, and Ben was overcome by what he kept explaining was a sudden and unforeseen attack of seasickness, and was violently and unendingly sick over the metal railings, into the black sea below . . .

After that it all got a bit odd.

Ben Lassiter awoke on the cold hillside with his head pounding and a bad taste in his mouth. His head was resting on his backpack. There was rocky moorland on each side of him, and no sign of a road, and no sign of any village, scenic, charming, delightful or even picturesque.

He stumbled and limped almost a mile to the nearest road, and walked along it until he reached a petrol station.

They told him that there was no village anywhere locally named Innsmouth. No village with a pub called The Book of Dead Names. He told them about two men, named Wilf and Seth, and a friend of theirs, called Strange Ian, who was fast asleep somewhere, if he wasn't dead, under the sea. They told him that they didn't think much of American hippies who wandered about the countryside taking drugs, and that he'd probably feel better after a nice cup of tea and a tuna and cucumber sandwich, but that if he was dead set on wandering the country taking drugs there was a magic mushroom patch behind the McGillicuddys' barn, and that young Ernie who worked the afternoon shift would be all too happy to sell him a nice little bag of home-grown cannabis, if he could come back after lunch.

Ben pulled out his *Walking Tour of the British Coastline* and tried to find Innsmouth in it, to prove to them that he had not dreamed it, but he was unable to locate the page it had been on, if ever it had been there at all. Roughly half-way through the book, however, most of one page had been ripped out.

And then Ben telephoned a taxi, which took him to Bootle railway station, where he caught a train, which took him to Manchester, where he got on an aeroplane, which took him to Chicago, where he changed planes, and flew to Dallas, where he got another plane going north, and then he rented a car and went home.

He found the knowledge that he was over 600 miles away from the ocean very comforting. Later in life he even moved to Nebraska to increase the distance from the sea: there were things he had seen, or thought he had seen, beneath the old pier that night, that he would never be able to get out of his head. There were things that lurked beneath grey raincoats that man was not meant to know. *Squamous*. He did not need to look it up. He knew. They were *squamous*.

A couple of weeks after his return home Ben posted his annotated copy of *A Walking Tour of the British Coastline* to the author, care of her publisher, with an extensive letter containing a number of helpful suggestions for future editions. He also asked the author if she would send him a copy of the page that had been ripped from his guidebook, to set his mind at rest. But he was secretly relieved, as the days turned into months, and the months turned into years and then into decades, that she never replied.

A Cocoon of Oldies

LOOKING-GLASS LAND

Lewis Carroll

I couldn't complete this anthology without including at least a sample of work from the two men who really created humorous fantasy. There had been satirical fantasies long before the Victorian era. Jonathan Swift's Gulliver's Travels *(1726), for instance, is a very clever political and social satire. François Rabelais's bawdy* Pantagruel *(1532) and* Gargantua *(1534) were also exuberant satires, in these instances of French society. In fact, we can go back at least as far as the Greek writer Lucian of Samosata who made a living from lampooning Greek and Roman beliefs in the 2nd century, and often got chased from town to town for doing so. But enough of history. Despite all these roots, something has to start flowering somewhere, and I believe that it was the two Alice novels by Charles Lutwidge Dodgson (1832–98), Oxford don and mathematician, better known as Lewis Carroll, where comic fantasy really began. He produced other stories and poems besides the Alice books, but they don't come within a Jabberwock's burble for the sheer ingenuity and invention of either* Alice's Adventures in Wonderland *(1865) or* Through the Looking-Glass *(1871). Although most people remember the first, I think the second is the more ingenious, and it is from that book that I have selected the following extract.*

Of course the first thing to do was to make a grand survey of the country she was going to travel through. "It's something very like learning geography," thought Alice, as she stood on tiptoe in hopes of being able to see a little further. "Principal rivers – there *are* none. Principal mountains – I'm on the only one, but I don't think it's got any name. Principal towns – why, what *are* those creatures, making honey down there? They can't be bees – nobody ever saw bees a mile off, you know—" and for some time she stood silent, watching one of them that was bustling about among the flowers, poking its proboscis into them, "just as if it was a regular bee," thought Alice.

However, this was anything but a regular bee: in fact, it was an elephant – as Alice soon found out, though the idea quite took her breath away at first. "And what enormous flowers they must be!" was her next idea. "Something like cottages with the roofs taken off, and stalks put to them – and what quantities of honey they must make! I think I'll go down and— no, I won't go *just* yet," she went on, checking herself just as she was beginning to run down the hill, and trying to find some excuse for turning shy so suddenly. "It'll never do to go down among them without a good long branch to brush them away – and what fun it'll be when they ask me how I liked my walk. I shall say, 'Oh, I liked it well enough—' (here came the favourite little toss of the head), 'only it *was* so dusty and hot, and the elephants *did* tease so!'"

"I think I'll go down the other way," she said after a pause, "and perhaps I may visit the elephants later on. Besides, I *do* so want to get into the Third Square!"

So, with this excuse, she ran down the hill, and jumped over the first of the six little brooks.

"Tickets, please!" said the Guard, putting his head in at the window. In a moment everybody was holding out a ticket: they were about the same size as the people, and quite seemed to fill the carriage.

"Now then! Show your ticket, child!" the Guard went on, looking angrily at Alice. And a great many voices all said together ("like the chorus of a song," thought Alice), "Don't keep him waiting, child! Why, his time is worth a thousand pounds a minute!"

"I'm afraid I haven't got one," Alice said in a frightened tone: "there wasn't a ticket-office where I came from." And again the chorus of voices went on. "There wasn't room for one where she came from. The land there is worth a thousand pounds an inch!"

"Don't make excuses," said the Guard: "you should have bought one from the engine-driver." And once more the chorus of voices went on with, "The man that drives the engine. Why, the smoke alone is worth a thousand pounds a puff!"

Alice thought to herself, "Then there's no use in speaking." The voices didn't join in, *this* time, as she hadn't spoken, but, to her great surprise, they all *thought* in chorus (I hope you understand what *thinking in chorus* means – for I must confess that *I* don't), "Better say nothing at all. Language is worth a thousand pounds a word!"

"I shall dream about a thousand pounds tonight, I know I shall!" thought Alice.

All this time the Guard was looking at her, first through a telescope, then through a microscope, and then through an opera-glass. At last he said, "You're travelling the wrong way," and shut up the window, and went away.

"So young a child," said the gentleman sitting opposite to her (he was dressed in white paper), "ought to know which way she's going, even if she doesn't know her own name!"

A Goat that was sitting next to the gentleman in white, shut his eyes and said in a loud voice, "She ought to know her way to the ticket-office, even if she doesn't know her alphabet!"

There was a Beetle sitting next the Goat (it was a very queer carriage-full of passengers altogether), and, as the rule seemed to be that they should all speak in turn, *he* went on with, "She'll have to go back from here as luggage!"

Alice couldn't see who was sitting beyond the Beetle, but a hoarse voice spoke next. "Change engines—" it said, and there it choked and was obliged to leave off.

"It sounds like a horse," Alice thought to herself. And an extremely small voice, close to her ear, said, "You might make a joke on that – something about 'horse' and 'hoarse', you know."

Then a very gentle voice in the distance said, "She must be labelled 'Lass, with care', you know—"

And after that other voices went on ("What a number of people there are in the carriage!" thought Alice), saying, "She must go by post, as she's got a head on her—" "She must be sent as a message by the telegraph—" "She must draw the train herself the rest of the way—", and so on.

But the gentleman dressed in white paper leaned forwards and whispered in her ear, "Never mind what they all say, my dear, but take a return-ticket every time the train stops."

"Indeed I shan't!" Alice said rather impatiently. "I don't belong to this railway journey at all – I was in a wood just now – and I wish I could get back there!"

"You might make a joke on *that*," said the little voice close to her ear: "something about 'you *would* if you could', you know."

"Don't tease so," said Alice, looking about in vain to see where the voice came from. "If you're so anxious to have a joke made, why don't you make one yourself?"

The little voice sighed deeply. It was *very* unhappy, evidently, and Alice would have said something pitying to comfort it, "if it would only sigh like other people!" she thought. But this was such a wonderfully small sigh, that she wouldn't have heard it at all, if it hadn't come *quite* close to her ear. The consequence of this was that it tickled her ear very much, and quite took off her thoughts from the unhappiness of the poor little creature.

"I know you are a friend," the little voice went on: "a dear friend, and an old friend. And you won't hurt me, though I *am* an insect."

"What kind of insect?" Alice inquired, a little anxiously. What she really wanted to know was, whether it could sting or not, but she thought this wouldn't be quite a civil question to ask.

"What, then you don't—" the little voice began, when it was drowned by a shrill scream from the engine, and everybody jumped up in alarm, Alice among the rest.

The Horse, who had put his head out of the window, quietly drew it in and said, "It's only a brook we have to jump over." Everybody seemed satisfied with this, though Alice felt a little nervous at the idea of trains jumping at all. "However, it'll take us into the Fourth Square, that's some comfort!" she said to herself. In another moment she felt the carriage rise straight up into the air, and in her fright she caught at the thing nearest to her hand, which happened to be the Goat's beard.

But the beard seemed to melt away as she touched it, and she found herself sitting quietly under a tree – while the Gnat (for that was the insect she had been talking to) was balancing itself on a twig just over her head, and fanning her with its wings.

It certainly was a *very* large Gnat: "about the size of a chicken," Alice thought. Still, she couldn't feel nervous with it, after they had been talking together so long.

"—then you don't like *all* insects?" the Gnat went on, as quietly as if nothing had happened.

"I like them when they can talk," Alice said. "None of them ever talk, where *I* come from."

"What sort of insects do you rejoice in, where *you* come from?" the Gnat inquired.

"I don't *rejoice* in insects at all," Alice explained, "because I'm rather afraid of them – at least the large kinds. But I can tell you the names of some of them."

"Of course they answer to their names?" the Gnat remarked carelessly.

"I never knew them do it."

"What's the use of their having names," the Gnat said, "if they won't answer to them?"

"No use to *them*," said Alice; "but it's useful to the people that name them, I suppose. If not, why do things have names at all?"

"I can't say," the Gnat replied. "Further on, in the wood down there, they've got no names – however, go on with your list of insects: you're wasting time."

"Well, there's the Horse-fly," Alice began, counting off the names on her fingers.

"All right," said the Gnat. "Half way up that bush, you'll see a Rocking-horse-fly, if you look. It's made entirely of wood, and gets about by swinging itself from branch to branch."

"What does it live on?" Alice asked, with great curiosity.

"Sap and sawdust," said the Gnat. "Go on with the list."

Alice looked at the Rocking-horse-fly with great interest, and made up her mind that it must have been just repainted, it looked so bright and sticky; and then she went on.

"And there's the Dragon-fly."

"Look on the branch above your head," said the Gnat, "and there you'll find a Snap-dragon-fly. Its body is made of plum-pudding, its wings of holly-leaves, and its head is a raisin burning in brandy."

"And what does it live on?" Alice asked, as before.

"Frumenty and mince-pie," the Gnat replied; "and it makes its nest in a Christmas-box."

"And then there's the Butterfly," Alice went on, after she had taken a good look at the insect with its head on fire, and had thought to herself, "I wonder if that's the reason insects are so fond of flying into candles – because they want to turn into Snap-dragon-flies!"

"Crawling at your feet," said the Gnat (Alice drew her feet back in some alarm), "you may observe a Bread-and-butter-fly. Its wings are thin slices of bread-and-butter, its body is a crust, and its head is a lump of sugar."

"And what does it live on?"

"Weak tea with cream in it."

A new difficulty came into Alice's head. "Supposing it couldn't find any?" she suggested.

"Then it would die, of course."

"But that must happen very often," Alice remarked thoughtfully.

"It always happens," said the Gnat.

After this, Alice was silent for a minute or two pondering. The Gnat amused itself meanwhile by humming round and round her head: at last it settled again and remarked, "I suppose you don't want to lose your name?"

"No, indeed," Alice said, a little anxiously.

"And yet I don't know," the Gnat went on in a careless tone: "only think how convenient it would be if you could manage to go home without it! For instance, if the governess wanted to call you to your lessons, she would call out 'Come here—', and there she would have to leave off, because there wouldn't be any name for her to call, and of course you wouldn't have to go, you know."

"That would never do, I'm sure," said Alice: "the governess would never think of excusing me lessons for that. If she couldn't remember my name, she'd call me 'Miss', as the servants do."

"Well, if she said 'Miss', and didn't say anything more," the Gnat remarked, "of course you'd miss your lessons. That's a joke. I wish *you* had made it."

"Why do you wish *I* had made it?" Alice asked. "It's a very bad one."

But the Gnat only sighed deeply while two large tears come rolling down its cheeks.

"You shouldn't make jokes," Alice said, "if it makes you so unhappy."

Then came another of those melancholy little sighs, and this time the poor Gnat really seemed to have sighed itself away, for, when Alice looked up, there was nothing whatever to be seen on the twig, and, as she was getting quite chilly with sitting still so long, she got up and walked on.

She very soon came to an open field, with a wood on the other side of it: it looked much darker than the last wood, and Alice felt a little timid about going into it. However, on second thoughts, she made up her mind to go on: "for I certainly won't go *back*," she thought to herself, and this was the only way to the Eighth Square.

"This must be the wood," she said thoughtfully to herself, "where things have no names. I wonder what'll become of *my* name when I go in? I shouldn't like to lose it at all – because they'd have to give me another, and it would be almost certain to be an ugly one. But then the fun would be, trying to find the creature that had got my old name! That's just like the advertisements, you know, when people lose dogs – '*answers to the name of "Dash": had on a brass collar*' – just fancy calling everything you met 'Alice', till one of them answered! Only they wouldn't answer at all, if they were wise."

She was rambling on in this way when she reached the wood: it looked very cool and shady. "Well, at any rate it's a great comfort," she said as she stepped under the trees, "after being so hot, to get into the—into the—into *what*?" she went on, rather surprised at not being able to think of the word. "I mean to get under the—under the—under *this*, you know!" putting her hand on the trunk of the tree. "What *does* it call itself, I wonder? I do believe it's got no name – why, to be sure it hasn't!"

She stood silent for a minute, thinking: then she suddenly began again. "Then it really *has* happened, after all! And now, who am I? I *will* remember, if I can! I'm determined to do it!" But being determined didn't help her much, and all she could say, after a great deal of puzzling, was "L, I *know* it begins with L!"

Just then a Fawn came wandering by: it looked at Alice with its large gentle eyes, but didn't seem at all frightened. "Here then! Here then!" Alice said, as she held out her hand and tried to stroke it; but it only started back a little, and then stood looking at her again.

"What do you call yourself?" the Fawn said at last. Such a soft sweet voice it had!

"I wish I knew!" thought poor Alice. She answered, rather sadly, "Nothing just now."

"Think again," it said: "that won't do."

Alice thought, but nothing came of it. "Please, would you tell me what *you* call yourself?" she said timidly. "I think that might help a little."

"I'll tell you, if you'll come a little further on," the Fawn said. "I can't remember *here*."

So they walked on together through the wood, Alice with her arms clasped lovingly round the soft neck of the Fawn, till they came out into another open field, and here the Fawn gave a sudden bound into the air, and shook itself free from Alice's arm. "I'm a Fawn!" it cried out in a voice of delight. "And, dear me! you're a human child!" A sudden look of alarm came into its beautiful brown eyes, and in another moment it had darted away at full speed.

Alice stood looking after it, almost ready to cry with vexation at having lost her dear little fellow-traveller so suddenly. "However, I know my name now," she said: "that's *some* comfort. Alice – Alice – I won't forget it again."

THE STORY OF THE FOUR LITTLE CHILDREN

Edward Lear

As with Lewis Carroll, Edward Lear (1812–88) established a standard for nonsense fiction that few equalled until the time of Spike Milligan and the Monty Python team. Lear is best known for his limericks and for his nonsense poems, although many of these, especially "The Jumblies" and "The Dong with the Luminous Nose", are tinged with pathos, reflecting Lear's rather sad and lonely life. Less well known are his short stories, of which he wrote only a few. The following comes from Nonsense Songs and Stories *(1871), and apart from a few references that suggest its age it could just as easily have been written in 1971.*

Once upon a time, a long while ago, there were four little people whose names were Violet, Slingsby, Guy and Lionel; and they all thought they should like to see the world. So they bought a large boat to sail quite round the world by sea, and then they were to come back on the other side by land. The boat was painted blue with green spots, and the sail was yellow with red stripes; and when they set off, they only took a small Cat to steer and look after the boat, besides an elderly Quangle-Wangle, who had to cook the dinner and make the tea; for which purposes they took a large kettle.

For the first ten days they sailed on beautifully, and found plenty to eat, as there were lots of fish, and they had only to take them out of the sea with a long spoon, when the Quangle-Wangle instantly cooked them, and the Pussy-Cat was fed with the bones, with which she expressed herself pleased on the whole, so that all the party were very happy.

During the daytime, Violet chiefly occupied herself in putting salt-water into a churn, while her three brothers churned it violently, in the hope that it would turn into butter, which it seldom, if ever, did; and in the evening they all retired into the Tea-kettle, where they all managed to sleep very comfortably, while Pussy and the Quangle-Wangle managed the boat.

After a time they saw some land at a distance; and when they came to it, they found it was an island made of water quite surrounded by earth. Besides that, it was bordered by evanescent isthmuses with a great Gulf-stream running about all over it, so that it was perfectly beautiful, and contained only a single tree, 503 feet high.

When they had landed, they walked about, but found to their great surprise that the island was quite full of veal-cutlets and chocolate-drops, and nothing else. So they all climbed up the single high tree to discover, if possible, if there were any people; but having remained on the top of the tree for a week, and not seeing anybody, they naturally concluded that there were no inhabitants, and accordingly when they came down they loaded the boat with two thousand veal-cutlets and a million of chocolate drops, and these afforded them sustenance for more than a month, during which time they pursued their voyage with the utmost delight and apathy.

After this they came to a shore where there were no less than sixty-five great red parrots with blue tails, sitting on a rail all of a row, and all fast asleep. And I am sorry to say that the Pussy-Cat and the Quangle-Wangle crept softly and bit off the tail-feathers of all the sixty-five parrots, for which Violet reproved them both severely.

Notwithstanding which, she proceeded to insert all the feathers, two hundred and sixty in number, in her bonnet, thereby causing it to have a lovely and glittering appearance, highly prepossessing and efficacious.

The next thing that happened to them was in a narrow part of the sea, which was so entirely full of fishes that the boat could go no further; so they remained there about six weeks, till they had eaten nearly all the fishes, which were Soles, and all ready-cooked and covered with shrimp sauce, so that there was no trouble whatever. And as the few fishes who remained uneaten complained of the cold, as well as of the difficulty they had in getting any sleep on account of the extreme noise made by the Arctic Bears and the Tropical Turnspits, which frequented the neighbourhood in great numbers, Violet most amiably knitted a small woollen frock for several of the fishes, and Slingsby administered some opium drops to them, through which kindness they became quite warm and slept soundly.

Then they came to a country which was wholly covered with immense Orange-trees of a vast size, and quite full of fruit. So they all landed, taking with them the Tea-kettle, intending to gather some of the Oranges and place them in it. But while they were busy about this, a most dreadfully high wind rose, and blew out most of the parrot-tail feathers from Violet's bonnet. That, however, was nothing compared with the calamity of the Oranges falling down on their heads by millions and millions, which thumped and bumped and bumped and thumped them all so seriously that they were obliged to run as hard as they could for their lives, besides that the sound of the Oranges rattling on the Tea-kettle was of the most fearful and amazing nature.

Nevertheless they got safely to the boat, although considerably vexed and hurt; and the Quangle-Wangle's right foot was so knocked about that he had to sit with his head in his slipper for at least a week.

This event made them all for a time rather melancholy, and perhaps they might never have become less so, had not Lionel, with a most praiseworthy devotion and perseverance, continued to stand on one leg and whistle to them in a loud and lively manner, which diverted the whole party so extremely, that they gradually recovered their spirits, and agreed that whenever they should reach home they would subscribe towards a testimony to Lionel, entirely made of Gingerbread and Raspberries, as an earnest token of their sincere and grateful infection.

After sailing on calmly for several more days, they came to another country, where they were much pleased and surprised to see a countless multitude of white Mice with red eyes, all sitting in a great circle, slowly eating Custard Pudding with the most satisfactory and polite demeanour.

And as the four Travellers were rather hungry, being tired of eating nothing but Soles and Oranges for so long a period, they held a council as to the propriety of asking the Mice for some of their pudding in a humble and affecting manner, by which they could hardly be otherwise than gratified. It was agreed therefore that Guy should go and ask the Mice, which he immediately did; and the result was that they gave a Walnut-shell only half full of Custard diluted with water. Now, this displeased Guy, who said, "Out of such a lot of Pudding as you have got, I must say you might have spared a somewhat larger quantity!" But no sooner had he finished speaking than all the Mice turned round at once, and sneezed at him in an appalling and vindictive manner (and it is impossible to imagine a more scroobious and unpleasant sound than that caused by the simultaneous sneezing of many millions of angry Mice), so that Guy rushed back to the boat, having first shied his cap into the middle of the Custard Pudding, by which means he completely spoiled the Mice's dinner.

By and by the Four Children came to a country where there were no houses, but only an incredibly innumerable number of large bottles without corks, and of a dazzling and sweetly susceptible blue colour. Each of these blue bottles contained a Blue-Bottle-Fly, and all these interesting animals live continually together in the most copious and rural harmony, nor perhaps in many parts of the world is such perfect and abject happiness to be found. Violet, and Slingsby, and Guy, and Lionel, were greatly struck with this singular and instructive settlement, and having previously asked permission of the Blue-Bottle-Flies (which was most courteously granted), the boat was drawn up to the shore, and they proceeded to make tea in front of the bottles; but as they had no tea-leaves, they merely placed some pebbles in the hot water, and the Quangle-Wangle played some tunes over it on an Accordion, by which of course tea was made directly, and of the very best quality.

The Four Children then entered into conversation with the Blue-Bottle-Flies, who discoursed in a placid and genteel manner, though with a slightly buzzing accent, chiefly owing to the fact that they each held a small clothes-brush between their teeth, which naturally occasioned a fizzy extraneous utterance.

"Why," said Violet, "would you kindly inform us, do you reside in bottles? and if in bottles at all, why not rather in green or purple, or indeed in yellow bottles?"

To which questions a very aged Blue-Bottle-Fly answered, "We found the bottles here all ready to live in, that is to say, our great-great-great-great-great-grandfathers did, so we occupied them at once. And when the winter comes on, we turn the bottles upside-down, and consequently rarely feel the cold at all, and you know very well that this could not be the case with bottles of any other colour than blue."

"Of course it could not," said Slingsby; "but if we may take the liberty of inquiring, on what do you chiefly subsist?"

"Mainly on Oyster-patties," said the Blue-Bottle-Fly, "and when these are scarce, on Raspberry Vinegar and Russian leather boiled down to a jelly."

"How delicious!" said Guy.

To which Lionel added, "Huzz!" and all the Blue-Bottle-Flies said "Buzz!"

At this time, an elderly Fly said it was the hour for the Evening-song to be sung; and on a signal being given all the Blue-Bottle-Flies began to buzz at once in a sumptuous and sonorous manner, the melodious and mucilaginous sounds echoing all over the waters, and resounding across the tumultuous tops of the transitory Titmice upon the intervening and verdant mountains, with a serene and sickly suavity only known to the truly virtuous. The Moon was shining slobaciously from the star-bespangled sky, while her light irrigated the smooth and shiny sides and wings and backs of the Blue-Bottle-Flies with a peculiar and trivial splendour, while all nature cheerfully responded to the cerulean and conspicuous circumstances.

In many long-after years, the four little Travellers looked back to that evening as one of the happiest in all their lives, and it was already past midnight, when – the sail of the boat having been set up by the Quangle-Wangle, the Tea-kettle and Churn placed in their respective positions, and the Pussy-Cat stationed at the helm – the Children each took a last and affectionate farewell of the Blue-Bottle-Flies, who walked down in a body to the water's edge to see the Travellers embark.

As a token of parting respect and esteem, Violet made a curtsey quite down to the ground, and stuck one of her few remaining parrot-tail feathers into the back hair of the most pleasing of the Blue-Bottle-Flies, while Slingsby, Guy, and Lionel offered them three small boxes, containing respectively Black Pins, Dried Figs, and Epsom Salts; and thus they left that happy shore for ever.

Overcome by their feelings, the four little Travellers instantly jumped into the Tea-kettle, and fell fast asleep. But all along the shore for many hours there was distinctly heard a sound of severely suppressed sobs, and a vague multitude of living creatures using their pocket-handkerchiefs in a subdued simul-taneous snuffle – lingering sadly along the wallopping waves, as the boat sailed farther and farther away from the Land of the Happy Blue-Bottle-Flies.

Nothing particular occurred for some days after these events, except that as the Travellers were passing a low tract of sand, they perceived an unusual and gratifying spectacle, namely, a large number of Crabs and Crawfish – perhaps six or seven hundred – sitting by the waterside, and endeavouring to disentangle a vast heap of pale pink worsted, which they moistened at intervals with a fluid composed of Lavender-water and White-wine Negus.

"Can we be of any service to you, O crusty Crabbies?" said the Four Children.

"Thank you kindly," said the Crabs, consecutively. "We are trying to make some worsted Mittens, but do not know how."

On which Violet, who was perfectly acquainted with the art of mitten-making, said to the Crabs, "Do your claws unscrew, or are they fixtures?"

"They are all made to unscrew," said the Crabs, and forthwith they deposited a great pile of claws close to the boat, with which

Violet uncombed all the pale pink worsted, and then made the loveliest Mittens with it you can imagine. These the Crabs, having resumed and screwed on their claws, placed cheerfully upon their wrists, and walked away rapidly, on their hind legs, warbling songs with a silvery voice and in a minor key.

After this the four little people sailed on again till they came to a vast and wide plain of astonishing dimensions, on which nothing whatever could be discovered at first; but as the Travellers walked onward, there appeared in the extreme and dim distance a single object, which on a nearer approach, and on an accurately cutaneous inspection, seemed to be somebody in a large white wig sitting on an arm-chair made of Sponge Cakes and Oyster-shells. "It does not quite look like a human being," said Violet doubtfully; nor could they make out what it really was, till the Quangle-Wangle (who had previously been round the world) exclaimed softly in a loud voice, "It is the Co-operative Cauliflower!"

And so in truth it was, and they soon found that what they had taken for an immense wig was in reality the top of the cauliflower, and that he had no feet at all, being able to walk tolerably well with a fluctuating and graceful movement on a single cabbage stalk, an accomplishment which naturally saved him the expense of stockings and shoes.

Presently, while the whole party from the boat was gazing at him with mingled affection and disgust, he suddenly arose, and in a somewhat plumdomphious manner hurried off towards the setting sun – his steps supported by two superincumbent confidential cucumbers, and a large number of Waterwagtails proceeding in advance of him by three-and-three in a row – till he finally disappeared on the brink of the western sky in a crystal cloud of sudorific sand.

So remarkable a sight of course impressed the Four Children very deeply; and they returned immediately to their boat with a strong sense of undeveloped asthma and a great appetite.

Shortly after this the Travellers were obliged to sail directly below some high overhanging rocks, from the top of one of which a particularly odious little boy, dressed in rose-coloured knickerbockers, and with a pewter plate upon his head, threw an enormous Pumpkin at the boat, by which it was instantly upset.

But this upsetting was of no consequence, because all the party knew how to swim very well, and in fact they preferred swimming about till after the moon rose, when, the water growing chilly, they sponge-taneously entered the boat. Meanwhile the Quangle-Wangle threw back the Pumpkin with immense force, so that it hit the rocks where the malicious little boy in rose-coloured knickerbockers was sitting, when, being quite full of Lucifer-matches, the Pumpkin exploded surreptitiously into a thousand bits, whereon the rocks instantly took fire, and the odious little boy became unpleasantly hotter and hotter and hotter, till his knickerbockers were turned quite green, and his nose was burned off.

Two or three days after this had happened they came to another place, where they found nothing at all except some wide and deep pits full of Mulberry Jam. This is the property of the tiny Yellow-nosed Apes who abound in these districts, and who store up the Mulberry Jam for their food in winter, when they mix it with pellucid pale periwinkle soup, and serve it out in Wedgwood China bowls, which grow freely all over that part of the country. Only one of the Yellow-nosed Apes was on the spot, and he was fast asleep; yet the Four Travellers and the Quangle-Wangle and Pussy were so terrified by the violence and sanguinary sound of his snoring, that they merely took a small cupful of the Jam, and returned to re-embark in their boat without delay.

What was their horror on seeing the boat (including the Churn and the Tea-kettle) in the mouth of an enormous Seeze Pyder, an aquatic and ferocious creature truly dreadful to behold, and happily only met with in those excessive longitudes. In a moment the beautiful boat was bitten into fifty-five-thousand-million-hundred-billion bits; and it instantly became quite clear that Violet, Slingsby, Guy, and Lionel could no longer preliminate their voyage by sea.

The Four Travellers were therefore obliged to resolve on pursuing their wanderings by land, and very fortunately there happened to pass by at that moment an elderly Rhinoceros, on which they seized; and all four mounting on his back, the Quangle-Wangle sitting on his horn and holding on by his ears, and the Pussy-Cat swinging at the end of his tail, they set off, having only four small beans and three pounds of mashed potatoes to last through their whole journey.

They were, however, able to catch numbers of the chickens and turkeys and other birds who incessantly alighted on the head of the Rhinoceros for the purpose of gathering the seeds of the rhododendron plants which grew there, and these creatures they cooked in the most translucent and satisfactory manner, by means of a fire lighted on the end of the Rhinoceros's back. A crowd of Kangaroos and Gigantic Cranes accompanied them, from feelings of curiosity and complacency, so that they were never at a loss for company, and went onward as it were in a sort of profuse and triumphant procession.

Thus, in less than eighteen weeks, they all arrived safely at home, where they were received by their admiring relatives with joy tempered with contempt; and where they finally resolved to carry out the rest of their travelling plans at some more favourable opportunity.

As for the Rhinoceros, in token of their grateful adherence, they had him killed and stuffed directly, and then set him up outside the door of their father's house as a Diaphanous Doorscraper.

THE DISADVANTAGES OF MIND

James F. Sullivan

To complete our trilogy of ancient tomes, here's a story by a long-forgotten writer from the turn of the century, James F. Sullivan (1853–1936). He was a regular contributor to the popular magazines of the day, especially The Strand *Magazine, and was also an excellent illustrator, occasionally producing eccentric pictures to accompany his stories and articles, making him something of a precursor to Heath Robinson. Sullivan wrote a series of amusing stories and articles for* The Strand *under the collective title of "The Queer Side of Things". When these were collected as* Queer-Side Stories *in 1900 he added a few new ones, including the following, which has never been reprinted in all those years.*

It was the heyday of the Pleistocene period. Mrs Elephas Primigenius sat up and yawned. Then she washed the children in a pond, and untied the rushes with which she curled the hairs at the ends of their tails every night, and brushed down the little ones with a bunch of thorns. Then she went and kicked Mr Primigenius as hard as she could.

"What a healthy sleeper George is, to be sure!" she said.

Snatching up one of the children with her trunk, she hurled it in the air, so that it descended with a resounding bump on its father's head: but Mr P only grunted and turned over in his sleep.

So Mrs P jumped as high as she could, and came down bang on her spouse. Yet the result was only a larger grunt.

"Gee-orge!" she screamed; "get up, will you? It's past breakfast time. Geee-horge!"

No use. Then she found a boulder weighing a ton or two, carried it to the top of the rock above Mr P's head, and dropped it over. It descended on Mr P's head with a shock that shook the surrounding cliffs; and Mr P opened his eyes, said, "Eh, my dear?" and slowly sat up and yawned.

"What a dreadful nuisance you are to wake!" said Mrs P crossly. "With thousands of ants boring into your hide, and you asleep like an idiot right in that puddle – enough to lay you up with rheumatic fever, and there I shall be a lone widow with these seven children to support, and it's a pity you can't be a little more considerate!"

Mr P sat chuckling in a way that frightened the ichthyosaurus, who lived next door, nearly into a fit.

"Ho! ho! Roo-matic fever!" roared Mr P. "Roo-matic fever! I hain't delicate, my dear – don't you bother yourself about *me*. I'm a 'ealthy sleeper, Jane; that's what I am."

"You're a horrid rough lump; *that's* what you are!" said Mrs P, thoroughly angry. "A rough, lumping, clumping, lumbering, pachydermatous mass of material, without any mind or sensibilities. It's a pity you don't cultivate some sensibilities by improving your mind a bit; *that's* what I think!"

And Mrs P stamped away to pull down a few trees for the children's breakfast.

Mr Elephas Primigenius sat where he was. He appeared to be trying to think. He was moody, and not in his usual spirits.

"Horrid rough lump!" he murmured, and sat stroking his trunk with his paw. Presently he muttered: "'Pachydermatous mass,' eh? 'No sensibilities.' 'Improve my mind a bit.' Humph!"

And when Mrs P returned he was still sitting there pondering.

"Whatever on earth *is* the matter, George?" said Mrs P. "You're not in spirits this morning. Have you eaten anything that disagrees with you?"

"Disagrees with me!" said Mr P, with deep derision. "Dis-a-grees with *me*!" Dj'yer ever know anything disagree with *me*? It'd have to be a toughish morsel, my dear!"

Yet he certainly was *not* in his wonted spirits. Instead of partaking of his usual breakfast of half an acre of forest and a few tons of grass, he strayed moodily by the river all the rest of the day, deeply pre-occupied about something; and towards evening he hastily masticated a few trees, and then sat gloomily with his back against a rock until the small hours of the morning; after which he fell into a troubled slumber, punctuated by grunts.

When he woke next morning he went straight off by the river; and Mrs P saw no more of him until, going in search of him, she found him minutely inspecting a small plant – sitting and watching it intently.

"Whatever on earth *are* you doing, George?" said Mrs P impatiently. "What's the matter with that little plant, that you're sitting glowering at it like that?"

"Trying to improve my mind, Jane," replied Mr P. "It struck me you were about right in what you said yesterday morning; so I'm looking into things a bit to see 'ow they're done. I've been watching this plant grow – most interesting, my dear, although, o' course, it's rather slow work. But I feel it's doing me good, Jane; and that's fact. There's a lot of wonderful things a-going on which never struck me before. What makes that plant grow? How does it do it? *Why* does it do it? Dear me? Most absorbin'.""

"Poor George," said Mrs P to herself, "I really didn't mean it. I'm sure I wouldn't hurt his feelings for the world; but perhaps it'll be good for him; he'll be all the better for something to occupy his mind all day while I'm looking after the children. I'm afraid I don't look after him so much since little James, and Maria, and Henrietta came," and she sighed, and went back to busy herself about a new bandage of grass for little James's foot, which had been bitten by a plesiosaurus that objected to children.

Mr Primigenius seemed very much changed; every day he would bring home a lot of plants which he was studying, and litter the domestic turf with them. One day he suddenly got up, selected two flints, laid one of them on a granite boulder, took the other with the end of his trunk, and sat patiently tapping it on the first. The little Ps, who thought it must be some new game, gathered round and watched.

"What are you making, George?" asked Mrs P.

"A knife, my dear – a dissecting-knife, to cut up the specimens with," said Mr P, and he chipped patiently until he made a keen edge, while Mrs P meditated wonderingly on this change from his old impatient way of tearing and rending anything which offered any resistance to his efforts.

It was a few days after this that Mrs P heard dismal wails proceeding from one of the children, and, with a mother's anxiousness, ran hastily up, to find Mr P birching little James with a young pine-tree.

"Oh, George! What has he done?"

"Bin eatin' them plants!" roared Mr P.

"Plants!" said Mrs P indignantly. "Of course. Don't you expect your lawful, innocent offspring to eat plants like their father did before 'em, you unnatural parent? Perhaps you look for 'em to go eating mud like the slimyosaurus and such-like low characters? They'd better let me catch 'em at it – that's all."

"But, my love," said poor Mr P, "they're my specimens he's bin eating, and all after me a-layin' them out so careful on the shelf! Tell you what; if I'm to improve my mind, I shall have to have a study to myself; and that's all about it!"

So Mrs Primigenius went and stroked her husband gently with her paw, and led away little James, still howling; and then she helped her husband to build a wall of boulders round a space of green turf, at the foot of a rock conveniently formed in shelves for the specimens; and this was Mr P's study; and the youngsters were warned not to set foot in it.

Time went on, and Mrs P began to get dissatisfied. She missed the society of her husband, once so cheering to her amid the cares of a family. She sat down by him on the study wall, and took his paw.

"Don't you think, George, dear, that – that you've improved

your mind enough now?" she said ruefully. "I never thought
you would take what I said so seriously to heart; and I'm sure
you're looked upon as quite a superior person now by the
mastodon and hippopotamus major, and megaceros hibernicus,
and anoplotheriun, and all those. They're always talking about
your learnedness; and what's more, I'm not sure they're quite
pleased about it. They seem to feel hurt; they say prehistoric
mammalia were intended to be prehistoric mammalia and
behave themselves as such with proper palaeozocism, and
not go making superior, conceited, stuck-up philosophers of
themselves. I heard the hippopotamus say as much to the
whatdyecallit vulpiceps only yesterday."

Mr P shook his head. "I feel I ought to keep on," he said.
"I think it's my mission. Every day I feel more and more how
horribly ignorant I am."

"You're not looking so well as you used to," said Mrs P,
with a tear in her eye. "You're paler; and I believe you're
thinner. You never trumpet now, like you used to when you
were merry; and the children miss it; and I miss the walks we
used to take together through the palaeodendric glades. You
never come and paddle in the lake now. I'm sorry I ever said
that about improving your mind!" And she wept.

"I am convinced that study is the right thing – the proper
pursuit even for a prehistoric mammal," said Mr P, thoughtfully;
and she could not but notice the remarkable improvement in his
method of speech.

It was useless to attempt to stop the ball which she herself
had set rolling; and bitter regret alone was left to her.

One evening, some years after this, Mr P arose from his
studies, and sank wearily down on a knoll outside.

"You're tired, George, dear!" said Mrs P, passing her paw
over his brow. "And I never saw you so pale!"

"Tired? Pale?" began Mr P, in a voice of derision; but he
paused; and when he went on it was in quite a different tone:
"I do believe I *am* tired, Jane! Just fancy my getting tired. To
tell the truth, I have a bit of a headache, and a sort of a pain
in my chest."

"Ah, I thought so – indigestion!" said Mrs P.

Mr P looked towards the children, who were trying to pull

down a large bulkeyodendron thousandfeetium Jonesii to play with; and they came trooping to their father to beg him to pull it down for them; and Mr P rose wearily and plodded towards it.

Seven times he tried to pull down that tree, but without success.

"I'm— I'm afraid I'm not quite the elephant I used to be, Jane!" he said sadly. "A few years ago I should have thought nothing of pulling down a bigger tree than that – and now—"

"Oh, you're out of sorts, George; that's all. Why, you're quite young yet, as I told that horrid, rowdy hippopotamus the other day when he had the impertinence to suggest that he could pull harder than you – quite young and worth twenty of him!"

But in spite of the forced gaiety of Mrs P's tone, a little sigh betrayed her inward anxiety; and she gazed furtively and sadly at her husband as he went slowly and wearily back to his seat on the knoll.

At that moment the hippopotamus strolled up.

"Hullo, Primy!" he shouted. "Why, you're looking off colour! Lost flesh too, old chappie – lost flesh. Why, I'll wager you don't weigh as much as me now!"

"Impertinence! He weighs as much as ten of you, so there!" said Mrs P angrily; but the moment after she regretted that she had said it; for the hippopotamus told the young elephants to balance a convenient log on a boulder, and invited Mr P to sit on one end while he sat on the other, and it was with intense mortification and misgiving that Mrs P saw the hippopotamus's end go down.

"I do wish those pterodactyls wouldn't keep up such a shrieking!" said Mr P. It was in the early hours of the morning; and he had lain, vainly trying to sleep ever since he had retired the evening before.

"What with one row and another in this miserable prehistoric forest, I'll be hanged if I can get any sleep! As soon as the bos antiquus leaves off bellowing, the confounded bubalus moschatus begins; then the palaeontological carnivora of Cuvier take it up; then the beastly machairodus palmidens begins his yelling; and the batrachians begin whistling all out of tune! and— hang it all, I can't get a wink!"

"You didn't mind noises once!" said poor Mrs P. "You could sleep through anything. Noises are unavoidable in the palaeozoic era."

"Why?" said Mr P irritably. "Why on earth? Noise is not a necessity, surely? I hate noise. Why can't these fools of animals have a little consideration for their neighbours?"

"Well, dear; you know their other neighbours don't mind noise, and can sleep through it. Your nerves are really getting dreadfully acute. I wish you had never, never taken up this miserable improving of your mind. You'll be a confirmed invalid – mark my words, George."

He was growing daily more irritable, especially during his fits of indigestion, which were becoming more and more frequent: his appetite had fallen off dreadfully, and he had to be careful about what he ate, being no longer able to digest anything but the tenderest shoots of a few plants. After a time he began to find that his sight was not so good as it had been; and he had to look about for some rock crystal, and slowly and painfully grind down two pieces into convex form, and fix them on each side of his trunk in front of his eyes.

He slept worse and worse, until he found himself the victim of confirmed insomnia.

Poor Mrs P would hide herself behind a mountain and sob for hours after she had seen the other prehistoric fauna whispering in corners and pointing at her husband: she knew the malicious delight those uncultivated specimens found in the misfortunes of a fellow-creature.

Mr P was becoming alarmingly emaciated and bald, and his nerves were dreadful; he suffered acutely from neuralgia and jumps. He knew a great deal by this time, having, in addition to his earnest study of botany, devoted much time to mineralogy and zoology; the latter being a very favourite pursuit, as it gave him much pleasure in his present unamiable and irritable state of mind to catch the smaller vertebrata and subject them to vivisection with that flint knife he had made.

Every day the ravages made by brain upon body became more noticeable; Elephas Primigenius was a physical wreck.

The acutest form of melancholia set in, resulting from complete nervous exhaustion.

Mrs P sat with the little Ps in the study – they were all sobbing as if their hearts would break. The hippopotamus-major looked in.

"Hullo!" he said, awkwardly. "I say, I *do* hope there's nothing serious, Mrs P? I'm a rough, thoughtless fellow, I know; but if there's any blessed thing I can do for you—"

"He's gone!" sobbed poor Mrs P. "Wandered away! I've searched for him everywhere! Oh, I'm afraid— afraid that— oh, what *shall* I do?"

"Deary, deary!" blurted out the hippopotamus, hurriedly brushing his eyes with his paw. "It's all right, ma'am – believe me, it's all right. I'm a rough fellow, I know – but—"

He hurried away, and searched tirelessly high and low; and at length he came upon the emaciated form of Mr P standing gloomily in a shallow pond. In an instant the hippopotamus had dragged him out and was standing over him on the grass.

"P!" he roared, stamping all his feet with indignation, "what were you doing?"

"Going to put an end to it – drown myself," said Mr P sullenly.

"P!" said the hippopotamus, "you're a coward – a coward and a criminal! Be an elephant, P! Only to think of it, and her at home, crying her eyes out! Just look here, P – I've known her and you for many years, and I tell you I *won't* stand by and see any more of this tomfoolery. Now you just mind what I say – you go away home right now, and you smash up every blessed one of them blessed specimens o' yours, sharp – d'ye hear? And if I ever see you studying any blessed thing again, I'll give you such a lathering that— confound my eyes, if I don't break every bone in your body! Now hustle!"

Elephas Primigenius looked at him, and saw the strange fixed determination in his eye, and the scorn and indignation in it; and rose, and gripped his rough paw.

"Hippy!" he said, in a new voice, "I never knew what a good fellow you were till this moment. You have changed me! You are right – I'll do it, every letter of it! You are right – a palaeozoic specimen should *be* a palaeozoic specimen and act as such, instead of inventing nerves. Don't speak, old chap!"

Elephas Primigenius was never the same fellow he had once been; but he picked up somewhat under careful treatment, and could get about.

He forbade his children to take to any form of study.

Hippopotamus-major called a meeting of the palaeozoics, at which it was unanimously carried that "This meeting unreservedly condemns all cultivation of the mind, as tendering to injure and undermine the physical health and well-being, and to introduce a most undesirable and disastrous innovation known as nerves: and it considers it the highest duty of the creatures of the palaeozoic era to discourage and oppose all undertakings in the direction indicated, and to leave all such foolishness to races of inferior intelligence and wisdom."

So there were no more nerves nor debility until a creature called "man" arrived on the earth.

A Quiver of Spooks

THE RETURN OF MAX KEARNY

Ron Goulart

Ron Goulart (b. 1933) began contributing short stories to The
Magazine of Fantasy & Science Fiction *in 1952 and, for
a period, was one of the few writers consistently producing
humorous stories – rather a lone voice. These did not generally appear in book form until years later, by which time
Goulart had diversified into a wide variety of space adventure and hero-pulp adventure novels, including most of the
work on William Shatner's* Tek War *(1989) and sequels.
Some of his more amusing stories will be found in* What's
Become of Screwloose? *(1971),* Broke Down Engine and
Other Troubles with Machines *(1971) and* Nutzenbolts and
More Troubles with Machines *(1975). Goulart first introduced the occult investigator with a penchant for bizarre cases
in "Time Was" in 1961, and several stories were brought
together as* Ghost Breaker *(1971). The following is a later
addition.*

At just a minute short of midnight the bathtub started screaming again.

On his side of the fourposter the big, bear-shaped man
clenched his paw-like fists and feigned deep untroubled sleep.
On the opposite side his lovely blonde wife sat bolt upright, her
frilly diminutive nightie twisting around her smooth body, and
gave him a punch in the kidneys.

"Oh, shoot. There it is all over again," said Tinkle Snowden.
The moonlight knifing into the second-floor bedroom made her
deeply tan skin shimmer in a highly provocative way.

Still huddled in one of his hibernating poses, Boswell Snowden
bit his tongue and waited for the pain in his lower back to
subside.

"This is really gross, Boz," said Tinkle, full lips next to
his shaggy ear. "A bathtub that wails like a banshee is . . .
gross."

"Hum?" He faked a mumbled yawn.

"What sort of impression must we be making on the other
people who live here in Hollow Hills Circle?" She placed
an icy hand on his naked shoulder. "Our bathtub screams,
our furnace chuckles like a madman, our . . . what the heck
is that?"

Down the hall the toilet had begun yodeling.

"Houses make noises at night," said Snowden.

Tinkle said, "It's not just noises, Boz, as you know darn
well."

"You're not used to being on the ground so much," suggested
her husband, trying not to hear the awesome noises rolling down
the hall from the bathroom.

"Well, no, I never heard a biffy yodeling when I was a flight
attendant for TransAm Airways, no." She swung one long
handsome leg over the bed edge. "I'm going to march right
down to the John and—"

"Listen, some things you ought not to fool with, hon."

"No darn bathtub's going to spoil my . . . oh, ugh!"

He lumbered into a sitting position. "What now?"

"I just stepped in something horrible and slimy. It's all over
the bedchamber floor," his wife said. "Oh, how gross . . . it's
blood. Our lovely rug's awash with blood, Boz."

"Probably only a leaking faucet." He elbowed over to Tinkle's side of the bed to stare down at the dark floor.

"What sort of faucet would leak blood?"

"Moonlight plays strange tricks on your eyes," suggested Snowden, striving to put a soothing note into his rumbling voice. "That stuff looks more like chocolate than blood to me anyway."

"Well, it's not fun putting your bare foot down in lukewarm chocolate either," she said. "And where'd gallons of it come leaking from?"

"Oh, there has to be a simple explanation."

"Heck, that's what you always say," she complained, making a tentative swipe at her toes with her forefinger. "One would think, Boz, that you, of all people, the nation's leading author of supernatural fiction would—"

"I'm not exactly the leading writer of weird stuff," he corrected. "There are three guys ahead of me."

"But *Curse of the Demon* has been number nine on the darn *New York Times* list for weeks and weeks."

"Meaning eight books are ahead of us."

"But it's been optioned by Mecca-Universal for a six-figure advance," persisted Tinkle. "On top of which you're dead sure to win the Grisly Award from the Occult Writers of America at the banquet at the Biltmore in New York City next—"

"That's Ghastly, not Grisly."

"Well, grisly or ghastly, you ought to believe in a real occult phenomenon when it happens right smack . . . darn, that is so blood." She'd clicked on her frill-shaded bedside lamp.

Her fingertip was red-smeared. The bedroom carpet, usually a sedate buff color, was now a soggy crimson across most of its four hundred square feet.

"Aw, looks more like rusty water to me."

"Rusty water? You could use this stuff to give sick people transfusions, Boz," his wife said. "I'd like to see you phone up Burt Nostradamus the plumber and tell him you've got twenty gallons or so of blood spilled on the rug and you think a rusty faucet did—"

"We won't be using Nostradamus anymore."

"Simply because he wanted to interview you?" Tinkle

continued to study her fingertip. "Personally I think it's darn admirable that he doesn't want to be a plumber all his life and aspires to become a writer of—"

"Your average plumber in this part of Connecticut makes more money than 97 percent of the freelance writers in the country," said Snowden. "Furthermore, Nostradamus writes for the *National Intruder*, which ain't my idea of the main current in American—"

"It'd be nice publicity for you, Boz."

"Sure, 'Crazed Author Plagued by Real Life Horrors!' I don't need that sort of publicity, honey."

"Before you had this fantastic success with *Curse of the Demon*, Boz, before you'd gotten that $100,000 advance from Usher House Books for the hardcover and the $230,000 from Midget Books for the paperback, before we'd met when you took that TransAm flight out to Hollywood to talk turkey with the movie moguls, back then you'd have jumped at—"

"Exactly. Now I don't need cheap publicity. Turn off the damn light."

"The bathtub is still screaming. Boz, this has been happening almost every night for the past three weeks," persisted Tinkle. "This house has to be haunted or possessed. I bet it's the site of a long-forgotten murder."

"This house is not even a year old."

"You absolutely have to find out what is wrong, what evil force holds our house in its sway."

"Ignore it," he advised, rubbing at his beard and then pretending to assume a ready-to-sleep position.

"You keep saying that and it keeps getting worse. First it was only an occasional maniacal laugh in the middle of the night or a few drops of blood forming on a wall." She paused to take a breath. "The whole dreadful process is accelerating. I really believe this horrible house wants to drive me goofy, the same way the mansion in *Curse of the Demon* did to poor Alice."

"Alicia," he corrected.

"Well, whatever. It's a silly name for a girl. Boz, maybe we ought to move before the house destroys—"

"I've been writing professionally for eleven years, Tinkle," he said, rising up on one shaggy elbow. "I'm nearly thirty-eight and this is my first real taste of success. This damn house represents something to me, a goal I've reached. No one is going to take it away or scare me into . . . never mind. Let's go to sleep."

"What do you mean no one? Do you know what's behind these ghostly manifestations?"

He waited a few seconds before answering, "No."

The screaming was waning, growing weak. So was the yodeling.

"What about the blood?" asked Tinkle.

"It'll be gone by morning."

She punched him in the side. "See? You *do* believe it's supernatural. Real blood wouldn't possibly go away just—"

"If you're not in the mood for going to sleep, what say we make love?"

"With the house full of demons and goblins and lord knows what else?" Shivering, Tinkle folded her arms across her breasts.

Her husband turned his massive back on her, and soon began producing snoring sounds.

"I think we're not the only ones," Tinkle said after a moment.

"What?"

"Not the only ones with a haunted house. Nobody's said anything directly to me, yet I suspect . . . well, it's possible all the houses in the circle are haunted," she replied. "Isn't that a really gross possibility? Something really terrible must've happened here a long time ago."

"More recently than that," murmured Snowden into his pillow.

The smell of sulfur awakened Max Kearny seconds before his bedside clock commenced bonging in impossibly loud and sepulchral tones. The brimstone scent was a familiar, though not recently experienced one. Wide awake, he hopped out of bed and made his way across the unfamiliar moonlit room. As he reached his trousers on the wicker armchair where he'd tossed them, an unearthly wailing came drifting up from the patio below.

Pants in hand, Max sprinted to a window.

There was a dark figure crouched next to the barbecue pit. Ducked low, it went scurrying away into the shadowy brush beyond the flagstones.

Max narrowed one eye. Turning away from the window, he tugged his pants on. "I think I see the real reason I'm a house guest," he said to himself. He shed the pajama top he'd been sleeping in, pulled on a rugby shirt and moved to the doorway.

He was a middle-sized man, slim and forty-one. He wore his grey-spattered black hair in a sort of shaggy crewcut.

Three steps into the upstairs hall and he stepped in something warm and slick, and went sliding and skidding.

He hit the balustrade, teetering on the brink of plummeting over into the yawning stairwell. Saving himself, he pushed back and stopped when he was leaning against the wall.

"That you out there, Max?" called a female voice.

"Yeah, it is." He wiped two fingers across his bare sole. "So you can come on out."

The other bedroom door opened and a plump red-haired woman in a terry robe peered out. "Can't sleep, huh?"

A thin-faced man, his sandy blond hair sleep-tousled, looked out over the redhead. "Nightmare, Max?"

Inspecting his fingers, Max said, "Blood."

"Wake up," urged the red-haired woman, "you're still dream—"

"C'mon, Nita," said Max as he wiped his hand on a pocket tissue. "I don't mind being conned now and then, but it can cease now."

"Sometimes when you mix pills and booze," suggested Nita McNulty, eyes not meeting his, "it causes . . . oh, hell, we do love you, Max, and we're sorry Jillian didn't come east with you on this trip. And we're happy you're our house guest while your advertising work keeps you back here."

"You're one of our favorite California people," picked up her husband, "and I miss you more than almost any other friend we left out there when we moved to Connecticut six years ago and I went to work for *Muck* magazine."

"But?" supplied Max.

"Let's go downstairs into the living room," suggested Nita.

"I'll brew a pot of coffee and . . . oh, you're into herb teas now, aren't you."

"I can forgo beverages of any kind, if you give me an explanation."

"Downstairs," said Gil McNulty, coming out into the hallway and taking hold of Max's arm. "Safer . . . that is, easier to chat down there."

"Watch out," warned his wife. "Don't step in the blood."

"Ah, so you folks do see it, too."

Wrapping her yellow robe more tightly around her wide body, Nita led the way down the stairs.

Before any of them reached the ground floor, the upstairs toilet started yodeling.

Max was the only one who flinched. Noticing, he asked, "This happens regularly?"

"Most nights," answered Gil, yawning. He'd pulled khaki slacks on over his paisley pajamas, giving himself makeshift anklets. "Around midnight or thereabouts."

"We're, sort of, used to it."

When they were settled in the living room, Gil said, "We would've invited you out for this weekend anyway, Max."

"Sure, I know." He glanced up at the ceiling.

A glistening black patch was forming on the white plaster; some thick black liquid was oozing through.

"The houses here in Hollow Hills Circle are all good houses, well-built, all ten of them." Nita was watching the growing black puddle. "Working for the Hollow Hills Realty Agency I could be a mite prejudiced, since I have to sell them. But, honestly, Max, there is nothing technically wrong with any of the ten. What's been happening isn't due to shoddy materials or faulty construction."

"No, that wouldn't account for blood-curdling wails and corridors of blood," he said, remembering to sip his peppermint tea.

"I told you he'd be sympathetic," said Gil across to his wife.

Nita held her mug of coffee tightly in both plump freckled hands. "Part of the problem, Max, is my being responsible for the selling of the particular houses. They go for $200,000, which is a damn good price for this part of Connecticut. Little over an hour from New York City, really wonderful shopping mall only a few minutes downhill, brand-new middle school and a whole new high school complex planned for—"

"Spiel," mentioned her husband.

"Yes, I'm sorry. Anyhow, Max, I have four more yet to sell. That's $800,000 worth of houses and my commission will be . . . quite nice."

"But something is wrong with one of the houses, with this one?"

Gil gave a bitter laugh. "If it were only this one."

Sitting up and putting his cup on the glass coffee table, Max said, "You mean people are experiencing similar stuff in other house in the circle?"

"In all of them," Nita replied, staring sadly into her coffee.

The black splotch in the ceiling began to drip.

Max rose, crossed to where the drops were hitting the rug and probed with a finger. "Some kind of foul-smelling sludge."

"It always disappears in an hour or two," said Gil.

"How long has all this been going on?"

"Nearly three weeks," answered Gil. "At first there were only small things. Odd gurgles from the pipes, modest little drippings. We had our friend Burt Nostradamus the plumber in to check out most of the early complaints. Thing is, it's been growing increasingly worse. Now we also get screams, wails and howlings."

"Blood dripping in big puddles, toilets glowing in the dark, little fuzzy creatures lurking under tables . . . Oh, Max, you must realize how awful things like this will affect the property values."

"Every single resident of the circle has complained?"

"That's right, every . . . well, no," said Nita, thoughtful. "For some reason the Snowdens haven't uttered a negative word. Which is odd, considering."

"He's Boswell Snowden," added Gil.

Max said, "Guy who wrote *Curse of the Demon*?"

"The same," replied his friend. "This ought to be right up his alley, but he and his nifty . . . well, she is pretty attractive, Nita, don't scowl . . . he and his wife are acting as though nothing is wrong."

"Acting?"

"I've done a couple of midnight prowls," said Gil, "while the . . . manifestations were in full swing. I'm just about certain every damn house in Hollow Hills Circle is suffering from the same sort of haunting or whatever. That includes the Snowden place as well as the homes Nita hasn't even sold yet."

"I'll never sell them," she sighed. "The poor people I conned into buying into this beautiful spot are barely speaking to me now; we all know if something isn't done soon, some of them will try to unload. For a lot less than they paid."

"So far, to anticipate your next possible question, Max, we haven't gone to the local cops," Gil told him. "Because, frankly, I don't see any way this could be a prank or vandalism. We could maybe ask some sort of environmental agency to come in and make a study, except this is unlike any contamination I've ever investigated. And on *Muck* I've investigated plenty of cases."

"Nobody else has gone for outside help?" Max tried his tea again.

"The Snowdens won't admit they're being tormented; the Milmans are away in Europe and have been since before this mess started," explained Nita. "As for the rest of them, the Steffansons, the Silvas and the Sanhammels, they—"

"All afraid," took up Gil. "See, they don't want to be laughed at or have the circle turn into a damn tourist attraction. Besides which, should word get around this area's contaminated by spooks or devils or whatever, well, Nita's right . . . the property values'd plummet, Max. The housing market is lousy enough without adding a supernatural element."

"You can't keep something like this quiet forever, though," said Nita. "Little rumors are already leaking, and if something isn't done soon, darn soon, it could really turn out terrible for all of us."

"When you phoned that you were in New York to supervise the filming of some commercials for . . . what was the product?"

"*Slurp!*," he replied. "Instant soup in a plastic mug. Our slogan is, "I'd rather *Slurp!* than eat!" Which brings me to an important point, folks. I am, in real everyday life, a full-fledged advertising person. When we were all chums out in San Francisco years back, I worked for someone else. The past four years and more, I've been president of Kearny & Associates, with an annual billing of $27,000,000. Jillian and I, along with Stephanie, live a fairly affluent life in the wilds of Marin County, and so. . . . well, I haven't done any occult detective work for years. Far as that's concerned, I'm retired."

"You did such brilliant work," said Gil. "I was always writing your exploits up when I was with the *Chronicle*. That invisible antiporn group and the guy with the haunted TV set and the lycanthrope who turned into an elephant on national holidays and the suburban gnome who—"

"Decade and more ago," reminded Max as he stood.

The black spot was fading, the toilet had grown silent.

"If this whole area goes under, it'll be awful," said Nita. "Not just because of the financial thing, but because of the brave families who've settled here, Max, put down roots, fought against all sorts of—"

"C'mon, you make us sound like something out of a John Jakes saga," said her husband. "Really, though, Max, we'd appreciate some help from you."

He was gazing out at the moonlit front acre. Turning to face his old friends, Max said, "Okay, I'll come out of retirement."

Gil said, "Great!"

"You're lovely," said Nita, coming over to hug him.

"For a couple of days anyway," he added.

The young woman on the ten-speed bicycle said, "You're Max Kearny."

Nodding, Max kept on running. "And you're a neighbor of the McNultys."

The dark blonde said, settling into a speed which kept her beside him on the early morning lane, "I'm Kate Tillman, my husband is Bronco Sanhammel."

"Used to play . . . football, didn't he?"

"That's him," she said. "Reason I'm Tillman and he's Sanhammel is I believe a woman ought to maintain her identity in marriage. Bronco doesn't exactly agree, but he's too busy at Malfunctions to argue."

"What sort of malfunctions?"

"No, it's the name of a company, Malfunction Studies

International. A research organization based over in Stamford. They study companies and institutions and explain why they're screwed up. Lots of clients these days. Your wife didn't hold on to her own name."

"No, she foolishly abandoned it years ago. How'd you know?"

"Read a frothy piece on you two in *People* last year. Do you find advertising a compromising trade?"

"A compromise with starvation." As far as Max could recall, the half page of copy in *People* hadn't mentioned his one-time ghost-breaking sideline. "I'd like to come over and talk to you and your husband sometime today. A sort of research thing I'm—"

"Bronco's in Ethiopia," Kate told him. "Looking into a donut factory that's been turning them out square instead of round. We're both individuals, though, and I can talk to you while he's away. Do you always wheeze like this when you jog?"

"Only on the fifth and final mile," Max admitted.

The young woman was frowning, studying him out of the corner of her eyes. "How old are you?"

"Forty-one."

"That explains it, I'm twenty-nine. We come from different generations."

"Is that still going around, generation gap?"

Kate's frown deepened. "I'm trying to remember something else about you. Something from when I was a kid."

"Way back in the dim and distant sixties?"

Her head bobbed in affirmation. "It was in some strange and sleazy magazine Uncle Alfie used to get . . . Right! You were a ghost detective, an occult investigator."

"According to Nita and Gil, I still am."

Downhill loomed the landscaped entryway to Hollow Hills Circle.

"Then I very much do want to talk to you, Max," she said. "You don't mind if I call you Max right off?"

"I expect such familiarity from your generation."

"You're teasing but I'm serious," she said. "Why don't you drop in for breakfast now? I'm a vegetarian, so I can't offer you ham and sausage or any other dreadful traditional Sunday breakfast fare. We can talk, though about . . ."

"About what?"

"The hauntings."

Max sat on the brick front porch of the Tillman-Sanhammel colonial, watching a carrion crow circle a nearby wooded area and aware of various thumpings coming from inside the house. A scruffy terrier cut across the vast front lawn, pausing to gruff once at him.

"Okay, all shipshape. You can come on in," invited Kate from the now open front door.

Stretching up, his left knee making a creaking, Max went into the cool, spotless living room, which was furnished with stark functional furniture and tropical plants. There were bookcases built into one wall, and he noticed, while following her through to the kitchen, a gap of about two feet on the otherwise crowded shelves. "How long have you lived here?"

"I suppose that was an old-fashioned stereotyped female thing to do," said Kate over her shoulder. "Tidying up before letting you in."

"Warms the heart of us senior citizens."

The kitchen was yellow, black and white, as angularly furnished as the living room.

Nodding at a square yellow table, Kate said, "What were you asking, Max?"

"How long you and Bronco have lived here in Hollow Hills."

"Oh, just a bit over two months," she said. "Before that we had a place over in Weston, but when Bronco got promoted to Assistant Foul-Up Field Research Man, we decided to move up the ladder a rung or two. Not that I'm into status."

"Did you hear about this area through someone?"

She placed a glass teakettle on an electric burner of the stark black stove. "Rose hip or Red Zinger tea?"

"Dealer's choice."

Kate reached up and took a box of rose hip tea from a cabinet shelf. Her navy-blue jersey hiked, showing a smooth stretch of tan back. "Matter of fact, we knew some of the people who were already living here," she said, busying herself with getting out two teabags and dropping them into a fat black teapot. "Actually I knew Boz Snowden and he'd spoken highly of Hollow Hills Circle."

"You're friends of the Snowdens?"

"Not exactly, I used to be Boz's typist." She turned, leaned against a counter. "He had a small place in Weston, too, before the tremendous success of *Curse of the Demon*."

"You type the manuscript on that?"

Kate lifted the whistling kettle off the heat. "Yes, a good part of it," she answered as she poured steaming water into the teapot. "How do soy pancakes sound? As the main course? Along with hashbrown rutabagas?"

"Yum-yum."

"I suppose, depending on the mass food business for your livelihood, you have to pretend to enjoy eating garbage."

"It's required, yes. Garbage, sewage, all sorts of other unspeakable stuff. That's what they pay me for." He took the cup of tea she handed him. "You ready now to talk about the unusual things that've been going on hereabouts?"

Bending from the waist, bare back flashing again, she took a black mixing bowl from a low shelf. "Everyone has been bothered by strange things, Max, all the houses," Kate said. "Strange noises during the witching hour, occult manifestations, ghostly materializations."

"What do you think causes it all?"

She faced him again, bowl clutched to her chest. "I haven't done as much digging into local history as I'd like," she said. "I do know, though, that centuries ago there was some kind of devil-worshipping cult that flourished in these parts, Max. It seems most likely that what we're experiencing is some sort of residual evil, a kind of supernatural toxic waste that's built up."

"What do you and your husband intend to do?"

Kate fetched two eggs from the squat yellow refrigerator. "Oh, Bronco isn't here enough to be much bothered. And, as you may recall, when he played pro ball they dubbed him the Salinas Stoic." She broke two eggs into the bowl. "Gibbering bathtubs and blood dripping from doorknobs doesn't much faze him. I guess we'll just sit it out. Sometimes, from what I've heard, these ghostly things end as suddenly as they began."

"In Boz Snowden's book it took two cardinals, a bishop and a psychic investigator to exorcize the demon who'd been dwelling in that old mansion on the Long Island Sound."

Kate sniffed. "That's fiction, Max." Picking up a mixing spoon, she began working on the contents of the bowl.

The white wallphone rang.

She caught it on the second ring. "Yes?" Kate paused, listening. "I can't talk to you now . . . It doesn't sound as though you have anything new to say to me anyway . . . Oh, really? I . . . I'll phone you later." She hung up carefully. "Relatives, even distant ones, can be a pain."

Max eased to his feet. "Can I wash up someplace before breakfast?"

"Downstairs bathroom's through the living room and along the hall on your right."

"Thanks." On his way there, Max stopped in the stark living room to take a look at the gap on the book shelf.

Shaved, showered and wearing old tennis shoes and denim slacks, Max cut across a grassy acre between the houses which ringed, informally, the circle. The sun was nearly at its midday mark in the clear blue sky.

On the close-cropped lawn directly in front of the Snowden house a long, tanned young woman in a fawn-colored bikini was spread-eagled on an air-cushion. Near her fluffy blonde head a tiny transistor radio was gurgling.

At the sound of Max's sneaker on the gravel path leading to the front door, the blonde sat up. "Are you coming over to complain?"

He shook his head. "I'm Max Kearny, staying with the McNultys for a few—"

"Boz, my gifted husband, is very class-conscious. He's got the dopey notion sunbathing annoys people and that I ought to do it out back in the privacy of our patio, except the sun's better out front this time of day. It isn't, besides, that I'm mother naked or indecent. He's Boswell Snowden, author of *Curse of the Demon*. It's a bestseller."

"I know." Max approached Tinkle Snowden across the bright grass. "Reason I dropped over, Nita McNulty, in her capacity as a real estate agent, has asked me to check out some complaints she's been getting. Always anxious to keep all the residents of the circle as content as—"

"Complaints, maybe, about spooky noises?"

Halting, Max squatted at the edge of the polka-dot air mattress. "Have you been suffering from such disturbances, Mrs Snowden?"

". . . climbing right up to the top of the charts, baby . . ." murmured the tiny radio.

"I guess you could say so. I mean, golly, the bathtub screams like a hooty owl, the toilet sounds like there's a fat man drowning in it, and . . . well, well, and how do you like Connecticut, Mr Kearny?"

"Hum?"

"Nix, nix." She hunched one bare shoulder at her colonial-style house, then whispered, "The electric typewriter's stopped clacking. He's probably watching us. From his studio."

"Does he read lips?"

"Boz has a wide range of unusual talents. I don't know, but he doesn't want me to admit we've been having any trouble with our house."

"Does he now? I'd have thought, since this is exactly the sort of thing he writes about in his novels, that he'd be eager to—"

"Heyo!" The front door flapped open, and while it was still quivering, the huge bearded Snowden emerged to stand squinting on the front porch. "What are you selling, buddy?"

"Slurp!" called Max. "But not to you. I'm a guest of the McNultys. Nita's asked me to—"

"No comment." Snowden came lumbering down across the lawn, a ballpoint pen gripped between his teeth.

"Nita's very anxious to make certain the folks residing here are trouble-free and—"

"No comment," replied the bear-like author. "I can emphasize that with a poke in the snoot."

"Boz, don't beat up Mr Kearny." Tinkle hopped up. "He's much dinkier than you."

"Kearny? Kearny? I read about you someplace, saw a picture."

"No doubt in *People*. About my wife and me, and my advertising agency."

"Naw, this was when I was a kid and first got hooked on the supernatural . . ." His thick shaggy eyebrows tilted toward each other. "Yeah, you used to be a ghost breaker, a demon buster, an occult busybody."

"In my vanished youth," said Max. "Right now I'm just doing Nita a favor by—"

"We have nothing to say, Kearny." Snowden raised a shaggy fist.

"But, Boz, maybe we ought to—"

"Shut your yap," advised her husband.

"If you are suffering from any sort of occult manifestations, the publicity from that could only help your—"

"You're going to suffer from a busted snoz if you don't haul ass out of here."

"Really?" Max remained facing the larger man.

After a second Snowden dropped his fist. "Tinkle's right, I can't smack a wimp like you."

Grinning at them, Max said, "If either of you change your mind, I'm staying at the McNultys through Tuesday." He walked away.

"Nice meeting you, Mr Kearny," called Tinkle.

Max leaned his elbows on the metal patio table, studying the notes he'd scribbled on the pages of a yellow legal tablet after talking with all the beleaguered residents of the circle, shuffling through the maps and floorplans Nita'd provided. "Demonic possession . . . some sort of residual evil . . . an unsolved murder in the past . . . none of the above?"

Pipes and wrenches rattled. "Courting the muse?"

Glancing up, Max beheld a man in a tan suit at the edge of the flagstone patio, a tool chest dangling in one hand. "You must be Burt Nostradamus," he said, pushing back in his deckchair.

Nostradamus was tall and lean, wearing dark glasses. "The village plumber." He came over and sat opposite Max unbidden. "Yet in my heart dwell deeper yearnings."

"Toward me?"

"I'm alluding to my dream of being some day a full-time professional writer," the plumber explained. "The ambition first struck me one chill winter's eve some years since while I labored to unearth the frozen pipe leading to the Hungerford's cesspool. Flurries of snow assailed my slim frame, making white smudges across the black slate of the night. 'Nostradamus,' I exclaimed at that moment of insight, 'there is more to life than dibbing into cesspools in the middle of the night.' From that day I was dedicated to becoming an author."

"How've you been doing?"

"Thus far I've sold seven articles to the *National Intruder*," the plumber said, smiling faintly with pride. "I know I could get a full page in there if only Boz Snowden would cooperate."

"You want to interview him?"

"This yarn is big enough to hit maybe even the wire services. If, that is, I can persuade Snowden to speak frankly and openly with me."

"This all has something to do with the strange midnight happenings?"

The gaunt plumber dropped his toolkit with a thunking rattle. "I know of your work in the field of occult investigation, Mr Kearny," he said in a confiding tone. "When I was but a small lad I read of your daring exploits in the very pages of the *Intruder*. Little did I dream that some fine day my own work would be gracing those selfsame pages, or that I'd meet such a—"

"You're around the Circle a lot, aren't you?"

"More than some realize," replied the plumber. "In the interest of gathering material, I've been paying nocturnal visits. Indeed, I was here last night when the demonic manifestations occurred. Perhaps you noticed me, being more perceptive than the rest, as I moved hither and yon on the track of the unknown."

"Were you out here on the patio?"

Nostradamus nodded. "It's risky being out in the open when this devilish work is going on, yet for a story—"

"What about the empty house two houses to the left of us? You been in there?"

Shaking his head, the plumber said, "Not since we installed the plumbing some time since. Why? You don't think a fellow occult investigator would stoop to housebreaking on the side."

Max said, "What's your theory as to what's behind this all?"

"Boswell Snowden's novel is a runaway bestseller, yet he writes little better than I do," said the plumber. "His earlier novels, all of which I've read, are much worse even. Poorly plotted, filled with trite conventionalities and stilted prose. They did not sell."

"*Curse of the Demon* is pretty well written."

"The explanation is childishly simple, Mr Kearny," said Nostradamus, leaning. "In order to insure himself a better prose style and to guarantee impressive sales, I am certain what Snowden did. He did what greedy and ambitious men have done through the ages, entered into a pact with the devil."

"You have any proof?"

"Nothing concrete, no," admitted the gaunt plumber. "Yet, from all I've seen and heard here during the grim watches of the night, I know I am right. As soon as I can prove my case, then have I got a story for the *Intruder*."

"What about all the things that are happening to the other houses?"

"Side effects," said the plumber, sitting back.

Phone on his lap and receiver to his ear, Max sat alone in the McNulty living room and watched the twilight come sweeping slowly across Hollow Hills Circle.

"Hello?"

"We have a collect call from the Bowery, New York," he said. "A Mr Maxwell Kearny Jr claims, as far as we can make out from his babbling, that he is your common-law spouse. Will you accept charges?"

"Oh, him. No, toss him back into his gutter and mention I'm on the brink of running away with the college boy who seeds the lawn."

Max said, "Otherwise how are things, Jill?"

Jillian Kearny said, "Stephanie got a homer and a double today."

"Admirable. Is she still the only girl in the Little League?"

"The only one on the Mill Valley Brewers. She's out at practice this very moment, so you can't talk to her. Did you buy her something?"

"It's in my suitcase."

"How are Nita and—"

"Listen, Jill, there's something going on here."

"Such as?"

He told her.

When he'd concluded she asked, "What's this Kate Tillman look like?"

"Oh, your usual long-legged blonde, beautiful and highly intelligent. Just like most wives in Fairfield County," he answered. "Little dinky auburn-haired ladies in their waning thirties they turn back at the border."

Jillian said, "You're investigating this whole frumus, huh?"

"Apparently so."

"Couldn't stay retired."

"Nope."

"So what do you think is afoot?"

"Somebody's summoned up a demon," he said. "All the manifestations point to that."

"Sounds like, yes," she agreed. "Which prompts me to suggest you go easy, Max."

Pushing aside the three library books on the coffee table, he moved the legal tablet into writing range. "Listen, Jill, all of my occult reference books and manuscripts are still up in the attic, aren't they?"

"I bumped into them only last night when I was hunting for Stephanie's bingo game, which she had a sudden wild urge to play."

"Can you pop up there and copy off a few of the strongest spells for getting rid of a demon?"

"Sure. Are we talking about a demon summoned to aid somebody?"

"No," he said, "one brought forth to get revenge."

A soft night rain was falling. Max zipped up his windbreaker, went edging along beside the McNulty house. He carried an unlit flashlight in his hand.

He waited in the bushes, watching the empty, rain-slick road which curved around the circle. After a few damp moments, he jogged across a slanting lawn, ran along a white driveway and, slowing, approached one of the unoccupied houses.

Moving along close to the side of the house, he halted near the window of the den. As he'd anticipated, there was a flickering light inside.

His watch face wasn't in the mood to glow, so he had to squint to make out the time. Three minutes in front of midnight.

He crept around to the rear of the house, let himself in by way of the kitchen door he'd left open during his afternoon visit.

The part of the house he'd entered still smelled of fresh paint and new wood. As he walked, silently, toward the den, though, new odors hit him. The smells of brimstone, sweet strong incense, damp earth, decay. Not your usual suburban household scents.

The whole house began to shudder.

Windows rattled, floors creaked.

It was like being directly over a quake.

From the den came a woman's voice. "You've got to go back!"

There was a rumbling, rasping laugh. "The gate has been opened! I am unleashed."

"Yes, but you were only supposed to do one simple thing and then go back . . . home."

Again the awful booming laughter.

All the pipes in the empty house began to shriek. Strange gurglings commenced underfoot. All the toilets were chortling.

"You haven't even succeeded in doing what I summoned you for. You've been making all sorts of annoying trouble for innocent people. It's stubborn and . . . mean-minded."

"You should have reckoned on that when you allowed Morax into this world again."

"I looked up another new spell, and this one'll bottle you up again."

Another evil laugh. "Your magic is not strong enough to stop me, foolish wench."

In the den Kate Tillman began, a shade nervously, to recite a spell in Latin.

Max was standing quietly next to the oddly glowing doorway. He shook his head. "Outmoded spell, not a chance of working."

"I heed it not! It has no effect!" roared Morax. "Now I'll once again torment your fellows."

"I really wish you'd go away. This hasn't worked out at all. He's even more stubborn than you."

"There is no way to stop me now. Each night at this enchanted hour I shall return to have my way."

"That's another thing, you keep doing these silly things to people. Can't you zero in on him, give him a real scare. I wouldn't mind your messing up the rest of us if—"

"Morax does as he pleases. None can stop such an all-powerful demon!"

"Correction." Max crossed the threshold, unfolding a sheet of yellow paper from his pocket. "This is a very effective spell, worked out by a demonologist working in tandem with a computer. Been tested on a lot tougher demons than you, always works."

Crouched just outside the magic circle, face illuminated by the flickering flames of the ring of votive candles, was Kate. A patch of smooth tan skin showed between the top of her white slacks and her green jersey. A hand pressed to her left breast, she was staring at the demon who stood within the circle.

He was impressive. Over nine feet high, muddy green in color, covered with dry scales, his growling mouth packed with needle-like teeth. His bulging eyes glowing with an unsettling yellow light.

"Impotent fool!" he warned Max. "I will visit numerous annoyances upon you."

Clearing his throat, Max said, "Okay, here we go. Zimimar, Gorson, Agares, Leraie, Zenophilus," he read slowly and carefully.

"Bah, this has no . . . I do feel decidedly . . ." Morax brought his terrible clawed paws up to his scaly face. "Gar . . ."

"Wierus, Pinel, Belphegor," continued Max.

The demon was panting, snarling, spewing greenish smoke from his mouth and ears.

Max kept on reciting the spell.

Morax shook, huddled in on himself, began to fade. Another moment and he was gone, even the smell of him.

The candles sputtered and died, the house was silent again.

Folding up the spell and slipping it away, Max crossed and touched Kate's shoulder. "I'll see you home."

Taking his hand, she got to her feet. "I . . . I wrote that book, you know."

"*Curse of the Demon*. Yeah, I figured that out," he said, as he guided her to the doorway. "After comparing his earlier works with it."

"I was so dumb, I signed some wretched agreement with Boz that gave him 90 percent of all the profits and 100 percent of the credit," she said. "Demonology has always been a hobby of mine. I did a really splendid job on that book. Thing is, I was timid and figured I needed someone like Boz Snowden to help me break into print."

They left through the back door. "So when he moved here, you followed. Deciding to go after a bigger share of the money the book's earning."

"Yes, although Bronco doesn't know that part of it," she said. "He's off in Ethiopia and Portugal and such places, never even knew I did the damn book."

"When you confronted Boz Snowden, he wouldn't give in?"

The rain was falling harder. Max put his arm around her slim shoulders.

"He simply threatened me, wouldn't listen at all," she said. "He's pretty vain; I think he's convinced himself that *Curse* wasn't a collaboration at all and that the book is entirely his. Well, I can get pretty mad and I decided to fix him good. The reason *Curse* is so good, Max, is because I really believe in demonology. And, damn it, it works."

"Somewhat too well."

"I summoned up Morax, that was easy, and ordered him to plague Snowden," she explained. "Except the demon started plaguing the whole area, all the houses. I suppose, giving him the benefit of the doubt, it's difficult to zero in on a small target. When I realized what was going on, I tried to send him off. Except, as you saw, I couldn't control Morax. He kept coming back night after night to play his pranks. On top of which, Boz has been very stubborn and, even though I told him the weird happenings were happening because he'd cheated me, he hasn't given in. All in all, it's been an awful mess."

"Your library of occult literature isn't broad enough for you to fool around with this sort of thing."

"How'd you know about my—"

"You hid the books in the hall closet this morning before you'd let me in the house," he replied. "I found 'em when I went to wash my hands."

"I should have expected that, you being a detective."

"Why'd you use the empty house as a base?"

"I didn't want to summon up a demon in our own place," she said as they neared her home. "There might have been a mess, and Bronco is very fastidious. How'd you know I'd been using that particular place?"

"I went through all the houses today, even the unoccupied ones. The remains of your magic circle showed on the floor," he told her. "My guess was we had a demon who'd gotten out of hand and that you'd be going back each night to try to keep him from reappearing."

"I'm sorry, more or less, that Morax made trouble for all the Circle people," Kate said, moving free of him and climbing to her front door. "But I'm not at all sorry about Boz Snowden. I'd still like to put a few more curses on him."

Max said, "I know a good literary attorney in Manhattan. Suppose we go in and talk to him tomorrow."

"You mean I ought to use legal means instead of supernatural to get what's rightfully mine?"

"Slower but sometimes more effective."

She shrugged, resigned. "Well, since demons turned out to be so unreliable, I may as well go to the law."

"I'll be driving into Manhattan tomorrow; you can come along."

"I'll do that." She opened the door. "Can I offer you a cup of tea?"

He hesitated before answering, "You can."

THE UNPLEASANTNESS AT THE BALONEY CLUB

F. Gwynplaine MacIntyre

The second of our two ghost stories is an affectionate tribute to the club story, especially the Jorkens tales by Lord Dunsany. It's also a slight nod to the Lord Peter Wimsey stories by Dorothy Sayers. F. Gwynplaine MacIntyre (b. 1948) – Froggy to his friends – is a Scottish-born, Australian-raised, American-resident author who has contributed a number of amusing stories to Isaac Asimov's Science Fiction Magazine *since his first sale in 1979. He is the author of the excellent Victorian science-fiction novel* The Woman Between the Worlds *(1994), as well as several pseudonymous novels.*

A waiter arrived with our brandy and cigars, and someone raised the subject of ghosts. My friend Maltravers had the first go, and we listened in hushed astonishment as he recounted an eerie incident that had befallen him one night during his years as a rubber-trader along the Burma Road, where he encountered a beckoning wraith that attempted to sell him some double-glazing.

It then fell to Smythe-ffolliott to regale us with his account of the ancient Saxon curse that has blighted his ancestral home and preyed upon his family for twenty-seven generations: something to do with a haunted jar of Vegemite, which apparently has *also* been in his home for twenty-seven generations. The hideous jar of unholy Vegemite follows its victims up and down the stairs at night, calling out to them in a sepulchral voice and demanding a loaf of sliced bread so that it can turn itself into haunted sandwiches.

The next supernatural tale was that of our club's newest member, young Chundermutton, who proceeded to describe his nocturnal encounter with a strange headless apparition that crept towards him on twisted limbs in the moonlight and made piteous moans. At this point I interrupted him to ask how a headless apparition – having no head, and therefore lacking a mouth – could possibly make any sort of moans, piteous or otherwise. This led to a brief exchange of opinions between Chundermutton and myself, during which his throat found itself lodged in my Masonic handshake, and he attempted to employ certain oriental techniques in a campaign to dislodge my pancreas from its rightful position. Maltravers and Smythe-ffolliott were obliged to come between us with the soda-water siphon and the smoking-room's third-best spittoon, and eventually a truce was negotiated.

"What we want here is Blenchcroft," said Maltravers, nodding towards the nearby armchair customarily occupied by our club's most distinguished member. Tonight, the fabled armchair was unaccountably empty . . . although its antimacassars could be seen moving eerily of their own accord, as if possessed by either poltergeists or blackbeetles. "Good old Blenchcroft always has a cracking good ghost story for us, what?" As he spoke, Maltravers applied marmalade to a kipper, and tucked it away in his waistcoat for future reference. "Pity that Blenchcroft isn't here just now. What d'you suppose could have happened to him?"

At that moment, a distant rattling of chains was heard within the walls. This could mean only one thing: someone was coming up in the lift. Our club's passenger-lift has not been repaired since the Siege of Mafeking, and the chains which support the elevator's counterweight have rusted nearly all the way through. Now, without rising from our chairs, we all turned our heads towards the lift's glass-paned doors, knowing that soon they would slide open – the doors, I mean; not our heads – and the lift's unknown occupant would arrive to confront us.

As the elevator's doors wheezed open, I glimpsed a familiar figure dressed in our club's livery: old Staveacre, the ancient lift-attendant who has served our distinguished club these past fifty-nine years. Reflecting upon the elderly retainer's long and faithful service to our club, it occurred to me that we really ought to start paying him wages. "Your floor, sir," old Staveacre croaked, and the lift's passenger stepped forth into the clubroom. As the doors slid shut and the elevator descended, I rose to greet the newcomer . . . and gasped.

It was Blenchcroft. Yet I barely recognized him. His face was all pale, like parchment. His hands trembled, his knees shook like castanets. His eyes were like two hollow sockets. (I keep a hollow socket handy at all times, for purposes of comparison.) With an effort, Blenchcroft staggered across the clubroom to his accustomed armchair, and sank into it gratefully. "A drink!" he quavered, shuddering spasmodically. "In heaven's name, man! Someone fetch me a drink!"

"Spot of whisky and soda?" asked Smythe-ffolliott brightly. He reached into his pocket and took out a sheet of A4 writing-paper. In its centre was a spot of whisky and soda. Blenchcroft ignored this, preferring to invert the communal jeroboam of brandy and drain its contents into his gullet. At last, when he seemed to have regained his nerve, he let the bottle fall empty upon the Axminster carpet, and he sat gazing wordlessly into the fireplace. He did not speak. A vein twitched in his forehead. A peculiar expression played across his face, flickering from his lips to his eyebrows and back again without a return ticket.

Chundermutton broke the silence: "What is it, man? You look as if you've seen . . ."

"*I have,*" said Blenchcroft mournfully, in the tones of a man who has met his own doom. We all kept still, and waited for him to continue.

The dying embers of the coal-fire cast weird shadows across

the clubroom's walls. I should mention that ours is one of the oldest clubs in Pall Mall, and in consequence the rooms are furnished with several centuries' worth of trophies and memorabilia collected in far outposts by our club's distinguished members. From my vantage point in the centre of the clubroom, I had a fine view of the east wall, from which a splendidly preserved Anglo-Norman battleaxe hung check by jowl with an *asagai* war-spear which had briefly festooned the chest cavity of our club's best yachtsman during the last Zulu uprising. Beneath these items were two display cases. The left-hand case contained a breech-loading harquebus which had seen duty during the War of Jenkins' Ear. The right-hand case contained Jenkins' ear. Not his *famous* ear, the one that caused so much bother; the Reform Club, I think, has got *that* one. This was Jenkins' *other* ear; one of our club's secretaries had obtained it at auction from Sotheby's, and now it was stuffed and mounted in the clubroom.

At long last, when all the world was silent as the tomb, Blenchcroft began to speak: "The day went normally enough, at first," he told us. "I spent the morning in my usual fashion, evicting widows and orphans from my various properties. At noon I had rather a heavier luncheon than usual, and I went back to my office for a quick nap. That was when I had the nightmare . . ."

"Objection!" Maltravers leapt out of his armchair and was on his feet at once, brandishing his leather-bound copy of the club's regulations. "'Rule Forty-Two: members telling ghost stories in the clubroom must confine their narratives to authentic paranormal encounters. Nightmares, being imaginary, are expressly forbidden.'" Maltravers snapped shut the booklet and sat down again. Unfortunately, he ruined the effect by missing his armchair, and landing headlong in an inglorious sprawl amidst the half-eaten scones of our previous meal.

"If I may continue . . .," said Blenchcroft irritably. "I was napping in my upstairs office. All of a sudden, I was awakened by the distant sound of hoofbeats – approaching slowly, steadily – and the rumble of wheels against cobblestones. Some horse-drawn conveyance was coming towards me. I heard the wheels and the hoofbeats draw closer, and soon I could hear the contraption rattling in the street directly underneath my window. I expected the unseen vehicle to continue past, but just then the wheels and the hoofbeats abruptly went silent. For some reason, the unknown conveyance had *stopped* directly in front of my rooms. I got up from my chair, and went to the window.

"I expected to see a dustman's cart, or somesuch. Would to heaven that I had." Blenchforth shuddered, and went on: "It was a black coach, pulled by a single black horse. There was a black plume in the horse's browband. The coachman was wearing an old-fashioned undertaker's rig: black frock coat, tall black hat, with a long black crepe ribbon dangling from the brim. He was seated sidelong on the driver's board, so that I couldn't see his face. But I saw that the coach was a *hearse*: in the rear compartment was a black coffin with silver handles. The lid of the coffin was missing. Looking down from my office window through the windows of the hearse, I could see that the coffin was lined with black satin . . . and it was empty. The coffin had no occupant.

"Suddenly the driver of the hearse turned round, and looked up at my window. *I saw his face . . .*" At this point, Blenchforth broke off his narrative. He shuddered violently for a moment, then resumed: "I saw the undertaker's face. It was ghastly, I tell you. His face looked very like a living skull. His limbs were thin, cadaverous. His eyes gazed into mine relentlessly, and he pointed one bone-fingered hand towards the empty coffin in his hearse. '*Just room for one inside, sir!*' he intoned, in a voice like something from beyond the grave."

"Good heavens!" gasped Chundermutton, filching the marmalade-pot whilst he glanced at his pocket-watch to ascertain if the pawnshops were still open. "And *then* what happened?"

"Well, then I woke up," said Blenchforth, sounding vaguely embarrassed. "Turned out that it had all been a nightmare. I'd slept all afternoon, and now evening was coming on. So I decided to come down here to the club for my usual session of drunken debauchery. I rung to have my car brought round, but the garageman told me it wasn't working. I should have to walk to the club." Blenchforth paused, and fortified himself with several stiff bourbons before resuming his tale: "I walked to the nearest bus-shelter, and I saw that one of the bus routes – number thirteen – would take me directly past the club's entrance. So I decided to wait for the bus.

"It was a long wait, and as I stood there I noticed that the bus-shelter was built on top of an embankment. I was a sapper in the last war but one, so I know a bit about structural engineering. Well, whoever built that embankment didn't know his business. It was top-heavy, with substandard revetments. There was a building site near by, and I saw that the builders didn't know their business either: they had dug a pit directly underneath the embankment, but neglected to shore it up properly. The slightest bit of weight in the wrong place, and the entire street would collapse into a crater. It was an accident waiting to happen.

"Just then a bus came looming out of the darkness, and on its destination board I saw the number 13. The bus was one of those double-decker jobs, of that new design I've never really trusted. Top-heavy, and improperly balanced. If the driver should have to stop suddenly, the whole affair could pitch over. As the bus came closer, I caught a whiff of petrol: there was a blockage in the fuel line. A clear violation of London Transport's safety rules. The slightest disturbance could ignite the petrol tank, and the bus would explode into a raging inferno.

"That wasn't the only safety violation: the lights were out inside the bus. As it stopped in front of me, I could see that all the seats were occupied, but I couldn't get a proper look at the passengers: they were only muffled silhouettes within the darkness. There was one empty seat, behind the driver. Then I looked up, and I saw the driver's face."

Blenchforth's voice suddenly went cold. He deftly reached for the sherry, and steadied his nerves with a long drink before he continued: "Where was I? Yes. I saw the bus-driver's face. It was ghastly. His face looked like a living skull. His limbs were thin, cadaverous. His eyes gazed into mine, and in sudden terror I realized that he was *the hearse-driver I'd seen in my nightmare*. Just as I thought of this, the driver pointed his long bony hand to the empty seat behind him and, with a voice from beyond the grave, he spoke to me: '*Just room for one inside, sir!*'"

Blenchforth fell silent. For a long moment, the only sound in the clubroom was the deep steady ticking of the antique clock. The fading embers in the fireplace sent flickering shadows across the battleaxes, spears and thumbscrews decorating the walls of the clubroom. Finally, Smythe-ffolliott plucked up the courage to speak: "Good heavens, man! *What happened next?*"

"Oh, nothing much," said Blenchforth, casually lighting a cigar and guzzling the last of our sherry. "I got on the bus, rode two stops, got out at the club's entrance, and now here I am. If the bus explodes between here and Stoke Newington, fat lot I care. Hullo! Any kippers left?"

I saw Maltravers draw a Webley-Vickers cavalry pistol from beneath his Norfolk jacket, whilst Chundermutton surreptitiously unlocked the safety of his Purdy twelve-gauge. "But the hearse-driver!" I protested. "The nightmare!"

"Oh, *that*," yawned Blenchforth. "I just put *that* rubbish in to make the story more interesting. Isn't it high time you chaps stopped believing in ghosts?"

With a bound, I seized the battleaxe on the wall and tore it loose from its bracket, whilst Smythe-ffolliott broke open the nearest display case and selected a Thuggee death-blade. " 'Rule Ninety-Three,' " the four of us recited in unison, closing in on Blenchforth from all sides. " 'Ghost stories told in the clubroom must contain at least one genuine supernatural incident, or else a good deal of bloodshed.' "

Blenchforth squealed in terror as we descended upon him. Somehow he broke through our onslaught, and made straight for the lift. Just as he reached it, the lift's doors wheezed open. The lift-attendant, faithful old Staveacre, was nowhere inside. In his place stood a grotesque stranger, dressed in the club's livery. His face was like a living skull. His limbs were thin, cadaverous. With one long bony hand he beckoned Blenchforth to enter the elevator, as he spoke in a weird death-like voice: "*Just room for one inside, sir!*"

Thumbing his nose at us, Blenchforth bounded into the lift. Its doors slid shut before we could reach him. Suddenly there was a hideous screech, as all of the chains supporting the lift's counterweight snapped simultaneously. Through the glass-paned doors, I caught a glimpse of Blenchforth's ashen face as he plunged to his doom. Moments later, an explosion at the bottom of the lift shaft reached our ears, and the air was suffused with thick billows of smoke and the odour of brimstone. For an instant, I fancied that I heard distant voices intoning the Black Mass.

Blenchforth was never seen again. Nor was the club's elevator. The charred walls of the empty lift shaft are the sole remaining evidence of what transpired that night. We found out afterwards that faithful old Staveacre had sold the elevator's safety mechanism to a scrap-metal dealer, shortly after he absconded with the club's silverware. As for Blenchforth, his ghastly fate saved us the trouble of striking his name off the club's membership rolls. Served the blighter right, for telling us a ghost story without any ghosts in it. Not the done thing at all. *Really!*

A FORTNIGHT OF MIRACLES

Randall Garrett

The following story was the one that made me realize that humorous fantasy works. Back in the early 1960s I was rather traditional about fantasy fiction. It had to be serious. I didn't like anyone taking the mickey out of the field. And then I read this and was immediately converted. Randall Garrett (1927–87) was an extremely prolific writer – mostly of science fiction – in the 1950s, often working in collaboration with Robert Silverberg. He reduced his output in the 1960s and, not surprisingly, the quality of the work increased. It was at that time that he wrote his best work, the Lord Darcy series, featuring a court detective who operates in an alternate twentieth century where the Reformation never happened and where magic operates as a science. The stories were collected as Murder and Magic *(1979) and* Lord Darcy Investigates *(1981). There is also a novel,* Too Many Magicians *(1967). Garrett had an excellent sense of humour, although it surfaced all too rarely in his fiction, which makes the following even more special. He did produce an early comic fantasy with Laurence Janifer,* Pagan Passions *(1959), and some of his clever parodies were collected as* Takeoff! *(1980) and* Takeoff Too *(1987). It was a tragic loss when Garrett died of meningitis after several years of memory degeneration. Stories like this one can help keep our memory of him alive.*

I

Magus MacCullen patted the neck of his mule, and the gesture made the pouch at his belt jingle pleasantly. "Gold and silver and two good mules," he said, with a smile that was almost hidden by his moustaches and his huge, fiery red beard. "The Count du Marche is most generous if you tap him at just the right time."

The hooded figure on the other mule might have been mistaken for a traveling monk except that no Order of the Church wore dark blue robes. In spite of the warmth of the late summer day, the hood of the habit was up, concealing the face in shadow. The voice which came from beneath the hood was not unpleasant, but the low tenor notes seemed to resonate as though the speaker were in a cavern or at the bottom of a well. "We could have stayed another five days or a week, Master Magus. Not that *I* need the rest, but you have a long way to go, and . . ."

"My dear Frithkin," Magus MacCullen interrupted, "if we had stayed an extra week we would have saturated the market. Always leave early. That way, they bribe you to come back. The Count and his Lady and his court were entertained for a week by the greatest magician in Christendom. They can hardly wait for us to come back – say in a year. But a fortnight of miracles would satiate even the most ardent of miracle-lovers. As it is, I keep my reputation."

"A reputation as a phony," said Frithkin glumly.

"Of course!" said the Magus. "What happens to sorcerers? What happened to Magus Prezhenski? That Baron Whatsis – the one with the unpronounceable name – wanted gold, so he decided to force Prezhenski to make the stuff for him. Laymen are always inclined to think a sorcerer can do anything God can do, I suppose. The Magus failed, of course, and the corbies were well fed for a week."

"He had it coming to him," Frithkin pointed out.

"Sure he did," the red-bearded man said agreeably. "Only a fool plays around with black magic. But does a layman know the difference? No. So I have a reputation as a clever trickster and nothing else. I'll live longer that way." He chuckled deep in his chest. "Remember that time the Earl of Weffolk tried to trap me by getting Father Finn to pull an exorcism while I was present?"

Frithkin's echoing chuckle joined that of his master. "And all the good Father could do was testify that you weren't a practitioner of black magic? I remember. If Magus Prezhenski had had—" He stopped and turned his hooded head. "What's that?"

Magus MacCullen had heard the noise, too. Both of them turned their mules to face whatever was galloping down the road behind them.

"He's coming from the direction of the Count's castle, whoever he is," said the magician. All he could see was a cloud of dust rising in the summer heat, but from it came the sound of hooves moving at a gallop. "A messenger sent by the Count, perhaps?"

"More likely he's changed his mind and wants his gold back," said Frithkin. "I suggest we head in the opposite direction."

"There's only one of him," the magician said calmly. "Besides, these mules couldn't outrun a warhorse – which, as you can plainly see, that is."

Over the little rise that had blocked their view, the two saw their pursuer charging toward them at full tilt. A knight and his horse, both in full armor, came thundering down from the crest of the rise, the horse in full gallop, the knight in a forward crouch, his lance aimed directly at Magus MacCullen.

The Magus was already in motion. He tossed the reins of his mule to Frithkin, who caught them dexterously with bony fingers. Then he vaulted out of the saddle, his long oaken staff in one hand. While Frithkin galloped the two mules off to one side of the road, Magus MacCullen took his position in the center, his brawny legs braced, his six-foot staff of one-inch-thick oak held firmly at an angle across his body. Then there was nothing to do but wait.

Magus MacCullen made a fine target for the oncoming lance point. He stood six feet two and was broader in proportion than he ought to be. The powerful hands gripping the staff were half again as big as an ordinary man's, and, like his arms, were corded with heavy muscle. With his light blue, silver-decorated robes and his bright red mane of hair and beard, he stood out against the brown of the road and the dusty green of the surrounding meadow.

The oncoming knight ignored Frithkin. He charged right on down the road toward the unmoving, blue-and-silver-clad figure of the sorcerer. The knight said nothing. There was no war cry, no insult, no warning – only that deadly, straightforward charge. He intended to spit Magus MacCullen on the lance and – perhaps – talk about it afterwards. MacCullen didn't move. He might have been a statue.

The steel-clad point of the lance was within inches of the Magus' breast before he moved. Almost too fast for the eye to see, and certainly too fast for the knight to react in time, the magician leaped to his right, holding the quarterstaff out to his left to fend off the lance. The heavy spear slid along the staff, deflected from its target by a full eight inches.

The great charger, unable to alter its course in the few feet it still had to travel, thundered by the Magus in full gallop. With his two hands still braced on the quarterstaff, Magus MacCullen pulled the left hand toward himself and pushed the right hand away. The lower end of the staff swung in a vicious arc and struck the horse just under the jaw.

It was like watching a mountain collapse. The horse, knocked unconscious by the blow, stumbled and fell. The armored figure in the saddle dropped the lance, did a complete somersault in the air, and landed in the road with a clatter and clang of steel armor.

Neither he nor the horse moved.

"Well, now," said Magus MacCullen. "Let's take a look at this brave, chivalrous gentleman who runs down unarmed people on the road without so much as a by-your-leave."

"It looks to me," said Frithkin from the side of the road, "as if you've done him in pretty well. Broke every bone in his body, apparently."

The fallen knight did, in fact, look as though he had suffered disastrously from his fall. His legs and arms were at angles that indicated terrible damage, and his body was twisted in a way that looked as though it had been wrung like a dishrag.

Magus MacCullen walked over and inspected the wreckage for a moment. Then he knelt down and opened the visor of the helm.

"Ha!" he said. Then he took the helmet completely off.

Frithkin had brought the mules up close and was looking over the sorcerer's shoulder. When the helmet came off, Frithkin said: "Ho! Nobody home?"

"Nobody home," said the Magus in agreement. "This suit of armor is as empty as a bride's nightgown." He poked his staff inside and rattled it around to indicate the emptiness behind the breastplate.

Frithkin slid off the saddle of his mule. Afoot, he stood a scant four feet high, and his legs were so abnormally short, his arms so abnormally long, that he might have been taken for a chimpanzee. He went to the suit of armor and bent over it; with one hand, he pushed back the cowl that had covered his head. His head was as hairless as his face, and his skin was of a brownish color that reminded one of fresh-turned earth. His eyes were large, much too large to be human, making him look like a pop-eyed owl. His mouth was wide and almost lipless. His nose, like his cat-pupiled eyes, was much too large for his face. It was a magnificent nose, a huge eagle beak of a nose, a nose that jutted out a full three inches from his face. That nose was making audible sniffing sounds as its owner inspected the armor.

"Ho!" said Frithkin after a moment. "There's black magic here, all right!" He tapped his great beak with a bony finger. "'What a goblin knows, he knows by his nose,' as the old saying goes."

"That's fine doggerel verse," said the Magus, "but let's be a little more specific. What *kind* of black magic? Any specific spell?"

Frithkin sniffed some more. "Well, Master Magus, I would say it's nothing *we* need worry about. I should say that the spell has been directed against the unfortunate gentleman who owns this armor. Or once owned it, since he doesn't seem to be around himself." More sniffing. "Nothing malignant about it. Not as far as we're concerned. The spell's still here, though, which is odd. Seems to be in abeyance, but not broken."

"Find out what you can," said Magus MacCullen. "I'm going to take a look at that poor horse. Hate to hit a horse that way, but it's the only thing to do when some high-born sorehead takes it in his noggin to do a fellow in with a lance." He strode over to where the great black destrier lay on the road, breathing quietly.

"Hmmm," murmured the Magus, "doesn't look like any damage done. Legs not broken, at any rate." He knelt down and checked the legs one at a time to make sure. Then he went over to the head.

"How's your jaw, friend? Mmmm. No fracture. Just a lump. You may find it a little difficult to chew your oats and hay for the next day or two, but you'll be all— *oops!* Steady, boy! Steady!" He gripped his staff tightly. The warhorse had opened a large brown eye and was looking at him reproachfully. A huge stallion like this could be dangerous with teeth and hooves if he decided that the red-bearded man deserved to be punished for that oaken uppercut.

The Magus hoped it would not be necessary to bat the poor creature over the head with the quarterstaff. He kept talking soothingly to the horse.

"*Yike!*"

Magus MacCullen turned his head at the sound of Frithkin's voice.

The suit of armor, *sans* helm, was climbing to its feet for all the world as though there was a man inside it. Frithkin was backing away rapidly, his own quarterstaff at the ready in his goblin hands.

At the same time, the great stallion rolled to his feet and stood up.

For a moment, Magus MacCullen wondered whether it mightn't be the smart thing to club the horse again so that both he and Frithkin could give their full attention to the Empty Knight. If the steel-clad vacancy decided to draw the great sword at his side, he might be a little difficult to take care of.

But the horse stood quietly, and the armored figure did nothing but bend over and pick up the helm from the ground and put it in its proper place.

"There!" boomed a hollow voice from the interior of the armor. "First off, I want to apologize. Terrible mistake and all that. Thought you were someone else, you see. Please accept my heartfelt apologies, Master Magus – for I see you are a magician."

"Your apology is accepted, Sir Knight," said the Magus, easing his grip on his quarterstaff a little. "But I think such precipitate behavior requires an explanation, don't you?"

"Yes, I suppose it does. Here, would you mind fastening this helm back on? It's difficult to get at, and besides, gauntlets aren't exactly built for delicate work. Yes, that's it. Thank you very much." The Empty Knight grasped the helm in both gauntlets and tested its firmness. "Fine," he said. "Thank you again, Magus."

Then he walked over to his horse and examined the jaw. "Painful, but no real injury," he said gently. "That's quite a trick you have there, Magus. Last time I'll try to ride down a man who has a quarterstaff, I'll tell you."

"About that explanation, Sir Knight . . ." the Magus prompted.

"Oh, yes. Well, it's rather a long story – and I must warn you that I can't tell you all of it, anyway. I've got a curse on me, as you may have gathered."

"I had surmised as much," said the Magus dryly.

"Yes, of course you had, being a magician and all that. Well, since we all seem to be going in the same direction, what do you say we mount up and go ahead while I make my explanation."

"That's agreeable with me," said MacCullen. "Let's go, Frithkin. By the way, Sir Knight, I am the Magus MacCullen. This is my assistant and familiar, Frithkin."

"Happy to make your acquaintance, Magus. Frithkin? Not a Christian name, I think?"

"No, my lord," said Frithkin. "Fey. Faerie. I am an earth elemental, my lord. A goblin."

"Really? Don't believe I've had the pleasure of meeting a goblin before. Met a tree elemental once – a dryad named Naaia. Very nice girl. Most beautiful green hair you ever saw. I guess I'm pretty much of an elemental myself, eh? Mostly steel and air, eh?" He chuckled sadly.

"I don't believe you gave us your name, Sir Knight," the Magus said pointedly as the three mounted their animals and moved on down the road.

"Well, that's the sad part about it," said the Empty Knight. "You see, I don't have a name, really. I'm not quite all here, if you see what I mean. I mean to say, I don't know *who* I am. I'm just – well, sort of *here*, if you see what I mean."

"Um," said Magus MacCullen thoughtfully. "How long has this been going on? I mean – tell me everything you can remember, from the beginning. As a white magician, I may be able to help you."

"Would you really?" There was a rather pathetic note of joy in the Empty Knight's booming voice. "That's awfully good of you. What do you need to know?"

"Begin at the beginning, as far back as you can remember. I think I know what has happened here, in a general way, but I need more evidence before I can decide what to do about it."

Magus MacCullen was in the center of the little party, with the Empty Knight on his left and Frithkin on his right. The goblin leaned over and whispered, in a voice that the knight couldn't hear, "Ask him why he tried to spit you on that pig-sticker of his."

"Later," the Magus whispered. "He'll get to it in time."

The Empty Knight was silent for several minutes. Then he said: "I can't seem to remember." His voice was gloomy. "I've just been touring the countryside for – I don't know how long. Weeks? Months? Years? I can't remember. Time just keeps moving on. Always does, I suppose. But still I keep looking." He sighed. "I go from castle to castle, from town to town, looking. It seems like a long time in some ways, but maybe not so very long. Of course, I don't eat, and that's pretty handy, for I haven't any money. Haven't had for a long time. Not ever, I think. Fortunately, someone is always ready to give Roderick food and a stable. Nobody'd let a horse starve. I always tell people that I've taken an oath not to take off my armor until I've fulfilled my vow – which is perfectly true. And since I only stop one night, I can tell them I'm fasting that day – which is true, if misleading. It gets lonely at times, but knight errantry is a lonely job, anyway. I'm not complaining, you understand. I just go on looking."

"Looking for what?" the Magus asked cautiously.

"Why, the magician, of course. Didn't I tell you? No, I guess I didn't. Well, that's who I'm looking for. The magician."

"*Which* magician?" Magus MacCullen asked. "Not just any old magician, I gather."

"Oh, rather not!" said the knight. "No, indeed. You see, that's where I made the mistake about you. I asked for food and lodging for my horse at that castle back there. The Count du Marche welcomed me and asked my name. I gave him the old wheeze about my being under a vow not to reveal my name or doff my armor until I'd fulfilled my quest. I said I couldn't tell him anything about the quest, either, you understand. Can't tell a fellow you're just out to catch yourself a magician, can you now? Anyway, I asked him if he'd seen any magicians lately, and he said he had, that you'd just left, as a matter of fact. By George, I thought I'd got him this time. But no. Turned out to be only you. Still, maybe you can help me find him."

"Maybe, Sir Knight," the Magus said agreeably. "Why are you looking for him?"

"Why, he's the one who did this to me, whatever it is he did. Nasty trick, I call it, leaving a man just a shell of his former self, as it were."

"Oh, you remember that, do you?"

"Well, no," the Empty Knight said after a short pause, "I can't say I really *remember* it. I just *know* it."

"I see. What does this magician look like? Do you know his name?"

"No. I don't know his name. No. But he looks . . . Hmmm. Well. Now, you know, that's awfully odd, but I really don't know what he looks like."

"Tall or short? Young or old? Haven't you any idea?" asked the Magus.

"Well, now, you know, I *don't*." The knight laughed hollowly.

"Isn't that funny? I mean, come to think of it, I haven't the foggiest notion what the fellow looks like. None at all."

"Then how do you know I'm not him?" asked Magus MacCullen.

The Empty Knight turned, and Magus MacCullen saw nothingness staring at him from the darkness beyond the bars of the visor of the helm. Then the knight faced forward again. "Well, because you're not at all like him, you see," he explained. "I mean, I don't know what he looks like, but I know what he *doesn't* look like, if you follow me. I'm quite certain I shall recognize him when I see him."

"Good. But if I were you, Sir Knight, I wouldn't go around trying to run a lance through every magician I came across. Some magicians are very touchy about that sort of thing and have a tendency to cast a fast spell that wouldn't do you any good. Besides, what if you kill the man you're looking for? He couldn't undo the spell if he were dead."

"That's so," the Empty Knight said complacently, "but I wasn't going to run you through, you know. I'm an expert with a lance; I was just going to catch your robe with the point and hoist you into the air. Then, if you'd turned out to be the magician I was looking for, I'd have you at my mercy, and you'd have had to take the spell off before I'd have let you down."

"Suppose he just threw another spell? Changed you into a toad or something?"

"Oh, that. Well, he couldn't, you see. I've got a protective spell on me. Very powerful. I'm proof against any magic spell except the one that will restore me to what I was before. Whatever I was. I wish I knew, but I can't remember for the life of me. If I have any life. You don't suppose I'm dead, do you? That would be a cruel joke to play on a fellow. But I *think* I'm alive. Don't you?"

"I'm pretty certain of it," said the Magus. "Look here, do you mind if I try something? I want to check on that protective spell."

"Certainly," the knight said agreeably. "If you think it'll be of some help, go right ahead."

"Not just yet," said MacCullen. "I'll let you know. Where are you headed now?"

"Oh, wherever you're going, my good Magus. It doesn't make a particle of difference to me. A knight errant doesn't care where he's going; he just goes, you know. I'll tell you what: in return for your help in finding this magician or getting rid of the spell on me or whatever it is you can do, I'll go along with you and protect you from danger. How's that?"

Magus MacCullen looked at Frithkin, and the goblin whispered softly: "Go ahead, Master; take him up on it. He may be of some use to us, and, after all, he won't cost much. It's not as if he was a regular knight, who'd expect to be fed the best foods, poured the best wines, and given the best bed, and expect somebody else to pay for it into the bargain. Here we've got a perfectly good knight, cheap. Remember, Master, we've got a long way to go to the Convention, and this fellow may come in handy in a pinch."

"You're right, of course," said the Magus. He liked to think that he could take care of any danger himself, but there was no use letting pride keep him from taking advantage of a good thing.

"Very well, Sir Knight," he said aloud, "that's a bargain. You go along with us and protect us from evildoers, and I, in turn, will do my best to relieve you of that spell, either by finding the person who laid it on you and forcing him to remove it, or, failing that, solving the spell and nullifying it myself. Fair enough?"

"Fair enough, my good Magus!" the Empty Knight boomed happily. "Let us go forward, then! We shall seek adventure and take it as it comes! Comrades three, whatever may befall!"

"Oh, *brother*!" muttered Frithkin under his breath.

II

"Frithkin!" bellowed Magus MacCullen. "Where the devil are you?"

"Right here, Master Magus," said the goblin voice from the next room. "I've got the wine, just as you ordered."

"Then bring 'em in. I'm thirsty as Satan himself."

"I'm opening them now," said Frithkin, dexterously plying a corkscrew. He shivered a little and told himself he was lucky to have the great MacCullen for a master. Only a very powerful sorcerer could speak of His Satanic Majesty with such familiarity and get away with it.

They were lucky, Frithkin thought, to have found rooms in an inn at this hour of the evening. After dark, many inns bolted their doors and kept them bolted, and the three travelers had, in fact, come to the door of the inn just as it was about to be locked.

In the gloom, Magus MacCullen had peered up at the sign over the door and said: "What is it? The Archangel Michael?"

Frithkin, whose eyes could see as well in the dark as in the daylight, had said: 'No, Master. It's the George and Dragon."

The Empty Knight had said: "How can you tell? They're both pictures of a knight in full armor sticking a dragon with a lance."

"Yes, my lord," Frithkin agreed, "but the Archangel Michael has wings and St George doesn't. Shall I knock, Master Magus?"

"If you please, good Frithkin."

The goblin got down off his mule and rapped solidly on the door of the inn. Footsteps were heard from within, and a panel in the door flew open. A woman with a beak nose that looked small only in comparison to Frithkin's, and who looked as though she could bite the head off a crocodile, snapped out: "Who might you be and what d'ye want at this hour?"

"Is this the *George and Dragon*?" Frithkin asked mildly.

"That's what the sign shows, don't it?" snarled the woman. "What d'ye want?"

"I think I want to speak to George," said Frithkin.

"What? What? Who?"

"Never mind," said Frithkin.

"We desire food and lodging for ourselves and our mounts."

" 'We'? Who's 'we'?"

"My masters and I," Frithkin answered. "Sir Roderick the Black and the Magus MacCullen."

The woman paled visibly. She peered out, trying to see the face beneath the hood that effectively shadowed Frithkin's features. "Who? Roderick? And a magician?" She essayed a feeble smile which did not go well at all with her features. "Why didn't ye say so, good sir? Come in! Come in and welcome! I meant no harm, sir. No harm at all. There's sometimes robbers and thieves about. But I meant no harm, gentle sirs." And she had opened the door while she pattered out her apologies.

While Magus MacCullen went upstairs to inspect the rooms, Frithkin and the Empty Knight had taken the animals back to the stable under the guidance of a stable boy who looked as though he had been frightened out of his sleep by the harridan who had answered the door.

"My lord," Frithkin whispered in an aside to the knight, "I hope you don't mind my calling you Sir Roderick. I had to give her a name; it would have taken too long to go through that rigamarole about the vow. I needed a name of some kind, and the first one that came to mind was the name of your horse."

"Perfectly all right. Wonder I didn't think of it myself, long ago. Black horse named Roderick made you think of Sir Roderick the Black, eh? Very clever, my dear Frithkin. Of course, even if it *had* occurred to me, I couldn't have told a lie. Not chivalrous, you know. But that doesn't apply to you, naturally."

"No, my lord. We goblins are free from that particular limitation – though we have others."

Within twenty minutes, everything was secure. MacCullen had ordered wine, Frithkin had obtained it from the now obsequious landlady, and was now drawing the corks with a practiced hand. He took two brass goblets from the saddlebag which he had brought upstairs after taking his and the Magus' from the mules, put the goblets on a tray with the wine bottles, and brought them in to Magus MacCullen.

"Where is our vacuous protector?" the Magus asked, pouring.

"Down in the stable, Master Magus. He says he prefers to stay with his horse. No point in wasting a bed on him, he says. Perfectly comfortable in the hayloft, he says." The wine bottle gurgled pleasantly as the goblin poured himself a drink.

"Good. That'll give us a chance to discuss this problem and

turn it to our benefit if possible. What do you think of our knightly friend?"

"Not much brains," said the goblin, sipping at his wine.

The Magus glowered. "None at all. You saw the inside of that helm. What would you expect? According to my analysis – which, I admit, is only tentative – this knight has been partially disembodied. Part of his spirit is still in his body somewhere; the rest of it is activating that suit of steel. Neither by itself is a whole man. How does that fit in with what your nose tells you?"

Frithkin gently stroked that magnificent member with thumb and forefinger. "All I can tell you, Master, is that somebody put a black spell on him – and a real whopping powerful one, too. Then someone – maybe the same person, but I doubt it – put a white spell on him, which has partially, but far from completely, counteracted the black one. Laid over the whole is the protective spell he spoke of. It seems to be a pretty refractive spell, too. Strong and tough. The texture is smooth and the structure coherent. Whoever wove that protective spell knew what he was doing."

"So," said the Magus thoughtfully. "Three different spells, involving from one to three different sorcerers."

"I'd say two, Master, though there might be three."

"One black magician and at least one white one, you think?"

"That's the way it smells to me," said the goblin.

"He doesn't know who he is, and hasn't got sense enough to care," said MacCullen. "Did you notice his shield? A field sable. In other words, somebody took his escutcheon off and painted the shield black. And that black surcoat he wears. Someone didn't want him to find out who he was, so they got rid of every bit of identification. But if that's the case, why not just kill him and be done with it? There's something very screwy going on here, my dear Frithkin, and I want to get to the bottom of it. Besides which—" He smiled broadly behind his flaming beard. "—if our voided friend is returned to his rightful condition, it is likely that he'll reward us handsomely."

"True, he seems like a good sort," Frithkin said, blinking his great eyes slowly and solemnly. "But how do you know he has enough money to reward us, even if he wants to?"

"His armor, dear boy. Black enamelled, inlaid with gold and with red enamel. Armor like that isn't cheap. It looks pretty dingy now, but that's because he hasn't been able to polish it. Mark my word, that lad has riches in his own right, and if we can help him regain them we'll be well rewarded."

"How do you propose to go about it?" Frithkin asked.

"There are two ways to approach the problem," the Magus said. "We cannot analyze the spells from the evidence obtainable from Sir Empty alone; we need the complete evidence. The rest of what we need can be obtained from only two sources: the knight's body or the sorcerer who enchanted him. We have to find one or the other – preferably both."

"Succinctly put, Master, but it gets us nowhere," said the goblin. "Either one of 'em could be anywhere. We can eliminate Heaven and the Nether Regions, but that still leaves us all Christendom and Faerie to search. And that's an awful lot of territory, Master."

"If we combed it inch by inch, it would be an impossible task, I agree," said MacCullen. "Therefore, we must use our brains. First, the body. No clues there. It could be anywhere, as you say. It could be lying somewhere in a coma, in a vault, say, or even buried somewhere with a protective spell cast on it. Or, it might be working as a slave somewhere – that's a likely idea."

"Why?" asked Frithkin.

"Because all the qualities that the Empty Knight has would be missing from the spirit left in the body; the bravery, the initiative, the ambition, the determination, and part of the intelligence. It would retain the memory, of course, but that wouldn't do it much good. What good is memory if you haven't got the ability to put it to use? In that condition, he – whoever he is – would make a fine slave. Especially if he's big and strong, which, judging from the size and build of the armor, he is."

"That narrows it down a bit," the goblin agreed, "but we can't go around checking every slave and serf in Christendom and Faerie."

"Obviously not."

"So that leaves the magician," Frithkin continued. "And we can't go around trying to check every magician in Christendom and Faerie, either."

"True enough," agreed the Magus. "But it so happens that we know where every magician will be in two months' time."

Frithkin slapped the palms of his bony hands together. "The Convention!"

"Precisely. Any sorcerer, magician, warlock, or other practitioner of the Art who doesn't show up at the Convention is automatically deprived forever of his powers, and all his spells are nullified. He'll be there, all right, and our hollow friend can identify him. If he doesn't come, of course, the spell will vanish and we can take credit for that. We can't lose, Frithkin."

"I don't know . . ." the goblin said doubtfully. "That law applies only to mortals, you know. What if the enchanter is one of the Faerie folk, like myself, who just naturally have certain powers, instead of having to study for them, as you mortals do?"

"In that case, we will go directly to King Huon. If any of the Fey are involved, they have violated one of the basic laws of Faerie by using black magic. We will lodge a complaint in Court, and King Huon du Cor will find the culprit for us in a flash."

Frithkin looked thoughtful while he downed half a glass of wine, then his mouth spread in a grin until the corners were almost even with his earlobes. "It might work, at that, Master Magus! Back in the time of King Oberon, you might have had a rough time getting such a case before the Court, but King Huon du Cor has a tendency to be more lenient toward mortals, having been one himself once."

"Really?" said the Magus. "I didn't know that. I'm not up on Faerie history as much as I should be. King Huon was once a mortal?"

"That's right. Used to be Duke of Bordeaux. King Oberon had been promised translation to Paradise, but he had to pick a successor and Huon was his choice. He's made a pretty good King, too."

Magus MacCullen waved a huge hand. "Well, there you are, my good Frithkin! Luck is on our side! Here I have been griping because a Convention Year happened to fall during my lifetime. Once every century there is a Convention, and I had to get caught! But now we see that all is for the good. Without the Convention, I wouldn't have but a small chance of catching the Empty Knight's enchanter. Now, it is almost certain!"

"I'm glad you said 'almost', Master," said the goblin.

The Magus scowled. "You're a pessimist, Frithkin. Now let me get some sleep. We have a long way to go yet, and I want to start out fresh in the morning."

"Very good, Master. Have a good night."

"The same to you, good Frithkin. Wake me early, and we'll go down and fetch His Emptiness and be on our way."

Ten minutes later, the red-bearded sorcerer was snoring away, while Frithkin, who slept but once in thirty days, sat silently in the darkness, thinking goblin thoughts.

Magus MacCullen was dreaming peacefully about refurbishing his home with the money he would get from aiding the Empty Knight when someone shook his shoulder and startled him into sudden wakefulness.

"Sssst! Master Magus!" It was Frithkin's whisper. "Up and out! Wake up!"

Instantly awake, the Magus swung his legs over the side of his bed. "What the Hell's going on?" he whispered.

"I don't know," Frithkin said, "but whatever it is, I don't like it. A minute ago, four men came up the stairway, and they're outside the door right now. Quiet as mice, they were, but they can't fool a goblin's nose."

"Robbers," the Magus muttered. "Is there anyone outside the window?"

Frithkin moved silently to the window and looked out. There was nothing moving in the courtyard fifteen feet below, no one about anywhere. Frithkin whispered that information to MacCullen.

"All right," said the magician, "you get down below, and I'll drop the saddlebags to you. Then I'll come down myself, and we'll get out of here. Move."

The goblin went over the window-sill and down the side of the stone wall, his fingers and toes finding handholds that no mortal could have found so quickly – certainly not in the dark. MacCullen dropped one saddlebag and then another, and Frithkin caught them before they struck the flagstones of the pavement. The whole operation was almost as silent as the evening breeze.

Then there was a gleam of light from behind MacCullen, and he spun away from the window. The door to the hall had opened, and there was a shaft of firelight from the flickering torch at the head of the stairs.

There were men outside, armed and lightly armored in hauberk and steel cap.

"Come out, Roderick!" shouted one. "Come out cowering like the dog you are!"

"That's not him," said another.

"Nah!" said a third. "That's the red-haired swine who claims to be a magician."

"Might as well get him, too," chimed in the fourth.

They moved into the doorway.

MacCullen knew he couldn't get out the window in time. He'd break his neck trying to climb down fifteen feet before one of these thugs crossed the room. And he certainly couldn't jump for it.

Things looked bad, but there was one consoling fact. They had to come in through that door one at a time, with the light behind them.

Using his quarterstaff like a lance, he charged forward, driving the end of it into the pit of the first man's stomach. The chain-mail hauberk could stop a sword's edge, but it wasn't much good against a blow like the one MacCullen gave. The first man collapsed, retching.

The second man tried to get by the first. MacCullen shifted his big hands, and the end of the quarterstaff swung and slammed against the side of his opponent's head, just beneath the rim of the steel cap.

MacCullen aimed another blow at the third man. The man ducked, and the staff hit the steel cap, which came off and spun into the air, landing with a ringing clang. The end of the staff came down on the top of the unprotected head.

MacCullen was just about to congratulate himself on having disposed of three out of four when he heard more noise on the stair. A fifth and then a sixth man appeared. Reinforcements!

With a roar of rage that seemed to shake the walls, Magus
MacCullen leaped over the three fallen men and slammed his
oaken staff into the middle of the fourth man so hard that he
staggered backwards into the arms of the man at the head of the
stairwell. The stairs were full of men. MacCullen didn't stop to
count, but it looked like a dozen or more. The ones at the top
rocked back as their comrade collapsed into their arms.

MacCullen heard a movement behind him and ducked to one
side just in time. A fist with a club in it came down past his right
ear. MacCullen dropped to a crouch and grabbed the wrist. Up
and over! The flying mare sent the attacker in a somersaulting
arc toward the head of the stair. MacCullen noticed in passing
that the man had no helmet on. Considering the rap he had
been given, he must have had a fairly tough skull.

The arrival of a second body, with considerable momentum
behind it, totally upset the already precarious balance of the
men at the top of the stairway. They fell backwards.

It was like watching an avalanche.

Or, MacCullen thought, like watching a row of dominoes
fall after the first one has been knocked over.

The men on the lower steps could not support the weight of
the men falling from above, so they, in their turn, fell, adding
more weight to the burden of those below.

Halfway down the steps, the avalanche began to slow as a
few of the more quick-witted grabbed for the stair railing and
held on.

MacCullen turned and looked at the two fallen men by the
door of his room. Neither one seemed inclined to move. He
grabbed one by the scruff of his neck and the seat of his hauberk,
lifted, turned, and tossed him down the stair. Without looking
to see the result, he grabbed the second man and sent him after
the first.

The avalanche, prodded by two new arrivals, proceeded on
its merry way.

In the gloom at the bottom of the stairs, MacCullen saw
that his own reinforcements had arrived. The Empty Knight,
brandishing a gigantic mace in one steel gauntlet, was taking
care of those who were tumbling to the bottom of the staircase,

banging them on the head in order of their arrival. Frithkin was jabbing his quarterstaff between the uprights of the banister, tripping those who had not yet fallen, and rapping the fingers of those who sought to retain their balance by holding on to the rail.

Regaining his own quarterstaff, which he had dropped when he was attacked from behind, Magus MacCullen charged down the staircase, tumbling men before him.

It was all over before any of the three realized it. MacCullen and the Empty Knight were looking for more heads to knock when they suddenly became aware that all of the available heads had already been so treated.

"One, two, three, four . . ." Frithkin began counting, pointing a long bony finger at one fallen man after another.

"Are you all right, Magus?" asked the Empty Knight.

"Fine. And yourself?"

"Not one of them touched me," the knight boomed hollowly. "Which is fortunate," he added, "since I don't like to be knocked down. How are you, my good Frithkin?"

". . . sixteen, seventeen! I make it seventeen," said Frithkin. "How am I? Oh, fine, my lord. Just fine."

At that moment, the landlady, who had heard all the noise and waited quietly until it was over, flung open the door and said: "Did you get 'em?" Then, seeing only her three guests standing, she froze and turned pale as death.

Frithkin was angry. Goblins do not like fighting; still less do they like to see their mortal masters attacked. He drew a long, wicked-looking knife from beneath his robe and advanced on the woman slowly. "Did *who* get *whom*, Madam?" he asked in his reverberating voice.

The shattered harridan quivered and made strangling noises, but found herself unable to move from the path of the advancing, hooded figure.

MacCullen opened his mouth to speak. He wanted no throats cut this night. But he was too late.

Suddenly, when he was less than four feet from the woman, Frithkin swept back the hood from his head. He bugged out his great, glowing goblin eyes. He opened his huge mouth wide, showing formidable rows of grinding teeth. He stuck out a tongue whose tip came even with the tip of his nose. Then he roared horrendously.

"*Arrraghh!*"

The landlady rolled up her eyes and collapsed in a heap on the floor.

Grinning, Frithkin put away his dagger and replaced his hood. "I suggest we get out of here, Master, before others come."

"I agree," said the Magus. He tossed a silver piece on the floor near the fainted landlady. "That will take care of everything, though I don't know as she deserves it. Come along, Sir Knight; we have riding to do."

III

By the time another six weeks had passed, the Empty Knight was firmly convinced that he had "always" been traveling with the Magus MacCullen and his goblin familiar. His memory of events began to fade after a few weeks, and anything more than a month in the past – unless he was reminded of it regularly – was almost gone completely. This lack of memory never disturbed his placid equilibrium nor his ever-present good humor. The only thing he never forgot was the reason for his quest: the discovery of the magician who had enchanted him.

Other than that one thought, nothing disturbed him. Not even the seeming disaster that occurred in the third week. The three travelers had spent their nights in various odd places – sometimes in barns of well-to-do peasants, sometimes on the grass of open meadows, sometimes beneath spreading trees. Two or three times, when one was handy, they stayed overnight in an inn – without further trouble. Once, they had spent three days in a castle, fed and lodged well by its genial baron.

On the twentieth day, they were riding through a pleasant wood, shaded from the summer sun by the leaves and branches overhead. There was no road as such; it was easy to go in a fairly straight path between the widely spaced trees. At noontime; they stopped and, while Magus MacCullen spread out a linen tablecloth, Frithkin unpacked dishes, goblets, wine, and food. The Empty Knight tethered the mules and his great warhorse Roderick to a nearby tree to cool off before they were led to the nearby brook to be watered.

"Nothing like a bottle and a cold bird," said the knight, seating himself on the grass near the tablecloth. "I'm sure I must have enjoyed a repast such as this many times," he added sadly. "I wish I could remember it."

"You'll enjoy it again, Sir Knight," the Magus promised as he tore a leg off a cold chicken. "Pour me some of that wine, Frithkin."

When the meal was finished, Frithkin got out his pipes and began to tootle a goblin tune.

"My good Frithkin," said the Empty Knight when the tune was finished, "do you know 'I Sing of One so Fair and Bright'?"

"Certainly, my lord," said the goblin. "Like this?" He began to play.

"That's it! Begin again, and I'll sing."

Frithkin complied, and the knight sang:

> I sing of one so fair and bright,
>   *Velud maris stella*,
> Brighter than the noonday light,
>   *Parens et puella*;
> I cry to thee, thou care for me,
> Lady, pray thy Son for me,
>   *Tam pia*,
> That I might come unto thee,
>   *Maria!*

Magus MacCullen sipped a final goblet of wine while the pleasant baritone of the Empty Knight mingled with the eerie notes of the goblin pipes. When the fifth verse was finished, he clapped his big hands in appreciation. "Well sung, Sir Knight! Well played, Frithkin! And now, let's finish up and be on our way."

By this time, they had worked out a routine for themselves. The Magus tidied up the place and packed things in the saddlebags, while Frithkin went to the shallow stream nearby to wash the goblets and plates, and the Empty Knight took the mules and Roderick upstream to water them.

MacCullen heard the drumming of hoofbeats a minute or so later and paused to listen. Then he saw the cavalcade of brightly caparisoned horses and knights in surcoats and armor moving at a fast canter through the trees in the distance. Obviously heading for a ford in the stream ahead, the Magus decided. Then they were out of sight.

A minute or so later, he heard Frithkin's screech. He dropped everything, grabbed his quarterstaff, and went running.

Frithkin had gone to the edge of the stream, and kneeling down, had began to scrub the greasy plates with the clean, wet sand from the bottom of the stream. He, too, heard the thunder of hooves and lifted his head to look.

The cavalcade rode into sight and splashed across the stream almost where Frithkin was sitting. He sprang to his feet, but just a little too late. One of the horsemen practically ran him over.

Frithkin stepped backwards, slipped on a wet rock, and fell splashingly into the water. The dozen or so knights roared with laughter and kept on riding as Frithkin came up out of the shallow water with a scream of rage. He still held a brass goblet in one hand. Without really taking aim, he flung it at the head of the man who had almost ridden him down. It missed, went sailing by, and hit with a loud clang on the coroneted helm of the man who was obviously the leader of the troop.

The laughter stopped suddenly. So did the horses as the man reined up.

The knight with the ducal coronet turned slowly in his saddle and looked at Frithkin. Then he said, in a snarling baritone: "Sir Griffith, kill me that base-born peasant! Teach him that a commoner does not throw things at the Duke of Duquayne! The rest of you come along. Let Sir Griffith have his sport."

Sir Griffith happened to be the man who had almost run Frithkin down. He evidently enjoyed such witty pranks. As he turned his horse about, Frithkin took off for the woods as fast as his goblin legs would carry him. With a coarse laugh, Sir Griffith set his bay gelding in an easy trot after the scampering Frithkin.

The goblin knew that his only chance was to get up a tree, so he headed for the nearest one. But the bay gelding was too fast. One glance behind him told the goblin that he'd never make it high enough to be out of reach of that lance, not in the seconds he had left. He dodged around the tree and headed for another one. The horse had to make almost a right-angle turn around the tree, and Frithkin gained a few yards – but not for long. Again he dodged around a tree, but this time Sir Griffith was ready for him and had the horse ready to make that turn. But Frithkin changed tactics, too. He made a complete circle around the tree, crouched, ran under the belly of the horse, and shot off in the opposite direction.

Sir Griffith got his steed turned around, and, with a curse, charged off after the running goblin. The time for sport was over; Sir Griffith was mad now.

Frithkin thought he could make it this time. But he was only eight feet up the trunk of the tree when the lance point got him in the back and went straight through his chest.

Sir Griffith flipped the lance up straight and Frithkin's body flew off in a high arc and crashed down among some bushes.

"Ho!" bellowed a booming, hollow voice. "Base knight! Stand to and fight! Lower your lance against an armored man if you dare, coward!"

The Empty Knight, astride the mighty Roderick, his black shield held at the ready, his lance aimed at the heart of Sir Griffith, charged across the clearing toward his enemy.

Sir Griffith had no choice. He lowered his own lance again, spurred his bay gelding, and charged toward the oncoming figure in black armor.

Magus MacCullen came running up a few seconds before the two met. In one glance, he saw that the Empty Knight should have the better of the encounter. His lance was steady and his aim was true, while the other knight was having trouble holding his aim. The Empty Knight sat a horse better and held his position better. There should have been no doubt of the outcome.

Part of MacCullen's prediction was true. Sir Griffith's lance point slid off the Empty Knight's shield, missing the fesse point by six inches, while the Empty Knight's lance struck solidly, full on.

To the amazement of both Sir Griffith and the Magus, the Empty Knight, still clinging firmly to his lance, came to almost a dead halt. Roderick, who could not stop so quickly, charged on. As a result, the Empty Knight was catapulted backward out of his saddle and came crashing to earth with a clash of steel.

Sir Griffith, still firmly seated, much to his own amazement, charged on by and then wheeled his horse to attack the fallen knight. But he reckoned without the great black stallion.

Roderick reared his mighty bulk into the air and struck with his forefeet. His heavy hooves struck. One hit the armored Sir Griffith, jarring him to his teeth. The other hit the bay gelding.

That was enough for the gelding. He took one look at that huge stallion, turned, and took off at a gallop. Sir Griffith had dropped the reins and could do nothing to control his horse. It was all he could do to hang on.

Great Roderick thundered along behind and would have caught the bay if he hadn't heard the Empty Knight's voice bellowing behind him.

"Roderick! Come back here!" He knew that if the horse kept on Sir Griffith's heels he would eventually have the whole troop of the Duke's men to deal with.

Roderick came back, his nostrils snorting angrily.

Sir Griffith regained the reins and finally got the bay gelding under control, but he decided not to go back. He had done as the Duke had ordered and had unhorsed the knight in black in the bargain. He had won, hadn't he? Besides, he felt safer with the troop.

The Empty Knight had leaped to his feet and was ready to remount Roderick and ride after the fleeing Sir Griffith, but Magus MacCullen yelled: "Hey! Where do you think you're going?"

"After that catiff swine! He's murdered Frithkin! I loved that goblin like a brother!"

"Wait a minute! There's a dozen of them! They can't kill you, but they'd knock you to pieces and scatter your armor all over the place. What do you mean, he murdered Frithkin? Don't be ridiculous!"

"Ridiculous am I?" bellowed the Empty Knight in a high

dudgeon. "Come over to these gorse bushes and take a look! Caught him right in the chest from behind!"

The Magus ran over to the bushes, reaching them before the knight did. "Frithkin! Frithkin! Are you hurt?"

"Damn right I am," said Frithkin feebly from the bushes.

The Magus parted the bushes and looked in. "What happened?"

Frithkin lay still, his hands over his chest, his body twisted, his goblin eyes glazed with pain. "He ran me through. My neck's broken, and so's my back. I think my head's busted."

The Empty Knight looked down at the goblin. "You're still alive, good Frithkin?" He paused, then said in a wondering voice. "And no blood?"

"Of course he's still alive," said MacCullen. "You can't kill an earth elemental. And who ever heard of a goblin with blood?"

"That's right, my lord," said the goblin with a feeble grin. "It'll take all night to heal, but I'll be all right in the morning." Then he winced. "Being immortal is all right, I guess, but dammit, this sort of thing *hurts*!"

Frithkin was obviously in great pain. "Help me get him out of there, Sir Knight," said the Magus. "Careful, now! Easy! There! Now let's get busy and bury him."

"But he's not dead," protested the Empty Knight, reasonably enough.

"No," said MacCullen patiently, "but that's the best way to cure an earth elemental of anything that's wrong with him. Put him in the earth."

"Aye," muttered Frithkin with a faint attempt at a smile. "It's back to the Auld Sod for me!"

They dug the grave and buried Frithkin. And all that afternoon the magician and the knight discussed in angry tones what they would do with the recreant knight when they caught him.

"I'll know his coat of arms when I see it again – a row of four red diamonds across a silver shield," said the Empty Knight.

MacCullen nodded. "Argent in fesse four fusils gules. We'll find out who that butcher is all right!"

They talked until the moon rose, then Magus MacCullen lay back on the grass and fell into fitful slumber. The Empty Knight sat up and tended the fire, having nothing else to do.

Just before dawn, he heard a scrabbling, digging noise and looked over at the grave. Frithkin was digging his way out. He stood up, brushed the crumbs of soil from himself, then looked over at the Empty Knight and grinned. "Good as new, my lord."

"I'm glad, good Frithkin," the knight said simply. "Very glad."

Three weeks later, they had reached the border of Faerie.

IV

The curious dimensional interface which constituted the "border" of the Land of Faerie was not always easy to find. It was computed by astrologers who knew their business that Faerie would drift further and further away until at last the interface would no longer exist, and knowledge of the Land of Faerie would fade from the memories of men and the stories of Faerie would be discounted as childish twaddle. "Nothing but a Faerie story," would become a catch-phrase until, after cycles of time, the drift reversed itself and Faerie came once again within the ken of mortal men.

For Frithkin, finding the exact location of the borderland was childishly simple; as a subject of the Faerie King, he had a homing instinct that was infallible. The goblin took the lead, followed by Magus MacCullen and the Empty Knight, and they threaded their way through a thick forest of gnarled, ancient oaks. The sky was shrouded with a light overcast, and the light filtered down through the leaves and branches to fill the air with greenish gloom.

There was danger here, for trolls, dragons, basilisks, and other horrendous denizens of Faerie often found their way through the border and lurked in wait for travelers – especially during a Centennial Convention year, when so many would be coming this way.

The Empty Knight had wanted to ride up front, by Frithkin – to protect them, he said – but Magus MacCullen would have none of it.

"They're more likely to sneak up on us from behind, anyway, Sir Knight," he said. "You'll be of much more use in the rear.

And if anything happens, for the love of Heaven use your mace or your sword, not your lance."

Mollified by having been put in the position of what the Magus said was of greatest danger, the Empty Knight rode behind.

As a further precaution against danger, MacCullen had previously conjured up a series of spells ready for casting should the occasion arise. The real reason he wanted the Empty Knight in the rear was that if a dragon, say, were to challenge them from ahead, the knight would most likely lower his lance and charge from force of habit. And, of course, get knocked out of his saddle as a result.

He had explained the whole thing to Frithkin on the day after the attack by Sir Griffith.

"He's strong enough and skilled enough, but he doesn't have the weight behind him. Oh, he *looks* heavy enough, but that's because we tend to think there's a man inside that armor. There's a common rumor, among peasants who don't know any better, that a knight in full armor can't get up again if he's knocked flat. The heaviest plate armor made doesn't weigh over ninety pounds, and any knight that can't get to his feet, with only ninety pounds of armor distributed evenly over his body, doesn't deserve to wear it.

"Now, Sir Empty's armor is fairly heavy, but it isn't of the heaviest kind. He doesn't weigh more than eighty pounds – eighty-five at the most. What chance does he have of driving his lance point home? How can he unhorse a man who, with armor, weighs close to two hundred and fifty pounds?"

"I see," Frithkin had said. "I remember when that ba— er, gentleman was chasing me, I wished I were a rock elemental – a gnome or a kobold. No fear of lances, then! A friend of mine named Gwuthnik is a little gnome who stands three feet high if he stretches, weighs a good four hundred pounds, and he's so hard that a lance point wouldn't do more than scratch him."

"Four hundred pounds, eh?"

"Since he's a rock elemental, I should have said he weighs close to twenty-nine stone."

*   *   *

A mace or a sword was something else again, MacCullen decided. A mace has weight of its own and a sword has a sharp edge and you don't depend so much on your own weight to wield them. Besides, the Empty Knight could hold on to the pommel of his saddle with one gauntlet while he used a sword or mace with the other.

Nevertheless, the Magus had charged himself up with a horde of good spells, just in case.

They came to a bridge over a wide, sluggish stream, and Frithkin stopped, his nose twitching. "Smells all right to me," he said after a moment. "Come along."

They went on across the stone bridge, but the Magus and the Empty Knight kept a sharp watch all the same. There was, as far as anybody knew, no reason for trolls to prefer bridges to hide under, but they did. Fortunately, none had discovered this particular bridge. The three travelers crossed without incident.

There was no precise moment when the interface was crossed. The border of Faerie was like any other border; unless it has been marked out by a surveyor and clearly marked, there is no way of knowing at which precise moment the border is passed. But one minute the three were in the mortal world – and a few minutes later they knew they were in Faerie. It was hard to tell how they knew. Partly it was the luminous appearance of everything; the colors of grass and leaf and flower seemed to have a fluorescent quality about them. And the quality of the light itself was different. Since the sky had been overcast before they crossed the border, the change in the sky had not been obvious, and the leafy branches overhead made it even more difficult to tell, but all three knew that the sun was gone. The sun never shines in Faerie; there is only the blue of the sky, a darkling blue which permeates the very air with a silvery twilight.

After an hour or so, the heavy forest began to thin out. The trees were still as big, but there was more room between them. The place might have been a well-tended park instead of a woods. If nothing else, the Faerie folk took care of their countryside.

"How does this place smell to you, Frithkin?" the Magus asked.

The goblin tilted back his head and tested the air with his

nostrils. "All right," he said. "Nothing dangerous. There's a griffin several miles to the south, but he's digesting a meal, not hunting."

"Fine. Let's take a rest, then. Unpack some sandwiches. And some beer. Be sure to take the cold spell off the beer or we'll chill our insides when we drink it."

Frithkin narrowed his eyes – as much as he could narrow those huge orbs – and said: "Where are you going?"

"For a walk. I'll be back in a few minutes."

Without waiting for an answer, he got down off his mule and strode off through the woods until he was well out of sight of the goblin and the Empty Knight. Then he walked over to the nearest oak, traced a peculiar symbol in the air, murmured three lines of potent verse, and knocked briskly on the tree.

"Who is there and what do you want?" said a contralto voice from the tree.

"Let's not play guessing games, my lady," he said; "I am the Magus MacCullen, as you well know. You and your sisters have been keeping a watch on us for a long time. I'm not a magician for nothing, you know."

"Very well, Magus MacCullen," said the voice, sounding rather miffed. "What is it you want?"

"Who is the Elder Sister in this grove?" MacCullen asked.

"It so happens that I am. Now, what do you want?"

"I thought my intuition was working pretty well," said MacCullen. "Picked you out right away."

"What do you want?" The voice sounded angry.

"I said, let's not play guessing games, my lady. You know what I want. Information. But if you want to play another kind of game, I have one for you."

"Which is?"

"First I tell you a story, then you tell me one."

"It had better be a good story," said the voice. "I'm not in a mood for games."

"Oh? I thought you were. Well, I'll do my best to interest you. First, I will begin my story by reminding you that it is against the Law of Faerie for any of the Faerie folk to fall in love with a mortal."

There was a gasp from the tree. Then the voice said: "Go
on, Magus."

"Fine. Now, we will mention no names. We both know what
we're talking about, don't we?"

"Yes, Magus."

"Thank you, my lady. Then I shall say that I know what
your sister did and I think it was very good of her. I want to
help. I know that she partially averted a very serious crime, a
breaking of both the laws of Faerie and the laws of Christendom.
In order to set right that situation, I am willing to overlook a small
infraction of the law, such as falling in love. More; with your help,
I am willing to aid and abet this minor misdemeanor." He was
bluffing. Most of what he was saying was guesswork, but it was
guesswork based on knowledge and observation.

"Do you swear by the Most Holy?" the voice asked.

"I swear by His Name," replied the magician.

"I believe you, Magus. I know you to be a good man. We
would not want to get our sister in trouble. Though I don't
know how you knew."

"Someday I'll tell you," the Magus promised, "but there
are more ears in this grove than ours." Again he mentioned
no names, but the air elementals were notorious for spreading gossip.

"I don't think there are any of the wind sprites about just
now," said the voice, "but let's keep it confidential, as you say.
Now, Magus, I honestly don't know all the details. None of us
does. Other information I am forbidden to give. What I tell
you now is all I *can* tell you. Ask no further questions."

"All right, my lady. I'll do the best I can with what I have to
work with. Speak on."

"Very well. You have heard of the Great Chalice?"

MacCullen raised his red eyebrows in surprise. "I have. Don't
tell me *that's* mixed up in this."

"It is."

The Magus pursed his lips for a silent whistle. The Great Chalice
was the symbol of the Kings of Faerie. Whoever rightfully owned
it was, by law, King of Faerie. It could not be stolen or taken
by force; each King had to give it willingly to his successor. To

mortals, it conveyed immortality; to all, it gave the power to rule Faerie.

"Someone is after it," said the voice from the tree. "I don't know any of the details of the plot, but if you solve it, you will solve your own difficulties and ours as well. Now, the man to watch is the Duke of Duquayne!"

"*That* son of—Pardon me, my lady. I have no love for the Duke; he ordered one of his knights to run through my familiar."

"Sounds like him," said the tree. "The point is, you have to get to King Huon's court before he does, and he's three days ahead of you. We were going to use subtle pressures and misguidance to get you to take the shortcut, but now that won't be necessary."

"The shortcut. You mean across the Blistering Desert?"

"Exactly. If you take the long way round, the Duke will be at King Huon's court before you."

"But nobody can carry enough water to cross that desert and live!"

"Arrangements have been made. Go directly to the edge of the desert from here. You will find a golden ring in the sand. We had arranged things so that you would find it accidentally, but there's no need of that now. With it, you will be allowed to ask for water three times as you cross the desert. Three times only, so don't waste your requests. Do you understand?"

"I understand, my lady."

"That is all, Magus MacCullen. I can tell you no more. Further, I bind you to say no word of this to anyone."

"I cannot promise that, my lady. The goblin Frithkin is my familiar; we have no secrets from each other."

"You may tell Frithkin when you judge the time is ripe. But no one else. Above all, not to the one you call the Empty Knight."

"Who is he, my lady?" the Magus asked. "Do you know?"

"I said no questions. But. . . I'll answer that one and no more. No. None of us knows. We suspect, but that is not enough. But the signs tell us that you will discover his identity."

"That's all I need to know, then. Thank you, my lady."

"Thank *you*, Magus MacCullen. May God go with you."

V

"Look here, Master Magus," said Frithkin pleadingly, "I'm not asking for my own sake. Lack of water makes me wither up, but I could still make it across that desert. So could his lordship, here. But you need water. And what about the mules and Roderick?"

"Don't you trust me, Frithkin?" the Magus asked gently.

"Yes, Master! Of course, but—" He clamped his lips together for a moment and looked out over the sandy waste that stretched before them. "Well, then, let's go, Master. Whatever you say."

"What about you, Sir Knight?" MacCullen asked.

"Lead on, Magus. I follow," the knight said boomingly.

Magus MacCullen had been surveying the edge of the desert. It began abruptly, as though a knife had been drawn across the landscape. On one side there was grass, on the other side, rock and sand. There was no heat from the sun, for there was no sun, only the blue sky overhead. But the sands of the Faerie desert were hot, and it was said that the fires of Hell itself were near the surface here.

Then MacCullen saw what he had been looking for. Something gleamed in the sand at the desert's edge, a few feet away. He couldn't have missed it, even if he had not known it would be there. He stooped, picked up a handful of sand, and let it run through his fingers. When the sand was gone, the ring remained in his palm. He got up on his mule, then, and said: "Let's go. We have a long ride ahead of us, and we must make good time."

All that day they plodded across the Blistering Desert. The hooves of the animals had been wrapped with cloth to protect them from the heat of the sand, which would have blistered their hooves in time.

Night came. The sky darkened to a royal blue, and a glimmer of light appeared on the horizon. Faerie has no sun, but its moon, three times the size of the moon mortal men were used to, was always full and shone with a yellowish light.

At midnight, when the moon was overhead, they stopped to rest the animals. The Magus conjured up a cold spell that

chilled the sands for a little while so that he and the mounts
could lie down without getting feverish from the sand's heat.
When the moon sank in the west, and the sky lightened again,
they all rose and went on.

At midday, Frithkin said: "Well, Master Magus, that's the
last of the water." He had just given a drink to the mules and
Roderick. The leathern water bag was empty.

"Well, we must do something about that," said Magus
MacCullen. He put his hand in the pocket of his blue-and-silver
robe and muttered something.

For a moment, nothing happened. Then, nearby, two small
whirlwinds began to form. They whirled faster and grew taller,
until they had become whirling cones of sand nearly as tall as a
man. Then they changed shape subtly, and the spinning sand
took the form of two girls, tan and shapely.

"Sand sprites," muttered Frithkin. "I wouldn't have believed
it if I hadn't seen it with my own eyes."

The sprites said nothing. There was only the swishing sound of
the little whirlwinds that held them together. Their arms were
uplifted to the sky, and their writhing fingers became long and
tenuous and seemed to reach upward to the sky itself.

Where a mortal woman would have had feet, the sand sprites
had only twisting whirls of sand. The spinning winds had lifted
the sand grains that formed their bodies from the desert itself,
leaving a shallow depression in the desert floor. Their hands,
reaching higher and higher, found what they sought. They
brought water down from the clouds themselves, letting it flow
through the interstices in their granular bodies and spreading
it like a blanket on the ground below. Within minutes, the
depression was full of cool water.

The two sand sprites, their work done, whirled away to a
point several yards distant. The winds slowed. Stopped. The
sand that had made up their bodies collapsed and became
two ordinary piles of sand, like any other little dunes in
the desert.

"You never cease to amaze me, Master," Frithkin said
thoughtfully, studying MacCullen's face. He knew perfectly
well that sand sprites cannot be commanded to do anything,

except perhaps by the King of Faerie himself. There was more to this than met the eye. But he said no more.

"That pool will warm up and evaporate pretty quickly," said MacCullen. "Fill up the water bags; let the animals drink. Then I'm going to take a bath and wash off the mules and Roderick."

"I hope you can do that trick again," said Frithkin. "We're only a quarter of the way across this desert."

"We'll make it, Frithkin," the Magus said shortly.

"I never doubted it, myself," said the Empty Knight complacently. "If Magus MacCullen says he'll do a thing, he does it."

"That's true, my lord," said Frithkin. "He always comes through. But sometimes I wonder *how*."

It took the travelers four days to cross the Blistering Desert. Twice more, at MacCullen's call, the sand sprites brought them water. They were just running short of the last of it when they reached the other side. The moon had just set and the Faerie dawn had brightened the sky.

As they crossed the edge and their mounts trod on grass again for the first time in four days, Magus MacCullen quietly flipped the gold ring behind him. Out of the corner of his eye, he saw a small swirl of sand surround it and it was gone.

"Thanks," said the Magus in his softest voice.

"You are welcome, Magus MacCullen," whispered a dry, slightly gritty voice in his ear.

Three days later, weary but pleased with themselves, the three travelers arrived at the Nameless City near which stands the great white castle of King Huon du Cor, the Sovereign Ruler of Faerie. They were fully a week ahead of time. And, since they had gained six days by taking a shortcut across the Burning Desert, they should be three days ahead of the Duke of Duquayne instead of three days behind.

"Now what do we do?" asked Frithkin.

"Do?" said the Empty Knight. "Why we go straight to the Palace, of course, and announce ourselves."

"Not just yet," said the Magus. "Let's not be too hasty. I want to look things over first. Is there a good reliable inn within the City gates, Frithkin?"

"Several. We're still solvent, Master Magus; how good a suite do you want?"

"Roomy, but nothing too showy. Not the best in town, certainly."

"You don't want the Queen Titania, then. How about the Hermes Trismegistus? A reliable place, and they cater to the magician trade, anyway."

"They'll be all booked up for the Convention, won't they?" the Empty Knight asked.

The goblin grinned and shook his head. "You're in Faerie now, my lord, and any Faerie Inn always has room for one more."

"All right," said the Magus. "We'll go there. And then I want you to scout around and find out what the news is, if any."

They went through the gates of the Nameless City, and through streets filled with shops and stores of all kinds. The people in the unnaturally clean streets were of all kinds and descriptions. Besides the near-human folk, who differed only by their pointed ears and their pale, translucent skin, there were goblins and gnomes and elves and brownies, and some odd-looking folk that even the Magus didn't recognize.

They got a suite of rooms at the Hermes Trismegistus, and Frithkin went out to search for news. He returned in the middle of the afternoon.

"Not much in the way of news, Master," he said. "The Duke of Duquayne hasn't arrived yet. I checked with the guards at the City gates and with the guards at the Palace. No sign of him, though he's been invited to stay at the Palace by the King himself."

"I don't understand it," the Magus said musingly. "The Duke and his troop aren't magicians. Or are they? Why should they be coming to Faerie at Convention time?"

"Oh, didn't you know? There's to be a tourney. Jousting and mock battles and everything. A big show that His Majesty is putting on for the entertainment of the visiting magicians. There'll be the usual prizes: a gold cup for the winner and a gold medal for the runner-up, plus lots of silver medals and ribbons for the others."

"By George!" said the Empty Knight enthusiastically, "I must enter!"

Frithkin grinned.

But Magus MacCullen nodded in agreement. "Indeed you must, Sir Knight! Indeed you must! Here—" He reached in to his belt pouch and brought out a silver piece. "—go down to the nearest armorer and get yourself a polish job. If they ask why you want the armor left on, give 'em your story about the vow. Make sure they do a good job, too. We want you to shine for this affair."

The Empty Knight stood up and took the silver piece in his gauntlet. "You've been very good to me, Master Magus," he said solemnly. "I shall repay you as soon as I come into my own."

"Think nothing of it. Now go down and get that polish job."

As soon as he was gone, Frithkin said: "What's got into you, Master? You know he won't last a minute in the first bout."

"Frithkin, let me do the worrying, will you? Here's another silver piece. Go down and get me a can of gold paint, a can of red paint, and a can of black paint. The quick-drying kind that isn't available outside of Faerie. And a brush and some solvent. Got it?"

"I've got it, but . . ."

"Go, Frithkin, go! I want you back here in fifteen minutes."

When Frithkin came back with the paint, he saw that MacCullen had very carefully cleaned the surface of the knight's shield.

"I am afraid to ask what you are up to, Master," said Frithkin.

"Then don't! Go to the public room and drink some beer or something! Come back when you're not so inquisitive."

Rather hurt, Frithkin did as he was told. He still had change from the silver piece, so he spent the next half hour drinking beer as he had been told. But his curiosity finally got the better of him, and he went back upstairs.

"There!" said MacCullen as soon as Frithkin opened the door. "How do you like it?"

Frithkin stared at the shield. It had been painted red, with a black chevron, like the letter A without the cross-bar, coming up to the center. Under this black inverted V was a round, gold disc, and there were two more on either side and just above the chevron.

Frithkin just stood there, open-mouthed.

"I know," MacCullen said gently, "you're going to say that I can't do that. Putting my older brother's arms on another's shield is a violation of the laws of heraldry, chivalry, and common decency. Well, you are perfectly right." He reached out and touched the shield. "It's dry now. Good. You win, Frithkin. I repent me of my actions."

And he took the brush and the black paint and painted the whole thing over black.

VI

The next day, the three travelers rode up to the Palace gates and asked to be admitted.

"You names and ranks, please," said the Captain of the Guard.

"I am the Magus MacCullen, Sorcerer of the Seventh Circle. This is my familiar, Frithkin, a subject of His Fey Majesty. This gentleman is a knight of noble birth who wishes to remain anonymous for the time being. He has taken a vow."

"You vouch for him, Master Magus?"

"I do."

"Sign here. Thank you. You may pass."

Others had come early, too. Around the great jousting field, several silk pavilions, blazing with the colors of their owners' coats of arms, had already been erected.

"Let's go on out there and pick a spot to put up our own tent," said Magus MacCullen with a chuckle. "Five will get you a hundred that there will be a herald along before the pavilion is up five minutes."

"No takers," said Frithkin. "Five will get you a hundred that—" He stopped. "No, no bet. I was going to say that they'll make us take it down in five more minutes, but you've got something up your sleeve."

"How often does a magician hear *that*?" the Magus asked

rhetorically. "But this time you happen to be perfectly right. Let's go."

Frithkin was perfectly right, too, in not betting either way. The Magus had sunk nearly all the money he had left in buying the big black silk tent that they put up, and four minutes after they had finished tightening the guy ropes, a gentleman in a herald's costume came by to investigate. The Empty Knight and Frithkin were inside the tent, rolling down the sides to insure privacy, but the Magus was standing outside. The gentleman in herald's costume walked all the way around the pavilion, then came over to MacCullen. He was short, with gray hair around a balding head, and had a rather mild smile on his face. Only the pointed ears and the fathomless sea-green eyes, which had no pupils, indicated that he was of Faerie stock. "Pardon me," he said gently, "I am Argent Wyvern Pursuivant. You are the Magus MacCullen?"

"I am, sir."

"It is a pleasure to meet you, Magus. The record of your distinguished family is well known to us here in Faerie."

Distinguished, but poor as churchmice, MacCullen said to himself. Aloud, he said: "It is good of you to say so, Argent Wyvern."

"Now, I understand," the Pursuivant went on, "that one of your companions is a knight who wishes to remain anonymous."

"That is correct. I vouched for him at the gate."

"Yes, yes, of course. But you can't put up a pavilion unless you intend to enter the tournament, and I can't permit anyone to enter the tournament unless I know his rank and status. Your friend can't remain anonymous if he wishes to enter the tourney. The others have a right to know that they are jousting against one of noble blood and not a— er— commoner."

"Of course they do," said the Magus, as though he were pondering the situation. "Ah! I think I see a way around this. Would it be possible for me to have a short audience with His Majesty?"

"Well-l-l . . . perhaps. I would have to arrange it through my superior, the Faerroi King of Arms, since it is a heraldic matter."

"Excellent. You see, the knight of whom we are speaking is under a vow not to reveal his identity. I, too, am unable to tell you who he is. But there are a few bits of information I *can* give – only to His Majesty, of course."

"What sort of information?" asked Argent Wyvern.

The Magus smiled. "Without breaking my vow, I can tell him what coat of arms lies under the coat of black paint on my friend's shield."

Argent Wyvern Pursuivant broke into a knowing smile. "Ah! That, of course, would solve the problem completely. I shall make arrangements, Magus."

"Thank you, Argent Wyvern."

An hour later, Magus MacCullen was in audience with His Sovereign Majesty, Huon, King of Faerie, and his chief herald, the Faerroi King of Arms. After making a low bow and going through the usual amenities, MacCullen waited for the King to speak.

"Magus," said King Huon, "what's all this about an anonymous friend of yours?"

The Magus explained, giving the story about the vow, which was perfectly true, as the Empty Knight had said, but misleading.

"So you see, Sire," MacCullen finished, "he does not want his identity revealed to anyone just at the moment."

"Then he can't fight," said the King. "Right, Faerroi?"

"Quite, Your Majesty," the herald agreed.

"If Your Majesty were to issue a statement saying that you guarantee that the Black Knight is of blood noble enough to engage the others without their losing their honor, wouldn't that suffice?"

"Why, certainly," said the King. "But how can I do that if I don't know who he is?"

The Magus looked at Faerroi King of Arms. "Without breaking my word, I can blazon for you the achievement beneath the black paint on the Black Knight's shield."

The Faerroi King of Arms smiled. "Aha! What is it?"

"This must remain secret."

"Certainly."

"The shield is blazoned thus: gules a chevron sable between three bezants – the whole debruised by a field sable."

"Only temporarily, I hope," said the herald.

"Gules a chevron sable between three bezants," King Huon repeated. "That's—"

"The Red MacCullen," said the King of Arms, who knew the coat of arms of every knight in Christendom and Faerie. "Head of the Clan MacCullen and older brother to the here present Magus MacCullen."

"The Red MacCullen! Why, his deeds are famous! One of the greatest knights in Christendom!" said King Huon.

"I shall be happy to tell my brother that you speak so highly of him, Sire," said the Magus, making a resolve to do so the next time he was home.

"He hasn't gone in much for tournaments, though," King Huon observed. "In fact, he has not done much of anything in the past five years."

"A matter of money, Your Majesty," said MacCullen. "I admit it for your ears only. It would be convenient for the family coffers if the Black Knight were to win a few ransoms of armor at this tourney."

"Ah, that's the Irish, all right," said King Huon. "Brave but poor. Very well, Magus. I will give my Royal Word that the Black Knight is of noble birth, that no man's honor would be sullied by a bout of arms with him."

"Thank you, Sire," said MacCullen with a low bow.

And that was that. As he left, MacCullen sighed with relief. He had managed to get what he wanted without telling one single lie.

Two days later, Magus MacCullen was having a less formal audience with His Majesty. The King had invited MacCullen and several other magicians who were early arrivals to an informal talk over a few glasses of mulled wine. MacCullen was being polite but saying very little. He left most of the talking to the others. He had some heavy thinking to do. There were still parts of this puzzle he did not understand.

One of the sorcerers, a Magus Ponzoni, was holding forth on the possibility of making a spell that would prevent Faerie gold from disappearing when touched by cold iron, when the door opened and a liveried servant approached the King. He whispered something in the King's ear. The King smiled happily. "Bring him in! Bring him in, by all means!" As the servant left, His Majesty turned to the eight magicians and said: "Gentle Magi, there is a friend of mine coming to whom I would like to present you. An old friend, whom I haven't seen for several years. He has come here to take part in the tournament, and that should make it a spectacle worth watching."

At that moment, a tall, handsome man, with jet black hair and a jet black, neatly trimmed beard, entered the room. He stopped and bowed low. "Your Majesty, it is a pleasure to see you again."

"My dear Duke!" said His Majesty. "Permit me to present to you some of our guests." Each of the magicians was named; each made a proper bow to the Duke. MacCullen watched narrowly, but the Duke showed no reaction when the King said: "Magus MacCullen."

And MacCullen was not at all surprised when the man turned out to be the Duke of Duquayne.

"My lord King," said the Duke when the introductions were over, "I am the bearer of unhappy tidings. There is a demon loose in your realm."

The King shot to his feet. "*What?* I shall complain to His Satanic Majesty at once! This sort of thing cannot be tolerated!"

"Your pardon, Majesty," said the Duke hurriedly. "My terminology was inexact. I should have said 'a fiend in human form'. A murderer and an impostor. A butcher of the worst sort. I, myself, saw him run down and kill a defenseless peasant, and there are other crimes against him which I can testify to. I have been unable to apprehend this monster thus far, but with your help it can be done. I happen to know that he is already within the borders of Faerie and is less than three days behind me."

"His name?"

"I don't know his name, Your Majesty. He gives none. But he wears black armor – which the base-born cur has no right to – and rides a black horse. A horse named, of all things, Roderick."

King Huon's face clouded over and he glanced at MacCullen, who looked as innocent as possible. The King looked back at the Duke.

"Three days behind you? Are you certain of that?"

"Quite certain, Your Majesty."

"Ah. I was worried for a moment. You see, we already have a knight here answering to that description. But I happen to know who he is, and he is neither base born nor a murderer. And his horse is called—" He glanced at MacCullen.

"Black Beauty," MacCullen said complacently. He had distinctly heard Frithkin call Roderick a black beauty. No lie there.

"Yes, Black Beauty," said the King. "Besides, this man has been here for three days now."

"Then he couldn't be the man we are looking for," said the Duke firmly. "But steps must be taken against the murderer."

"Have no fear, my friend," said the King. "Orders will be issued immediately. Your word is good enough for me. If he is found, he will be hanged instantly from the nearest tree."

"You will rid your realm of a monster," said the Duke. "Perhaps my own men could aid in the search. I would have taken him myself before this, but I have no right to do so in your realm."

"Very proper of you," said the King, "but you should have known that I would have forgiven you."

"You are most kind, Majesty. Oh, by the way, would you ask your men to be very careful not to harm the horse? The stallion belongs to me. It was a gift from a friend, and this cur stole it."

"Your horse? Yes, it would be, having your name. Well, we can just add horse stealing to the list of crimes which we shall hang this villain for."

MacCullen sipped quietly at his mulled wine. So the Duke's Christian name was Roderick, eh? The last piece of the puzzle had fallen into place.

The Duke had made a very bad mistake. He had assumed that he had outsmarted everyone.

VII

The third day of the tournament. For a week, now, the search had been going on for the "murderous villain" who was supposed to be following the Duke, and there had been no trace of him. It was conjectured that a troll or a dragon had disposed of him, since he was supposed to be traveling alone. MacCullen knew what had made the Duke wary of the knight in black armor. Sir Griffith de Beauville had heard the Empty Knight call out Roderick's name and had reported the unusual incident.

MacCullen had heard things, too. Duke Roderick of Duquayne was not well-loved in his duchy. In the past year, he had become a tyrant. That explained the attack in the George and Dragon. Those men had evidently thought that "Sir Roderick the Black" was the Duke. He was sorry now that he and the Empty Knight had dealt so harshly with them. Still, what they had attempted to do had been illegal, even if possibly justifiable. Besides, none of them had been killed. The punishment had been light.

MacCullen had been watching each day's jousting with a critical eye, and he saw that Duke Roderick was out to win by fair means or foul.

Well, let him try. The Magus MacCullen had tricks of his own.

"Look here, good Magus," the Empty Knight said on the third day, "why haven't you let me get out there? Am I to sit in this pavilion all through the jousting?"

"No, Sir Knight, you fight today. I have matched you against your old friend, Sir Griffith de Beauville – he of the 'Argent in fesse four fusils gules'. That will qualify you for the final round."

"Ahh-*ha*! I'll slaughter him."

"I'll say you will. Frithkin, have you got that sand ready?"

The goblin chuckled. "All ready, Master Magus."

"Very well. Let's get started. You'll be called in fifteen minutes, Sir Knight."

"What are you going to do?" the knight asked.

"Well, one of the things I'm going to do is give you a head. It will just be a simulacrum, but when the herald asks you to raise your visor, there will have to be a face behind it. I'm going to make you look like my older brother."

"Your brother? But why?"

"Because it's necessary. Besides, I have to give you *some* face, and it is a law of magic that a simulacrum has to be a copy of some living person. It can't be imaginary, and the person can't be dead, do you see?"

"I see. Very well, good Magus. Go ahead."

Fifteen minutes later, the Black Knight rode to the lists on "Black Beauty" – who had had a small white blaze painted on his forehead. MacCullen did not want the Duke to recognize the horse too soon.

MacCullen and Frithkin watched expectantly as the two knights, Sir Griffith and the Black Knight, faced each other across the jousting field. They had met in the center, raised their visors, and cantered back to the ends of the field.

Now, visors down, they prepared to charge.

The signal was given. The herald dropped his flag. The two great warhorses began to move. Faster and faster they gained momentum until, at the moment of impact, they were hurtling along at a full gallop.

Like the first time they had met, Sir Griffith's aim and poise were not as good as his black-armored opponent. His own spear struck just off the fesse point, while the Black Knight's lance struck dead center.

But this time, it was Sir Griffith who shot out of his saddle as though he had been propelled from a gun. The Black Knight hardly budged in his saddle as his lance cut through Sir Griffith's shield and pierced the armor. Sir Griffith landed crashingly in the sand of the jousting field. He wasn't quite dead, but he would be a very sick man for some time to come.

Frithkin had been avenged.

"Very beautifully done, Sir Knight!" said the Magus as the Black Knight rode back into the pavilion. "Beautifully done! Listen! The crowd is still cheering! How do you feel?"

"Sort of stuffy."

"I don't blame you. Be careful getting down off Roderick. If you slip, I can't catch you."

Slowly and carefully – and some what stiffly – the Empty Knight dismounted.

Not really an empty knight any longer, for his armor had been filled with three hundred pounds of sand.

The next day, Magus MacCullen watched the jousting carefully. He was not interested in any bouts except those fought by the Duke of Duquayne.

The Duke was doing quite well, as a matter of fact. He had arranged to take on as many knights as possible on the last day, and he was knocking them over one by one.

Has to be a hero, MacCullen thought to himself. It didn't matter how many he jolted from their saddles; he would have to take on all who challenged him, and if he lost the last one, he lost the tourney. MacCullen was letting him do all the hard work he wanted to do, saving the Not-Quite-Empty Knight for the final round.

The Duke was not a particularly good jouster, though, and it took MacCullen a little while to see why he was winning. If one wasn't looking for it, it would have been easily overlooked. The Duke was using a confusion spell on his opponent's eyes. They saw him just a few inches to the right of where he actually was.

You are in for a surprise, my lord Louse, MacCullen thought grimly.

At last, the Duke of Duquayne reigned supreme in the field. No one appeared to challenge him. He rode up to the grandstand, to the King's box.

The herald blew a trumpet.

"If there are no further challenges," he cried in a loud voice, "His Majesty will award the golden cup to His Grace, Duke Roderick of Duquayne!"

"All right, Sir Knight!" MacCullen whispered. "You know what to do! Get out there and do it. And don't forget what I told you!"

"I'll follow your instructions to the letter, Magus," the knight promised.

Then he rode out into the arena and shouted in his booming voice: "*I challenge!*"

*   *   *

Duke Roderick, who had been about to take the cup from King Huon's hands, looked around at the sound of the voice. "Who *is* that man?" he asked the King. "Or doesn't anyone know?"

"I can assure you, my friend, that he is worthy of your steel."

"Very well. One more."

And the two knights took their positions.

And thirty seconds later, the Duke of Duquayne was lying unconscious on the ground.

As his seconds came out and dragged him off to his pavilion, the Black Knight rode up to the King's box. Again the herald sounded his trumpet. Again challengers were asked for.

And this time there were none.

The King stood up, the golden cup in his hands. "My lord," he said, "you have done well this day. You have defeated the champion. In token of which, I give you this cup."

The Black Knight took the cup in his hands.

Instantly, it changed. Before, it had been a chalice of carved gold. Now, it was encrusted with dazzling gems – diamonds, rubies, sapphires, and emeralds in a coruscating array.

The onlookers gasped. King Huon had, of his own free will, given away the Great Chalice! He was King no longer; he was just Huon du Cor, sometime Duke of Bordeaux.

And then the new King, the Black Knight, did a strange thing.

"Huon of Bordeaux," he said in his booming voice, "I, of my own free will and pleasure, return to you the Great Chalice, symbol and instrument of the Sovereignty of Faerie!" And he put the cup back in Huon's hands. Huon was King again.

MacCullen had been working his way through the silent, shocked crowd to the King's box.

"My lord King," he said, "perhaps it would be best if you come with me. I can explain this whole thing. It was a plot of the most dastardly kind. Will you come with me to the pavilion of the man who calls himself Duke of Duquayne?"

Dumbfounded, the King could do nothing but follow.

The Duke was just regaining consciousness when the King, MacCullen, and the Black Knight, followed by a score of Royal Guardsmen, entered his pavilion.

"What happened?" he asked feebly. Then his eyes focused on the stern face of the King.

"Yes. That's what I want to know," said the King. "What happened?"

"Permit me to show you, Your Majesty," said the Magus MacCullen. His fingers made intricate patterns in the air, and he constructed, syllable by syllable, a sestine of great power.

And the Duke's face changed. The hard-eyed, wrinkle-faced wretch who lay on the pallet was quite obviously not the Duke of Duquayne.

"The Magus Prezhenski!" said the King. "But he's supposed to be dead!"

"A hoax," said MacCullen. "He wanted everyone to think he was dead. You see, he had to come as Duke Roderick to pull off his plot against the Throne of Faerie. He put an enchantment on the Great Chalice so that you would think it was the prize cup and give it to him. Not content with usurping the place of the real Duke of Duquayne, he wanted to be King of Faerie."

"What did he do with my friend, Duke Roderick?" King Huon asked in a cold voice. "Kill him?"

"No. The Duke had to be alive in order to allow Prezhenski to use a simulacrum of his face." The Magus MacCullen pointed a finger at the Magus Prezhenski. "You have bartered your soul, Prezhenski. You have dealt with His Satanic Majesty and signed away your life in eternity. Shall we call him and tell him to collect, or will you remove the enchantment on the true Duke of Duquayne?"

"I'll remove it!" the frightened Magus Prezhenski quavered. "Give me a chance."

"Very well. And remember, I know as much magic as you and a great deal more. Don't try any trickery."

"I won't! I won't! I promise!" He began moving his fingers and mumbling verses.

And, quite suddenly, the suit of armor which had been the Empty Knight collapsed to the floor of the pavilion.

"What's this?" said the King.

Outside, there was a commotion.

And then, with Frithkin by his side, in walked the Duke of

Duquayne, stark naked except for the horse blanket he had wrapped around him.

"It worked!" he said happily. "It worked, Magus MacCullen! I remember everything!"

"It must be a sort of double memory," the Magus said with a grin. "You should remember being both horse and knight."

"I do! Very odd sensation, I must say."

MacCullen started to say something, but he noticed out of the corner of his eye that Prezhenski was muttering and moving his fingers. MacCullen made one gesture, and the evil magician froze, paralyzed.

"I suggest you put that man under arrest, Your Majesty. Duke Roderick, I should like to speak to you later."

It was only an hour later. Prezhenski had been safely locked away, and a team of three magicians had put tight binding spells on him that he could never throw off by himself.

The King, the Duke, and Frithkin listened to MacCullen explain.

"The Empty Knight, you see, could only remember things that were extremely important to him, things that had registered strongly *after* the enchantment. I thought it odd from the first that he couldn't remember his own name, but could remember the name of his horse.

"By the way, Your Majesty, I should like to call it to your attention that you owe the Duke a boon. He gave you back your kingdom. Legally, he could have kept it."

"Really, Magus," the Duke said, "Huon knows I wouldn't do anything like that to an old friend."

"Nevertheless," said the King, "what he says is true. If you have a boon to ask, I will grant it if it is within my power."

"Well-l-l . . ." the Duke began. "You tell him, Magus."

"He wants a pardon for a certain dryand named Naaia," said the Magus. "That was another name he remembered. What happened was this: Prezhenski, using black magic of the blackest kind, transformed Duke Roderick into a horse. A magnificent black stallion. Naaia, as far as I know, must have seen him do it."

The Duke nodded. "We were out hawking together. I trusted

him, and he got me in the woods – near a big oak – and . . . well, suddenly I was a horse. I was too confused to think of what to do. He tied me to the tree and went away."

"And Naaia," said the Magus, "didn't know who you were, but she had seen you as a man and had fallen in love with you. She came out of her tree and tried to help you. She couldn't reverse the spell, but she could modify it. She partially disembodied your spirit, leaving enough in the horse's body to make a good horse – all the horse sense, as it were – and put the rest into the armor. At least, that way you could go out to find the magician who had wronged you.

"Prezhenski, meanwhile, took your place. He must have been worried, though, when he found that the horse he had tied so well to the oak tree was gone when he came back to get it."

"Magus MacMullen," said Duke Roderick, "I shall never forget what you have done for me. You have saved my dukedom."

"And my kingdom," said King Huon.

"Oh, by the way, Your Majesty," the Magus said, "I want to apologize for misleading you into thinking that the Empty Knight was my brother, but all I asked you to do was give your Royal Word that the Black Knight was worthy of any man's steel – which he is."

"You are forgiven, Magus. And so is Naaia. Do you love the wench, Roderick?"

"I do, Huon."

"Then we'll see if arrangements can be made. And now, I trust I will see you all at the banquet tonight. This is a story that will make good telling for centuries to come. Will you come with me, Duke Roderick? We'll have to find something for you to wear besides that horse blanket. Oh, and, Magus— between us we will decide upon a suitable reward, though we can never pay what we owe."

"Your Majesty," said Magus MacCullen, with a wink at Frithkin, "You once said the Irish were brave but poor. It is within your power to correct that to some extent – without, of course, removing the bravery."

APHRODITE'S NEW TEMPLE

Amy Myers

Amy Myers (b. 1938) is best known for her books featuring Auguste Didier, the Victorian/Edwardian master-chef with the remarkable deductive powers, who first appeared in Murder in Pug's Parlour *in 1987 and has built up a dedicated following. She was previously an editor for the publisher William Kimber, for whom she edited the* After Midnight Stories *series of anthologies. Her humour is evident in the character of Didier, but she gives it full rein here in a story which is a sequel of sorts to "Aphrodite's Trojan Horse", published in my anthology* Classical Whodunnits *(1996).*

"I've got my new temple licence," Artemis crowed, waving a scroll in the air. (We gods and goddesses have to apply for planning permission for new temples.)

I was not pleased to find my half-sister smirking in the Golden Hall of Olympus. Supposedly Artemis is the virgin goddess of the bow and chase – huh! There is nothing she likes more than to shoot herself a man, and it's my belief she's kinky. All her young men seem to meet mysterious deaths, and she's had a whole string of them to her bow.

"It's for the island of Albion," she boasted. "Where New Troy is to rise."

"*What?*" I shrieked. "New Troy is *mine*. Destiny has decreed it, and my darling son, pious Aeneas, is in Hisperia about to found it any moment." (Hisperia is that odd peninsula with a boot at the end of it.)

The lady laughed through her wolfine teeth. (That's what hunting does for you.) "Destiny also decreed Aeneas's children's children should rule New Troy."

Madam Snake Sister obviously had something up her sleeve other than those spotty brown arms with the overdeveloped muscles, and she couldn't wait to tell me about it.

"I've promised your great-great-grandson Brutus that he can found New Troy on a riverbank in Albion. Daddy's promised me that if I make a go of my temple, New Troy will become famous." She sniggered at my look of horror.

"Daddy? Do you mean Great Zeus of the Sable Brows, Mighty Son of Cronos?" I enquired dangerously, while thinking furiously. Father likes us to be formal.

I was much annoyed to learn that I was a great-great-grandmother. As laughter-loving Aphrodite, goddess of love, nothing could be worse for my image. Believing my duty as a mother done, I had forgotten all about Aeneas, when the rat left the sinking ship of Troy. Take your eyes off any man, mortal or immortal, and something goes wrong.

Prompt action was needed. I whirled round on my dancing golden feet. I ordered the chariot, without Father's permission, aware that thanks to my girdle Zeus was spending the afternoon tucked up with a shepherdess who was under the impression she was nursing a sick lamb. I would pay a flying visit to my beloved son.

I burst in with all my goddess glory upon Aeneas, as he was taking his afternoon nap with his second wife Lavinia, landing on his fat stomach to be sure he woke up. He'd aged in all directions; not surprising, since he must be well into his mortal eighties now.

"Can't you keep tabs on your own great-grandson?" I

demanded without preamble, stepping daintily to the floor. "Artemis has told Brutus he can found New Troy."

Lavinia woke up and started screaming at finding a goddess in the middle of her best mosaic, so I sent her back to sleep.

Aeneas burst into tears. "But *I'm* founding New Troy. It isn't fair."

Aeneas is my son, and they never grow up. I sighed and stroked what remained of his hair. "I'll see what I can do." Be Hadesed if I'd let my sister Artemis get the better of me.

I was back on Olympus in the nick of Ambrosia Time. Cup-bearer Hebe was already hopping around like a demented grasshopper. Father strode in, sable brows twitching, as he recited the Ode of Thanks to himself for providing us with this eighty millionth (or thereabouts) dinner of ambrosia and nectar.

"Where's Artemis?" he thundered, after his tenth glass of nectar.

I looked round the table at the illustrious assembly of gods and goddesses, which included Ares, god of war, my current flame, staring at me, cannon at the ready as usual.

"Oh," I wailed. "She's gone already. You gave her permission to found a new temple, Father, and she's going to call it the Temple of New Troy on an island called Albion." I let one piteous sob roll down my cheek. "You promised New Troy to Aeneas."

His brows looked comfortingly sable. "She didn't tell me what she was planning to call it."

"There's daughters for you," I sighed. "I do try, myself, to keep you fully informed."

Mighty Zeus rose to full majestic height, and his mighty wife Hera (but in girth not power) cast me a venomous look for disturbing his dinner. "Albion?" Father's brows grew sabler. "I can't stop her now. I have no jurisdiction there." The whole world is supposed to be in his jurisdiction, but if it suits him he pretends some places are exempt.

"But you can watch what's happening?" He wasn't going to get away so easily. We lesser gods have to apply for an international viewing permission; only Zeus has the power to see everyone, everything, everywhere.

He stomped off to visit his Sighting Room while the rest of us looked at each other and tried to decide which side was winning so they could join it. Father came stomping back, even crosser.

"She's in her temple on Leogicia. Your great-great-grandson Brutus is there with all those blasted refugee Trojans trailing behind him. She's told him to sail off into the sunset and find an island lying beyond Gaul. He's on his way."

"How dare she tell *my* great-great-grandson what to do."

"You haven't taken much interest in his career yourself," he pointed out.

"That's beside the point." I could hardly say I'd only just heard of his existence.

Father stomped around some more. "It's out of my hands," he roared, sweeping out regally. Laughing her silk socks off, Hera swept out regally after him.

I sulked for a while and then had a brilliant idea. When Apollo came up to me to ask for my magic girdle to chase a nymph called Daphne, I refused. I'd refuse *all* such requests, save from Father, who wasn't going to know anything about it.

I announced sadly to them all that I was too distraught to consider mundane requests for my girdle, and then I tottered tragically out. There was instant consternation. I could hear it. I gave them twenty-four hours.

Two was all it took. A deputation to me was spearheaded by Apollo; Ares, Dionysus and Poseidon followed in his wake. It wasn't much, but it was something.

"We'll come with you to Albion," Apollo declared.

I hadn't been planning a trip abroad, but I could see the advantages, so I sweetly agreed that was just what I needed.

Apollo shuffled his elegant little feet. "Hera, Athene, Hephaestus, Hermes and Iris are coming too."

"Oh, good." I was surprised, since their love lives were on the lacklustre or non-existent side.

"To fight us," he amplified.

I shrieked. "*Fight?*" I only once got mixed up in a battle, and it was most disagreeable.

"We'll bring Paean along," Apollo added hastily.

"A fat lot of use that dodderer is," I wailed. The gods' doctor can't tell a *pharmaka* from a flower-pot any more.

Apollo got tough. "Do you want my darling sister Artemis to have her new temple?" Apollo can't stand his sister, who, hypocrite that she is, is always sermonizing about his reckless love life.

Ares piped up: "Go on, Aphrodite, please. I haven't had a good fight for a long time."

I was tempted to say that if he didn't mind his alphas and betas he could have one in bed tonight, but managed to retain my expression of reluctant compliance. Zeus has strictly forbidden any fighting on Olympus, which means that if anyone feels like a battle royal they have to disguise themselves as mortals. So if Albion proved to have no native mortal inhabitants of its own, the fight was going to be one-sided to say the least. I'd be on the losing side, and I could say goodbye to my temple.

I packed carefully for the trip. You never know what the weather will be like on unknown islands. I ordered the Three Graces to run me up a few pretty muslin *chitons* in saffron and red and a travelling wool *himation*, and I was ready for a showdown.

There was one snag. Uncle Poseidon whispered to me that Brutus had lost his way and gone to Gaul by mistake, where he was experimenting with fighting a few natives. When at last Uncle reported that Brutus had left Gaul, I was horrified to hear that he was heading straight for Madam Artemis's temple site in East Albion. There was only one person who could stop him.

Aeolus, god of the winds, prefers to live in a cave where he can keep his eye on his precious winds, rather than mooch around on Olympus. He is so old now I would have thought he was past sex, be he pinched me as soon as I arrived, breathless and longing for a cup of nectar.

"You're a naughty man, Aeolus," I giggled delightfully. "Would that I could be unfaithful to Ares, but I simply daren't."

Aeolus comes of a generation that believes in faithfulness, so the hand was removed, much to my relief.

"Do you feel like a good blow, Aeolus?"

Unfortunately he mistook my meaning, so it was some time

before we got down to bronze tacks. After that he was undried brick-mud in my hands, and obligingly trotted out of the cave, taking a blustery strong wind on its lead with him.

He came back highly satisfied. "I've blown all the Trojan ships away from the east of the island and round to the west. There's a piece of land sticking out from Albion like a fat thigh and boot, and I've selected a nice river half-way down the thigh."

"How clever," I said admiringly, quickly donning my *chiton* again, in case he felt refreshed after his work.

As luck would have it, Zeus called an emergency meeting of the gods to discuss the political situation in the House of Atreus, and as he might have noticed if we'd none of us been present and all the chariots had been out on hire, we had to postpone our travel arrangements yet again. So when we finally hovered over Albion's fat thigh, Brutus and his New Trojans had already ensconced themselves, although some kind of mist hid the earth beneath us.

"I think it's called drizzle," Apollo said doubtfully. "It's a kind of rain."

Whatever it was called, I didn't like it. True, it had the effect of making my gauze cling to me most attractively, but it gave a most unpleasant feeling.

There wasn't even a useful mountain like Olympus to camp on, merely a wide high moor – although when the drizzle finally decided to stop we had a good view over the plain and the valley. Poseidon informed us that the settlement we could see below, by the river up which Brutus had been blown, was called Totnes. What a pity it was already founded and so couldn't be the New Troy. It looked a nice little place, and I rather fancied fortifying it with walls and a castle, then building my temple in the centre, surrounded by plenty of little nectar shops for my worshippers. Ah well, at least its presence meant there were natives around, for if Brutus was anything like his great-grandfather at do-it-yourself he couldn't have built Totnes in two days.

From the smell of travelling nectar, the opposition was near by, and I didn't have far to look. Madam Artemis was busy setting up her altar regalia on a pile of rough stones. I was delighted that this drizzle, which had begun again, kept putting out her sacred flame.

"Darling, we're here," I called sweetly, and Madam Snake jumped.

"Oh, it's you, Aphrodite."

Her fighting troops appeared, and we surveyed the hostile army. They might outnumber us, but at least my troops were all men. Artemis's included three women and I've always had my doubts about Hermes.

"Is this what you call a temple, darling?" I enquired, looking at the stones.

She's got no sense of humour. "No, I'm going to build that in New Troy."

"Any local gods who might object?"

She hadn't thought of that, and she blanched a little.

"Are there any natives here?" I continued, while she shuffled stones around.

"None," she chortled.

"Don't crow too loudly," I replied sweetly. "Look down there . . ."

Below us in the valley, the Trojan camp – in other words Brutus, his second in command, Corineus, and a rag-tag collection of expatriate Trojans – was waking up for the morning.

At last what appeared to pass for sun in this island condescended to appear – Apollo gave me a weak smile and pointed out that his authority as sun-god was limited outside Greece. I told him that would apply to me too, just in case he had any ideas about chasing native wenches, and he promptly decided he could make the sun shine a little brighter.

I was almost sorry I'd asked. I had been watching Brutus exhorting his troops with the usual boring speeches – so like his great-grandfather – when I observed that some very long shadows were creeping towards them from behind. They emerged from the large round dwellings like beehives, and they belonged to the biggest bees I'd ever seen . . .

Albion appeared to be inhabited by giants, which was most pleasing. Besides my taking a professional interest in these tall gentlemen, it looked as though our battle would be won for us, and I could sit back and enjoy the show.

And show it was. At least fifty giants, clad in leathers and skins, four times the size of Brutus, were striding towards the unsuspecting Trojans, who were making so much noise with their hollas and cheers of encouragement to their leader that they didn't hear their visitors' approach.

When they at last noticed, their hollas redoubled and they hastily backed towards their tents. Unfortunately, the tide was out, so there was to be no quick getaway to their ships. Instead, they cowered back, protecting their goods (typical of Aeneas's family) as the dread shadows advanced.

Artemis began wailing her head off, threatening to take her forces and leap inside Brutus and his officers to see these rebels off. Her temple looked less certain by the moment.

"If you do," I informed her with great delight, "we'll take over the giants' bodies."

That stopped her in her merry chase. Giants without gods inside them she can manage. She had quite a success slaughtering Otus and Ephialtes. These twin brothers were rather nice young giants, until one of them made the mistake of falling for Madam Artemis, who naturally (or unnaturally according to the way you get your kicks) arranged for them to slaughter each other in her woods while under the impression they were shooting at a white hart. I'm *never* so deceitful.

One thing interested me about these giants. I didn't recognize any weapons. Maybe they were cannibals. Now that was a nasty thought. Zeus wouldn't thank me if I returned with five or six gods who had to be reconstructed by Paean. At last the leader, an enormous fellow, even taller than the others, produced a weapon, and I relaxed.

To my surprise, the leader set down his fearsome weapon, a round hairy boulder, in the midst of the space between the two hostile armies, and then retreated. Was he the local god, I wondered, and this his portable altar? Was he going to sacrifice the Trojans, ritually disembowelling them before our very eyes?

The giant took a loping run, and with the point of his huge leather boot kicked the boulder towards the opening of the foremost Trojan tent. Immediately a brave hero (not my grandson I noticed) stopped it. Did it have a sacred explosive flame in it? Puzzled, I watched our Trojan hero proceed to kick it all the way back to the giants, intent on demolishing one of the beehives. And so it went on.

I was immortified when Artemis cried with delight: "They're playing a game!"

"But that's *terrible*," wailed Apollo, seeing his chance of an Albion nymph diminishing every minute. Even Ares stopped sulking at the size of these magnificent specimens of manhood – I wonder— no, Aphrodite, temples first, love life later.

"They can't do that," I shrieked. "Fight, you giants, fight."

After the mortals below us had stopped cavorting around with what we realized were hide water-bottles filled with mud (no problem in this nasty wet little island), Apollo suggested timidly: "Why don't you appeal to Brutus's better nature over the temple?"

"He won't have one if Aeneas is anything to go by."

"Then disguise yourself as the giants' leader," Apollo urged. "Tell him there are plenty of fierce local gods around, and they don't need another."

I brightened up. Sometimes Sun-God Apollo, when he can raise his brains from his lower region, has flashes of brilliance.

Disguising oneself as a giant is an interesting experience. This one, the leader, was called Gogmagog, and I rather took to his boots as I pranced around getting the hang of giant strides.

I materialized in front of Brutus (or rather in front of his tent since I was three times its height), just as he was finishing his supper, a pile of something which looked unmentionable. His batman proudly informed him they were called blackberries. Brutus came to the door of his tent with a mouth stained red, and I shuddered till I realized Gogmagog would not possess such delicate sensibilities as mine.

"Good game, wasn't it?"

I impatiently waved aside the accompanying pantomime. "Gogmagog speaks," I began, adjusting my international language calculator, in case he wasn't brought up bilingual. "Now we friends you go home. Or stay in Totnes. Plenty games. Much fun."

Brutus looked wistful. "We'd like that, but unfortunately I'm on my way to found a new city."

"Take no gods with you. Me Gogmagog god of Albion. Only god wanted here is goddess of love. Build plenty temples to her."

He looked obstinate. Goodness, how like Aeneas he was.

"Alas, Great Gogmagog, I'm already spoken for. I am follower of the goddess Artemis, and she wants her temple in New Troy."

"Gogmagog forbid this new temple," I declared unpleasantly, folding my enormous arms across my enormous chest.

"Try and stop me!" Pygmy Brutus made the unsporting gesture of producing a sword, and he wasn't joking. He dispensed with any official warnings, and decided to kill me there and then, regardless of my claim to be a British god. He ran at me with his sword held high. Even though he could only reach my knee, he could do considerable damage, and I hastily backed away, shrieking: "Don't kill me. I'm your great-great-grandmother."

He lowered the sword, appearing somewhat surprised at this claim from an animal-skin-clad giant.

It was time to impress: I promptly materialized into my goddess form, glad I'd been wearing my best saffron *chiton* which flattered my flowing blonde tresses. "Don't you know *any* family history, darling Brutus?" I asked winningly. "I'm the goddess of love and your great-grandfather is my son."

Brutus was suddenly ashen-faced. "Noble King Aeneas was always boasting about having immortal blood in his veins, but I thought he was just spinning a line, you know the way he does."

"For once, he wasn't." I looked more graciously on him. "So now you know the truth—"

He interrupted me. He'd been thinking. "Once I've founded my city, does that mean you'll find me another Helen of Troy to be my queen?"

Oh yes, a chip off the old block all right. Self, self, self.

"If you dedicate your city to me by building my temple, of course, dear great-great-grandson."

His face fell. "I can't, goddess. I've already promised Artemis. My honour—"

"What about mine?" I snapped.

He drew himself up, looking as though he were in search of an epic poet to do him justice. "Perhaps, after New Troy, I could go on to found another city, a greater, more worthy—"

Smoothie. "New Troy is what I deserve, after all I did for the old one," I shouted. "It's war."

In an instant my four immortal supporters had each leapt inside a giant, and Sister Artemis's quintet rushed into Brutus's merry band. Her stalwart heroes swept into action as though we were going to fight the Trojan wars all over again. Just you wait, sister dear, I thought, as I climbed inside Gogmagog again after rousing my followers. Artemis saw me and leapt inside Brutus's second in command, Corineus. Once she was out of sight, I cunningly swapped giants with Ares, who was delighted to be Gogmagog. Brutus was left playing himself, it appeared, for he stayed right out of the way. Typical!

Weapons were real boulders this time, with the odd axe or bow and arrow. Both sides seemed to be enjoying playing Trojans versus giants (even Queen Hera was jumping up and down like a water nymph in big boots – I found out later she'd changed sides because giants were more fun), and I had to remind my followers that this was serious business.

Three full hours the battle raged; many the stone that was thrown and many the brave warrior who fell. Paean hadn't done so much work in millennia, and was run off his feet rushing from fallen body to fallen body shouting, "Don't hit me." Then fallen bodies would leap up to rejoin the fight once their wounds had had a *pharmaka* applied. Rivers of ichor ran on that mighty day of battle. I kept out of the way, of course, but it was fun watching Artemis as Corineus, assuming she would get the better of Gogmagog because he was only fragile, delicate old me.

Eventually we ran out of boulders, most of which had been tossed into the sea or down to the far end of the peninsula, and the battle descended to a wrestling match between Gogmagog and Corineus. This I really looked forward to, for Ares had promised to thrash darling sister. I'd stolen a signed planning permission before I came, so I'd have my temple before Artemis could shout "Give me a hunk!"

The wrestling match looked ridiculous, with Gogmagog (Ares) being three or four times the size of Corineus (Artemis), but my sister had developed a rather fine flying jump on to Ares's knees in the hope of toppling him over, and I had to admit he looked rather silly, hopping along with his legs fastened together, trying to throw her off. However, might is might, and Ares managed to shake her off into the air, catch her, and drop her flat on the ground. Then he thoughtfully sat astride her and raised his arm in triumph. I clapped.

It was premature.

Suddenly something strange happened. Corineus heaved up his body, throwing Gogmagog off to sprawl on the ground, then sprang up and kept his tiny foot on Gogmagog's vast body. Ares lay there, looking as if he were wondering how a girl only a quarter of his size could overturn him. Being so very masculine, he would be touchy on the point.

"Victory is ours," piped up Corineus. He bent down and picked up Gogmagog in his arms. How furious Ares's face looked at finding himself cradled in darling Artemis's arms, as she ran with him to the cliff edge and then threw poor old Gogmagog over.

"I've won my temple!" It was Snake's voice, but to my horror it was chortling in my ear from *behind me*.

"If you're there – then who . . .?" I pointed in horror at Corineus, now puffing himself up with pride and shaking everyone by the hand. Then I realized with sinking heart who was inside him.

"Aphrodite!" Father roared in fury, materializing in all his sable-browed thundery might.

"How did you know where we were?" I wailed, falling on my knees. One is apt to ask silly questions in times of stress.

"I am the All-Seeing Eye."

In fact, I discovered later, because I was temporarily missing and couldn't arrange any love trysts for him, he went in search of his own wife, prepared to put up with her for once. Of course he couldn't find her either, for she was having the time of her life inside a giant.

"How dare you disobey my ruling, child?" he continued to roar, as Sister Artemis smirked her head off.

"Because it wasn't fair," I said meekly. "You said Aeneas could found New Troy."

"Certainly," he agreed grandly. "And I always keep my word. But I never said how *many* New Troys there would be, did I?"

I wonder how he thought that one up?

Father put on his "I am All-Powerful" look, thundering, "Aeneas is busy founding a New Troy. The name Hisperia will change to Italy, and New Troy to Rome. In due course," he added hastily, seeing my tears welling up.

"Then what's Brutus doing *here*, if Aeneas's children are going to inherit this Rome?"

He explained it to me kindly, as if to an idiot child. "Brutus is going to march up to the eastern side of this island where it was always intended he should land until someone—" he said meaningfully, "arranged he should be blown here. He will found New Troy, and – here's the part you'll like, Aphrodite – in years to come New Trojans from Rome will conquer it. It, too, will change its name. Perhaps London, that has a nice ring to it."

"Oh, Father," I said delightedly, clapping my hands. "You *are* kind."

"But *my* temple will remain there," jeered Artemis.

Dolefully, I turned to Father. He shook his head regretfully. "I'm afraid so, Aphrodite. At least until such time as the Britons get some decent gods of their own."

He cast a scathing look at Gogmagog, whose head was dolefully appearing over the top of the cliff, though Ares had hopped out of him long ago.

"So it won't be there for ever," I said smugly.

"Oh yes it will," Artemis shouted, and Father continued hastily:

"Yes, but over it a new temple will be built called St Paul's."

I thought she was going to howl, and so did Father for he

added soothingly: "How would you like some trophies from this day's sport, Artemis?"

"Oh goody." Artemis cheered up: she likes a nice bloody stag to hang up in her bedchamber. "What can I have?"

Zeus pointed. Over the clifftop came Gogmagog. I thought I was seeing double at first, so I looked again. Then I realized I was. There were two of them, identical twins, both giants.

"Twins," Artemis cried in ecstasy. "Oh, I *like* twins."

It's a good job Gogmagog claimed immortality – I wouldn't give much for his chances otherwise.

"I'm Gog," announced one gloomily.

"I'm Magog," announced the other.

Zeus looked pleased. He always does when he performs a party trick successfully. "I'm appointing them sub-gods for Britain – under your command, of course, Artemis. You can march them up to London with your Trojans."

"Mighty Father, son of Cronos, thank you." She grovelled on the floor. "I'll build a very small temple for them in the public market-place, and call it the Guildhall. They will worship me above all goddesses."

Not if I have anything to do with it.

"Father, may I join the triumphant march to New Troy?" I asked humbly. Artemis eyed me suspiciously, but I can put on a good show when I need to.

I was forced to walk quite a lot of the way, partly to catch up on the family news that I'd missed for a few generations, and partly so that I could chat to that friendly pair of oversized mortals, Gog and Magog, who were happily striding towards their new home.

Some way along the route to London I spied a suitable place and suggested it as a campsite. Morpheus, who'd joined us for a day or two, obliged me by putting the rest of the party to sleep, leaving me, Gog and Magog to discuss the responsibilities of immortal status. It takes a lot to get these Albionites started. Eventually I had to come straight to the point, stripping off in all my womanly immodesty and saying: "As goddess of love, I do feel I have a professional responsibility to the New Trojans in view of the size of you Albions, but I don't know which of you to choose."

The message slowly percolated and they both began to look satisfactorily interested. "Me." They both thumped themselves on the chest.

"Alas, I can't love you both," I said regretfully (give me a chance).

"Then we fight."

"Over little me?" I opened my wondrous eyes wider. "Well, if you insist. You see that big pile of large, rough-hewn stones over there? Perhaps you could have a contest as to who could throw them furthest?"

Men are so simple-minded. The mutts did it. I stood, goddess-like, on a mound watching them toss those huge stones as if they were flower petals. From time to time I gave them a little encouragement, but they were so keen on their "fight" they hardly needed it. All the same they needed some direction.

"Darling Magog, why don't you try to throw one across those stones Gog has so clumsily dropped upright?"

"Dearest Gog, it's really you I want. Why don't you drop a couple more upright if you can?"

That night, somewhat tired after rewarding both my giants' efforts (it seemed so mean to favour only one when both had done so well, so I declared it a draw), I staggered out of our sheltering bower and walked down to the plain beneath the mound, where I could admire my new temple set so prominently against the skyline. Built by my henchmen giants, it would stand for ever – unlike the one to Artemis, ho, ho!

What should I call my glorious stone temple? I like to reward effort, so then the perfect name came to me.

I'd call it Stonehenge.

THE FIFTY-FIRST DRAGON

Heywood Broun

Heywood Broun (1888–1939) is another pretty much forgotten humorist, who was always better known in his native United States than he ever was in Britain. He was a columnist and critic for several New York newspapers, particularly the World *and the* Telegram. *An ardent socialist, he became famous for his outspokenness and his crusades for or against causes. His work is seldom reprinted today, but I think you'll find the freshness and vivacity in the following story, which first appeared in 1921, a pleasant surprise. It also gives me an opportunity to include an Arthurian fantasy. My thanks to F. Gwynplaine MacIntyre for securing a copy of the story for me.*

Of all the pupils at the knight school Gawaine le Cœur-Hardy was among the least promising. He was tall and sturdy, but his instructors soon discovered that he lacked spirit. He would hide in the woods when the jousting class was called, although his companions and members of the faculty sought to appeal to his better nature by shouting to him to come out and break his neck like a man. Even when they told him that the lances were padded, the horses no more than ponies and the field unusually soft for late autumn, Gawaine refused to grow enthusiastic. The Headmaster and the Assistant Professor of Pleasaunce were discussing the case one spring afternoon and the Assistant Professor could see no remedy but expulsion.

"No," said the Headmaster, as he looked out at the purple hills which ringed the school, "I think I'll train him to slay dragons."

"He might be killed," objected the Assistant Professor.

"So he might," replied the Headmaster brightly, but he added, more soberly, "we must consider the greater good. We are responsible for the formation of this lad's character."

"Are the dragons particularly bad this year?" interrupted the Assistant Professor. This was characteristic. He always seemed restive when the head of the school began to talk ethics and the ideals of the institution.

"I've never known them worse," replied the Headmaster. "Up in the hills to the south last week they killed a number of peasants, two cows and a prize pig. And if this dry spell holds there's no telling when they may start a forest fire simply by breathing around indiscriminately."

"Would any refund on the tuition fee be necessary in case of an accident to young Cœur-Hardy?"

"No," the principal answered, judicially, "that's all covered in the contract. But as a matter of fact he won't be killed. Before I send him up in the hills I'm going to give him a magic word."

"That's a good idea," said the Professor. "Sometimes they work wonders."

From that day on Gawaine specialized in dragons. His course included both theory and practice. In the morning there were long lectures on the history, anatomy, manners and customs of dragons. Gawaine did not distinguish himself in these studies. He had a marvelously versatile gift for forgetting things. In the afternoon he showed to better advantage, for then he would go down to the South Meadow and practice with a battle-ax. In this exercise he was truly impressive, for he had enormous strength as well as speed and grace. He even developed a deceptive display of ferocity. Old alumni say that it was a thrilling sight to see

Gawaine charging across the field toward the dummy paper dragon which had been set up for his practice. As he ran he would brandish his ax and shout "A murrain on thee!" or some other vivid bit of campus slang. It never took him more than one stroke to behead the dummy dragon.

Gradually his task was made more difficult. Paper gave way to papier-mâché and finally to wood, but even the toughest of these dummy dragons had no terrors for Gawaine. One sweep of the ax always did the business. There were those who said that when the practice was protracted until dusk and the dragons threw long, fantastic shadows across the meadow Gawaine did not charge so impetuously nor shout so loudly. It is possible there was malice in this charge. At any rate, the Headmaster decided by the end of June that it was time for the test. Only the night before a dragon had come close to the school grounds and had eaten some of the lettuce from the garden. The faculty decided that Gawaine was ready. They gave him a diploma and a new battle-ax and the Headmaster summoned him to a private conference.

"Sit down," said the Headmaster. "Have a cigarette."

Gawaine hesitated.

"Oh, I know it's against the rules," said the Headmaster. "But after all, you have received your preliminary degree. You are no longer a boy. You are a man. Tomorrow you will go out into the world, the great world of achievement."

Gawaine took a cigarette. The Headmaster offered him a match, but he produced one of his own and began to puff away with a dexterity which quite amazed the principal.

"Here you have learned the theories of life," continued the Headmaster, resuming the thread of his discourse, "but after all, life is not a matter of theories. Life is a matter of facts. It calls on the young and the old alike to face these facts, even though they are hard and sometimes unpleasant. Your problem, for example, is to slay dragons."

"They say that those dragons down in the south wood are five hundred feet long," ventured Gawaine, timorously.

"Stuff and nonsense!" said the Headmaster. "The curate saw one last week from the top of Arthur's Hill. The dragon was sunning himself down in the valley. The curate didn't have an opportunity to look at him very long because he felt it was his duty to hurry back to make a report to me. He said the monster, or shall I say, the big lizard? – wasn't an inch over two hundred feet. But the size has nothing at all to do with it. You'll find the big ones even easier than the little ones. They're far slower on their feet and less aggressive, I'm told. Besides, before you go I'm going to equip you in such fashion that you need have no fear of all the dragons in the world."

"I'd like an enchanted cap," said Gawaine.

"What's that?" answered the Headmaster, testily.

"A cap to make me disappear," explained Gawaine.

The Headmaster laughed indulgently. "You mustn't believe all those old wives' stories," he said. "There isn't any such thing. A cap to make you disappear, indeed! What would you do with it? You haven't even appeared yet. Why, my boy, you could walk from here to London, and nobody would so much as look at you. You're nobody. You couldn't be more invisible than that."

Gawaine seemed dangerously close to a relapse into his old habit of whimpering. The Headmaster reassured him: "Don't worry; I'll give you something much better than an enchanted cap. I'm going to give you a magic word. All you have to do is to repeat this magic charm once and no dragon can possibly harm a hair of your head. You can cut off his head at your leisure."

He took a heavy book from the shelf behind his desk and began to run through it. "Sometimes," he said, "the charm is a whole phrase or even a sentence. I might, for instance, give you 'To make the'— No, that might not do. I think a single word would be best for dragons."

"A short word," suggested Gawaine.

"It can't be too short or it wouldn't be potent. There isn't so much hurry as all that. Here's a splendid magic word: 'Rumplesnitz.' Do you think you can learn that?"

Gawaine tried and in an hour or so he seemed to have the word well in hand. Again and again he interrupted the lesson to inquire, "And if I say 'Rumplesnitz' the dragon can't possibly hurt me?" And always the Headmaster replied, "If you only say 'Rumplesnitz', you are perfectly safe."

Toward morning Gawaine seemed resigned to his career. At

daybreak the Headmaster saw him to the edge of the forest and pointed him to the direction in which he should proceed. About a mile away to the southwest a cloud of steam hovered over an open meadow in the woods and the Headmaster assured Gawaine that under the steam he would find a dragon. Gawaine went forward slowly. He wondered whether it would be best to approach the dragon on the run as he did in his practice in the South Meadow or to walk slowly toward him, shouting "Rumplesnitz" all the way.

The problem was decided for him. No sooner had he come to the fringe of the meadow than the dragon spied him and began to charge. It was a large dragon and yet it seemed decidedly aggressive in spite of the Headmaster's statement to the contrary. As the dragon charged it released huge clouds of hissing steam through its nostrils. It was almost as if a gigantic teapot had gone mad. The dragon came forward so fast and Gawaine was so frightened that he had time to say "Rumplesnitz" only once. As he said it, he swung his battle-ax and off popped the head of the dragon. Gawaine had to admit that it was even easier to kill a real dragon than a wooden one if only you said "Rumplesnitz".

Gawaine brought the ears home and a small section of the tail. His schoolmates and the faculty made much of him, but the Headmaster wisely kept him from being spoiled by insisting that he go on with his work. Every clear day Gawaine rose at dawn and went out to kill dragons. The Headmaster kept him at home when it rained, because he said the woods were damp and unhealthy at such times and that he didn't want the boy to run needless risks. Few good days passed in which Gawaine failed to get a dragon. On one particularly fortunate day he killed three, a husband and wife and a visiting relative. Gradually he developed a technique. Pupils who sometimes watched him from the hilltops a long way off said that he often allowed the dragon to come within a few feet before he said "Rumplesnitz". He came to say it with a mocking sneer. Occasionally he did stunts. Once when an excursion party from London was watching him he went into action with his right hand tied behind his back. The dragon's head came off just as easily.

As Gawaine's record of killings mounted higher the Headmaster found it impossible to keep him completely in hand.

He fell into the habit of stealing out at night and engaging in long drinking bouts at the village tavern. It was after such a debauch that he rose a little before dawn one fine August morning and started out after his fiftieth dragon. His head was heavy and his mind sluggish. He was heavy in other respects as well, for he had adopted the somewhat vulgar practice of wearing his medals, ribbons and all, when he went out dragon hunting. The decorations began on his chest and ran all the way down to his abdomen. They must have weighed at least eight pounds.

Gawaine found a dragon in the same meadow where he had killed the first one. It was a fair-sized dragon, but evidently an old one. Its face was wrinkled and Gawaine thought he had never seen so hideous a countenance. Much to the lad's disgust, the monster refused to charge and Gawaine was obliged to walk toward him. He whistled as he went. The dragon regarded him hopelessly, but craftily. Of course it had heard of Gawaine. Even when the lad raised his battle-ax the dragon made no move. It knew that there was no salvation in the quickest thrust of the head, for it had been informed that this hunter was protected by an enchantment. It merely waited, hoping something would turn up. Gawaine raised the battle-ax and suddenly lowered it again. He had grown very pale and he trembled violently. The dragon suspected a trick. "What's the matter?" it asked, with false solicitude.

"I've forgotten the magic word," stammered Gawaine.

"What a pity," said the dragon. "So that was the secret. It doesn't seem quite sporting to me, all this magic stuff, you know. Not cricket, as we used to say when I was a little dragon; but after all, that's a matter of opinion."

Gawaine was so helpless with terror that the dragon's confidence rose immeasurably and it could not resist the temptation to show off a bit.

"Could I possibly be of any assistance?" it asked. "What's the first letter of the magic word?"

"It begins with an 'r'," said Gawaine weakly.

"Let's see," mused the dragon, "that doesn't tell us much, does it? What sort of a word is this? Is it an epithet, do you think?"

Gawaine could do no more than nod.

"Why, of course," exclaimed the dragon, "reactionary Republican."

Gawaine shook his head.

"Well, then," said the dragon, "we'd better get down to business. Will you surrender?"

With the suggestion of a compromise Gawaine mustered up enough courage to speak.

"What will you do if I surrender?" he asked.

"Why, I'll eat you," said the dragon.

"And if I don't surrender?"

"I'll eat you just the same."

"Then it doesn't make any difference, does it?" moaned Gawaine.

"It does to me," said the dragon with a smile. "I'd rather you didn't surrender. You'd taste much better if you didn't."

The dragon waited for a long time for Gawaine to ask "Why?" but the boy was too frightened to speak. At last the dragon had to give the explanation without his cue line. "You see," he said, "if you don't surrender you'll taste better because you'll die game."

This was an old and ancient trick of the dragon's. By means of some such quip he was accustomed to paralyze his victims with laughter and then to destroy them. Gawaine was sufficiently paralyzed as it was, but laughter had no part in his helplessness. With the last word of the joke the dragon drew back his head and struck. In that second there flashed into the mind of Gawaine the magic word "Rumplesnitz", but there was no time to say it. There was time only to strike and, without a word, Gawaine met the onrush of the dragon with a full swing. He put all his back and shoulders into it. The impact was terrific and the head of the dragon flew away almost a hundred yards and landed in a thicket.

Gawaine did not remain frightened very long after the death of the dragon. His mood was one of wonder. He was enormously puzzled. He cut off the ears of the monster almost in a trance. Again and again he thought to himself, "I didn't say 'Rumplesnitz'!" He was sure of that and yet there was no question that he had killed the dragon. In fact, he had never killed one so utterly. Never before had he driven a head for anything like the same distance. Twenty-five yards was perhaps his best previous record. All the way back to the knight school he kept rumbling about in his mind seeking an explanation for what had occurred. He went to the Headmaster immediately and after closing the door told him what had happened. "I didn't say 'Rumplesnitz'," he explained with great earnestness.

The Headmaster laughed. "I'm glad you've found out," he said. "It makes you ever so much more of a hero. Don't you see that? Now you know that it was you who killed all these dragons and not that foolish little word 'Rumplesnitz.' "

Gawaine frowned. "Then it wasn't a magic word after all?" he asked.

"Of course not," said the Headmaster, "you ought to be too old for such foolishness. There isn't any such thing as a magic word."

"But you told me it was magic," protested Gawaine. "You said it was magic and now you say it isn't."

"It wasn't magic in a literal sense," answered the Headmaster, "but it was much more wonderful than that. The word gave you confidence. It took away your fears. If I hadn't told you that you might have been killed the very first time. It was your battle-ax did the trick."

Gawaine surprised the Headmaster by his attitude. He was obviously distressed by the explanation. He interrupted a long philosophic and ethical discourse by the Headmaster with, "If I hadn't of hit 'em all mighty hard and fast any one of 'em might have crushed me like a, like a—" He fumbled for a word.

"Egg shell," suggested the Headmaster.

"Like a egg shell," assented Gawaine, and he said it many times. All through the evening meal people who sat near him heard him muttering, "Like a egg shell, like a egg shell."

The next day was clear, but Gawaine did not get up at dawn. Indeed, it was almost noon when the Headmaster found him cowering in bed, with the clothes pulled over his head. The principal called the Assistant Professor of Pleasaunce, and together they dragged the boy toward the forest.

"He'll be all right as soon as he gets a couple more dragons under his belt," explained the Headmaster.

The Assistant Professor of Pleasaunce agreed. "It would be a shame to stop such a fine run," he said. "Why, counting that one yesterday, he's killed fifty dragons."

They pushed the boy into a thicket above which hung a meager cloud of steam. It was obviously quite a small dragon. But Gawaine did not come back that night or the next. In fact, he never came back. Some weeks afterward brave spirits from the school explored the thicket, but they could find nothing to remind them of Gawaine except the metal part of his medals. Even the ribbons had been devoured.

The Headmaster and the Assistant Professor of Pleasaunce agreed that it would be just as well not to tell the school how Gawaine had achieved his record and still less how he came to die. They held that it might have a bad effect on school spirit. Accordingly, Gawaine has lived in the memory of the school as its greatest hero. No visitor succeeds in leaving the building today without seeing a great shield which hangs on the wall of the dining hall. Fifty pairs of dragons' ears are mounted upon the shield and underneath in gilt letters is "Gawaine le Cœur-Hardy," followed by the simple inscription, "He killed fifty dragons." The record has never been equaled.

THE BOSCOMBE
WALTERS STORY

Robert Rankin

*Robert Rankin (b. 1949) crept into the book arena in 1981 with
the first of his Brentford trilogy,* The Antipope. *Since the same
publisher had recently invested hugely in Douglas Adams's* The
Hitchhiker's Guide to the Galaxy, *Rankin's book was a little
overshadowed, but by the time the trilogy was complete, with* The
Brentford Triangle *(1982) and* East of Ealing *(1984), his work
was being noticed. Although it inevitably came to be compared to
that of Terry Pratchett, there is little similarity. Rankin's work is
closer to Spike Milligan's* Puckoon *or Flann O'Brien's* The Third
Policeman, *although removed to an anarchic and bewildering
London. Rankin later added a fourth novel to his "trilogy", the
superbly entitled* The Sprouts of Wrath *(1988). He has since
produced his Armageddon trilogy, the Cornelius Murphy series,
and such one-off books as* The Most Amazing Man Who Ever
Lived *(1995),* The Garden of Unearthly Delights *(1995) and*
A Dog Called Demolition *(1996), from which the following
story comes.*

"The cruel fact of the matter," sighed the sympathetic dermatologist, "is that some people are simply born – how shall I put this? – ugly. While some have complexions like peaches and cream, others resemble glasspaper, or places of acute volcanic activity. Sadly you are one of the latter."

And there was no doubt about it, Boscombe Walters was one ugly bastard. And it wasn't just the pustules. It was the entire physiognomic caboodle. The heavy jowls. The flaccid mouth. The bulbous nose. The terrible toad-like eyes.

These now glared balefully at the handsome dermatologist.

"But it needn't be a handicap," this fellow was saying. "Many a man born without the advantage of conventional good looks has gone on to find fame and celebrity. Has won the respect of his peers and the love of a good woman. Think of, well . . ." He paused for thought. "Think of Sidney James, or Rondo Hatton.*"

Boscombe thought of them. Both were dead, he thought.

"It's not what a man looks like. It's what he has inside him."

Boscombe raised a grubby mit to squeeze a prominent boil on his neck and release a little of what *he* had inside *him*.

"Oh, please *don't*," implored the doctor. "The surgery has just been redecorated."

Boscombe returned his mit to his lap and scratched his groin with it. "So what you're saying," he growled, "is that you can do sweet sod all to help me."

Dr Kinn, for such was the physician's name, coughed politely. He had come to dread the weekly sessions with this unsavoury little man. An aura of evil surrounded him, which made him about as welcome as King Herod at a baby show. "Go out and live your life," the doctor advised. "Rejoice that you are alive. Revel in your existence. Think positively."

Boscombe rose negatively from his chair. "Bloody quack," said he.

"Excuse me?"

* Now legendary star of *The Creeper* and *The Brute Man*.

"I said, bloody quack. As in doctor, rather than duck."

"You can collect your usual prescription at the reception area," said Dr Kinn, moving papers around on his desk. "And, er, come back and see me in, what shall we say, six months?"

Boscombe hawked up a green gobbet of phlegm the size of a glass eye and spat it onto the carpet. "That to you," said he.

"Make that *one year*," said the doctor. "And see yourself out."

Boscombe had recently taken to wearing tropical kit, as it made the mosquito net he had stitched onto his solar toupee in order to conceal his face seem a little more in keeping. The khaki shorts, however, flattered neither his beer belly nor his bow legs.

From the surgery in Abaddon Street to the chemist's on the main road is a fairly short shuffle, and as it was term time there were no children about for Boscombe to cuff as he passed upon his dismal way.

A cat or two to kick at though.

Beneath his breath the ugly man cursed darkly. He would do for that bloody quack. Pop around at lunch-time and loosen his bicycle brakes, watch him sail down the hill towards the traffic lights, then—

Boscombe Walters sniggered. "Then *splat* and physician heal thyself."

There was no spark of goodness in Boscombe. He was ugly through and through. From the outside to the in and out again. Boscombe cared for no one and no one cared for him. And that was just the way he liked it. Ugliness suited him fine. He'd made a career out of it (although not one that was likely to bring him fame and celebrity and the love of a good woman). Boscombe's problem was the spots. The boils! The buboes! If only he could rid himself of these, then everything would be as fine as it was ever likely to be. Which, though far from perfect, was perfect enough for him.

Boscombe took a short cut down an alleyway, on the off-chance that there might be dustbins to ignite, or ladies' items upon a line that he might add to his collection.

Sadly there was neither, but as he slunk along, muttering

sourly, he did chance to notice a bright little card that was pinned to a back entrance gate.

It had the look of those printed postcard jobbies which always add that essential touch of colour to the otherwise drab interiors of telephone boxes.

This one, however, did not promote the skills of some lady "trained in those arts which amuse men". This one bore a mysterious logo and the words:

> DR POO PAH DOO. OBEAH MAN.
> HERBALIST. SKIN SPECIALIST.
> BMX CYCLE REPAIRS.

Out of habit, born from badness, Boscombe plucked the little card from the gate and crumpled it between the fingers of his rarely washed hands. He was about to cast it groundward when a little voice inside his head said, "Hang about there, pal."

Boscombe sniffed deeply, brought up another ball of phlegm and sent it skimming back along the alleyway. And then he uncrumpled the card. DR POO PAH DOO. *SKIN SPECIALIST!*

"Luck," said the ugly man. "Luck indeed."

But was this luck? What was an Obeah Man? Something to do with voodoo, wasn't it? And that was all crap, that kind of thing. "Nah," said Boscombe, recrumpling the card. "Waste of time."

But then, DOCTOR. SKIN SPECIALIST. HERBALIST? It had to be worth a try. It couldn't hurt. And a spotty man *is* a desperate man.

Boscombe thrust the card into a pocket of his safari jacket and pressed open the gate. It moved upon groaning hinges to reveal a squalid backyard. There was a mound of mouldy papers and a black cat.

Boscombe skirted the mound and kicked the cat.

"Meoooow!" it went.

The back door was open. Boscombe didn't knock.

It was dim and dank within. A dour hallway led to a flight of uncarpeted stairs. A sign on the wall read, "Dr Poo Pah Doo.

First Floor." Somewhere in the distance a dripping tap spelt messages in morse.

Boscombe trudged up the stairs. This house smelled none too good. This house smelled of dampness and old bed linen.

This house smelled like Boscombe's house.

On the first floor was a single door and upon this a brass plate which bore the name of Dr Poo Pah Doo.

Boscombe knocked.

"Come on in then," called a deep, brown voice. "And bring yo' bike."

Boscombe entered.

The room was souped in ganja smoke. A single bulb, yellow-hued and naked, cast a wan crepuscular glow.

Bits and bobs of bicycles brought an occasional glitter. But there was nothing here that really offered welcome.

"Welcome," said something.

Boscombe strained his toad-likes. Close by in the fug something sat. It was a beefy-looking something and it wore a top hat decorated with chicken feathers. Two large dark hands tinkered with an alloy chainset.

"What de trouble?" asked Dr Poo Pah Doo, for such was this something. "Bin doin' de bunny-hops and done twisted yo' frame?"

"I don't have a bike," said Boscombe.

"Well, I don't do skateboards. Trucks too damn expensive."

"Don't have a skateboard either." Boscombe turned to take his leave. This obviously *was* a waste of time.

"Where yo' damn well goin'?" asked the Obeah Man. "What yo' problem anyhow?"

"Skin." Boscombe had one hand on the door. "I saw your sign. Skin specialist, it said."

"And in capital letters." The tall top hat rose to expose the face beneath. It was an African face. A noble warrior's face. Fierce, with piercing almond eyes, but smiling a mouthload of golden teeth. "Come here. Let's have a look at you."

Boscombe did a two-step shuffle, raised his mosquito net and inclined his head towards the sitter.

"Whoa!" went this body. "Not so god-damn close. Yo' got a

real rake of trouble and grief there, boy. Yo' should get someone fix that for you."

"Someone?"

Dr Poo Pah Doo sniffed at Boscombe. "I can smell yo' aura, boy and it don't smell good. It smell wicked. Yo' wicked 'cos yo' ugly, or ugly 'cos yo' wicked? Which it be?"

"You spades know bugger all!" said Boscombe, who numbered racism amongst his more appealing qualities. "I'm off."

"Yeah. Yo' do that. Come in here, uglying up my workshop. I not make yo' pretty."

"As if you could."

"Oh, I could do it, wicked man. I could do it. But I won't. Go on now. Scoot."

Boscombe stood his ground. "What *could* you do?" he asked.

"I could fix up that face of yours. Make that face as smooth as a baby's bum bum."

"How?"

"There's ways."

"What ways?"

"Old ways."

"Mumbo-jumbo."

"If yo' think it's that, then that's what it is. It don't work unless yo' believe. Why do yo' think I sit here fixin' bikes all the damn day?"

"Probably because your old ways ain't worth shite," Boscombe suggested.

"Then reckon yo' know best, wicked man. Go on now, scoot. Believe in nothing. Be wicked ugly man all yo' god-damn life. See if I care."

"How much?" Boscombe asked.

"How much I care? Not much. Not damn all."

"How much to make my face as smooth as a baby's bum bum?"

"Hundred pounds."

"How bloody much?"

"Hundred pounds. How much it worth to yo'? I charge you two hundred pounds and that's my final offer."

"Done!" said Boscombe, who didn't intend to be.

★　　★　　★

An hour passed and during this time various prayers were offered up to less-than-Christian deities. Some salt was thrown. A frozen chicken was symbolically sacrificed.

A cheque for two hundred pounds changed hands and a bottle of yellow pills came into Boscombe's possession.

"Trust it must be," said the Obeah Man. "Now go, wicked man. Take one pill each day at dawn and look not into a mirror until the seventh day. Then all be done."

"As smooth as a baby's bum bum?" Boscombe asked.

"As smooth as a baby's bum bum."

Boscombe went off whistling: he had omitted to sign the cheque.

The days dragged into a week. Boscombe took one pill each dawn and on the seventh he rushed to his mirror.

And there a great wonder was to be revealed.

Boscombe blinked and blinked again. The hideous pustules had vanished without a trace. The skin, so long pitted and ghastly was now pure and unsullied, sensuous and soft.

The horrible pimples were gone.

So too were Boscombe's nose, ears and eyebrows.

And as he stared, his left eye smoothed over, closely followed by his right.

Boscombe was about to remark upon the somewhat Gothic turn that events had suddenly taken, when his mouth vanished, leaving his entire visage as smooth as a baby's bum bum.

And he suffocated.

Little Epilogue Bit

Dr Kinn, who viewed the spot-encrusted face of the deceased, said that he "appeared to have died from natural causes", but declined further examination of the body on the grounds that he was "far too ugly to look at closely".

"Quack indeed," said he, as he rode off on his BMX to his chess evening with Dr Poo Pah Doo.

FALL'N INTO THE SEAR

James A. Bibby

James Bibby has been contributing jokes and sketches to such television series as Not the Nine O'Clock News, Three of a Kind *and the* Lenny Henry Show *for twenty years, but has only recently entered the comic fantasy book world with his spoofs on Robert E. Howard's Conan stories,* Ronan the Barbarian *(1995) and* Ronan's Rescue *(1996), both translations from the Gibberish. The following is a brand-new story set in the same world and specially written for this anthology.*

Mavol watched with a frown on his face as the half-orc landlord slouched across the malodorous dining-room with a tray of food and dumped it sullenly on the table in front of him. He rubbed his eyes tiredly and stared down at the revolting mess that was apparently supposed to be breakfast. There was a slab of grey bread that had the appearance and consistency of pumice, a mug of muddy brown liquid that looked and smelt as though yesterday's bedding had been washed in it, and a single cracked egg that had reputedly been boiled, although what it had been boiled in was anybody's guess, for it had turned a malevolent shade of orange, and pale green fumes were eddying from the crack in the shell.

Although he had been in Malvenis for less than fifteen hours, Mavol was feeling seriously pissed off with the city and, more especially, with this foul, verminous hovel in which he had been forced to stay. He had travelled a long, long way to get there and the four-week journey had been tiring, especially as he had been forced to finish it on foot. His horse had spread a plate as he left the elven-realm of Nevin and, misguidedly, he had tried to fix it himself, for he was the proud owner of a signed copy of *Delia Cook's Smithery Course*, the best-selling pamphlet that had put half of Midworld's blacksmiths and farriers out of business. Unfortunately, he was no Delia, and his horse had developed a gangrenous pastern and had died shortly afterwards.

He had eventually trudged into Malvenis the previous evening, hot, dusty and tired, and looking forward to a bath and a good meal in a comfortable tavern. But, to his chagrin, he had found that the Millennium Midsummer Games were taking place in the city, and nearly every lodging-place was fully booked. In the end he had managed to find a bed in this run-down slum in the orcish quarter, but he had seen better facilities in a pigsty. The place had no bath, the food had no taste, and the bed had no sheets, just a stained and lumpy mattress. And then he had woken in the middle of the night to find that the lumps were moving, and were in fact huge bed-bugs. Luckily, they must have been feeding off orc-blood recently, for they were all as pissed as farts, and not one of them had managed to get it together long enough to puncture his skin. But their drunken, tuneless singing had kept him awake for the rest of the night.

Mavol stared apprehensively at his egg and then, with a sinking heart and a rising stomach, he picked up the stained spoon and hacked off the top of the shell. Green fumes billowed out and he gagged at the mephitic smell. The semi-liquid matter inside was green and rancid, and whatever the small foetus nestling beside the yolk had been destined to turn into, it wasn't any variety of bird. For a few moments he stared disgustedly at the contents of the egg, and then he looked across to the half-orc landlord, who had stopped beside a recently vacated table and was scraping bits of food debris off the stained, yellowing tablecloth with a filthy talon and popping them into his mouth.

"Hey, dung-face!" called Mavol.

The landlord looked up, and Mavol hurled the egg at him with unerring accuracy. It smashed into fragments against the half-orc's cavernous nose, and Mavol followed it with the bread, the mug, and (just for good measure) the table. Then, picking up his backpack, he strolled across the room, stepped over the landlord's unconscious body, and went in search of a clean, well-run bath-house and a decent meal.

It was the fifth day of the Midsummer Games, and the sun was hammering down on Fadbasrad, a private of the Malvenis City Guard, as though it couldn't stand the man. The first four days had been wet and misty: typical Malvenis weather, for the city was set high in the foothills of the Irridic Mountains and seemed to attract clouds like a magnet. But today of all days the sun had decided to show just what it could do when it really tried.

Fadbasrad was on sentry duty at the entrance to the Games, which were taking place in the fields outside the Malvenis city walls, but his mind wasn't really on the job. His head was thumping like a bass drum, his legs were shaking like those of a minute-old foal, and his breakfast seemed to have quarreled with his stomach and was threatening to walk out on it any second now.

In fact, Fadbasrad could really have done with sneaking off home for an hour or two, but he knew full well that to desert his post would be to end up spending several days on fatigues under the vengeful eye of Sergeant Haydest, known throughout the Guard as Haydest the Sadist, and so Fadbasrad stood there clinging to the upright haft of his spear like ivy to a tree, cursing his stupidity and praying for some nice, cool, soothing rain.

It was his own damn fault, he knew that. Only someone who was tired of living would have gone on a pub-crawl with a gang of orcs the night before a morning sentry duty. Orcs were creatures with such a high habitual intake of alcohol that their physiology had evolved to become dependent upon the daily consumption of at least the equivalent of a bottle of brandy. Nor was it merely their appetite for drink that was life-threatening to a human:

orc party games tended to be so violent and bizarre that the average orcish week-long drinking spree had a mortality rate of more than 15 per cent. Fadbasrad had been lucky to wake up that morning with his head still attached to his shoulders.

He winced and closed his eyes against the blinding glare as the sun turned the heat up an extra notch. Maybe he hadn't been so lucky, after all. His gleaming metal helm seemed to be frying his brain, and his head felt as though it was going to burst. *By the Gods*, he thought, miserably. *Surely I didn't drink enough to merit such a bastard of a hangover?*

The trouble was, he'd got a bit out of practice lately. In fact, he hadn't been drinking at all for the past couple of months in an effort to lose a little weight and get a bit fitter. He'd decided he needed to do something when the Sergeant had started calling him Fatbastard. And he had to admit his wife had a point when she said he was an overweight, out-of-condition slob. These days, sex left him panting and exhausted – and that was just climbing the stairs to the bedroom.

In fact, had he but known it, Fadbasrad was absolutely right when he thought that he hadn't drunk enough to merit the reaction he was suffering. But, unfortunately for him, Rettch, the Goddess of Hangovers, had had her eye on him for quite a while. This diet of his had caused her no end of inconvenience, and on seven separate occasions she had been forced to cancel the hangovers she'd had lined up for him when he had backed out of a prospective night out with the boys at the very last minute. Rules are rules, even for the Gods, and when Rettch had one night threatened to visit a long-overdue hangover on this recalcitrant human, despite the fact he was only having a quiet night in with a cup of cocoa, Gomal (the God of Gods) had given her a right old ticking off. And so, when at last Fadbasrad had decided to drown his sorrows the previous evening after the Sergeant had made his day a particularly miserable one, the vengeful Rettch had visited all seven hangovers on him in one vast, economy-sized maelstrom of pain.

A loud *Crash*! and a burst of drunken cheering from one of the nearby beer tents caused Fadbasrad to open his eyes and peer blearily across. Most were doing good business, for the day's programme of events was close to starting, but the tent specializing in orcish beers was packed out with revelling orcs and was bulging and writhing like a sackful of eels. Malvenis was twinned with High Meneal, the orcish city in far-off Frundor, whose visiting delegation of town dignitaries had spent the entire first four days of the Games in the beer tents. Malvenis had quite a sizeable orc population of its own, being so close to the Irridic Mountains, and things were beginning to liven up quite nicely. Fadbasrad could scent trouble brewing.

But then his nostrils caught a faint waft of ale from the tents, and his throat started to go into spasms. Clamping one hand over his mouth and fighting desperately to keep the contents of his stomach where they belonged, Fadbasrad turned and concentrated on watching the stream of spectators who were arriving for the day's events. He recognized quite a few, but there were many faces that were unfamiliar, for folk had travelled from towns as far afield as Ilex and Far Tibreth to watch or participate in the Games.

He nodded a greeting as his next-door neighbour went past, and immediately regretted it for the throbbing in his head had started up again. He lifted a hand to shield his eyes from the burning sun, and it was then that he realized he was being watched. A man had stopped just inside the gates, and was peering at him with a thoughtful expression on his face. Fadbasrad peered back, wondering why he was being stared at, for he was certain he had never seen the other man before. The guy was no more than average height, with long, dark hair and a thin, deeply tanned face, but there was something about his poise and muscle-tone that hinted he was a warrior. Mind you, the dirty great sword that he wore slung down his back, Southern-fashion, was a bit of a give-away as well.

Fadbasrad straightened uneasily and stared rigidly ahead of him, trying to give the impression that he was a sentry who was right on the ball. The guy might just be a passer-by, but then he might also be another of Haydest's little spies. For a full minute Fadbasrad stood there at attention, peering straight ahead, but then he flicked his eyes nervously sideways to see if he was still being watched. The man had switched his attention to the small group of picketing pedants by the gate, but even as Fadbasrad glanced at him he turned back and stared straight at him. And then, to Fadbasrad's dismay, a small, rather cruel smile started to play about his lips and he began to walk decisively towards the perspiring, hung-over sentry.

After a long, slow, luxurious bath, Mavol had discovered that, as it was the week of the Midsummer Games, nearly every tavern in the city was opening early and serving breakfast. He had eaten in a wine-bar called Dipso Facto in Blood Lane, and had then spent an hour browsing through the local news sheets and reading about the day's events. Some of them sounded quite interesting and so, although he was now just a couple of days' travel away from the culmination of his quest, he had reckoned that he could spare a few hours and had decided to spend an afternoon watching the gladiators.

With his hunger sated he had felt much happier, but he was still in just the right mood for a little devilment. He had been delighted to discover a small group of protesting pedants near the entrance to the Games, waving their placards and chanting dejectedly. They were objecting to the fact that the Millennium Games were being held in the year 1000, when in fact (they insisted) the Millennium didn't really begin until 1001. But they hadn't got very far. The vast majority of people merely laughed at them, and they had quickly become objects of ridicule. Folk had started bringing decaying fruit and vegetables to the Games to throw at them on the way in, and Mavol had joined in with a will. A couple of direct hits had left one of them with a face that was covered in bits of rotten tomato, and Mavol had turned away feeling a good deal more content. But then he had seen that the sentry on duty by the gate was looking distinctly nauseous and had decided that perhaps it was time for a little more light relief.

Mavol stopped in front of Fadbasrad and gave him one of his brightest smiles. He took in the bloodshot eyes, the sheen of sweat, the pasty, yellow tinge to the skin and the foul breath. *I was right*, he thought to himself. *The guy has one mother of a hangover.*

"Good morning," he said, brightly. "I couldn't help noticing that you look a little unwell. That poor man must have been on sentry duty all morning, I thought to myself, he must be faint with hunger. I wonder if he'd like me to fetch him a little snack. Perhaps some fat-pork lightly fried in lard . . . ?"

"Hurp!" said Fadbasrad.

"Or maybe a nice runny egg sandwich? Here, are you all right? You've gone a very strange colour . . ." Mavol paused, apparent concern written all over his face, and tried not to grin. The guard's face had turned the colour of old cheese, and his throat was jerking convulsively like that of a lizard.

"I know," Mavol continued. "I've got just the thing for a hungry soldier!" Grinning, he hauled an old *pasaroni** out of his backpack and held it under the sweating guard's nose.

"How about some nice, ripe garlic sausage?" he asked, wafting it gently to and fro, and then he leapt smartly backwards and contemplated the resulting eruption with something approaching awe.

If the Midsummer Games had included an event called the Chucking-up Cup or the Marathon Hurling Championship, then Fadbasrad would have been a certainty for the gold medal. Once he had got started, there was simply no stopping him. He seemed to be putting his whole heart into the performance – and several other organs as well, to judge from the vocal accompaniment he was providing.

"Ah, the poor man," sympathized an elderly matron who had stopped near by. "He must have a weak stomach."

"Weak?" muttered her husband. "You must be joking! Look how far he's chucking that stuff!"

Mavol watched from a safe distance, but as he did so, the slow realization crept over him that he wasn't getting the same pleasure from such a successful prank as he used to. In fact, as he viewed the wretched guard's discomfort, he realized that he was feeling pity more than anything else; pity mixed with another unaccustomed emotion that left him feeling vaguely uncomfortable and unclean, and made him want to creep quietly away. With astonishment, he realized that it was guilt.

He swore quietly under his breath. To his disgust, he seemed

* *Pasaroni* is a Behanian garlic sausage which smells rather like the inside of a gladiator's jockstrap. Unfortunately, it is nothing like as pleasant to chew.

to have developed something of a conscience in the past few months, and he was beginning to feel a bit concerned. If he was to accomplish the quest that he had set himself, and for which he had travelled all the way to Malvenis, a conscience was going to be about as much use as a chocolate condom.

Frowning, he turned to push his way through the crowd of onlookers when a sudden fanfare of orc trumpets blasted out, making his head ring. It was a wonderfully discordant fanfare, and the trumpets seemed to be treating it more like a test of stamina than a musical event. Beginning more or less together, they set off at different paces and in different keys. The clear winner was the one that began in B flat and accidentally moved into F sharp near the end. C sharp pushed it all the way and actually took over the lead at the half-way point, but then ran out of puff and died away with an agonized glissade in the finishing straight. The others trumpeters either gave up completely or trailed in at intervals afterwards, with E sharp vibrato bringing up the rear and finishing some distance behind after a bad attack of hiccups.

The final wavering notes died away and there was a stunned silence which lasted a good thirty seconds. Orc fanfares were notoriously uneven, but this had been something truly spectacular. Fadbasrad, had he been capable of speech, could have explained why: it had been the orc trumpeters with whom he had got so drunk the previous night. But then the silence was broken by the town crier, who began to announce the start of the afternoon's events. A thickening stream of people began to flow towards the gladiatorial arena that had been set up in the field ahead, and Mavol, after one last guilty glance at the now prostrate sentry, went with them.

Algin Bonecrusher, the undefeated champion gladiator, was not the sort of person who anyone would want to take to tea at grandma's house − not unless they wanted grandma to be disembowelled, flayed, trimmed and stapled to the kitchen ceiling. Standing well over 6 ft tall, he looked like the result of an illicit liaison between a gorilla and a bear. His chest appeared to have been constructed using barrel-staves as ribs, and his strong, powerful arms reached almost to his knees. His head was bald and gleaming, and a thick, black, bushy beard covered his chin. From one ear hung a gold earring so large that a chicken could have roosted in it, and his eyes glittered with a red, malevolent fire, like a demon that has had a few whiskies too many and is looking for trouble. He was clad only in leather trousers, but his body-hair sprouted so thickly that from a distance he appeared to be wearing something that had been very badly knitted.

Algin glowered round at the spectators crammed onto the tiers of wooden benches encircling the temporary arena and growled threateningly, then snorted with satisfaction at the chorus of boos that greeted him. Reaching down, he jerked his sword free from the mangled remains of his latest victim and brandished it above his head. The chorus of boos redoubled, but Algin just smiled coldly and began to strut round the arena, waving his blood-stained sword and taunting the spectators. He was exactly the sort of gladiator that the paying public loved to hate, for he was fast, brutal, totally unsporting and he knew how to wind up a crowd. There had almost been a riot when he had shaken his opponent's hand after his previous bout, for it had no longer been attached to his opponent's arm, and the blood had splattered over quite a few of the ringside spectators.

From a seat in the second tier, Mavol watched the victorious gladiator thoughtfully. The man would have been lethal enough bound by Warrior Codes, but as a gladiator he was unfettered by such conventions, and he seemed to know every dirty, underhand, sordid trick that there was. Mavol had come to the rapid conclusion that Algin was by far the most dangerous fighter he had ever seen.

As Algin continued his lap of dishonour, the Master of the Games signalled to his assistants from his position on a podium beside the arena. Immediately, three of them scurried across the trampled, muddy turf to where the bloody remains of the last victim lay, and began to drag them out of the arena. The Master winced at the sight of one of them carrying a severed arm slung over one shoulder, then raised his megaphone to his mouth to announce the final results.

"Ladies and gentlemen, for the fifth year running, the champion gladiator is Algin Bonecrusher." He paused to allow the booing to reach a crescendo and die away a little.

"In a moment," he continued, "I will ask Mellodie, the reigning Malvenis Carnival Queen, to step forward and present Algin with the Victor Ludorum crown." He looked down to where Mellodie was standing, shaking with fear, and made a mental note to recommend to the committee that next year they change the presentation ceremony. Algin was always unpleasantly enthusiastic about thanking the carnival queen, and the poor girl last year had ended up having hysterics. Presenting him with the trophy was such an abhorrent and unwelcome job that there had only been five entrants for the carnival queen competition this year, and two of them had been totally batty old crones.

"But firstly," continued the Master of the Games, "as tradition demands, any spectator here present is entitled to challenge Algin to defend his title. To do so will cost a single gold *tablon*, but should the challenger be victorious, he will receive the whole of the winner's purse! Is there a challenger?"

The arena fell silent as the crowed waited, hoping against hope that someone would step forward. The Master of the Games gave the crowd a cursory glance, knowing full well that there would be no takers. One person had dared to challenge Algin in his first year as champion, and he had died so horribly that even the orcs in the crowd had been taken aback. After the initial flurry of blows, the poor man had turned and run, but Algin had caught him when he tripped over his own intestines, and had dispatched him in a way that still made the Master of the Games feel queasy when he thought about it. He shook his head to dispel the memory, and was just drawing breath to continue when another voice broke the silence.

"I will challenge him."

Mavol's voice rang out around the arena, and the whole crowd turned their heads as one, craning their necks to see who this suicidally brave volunteer could be. Then, as he rose from his seat, they began to cheer. Although he was no more than average height and build, it was obvious from the sword slung casually down his back that he was a fighting man, not some drunken out-of-towner who didn't know what he was letting himself in for, and so, in the hope that at last someone might give Algin a run for his money, they cheered him unreservedly.

Mavol stepped forward onto the muddied grass of the arena and turned, acknowledging their approbation with a wave of his hand. He had been as surprised as the rest of the crowd to hear the challenge issuing forth from his mouth, for this was not the reason he had travelled to Malvenis. But he had always been keen to test himself against the best, and Algin Bonecrusher was without doubt the best fighter he had ever seen.

Above him, the Master of the Games was staring down at him with a mixture of surprise, awe, and obvious doubt about his sanity.

"Are you sure you wish to challenge the Victor Ludorum?" he called.

"I am."

The Master of the Games shrugged and turned to the far end of the arena, where Algin was staring towards his challenger like a hungry gorilla that has just noticed a small monkey stealing its last banana.

"Algin Bonecrusher, Champion of Gladiators, do you accept this challenge?"

From the roar of anger and the vigorous gestures he was making with his sword, it was obvious that Algin had every intention of accepting. The giant gladiator began to stride purposefully towards Mavol, growling threats as he came, and the crowd fell silent as the challenger drew his sword and stood calmly waiting, poised and ready, feet widely spaced on the damp, scarred sward.

To the onlookers it seemed that Algin would quite simply steamroller his foe into the ground, but when he was a few yards away he paused, his sword held motionless in front of him in a two-handed grip, his burning eyes staring balefully down at his rival. He liked to give new opponents a chance to examine his massive bulk and his vast reach from close up. It started their nerves fraying, and sometimes he had known them to turn and run. But for once the tactic seemed not to be working. His challenger just stared back, his flint-grey eyes steady, his mouth slightly bent in an annoying smirk. Algin decided that a bit of sledging might do the trick.

"Okay, sonny. You'd better know how you're going to die. I'll be aiming for your groin, and this sword is gonna carve straight through your . . ."

"Ah, blow it out of your wobbly great backside, fat-boy," interrupted his opponent, and Algin stared down at him in open disbelief.

"You what?" he roared.

"You heard me, lard-arse. Now, why don't you stop poncing around like some bloated great queen, and then maybe we could get this thing sorted."

For a moment Algin was so taken aback that he was rooted to the spot, his mouth opening and shutting wordlessly. Then, as a murderous rage flooded through him, his face darkened and he began literally to shake with anger.

Mavol beckoned to the huge gladiator.

"Come on, then," he invited. "I haven't got all day. Or is your mouth even bigger than that mountainous great belly . . ."

With a roar that could have been heard several planets away, Algin threw himself forward, slashing and hacking furiously with his lethally fast sword, and Mavol gave ground, forced rapidly backwards by the sheer weight of blows. The crowd gasped, giving vent to a collective expression of fear for the challenger, as such was the speed and savagery of the attack that it seemed he must surely be overcome in seconds.

But although Mavol was forced backwards, he defended himself with fluent, practised ease, deflecting the murderous blows with a deftness and subtlety that, to the onlookers, was almost beyond belief. Gradually, Algin's attack began to slow, and a look of almost comical concern planted itself on his face. He had fought many, many people over the past five years, and in every contest he had known that he was the stronger, faster man. Every contest until this one.

All of a sudden, Mavol switched to the attack. His broadsword flashed and glinted in the brilliant sunshine as it weaved through a complicated tracery of probing, testing attacks. Now it was Algin's turn to defend himself, but there was nothing deft about the desperate, panic-stricken parries with which he somehow contrived to fend off his challenger's blows. Slowly but surely he was driven back across the churned-up, treacherous turf, until his back was to the wooden fencing of the arena.

For perhaps a minute the huge gladiator managed to keep his challenger at bay, but then Mavol suddenly feinted and spun round, delivering a lethal back-hand slice towards Algin's stomach which curved upwards at the last moment to graze across his throat, leaving a thin red line across the bare flesh. Algin's sword drooped, and he stared at his challenger in baffled incomprehension. Then his eyes glazed over, his head sagged backwards and the red line widened to a gash, then a grinning chasm. Blood fountained out in a crimson tide, and Mavol stepped backwards as Algin crumpled lifelessly to the ground.

For an instant there was total silence, and then the entire arena erupted. For five years the crowd had waited for someone who could rid them of the brutal, leering champion that they had come to loath. Now, out of the blue, this stranger had challenged him and had beaten him, not by luck but by vastly superior skill, and they stood and cheered him to the echo.

Mavol stood staring round, taken aback by this reception. Hesitantly, he lifted his sword in a salute to the crowd, and was met by an immediate increase in the cheering. In something of a daze he began a lap of honour, and to his astonishment, people began to throw flowers into the arena as he passed them. Even more astonishingly, amongst the flowers were several small, wispy items of extremely feminine underwear. Resisting the almost overwhelming urge to pick up the underwear and stuff it in a pocket, Mavol blinked, and tried to not to smirk. Popularity was a new experience for him, and he was finding it extremely pleasant.

From his position on the podium, the Master of the Games watched with satisfaction. An exciting new champion was just what the Games needed. Waiting until the applause began to die down a fraction, he lifted his megaphone and began to speak.

"Ladies and gentlemen! By virtue of our traditional Right of Challenge, and through his strength and guile, the title of Victor Ludorum has worthily been taken by the challenger!"

He paused to lead a fresh round of applause, then signalled to the officials clustered around Mellodie that they should get ready for the presentation of the trophy. As they fussed and hurried her out into the arena, he raised the megaphone once again.

"Champion," he boomed. "Will you give us your name?"

Deciding that maybe a little formality wouldn't go amiss, Mavol turned and bowed deeply to the podium, and the crowd quietened to hear him speak.

"I am Mavol. I come from Vandor," he called.

"Then, Mavol, may it please you to accept the title and the crown from the fair hand of our Carnival Queen."

Mavol watched as Mellodie walked towards him, flanked by several nervous officials. Her face was flushed with excitement, and her eyes sparkled as she stopped in front of him and looked up into his face. He stared back, feeling definite stirrings of interest. She was beautiful! It had been a long time since a girl had looked at him like that . . .

All of a sudden he realized that one of the officials was gesturing for him to kneel. He did so, resting one knee on the grass, and Mellodie stepped forward and placed a golden laurel wreath on his head. Then, bending, she kissed him on each cheek, lingering over the kisses slightly longer than was necessary. Her long, raven-black hair brushed his shoulder, and the smell of her perfume washed over his senses.

"Thank you," she whispered, and amidst the roar of the crowd he knew he was the only one who could hear her words. "Thank you for saving me from that . . . that beast! I am *very* grateful."

She stared directly and meaningfully into his eyes, and Mavol suddenly realized just how grateful she was. But before he had time to do anything sensible, such as asking her what her star sign was, or whether she was doing anything that evening, the Games Master's voice boomed out again.

"Ladies and gentlemen . . . Champion's Bane and Victor Ludorum, Mavol of Vandor!"

The crowd gave a huge shout of approbation, and Mavol stared round in astonishment as people began scrambling over the wooden fences into the arena and came flooding towards them. Seconds later he was surrounded by a cheering, grinning mob, although they kept at a respectful distance. One thing they had learned after five years of having Algin as champion was that if you upset a gladiator, he was quite capable of turning your entrails into your extrails in one flash of his sword.

For much of his life, Mavol had dreamt of being the focus of an adulatory crowd of spectators, but now that it was happening, he was finding it a bit of a pain. Right now, the one thing above all that he wanted to do was to have a quiet private conversation with Mellodie, but instead he found himself forced to speak to her in front of an audience of several hundred interested, eavesdropping people.

"My lady!" he began, groping desperately for an innocent-sounding way of phrasing a leading question. "I thank you for your kind words. Your beauty renders me almost speechless . . ."

There was a low murmur from the crowd, and somebody whistled. Mavol could feel himself going red.

"I would dearly like to meet with you again," he stumbled on, "to show you my appreciation."

"I bet that's not all he shows her," muttered a voice from the crowd.

"I realize that, as the Carnival Queen, you must have a busy schedule," Mavol continued, through gritted teeth, "but I was hoping that you might find a moment to squeeze me in."

"You dirty old gladiator!" said the voice in the crowd, and the crimson-faced Mavol stared around furiously.

"For the next three days my time is taken up with my official duties," Mellodie answered. Her voice was low and deliciously throaty, and sent hormones stampeding round his bloodstream like runaway horses. "But after that I would be delighted to . . . receive you."

"Wha hey hey!" cheered the voice in the crowd, but Mavol was no longer bothered. *Three days*! he thought, sadly. *It might as well be three years*!

"Alas, my lady," he said ruefully, "in three days I will be gone. I am just passing through your fair city, for I am on a quest. A quest that I have waited half my life to undertake. Tomorrow I take the high road through the mountains that leads to Easterndelve."

Mavol paused, for a sudden hush had fallen over the entire arena. It had gone so quiet that the only sound he could hear was his own breathing. Wherever he looked, horrified faces were staring at him.

"You are plainly a stranger here," said Mellodie, "for were you not, you would surely know that it is impossible to use that road."

"How so?"

"That is the road which is guarded by Koban Bloodsword. He was once champion of this city, and some say he was the greatest warrior to have lived, for he was never defeated in single combat. But then he fell out with the city over some trivial matter, and swore revenge. Since then he has lived wild in the mountains, challenging all who use the Easterndelve road to combat and never losing. Many brave fighting men have gone to face him, but none have come back. All folk know that it is death to travel on that path, and no one has been foolhardy enough to use it for many moons."

"But that is the road I must travel, for it is Koban whom I seek."

"Then you too will die," said Mellodie, and turning her face from Mavol she pushed her way through the solemn, silent crowd.

Mavol paused to get his breath back and turned to look down at the lights of Malvenis twinkling in the valley below him. The night was closing in now, and although the bright moonlight would have made travelling easy, he felt a strange reluctance to leave the city behind him.

The air was heavy and still, and the scent of mountain honeysuckle pervaded everywhere. The only sound that could be heard was a single Cydorian flocking goat that was bleating morosely as it picked its solitary way up the mountainside near by.*

Removing his pack, Mavol sat on a rock at the side of the road and delved into it in search of some food. He had bought fresh bread and cheese before leaving Malvenis, and his water bottle

---

* The Cydorian flocking goat is so named because it is usually found in large groups. As this one was alone, its mates had presumably flocked off and left it.

was still full. Munching on the bread, he peered wistfully down at the twinkling city lights, then turned to stare up at the full, bright disc of the moon. When he was young, his grandmother had told him that if you made a wish when you saw the full moon, the Moon-fairy would grant it for you. She had also told him that the stars were the souls of dead bunny-rabbits, and that if you washed your face with butter, you'd never get acne. No wonder they'd locked her up in that special hospital with the high walls!

Sighing, he shook his head and stood up, ready to travel onwards. But for some reason his feet were reluctant to move, and his eyes were drawn irresistibly back to the distant city lights. Down there in the valley were hundreds of people who had seen him as a hero, and a single beautiful girl who had wanted to get to know him better. For virtually the first time in his life, Mavol had been popular, and it had proved a heady experience. All of a sudden there was a place where people liked him and wanted to see him, yet he was leaving it behind. But Mavol knew that he had to do so, for he was mere hours away from the culmination of his quest, and so dragging his head round to face the east, he set off once more along the steep and winding Easterndelve road in pursuit of a destiny that he knew full well might end with his death.

For as long as he could remember, Mavol had never quite fitted in with society. Although he had been a good-looking and happy child, new acquaintances had rapidly come to regard him with suspicion and distrust despite his friendly facade, for there had always been a basic and deep-rooted flaw in his character: Mavol was a natural practical joker, revelling in the discomfort and misfortune of others. From an early age, his easy-going manner and pleasant smile had attracted folk, but every potential friend had been forced to run a gauntlet of drawing-pins on seats, itching powder down the neck and buckets of horse urine on top of the door, until invariably they had decided to steer clear of him after all.

This antisocial sense of humour hadn't been too unusual, for many children have a cruel streak, but what had made Mavol stand apart was that he was also a naturally gifted fighter. In his first week at school, after he had initiated a stream of such pranks, the two biggest boys in the class decided to teach him a lesson. Mavol had wiped the floor with them. The same thing happened every time anyone dared to retaliate. The rest of the children had soon discovered that it was wiser to turn the other cheek, and so instead of learning to temper his cruel humour with a little reserve, Mavol had been allowed to continue unchecked.

As he grew older, Mavol's fighting ability had been noticed and fostered by his teachers, and he had gained a scholarship to Faramir's Warrior School in the city of Ged. He had taken to swordplay like an orc to vodka, and within a year there hadn't been an instructor in the school who could beat him. By the end of his second year even Rangvald Ironteeth, the grizzled old veteran of a hundred contests in the Cumanceum who was the school's gladiatorial tutor, had said that he had never seen a better fighter. But despite his undoubted skill, Mavol had not been popular with the other students. His penchant for practical jokes had alienated them and he had become a solitary, isolated figure, an efficient, smiling, friendless killer.

It had been during his second year at Faramir's that one of his tutors had told him that he was a good enough fighter to beat Koban Bloodsword himself. It had been the first time that Mavol had heard the name, but as the weeks passed and several other tutors also compared him to this mysterious warrior, his curiosity had been raised. During half-term he had spent some time in talking to experienced fighters and researching in Ged's city library, and had discovered that this Koban was generally held by the fighting fraternity to be the greatest warrior alive.

It was then that his quest had taken shape in his mind, and he had suddenly found an aim in his life. He would graduate from Warrior School and spend a few years as a professional fighting man, doing gladiator or bodyguard work and honing his skills. And then, when he was as good a fighter as he could possibly become, he would seek out this legend and defeat him. And in doing so he would prove that he, Mavol, was the best.

And now, after four long years, he was as ready as he would ever be. He had made the long journey north to Malvenis, and he was about to fulfil his destiny. Within a few hours, he would carve a niche for himself in the chronicles of Midworld as the man who killed Koban Bloodsword. That is, as long as Koban didn't kill him instead . . .

It was past noon the next day when the road eventually levelled out to run through the high pass that cut through the Irridic Mountains, leading down towards the Dwarven settlement of Easterndelve. Mavol could tell that few if any people had passed this way for many a month. Mosses, ferns and weeds covered the bare, compacted earth, and in places sweet-briers had writhed across the track and lay there undisturbed. He was travelling cautiously now, sword in hand, but so far he had found no evidence of life. Just the opposite, in fact, for there were signs of death everywhere.

Human bones and skulls were scattered around where the scavenging beasts of the mountains had left them, and broken swords, cloven shields and discarded armour were strewn along either side of the road. Much killing had taken place here, but it had plainly happened a long while ago. The weapons and armour were rusted and dull, and the bones were brittle and greying with age.

Mavol paused and wiped his brow. He was sweating, not from heat or exertion, for he was fit and the mountain air was cool, but from nerves. If the myths and stories were to be believed, Koban was waiting somewhere ahead of him, but where? What was the routine of a man who set himself up in an isolated mountain pass and challenged all-comers to combat? Did he get up every morning and sit at the side of the road, waiting for challengers? Did he lie in wait and ambush the unwary? Was there a bell hanging at the side of the road which people were meant to ring if they wanted to take him on? The more that Mavol thought about it, the odder the whole set-up seemed to be.

I mean, he said to himself as he picked his way past the clutching tendrils of the sweet-briers, *why would anyone want to leave a nice place like Malvenis to live for years in the wilderness, fighting total strangers just because they wanted to pass through the mountains? You'd have to be mentally unstable at the very least, if not downright insane. And what would you do to pass the time? Stuck up here for years, with just the occasional passer-by to butcher, you'd go out of your mind with boredom! I reckon he must have jacked it in years ago. That's what I'd do. Stay here long enough to get myself a reputation, then slide quietly off to an eastern city where no one knew me and . . .*

Mavol froze in mid-step, jerked back to reality with a bump, for someone had coughed ahead of him. It was difficult to judge how far away they were, for sound travelled a long distance through the clear air of the mountains, but Mavol guessed that they were not more than fifty yards ahead, probably just over the small rise in the ground that he was starting to climb. Of course, it might be another traveller, but somehow he thought it unlikely. Anyone passing this way would know all about Koban Bloodsword and would be keeping as quiet as a mouse. And not a normal mouse, either, but a dead one wrapped in swathes of cotton wool after its voice-box had been removed. No, there could only be one source for the cough. Koban himself!

Twin waves of exhilaration and fear swept through him, and he swallowed painfully as his stomach threatened to rebel. Then, clutching his sword in his damp hands and hardly daring to breathe, he crept forwards. Pace after silent pace he climbed the rise, craning his neck to peer ahead, until he had reached the top and could see the track as it wound its way down to disappear between two outcrops of rock. At first he saw nobody and thought he must have misjudged the distance of the cough, but then a slight movement caught his eye and he realized with a thrill of excitement that someone was sitting on a boulder in front of the right-hand outcrop.

It was a very old man dressed in tattered remnants of clothes. Once he must have been tall and strong, but now his shoulders were stooped and the wrinkled skin hung loosely on his thin, lanky frame. Ragged tendrils of sparse white hair draped round his shoulders and long, bent fingernails protruded from hands that shook uncontrollably. Beside him, a massive sword was stuck point first into the soil, but it must have been planted there for a long, long time, for ivy had crept up the blade to hang loosely from the pommel, almost 5 feet from the ground.

Mavol crept forwards, but the old man didn't notice him. He was staring blankly into space, lost in the imaginings of his ailing mind, and his lips moved incessantly as he conducted a silent conversation with himself. Mavol paused as something shifted beneath his foot, and looked down. The ground here was thickly strewn with crumbling old bones and half-rotted armour, and Mavol sighed and lowered his sword, smiling wryly. He had found Koban Bloodsword.

Now that he thought about it, it made perfect sense. He had read a lot about Koban's exploits, but nothing much had been written about his age. However, if you stopped to work it out, the guy must have been at least fifty when he left Malvenis. How long had he been living up here in the mountains? Ten years? Twenty? By the Gods, the guy must be at least sixty-five, and probably older. But then that was the problem with being a famous warrior. You attained super-hero status and people believed the myths. They would think of you as you were at your peak, even when the ravages of time were taking their cold-blooded toll. With a shiver, Mavol was suddenly uncomfortably aware of his own mortality, and he looked at the stooped old warrior with a new fear.

"Oh, hello," said a voice behind him, and Mavol twitched so violently he nearly cut his own foot off. Whirling round, he found he was being studied by a grimy, rag-clad figure even thinner and scrawnier than Koban, although a good deal younger.

"Come to challenge the old sod, have you?" the figure continued, smiling to expose teeth that looked as though they had been made out of mouldy cheese. "I'm not surprised. I knew that sooner or later someone would figure out that he must have got so decrepit that he would be ripe for the chop."

It shoved a filthy hand into its matted mass of hair and scratched with enthusiasm. Mavol watched with horror as several small, multi-legged creatures were dislodged and fell to the ground. Then the hand emerged holding a plump head-louse between its filthy fingers.

"It must be four years since the last guy challenged him," the figure continued, "and the daft old codger has really lost it since then. Can't even remember who he is, most of the time. Just sits on that rock all day long. Thinks he's waiting for visitors."

The figure paused to inspect the louse, then burst it with a quick squeeze of the fingers, wiped the remnants from its hand onto a filthy sleeve, and held out the hand in greeting.

"By the way, my name's Norman," it smiled. "How do you do?"

Mavol took the hand reluctantly and tried to shake it without actually touching it.

"Er . . . hello," he managed.

"So. You're a warrior, I take it?" continued Norman. "I'm a hermit, myself. Have been for eight years. I used to be a scrivener in a bank in Derchey, but I hated it. Absolutely hated it. I'd always fancied the country life, so when my wife ran off with a jongleur, I thought now's your chance, Norman. And I've never regretted it. Never."

He looked across at Koban, who seemed to have nodded off on his boulder and was making slight snoring noises.

"Mind you," he continued, "I'm going to miss that cantankerous old bugger after you've topped him. He's kept me busy these past few years looking after him, I can tell you. If it wasn't for me he'd have starved or frozen. Still, what are neighbours for, eh?"

He paused again to give his hair another good scratching, rendering several more small creatures homeless, and then held his hand out to Mavol a second time.

"Well, it's been nice meeting you, but I must be running along. Its almost lunch-time, and I haven't gone scavenging yet. I'd ask you back for a few locusts and some wild honey, but I know you've got a job to do, so I'll leave you to it. Say goodbye to him for me, would you, before you lop his head off?"

With that the hermit pumped Mavol's hand up and down again before turning and trotting off along the track. Mavol watched him go, then wiped his hand gingerly on his jerkin and turned his attention back to Koban.

The old man had woken up, and was staring around him with the bemused air of someone who had expected to wake up in bed but has found himself sitting on a boulder in the middle of nowhere instead. Mavol gazed at him, and the full import of the situation suddenly struck home. The old guy was defenceless! It was going to be a piece of cake! After all these years, he was about to attain his dream of becoming the man who killed Koban Bloodsword, the greatest fighter in Midworld. He would be renowned throughout the land! But it was strange how little enthusiasm he seemed to be able to dredge up for the task . . .

And then he thought of the crowds at the Malvenis Midsummer Games who had cheered him to the echo. He thought of Mellodie, of how her hair had brushed against his shoulder, and of the way she had kissed him on the cheek. He thought of the friendly wine-bars and taverns in the city, and of the strangers who had come up to him in the street and congratulated him on his defeat of Algin Bonecrusher. And then he thought of the sentry who had been the last victim of one of his practical jokes. Somehow that seemed like the work of a different person.

All at once, his mind was made up. Sword in hand, he strode decisively across to the old man.

Koban peered blankly up at him for several seconds, but then, as his rheumy eyes focused on the sword, they seemed to fill with a clear lucidity. His back straightened, his head lifted proudly, and suddenly Mavol could see an echo of the mighty warrior that the old man had once been.

Koban looked from the hovering sword back to Mavol, and his face filled with understanding. Then he nodded with a tired acceptance.

"I am Koban Bloodsword," he said almost with wonder, as though it was a secret that had been long hidden from him. "Have you come to kill me?"

"No," answered Mavol, grinning down at him. "I've come to guide you home."

And taking the ancient warrior by the arm, he helped him up and began to lead him slowly down the road that led back to Malvenis.

THE CUNNING PLAN

Anne Gay

*Anne Gay (b. 1952) sold her first story in 1982 but only began writing regularly after the success of "Wishbone" in the Gollancz/*Sunday Times *best sf story competition in 1987. Her novels include* Mindsail *(1990),* The Brooch of Azure Midnight *(1991) and the much-acclaimed* Dancing on the Volcano *(1993). She also wrote the Masked Rider sequence, starting with* Escape from Edenoi *(1996). The following story was written specially for this anthology.*

Sunset painted the tops of the mountains, but on the alpine meadows no goats whatsoever gambolled. Nobody, absolutely nobody, yodelled. Cheerfulness was not allowed.

Crimson light rivered from the sky, seeping like blood into the valley. At the edge of the shadowed village, lights twinkled merrily through diamond-lattice windows. A creaking sign at the front and a stack of empties at the back showed what this place was. As soon as it was full night, dark-cloaked figures began to make their way to the tavern.

Four customers slummocked along close behind. The bright wedge of firelight from the door swallowed them up. Tossing their cloaks over the pegs on the wall, they made their way to their usual table. They sat with an air of cheerful expectancy, watching through the crowd as alleged maidens in black-laced bodices ploughed a path with their ample, up-thrust bosoms.

It was happy hour at the Carpathian Arms.

One such mock-virgin plonked down a tray of tankards for the quartet. Foaming liquid splashed from the steins, staining the table red. Four hands reached eagerly for the scarlet drinks, four sets of pointed eye-teeth plunged into the fluid. Over the rim of their drinks, Sleepless MacBride, Mack the Fang, Long-Tooth McGurky and Kevin the Killer leered at the wench.

Fraulein Liesl smiled nervously.

Then Sleepless MacBride lifted his face from his tankard to glare around in disgust. Without warning, he hurled his glass at the wall. "Bleedin' Ribena!"

Crash, tinkle, silence. You could have heard a needle drop – except someone would have caught the syringe to suck out the dregs.

But the waitress was indignant. Worse, she owed Sleepless for getting her into trouble. Hadn't he tripped her up the day before when she was carrying a bun full of raw meat and Emmental? She'd fallen on Long-Tooth and the Fang, covering them in goo and soggy lettuce to the detriment of their tempers and her health. And what had he said? "Big Mack is served with cheese and Gurkl."

Now everyone was listening, Liesl grinned vindictively. "Is it my fault you emptied the cat?"

The other three vampyres stared at Sleepless. The rest of the throng came to mill threateningly around him.

"So that was you, was it?" hissed Long-Tooth von Gurkl.

A chorus of "You selfish bastard!" followed Gurkl's refrain.

Never very tall, Sleepless shrank down even further beneath the weight of the Carpathians' united opprobrium. If it went on for much longer, he felt he might disappear altogether. Licking suddenly paler lips, he babbled, "Er . . . um . . . I, er, thought it would give us more rats' blood!"

"Berk! Fang had the last rat weeks ago, didn't you, Fang?"

Next to Sleepless, Mack the Fang leaned forward, shoving his chin out aggressively. He was so muscular he looked like he had whole packs of rodents sliding around under his skin rather than the contents of one scrawny rat in his tum. "So?" he said. "I told you it was an accident. I didn't know it was the last one, did I?" His eyes slid pugnaciously round the room. Before they could fall off the table, Fang grabbed them and popped them back in.

"Eurgh!" said Liesl. "I wish you wouldn't do that!"

"Never mind his blasted eyes!" Gurkl grated. "When's this damned boozer goin' to get some more blood?"

Other customers called out, "Yeah! Can't have a boozer with no blood!" "Come down here for a quiet pint and you can't even get one!" It was bedlam.

Liesl stammered, "I ordered a barrel of type O at the dark of the moon but it hasn't come yet! And someone—" she stared at Kevin the Killer "—drank my last messenger-bat. There isn't even a Tampax to make a cup of tea."

The crowd, always fickle, was turning uglier. She backed up against the wall, her hands protecting her throat. Not that she could have stopped the baying mob of undead who swarmed towards her.

An unholy thud echoed through the room like a coffin-lid falling into place in a crypt. Again, silence. Except Sleepless stage-whispering to Kevin: "Now you've done it!" But had he managed to shift the blame?

Toe Knee the barman let the flap drop back onto the counter and stepped through the hatch, the magnet of everyone's gaze. Mack had to peep through his fingers to stop his eyeballs wandering off and getting trampled on.

Shuffle, scrape. Shuffle, scrape. The barman came ponderously forward. Patrons melted out of his path, some of them too nervous to put themselves back together again after he had passed. Beneath his bulk the floorboards creaked. Splinters flew as the claws at the end of his thighs raked the wood. Bears had been known to break their teeth on the monstrous muscles of his arms. He had been known to toss horseshoes with the horse still attached, back in the nights when there had still been living creatures in the valley. He had never been known as patient.

Sleepless's ploy hadn't worked. The blame stayed firmly where it belonged.

"Oi, you!" Toe Knee stabbed a finger at him. "You're the one that's brought us to this! My poor Tibbles! No wonder she stopped chasing her little tinkly ball. So you—" jerking away from the sickle-nailed digit, Sleepless banged his head on the wall "—you're going to fix it."

"But— but I can't bring a cat back to life! I couldn't even make it come back to death!"

"Just as well, really," muttered the Fang, "or there'd be blood-sucking badgers, killer cattle and deadly ducks on the loose. Some people just have no standards at all."

But Toe Knee didn't see it that way. The barman's roar reverberated from the peaks high above. A couple of avalanches crushed passing lycanthropes and clouds of vultures flapped across the star-sprinkled sky. "Then get fresh blood!" he bellowed. "Lots of it, you selfish sod! D'you think I don't know what happened to my drayman?"

"Gluh—" said Sleepless. Actually he was fairly sure Toe Knee didn't know what had happened to the drayman. If Toe Knee suspected there was a pile of bones under a certain pine-tree in the woods, Sleepless wouldn't be sitting here now quivering.

"So it's up to YOU," the mammoth barman gritted, "to make sure there's plenty of drink. You wouldn't want the Carpathian Arms to go down the tube, would you?"

"N-n-n—"

"I'll give you forty-eight hours. After that, you're juice. Got me?"

Sleepless nodded, feeling the eyeballs rattling in his skull. It was long after Toe Knee had gone back to his subterranean lair that they settled into anything resembling a viewing position. But the outlook wasn't good.

"What am I going to do?" he wept, since Ribena was no good at all at stiffening up the sinews, let alone summoning up the blood.

Gurkl said mournfully, "Trouble is, Sleepless, the minute you get out of the valley there's all these gits with garlic earrings and silver bullets and damn' great chunks of sharpened wood just waiting to turn us into a barbie."

"Besides which," Kevin added, "there'd be no point sending you out to bring back supplies. You'd drink the bleedin' lot before it got here."

"Even if I could cross the . . . the stream," Sleepless said, just to remind them that he couldn't. None of them could. Creatures of the twilight world would fall apart if they crossed running water. Hence the shortage, since the stream crossed the only way in or out of the valley.

"See, what we need," Kevin said, tucking his fetid feet further under his seat and spreading his hands on the table, "is loads of people coming here."

Gurkl shook his head pityingly. "You're not going to get that, though, are you? Stands to reason nobody's going to come here from outside." He pushed back his long, lank locks and scratched the great gherkin of his nose. "People come here—" his voice sank to a menacing whisper "—they don't go back."

Sleepless grasped at straws. "Isn't there another film-crew coming soon?"

"Nope."

"Not even David Attenborough?"

A mass of tongues clicked in disgust.

The quartet sat on in thirsty silence. Mack picked his teeth with a dagger. "What we need," he said reflectively, "is bait."

"Oh, brilliant!" Kevin sneered. "Come to the Carpathian Arms and get sucked dry."

Thud! He looked down aghast as the dagger sliced into the wood between his fingers. Mack smiled a smile that turned the Ribena dripping down the walls into crimson glaciers. "Got a better idea?"

The odour of Kevin's deadly extremities got suddenly stronger. "No. No, no, no, no, no, Mack. Great idea. Fab. Super."

Mack swung around to squint threateningly at Sleepless. "You got us into this mess. Don't think I never seen you creeping through the pinewood. I had my eye on you and you never spotted it. Took me days to pick the pine-needles out of it after."

Sleepless's jaw dropped in astonishment, then firmed with anger. (If asked, it would also thrust forward so the teeth could do a chorus-dance, no reasonable offer refused. Sometimes after parties, Sleepless had a heck of a job getting it back again.) He forced his eyeballs to glare balefully at Mack. "So you're the son of a witch who nicked the barrels from my cellar!"

"I had to. It was coagulating."

"Clot!" Gurkl said.

"But the question is," Big Mack said heavily, "*how* are we going to lure lots of people to the valley?" Mack lowered at the little man. "It's your fault my glass is empty. So *you* think of a lure."

Sleepless's nose began to run under pressure. Automatically jamming it back, he sniffed. Spiders swinging in the rafters were sucked into that mighty gale.

Sleepless dripped and thought by turns.

They sat and watched him for a while. Then they slumped and watched him for another while.

"How about writing to a university to come and study us?" he asked eventually.

"Pillock! Professors and that, they'd miss their students. Then we'd have the stake and chips brigade on our necks."

"Well how about tourists?"

They stared at Sleepless, aghast. "They'd— they'd have to have *running water*!"

"Okay, okay! You don't need to bite my head off!"

"Oh, bloody hell, we'll just have to think of a load of people that no one would miss."

"Tele-sales callers," said Kevin.

"Double-glazing salesmen," said Mack.

"Politicians," said Sleepless. Just before they hit him.

But when the candles had guttered low in their sconces and Liesl was pointedly not putting out the cat, Sleepless woke up.

"I've got it!" he yelled. "Football hooligans!"

Even Gurkl spent a microsecond in reverential awe. "It's a great, shining, incandescent jewel of an idea, Sleepless. A coruscating nugget encapsulated in crystal clarity. A glorious gobbet of genius. But there's just one fatal flaw."

Sleepless beamed happily. "Only one?"

"Well up on your usual score, Sleepless. Football hooligans it is. But *how* are we going to get them here?"

"Coach."

They hit him again.

Liesl threw a bucket of Ribena over him as he lay on the floor. He propped himself up on one elbow, sputtering, "No, really, though. Football hooligans travel on coaches 'cause they get chucked off everything else. What we need is a load of fans—"

Kevin stood on Sleepless's head, his hobnails sticking into the little man's tongue. Sleepless tried hard not to breathe as his vast nostrils found themselves under Kevin's fatal feet. Kevin said, "Which means advertising a stadium they could see we haven't got. And we can't exactly pay Saatchi and Saatchi, can we?"

Mack nodded. "Specially not within—" he consulted the moondial on his wrist "—forty-two hours."

"Well a pub football team, then!" mumbled Sleepless, having emptied his mouth by the simple expedient of chewing off Kevin's toe. "They're always bragging about how their centre forward used to play in the Fifth Division of the Coronation Cup while they pour another pint of that nasty 'orrible beer stuff into their nasty bloated beer guts."

"Yeah," muttered Kevin, "they used to be a contender. Nearly had a trial with Tranmere Rovers' youth team. Long ago, like, when they were footloose."

"Like you, old son." Sleepless bit Kevin's toenail. Then slurped on the juicy bone. The way Kevin tasted, he didn't need any parmesan. "So what we want now is a prize."

"Like what?"

"Big enough to lure the ageing footie-freaks."

"Like what?"

"But not so big that real players will want to stick their oar in."

"*Like bloody what?*"

Sleepless pulled himself up onto the bench. Wriggled nonchalantly, a self-satisfied smirk scooting across those all-singing, all-dancing mandibles. "Like a barrel," he said, "of beer."

Mack sent a drowsy eye across to peer at him. "That," he said, "is the best idea yet."

"But how am I going to get there? I can't cross the stream – I'd disintegrate!"

Mack laid a heavy arm around Sleepless's shoulders. "Disintegrate, shmisintegrate. I have a Cunning Plan . . ."

Kevin had often played doctors and nurses but he'd never played dentists before. Or, come to think of it, football. However, he did a fine line in sharpening up daggers, and at least he had the right tools. So the next night, when they had dragged Sleepless from his hiding-place under a rotting haystack, Kevin waved his long, metal rasp optimistically. "'Sokay," he said, while McGurk and Mack crowbarred Sleepless's jaws apart and then stopped them scuttling off. "These particular files have the sharp bits cut in the shape of an X. Makes them extra popular. You know, they're X-rasps."

"Anyway," said Mack, "losing an inch or two off your gnashers is nothing to worry about."

"Nah," MckGurk drawled. "'Specially when you're going to lose a foot or two crossing the stream."

"Mfuh gruh!" expostulated Sleepless in a spray of tooth-shards. But they ignored him anyway.

Soon his prize incisors would never win a show again. "My victims will have to be catheterized!" he wailed, but McGurk and Big Mack were already dragging him across the valley and up to where the— the *stream* ran gurgling in the light of the all but full moon.

"I can't cross that!" he protested, but Long-Tooth proudly showed him a length of giant-sized elastic tied between two trees on the river-bank. Sleepless stared, appalled. "That's not a Cunning Plan!" he said. "It's a catapult!"

"Pre-zackly." Kevin helped him ungently into position and tucked a bundle of posters under his belt. "Correct. So you'll only be above the . . . the running water for about half a second. Stirring deeds are afoot, lad. This is no time to go to pieces."

As he spoke, Mack nodded, and the combined strength of three large vampyres propelled their small comrade rapidly across the river. He landed in a tangle of his own bodily organs, only some of which were still attached. Replacing his ear with dignity and a blob of plasticine which Mack thoughtfully fired across after him, Sleepless set off disconsolately with the bundle of posters.

He trudged along the gravel road the Gammer film-crew had made for Christopher Flummer's caravan. The silver star had almost faded from the caravan's door and spiders now inhabited the immobile dressing-room, but at least it had been fun. Except for the guys from Gammer.

Bright under the light of the big, almost spherical moon, the road passed through the only pass out of the valley. Soon Sleepless's feet hurt, and a large blister was developing quite a relationship with his corns. "Oh, joy," he muttered, "pain."

By the time Sleepless had descended the forty-one hairpin bends, it was worryingly close to dawn. Once he'd finally reached the town below, he rushed around pasting his posters on every wall and door in sight. Soon he had only one left: the biggest one, meant for the door of the inn where the prey were bound to see it. But the inn was damned elusive.

Ugly golden light was plastering the fleecy clouds overhead as he raced up and down the crooked streets. Overhanging gables provided some relief, but there was a nasty azure lightening on the horizon. Disgusting birdsong almost made him want to throw up. Already he could feel the first motes of sunlight ricocheting out of the sky and peppering him with unpleasant sensations, and however hard he looked, there wasn't a convenient cellar or crypt in sight. The nice, helpful darkness had all but disappeared as he skidded around a corner and into the village square.

At last! There was the alehouse, with a red flower painted on the sign. He just had time to slap the sign up below the lettering which read, "The Pimpernel Bier Keller and Meat Mart". Then he dived down a manhole cover as the sun peeped nosily into the village.

Gnawing vermin in a sewer wasn't Sleepless's idea of fun, but it helped to pass the time of day. Above him in the square, rosy-cheeked peasant women gabbled in the market, kerchiefs wagging as they gossipped. More to the point, rosy-nosed men with beer bellies sat drinking anaemic lager and jabbing their thumbs at the notice:

COME ONE, COME ALL
OVER-FORTIES FOOTBALL MATCH AND

BARBECUE
WITH THE MIGHTY CARPATHIAN WANDERERS
FREE BARREL OF BEER TO THE WINNERS
CARPATHIAN ARMS, SUNSET TONIGHT
BE THERE OR BE BORING

And by late afternoon there was an air-conditioned Van Hool fifty-two-seater horseless coach parked encouragingly over a certain manhole cover right outside the pub. Someone was cutting out very large letters to stick in the back window. Through the gap in the manhole cover, Sleepless could just make out an O, an L, a V, and that was an E, wasn't it? Maybe he should have paid more attention in school but that snaky one, it was definitely an S.

Men were saying, "I had a trial with Negoi Rangers once," and, "See, there was this talent scout from Hategului City but me dad wouldn't let me go," and thumping each other bluffly on the back in the sunset.

Sleepless wasn't sure the folks at the Carpathian could manage fifty-two plus driver, but he needn't have worried. Twenty of the seats were piled with cans of Pilsner, and half a dozen with onion and black pudding crisps. Only a score or so men shook the coach with their stumbling footsteps as they poured themselves aboard. They were deep in an argument about who'd be the next manager of Focsani Tuesday. They didn't even notice Sleepless creeping into the driver's mate's coffin, the little alcove down by the luggage lockers.

Stopping only twice for pee-breaks, the coach ground its gears noisily up towards the twilit pass. Sleepless heard the visitors singing, "With a T and an R and an A N S," but he was in no position to care. Faint with malnutrition, he found the swaying around the hairpin bends nauseating. He almost lost the contents of his stomach, and when the coach splashed through the ford, he did lose his other ear. In the seconds it took to cross that fiercely running water, his agony made him deaf to what might be happening to the visitors sitting suddenly quiet above.

But it was worth it. It was all worth it when the twenty-seven strangers drew up outside the twinkling windows of the

Carpathian Arms. Sleepless slipped out and found himself being hugged gratefully by his mates. With tears in his eyes, Long-Tooth said, "Talk about drinks on the hoof!" Even Mack the Fang whispered, "Nice one, son," while pretending to welcome the cocktails.

"There's too many of 'em just to dig straight in," Toe Knee murmured. "Better pretend we're going to start the match. Take a few cressets over to my mandrake field, will you? I harrowed it last spring so it should be reasonably level." Louder he added, "Have a drink or two on the house, lads. Who's the captain?"

A large, fat, balding man pushed his way forward. "Pleased to meet you. I'm Hans, and that's Nies, and that's Igor, and that's Bumsidasi Junior," and as introductions do, they went on confusingly for far too long for anyone to find out who anyone else was. But Sleepless hid a mocking smile when he heard the away team's title. Even if they'd brought their own ref, they'd had it if they had to make up a phoney name like that.

The challengers were taking it seriously. Some of them had real boots with real studs, and a few of them wore shorts on surprisingly hirsute legs. Once people started taking up their positions, there was a fair bit of pushing and jostling. The opposing goalie jabbed an elbow in Big Mack's ribs. "We're gonna slaughter you, mate," he bragged.

"Yeah, we're gonna massacre you," echoed his friend, one of the Hansis.

Now Mack came to look, Hansi was nearly as tall as he was, but still he managed to stare down at the interloper. "Oh, yeah? You and whose army?" he grated. Sweeping his opponent into a crushing bear-hug, Mack leaned his head in close to the other man's neck, jaws beginning to open.

"Break!" Toe Knee shouted. "No cheating now, lads. Remember," he said meaningfully, "the barbecue's not 'til after."

Reluctantly, Mack stopped, but only because he knew the Carpathianites couldn't take on the team and the spectators all in one go. They'd have to wait until the other side were dead drunk and knackered . . .

Rudolf tossed a coin, Kevin guessed wrong, and the

visitors took the downhill goal. Or at least, downwind from Kevin's feet.

The moon wasn't up yet as the players took their positions. Her light was only a dim platinum glimmer on the snow-capped peaks. Still, there were four cressets blazing away to mark the goal-mouths, and the driver helpfully left his coach-lights on to flood the pitch while he snoozed over a crate of beer on the back seat.

Sleepless gave up trying to work out what those letters spelt: W – O – L – or something, and stood sniffing up the odours of fresh grass and living flesh. This was a moment that made him proud to be dead. On the sidelines, Liesl was flourishing her dishmop and yelling, "Come on you Carps!" While on the other side of the pitch, the visitors were chanting, "You'll never walk alone."

Then the Big Match started. The hollow crump of boot on bladder rang out as Nies belted the ball off the centre spot. There was a moment of confusion as everyone raced the same way, and Rudolf the ref blew his whistle at the Carps. "You lot are going that way!" He pointed sternly at the Carps' goal and the home side drifted sadly away from the men they were marking.

Ten seconds later, he blew it again. "Foul!"

Sleepless had chopped a visitor's shin. A crowd gathered round the man who was writhing dramatically on the turf, a trickle of blood barely oozing out of the graze on his leg. All the same, Sleepless was down on his hands and knees, licking his lips and bringing his head down towards the infinitesimal gore.

Toe Knee, who'd appointed himself team coach, rushed across with a bucket and sponge. He mopped the man's shin and carefully wrang the sponge out into the empty bucket. It was turning into a right needle match.

One of the Hansis threw the ball from the sideline, yelling, "On the 'ead!" and the ball went flying into the penalty box. Igor belted it into the back of the net with total disregard for the off-side rule.

The Wolves went wild. With their supporters roaring, they ran to hug Igor. And found that the Carps were also swarming around him. Indeed, Long-Tooth was kissing him warmly on the neck.

Rudolf got busy with his whistle. "'Ere! You lot aren't supposed to kiss our lot. Do it again and it'll be the red card, right?"

But the Carpathians couldn't help themselves. The game got bloodier and bloodier. Fouls grew fouler and tempers frayed. Already the Carps were three men down, and the Wolves were fielding a grandfather with a pacemaker – their "secret weapon", Grithi having mysteriously vanished, presumed drunk. At 17–0, with the Wolves fans chanting, "We're gonna kick your blasted 'eads in," even Kevin was getting narked.

"We're gonna make you into mincemeat," he hissed at the Wolf who'd just chinned him.

"Bugger off, giblet-brains." The Wolf stamped down with his spikes and Kevin lost a toe he could ill afford. In seconds, fists were flying and the whole thing had turned into a free-for-all with whistle accompaniment.

"Get 'em, lads!" yelled Mack, and the vampyres dropped all pretence of football. The visitors were trounced. Then trussed. Then treated to toothy torment, except for the ones who had to wait their turn. Their bodies shrivelled as bit by bit the blood was drained. Most of it, of course, went straight into the vampyres' stomachs. Sleepless, one eye as ever on the main chance, siphoned a bit off into the football for later. Now his eye-teeth weren't the right shape any more, it'd be easier that way. He drank the dregs from the body then stole away with his booty to enjoy it in the privacy of the woods. But he stayed where he could see the field in case there were afters.

Even the driver was not exempt, though he kept pleading that he supported Man U. Lucky for him the pneumatic doors worked quickly. He threw his Van Hool into reverse and scarpered. The coach turned into a little white dot at the crest of the pass then vanished forever down the other side. The hapless visitors were stranded.

Except just then the moon rose over the mountains, fat and white and full.

As one, the surviving opposition howled. Claws burst out from their boots. Shirts ripped apart as hairy chests boiled out of them. Their faces grimaced into lupine masks with dentistry that blinded Sleepless with envy. With several mighty bounds, they were free. Sleepless was glad he was under cover in the pinewood.

The Transylvanian Werewolves thought it was all over, but the Carps fought back. Finally, the survivors were thrashed to a standstill. In the first grey light of pre-dawn, the whole lot of them were panting helplessly, some with their tongues out further than others.

Stalemate.

Igor and Toe Knee both held the other's gaze.

"We won," Igor said thickly.

Toe Knee cracked his knuckles. "Yeah, but you're still stuck in the valley. Without the coach, none of us can get out of here. Didn't you notice the pain when your coach crossed the river?"

The Werewolf captain stood on the penalty spot and shrugged all four of his shoulders hopelessly. He nodded. It hurt. "What are we going to do? What are we going to eat?"

Slumped on the grass, Mack the Fang groaned and turned towards them. "'S'all right," he said. "No problem. It was all Sleepless's fault so I . . . I thought up this Cunning Plan . . ."

As the moon eavesdropped on his tale, Toe Knee smiled for the first time since his cat had been nailed up behind the bar. Slowly he peered out into the trees, where he could just make out the flash of dancing teeth.

"Sleepless," he crooned. "Oh, Sleepless . . ."

WAR OF THE
DOOM ZOMBIES

Richard A. Lupoff

*Richard Lupoff (b. 1935) is another of those writers whose work
is so diverse that he defies categorization. Most of it is probably
best defined as science fantasy rather than science fiction, including*
Into the Aether *(1974)*, Sword of the Demon *(1978)*, Space
War Blues *(1978)*, The Crack in the Sky *(1976)*, Lisa Kane
(1976), Circumpolar! *(1984) and its companion* Countersolar!
(1986), and Lovecraft's Book *(1985). He has since moved into
the mystery field, starting with* The Comic Book Killer *(1988),
the first of his series featuring insurance investigator Hobart Lindsey.
Comic books are a special enthusiasm of Lupoff's and one on which
he wrote extensively in* All in Color for a Dime *(1970), and
which also feature in the psychological thriller* The Triune Man
*(1976). In the 1970s Lupoff produced a series of parodies under the
alias of Ova Hamlet, lampooning various sf and fantasy writers;
some of these were collected as* The Ova Hamlet Papers *(1979).
Incidentally, the title "War of the Doom Zombies" was dreamed
up by Lupoff in the 1960s as the ideal (if rather tongue-in-cheek)
title for a science-fiction novel for Ace Books, at the time the most
prolific publisher of space adventure novels. The outline he wrote
for that book eventually surfaced as* One Million Centuries

(1967), but the title stayed with him and later re-emerged with this story.

Aye, men call me Upchuck and tremble. Upchuck the Barbarian I am, am I, and my fame is spread from the ancient lands of the Delwara Basin to the Valley of the Terraplane, and rare it is for the immortal Upchuck to flee from any foe, be he man or beastie.

But flee I did, I, Upchuck, tumbling and panting down the face of Pappalardi Mountain, scrambling before the broken pottery and dirty water flung after me by yon harridans in the Cave of Women high on the western face of the mountain. "Out, amscray!" their shrill voices rang yet in mine beet-colored ears, "come back when you get some meat on your scrawny frame and some hair on your pimply cheeks!"

Shaking my fist at the Cave I vaulted upon the splendid shanks of my she-horse Heroine and spurred away from this place of shame and wickedness. Aha, though, laughed I to myself, taunt me though they may for my seeming youth, yet will those wenches grow feeble with age, their magnificent breasts (O, slobber!) withered and their voluptuous hips (aye, grind and grimace!) softened and spread ere grow locks upon the cheeks (or the belly!) of Upchuck!

Such be's my secret, and secret 'twill remain, mine only and thine, thou reader of mine screed!

As Heroine carried me sedately along the rock-bestrewn path leading away from Pappalardi I stopped to pop a particularly noisome carbuncle from between my eyes, listing with glee to the merry sound as pus parted from Upchuck and sailed to land with a tiny *plop* in the dirt beside Heroine's ill-shod hoof. I dug spurry heels into Heroine's bony flanks and proceeded to check my accouterment as the gallant mare advanced from her plodding walk into an exhilarating trot.

Atop my somewhat dusty pate perched my ancient peaked cap Skullwarmer. About my splendid torso there hung limply my ancient leather jerkin Lotion. Athwart my fine legs there clung my ancient trousers Gravyshedder. Upon my athlete's feet were snugly laced my ancient boots, upon the left foot Ed and upon the right Fred.

I was well satisfied with the completeness and good condition of my garb, and had nigh begun to burst into a song of my own improvisation when there appeared before me on the trail a sight of such imposing mien as to make me rein in and reach for my trusty weapons, survivors both of the ancient times before the unspeakable cataclysm of which we moderns are wont so often to speak. Gladly felt I Hoodsticker my ancient gravity knife and Punkzapper my ancient zip gun!

"Ho, fellow!" challenged I, backwards speaking ever as. "Thy garb marks thee a sorcerer as! Be'est though one of white or of black sorcery?"

"Tell I not the color of my tricks till I see the color of thy stash, youngun," rejoined the mage, nodding his peaked cap and gesturing significantly at the cashpurse (Ari) which dangled from my leathern belt (Hickock). A crafty one, this could I detect at once!

"I hie Upchuck," told I the necromancer, and "Upchuck hie I," repeated I, performing a courtesy in case he be hard of hearing and completing a palindrome into the bargain, a little trick which it pleases me occasionally to perform.

"That be no palindrome," challenged the stranger. "Madam, I'm Adam, *that* be such, or Sam, no toot-toot on Mas, though I admit I ken not the meaning of such."

"Ay, well," quoth I, demolishing his feeble argument, " 'tmay be as 'tis, 'tis still as 'twas!" This logic have I found ever proof against the sophistry of wise and pseudo-wise disputers.

"Seemst troubled, youth," mumbled yon mage. "Mayhap can I aid thee in thy need, canst but pay some modest price to sustain an ancient wise man. Tax deductible as well, be I non-prophet as I be."

"Well, tell who arst," quoth I.

"I heit Mus Domesticus, once apprentice now sorcerer in full," he proclaimed. "Philtres and spells deal I to all and sundry, aye, with quantity discounts and student's specials. Looketh to me as if thou couldst use a magicke of pimple cream, lad, following which I swow as thy lady love may look upon thy suit more kindly than she has."

Now we were to serious business, but evening as well was in its approach, and dark clouds too seemed to be bellying up from the Bay of the Jam-makers, so I courteously suggested that Master Mus and I dismount and make camp beneath a sheltering rock which I noticed conveniently beside our trail. We dislodged a nesting firedrake and roasted her eggs for dinner while we bargained over Mus's services.

"You be a mere lad seeking the pleasures of manhood, be you not?" quoth the sorcerer.

"Nay, O wizened one," rejoined I. "Stranger than that be my tale, nor could seer's potion give you vision of my truth. What number of summers think you I have seen?"

Deep peered he into my eyes, his own blazing with a strange and sinister inner flame. "Some fifteen summers," quoth he, "since first peeped thine orbs at thy dam's adoring phiz, and fifteen winters since thy lips sought warm and nourishing pap."

Roaring with laughter and pulling another roasted egg from the campfire I clapped the ancient on the shoulder and wiped my tear-wettened eyes with my other hand, while rubbing my belly merrily with the other and loosening my jerkin Lotion for greater comfort. With singed fingers I proceeded to peel away the shell of my roast egg, reaching for Mus's generously proffered wineskin with my free hand and pointing gleefully at his astounded countenance with the other.

"Eh, that be a neat trick with thy hands," he said. "Wouldst teach it to an old man in need of every shtick he can learn?"

"For a price, mayhap," intimated I, "but first my tale, and to see what canst do to aid my need."

Now launched I into mine standard autobiography, which manufacture I an excuse to cram into every Upchuck story, which the experienced reader will skip over with a groan but which the neophyte will devour with incredible enrapturement.

"Men think me a stripling youth of fifteen, and so seem I to all. And yet for as long as memory serveth have I looked as I look now. My skin as ever marked with the eczema, my voice as ever cracking and high, my cheeks sprouting irregular

patches of fuzz and my pubes giving forth a call which no wench
has yet deigned to satisfy.

"Fifteen, am I? I, Upchuck, was fifteen when thou, ancient
sorcerer, were but a pewling tad. I was fifteen when thy pa
was a tad. I was fifteen, by the god Yogh-Iberra, when the
ancient crone Doris Day was a fleshy and well-juiced maid of
but forty-five or fifty."

"'Ware blasphemy!" shouted Mus Domesticus. "The Madonna
Day hath been a virginal twenty-one for sixty years or more."

Angrily I leaped to my feet, prepared to draw my ancient
gravity knife Hoodsticker, only I cracked my pate upon the
overhanging rock and avoided a real ear-ringer only through
the good services of Skullwarmer my woolen cap. Calming
myself I reverted to iron-clad logic once again.

"Isn't!" I shouted at the sorcerer.

"Is too!" he countered.

"Isn't!"

"Is!"

"Isn't!"

"Is!"

Thus we struggled, our brilliant arguments and counter-
arguments continuing far into the night, and would have gone
on far longer had not a voice thundered from on high, "Two
cents a word is two cents a word, but get moving quick or giffs
der dejection shlipp!"

"Well then," the ancient one murmured, "sip a few drops of
this and you shall awaken in the morning an older man indeed."
Saying this he reached into his saddle bag and drew forth a vial
of greenish, glittering liquid.

I reached eagerly and took the vial from him. I held it before
my eye, studying it in the light of the campfire that crackled
and sputtered between the magician and myself. Through the
liquid the flames seemed living things and Mus Domesticus
seemed to waver and reform into a strange creature with huge,
round black ears, a mouth all on one side of his face, and
three fingers on each hand. "Drink it," he said in a mild,
tenor voice.

I unstoppered the vial and tilted back my head, swirling
the greenish contents around in my mouth before swallowing.

"Umm," I said, "tastes like toothpaste," and collapsed into the campfire.

Mus Domesticus must have been less than a total villain, for he pulled my unconscious head back out of the campfire before robbing me of Punkzapper, Hoodsticker, Ed, Fred, and my stash. He left me Heroine, Skullwarmer, Lotion and Gravyshedder.

I awakened with an angry firedrake kicking embers in my face, rose chagrined and began to make my way after the charlatan. Which way would the wily sorcerer Mus Domesticus head? He was riding toward Pappalardi Mountain when first we encountered. Would he proceed now, or, being wily, would he expect me to remember his original direction and follow, and would he instead double back across the Plain of Euclid whence he had come? Or, expecting me to second-guess his intention thusly, would he third-guess me and head toward Pappalardi Mountain? Or, expecting me to fathom his intention to third-guess me . . .

On and on it went, until I decided to assume a more powerful strategy and flip a coin. With my purse gone I was unable to do this, so instead placed one hand over my eyes, turned widdershins three times, staggered about a bit, and then opened my eyes to see which way the God Yogh-Iberra directed me.

Twas across the barren Plain of Euclid, toward the dire and malign and ill-famed, infamous and despised Dukedom of Poughkeepsie.

I climbed once more aboard Heroine's brawny withers and slapped her flank affectionately, whispering sweetly in her soft ear, "Move along, O noble she-horse, or to knackers you'll go."

Heroine, as ever, responded to kindness and persuasion, and soon we found ourselves gazing upward at the blazing orb that illuminated the Plain of Euclid.

O ye who read this chronicle, if yet in yon distant day men know the Plain of Euclid no more needst I say, but if it be sealed off and forgotten, read ye of that place of desolation. Flat it is as the face of a pond, its smooth surface broken only by the occasional rippling of the dreaded sine waves. Deadly tribes of isoceles and secants struggle endlessly for possession of the Obtuse and the Acute.

Terrifying tangents accompanied as ever by their cotangents drop perpendiculars at a moment's warning, impaling unwary tribesmen of the Geometers and Trigonometers amidships.

Far, far across the Plain saw I Mus Domesticus, or anyway a tiny black dot silhouetted against the blinding white of the Plain which I took to be the traitorous sorcerer. Onward urged I my faithful horse Heroine, she crying and moaning in her thirst as my eyes alternately scanned the Plain in search of drink and sought ever to keep visual touch with Mus.

At last there rose on the edge of the Plain greener woodlands and the towering towers of ill-starred Poughkeepsie. Long before Heroine and I could reach the city's walls the tiny dot that was Mus Domesticus disappeared, swallowed up into that city of darkness and sin.

Shades of evening were falling and the cool of that country's far-famed night had begun to descend ere my faithful mare and I reached the far edge of the Plain of Euclid. Approaching the city gate of towering and mystery-shrouded Poughkeepsie I drew back the mighty right fist that had been so oft the despair of foeman and friend alike and pounded thrice upon the city gate, hurling a resounding bell-like challenge through the guard posts and alleyways of Poughkeepsie.

Boom!

Boom!

Boom!

Boom!

From within the wall there came a scurrying and mumbling as of many hoofs and mouths, then opened there a peephole in the wall and down peered a baleful eye at me, balefully.

"Who are you, and what do you want?" it demanded.

"I be Upchuck the Barbarian," I responded. "Warlock of Secaucus, Master of the Galloping Pack and Champion of the Annual Intramural Track Meet. I seek a foully treacherous conjurer, the evil and ill-visaged Mus Domesticus."

"Very well," quoth the baleful eye. "Pay the toll and what you do inside is your own business."

"Listen fellow," bellowed I crisply, "the traitor Mus Domesticus hath drugged and robbed me of mine all, and made away with mine stash. Admit me to Poughkeepsie and once I capture the foul Mus pay I your Duke threefold his customed tribute, um, shall, uh, I, uh, I shall." Fough, how I hate these convoluted sentences. But, then, heroic chronicles are heroic chronicles and one must observe the customs of the trade.

The eye was withdrawn, the peephole slammed shut, then a door was opened in the city wall. "I've heard 'em all, a hundred times," the guardsman grumbled. "Look, buster, if you don't have the loot to pay the toll just sign this form FT37–6, Temporary Waiver of City Toll, in sextuplicate, explaining fully your reason for not paying the toll, retain one copy for your own records and come on in. I don't suppose that walking gluepot's registered either." He gestured meanly at Heroine, who ignored the impertinence.

As did I. I signed the waiver and entered ill-famed Poughkeepsie, seeking directions from this passerby and that until an ancient crone directed my path down a dark and foul-smelling alleyway off the Street of the Systems Programmers. At the end of the alley a dim-lit and dirt-encrusted sign proclaimed the Stagger Inn.

Taking care to tether and booby-trap Heroine in the manner long known to the members of my guild, I boldly thrust open the door of the Stagger Inn, finding it less securely bolted than I had anticipated, and stumbled into a smoky and alcoholic tavern populated by brawling townsmen, drunken visitors, loose wenches and long-fingered cutpurses.

I found a newly vacated table and, when a serving-maid clad in low-cut blouse and well-filled dirndl approached to ask my will, I grasped her fleshy wrist in an inconspicuous but painful grip known well to members of my guild and shot at her but three words: "Where be he?"

"Where be who?" she responded. O clever slut!

"The evil sorcerer Mus Domesticus," saith I.

"Oh, ah, aye, sir," wheedled the serving-maid, squirming in my iron-like grasp so as to give mine orbs a breathtaking tumble twixt her jollying twin *knockers* (as we call 'em in the guild). "Aye, oh, ah, well, ooh, aiie, if you don't let go my wrist, you squirt, I'll bash in your bloody skull like a grackle's egg!"

With that the high-spirited darling took her free hand and

clouted me on the ear so that my head felt as it had the time Heroine accidentally stepped on it whilst I slumbered.

"Well, maid, no need for me to hurt thee if thee'll just answer my questions," I told the lass.

"Thou," she said.

"Thou what?" I asked.

"Thou'll answer, not thee, thou knot-head," she chirped.

Ah, high-spirited womanhood, delight of the world!

"And if you mean the kind old gentleman in the magician's robe," she continued her abject explanation, "he said to take a snack and a tankard on his own tab, and he'll see you in the morning."

Could it be? Mayhap, thought I, the sorcerer Mus Domesticus was willing to come to terms. Perhaps he had realized that his victory over Upchuck the Barbarian was but a temporary one, that any man who durst place himself in opposition to the terror out of Secaucus was doomed. If Mus had so realized, mayhap he was seeking to make amends.

"Very well," quoth I to the serving wench. "Bring me a haunch of salmon and a flagon of fermented penguin's milk, and be quick with it. And by the by," I added quickly ere she was away, "what do they call you, my dear?"

She blushed cunningly and curtsied at that sharp sally, and said, "Betimes they calls me Blodwen and betimes they calls me other things, but I never me mind so long's they don't call me late for dinner!"

With that she burst into an uproarious tittering and made her way, both jiggling and giggling, to fetch my food and drink. I pointed mine naked feet toward the inn's fireplace to warmth. Sorely did they miss old Ed and Fred, held hostage by Mus Domesticus. Whilst awaiting mine refreshments I occupied myself with listing to the conversations of revelers and merry-makers athwart and abaft my unbroken oaken table.

Nearby a grimy cut-throat and his equally disreputable companion were discussing the local Shire Reeve, one Lawless Quinsana, whose latest exploit had been the arrest and imprisonment of an entire class of choir students *en route* from matins to midday devotions. Shire Reeve Quinsana had accused the younglings of thinking impure thoughts, and had sold them all off into bondage to the Geometers of the Plain of Euclid. None were expected to survive the ordeal.

Afore I could hear more sweet Blodwen returned with a steaming platter which she placed on the oaken board before me. I sampled the dishes thereon and offered her my gallant approval, adding a sly compliment to her maidenly charms. "Wouldst join me in a comfy room above, after thy service ends for the night?" I asked.

"Aye, fuzzycheeks," she assented, "Lord Domesticus's simoleons be as good than any, I'll close mine eyes and think on some fair foreign land whilst I earn my—ugh!—biastres."

Well, ye who read this chronicle, see you now the irresistible appeal with which she was smitten! I downed two, three, many tankards of fermented penguin milk in celebration of my coming disflowerment, then trembling with anticipation and somewhat nauseous from the amount of penguin's milk I had downed, I staggered barefoot up a narrow flight of stairs flickeringly lighted by a few greasy torches.

Upstairs I flopped across a mattress of straw ticking and hummed a brave tune to myself while I held down my stomach and awaited Blodwen. Here is how went the old folk ballad that I hummed:

Ay, diddle dizzy dilly dummy
  Dooby what a hack
Wrote about a dopy fellow
  By the name of Brak.
Sing swords and thews and beak-nosed Jews
It's very absurd but it's a penny a word.
Ay, decades ago there was a guy who wrote
About a goop named Jongor
But the passage of time brought a much worse crime
When another scribbler first invented Thongor.
Sing spells and bells and bottomless wells
And write any junk as long as it sells.
Ay, Kothar, Kandar and the resta them yuks
Can struggle along till things go wrong
And then, you see, if you don't know what to do

You can stop and vamp while someone sings a song.
This stuff is bunk though I guess the author needs it
But what kind of cretin is the idiot who reads it?

By now there were poundings upon the walls of my quarters and angry shouts of protest from other guests of the inn so I ceased my ballading. Admit I will that the meter was imperfect in one or two places, and mayhap the rhyming was a trifle obvious, but then it was an old ballad which I was making up as I went along, and my head was more than slightly bleared.

As well I had raised my dulcet voice in song, though, for now, with only a shy knock to announce her arrival, the voluptuous Blodwen slipped through my doorway, a large drinking-skin – I should guess of rehoboam size – coyly hidden beneath her already amply filled blouse. She bolted the heavily timbered door behind her and crossed the room lightly, seating herself beside me on the bed.

"Hoy there, Blodwen," quoth I, "welcome to my love nest."

"Ooh, fresh," she responded, holding the wineskin to my lips. Deeply quaffed I of its nectar-like contents, lying back with a sigh and beginning to toy with her skirt.

"Why Upchuck," she giggled, "art always so for'ard with the maidens?"

"Mmm," I replied archly. She offered me a bit more of the wineskin and I imbibed deeply, rubbing mine cheek sensuously against her neck.

A few more endearments and a few more sips from the skin and I lay back upon the ticking, struggling to free myself of Lotion and Gravyshedder. The now enchanted Blodwen gave me the wineskin to hold and pressed me down upon the ticking. I felt myself burp once or twice and then all was blackness.

The yellow rays of dawn crept through cracks in the wall of the Stagger Inn and wakened me still there upon the ticking. Lotion and Gravyshedder still clung to me. Mine head was filled with a myriad trolls pounding anvils. Mine stomach was as an angry swamp, sending upward distress signals and sour tastes. I sat myself upon the edge of the bed and found myself barely able to remain upright.

After a while I stumbled down the stairs and found a crew ready to confront me. There stood the tricksy Mus Domesticus, there stood the blowsy and delightful Blodwen, and between them a man of surly mien and foul disposition who introduced himself as the Shire Reeve Quinsana.

"Ay, Reeve," quoth I, "your goodwill is appreciated but I wouldst seek mine own revenge against these two foul traitors."

"He's the one," Blodwen broke in, "he ate and drank and filled a room, and now he must pay."

"Pay?" I gasped, amazed. "Pay? Twas the foul sorcerer who robbed my stash and who then offered me his hospitality at this inn!"

"Never heard of the bum," saith Domesticus, turning toward the Reeve. "I just dropped by to visit my cousin Blodwen and her old daddy, Quinsana."

"What?" I choked. "Then stand and defend your foul selves!" Thus saying I reached for Punkzapper and Hoodsticker, only to recall that they had been stolen from me along with my boots, Fred and Ed.

The Reeve siezed me by one shoulder, the sorcerer by the other. "Come along, kid," quoth Quinsana. "A little spell with the Trigs'll straighten you out. I'll see to it that they set you free as soon as you come to full manhood, so you can become a decent, bill-paying citizen."

I screamed, kicked and struggled all the way to the Shire Reeve's cart. The guardsman at the gate recognized me as we left Poughkeepsie and followed us screaming that the Duke would demand his tribute if ever I dared set foot in the city again.

My lovely she-horse Heroine was seized to pay my debts.

But Upchuck does not forget, nor will he be forgotten. Somehow I will endure my vile servitude until I am able to escape, and new chronicles of Upchuck of Secaucus will see print, if but ever again I can find an editor mad enough to purchase them!

THE TALE OF THE SEVENTEENTH EUNUCH

Jane Yolen

Jane Yolen (b. 1939) is a prolific writer of fantasies for both children and adults. She is a master of the fairy tale, having produced over a dozen such collections, of which perhaps the most representative are Tales of Wonder *(1983) and* Dragonfield *(1985). Many of her tales capture that essence of story and she can manipulate it to whatever ends she desires. The following amusing Arabian Nights entertainment is definitely not a fairy tale – at least, not for children.*

It is true that I am the seventeenth eunuch of the Lady Badroulboudour, and the last of the bed guardians chosen to serve her. Some of us were born so, some were created so by other men, and a few are self-made – or self-unmade. But none of the eunuchs had so odd a borning as I.

When I came to the Lady Badroulboudour, her husband The Aladdin was already some years dead. Their illustrious sons were the rulers of kingdoms, court viziers, and members of the advisory. Their daughters were wives to neighboring princes and caliphs and emirs. Exiled to her own apartments – for the new sultan, her eldest son, knew how mothers can interfere in the running of kingdoms – she had nothing better to do than practice such small magicks as her husband had instructed her in, read trashy tales of houris and kings, and care for her many cats. She had white cats with fur like the tops of waves, brown cats the color of the dunes at dusk, gray cats as dark as storms. And one brawling black cat just newly acquired.

The eunuchs cared for the rest. They tried to pleasure her – for do not think that eunuchs are devoid of sexual passion. It is just that we cannot father a child. And – truth be known – we take far less pleasures ourselves in our duties.

But the Lady Badroulboudour had no interest other than in her memories. Her husband The Aladdin had been a manly man, his black hair and beard long and luxuriant, his voice resonant and low. He had been gallant and frequent and manly in his loving – as attested to by their numerous progeny. The Lady Badroulboudour made many loud exclamations to that effect.

Why, then, did her son, the sultan, allow her so many eunuchs? Perhaps because he believed the stories fostered by the harem that no man can perform save he has all his parts. Or perhaps because he firmly believed that if his mother were satisfied in all ways, she would leave the running of the kingdom to him.

Now it was on the tenth day of the third month of Lady Badroulboudour's fiftieth year that she came upon the lamp that The Aladdin owed all his wealth and power to. She had been looking for it in desultory fashion ever since he died, as she was only partially convinced there was any such thing. No one but she had even believed the old stories of the lamp anyway, except her crazy mother-in-law, who was dead now as well.

The discovery of the lamp happened in this fashion. The eunuchs in their high-pitched voices had fallen to quarreling over some inconsequential and Lady Badroulboudour had banished them to the outer rooms. Then, wanting to feed the cats, she noticed that she was short one dish, for the black cat was but newly arrived, a present from her son, the sultan. She wanted to comfort the new black cat with sweetmeats and a dish of cream, that being her way.

So she went from inner room to inner room, then outer room to outer room, looking for a suitable container, rejecting rouge pots and flower vases and a basin containing rose petals in water. And at last, way down the hall, she looked into a storeroom that had been closed for years. There, in a corner, as if thrown by an angry or disinterested hand, was an unprepossessing copper lamp with a small wick and a handle with a chink out of the right side. It was the chink she dimly recalled, having handled it only once, when abducted by the Afrik magician long ago.

She pounced on it with a cry not unlike that of one of the brown cats, which brought the new black cat running into the room to twine around her legs. She picked up cat in one hand, lamp in the other, and made her way back to her rooms.

"Lady, your pleasure?" asked the fifth eunuch, a pudgy, hairless, whey-faced man much given to candies and flatulence.

She dismissed him and the others with a wave of her hand. And when they were all gone, exiled to the outer rooms, she settled herself down on her great bed with her pillows and white cats at her head and feet.

"Could it be?" she mused to herself. The black cat and two brown ones echoed her. "Could it be?" She remembered The Aladdin's hints about magic. Then she added, "If I could have a wish, surely I would ask for my dear Aladdin back."

At his name, all the cats but the black one jumped down to the floor and made themselves scarce for often the mere mention of the name caused Lady Badroulboudour to weep and wail and throw pots and bowls. Only the black cat did not run away. He was, you must remember, new to the palace. And not yet moving quite so fast as the rest.

"But," Lady Badroulboudour reminded herself, "I must attend to my dress." For it is true that since the death of The Aladdin she had lived in great neglect of her person, except for the occasional state dinner. So she took a long and luxuriant bath with soft oils and many powders after, filling the apartments with a heady aroma, not unlike that of nepeta, mintlike and pungent. The cats all rolled about and frisked with pleasure.

Then she put on a gown of silk the color of the sea – green and blue and black. Around her waist she placed a girdle of diamonds set in gold. She set about her neck the six-strand necklace of pearls. On her wrists she put bracelets of diamonds and rubies. Her eyes she outlined with kohl and she put rouge on her mouth and cheeks. She was a woman in her prime.

Then, taking the lamp in hand, she sat back down on her bed, leaning against the black cat. The cat did not complain, but purred both deep and low.

"If there is a genie," Lady Badroulboudour said aloud, "I shall set it free." And she turned the lamp this way and that, looking for a magical key. For though The Aladdin – and the Afrik magician – had both spoken of the lamp, neither of them in the telling had thought to mention how it worked.

She pulled at the wick. She tried to light it. She stuck her finger inside the spout. She blew across both top and bottom. At last, in frustration, she tried to shine the lamp as if by doing so she might find some written instructions on the side.

No sooner had she stroked it, then a strange bituminous smoke began to ascend from the spout, coalescing into a shape that was as rounded and hairless and large as a eunuch, only wafting about four feet above the bedclothes.

"Oh, I have had enough of you half-men!" she cried, sitting up.

"I am no man, lady," said the genie.

"I did not really believe it," said Lady Badroulboudour.

"I am ready to obey thee as thy slave," the genie answered.

"So it is true," Lady Badroulboudour replied.

And they would have gone on and on like this at cross-purposes and not actually corresponding, if the black cat had not been made so playful by the scent of nepeta that the feline took a swipe at the smoke where it was connected to the spout, all but severing the genie's legs from the lamp.

At that Lady Badroulboudour gathered up the cat to her bosom, where it was distracted by the six strands of pearls.

"Then, slave, restore to me my husband, The Aladdin."

The genie managed to look nonplussed, not an easy trick for a man of smoke. Then he laughed. "If you have me bring him back, lady, he would be nought but winding cloth and

bones. Is that your desire? For you must mind what you ask
for, mistress."

"Give him back to me as he was, not as he is."

The genie laughed again. "That I cannot. I can only bring
you what is, not what is no longer."

"I want Aladdin!" She pouted for a moment, looking just like
the princess whom The Aladdin had loved so long ago.

"Alas, that cannot be," said the genie. Somewhere a door
shut or opened and the breeze it let in made him sway gently
over the bed.

"Then what good is your magic?" Lady Badroulboudour
cried, and she threw the lamp, genie and all, across the room
where they fetched up against the north wall with a clatter and
a bang. Before the lamp actually hit, the genie managed to
disappear back down the spout, though there was a small,
pitiful cry from inside the lamp when it landed.

Lady Badroulboudour did not come out of her room the entire
day, nor did she pick up the lamp. She lay on her bed, angry and
speechless, until the sixth eunuch, who was given to honeycakes
and moist eyes, threatened to call her son the sultan. And the
ninth eunuch, who was given to candied dates and belching,
threatened to call her son the vizier. When the sixteenth eunuch,
who was given to buttered toast and tears, bent over to pick up
the lamp, Lady Badroulboudour sat up in the bed and screeched
so loudly that all of the bed guardians left the room at once, the
last slamming the door behind him.

Then Lady Badroulboudour rose from her bed and looked
at herself in the mirror. She drew more kohl around her eyes
and pinched her cheeks until they were red. She took off the
dress the color of the sea, took another long bath, then put on
a dress the color of sand – brown and white and gray. She
rearranged the diamond girdle, the necklace of pearls, and the
bracelets. She put red jewels in her ears. She was a woman in
her prime.

Then she picked up the lamp and stroked its side with a
feather touch.

This time a strange ocherous smoke ascended from the spout,
coalescing into a shape that was as rounded and hairless and *twice*

as large as any eunuch. The genie wafted about three feet above the lamp.

"So," Lady Badroulboudour said.

"What one wish wouldst thou have?" asked the genie.

"Can you bring back my husband any better than your brother can?" she asked.

"No more than he, mistress," said the genie. "Save in winding cloth and bones. Oh— and a bit of wormy matter as well. I have taken the opportunity to check."

"That is all?" Lady Badroulboudour asked.

"That is all," said the genii. "But . . ." he wavered a bit, right hand raised. "I *could* bring you a substitute. One who is like and yet not like your former master, The Aladdin."

"And by this you mean . . . ?" asked Lady Badroulboudour.

"I can bring you a dark-bearded man from the streets of your city, or a deep-throated man from the gateposts of a neighboring town, or a well-muscled man from the taverns of another kingdom, or from the Antipodes for that matter."

"Where they walk upon their hands and eat the dust of the road?" shouted Lady Badroulboudour. "Never!" And this time she threw the lamp, genie and all, against the south wall with a clatter and a bang. The genie managed to disappear – all but his left foot – back through the spout before the lamp actually hit the wall. But there was a rather loud pitiful cry from inside the lamp and a bit of strange muck ran down the lamp's side.

This time Lady Badroulboudour did not come out of her room for a week, nor did she pick up the lamp. She lay on her bed, angry and speechless – and hungry – though the eunuchs fed all the cats. All but the black cat, who refused to eat till she did. The eighth eunuch, who was given to tippling and weeping late at night, threatened to call her daughters. And the second eunuch, who had no faults at all, save he stared with popped eyes and so always managed to look startled, threatened to call her father's maiden aunt, and she, dear lady, was well into her nineties and had a voice like an angry camel. Still nothing worked until the thirteenth eunuch bent over to pick up the lamp. At that, Lady Badroulboudour screeched so loudly that they all left, slamming the door behind them.

Then Lady Badroulboudour rose from her bed, scattering cats white and brown and gray, and looked at herself in her mirror. She drew yet another circle of kohl around her eyes, but left her cheeks white. She took off the dress the color of sand, took a long bath with many new oils, and put on a dress the color of fire – yellow and orange and red. She rearranged the diamond girdle, the necklace of pearl, the bracelets, and the red jewels in her ear. She placed a chain of gold on her left ankle. She was a woman in her prime.

Then she picked up the lamp, thoughtfully rubbing it on both sides and vigorously down the middle.

This time a strange opalescent smoke ascended from the spout, coalescing into a shape that was rounded and hairless and *three* times larger than any eunuch. It wafted fully five feet above the lamp.

"No tricks," said Lady Badroulboudour.

"What one wish wouldst thou have?" asked the genie.

"I assume you cannot bring me back Aladdin whole either?"

The genie shook his head, though whether from dismay or from a passing breeze it was hard to say. "We cannot bring back what is no longer, mistress."

"And you have only men from the street or the taverns or the Antipodes to offer me?"

"My brothers of the lamp are good and they are kind," said the genie. "But I understand your reluctance, O princess, daughter of the mighty sultan, wife of the late great Aladdin, to take a lesser man."

Lady Badroulboudour nodded.

"And my brothers of the lamp are young, both in their time in this copper prison and their magic," said the genie. "I, on the other hand, can offer an exchange."

"An exchange?" Lady Badroulboudour asked. "Do you mean a trade? A swap? A bargain? Like camel merchants at a bazaar?"

"I can make you a man out of a camel, mistress."

"To spit in my face?"

"Or a bird . . ."

"To peep and preen?"

"Or a dog . . ."

"To water my bedposts?"

"Or . . ."

Just then the black cat stretched and arched its back.

"He must have luxurious black hair and beard and a deep, soothing voice," said Lady Badroulboudour, as the black cat purred under her hand.

"If those are the characteristics of the animal," the genie said. He held up his opalescent hand. "This one wish, my mistress, and no other."

She gathered the black cat up from the bed, and held it out to the genie. "This cat, then."

"I ask again, my mistress, to be absolutely certain. And you must mind how you ask. What wouldst thou have?"

A smile played about Lady Badroulboudour's mouth. Two dimples which had not been seen since the death of her husband suddenly appeared in her cheeks. "I wish, genie, that this cat, this black cat that I hold in my arms . . ." and the cat purred loudly in a low, deep tremolo. "That this cat were exchanged into a man."

The genie nodded and moved his great hands above the cat. The cat stretched, yowled once, stretched again, and shook itself free of Lady Badroulboudour's hands. As it touched the floor, its back legs lengthened and she could hear the creaking and groaning and unknotting of its bones.

Closing her eyes contentedly and only listening to the sounds of her bargain being made, Lady Badroulboudour waited a moment or two longer than necessary. When she opened her eyes again, a handsome, dark-bearded man was kneeling before her, naked and unashamed.

"My lady," he said, his voice low and with a kind of deep, dark burr in it.

Lady Badroulboudour looked at that face, at the green eyes staring up at her, at the curl of his dark beard. She looked down at his well-muscled shoulders and chest. She looked further down . . .

"Genie . . ." she said, her voice suddenly stony.

"I told you to mind what it was you asked for," said the genie. And he was gone back into the spout.

Lady Badroulboudour suddenly remembered what she should have remembered before. All the cats in her apartments – male and female – were neutered, some as kittens and some rather later on.

"My lady," the low, purring voice came again. She looked down into his handsome dark-bearded face.

"Well, two out of three ain't bad," she said, affecting the language of the camel market. Then she lifted me up to clasp me in her arms.

I took her eagerly, for the memory of my recent maleness was still upon me, she smelled deliciously of nepeta, and she was, after all, a lady still in her prime.

AN EYE FOR AN EYE, A TOOTH FOR A TOOTH

Lawrence Schimel

Lawrence Schimel (b. 1971) is an American writer with a remarkable facility for producing short, sharp stories with refreshing twists on old ideas, and often with new ideas entirely. He has a most infuriatingly creative imagination (said without the slightest malice!) which I envy immensely. His first story collection, The Drag Queen of Elfland *(1997), contains a quote by Marion Zimmer Bradley which echoes my feelings entirely: "I wish I knew Lawrence Schimel's secret of getting so much character into so few words." You'll see what I mean in the following story, which is one of the examples of dark humour in this book.*

The alarm clock went off and I rolled over to slam down on it, hard. It stopped buzzing. I wanted to roll over and go back to sleep, but I knew I shouldn't. I debated whether to get up or not, arm still outstretched to the clock since I was too tired to pull it back into bed. Finally, I opened my left eye to check the time. 6:47. I could snooze ten more minutes.

I rolled over and pulled the covers up close, but I couldn't fall asleep. There was something lumpy under my pillow. I tried to ignore it, but it wouldn't go away. I couldn't imagine what it was, and for an absurd moment I thought of the fairy tale, "The Princess and the Pea". I knew I hadn't been eating peas in bed; I hate vegetables.

When I couldn't stand it any more, I rolled onto my stomach and reached under my pillow, keeping my eyes shut so I could go back to sleep when I rolled over again. My fingers closed on something hard and cold and round. Coin? Quarter? No, more like one of those Susan B. Anthonys they pulled out of circulation because they were so much like quarters.

I rolled over onto my back again and settled my head into the now comfortable pillow, wondering what the silver dollar was doing there. I hadn't seen a Susan B. Anthony in years, not since I was a little kid. And even if I had accidentally gotten one with my change, what would it be doing under my pillow?

My parents used to give me them whenever I lost a tooth, back when I still believed in the tooth fairy. Nervously, I felt around my mouth with my tongue to make sure I hadn't lost a tooth during the night, just in case the tooth fairy really did exist and this was the exchange I'd gotten. But I couldn't feel any gaps in my teeth.

I wondered what the tooth fairy did with all those teeth, anyway. Or how it got a hold of the Susan B. Anthony dollars and why that was how much it paid for teeth.

Stupid, I told myself. There's no such thing as the tooth fairy.

I nestled back into the pillow, ready to nap for a few more minutes, when I felt a weight land on my chest. Cracking my left eye open again I saw a little gnome-like creature sitting on my chest, with a million eyes all over its body. My heart pounding, I tried to sit up. I couldn't, though, because he was pretty heavy. Lifting my head to get a better look, I tried to open my other eye, but it refused to open.

I rubbed at my eyes with my hands. When my fingers pressed against the lid of my right eye I could feel that there wasn't anything inside the socket. I started screaming. Or at least I tried to. The guy was really heavy and having him sitting on my chest didn't make matters any easier. Not to mention the fact that he had clamped his hands over my mouth.

Wondering what he was doing there and what he wanted, I stared at the gnome-like creature again with my left eye. He had eyes all over his body, like that Greek god, whatever his name was. Only they weren't all human eyes. I could see a whole bunch of compound ones, like a fly's, as well as perfectly round ones, slit-pupiled ones, and other variations. I thought it was disgusting, so I closed my eye, then thought better of it; I'd rather know what he was doing so I could maybe have a few seconds warning if he tried anything.

When I reopened my eye I noticed he was wearing a T-shirt. There wasn't much of it left – he'd cut holes into it for all the eyes – but I still could make out a few letters. There was an "L" followed by an "X", then an "AL", and at the end was an "S". I had no idea what it meant.

I felt something moving around on the bed near my feet, and I risked looking away from the thing on my chest to see what it was. It was another gnome, like the one on my chest, but all teeth instead of eyes. He was wearing a T-shirt as well, and his was readable. It said: LEX TALIONIS.

"Hi!" the thing at the foot of the bed croaked. Its voice was really deep and scratchy. "I'm the tooth fairy. And this here's my brother."

I turned my head to look back at the thing on my chest, but it was too late; his hand was in my face. I could feel him pop my eye out of the socket and was surprised that it didn't hurt. It felt hot, like a water bottle when you're sick, but that was it, no pain or anything.

I reached out to grab him, but he was suddenly off me. I kicked around, but couldn't feel the thing at the foot of the bed either.

"My brother's always jealous," the deep, scratchy voice said. "I mean, who ever loses an eye and leaves it for him under their pillow?"

So this was his revenge. I expected I would be angrier, but I merely wondered if they would at least leave me another Susan

B. Anthony. A moment later, something cool was placed on the space my left eye had formerly occupied. I flailed around near my head, but aside from banging my hand against the bed boards couldn't grab whichever one of them had put it there.

As I was wondering why they had put the coin over my eye, I heard a thumping, like the pounding of blood in my ears. It's like the pennies to pay Charon, I realized, and my heart nearly froze. The pounding grew louder, *thump-thump, thump-thump*, and suddenly the deep, scratchy voice of the tooth fairy said from right beside my left ear, "And this is my other brother."

QUEEN OF THE GREEN SUN

Jack Sharkey

Earlier I mentioned that Ron Goulart was pretty much a lone voice amongst humorous sf and fantasy in the 1950s. By the 1960s a few new voices were joining the chorus, including Jack Sharkey (1931–92). For about six years, from 1959 to 1965, Sharkey was a prolific contributor of sf and fantasy to the specialist magazines, always with exciting and clever stories. Amongst them was a comic fantasy novel, "It's Magic You Dope", serialized in Fantastic *in 1962 but never published in book form, perhaps because it was too ahead of its time. He was really a short-story specialist, producing very few novels, although he did write a novelization of* The Addams Family *in 1965. After 1965 Sharkey turned to the theatre, writing over eighty stage plays and musicals, so fantasy's loss was the theatre's gain. The following story is one of Sharkey's earliest.*

Once there was a queen, in the Land of the Green Sun, who arose from the Royal Bed in the morning, looked into the Royal Mirror, and saw a stalk of celery growing out of the top of her head. Whether or not she screamed at the sight is still open to conjecture; as a queen, she had a certain reputation for *savoir-faire* to maintain, and a terrified bellow would have been far beneath her Royal Dignity. Besides, in the Land of the Green Sun, the appearance of celery atop one's head was not a sight to evoke terror, but rather, a contented delight, for the bearer of the Sacred Celery was considered the chosen of the gods. The persons fortunate enough to find the stalk sprouting upon them – it happened once every thousand apexes – were the beloved of the land. For one solid year, it was their privilege to live in the Royal Palace, as though they were royalty themselves, and to wine and dine and whoop it up with abandon, with no – well, hardly any – thought of tomorrow. At the end of the year, the person thus endowed would be taken in solemn procession to the top of Mahogany Mountain, and the stalk of Sacred Celery (along with the top of the person's head) would be removed, and ensconced in the Emerald Temple for the adulation and awe of posterity. It had been argued by some of the former celery-bearers that the loss of their craniums was going a bit too far, but it was pointed out to them (on their way to the top of Mahogany Mountain) that this was the only way in which they could be certain the Sacred Roots would not be damaged in the process. And so, in the Land of the Green Sun, each day on arising, the citizenry, male, female, young and old, would rush to their mirrors to see if they were the lucky ones. After a careful, and fruitless examination of their respective scalps, they would sit back with a sigh of bitter regret. (Some said that the sigh was more of relief, but that is undoubtedly a vicious rumor circulated by the Camps of the Carrot-Eaters, to the south.)

The queen, however, could not be truly said to be overjoyed by this sign of honor. After all, she lived like royalty *anyhow*, and rather than having a reward offered to her, she had nothing but the prospect of sudden curtailment of her normal activities in a year, and the mental image of her cranium, mounted upon a pedestal in the Emerald Temple with her glorious red-and-black-striped hair dangling in soft waves to the floor, brought tears to her Royal Eyes. And so, while it is uncertain as to whether or not she screamed, it is a fact that she did *something*, else why should her handmaidens all be rushing down the winding corridors of the palace toward the Royal Bedroom, with their wooden toeclips clacking frenziedly upon the glossy floor?

By the time they arrived, however, the queen had had enough presence of mind to wind her head (and the Sacred Celery) with a large orange turban, hiding her secret from prying eyes. She would not admit to having screamed, and the handmaiden who had been first to voice such a suggestion had had her back-scratching privileges suspended for a week. The queen, after the weeping girl had slunk miserably from the Royal Presence, commanded the handmaidens to fly quickly to the far end of the palace, and to arouse Havler Grem from his slumbers in his decadently comfortable feather-pit.

If anyone could help her, the queen reasoned, it was Havler.

Havler Grem was the Royal Minister of Interstate Commerce, and, since there was only one state in the Land of the Green Sun, some of the people thought that he had a pretty soft job. Be that as it may, Havler arrived in due time at the queen's bedroom, bowed solemnly to his Monarch, and remained in that subservient stance until the last of the handmaidens had fluttered away to have – at the queen's suggestion – a picnic in the Royal Gardens.

No sooner had the door closed behind the last of them, than the queen, with a brave, tragic smile, whipped aside her orange turban, and let Havler's eyes, as he straightened up from his bow, fall upon the pale green stalk atop her head. Havler, after a momentary uprising of his bushy eyebrows and the faint suggestion of a cynical smile curling the corners of his thin-lipped mouth, pointed out to the queen, with a certain sarcasm, how fortunate she was to be amongst the elite of the kingdom, a chosen one of the gods. There is no record of the queen's reply to Havler Grem, but the residents of the palace talk of the unaccountable rise in temperature that day for the space of a quarter of an hour. Havler, when the queen had finished replying, asked her what she intended to do about the celery: would she publish the news at once, or would she wait until the height of her birthday celebration, due to begin that very night?

The queen replied, with some frigid dignity, that she intended to get rid of the (the adjective here used has been thus far unable to be translated by historians delving into this period; from its context, they can only assume it was a rather nasty one) celery stalk, and the sooner the better. There were, she intimated, books on the subject, were there not? There were, of course, but all such books, dealing with the removal of Sacred Celery (the possession of which was such an honor) had naturally been banned from the kingdom, and the penalty for being caught with one of them was far worse than – as the townsfolk put it – being caught with the celery.

Havler, of course, had read all the books. And the queen knew it, and he knew that she knew, so there was little use beating around the bush any longer. What the queen wanted to know was how to divest herself of her unwonted (and unwanted) vegetation, and she wanted to know at once, or she might be tempted to adulterate the feathers in Havler's pit with a bushel of thorns, and confine him therein with nothing but slime lizards for company. Havler decided the wisest course – besides, he'd had his fun for the morning – was to tell the queen how to go about it.

Together (the queen having first replaced the turban) they hurried down the corridor to Havler Grem's room, to consult one of the forbidden books. The queen kept urging Havler to hurry; at any time, she felt, the palace residents would begin to ask questions about that turban – especially the Royal Hairdresser, who had that morning, for the first time since her employment, been told her services were not necessary, as the queen had decided to let her hair alone for a change, and there was the even worse – though remote – possibility that the celery would start going to seed (a turban can be wound only so hugely without inciting talk).

Havler, remaining calm despite the queen's frantic urgings for greater haste, thumbed through the pages of the Emerald Bible, a book written entirely on swatches of silk (reputedly from the original worm), by a malcontented high priest of the temple who had decided – before he was captured and destroyed – that people might as well know that obedience to the priest-sorcerors of the Emerald Temple was not necessary if you knew the counterspells. Havler paged idly through – the book's slithery pages gave him a certain sybaritic delight – the Emerald Bible, and finally, when the queen was nearing the verge of nervous collapse, opened the book wide to a certain passage inscribed in glittering golden ink. It dealt with "Celery, Sacred, Removal of".

The queen tore the book from his hands when he announced he'd located the countermeasures against encroaching celery, and read it carefully, and with fluttering heart.

The method was simplicity itself. All one had to do was to get – in writing – a request from any other person in the kingdom for a transference of celery, and, on the burning of the parchment (necromantic protocol called for parchment; paper or silk wouldn't do) the bargain became finalized, and the celery would transport itself instantaneously to the cranium of the person who had asked for it. The queen having read it twice over began to grow pale. More than the people of the kingdom suspected, she knew of their less-than-enthusiastic checkups at their morning mirrors, and the chances of finding a person stupid enough to be amenable to signing the request (or of finding a person literate enough to write their own name) were few and far between. And there was the further danger that if the person refused, they would (since they'd been approached by the turbaned queen) know of her possession of celery, and know further of the fact that she'd consulted the forbidden books. And the still further danger that even if they accepted the celery, they would somehow let slip the awful truth that the queen had been chosen by the gods and had fudged on the deal.

With a small Royal Sigh, the queen sank down into a chair and let the book close with a silken slam. How could she possibly go about losing that celery? Havler, sensing her dilemma, suggested, almost casually, that a person could possibly be made to sign something without knowing what it was that they signed. The queen started to emerge from her blue funk. Havler further insinuated that if the person knew not that there were any connection between the signing and the appearance of the celery, they would have to assume that the celery had –

since this was the period of the thousandth apex – appeared of its own volition, and that they were *naturally* the chosen one. The queen brightened even further. And, Havler pointed out, the queen had in her possession at that very moment a large volume entitled "Expendable Subjects" (which included all the populace but the queen and Havler) from which she might select a name at random.

The queen, moving so fast that Havler could barely keep pace with her, flashed down the corridor and back to her room, where she threw open the aforementioned volume and espied, at the head of the list of expendables, the name Leejee Lahl. And what made her task even simpler, Leejee was employed in the palace kitchen, a few short flights away from the Royal Bedroom. The queen closed the book and smiled a smile that even turned Havler's blood cold . . .

Leejee Lahl, unaware of her date with fate, was at that very moment down in the kitchen, peeling potatoes for the Royal Dinner Party that night, in honor of the Queen's Birthday Celebration. She peeled automatically, not watching her hands at all, and the peels, nearly a half-inch thick, thudded gently to the flagstoned floor of the immense kitchen, arising into a pile that hid her rather large bare feet. Leejee's eyes were focused on some middle distance, and to look upon her vapidly pretty face, one would think that she had not a thought in her head. And one would have only been off by one thought.

For Leejee thought solely of Garnel Ross. Garnel the Handsome, Garnel the Bold, who that very night was to meet her back of the Royal Garden Gate, and take her away with him (riding tandem on one of the swiftest desert frogs in the land) to the Camps of the Carrot-Eaters, to the south. Garnel was a warrior, tall and strong, and his rank amongst the Carrot-Eaters was nearly that of prince. Someday, if he could live longer than the other aspirants to the Teakwood Chair, he would be King of the Carrot-Eaters, and Leejee, as his wife, would be queen. She sighed, thinking of her lover, thinking of her future queenship, thinking of ruling over all those people, eating all those carrots. It was quite a step upward, socially, for the humble, beautiful and stupid daughter of a toeclip-maker. And as she was lost in her introspective reveries, dreaming always of Garnel, his muscular arms, his soft, creamy-blue hair, and wide-set pink eyes, she heard not the approaching toeclip-clacks of the queen herself, until the fuzzy shadow of a tall orange turban fell upon her pile of peels.

Leejee broke from her thoughts of Garnel and looked upward, into the smiling (and tense, though she didn't notice) face of the queen. She felt a bit less than subservient at the moment, since she, too, was in line for the throne, but she acted democratically polite when the queen spoke to her, and accepted the Seat of Honor at that evening's celebration without even asking herself why the queen of the land should choose the humble, beautiful and stupid daughter of a toeclip-maker as the Honor Guest of a Royal Party. And, after the queen – and the trailing, whispering, expostulating form of Havler Grem – had left the kitchen, Leejee reasoned that it was only right that she, a future queen, should have her first taste of Royal Living before she eloped with Garnel Ross. It would undoubtedly put her in good stead with the Carrot-Eaters if she had a little experience at Royal Living before she got to the Teakwood Chair.

Leejee sighed again, and returned to her labors, her mind dreaming of the night, when, after the party, she would be racing across the Crystal Desert with her lover, astride the sleek gray-green flanks of a bounding frog. It was an event not many girls had a chance to consider. A small frown creased her brow as she realized that the party would run beyond the hour at which she was to meet Garnel at the gate, but Garnel, if he truly loved her, would understand that she was doing it for him: that he might have a queen of whom he could be proud. He could certainly wait a few more hours for her. What did it matter that every moment he spent in the Land of the Green Sun was fraught with danger? What did it matter that there was a substantial price on his head . . . his creamy-blue curly-haired head? Was his love for her not strong enough to brave the additional risk? And what did it matter that the Royal Guard would be doubled on the rough log wall about the Royal Courtyard that night, to assure the merrymakers that no peasantry crept near enough to even hear the sounds of the fun? Garnel was brave, was he not? He would surely understand that she, even though a bit later than promised, would certainly be coming to him. Leejee sighed yet again, and kept on with her flaying of the hapless potatoes. Tonight, she thought to herself, will be a night to remember always . . .

The smoky green sun, having reached the center of the overhead dome of pallid gray sky, the point of its apex, began to reverse its direction and spiral in increasing circles toward the jagged circle of mountains that comprised the horizon of the Land of the Green Sun. One time it would circle completely about the kingdom, seemingly rolling along the uppermost peaks of those mountains, then it would dip out of sight behind the tallest – Mahogany Mountain – and a gray-green twilight would come upon the land. Then would the party begin. The rim of the smoky green fireball was just coming in contact with that very mountaintop when, from the tanglewood behind the palace, Garnel Ross, astride his slack-jawed, sleepy-eyed desert frog came riding stealthily up to the back gate of the palace. He let his soft pink eyes rove over the vicinity of that gate, giving them leave to seek out the object of his heart's desire: Leejee Lahl, the beautiful, the humble, the daughter of the toeclip-maker. His pink eyes roved in vain; no such object did they encounter. Garnel, shivering a bit (for the low-circumference period of the green sun was chill), dismounted from his steed, gave it a large rubber bug to chew upon, and crept carefully toward the distant wall of logs . . .

As he crept ever nearer, his heart thudding against his ribs when he espied the doubled guards upon the upper part of the wall, the sound of music came to his ears. He recalled then that this was the night of the queen's birthday celebration, and that all the palace residents would be on hand to indulge in the festivities. From the far side of the wall came the roaring lilt of drunken laughter, and Garnel smiled within himself, knowing that, thus occupied, none of them would think to guard the Garden Gate. Soon, whether or not they knew it, they would be short a potato-peeler in the palace kitchen. It was a cruel trick to play upon them, but Garnel steeled himself against any thoughts of mercy toward the hated royalty of the Land of the Green Sun. Let them seek out and find and train a new potato-peeler, he said to himself. It would serve them right. From his vantage point beyond a small scrub pine, he saw that the guards, rather than keeping an eye upon goings-on outside the wall, were concentrating their attention upon the doings in the courtyard itself. It wasn't every day they got to see such a splendid show. Garnel, more than confident that he wouldn't be observed, was prepared to skirt the courtyard proper and head for the garden gate when he heard another sound, somewhere between a whinny and a cackle, mingled with a fresh surge of Royal Laughter beyond the wall. The sound made his heart leap, his hackles rise, and his tongue go dry. He would know that voice anywhere: it was that of Leejee Lahl, his betrothed.

What might she be doing in the midst of a Royal Party? Garnel wondered this, and also wondered why she was doing anything other than waiting for him at the appointed place. Perhaps, he told himself, she was a prisoner? Mayhap the queen – plague upon her – had discovered their upcoming tryst and had taken steps to assure Leejee's remaining in humble servitude.

Garnel, throwing caution to the winds, felt a fierce anger rising within him. Rising along with it, from his crouch behind the scrub pine, he vaulted to the log wall, scrambled up its rough bark side, slid over the brink of it on his stomach, and plunged headlong into the waving fronds of unmown grass on the far side. Had he been unobserved? He hoped so, as he lay there, his face in the dirt, his body criss-crossed by the long pencil-shadows of the grass. The guards at the wall top made no outcry, nor did the boisterous sounds of revelry abate. Garnel, deciding he was safe, began to crawl stealthily through the clinging weeds and grass on his stomach, until he drew near enough the perimeter of the cleared courtyard to see the festivities themselves. But Garnel looked beyond the courtyard proper to the simple gilt-speckled couch on which Leejee sat, her simple, cowlike eyes wide and watery, observing the festive performers that cavorted in the arena. Or so she seemed to his eye.

Actually, Leejee's mind was not even aware of the goings-on. This was due both to a natural aptitude for blankness and a great quantity of fermented tomato juice which she'd been imbibing like water since early afternoon. And there was a third reason. Leejee, so much enamored of her tall, handsome king-to-be, could think of nothing but Garnel, whose bride she would become that very night.

The Royal Dancers bounded into the arena, and the band struck up a swiftly surging waltz as the lithe bodies of the men and women soared and spun and whirled to the fantastic rhythms of the dance. The women shrieked their delight aloud as their partners hurled them through the torch-lit night air, trailing a rainbow stream of gauzy finery behind them. Up, down, to and fro they wound, in an intricate pattern of insane color and fierce abandon, until, at the climax of the music, they all fell heavily prostrate upon the earth, some of the more dedicated ones never to rise again, being danced to death. But Leejee thought only of Garnel, his pink eyes glowing with love.

As the remnants of the dancers carried the bodies of the dead and dying away, the Royal Clowns appeared, somersaulting over one another, whacking themselves over the heads with petrified hollyhocks, tearing the very clothes off their backs, beating gongs, drums and cymbals, setting fire to their shoes, and throwing mud at the nearby guests. But Leejee, lost in her thoughts of Garnel, did not so much as smile, merely coming out of her reverie long enough to take another sip of her fermented tomato juice.

Why is she here? Garnel asked himself over and over. He knew that the couch on which she sat was the place of highest honor. How had Leejee, the Royal Potato-Peeler, daughter of a humble toeclip-maker, gotten herself into such an enviable situation? Garnel decided to wriggle closer and find out. At that moment, he heard a sound, and froze into immobility. Someone was walking through the tall grass and weeds, and coming his way. No, not just someone, two people. Garnel could hear their voices, a man's and a woman's, speaking in hoarse, nervous whispers. One of them sounded a bit like the queen, but Garnel, peering between stalks of grass, could see no crown, though he did get a glimpse of what seemed to be an orange turban. He'd almost turned his mind back to his loved one, when he heard them mention her by name. Listening much more closely, he realized, all at once, that this *was* the queen, after all. And she was going to— *What* did she say?!!

Garnel's stout heart turned quite cold as he heard the queen tell her confidante – who who just had to be Havler Grem, his voice was so oily and low and vile – how near her insidious plan was to its completion. He lost some of the words, but it became clear enough to him that the sooner he took Leejee away from this place, the safer she would be. He would wriggle around the courtyard, get behind the couch upon which Leejee sat, and then, drawing the fire-hardened oaken sword, he would hack the birthday guests to pieces, carry Leejee away on his shoulder, set fire to the log wall, and— No, that was no good; someone was sure to try and stop him. Maybe— Despite the dirt and grass-stains on his face, he found himself smiling as his plan entered, took hold, and grew in his brain. With scarcely a whisper of noise, Garnel humped himself quickly through the grass, carefully skirting the region where the queen and the Minister of Interstate Commerce were still talking – the queen was fishing for compliments on her birthday gown of the finest spun sand, and Havler seemed to be deliberately avoiding the bait – and wriggled determinedly toward Leejee, his love, the light of his life . . .

Leejee, in the midst of a large swallow of juice, was startled to hear the voice of her lover quite close at hand. At first she thought it was coming from within her mind, but an irritated rustling in the grass that almost overhung the back of the gilt-speckled couch convinced her that he was truly with her. Garnel, crouched uncomfortably behind her, told her of the fate that lay in store for her should she sign the parchment the queen had already prepared. Leejee thought about it a minute and decided that he was right. What could she do? Garnel told her. And, as he spoke, her face curved into a vengeful smile of flinty-eyed anticipation. His message completed, Garnel hitched himself around, and crawled back the way he had come. Many minutes later, Leejee observed his tall, magnificent body as he stood up on the far side of the courtyard and climbed back over the wall. None of the other guests seemed to have noticed him, but that may have been either because of the cleverness of the entertainers, or the fact that they were all too decadent to really care. The queen, seeming to come from nowhere, suddenly seated herself beside Leejee on the couch, and Leejee pretended once more to be engrossed in the evening's entertainment.

A battle to the death started. The Royal Gladiators were now in the arena, bowing their final obeisances to the queen, and then proceeding to brain one another with clubs, until only one man was left standing, and he fell over during the applause. But so intense and all-absorbing was Leejee's love for Garnel that she never even heard the plop as the gladiator fell from his victorious stance.

The yellow-and-violet-striped moon was beginning to lose its grip on the center of the sky, and to slide in a long spiral toward the mountain rims surrounding the kingdom. The sun would soon start its climb around the sky toward the next apex. The guests were all looking kind of furry-eyed and droopy, and even the final act – a man who held corn kernels in his mouth until (after judicious application of a torch beneath his chin) they began to pop – was unable to hold their attention. The queen yawned, stretched, and got up from the couch. Leejee followed the queen wearily toward the palace, not even looking back as the man, his feat accomplished, was rushed by a group of friends toward a waiting tub of butter, into which he plunged his head, valiantly forebearing shrieking.

The queen, leading the way up the Royal Staircase toward the sleeping chambers – Leejee had been given one for the night – was unaware that Leejee was "on to" her scheme, as she produced, almost casually, a square of parchment from somewhere within her gown, and Havler Grem materialized a pen, its point freshly inked, for Leejee to use in signing the document. It was, the queen told Leejee rather carelessly, merely a sort of receipt acknowledging that Leejee had had a good time at the party. Leejee, without hesitation, signed it. Instantly, the queen tore it from her grasp, and dashed down the staircase, heading for the Royal Basement where the Royal Stokers were keeping the Royal Furnaces in white-hot headiness. Havler, as Leejee looked after the queen, yawned elaborately and vanished into his sleeping chamber. A sort of swoosh of air and a gentle thump, just before his door swung closed, told Leejee that he was safely ensconced in his feather-pit for the night, or what remained of the night. All at once, Leejee grew tense. This was the moment she and Garnel had planned for.

For Garnel's plan was hideously simple. Rather than sign her own name, Garnel had explained, all she had to do was to sign another name, and *that* person would be the next sprouter of the Sacred Celery. And what better name to employ other than that of Havler Grem? Leejee giggled to herself as she tiptoed to the door of Havler's room. Hearing his rumbling snores from the depths of the feather-pit, Leejee crept silently but confidently across the room to the window, where Garnel was climbing a ladder, eager to claim his prize.

As he reached her, and would have lifted her over the sill, Leejee held back, and indicated by gestures that she wished to await Havler's shout of despair when he should first feel the growth on his cranium.

At that very moment, down in the Royal Furnace Room, the queen, with the aid of a long heat-proof pole (the fires were *very* white-hot), thrust the parchment, with its damning signature, full into the flames. It hissed, turned brown, then black, then flared into leaping needles of red fire and was gone. At that instant, the orange turban sagged, lost its contours, and fell about the shoulders of the happy queen.

Simultaneously with the immolation of the parchment, a horrified scream rang through the feather-pit room of Havler Grem. Leejee heard it and smiled, and then her smile turned uncertain and died. The scream did not seem to emerge from the dark recesses of the feather-pit. She listened more carefully, and tried to divine the source of that eerie, piteously hopeless noise. Ah! It came from behind her. Leejee turned about. There was none behind her save Garnel, her lover. But what had happened to him!?! Leejee's cowlike eyes widened even more than their usual width as she watched with horror the greenish, stiff, leafy thing that burgeoned gently upward through the blue curls of Garnel's hair. For, so all-absorbing and all-engrossing was Leejee's love for Garnel that she had written *his* name by mistake. Leejee, with a soft cry, swooned dead away on the floor of the room, while Garnel just kept screaming for the longest time . . .

Or, at least, that is the tale told nowadays around the campfires of the Carrot-Eaters (to the south), when their Bachelor King, Garnel of the Tall Hat, is not about the place . . .

WU-LING'S FOLLY

Alan Dean Foster

For a period Alan Dean Foster (b. 1946) was amongst the most prolific novelizers of movies, including Star Wars *(1976) and* Alien *(1979) and its sequels,* Clash of the Titans *(1981),* Krull *(1983) and* Pale Rider *(1987), yet despite this Foster has succeeded in developing and maintaining his own voice with a multitude of his own stories and novels since his first story was published in 1971. Probably his best-known fantasy books are the Spellsinger series, which started with* Spellsinger at the Gate *(1983). He has produced many short stories, of which those in* The Metrognome and Other Stories *(1990) contain some of his most humorous. He has also edited two anthologies of humorous fantasies,* Smart Dragons, Foolish Elves *(1991) and* Betcha Can't Read Just One *(1993). Back in 1982 he started a series of stories about a giant North American woodsman, Amos Malone, of which the following story was the first; the stories are available in book form as* Mad Amos *(1996).*

Hunt and MacLeish had worked for the Butterfield Line for six and seven years, respectively. They'd fought Indians, and been

through growler storms that swept down like a cold dream out of
the eastern Rockies, and seen rattlers as big around the middle
as a horse's leg. All that, they could cope with; they'd seen it all
before. The dragon, though, was something new. You couldn't
blame 'em much for panicking a little when the dragon hit the
stagecoach.

"I'm tellin' ya," Hunt was declaring to the Butterfield agent
in Cheyenne, "it were the biggest, ugliest, scariest-lookin' dang
bird you ever saw, Mr Fraser, sir!" He glanced back at his driver
for confirmation.

"Yep. S'truth." Archie MacLeish was a man of few words
and much tobacco juice. He was tough as pemmican and as
hard to handle, but the incident had turned a few more of
the brown-stained whiskers in his copious beard gray as an
old Confederate uniform.

"It come down on us, Mr Fraser, sir," Hunt continued
emphatically, "like some great winged devil raised up by an
angry Boston Temperance marcher, a-screamin' and a-hollerin'
and a-blowin' fire out of a mouth filled with ugly, snaggled teeth.
'Twere a sight fit t'raise the departed. I gave it both barrels
of Evangeline," he indicated the trusty ten-gauge resting in a
corner of the office, "and it ne'er even blinked. Ain't that right,
Archie?"

"Yep," confirmed the driver, firing accurately into the bronze-
inlaid steel spittoon set at a corner of the big walnut desk.

"I see." The Butterfield agent was a pleasant, sympathetic
gentleman in his early fifties. Delicate muttonchop whiskers
compensated somewhat for the glow the sun brought forth
from his naked forehead. His trousers were supported by over-
loaded suspenders which made dark tracks across an otherwise
immaculate white shirt. "And then what happened?"

"Well, both Archie and me was ready t'meet our maker. You
got to understand, Mr Fraser, sir, this varmint were bigger than
coach and team together. Why, them poor horses like t'die
afore we coaxed and sweet-talked 'em into town. They're
bedded down in the company stable right now, still shakin'
at the knees.

"Anyways, this ugly bird just reached down with one claw
the size o' my Aunt Molly's Sunday dress and plucked the

strongbox right off the top, snappin' the guy ropes like they was made o' straw. Then it flew off, still a-screechin' and a-brayin' like the grandfather of jackasses toward the Medicine Bow Mountains."

"God's Truth," said the driver.

"This is all most interesting," Fraser mumbled. Now, while known as a sympathetic man, the Butterfield agent would have been somewhat disinclined to believe the tale to which his two employees were swearing, save for the fact that MacLeish and Hunt were still standing in front of his desk rather than cavorting drunk and debauched in the fleshpots of Denver, spending free and easy the ten thousand in gold which the missing strongbox had contained.

And, of course, there was also the confirmation afforded by the stage's three passengers, a reputable Mormon rancher from Salt Lake and two of his wives. At the moment, the ladies were under the care of a local physician who was treating them for shock.

"Couldn't it have been a williwaw?" he asked hopefully.

"Nope," said MacLeish, striking with unerring accuracy into the spittoon a second time. " 'Tweren't the likes o' no wind or beastie I ever seed nor heard tell of, Mr Fraser. I kinna say more than the truth." He squinted hard at the agent. "D'ye doubt our word?"

"No, no, certainly not. It's only that I have no idea how I am to report the nature of this loss to the Company. If you'd been held up, that they would understand. But this . . . you must understand my position, gentlemen. There will be questions."

"And *you* should've been in ours, Mr Fraser, sir," Hunt told him fervently.

The agent was not by his nature an imaginative man, but he thought for a moment, and his slim store of inventiveness came to his rescue. "I'll put it in as a storm-caused loss," he said brightly.

MacLeish said nothing, though he made a face around his wad of fossil tobacco. Hunt was less restrained. He gaped at the agent and said, "But there weren't no storm where we was comin' through, Mr . . ."

Fraser favored him with a grave look. Hunt began to nod slowly. Meanwhile, MacLeish had walked to the corner and picked up the ten-gauge. He handed it to his partner. The two of them started for the door. And that was the end of that.

For about a week.

"Another month, boys, and I think we can call it quits." A bulbous nose made a show of sniffing the air. "Snow's in the wind already."

"Damned if you ain't right, there, Emery," said one of the other men.

There were four of them gathered around the rough-hewn table which dominated the center of the cabin. They were spooning up pork, beans, jerky, dark bread, and some fresh fowl. It was a veritable feast compared to their normal cold meals, but they had reason to celebrate.

Johnny Sutter was an eighteen-year-old from Chicago who'd matured ten years in the twelve-month past. "I," he announced, "am goin' to get me a room in the finest whorehouse in Denver and stay stinkin' drunk for a whole month!"

Loud guffaws came from the rest of the men. "Hell, Johnny," said one of them, "if'n yer goin' t'do that, don't waste your time doin' it in a fancy place. Do it in the streets and let me have your room."

"Dang right," said another. "You'll get yourself too stiff t'do what you'll want t'be doin'."

"Not stiff enough, mos' likely," corrected the mulatto, One-Thumb Washington. He laughed louder than any of them, showing a dark gap where his front teeth ought to have been. He'd lost those two teeth and four fingers of his left hand at Shiloh, and never regretted it. Two teeth and four fingers were a fair enough trade for a lifetime of freedom.

Wonder Charlie, the oldest of the four, made quieting motions with his hands. His head was cocked to one side, and he was listening intently with his best ear.

"What's wrong with you, old man?" asked Johnny, grinning at all the good-natured ribbing he was taking. "Ain't you got no suggestions for how a man's to spend his money?"

"It ain't thet, Johnny. I think somethin's after the mules."

"Well, hellfire!" Emery Shanks was up from his chair and reaching for his rifle. "If them thievin' Utes think they can sneak in here the day afore we're set t' . . ."

Wonder Charlie cut him off sharply. "'Tain't Utes. Ol' Com-it-tan promised me personal two springs ago when I sighted out this creekbed thet we wouldn't have no trouble with his people, and Com-it-tan's a man o' his word. Must be grizzly. Listen."

The men did. In truth, the mules did sound unnaturally hoarse instead of skittish as they would if it were only strange men prowling about the camp. If it were a grizzly, it sure would explain the fear in their throats. A big male could carry off a mule alive.

The miners poured out the cabin door, hastily donning boots and pulling up suspenders over their dirty longjohns. One-Thumb and Emery fanned out to search the forest behind the hitch-and-rail corral. The moon was swollen near to full and they could see a fair piece into the trees. There was no sign or sound of a marauding grizzly. One-Thumb kept an eye on the dark palisade of pines as he moved to the corral and tried to calm the lead mule. The poor creature was rolling its eyes and stamping nervously at the ground.

"Whoa, dere, General Grant! Take it easy, mule . . . Wonder, what the blazes got into dese mu . . ."

He broke off as the mule gave a convulsive jerk and pulled away from him. There was something between the camp and the moon. It wasn't a storm cloud, and it certainly wasn't a grizzly. It had huge, curving wings like those of a bat, and wild, glowing red eyes, and a tail like a lizard's. Thin tendrils protruded from its lips and head, and curved teeth flashed like Arapaho ponies running through a moonlit meadow.

"Sweet Lord," Johnny Sutter murmured softly, "wouldja look at that?"

The massive, yet elegant shape dropped closer. The mules went into a frenzy. Wonder Charlie, who'd been at Bull Run as well as Shiloh and had emerged from those man-made infernos with his skin intact, didn't hesitate. He fired at that toothy, alien face, a rifle *ka-booming* through the still mountain air.

The aerial damnation didn't so much as blink. It settled

down on wings the size of clipper ship toproyals and began digging with pitchfork-size claws at the watering trough just inside the corral. The mules pawed at the earth, at each other, at the railing in a frantic desire to crowd as far away from the intruder as possible.

One-Thumb ducked under the sweep of a great translucent wing and shouted in sudden realization, "Curse me for a massa, I think the monster's after our gold!"

Sure enough, several moments of excavation turned up a small wooden box. Inside lay the labor of four men sweating out the riches of a mountain for a year and a half, a glittering horde of dust and nuggets large enough to ensure each of them comfort for the rest of his life.

Monster bird or no, they'd worked too damn hard for any of them to give up so easily that pile they'd wrested from the icy river. They fired and fired, and when it was clear to see that guns weren't doing any good, they went after the intruder with picks and shovels.

When it was all over, a somber moon beamed down on a scene of theft and carnage. The gold was gone, and so were the bodies of young Johnny Sutter and One-Thumb Washington and a mule named General Grant . . .

There were not many physicians residing in Cheyenne at the time, and fewer still who knew anything about medicine, so it was not entirely coincidental that the one who treated the Mormon rancher's wives would also become conversant with the story related by the unfortunate survivors of the Willow Creek claim. He brought the information to the attention of Mr Fraser, the local Butterfield Line agent who had seen to the care of the distraught passengers. Now these two comparatively learned men discussed the events of the week past over sherry in the dining room of the Hotel Paris.

"I am at a loss as to what to do now, Dr Waxman," the agent confessed. "My superiors in Denver accepted the report I sent to them which described the loss of the strongbox on a mountain road during a violent, freak storm, but I suspect they are not without lingering suspicions. My worry is what to do if this should occur a second time. Not only would the cargo be lost, I should be lost as well. I have a wife and children, doctor. I have no desire to be sent to a prison . . . or to an asylum. You are the only other educated citizen who has been apprised of this peculiar situation. I believe it is incumbent upon the two of us to do something to rectify the problem. I feel a certain responsibility, as an important member of the community, to do something to ensure the safety of my fellow citizens, and I am sure you feel similarly."

"I agree. Something must be done."

"Well, then. You are positive these two men you treated yesterday were confronted by the same phenomenon?"

"There seems to be no doubt of that." The doctor sipped at his sherry as he peered over thick spectacles at the agent. "With two of their companions carried off by this creature, I should ordinarily have suspected some sort of foul play, were it not for the unique nature of their wounds. Also, they are Christians, and swore the truth of their story quite vociferously to the farmer who found them wandering dazed and bleeding in the mountains, invoking the name of the savior repeatedly."

The agent folded his hands on the clean tablecloth. "More than citizen safety is at stake in this. There is a growing economy to consider. It is clear that this creature has an affinity, nay, a fondness for gold. Why, I cannot imagine. What matters is that next time it may strike at a bank in Cheyenne, or some smaller community, when there are women and children on the streets.

"But how are we to combat it? We do not even know what we face, save that it surely is not some creature native to this land. I suspect a manifestation of the Devil. Perhaps it would be efficacious for me to have a talk with Pastor Hunnicutt of the . . ."

The doctor waved the suggestion down. "I think we must seek remedies of a more earthly nature before we proceed to the final and uncertain decision of throwing ourselves on the mercy of the Creator. God helps those who help themselves, whether the Devil is involved or not.

"I have had occasion in my work, sir, to deal with certain individuals whose business it is to travel extensively in this still-wild country. Certain acquaintances sometimes impress themselves most forcefully on these bucolic travelers, who are usually commonsensible if not always hygienic.

"In connection with unusual occurrences and happenings, with unexplained incidents and strange manifestations, one name recurs several times and is uttered with respect by everyone from simple farmers to soldiers to educated citizens such as ourselves. I have been reliably informed that this person, a certain Amos Malone, is presently in the Cheyenne region. I believe we should seek his counsel in this matter."

The Butterfield agent stared across at the doctor, who, having finished his sherry, was tamping tobacco into a battered old pipe. "Amos Malone? Mad Amos Malone? I have heard tell of him. He is a relic, a throwback to the heyday of the mountain man and the beaver hat. Besides which, he is rumored to be quite insane."

"So is half of Congress," replied the doctor imperturbably. "Yet I believe we need him."

The agent let out a long sigh. "I shall defer to your judgment in this matter, sir, but I confess that I am less than sanguine as to its eventual outcome."

"I am not too hopeful myself," the physician admitted, "but we have to try."

"Very well. How are we to get in touch with him? These mountain men do not subscribe to civilized means of communication, nor do they usually remain in one place long enough for contact to be made."

"As to that, I am not concerned." The doctor lit his pipe. "We will put out the word that we require his presence and that it involves a matter of great urgency and most unusual circumstance. I believe he will come. As to precisely how he will learn of our need, I leave that to the unknown and ungovernable means by which the breed of man to which he belongs has always learned of such things."

They waited in the doctor's office. Just before dawn, a light snow had salted the town. Now the morning sun, hesitantly glimpsed through muddy dark clouds, threatened to melt the serenely pale flakes and turn the streets into a quagmire.

Sitting in the office next to a nickel-and-iron stove were the

Butterfield Line agent and a distraught, angry, and bandaged-up Wonder Charlie. Wonder Charlie wasn't feeling too well – his splinted right arm in particular was giving him hell – but he insisted on being present, and the doctor thought the presence of an eyewitness would be vital to give verisimilitude to their story.

The clock on the high shelf chimed six-thirty.

"And that's for your mountain man," snapped Fraser. He was not in a good mood. His wife, an unforgiving woman, had badgered him relentlessly about risking an attack of colic by tramping outside so early in the morning.

Dr Waxman gazed unconcernedly at the clock. "Give him a little time. The weather is bad."

There was a knock at the door. Waxman glanced over at the agent and smiled.

"Punctual enough," Fraser admitted reluctantly. "Unusual for these backwoodsmen."

The doctor rose from his seat and moved to open the door, admitting a man who stood in height somewhere between six feet and heaven. He was clad in dirty buckskin and wet Colorado. Two bandoliers of enormous cartridges criss-crossed his expansive chest. In his belt were secured a Bowie knife and a LeMat pistol, the latter an eccentric weapon favored for a time by Confederate cavalry officers. It fit the arrival, Fraser thought.

The man's beard was not nearly as gray-speckled as Wonder Charlie's, but there were a few white wires scattered among the black. His eyes were dark as Quantrell's heart, and what one could see of his actual flesh looked cured as tough as the goatskin boots he wore.

"Cold out there this morning," he said, striding over to the pot-bellied stove. He rubbed his hands in front of it gratefully, then turned to warm his backside.

The doctor closed the door against the cold and proceeded to make formal introductions. Fraser surrendered his uncalloused palm to that massive grip gingerly. Wonder Charlie took it firmly, his age and infirmities notwithstanding.

"Now then, gentlemens, word's out that you folk have got yourselves a little gold problem."

"Bird problem, ye mean," said Charlie promptly, before Fraser or the doctor could slip a word in. "Biggest goddamn bird ye ever saw, mister. Killed two o' my partners and stole our poke. Took off with m'best mule, too. Out o' spite, I thinks, for surely One-Thumb and Johnny would've made the beast a good enough supper."

"Easy there, old timer," said Mad Amos gently. "It don't do to make your head hurt when the rest of you already does. Now, y'all tell me more about this gold-lovin' bird of yours. I admit to being more than a mite curious about it, or I wouldn't be here."

"And just why *are* you here, Mr Malone?" asked Fraser curiously. "You have no assurance we are able to pay you for your services, or even what extremes of exertion those services might entail."

"Why, I don't care much about that right now, friend." He smiled, showing more teeth than men of his profession usually possessed. "I'm here because I'm curious. Like the cat."

"Curiosity," commented Fraser, still sizing the new arrival up, "killed the cat, if you will remember."

The mountain man turned and stared at him out of eyes so black that the agent shrank a little inside. "Way I figure it, Mr Fraser, in the long run we're *all* dead."

With the doctor and the agent nearby to assist his memory, Wonder Charlie related his story of the devil-thing which had attacked his camp and killed two of his partners. Then Fraser repeated what his set-upon driving team had told him. He and Charlie argued a little over details of the creature's appearance, picayune disagreements involving color and size, but basically they and their respective stories were in agreement.

When they'd finished, Mad Amos leaned back in the rocking chair into which he'd settled himself. It creaked with his weight as he clasped both hands around a knee. "Shoot, that ain't no bird you're describing, gentlemens. I thought it weren't when I first heard about it, but I weren't sure. Now I am. What came down on you, old-timer," he told Charlie, "and what lit into your stage, Mr Fraser, weren't nothin' but a full-blood, gen-u-wine, honest-to-goshen member of the dragon tribe."

"Your pardon, Mr Malone," said the doctor skeptically,

"but a dragon is a mythical creature, an invention of our less enlightened ancestors. This is the nineteenth century, sir. We no longer cotton to such superstitions. I myself once had an encounter with a snake-oil salesman who guaranteed to supply me with some powdered unicorn horn. I am not unskilled in basic chemistry and was able to prove it was nothing more than powder from the common steer."

"Well, y'all better readjust your heads a mite, 'cause that's what got your gold, and those stealings ain't no myth."

"He's right, there," said Wonder Charlie sharply.

"I had thought perhaps a large eagle that normally resides only among the highest and most inaccessible peaks . . ." the doctor began.

"Haw!" Mad Amos slapped his knee a blow that would've felled most men. His laugh echoed around the room. "Ain't no eagle in this world big enough to carry off a full-grown mule, let alone twenty pounds of gold in a Butterfield steel strongbox! Ain't no eagle got batwings instead of feathers. Ain't no eagle colored red and yellow and blue and pink and black and everything else. No, it's a true dragon we're dealing with here, gentlemens. By Solomon's Seal it is!"

The Butterfield agent spoke up. "I cannot pretend to argue with either of you gentlemen. I have not your scientific knowledge, sir," he told the doctor, "nor your reputed experience in matters arcane, Mr Malone. The question before us, however, is not what we are dealing with, but how we are to be rid of it. I care not what its proper name be, only that I should not have to set eyes upon it." He eyed the mountain man expectantly.

Some said Malone had once been a doctor himself. Others said he was captain of a great clipper. Still others thought he'd been a learned professor at the Sorbonne in France. General opinion, however, held to it that he was merely full of what the squirrels put away for the Colorado winter. Fraser didn't much care. All he wanted was not to have to explain away the loss of another strongbox filled with gold, and there was a shipment of coin coming up from Denver the very next week.

"That's surely the crux, ain't it? Now you tell me, old timer," he said to Wonder Charlie, "how many appendages did your visitor have streamin' from his mouth? Did he spit any fire at

you? Was his howling high-pitched like a band of attacking
Sioux, or low like buffalo in the distance? How did he look
at you . . . straight on, or by twisting his head from one side
to the other?"

And so on into the late morning, until the old miner's head
ached from the labor of recollection. But Charlie persisted.
He'd liked Johnny Sutter and One-Thumb Washington, not
to mention poor ole General Grant.

Canvas tents pockmarked the sides of the little canyon, their
sides billowing in the wind. Piles of rails and ties were stacked
neatly nearby, along with kegs of spikes, extra hammers, and
other equipment. Thick smells rose from a single larger tent
while others rose from the far side of the railroad camp. One
indicated the kitchen, the other the end product.

The line from Denver to Cheyenne was comparatively new
and in need of regular repair. The crew which had laid the
original track was now working its way back down the line,
repairing and cleaning up, making certain the roadbed was
firm and the rails secure.

The muscular, generally diminutive men swinging the
hammers and hauling the iron glanced up with interest
as the towering mountain man rode into camp. So did the
beefy supervisor charged with overseeing his imported workers.
Though he came from a line of prejudiced folk, he would brook
no insults toward his men. They might have funny eyes and
talk even funnier, but by God they'd work all day long and
not complain a whit, which was more than you could say for
most men.

"All right. Show's over," he growled, aware that work was
slowing all along the line as more men paused to gaze at the
stranger. "Get your backs into it, you happy sons of Heaven!"

The pounding of hammers resumed, echoing down the
canyon, but alert dark eyes still glanced in the direction of
the silent visitor.

They widened beneath the brows of one broad-shouldered
worker when the stranger leaned close and whispered something to him in a melodic, singsong tongue. The man was
so startled he nearly dropped his hammer on his foot. The

stranger had to repeat his query more slowly before he got a reply.

"Most unusual. White Devil speaks fluently the tongue of my home. You have traveled that far, honored sir?"

"Once or twice. I'm never for sure how many. Canton's a nice little town, though the food's a bit thin for my taste. Now, how about my question?"

The man hesitated at that. Despite his size and strength, the worker seemed suddenly frightened. He looked past the visitor's horse as though someone might be watching him.

Mad Amos followed the other man's gaze, and saw only tents. "Don't worry," he said reassuringly. "I won't let the one I'm after harm you, or any of your friends or relatives back home. I will not allow him to disturb your ancestors. Will you trust me, friend?"

"I will," said the worker abruptly. "The one you seek is called Wu-Ling. You will find him in the third tent down." He leaned on his hammer and pointed. "Good fortune go with you, White Devil."

"Thanks." Mad Amos chucked his horse and resumed his course up the track. The men working on the line watched him intently, whispering among themselves.

Outside the indicated tent he dismounted, pausing a moment to give his horse an affectionate pat. This unique steed was part Indian pony, part Apaloosa, part Arabian, and part Shire. He was black with white patches on his rump and fetlocks, and a white ring around his right eye. This eye was unable to open completely, which affected the animal with a sour squint that helped keep teasing children and casual horsethieves well away.

"Now you wait here, Worthless, and I'll be right back. I hope." He turned and called into the tent.

"Enter, useless supplicant of a thousand excuses," replied an imperious voice.

Seated on a mat inside the tent was a youthful Chinese clad in embroidered silk robes and cap. He wore soft slippers and several jade rings. There were flowers in the tent, and they combined with burning incense to keep out the disagreeable odors of the camp. The man's back was to the entrance and he gestured with boredom toward a lacquered bowl three-quarters filled with coins.

"Place thy pitiful offering in the usual place and then get out. I am meditating with the Forces of Darkness. Woe to any who disturb my thoughts."

"Woe to those who meddle with forces they don't understand, progenitor of a hundred bluffs."

The genuflector whirled at the sound of English, only to find himself gaping up at a hairy, ugly, giant White Devil. It took him a moment to compose himself. Then he folded his hands (which Mad Amos thought might be shaking just a little) back into his sleeves and bowed.

Mad Amos returned the bow and said in perfect Mandarin, "Thy ministrations seem to have exceeded thy knowledge, unomnipotent one."

A hand emerged from silk to thrust demandingly at the tent entrance. "Get out of my tent, Devil. Get out! Or I will assuredly turn thee into a lowly toad, as thy face suggests!"

Mad Amos smiled and took a step forward. "Now let's just settle down, inventor of falsehoods, or you'll be the one gets done to. I can't turn you into a toad, but when I finish with you you'll look like a buffalo carcass a bunch o' Comanches just finished stripping."

The man hesitated but did not back down. He raised both hands and muttered an important-sounding invocation to the skies.

Mad Amos listened a while, then muttered right back at him.

The would-be sorcerer's eyes went wide. "How comes a White Devil to know the secret words of the Shao?"

"That's a long, nasty story. 'Course, I don't know *all* of 'em, but I know enough to know you don't know what the hell you're invoking about. I suspect that's what got you into trouble the last time. I know enough to know this is all a show to impress your hard-working kinfolk out there. You ain't no Mandarin, Wu-Ling, just as you ain't no Shao sorcerer. You're nothing but a clever amateur, a dabbler in darkness, and I think you got yourself in over your head with this dragon business."

"So that is what inflicts you upon me. That damnable beast!"

He threw his cap to the floor. "May its toenails ingrow a thousand times! I knew it would bring me problems from the moment the incantation expanded beyond my ability to control the signs." He sat heavily on a cushion, no longer bold and commanding, now just a distraught young would-be lawyer whose pact with the forces of darkness had been overturned by a higher court.

Watching him thus, Mad Amos was able to conjure up a little sympathy for him, no small feat of magic in itself. "How'd you come to have to call him up, anyways?"

"I needed something with which to cow my ignorant kinsmen. There had been mutterings . . . a few had begun to question my right to claim their support, saying that I was not a true sorcerer and could not threaten them as I claimed, nor work magic back in the homeland for their relatives and friends. I required something impressive to forestall such uncertainties once and for all."

"I see. How'd the railroad feel about your brothers supporting you in luxury while they worked their tails off?"

"The White Devil bosses care nothing for civilized behavior so long as the work is accomplished on time."

"So you finally had to produce, magically speaking, or risk going to work with your own delicate fake-Mandarin hands. That about right?"

"It is as you say." He turned and assumed a prideful air. "And I did produce. A dragon of whole cloth, of ancient mien and fierce disposition did I cause to materialize within the camp one night. Since then there have been no further mutterings among my kinsmen and my support has multiplied manyfold."

Mad Amos nodded and stroked his luxuriant beard. "Yup, you got a nice little racket going here. 'Course there might be some trouble if I were to stroll outside and announce that you've got no more control over this dragon than I do over a thunderbird's eye. I think your toiling kinsfolk would be a touch unhappy."

The young man's boast quickly turned to desperate pleading. "Please, you must not tell them that, White Devil! Please . . . they would linger over my killing for weeks if they once learned that I have no power over them." His gaze sank. "I confess all this to You Who Know the Words. I have no control over this dragon. I tried to make it vanish once its purpose had been accomplished. It laughed at me and flew off toward the high mountains. I have tried to call it back, to no avail. Now it does as it pleases, threatening your own people as well. I was an overanxious fool, determined to overawe my people. I should have settled for a less dramatic materialization."

Mad Amos nodded sagely. "Now you're learning, inheritor of troubles. It's always best to make sure you've put all the parts back into a disassembled gun before you go firin' it. I kinda feel sorry for you. The main thing is, the damage this dragon's already done wasn't by your direction."

"Oh, no, Honored Devil, no! As I confess before you, I have no control over it whatsoever. It does as it desires."

"Okay, then, I'll strike you a bargain. You quit dealing off the bottom of the deck with your brothers out there. Pick up a hammer and go to work alongside them. I promise it won't kill you, and you'll gain merit in their eyes by working alongside 'em when you supposedly don't have to. Tell 'em it's time for you to put aside wizardly things and exercise your body for a change. You do that, and I'll keep my mouth shut."

The young man rose to his feet, hardly daring to hope. "You would do this for me? My ancestors will bless you a hundred times."

"They'd damn well better. I'll need all the help I can gather if I'm going to do anything about this dragon you cooked up, Wu-Ling."

"But you cannot! It will surely slay you!"

"Sorry. I'm bound to try. Can't just let it wander about, ravaging the countryside. Besides which, this country of mine is a young one. It ain't quite ready to cope with dragons yet. Havin' enough trouble recoverin' from the war and the devils it spawned. Now, this ain't one of those types that likes to carry off women, is it?"

"It would be in keeping with its lineage if it chose to abduct and consume a virgin or two, I am afraid."

Mad Amos grunted. "Well, even so, that ain't a worry. There ain't a virgin between here and Kansas City. That means it's just this gold affinity we got to worry about. That's a new one on me, Wu-Ling. What's it want with this gold it keeps stealin'?"

"I thought one so wise as thyself would surely know, Honored Devil. Gold is a necessary ingredient in the dragon's diet."

"It eats the stuff? Well, I'll be dogged. And all this time I thought it was doin' something normal with it, like buying up spare souls or accumulatin' a memorable horde of riches or some such nonsense. Gulps it right down, you say?"

"Truly," admitted Wu-Ling.

"Huh! World's full of wonders. Well, gives me something to think on, anyways." He gazed sternly down at Wu-Ling. The would-be sorcerer paid close attention. A baleful look from Mad Amos Malone was something not to be ignored. "Now, you mind what I told you and quit leeching off your kinsfolk out there. They're good people and they deserve your help, not your imaginary afflictions. It's tough enough gettin' by in a foreign land. I know, I've had to try it myself. I've ways of knowin' when someone gives me his word and then backs off, and I don't like it. I don't like it one bit. You follow me, son of importunate parents?"

"I follow you, Honored Devil."

Wu-Ling allowed himself a sigh of relief when the giant finally departed. He wondered by what method the dragon would slay him.

Mad Amos worked his way up into the heights of the Medicine Bows despite the signs that winter was arriving early that year. It would be bad if he were caught out on the slopes by a blizzard, but he'd weathered out bad storms before and could do so again if compelled to.

Near a fork of the Laramie River he paused and made camp, choosing an open meadow across which the river ran free and fast. To the west the crests of the mountains already slept beneath the first heavy blanket of snow.

"Well, Worthless, I guess this is as good a spot as any. Might as well get on with it. Oughta be an interesting business, unless I've figured it all wrong. In that case, you hie yourself off somewhere and have a good time. These mountains are full of herds. Find yourself some fine mares and settle down. Bet you wouldn't be all that sad to see me go, would you?"

The horse let out a noncommittal whinny, squinted at him

out of his bad eye, and wandered off in search of a nice mud wallow to roll in.

Mad Amos hunted until he found a willow tree of just the right age. He cut off a green branch, shaped it, and trimmed off the leaves and sproutings. Then he sharpened the tip with his Bowie, fired it in charcoal, and used the white-hot, smoking points to etch some strange symbols in the earth around his kit. Some of the symbols were Chinese ideographs, some were Tibetan, and a few were not drawn from the lexicon of man.

Next he rummaged around in his battered old saddlebags, which some folk whispered held things it were best not to talk about. Out came an owl's head, a bottle of blue goo, several preserved dead scorpions, three eagle feathers bound together with Zuni fetishes, and similar debris. He reached in a little further and withdrew a shiny metal bar. It was five pounds of enriched tumbaga, a gold alloy made by the Quimbaya Indians of the southern continent, composed of roughly sixty-five percent gold, twenty percent copper, and the rest silver. This he set carefully down in the center of the inscribed symbols.

Lastly he pulled the rifle from its fringed and painted holster. The holster had been fashioned by one of Sacajawea's daughters. Good gal, that Sacajawea, he mused. Some day when they were both ruminating in the Happy Hunting Ground he hoped to meet her again.

The rifle had an eight-sided barrel, black walnut stock, and a breech large enough for a frightened cottontail to hide inside. It was a Sharps buffalo rifle, fifty caliber, with a sliding leaf sight adjustable to eleven hundred yards on the back. It fired a two-and-a-half-inch-long cartridge loaded with a hundred grains of black powder, and could drop a full-grown bull buffalo in its tracks at six hundred yards. The bandoliers draped across Mad Amos's chest held three-and-a-quarter shells packed with a hundred and seventy grains of black powder.

The Sharps was a single-shot. But, then, if you could fire it proper without busting your shoulder, you only needed a single shot. To Mad Amos's way of thinking, such built-in caution just naturally led to a man bettering his marksmanship.

He loaded it with more care than usual this time, paying special attention to the cartridge itself, which he carefully chose from the assortment arrayed on his chest.

Then he settled down to wait.

The moon was waning and the sky had been temporarily swept clean of most clouds when he heard the wings coming toward him out of the west, out of the mountaintops. Soon he was able to see the source of the faint whistling, a streamlined shape dancing down fast out of the heavens, its long tail switching briskly from side to side as it sniffed out the location of the gold.

It landed between the river and the camp and stalked toward the lonely man on feet clad in scales of crimson. Its neck was bright blue, its body mostly yellow and gold, its wings and face striped like the contents of a big jar stuffed with assorted candies. Moonlight marched across scimitar-like teeth and its heritage burned back of its great eyes.

"Whoa up, there!" Mad Amos called out sharply in the dragon tongue, which is like no other (and which is hard to speak because it hurts the back of the throat).

The dragon halted, eyes blazing down at the human who had one foot resting possessively on the golden bar. Its tail switched, flattening the meadow grass and foxgloves, and the tendrils bordering its skull and jaws twisted like snakes with a peculiar life of their own. Its belly ached for the cool touch of yellow metal, its blood burned for the precious golden substance which purified and helped keep it alive.

"Oh-ho!" it replied in its rasping voice. "A human who talks the mother-tongue. Admirable is your learning, man, but it will not save you your gold. Give it here to me." It leaned forward hungrily, the smell of brimstone seeping from its garishly hued lips and parted mouth.

"I think not, Brightbodyblackheart. It ain't that I resent you the gold. Everybody's got to eat. But you scared the wits out of some good people hereabouts and killed a couple of others. And I think you're liable to kill some more afore you're sated, if your appetite's as big as your belly and your desire as sharp as your teeth. I'm not fool enough to think you'll be satisfied just with this here chunk." He nudged the bar with his foot, causing the hungry dragon to salivate smoke.

"You are right, man. My hunger is as deep as the abyssal

ocean where I may not go, as vast as the sky which I make my own, and as substantial as my anger when I am denied. Give me your gold! Give it over to me now and I will spare you for your learning, for though gluttonous I am not wasteful. Refuse me and I will eat you, too, for a dragon cannot live by gold alone."

Casually, Mad Amos shifted the rifle lying across his knees. "Now this here's a Sharps rifle, Deathwing. I'm sure you ain't too familiar with it. There ain't the like of it where you come from, and there never will be, so I'll explain it to you. There ain't no more powerful rifle in this world or the other. I'm going to give you one chance to get back to where you come from, hungry but intact." He smiled thinly, humorlessly. "See, I ain't wasteful, neither. You git your scaly hide out of this part of the real world right now, or by Nebuchadnezzar's nightshade, I'm oath-bound to put a bullet in you."

The dragon roared with amusement. Its horrible laughter cascaded off the walls of the canyon through which the Laramie runs. It trickled down the slopes and echoed through caves where hibernating animals stirred uneasily in their long sleep.

"A last gesture, last words! I claim forfeit, man, for you are not amusing! Gold *and* life must you surrender to me now, for I have not the patience to play with you longer. My belly throbs in expectation and in my heart there is no shred of sympathy or understanding for you. I will take your gold now, man, and your life in a moment." A great clawed foot reached out to scratch contemptuously at the symbols so patiently etched in the soil. "Think you that these will stop me? You do not come near knowing the right ways or words, or the words you would have uttered by now." It took another step forward. Fire began to flame around its jaws. "Your puny steel and powder cannot harm me, Worm-that-walks-upright. Fire if you wish. The insect chirps loudest just before it is squashed!"

"Remember, now, you asked for this." Quickly, Mad Amos raised the long octagonal barrel and squeezed the trigger.

There was a crash, then a longer, reverberating roar, the thunderous double *boom* that only a Sharps can produce. It almost matched the dragon's laughter.

The shot struck Brightbodyblackheart square in the chest. The monster looked down at the already-healing wound, sneered, and took another step forward. Its jaws parted further as it prepared to snap up gold and man in a single bite.

It stopped, confused. Something was happening inside it. Its eyes began to roll. Then it let out an earth-shaking roar so violent that the wind of it knocked Mad Amos back off his feet. Fortunately, there was no fire in that massive exhalation.

The mountain man spat out dirt and bark and looked upward. The dragon was in the air, spinning, twisting, convulsing spasmodically, thoroughly out of control, screaming like a third-rate soprano attempting Wagner as it whirled toward the distant moon.

Mad Amos slowly picked himself off the ground, dusted off the hollow cougar skull which served him for a hat, and watched the sky until the last scream and final bellow faded from hearing, until the tiny dot fluttering against the stars had winked out of sight and out of existence.

From his wallow near the riverbank, Worthless glanced up, squinted, and neighed.

Mad Amos squatted and gathered up the tumbaga bar. He paid no attention to the coterie of symbols which he'd so laboriously scratched into the earth. They'd been put there to draw the dragon's attention, which they'd done most effectively. Oh, he'd seen Brightbodyblackheart checking them out before landing! The dragon might bellow intimidatingly but, like all its kind, it was cautious. It had only taken the bait when it was certain Mad Amos owned no magic effective against it. Mere mortal weapons like guns and bullets, of course, it had had no reason to fear.

He used his tongue to pop the second bullet, the one he hadn't had to use, out of his cheek, and carefully took the huge cartridge apart. Out of the head drifted a pile of dust. He held it in his palm and then, careful not to inhale any of it, blew it away with one puff. The dust duplicated the contents of the bullet which had penetrated Brightbodyblackheart: mescaline concentrate, peyote of a certain rare type, distillate of the tears of a peculiar mushroom, coca leaves from South America, yopo – a cornucopia of powerful hallucinogens which an old Navajo had once concocted before Mad Amos's attentive gaze during a youthful sojourn in Cañon de Chelly many years before.

It was not quite magic but, then, it was not quite real, either. The dragon had been right: Mad Amos had not had the words to kill it, had not had the symbols. And it wasn't dead. But it no longer lived in the real world of men, either. In a month, when the aftereffects of the potent mixture had finally worn off and Brightbodyblackheart could think clearly once more, it might wish it *were* dead. Of one thing Mad Amos was reasonably certain: the dragon might hunger for gold, but it was not likely to come a-hunting it anywhere in the vicinity of Colorado.

Carefully he repacked that seemingly modest pair of saddlebags and prepared to break camp, casting an experienced eye toward the sky. It was starting to cloud over again. Soon it would snow, and when it started it again it wouldn't stop until April.

But not for two or three days yet, surely. He still had time to get out of the high mountains if he didn't waste it lollygaggin' and moonin' over narrow escapes.

He put his hands on his hips and shouted toward the river. "C'mon, Worthless, you lazy representative of an equine disaster! Git your tail out of that mud! North of here's that crazy steamin' land ol' Jim Bridger once told me about. I reckon it's time we had a gander at it . . . and what's under it."

Reluctant but obedient, the piebald subject of these unfounded imprecations struggled to its feet and threw its master a nasty squint. Mad Amos eyed his four-legged companion with affection.

"Have t'do somethin' about that patch on his forehead," he mused. "That damn horn's startin' t'grow through again . . ."

MEBODES' FLY

Harry Turtledove

Harry Turtledove (b. 1949) is probably best known for his science fiction, particularly his long alternate-history sequence, the Videssos Cycle, starting with The Misplaced Legion *(1987), which exploits his deep knowledge of Byzantine history by creating an alternate Byzantine world where magic works. He began by publishing fantasy, starting with* Wereblood *and* Werenight *(both 1979) under the alias Eric G. Iverson, and he occasionally returns to the fantastic in his short fiction. He used the Iverson name on the first of his stories featuring Clever Rolf, "Blue Fox and Werewolf" (1983). This is the second story in the series.*

Viviane thought Clever Rolf the scribe was reckoning up accounts for the baron of Argentan. The baron thought he was doing the same for Herul, who owned the Blue Fox, the best tavern in town. Herul didn't know where he was, or care.

In fact, Clever Rolf was pleasantly horizontal in a little upstairs room at the local sporting house, for which he also kept accounts. He took his pay there, not in the baron's silver or Herul's ale, but in the place's stock-in-trade. Viviane talked too much, and it wasn't as if she owned him.

His pay sat up, jiggling prettily, and reached for the wine jug on the rickety nightstand by the side of the bed. *She* did not talk too bloody much, he thought, and certainly did not bring up the size of his belly, which dear Viviane was all too apt to do these days.

The girl offered him a cup of wine. "Thanks, Aila," he said, and reached over the edge of the bed for a coin from his trousers. The wine was not free. He found another small bit of silver. "This is for you, and don't tell that old harridan down below you got it."

She wrinkled her nose. "As if I would." They drank together, well pleased with each other. Aila's sandy hair flipped up and down as she suddenly nodded, remembering something. She put a warm hand on his arm. "Somebody was up here the other day, asking for you."

Clever Rolf scratched his head. "Easier ways to find me than that. Who was he? What did he want?" He wondered which one of his little schemes had gone wrong. Had the baron found out he was involved with the sporting house? Surely not – if old Bardulf wanted to make something of that, he knew well enough where the scribe lived.

Alia said, "I didn't see him myself, and I'm glad of it; from what Mintrud told us afterward, he was cruel. He looked it, too, she said: tall, skinny, somber, with a great hawk's beak of a nose. He spoke with an Easterling accent."

"A rogue born," declared Clever Rolf, who was no taller than Aila, pudgy (too much good beer at the Blue Fox, he always thought), and snub-nosed. "Not a rogue I know, though. What name did he use?"

"Wait. She said it. Let me think. Mi— Ma— Mebodes; that was it . . . Rolf, what's wrong?"

She sprang up quickly, but not as fast as Clever Rolf, who was already scrambling into his breeches. He put on his tunic back-to-front, and never noticed. A scheme had gone wrong, all right, but no little one – Mebodes was the wizard from whom he'd stolen Viviane. Having lived with her awhile, he was perfectly willing to give her back, but he feared that wouldn't be good enough. Nobody knew much about Mebodes, but his reputation was black. And wizards, black, white, gray – pink, for that matter – enjoyed revenge.

"What will I do?" he mumbled in despair. "What will I do?"

He took the stairs two at a time and dashed through the reception hall, angering the madam and frightening a couple of customers (which angered her more). He was past caring. In blind panic, he flung the door open, crashed it shut after him.

"How kind," a cold voice said. "The mouse runs into the cat's jaws."

Cruel, Aila had told him. He discovered how little weight a word has, next to reality. Mebodes loomed over him. The wizard's eyes were huge, yellow, and unwinking as a falcon's. Clever Rolf saw himself reflected in them. His reflection did not look clever; it looked small, disheveled, and scared. The reflection, he thought, did not lie.

"I m-meant no harm," he quavered. "I c-can explain—"

"What care I for your lies?" Mebodes' hands twitched in anticipation of the torment Clever Rolf would know. His fingers were long, pale, and many-jointed, like a cave spider's legs. He filed each nail to a point.

"But—" Clever Rolf squeaked.

The wizard spat in front of him; his spittle steamed, as if boiling hot. "Had you owned to your crimes, I might have given you a quick, clean ending. But as you snivel like an insect, I think it only just that insects bring you your fate. Sometime soon, they shall. Until then, your life will be—interesting." With a mocking bow, Mebodes stepped round the corner into an alley.

More terrified of standing frozen than of moving, Clever Rolf darted after him, to beg forgiveness one last time. The alley was empty.

He started for home, his knees still knocking. Halfway there a wasp buzzed out of its nest of mud, stung him on the back of the hand, and flew away. He yelped and cursed and plunged his arm into the cool water of a horse trough, none of which did much good. His head went up like a hunted animal's – was that the ghost of chilling laughter on the breeze?

He snarled at Viviane when he got back, and she screeched at him. It might have turned into a nightlong brawl, but the good smell of mutton stew was rising from the pot that bubbled over the fire. Viviane made a couple of pointed remarks about his caring more for his stomach than for her, but served him a big bowlful. Whatever her other faults, she could cook. *Maybe that's why I don't heave her out on her rump*, he thought, digging in with his spoon. He raised a big chunk of meat to his mouth.

Pleasure turned to horror as he began to chew. Instead of the savor of fat mutton, an acrid taste filled his mouth. He choked, gagged, spat, then gaped at the tabletop, his eyes bulging and stomach heaving. In place of the meat he had put into his mouth, there was a gob of little brown ants, most of them dead, but some still feebly moving. More tiny legs kicked against his tongue and the inside of his cheeks.

He rinsed his mouth again and again with ale, wondering each time if it would turn to scorpions as it passed his lips. Viviane was, for once, speechless. "Remind me not to go rescuing damsels in distress," Clever Rolf wheezed when he could speak again. "Your precious Mebodes has a sense of humor I don't care for." He told her what had happened.

She paled. "You wouldn't hand me back to him, would you?" She had come to know him well enough to make it a serious question.

"He didn't show any signs of wanting you back, my sweet," said Clever Rolf. Viviane glowered at him; no woman cares to hear she is unwanted. Clever Rolf was too caught up in his own fear to worry about her feelings. He went on: "And if he did try to take you, I don't know what I could do to stop him. No, he's after vengeance now, and all from me, all from me."

The scribe sat with his head in his hands, staring at the bowl of stew in front of him. "Do I dare?" he muttered. At last, with trembling hand, he raised another spoonful to his mouth. He gulped it down, as if hoping to swallow before he could find out whether it had turned dreadful.

Nothing happened. He ate more, with growing confidence – maybe Mebodes was still loosing warning bolts from his catapult. Then, with no warning at all, Clever Rolf bit down on a mouthful of beetles. They crunched between his teeth.

He kept shuddering long after the noxious taste was gone – he wouldn't be able to trust another bite of food for as long as he had left. This was no fun at all. Never had one of his finaglings come home to roost so disastrously.

He got through breakfast next morning without catastrophe, but only wondered what Mebodes had waiting for him. Jamming a disreputable hat onto his head, he hurried out the door. For one, he really did have to see to the baron's books.

Mebodes was waiting for him. "Why hello, my friend," he said, though his voice made the word a lie. "I trust you enjoyed your evening meal."

"Screw you," Clever Rolf said. It was not courage, or even defiance – more on the order of having nothing left to lose.

The wizard laughed. "Such spirit! Anyone would think you had the means with which to back up your insolence. Unfortunately for you, we both know that is not the case, do we not? No, I fear you must continue to savor your richly deserved punishment yet a while longer. For your pluck, though, I shall grant you a boon."

"Save it," Clever Rolf said.

"No, no, I insist – and who are you to say me nay?" Mebodes chuckled, a sound that made Clever Rolf want to hide. "Here is my boon: I grant it to you to know your end. You shall recognize the envenomed fly that bears your doom by its eyes, which shall be golden as my own, to remind me of you in your final moments."

The wizard stalked away, lifting his trousers to keep the muck in Argentan's dirt streets from soiling them.

Clever Rolf did not bother following him. All he had to be thankful for was that it was early, and no one had seen him cringing. His head hung; he muttered hopeless curses under his breath as he tramped past the Blue Fox.

An apple tree stood outside the tavern, its fragrant blossoms opening as the sun began to climb in the sky. Bees happily buzzed round the flowers. Or they did until Clever Rolf came by – then the buzz turned furious. As though they were so many hawks, they dove on the scribe.

He shrieked when the first one stung him. Ice ran up his back as he heard the rising, angry drone. Without conscious thought, he jumped through the Blue Fox's doorway.

The hour being so early – for everyone save Clever Rolf and, worse luck for him, the bees – the tavern was almost deserted. One old soak sat blearily at a table, nursing the mug of thin, sour beer to which Herul staked him every day until he cadged enough coins for a stronger fare. And Herul himself, an immensely fat man – fatter than Clever Rolf – with a black beard that reached what had once been his waist, but now might be called his equator, stood by the fire, stirring a pot of porridge. It was thick, strong stuff, and bubbled merrily as Herul dragged his long-handled spoon through it.

"Get out from there, Rolf, you whoreson!" he roared as Clever Rolf dove behind the bar. Save for a yip as a bee stung him on the forehead, the scribe did not answer. He grabbed a dipper, plunged it into the cask of mead that sat between red wine and porter, and sloshed a great sticky puddle of fermented honey over the polished top of the bar.

Herul roared again, louder this time. "Out, out, you dizzard, you loon, you crackbrained jobbernowl, and never come back! I'll make my own reckonings of profit from now on – you, you're a dead loss."

"Oh, put a cork in it, suet-chops," Clever Rolf said with dignity. His stings throbbed, but he was not getting any more of them. Next to the perfume of mead, Mebodes' magic was magic no more. The bees droned down to the puddle one by one. A couple flew away, weaving slightly from the potent brew. The rest stayed to gorge themselves. Clever Rolf crushed them all with a big skillet, then set to work digging the stings out of his flesh.

Herul bore down on him, fist clenched on the long-handled spoon. He realized he was brandishing it like a club, slowly lowered it. His eyes went back and forth from Clever Rolf to the smashed bees.

"Here." The scribe dropped a coin on the bar next to the puddle. "This should cover a dipper of mead. I always thought it was vile stuff, but it came in handy today." Leaving Herul and his solitary customer staring after him, he strolled out of the Blue Fox.

Though one eye was puffed shut, he was whistling as he reached the baron's keep. The half-victory his quick wits had won him gave him back his hope; maybe he could find some way to save his hide (however punctured) from Mebodes after all.

He did not, unfortunately, have any idea of what that way might be.

Bardulf was brusquely sympathetic to his lumps and bumps. "I got stung myself, a couple of years ago," the baron remarked. "Bees are nasty things."

"Yes, sir," Clever Rolf said. He hurried up the spiral stair to the castle's record room. Dust puffed under his feet as he made his way to the accounts – but for him, few people came here.

The parchment account-scrolls smelled of old dust. As a scribe, Clever Rolf found the odor as comfortable as the old shoes he wore. It was doubly welcome today: no risk that musty smell would draw any stinging bees, he thought. He bent above the scroll, frowning when he saw how much the baron had spent for horse leeching.

A silverfish scuttled over the parchment. One day, Clever Rolf thought, all of Bardulf's records would be bug turds, and a good thing, too. But this insect moved with malignant purpose. It darted onto Clever Rolf's hand, then scurried up his arm inside the sleeve of his tunic.

The scribe gave a stifled scream and swatted frantically. The silverfish might have been dipped in liquid fire. It drew a line of agony behind it everywhere it ran. Clever Rolf sprang up from the table, ripped the tunic off over his head. The silverfish was in the matted hair on his belly. Sobbing, he knocked it to the floor and stepped on it. Wherever it had touched him, his skin was an angry red. The pain remained fresh when he went home that evening.

He faced supper with a certain amount of dread, but Mebodes did not disturb his meal. But when he and Viviane went to bed, a horde of ants emerged from the mattress ticking and crawled all over them like an animated brown carpet. Naked but for ants, Clever Rolf and Viviane ran for the creek and plunged in, scrubbing at their hair and digging the insects out of their ears and noses.

When they looked up, Mebodes stood at the stream bank, a

glow of pleasure in his terrible eyes. He bowed mockingly toward Viviane. "Only fair you should have your share of enjoyment, too, my dear." Then to Clever Rolf again: "Not long now before the fly." He gestured, as if to make a sorcerous pass. Both his victims ducked under the water. When they raised their heads again, he was gone.

Viviane shivered, half from the chill of the creek, half from fury. "Ohhh!" she said, a long syllable of rage. "He is *such* a wicked man! Even the other wizards hate him."

"And I don't blame them—" Clever Rolf stopped in amazement. He stared at her with something closer to real affection than he had shown her for a long time.

"Let go of me!" she exclaimed a moment later. "Stop that, you shameless lecher! Stop it, I say – or at least let's get out on the grass. Let's— *mmglmph!*"

Clever Rolf was not listening anymore.

When he got an idea, he seized the bit in his teeth and ran away with it. He set out that very night, leaving a rolled-up blanket in bed in the hope that Mebodes might think he was still at home. He even left his mule behind and went by shanks' mare. By the time the sun came up, he was halfway to Estreby, which was a larger town than Argentan and boasted a wizard in residence.

Clever Rolf was footsore and yawning by the time he found the wizard's establishment on a side street between a farrier and an apothecary. The sign simply said "Rigord". Either one knew who he was, or not.

Rigord proved to be a tall, sleepy-looking fellow in his forties; his chamber was dustier than Bardulf's record room. He was not, however, lightly befooled. When Clever Rolf tried to present a circumspect version of his difficulties, the wizard drawled, "Ah yes, heard about you: the fellow who diddled Mebodes. Wants his own back now, does he?"

"Well— yes," Clever Rolf admitted.

Without haste, Rigord got up and dug out an astrological tome and an abacus. He cast a quick horoscope, flicking beads back and forth and muttering to himself as he calculated. At last, when Clever Rolf was quivering with anxiety, he said, "I can help, I reckon. Mebodes is strong, but so full of his affairs that he leaves himself vulnerable to magic. Now" – and Rigord's sleepiness fell away – "what's it worth to you?"

Clever Rolf had been waiting for that question, but not so soon. "Ah— three silver marks."

"This is your *life* we're speaking of," Rigord reminded him scornfully.

"Very well, then – a whole gold piece. I am not a rich man."

"No?" Rigord leaned forward. "What about the treasure you stole from Mebodes along with your leman?"

Clever Rolf quailed. "You know too much. I'll pay you six marks."

"I want the treasure – all of it."

"Would you beggar me? I'll give you two gold pieces, or even two and a mark."

"The treasure." Implacable, Rigord folded his arms and waited.

"I've spent some of it," the scribe said miserably.

"How much? The truth – I will know if you lie." The wizard made a quick pass.

"Maybe a quarter."

"The balance will do nicely – if, of course, you truly want my aid."

Clever Rolf yielded; as Rigord knew, he had to yield. "All right," he said, very low, the picture of a beaten man.

They dickered over terms after that; the scribe did not want to pay before Mebodes was driven off. At last he agreed to let Rigord lay a geas on him, compelling him to fetch the treasure once the magician had met his half of the bargain. The spell was quickly and competently cast. Clever Rolf's mercurial hopes began to revive; Rigord knew what he was about. He might well prove a match for Mebodes.

And deep inside, where it did not show, the scribe was chortling. Mebodes' treasure was largely brass, worth a mark and a half at the outside. Rigord would have done better for himself had he been a less steely haggler. That, however, Clever Rolf thought, was Rigord's problem.

When they went back to Argentan, Rigord rode a mule while Clever Rolf walked once more. The wizard's beast had as lackadaisical a disposition as that which he affected, so the scribe, sore feet and all, had no trouble keeping up.

It was almost evening when Rigord's nostrils started twitching; he and Clever Rolf were still a mile or so outside Argentan. The scribe sniffed, too. "Night-blooming jasmine," he said. "We have some of the finest in the duchy."

"Quiet, fool." As it did at need, Rigord's laziness disappeared. "It's the reek of evil sorcery I smell." He paused, considering. "Aye, likely Mebodes. The spells have an eastern flavor to them."

"Spells?" Clever Rolf's fears flooded back. "Are they done?" If they were, he was likely doomed no matter what Rigord did.

The wizard extracted a packet of whitish powder from his robe, poured a little into the palm of one hand. He mumbled an incantation, moving his other hand in small, jerky passes. Then he spat into the powder. It bubbled and turned a faint pink. "Close, but not quite," he told the anxiously waiting scribe. "Were it red, you could visit the undertaker now and save yourself the wait."

"Heh, heh," Clever Rolf said in hollow tones. "By the gods, then, find him and deal with him before it's too late." He had an inspiration. "If you don't, you'll never see his treasure, you know."

That seemed to stir Rigord. He sniffed again, worked a quick divination with a green twig. It hung suspended in the air. "That way," he said, squinting along it. He repeated the divination several times as they got into town. Night had fallen by then; hardly anyone was in the street to ask questions.

At last the floating twig pointed squarely at a two-story building bigger and finer than most. "He's in there," Rigord said decisively. "On the second floor, by the angle of things, behind that window there – here now, you idiot, what's so funny?"

"Angle of things, forsooth." Clever Rolf had to fight back hysterical laughter. "It's the town bawdy house."

"Is it indeed? So much the better; if Mebodes is with one of the wenches, he'll hardly be minding his wardspells. Like as not, this is what I saw back in my study."

"'Affairs', eh? So that's what you meant. Well, all right – now nail the bastard."

"Hush," Rigord said absently. He had lit a small lamp and was heating several strong-smelling potions and liquids over it. Then he poured them one after the other into a small, deep silver bowl. A puff of pungent steam rose from it. Clever Rolf sneezed.

"Hush," Rigord said again. He was chanting now, in Iverian dialect so thick Clever Rolf could hardly follow it. The hair rose on the back of the scribe's neck; he could feel the magical force Rigord was concentrating in that bowl.

The wizard's voice went harsh and deep: "Fiery spirit of the void, I summon thee! Come forth, O salamander; come forth, come forth!" A sphere of coruscating flame rose from the silver bowl. It threw sparks – red, gold, white – into the night. Clever Rolf's mouth fell open in awe.

At Rigord's urging, the salamander slowly floated toward the sporting house. It drifted in through the open second-story window. After a moment of silence, twin screams rang out, one soprano and frightened, the other a baritone roar of outrage that changed in mid-cry to a howl of pain.

"You did it! You did it!" Clever Rolf cried. Exhaustion forgotten, he capered about, hugging himself with glee. "I hope your fireball roasts him like a capon!"

"Then you'll likely be disappointed," Rigord said. "Wizards aren't that easy to kill. But you should be rid of him for a while."

As if to prove him right, Mebodes came diving out of the window by which the salamander had entered. He was a sadly different sorcerer from the one who had terrorized Clever Rolf. Landing in the muddy street with a bone-jarring thump, he got to his feet and ran, the salamander in hot – in both the literal and figurative senses of the word – pursuit. Mebodes would have fled faster had he not had to reach down every couple of strides to haul up his unbuttoned breeches. Each time he did, the salamander scorched his bare backside.

Aila appeared at the window through which Mebodes had crashed. "Serves you right," she shouted at him as he vanished into the night. Then she looked down toward Clever Rolf, who was still cheering in the street below. When she recognized him, she said, "Come on up. You can have this one free, for ridding me of that scoundrel." As she was wearing her working clothes – which is to say, nothing much – the invitation's appeal was immediate and urgent.

"Remember the geas," Rigord called to Clever Rolf, but the scribe's hearing could be very selective when he chose.

Afterward, in the comfort of a well-warmed bed, he gave Aila the whole story (though Viviane, had she heard, would have been furious at how small her role was). Aila giggled when he told how he had used Rigord's covetousness against him. "These wizards, they're not so much," he said grandly.

The candle by the bed lured moths and other insects into the little chamber. For the first time in days, Clever Rolf listened to their flutterings and dronings without a sense of panic. Then one buzzed down to settle on his arm. Aila's face twisted with fear. "Rolf," she quavered, "look at its eyes! That's— that's Mebodes' fly!"

The scribe reached out with a thumb and killed the insect, whose eyes were indeed golden like the wizard's.

Aila stared. "How could you—?"

"Nothing simpler, my sweet." He showed her the dead fly; it had no mouthparts. "For one thing, Rigord told me his spell wasn't finished. But I didn't need Rigord to know that. After all" – he leered at her, his sense of his own quick wit at last completely restored – "didn't you just watch Mebodes running away down the street with his fly undone?"

THE RETURN
OF MAD SANTA

Al Sarrantonio

Al Sarrantonio (b. 1952) has been selling fiction since 1978, and is best known for his horror fiction, including the novels Totentanz *(1985),* The Boy With Penny Eyes *(1987) and* October *(1990), although his most recent work is a massive science-fiction trilogy,* The Five Worlds. *His short fiction has appeared in many anthologies, but his humorous stories are less well known. This story sold itself to me on the title alone when I first encountered it in 1981. See what you make of it.*

The whole mess began on the afternoon of Christmas Eve. I was in the sleigh shed talking with Shmitzy, my chief mechanic, about some minor problems he'd been having with the front runners of the sleigh. Shmitzy's a little guy – about two-and-a-half feet tall, a good foot shorter than me – a solid, reliable elf with a grease-stained beard. The sleigh sat polished and clean in the center of the room, and Shmitzy was leaning against it with his arms folded, throwing unintelligible technical terms at me. I'd just gotten him to tell me in English what the heck was wrong with the sleigh when the doors to the shed burst open and Santa Claus bounded into the room.

"Gustav! Shmitzy!" Santa boomed. "How are my favorite helpers?" He was fat and pink, his beard fluffed, his eyes twinkling. He leaned over, patted our backs playfully, and brought his rosy cheeks down close to our faces.

I gave him the thumbs-up sign and rapped my knuckles on the side of the sleigh. "A-okay, Santa. Everything's right on schedule, and Shmitzy tells me he'll have this boat ready to roll by tonight."

"Good, boys! Good!" Santa threw back his head and gave us a hearty "Ho ho ho!" I was sick of that laugh – it usually started to get to me around this time of year, though I have to admit I'd have walked off a cliff for Santa, annoying laugh or no – but I gave him a big smile anyway. He patted us gently again.

"See you later, boys! I just came by to see how things were coming along. I'm supposed to be helping Momma with her baking for dinner tonight." His eyes sparkled. "Special cakes for everybody! Ho ho ho!"

I winced, then quickly gave him a grin and the thumbs-up sign as he turned to leave.

And then a strange thing happened. He was halfway out the door when he suddenly froze in mid-step. He stood locked like that for a few seconds. Then, just as suddenly, he unfroze. He turned back to us with a strange, confused look on his face.

"Boys," he said. But then he shrugged. "Oh, never mind. It was nothing." He turned and took another step.

Again he froze. Shmitzy and I started toward him to see if he was all right. All of a sudden, he gave an ear-piercing roar and spun around, plucking Shmitzy up off the floor beside me and tossing him through the air. Shmitzy gave a yell and sailed like a shotput about thirty feet, hitting the floor in the corner of the shed with a groan.

Santa turned to me, his hands reaching for my neck. There was a horrible look on his face – his eyes bulged whitely from their sockets, and he was beet red above his beard. "Gustav," he said, his voice a cold growl.

He opened his mouth in a gaping cartoon grin, grasped my neck with his white-gloved hands, began to squeeze . . . and then suddenly returned to his old self. It was like someone had flicked a switch. He dropped his hands and looked at me, completely mystified.

"Gustav, what happened?"

I was shaking like a belly dancer, but I managed to open my mouth. "I don't know, Santa. You . . . didn't look so good for a minute."

There was an expression of helplessness on his normally jolly face. "I don't know what came over me," he said. He turned to Shmitzy, who was sitting on the floor across the room, touching his head tenderly. "I'm sorry, Shmitzy. I . . . just don't know what happened."

I took Santa gently by the arm. "Don't worry about it," I said. "Why don't you go back to the house and lie down. Have Momma fix you something hot to drink. The rush must be getting to you."

He brightened a bit and let me lead him to the door. "Yes, I suppose I should. Now that I think of it, Momma has seemed a bit irritable today, also." He paused, trying to think of something. "And I seem to remember something . . . a long time ago . . ."

"Well, don't you worry about it, Santa. Go in and take it easy. You've been working too hard." I smiled and patted his arm, nudging him in the direction of the house. "Leave everything to me."

"Yes, I will. Thank you, Gustav." He smiled and patted his belly.

I watched him walk across the snow-covered courtyard to his cottage, open the door, and go in. I thought I saw him freeze again for a moment as he stepped through the doorway, but I couldn't be sure. He really must be working hard, the poor guy; I'd never seen him get mad before, never mind toss an elf across a room. I considered going over to the cottage and having a talk with him and Momma to make sure everything was all right, but then Shmitzy, now recovered, called me over to explain one more time what he was going to do with the front runners on the sleigh, and I soon forgot all about Santa.

That night everybody came marching into the dining room at the usual time for our special Christmas Eve dinner – a little celebration we have every year before all the craziness and last-minute work. They were all there: the wise guys from the Toy Shop, tripping each other and giggling and sticking each other with little tools; the gift-wrappers, lately unionized; the R&D boys with their noses in the air (big deal, so an elf can get a college education); the maintenance men; and assorted others. The dining room was decorated for the occasion: holly and tinsel, and red and green ornaments all over the walls, a "Merry Christmas" sign hung crookedly over the big fireplace behind the head of the table, fat squatty candles hanging from the low-beamed ceiling giving the place a warm, cheery glow. Though I know it sounds mushy, I have to say that getting that dinner organized always left a warm glow in me and was one of the high points of my year.

When everyone finally sat down I rose near the head of the table in my place as chief elf and raised my glass of wine to give the traditional toast to Mr and Mrs Claus, just as my father had done before me and his father before him. Every year it was the same thing: a simple toast, Mr and Mrs Claus come in, they bow, we bow, everybody drinks the wine, everybody sits down, we eat a great meal prepared by Momma Claus, we all eat too much, we all eat some more, and then we work like crazy getting ready for the big ride. All traditional. Smooth production. End of story.

This time I stood up and made the toast, and Mr and Mrs Claus entered, and everybody dropped his wine glass and gasped. Santa and Momma swaggered into the room like a couple of movie gangsters. Santa had a big cigar clamped in his teeth, and that evil grin I'd seen on his face that afternoon was now painted on both of them. I couldn't believe that the always-sweet, round-faced, bun-haired Momma Claus could ever look like a prune-faced dock worker, but she did. In the glow from the candles, they both looked pretty nasty.

Momma Claus stepped to the head of the table and raised her fist. There was a toy bullwhip in it. "Santa's going to talk to you now," she snarled, "and you'd better listen. Anybody who doesn't gets *this*." She cracked the whip down the length of the table, over our heads. It knocked Shmitzy's cap off, revealing the large bump on his head.

Momma stepped aside, and Santa took her place. He pounded on the table with a fist, then looked up, glaring into each of our faces up and down the table. "I like you boys," he growled, "so I'm going to keep you around." He opened his mouth in a horrid, toothy smile. "But from now on we're going to do things a little differently."

The heavy table shook from all our trembling.

Santa grabbed a full bottle of wine from the table and drank half of it in a gulp. He wiped his mouth with his sleeve. "Come on!" he roared, and, waving the bottle like a banner, he stomped out of the room into the courtyard.

We all sat rooted to our seats, eyes wide with terror; then Momma cracked her whip and we scampered out. As we marched out into the snow, old Doc Fritz, the physician here at the North Pole, a solemn fellow with the body and face of a miniature Sigmund Freud and a professorial manner to match, edged up to me. He leaned over unobtrusively and whispered into my ear.

"I believe I know what is happening," he said. "This has occurred before."

"What?" I said.

He nodded slowly and scratched at his beard. "It was a long—"

Just then, Santa came screaming down the line, waving his arms madly in the air. "Everybody to his station!" he shouted.

Fritz opened his mouth to continue, but Santa came charging toward us. We quickly separated. Fritz shambled off toward the infirmary, and I scooted to my office.

I sat drumming my fingers on my desk for a few minutes, and then decided I had to talk to Fritz again to find out what was going on. There was a lot of howling and yelling outside, but I climbed quietly out of my window and made my way to the infirmary, a small, neat cottage at the edge of the village.

The door was locked and the windows dark. As I stepped off the porch I nearly bumped into Santa as he ran wildly around the corner of the building, a wine bottle in his hand. "Gustav!"

he yelled. "Come with me!" And, dragging me along behind him, he went on a rampage.

He drank two and a half bottles of wine, and stumbled from building to building, department to department, shouting and breaking things. He started in the maintenance shed, went through the dining room and kitchen, and eventually made his way to the Toy Shop. There he told one of the master craftsmen that he didn't like the face on two thousand just-completed toy soldiers, lined them up in rows, and stomped them to sawdust.

At that point, one of the apprentices tried to shoot him with a replica Winchester rifle. Santa snatched it, batting the apprentice aside. He stumbled out into the snow.

"Where's Rudolph!" he roared. "I want to see my Rudolph!" Barely able to stand, laughing drunkenly, he found his way to the stables and threw open the wooden doors. "Rudolph!" he shouted, swaying from side to side. The interior of the stable was illuminated by moonlight. Rudolph, still in his stall, looked up and blinked, his red nose flashing. "Red-nosed bastard," Santa said, and as I watched in horror he raised the rifle, fumbling for the trigger.

As I leapt for him, he pulled the trigger; but as he did so he fell over backwards, out through the doors. He lay laughing in the snow, kicking his feet and howling, and firing the rifle at the moon and the weather vane on top of the stable. Then suddenly he stopped shooting, gave one long wolf-like howl, and instantly fell asleep.

The moment this happened, I gave a signal, and Shmitzy and a couple of other guys ran and got a long rope. We jumped on Santa and started to tie him up, but just as we got the rope around his waist, Momma Claus burst out of the Toy Shop and came running toward us, swinging a headless doll over her head and shouting, "Get away from him! Get away!" We scattered, and from a safe distance I watched as she dragged Santa's snoring body across the courtyard and into the house. Apparently he woke up, because a few minutes later all the lights in the house went on and I heard them laughing and breaking things.

I looked for Fritz but couldn't find him anywhere, so for the next couple of hours I tried to organize clean-up crews and estimate the damage. For all intents and purposes, the North Pole lay in ruins. There wasn't one building with its shingles and shutters intact, and the infirmary and elves' quarters were burned to the ground (Momma and Santa had danced around them as they blazed). The only structures left reasonably unscathed were the sleigh shed and the Toy Shop. I had no idea what we were going to do. There didn't seem to be any way to stop him, and I couldn't possibly let him make his Christmas Eve ride in his condition. It was almost too late to start, anyway. It looked as if there wouldn't be any visits from Santa this year.

As I was walking out of the Toy Shop I heard a commotion going on in the courtyard, and was just in time to see a great cheer go up as Santa walked out of his cottage. He looked like the old Santa we all knew and loved. He had a bright clean red suit and cap on, his cheeks were rosy and his beard was brushed and fluffed, his boots were polished to a high gloss and he was rubbing his belly. He even had a sack flung over his shoulder. Tough guy that I am, I almost started to cry for joy; but suddenly my eyes went dry and the cheer died in the middle when he got closer, because the wild look was still in his eyes and that twisted grin was still stuck to his face. When he opened his mouth and growled, we knew nothing had changed. He still looked like a bleached bluebeard.

"Get ready to roll!" he shouted.

We all looked at one another, mystified. Was he going to make his rounds looking like that?

"I said get ready to roll!"

Shmitzy stepped meekly out of the crowd. He was trembling like a leaf. "B-but Santa—"

Santa thundered, "Do what I say, or I'll string you all up like sides of beef!"

Five minutes later I had them buffing up the sled and loading piles of empty toy sacks onto the back of it, as per Santa's instructions. The Toy Shop remained untouched. The reindeer were groomed, the harness cleaned and rigged.

When all of this was finished, Santa assembled us by the sleigh, which had been pulled out into the courtyard. "Okay, boys," he said, chuckling sardonically. "It's time to make our rounds."

Momma was laughing, too.

Poor little Shmitzy stepped out of the crowd. He was still trembling uncontrollably. He pointed at the Toy Shop and the empty sacks in the sleigh. "S-Santa, we—"

Santa reached out and picked Shmitzy up by his feet, turning him upside-down. He brought him up very close to his face, and opened his mouth wide. For a moment it looked as if he were going to bite Shmitzy's head off. Then he put him down.

Shmitzy hurried back into the crowd.

"Gustav," Santa said in a low, mellow voice, rubbing his hands together and smiling evilly, "get your crew into the sleigh."

I was so scared I hustled the three elves nearest to me into the back with the empty bags. Santa threw his own half-filled sack into the front and climbed in after it. He cracked the reins.

"Ha ha ha," he said.

The take-off was fairly smooth, given the circumstances. Rudolph was still a bit shaken by almost having his nose blown off, but we got off the ground in one piece. It was a clear night with a bright moon, and I looked down as we made our turn over the North Pole. The jolly, festively painted little village of a few days before now looked like an abandoned amusement park: wreckage and near-wreckage everywhere. None of the Christmas trees along the perimeter had been decorated; none of the remaining decorations had been polished. None of the last-minute work had been done. The scene would have made a disheartening air-photo. I shook my head and put up my collar. It was cold in that sleigh.

Santa laughed diabolically and straightened the sleigh out for the ride south. I was depressed, and the three elves huddled back there with me surrounded by empty sacks didn't look too cheerful, either. I looked closely at them now: two shivering apprentices, and a third elf bundled up like a mummy with his face covered. I glanced up front; Santa was waving his arms madly, cracking the reins fiercely over the poor reindeer. I wondered what he was going to do.

The bundled-up elf inched over to me and pulled down the muff covering his face. I almost shouted; it was Fritz!

He motioned for me to be quiet, and leaned over to whisper in my ear. "Don't raise your voice, my friend," he said. "If

Santa finds me here I'm sure he'll throw me overboard." He whispered that we should move carefully to the back of the sleigh, and we did so. We piled up empty canvas sacks to form a sort of wall.

"I've been in hiding," Fritz continued. "I'm the only one who knows what's wrong with Santa and Momma Claus, and he knows that I know. I concealed myself in the basement of the infirmary, and, after the infirmary burned down, I hid in the Toy Shop trying to puzzle this out and come up with some sort of solution. Gustav," he said, stroking his chin thoughtfully, "to tell you the truth, I never believed the tale."

"Tell me everything," I said.

He nodded sagely. "Well, in summary form, this is the story. On Christmas Eve, eight hundred years ago to this night, when Santa and Momma Claus and their helpers still lived in Myra, in what is now southern Turkey, Santa and Momma lost their minds. It happened very suddenly. According to the story, they carried on like madmen all of Christmas Eve. The elves – my great-great-grandfather was the physician at the time – tried to stop them, but could not. They destroyed the village.

I was dumbfounded. "Why didn't I ever hear of any of this?"

"I'm coming to that. After the destruction, on Christmas Day, Santa went to sleep, and when he awoke it was as if nothing had happened. He could not believe what he and Momma had done. At that time, St Nicholas was just a local phenomenon. He hadn't made his Christmas Eve visits, but they were limited at that time to poor children in the area, so excuses were easily made and the local furor eventually died down. No one outside the village ever knew what had really happened. The following year, Santa moved to the North Pole. A solemn vow was taken among the elves that only the physician would ever be tainted with the knowledge of what had occurred. The story was passed down to me by my father. I thought it was just a nasty fairy tale; even my father told me he didn't really believe it."

"Did they ever figure out why it happened?"

Fritz sighed. "No. The only explanation my great-great-grandfather came up with was that Santa had been possessed by a demon, and that the demon had been driven out by Santa's extreme goodness." He paused. "Very backward of him, don't you think? But now I have my own theory."

I looked at him expectantly, and after some thoughtful beard-stroking he went on.

"I believe that after eight hundred years of extreme, selfless, total goodness, something happens within Santa's subconscious mind. I think there is a kind of reaction against all this goodness which builds and builds, a kind of ego-force, and when it has built to a sufficiently high point it bursts through to the surface volcanically. A similar reaction occurs in Momma Claus, also. That reaction is what we are seeing now." He paused, shook his head quickly, resolutely, and reached inside his coat. "But no matter what the cause," he said, producing a syringe, "we must now do something. Santa's actions have now taken an even wilder course than they did the first time this occurred. We have no idea what he will do, and we cannot allow him to continue. I decided today that if he tried to carry his violence beyond the North Pole he should be stopped at all costs. We must give him this strong sedative and turn the sleigh back."

"Should we get the two apprentices to help?"

"They are obviously in no state to be of assistance. We must—"

"Having a nice chat, boys?" Santa's demonically smiling face looked down at us over the little wall we had constructed. He reached over and pulled Fritz up by the collar, taking the syringe from his hand and throwing it overboard. I looked up front: the two apprentices were frantically trying to control the reindeer, and were being bounced all over the front seat by the reins.

For a terrible moment, I thought Santa was going to pitch Fritz over the side after the syringe, but after shaking him a few times he put him down. He held him with one hand while he reached up front between the bouncing apprentices and rummaged in his sack, producing a length of rope. He tied Fritz up and gagged him, then let him go and grabbed me by the collar. "And you, little Gustav, will be my special helper, just like always. Hold this," he growled, thrusting the sack into my hands. "And if you make one wrong move I'll toss you out like a sandbag." I threw a helpless look at Fritz, who was wriggling in his ropes, trying to tell me something, and followed Santa up front.

He retrieved the reins from the two apprentices and frightened them into the back. We made a long, slow turn and came in over North America.

Santa turned and showed his teeth. "And now," he said mockingly, "it's time for our Christmas visits. Ho ho! Ha ha ha!" He snapped the reins, and we swooped down to a landing on a snowy rooftop.

He bounded out of the sleigh, and drove me and the two apprentices toward the red-brick chimney. I took a quick look in the bag I was struggling with; it was filled with all kinds of tools. I groaned silently. Santa hustled us down the chimney.

We found ourselves in a cozy living room. There was a lot of comfortable-looking furniture, and the fireplace was big. I brushed past four small stockings as I stepped into the room. A Christmas tree was decorated and lit in one corner.

Santa grabbed the sack from me and opened it, removing a set of fine jeweler's tools, a heavy monkey wrench, a hammer, and a flashlight. He gathered them all into his arms, then turned to us. "Now let's be quiet, boys," he whispered, grinning. "We wouldn't want anyone to disturb us, would we?"

Santa Claus, the gift-giver, then set about taking everything of value and stuffing it into the empty bag. Whatever was fastened or bolted down, he lifted with the wrench or the back end of the hammer. He dragged me along beside him, making me hold the sack open as he dumped in all sorts of stolen goods.

When he was through with the furniture and the other valuables in the room, he tiptoed through the rest of the house looking for money and jewelry. He found a wall safe in the den, and chuckled sardonically when it popped open under his sensitive fingers, revealing a small horde of gems and gold jewelry to his flashlight beam. When we came back to the living room he hoisted the stuffed sack and drove us to the fireplace. The room was completely bare. We'd even taken the lights and ornaments from the tree, which now stood naked and forlorn in the corner.

Before hustling us back up the chimney he turned to the living room, put his finger to the side of his nose, and said, in a grotesque parody of his normal self, "Happy Christmas to all, and to all a good night – ha ha."

We loaded the sleigh, and with a slap of the reins we were off to the next rooftop. Santa took a fresh empty sack with him, and we went through the same routine.

We finished with the last house at about three in the morning. My arms ached from transporting stolen property. I dragged myself into the front seat, and we rose, the reindeer straining against the load, from the last snow-covered roof.

Santa kept an eye on me for a while, but as the sleigh turned up toward the North Pole he finally forgot about me. He sat with a bag filled with the biggest diamonds and silver pieces he'd taken, and after telling the reindeer he'd "roast them alive" if they didn't find their own way home, he put the reins aside and sat with all the precious stuff in his lap, scooping big handsful up and letting it run through his fingers.

I slipped silent as a shadow over the seat into the back. Fritz was wedged between a sack of paintings and a bag filled with patio furniture that Santa had spotted piled up on someone's back lawn. The two apprentices were exhausted, snoring in odd positions on top of two bags filled with bar stools. I pulled the gag out of Fritz's mouth and said in a low voice: "Is there anything we can do?"

He nodded. "There is in my left coat pocket another syringe which I brought for just such an emergency. If you could somehow give him an injection, we might still do something. But you must hurry." I took the syringe from Fritz's pocket and made my way back up front. Santa was still drooling over the jewels. I leaned over to push the needle into him, but as I did so my foot came down on a champagne glass that had rolled out of one of the bags.

He whipped around at the grinding noise. "More tricks!" he said, grabbing me and lifting me off the floor. I hid the syringe behind my back, but he saw it, and his face went red with anger. He reached around me with his free hand, and I kept it away from him by squirming this way and that. He stood up to get a better hold on me, and the sudden movement panicked the reindeer. They started weaving crazy patterns in the air. Santa lost his balance for a moment, and I gave him a kick in the belly. He said "Ooof!" and dropped me. I ran into the rear of the sleigh and hid behind a sack.

Santa came after me, blubbering and huffing, and climbing over filled sacks as I darted between and around them. The reindeer were still flying out of control. The apprentices woke up; they started screaming and tried to crawl up front to calm Rudolph and the rest down. Santa bounded over one sack and came down inches from Fritz's head; he was close behind me, his hands almost around me when I suddenly saw a tiny opening between two bags. I dove through it, scooting around to the right.

I found myself face to face with Santa's rear end.

I froze there in surprise, the needle held out before me, when suddenly the sleigh lurched ahead and I fell into Santa and the needle hit the bullseye. He yelped once, went stiff as a board, and fell over backwards.

I quickly untied Fritz as the two apprentices managed to calm the reindeer down and get them flying in a straight line again. Fritz examined Santa, nodded his approval, and then, at his instructions, we took Santa's suit off and tied him up with the rope that had bound Fritz.

When he finished, Fritz looked up into the night sky. "We have about two and one half hours of darkness left, Gustav," he said. "I suggest that if we are to save Santa's good name you put this suit on and go up front and take over." He then told me his plan, and I balked and screamed, but finally I gave in. The suit was forty sizes too big, but I put it on anyway and climbed into the front seat; we were soon heading at top speed back to the North Pole.

When we touched down in the courtyard everything was dead quiet. We were expecting the worst from Momma Claus, and while Fritz ran over to try to find another syringe in the wreckage of the infirmary I climbed out of the sleigh and cautiously began to look around. My feet kept getting tangled up in the too-long legs of Santa's suit, and I kept falling down. I looked in the toy shed, but found no one. When I tip-toed into the sleigh shed, hiking the suit up around me like a skirt, twenty-five elves jumped out of every crack and corner in the place, yelling like bandits and pummeling me with rubber toys. They wrestled me to the ground and had wound about two hundred feet of rope around my neck before one of them saw my face and shouted, "It's Gustav!"

They helped me to my feet, and I stood panting for a few minutes before I told them to go out and get Santa. They carried him off like triumphant hunters bearing a huge wild boar. I found Momma Claus already bound and gagged in their cottage; she'd passed out after drinking an uncounted number of bottles of claret while making everybody dance the rumba out in the snow. Good old Shmitzy had then rounded everybody up and set up the ambush for Santa's return.

After making sure the two of them were safely salted away, I got everyone together and quickly told them what had to be done. Their eyes all went wide, but they moved like jackrabbits. In fifteen minutes the sleigh, already packed solid, was piled twice as high with great sacks filled with toys. The Toy Shop was emptied. We harnessed a couple of back-up reindeer – Dintzen and Pintzen – to the rig for extra power. Fritz informed me that we had about an hour and a half to succeed. I pushed Shmitzy and the two apprentices who'd gone with me the first time into the front seat, and we made our take-off.

It was quite a ride. Everything went by in fast motion. The reindeer, though obviously straining under the mountainous weight, didn't offer a squeak of complaint as they moved like lightning from rooftop to rooftop. We hauled two bags down each chimney – one filled with toys and one filled with stolen goods.

I'm almost sure we got all the stolen stuff back in the right place, though somebody probably ended up with an extra golf bag or can opener. If something looked like it didn't belong in a particular place, I put it with the Christmas presents.

The only time we came close to being caught in the act was in one of the very last houses when a little girl walked sleepy-eyed into the room where I was madly stacking gifts. She took a long look at my baggy suit and dark beard, and stared suspiciously at me. "I've been dieting," I said, and darted up the chimney.

We finished as the first crack of orange sunlight broke on the horizon. I tumbled into the sled, and the reindeer just barely managed to pull off the last roof and into the sky. Shmitzy and the two apprentices fell dead asleep in the rear, and I had to fight to keep my eyes open to guide us home.

When we touched down at the North Pole there was a cheering

welcoming committee waiting, but I stumbled through them with a tired smile on my face and went to my office and fell asleep on top of my desk for twelve straight hours with the red suit still on, the legs and arms draped over the desk like a tablecloth. When I awoke it was broad daylight, and the North Pole had been pretty much cleaned up – at least, all the wreckage had been swept into high piles. I was proud of my elves.

Santa and Momma Claus, just as Fritz had predicted, awoke late in the day in apparently normal condition and were appropriately astounded by what they had done. Santa seemed quite depressed for a while, but I gave him the thumbs-up sign a few times and kept patting him on the back and before long he was rubbing his belly merrily once again and giving booming "Ho ho ho!s" that made me cringe. We drew up tentative plans to rebuild the North Pole.

We had a long conference with Fritz, who explained all the psychological implications and convolutions and repressed reasons why all of it had happened. None of us had the faintest idea what he was talking about, but the upshot was that he thought he understood why it had happened – why it *had* to happen – and that there was nothing wrong with Santa and Momma Claus. He assured us that according to all the scientific data he had it shouldn't happen again for at least another eight hundred years; he even said it might be possible to offset its happening again by the use of encounter sessions, mind expansion, and other ego-soothing measures.

"I am positive the effects are not cumulative, and that once this so-called volcanic gush of bad feelings is expelled, it will not build up again for centuries. And I believe that by using precise psychological techniques we can bleed off these feelings before they build. I am certain of this."

His lecture finally ended, Fritz gathered his notes together and prepared to leave.

Momma and Santa had sat very still through all of this, but when it was all over they nodded slowly in understanding. I saw them turn to one another and smile sheepishly, and this was all very touching until Santa's smile suddenly widened into that horrible toothy grin and both their eyes went big and white. I could swear I heard Santa say "Heh-heh-heh."

But it was all over in a second, and Fritz missed it, and the two of them were as normal and healthy as one of Momma's pies again. The sheepish smiles were back, and they even kissed and held hands.

I thought I'd imagined it until we were all leaving and Santa suddenly turned to me and winked, flashing his fangs. "Everything back to normal for another eight hundred years. Right, Gustav? All in my head, eh?"

I gulped, gave him the thumbs-up sign, and scooted by him as he whacked me on the can. His smile had turned back to normal by then.

That's why I'm getting out of the North Pole tonight while the getting's good. I've told Fritz and the rest of them, but they just won't believe me. They think everything's back on track.

Maybe I'll buy a house in Florida.

Wherever it is, it won't have a chimney.

RUELLA IN LOVE

Molly Brown

Chicago-born and now London-resident Molly Brown has rapidly established herself as a writer of science fiction, fantasy and thrillers. She wrote the historical mystery novel, Invitation to a Funeral *(1995), in which Aphra Behn and Nell Gwyn feature as investigators. This novel grew out of Molly's short story "The Lemon Juice Plot" in the anthology* Royal Crimes *edited by Maxim Jakubowski and Martin H. Greenberg, and she has now become something of an expert on Restoration London, developing her own website on the Internet (http://www.okima.com/) where you can explore late seventeenth-century London. Her other books include a novelization of the TV series* Cracker – To Say I Love You *and a science-fiction thriller for children,* Virus. *None of the above, however, prepares you for the following story.*

Queen Ruella of the combined kingdoms of Tanalor and Hala, twice-widowed and still a virgin, opened her eyes to bright sunlight streaming through her window. She yawned and stretched like a cat; then she sat up and planted a big sloppy kiss on the Lord of Darkness poster mounted beside her bed. Of course most of his features weren't visible – just a single red eye glaring out from beneath a dark hood – but she'd smeared a bit of glue where she guessed his mouth should be, so every time she kissed the poster, it stuck to her lips and made a satisfied smacking noise that made her giggle.

She'd just had the most wonderful dream: she'd married the Lord of Darkness, who was madly in love with her, and she'd gone to live in his huge black tower, where orcs waited on her hand and foot, granting her every wish, and everybody, but *everybody*, addressed her as "Your Dark Ladyship". She winked at the poster and hugged herself in delight – it had to be a premonition, it just had to be.

She was standing in front of the mirror, trying out some new devastating poses, when there was a knock at the door. "Come in," she said.

A tall, skeletal figure in hooded black robes loomed in the doorway. It pushed back its hood, revealing a head divided into two sections – one half was bare skull, the other covered with rotting flesh – and fanned itself with a batwing mounted on a stick. The creature had one eye loosely hanging from a socket on the fleshy side. One long black string of hair, twisted into a perfect corkscrew curl, sprouted from what was left of its scalp. An occasional maggot could be seen crawling down its face. "Oh honey, it's like an oven in here," the creature said, "mind if I open a window?"

"Go ahead."

The creature crossed the room, pushed the shutter open, and sighed. "That's better." It turned back to Ruella, the fleshy side of its mouth raised into a smile. "So how's the birthday girl?"

Ruella shrugged. "I'm okay."

The creature grabbed her by the shoulders and planted a huge kiss on her cheek. "I could just eat you up! You know that?"

Ruella sighed and rolled her eyes, wiping bits of rotted lip off her face. "Oh please. Can we just get on with it?"

"Tetchy tetchy," said the creature. "All right, sit."

Ruella sat down in front of the mirror. The creature positioned itself behind her. It shook its head, *tsk tsk*'ing and clucking disapproval. "Your ends are dry as dust! Girlfriend, you need some long-term intensive conditioning and you need it bad." Like so many of the hangers-on around the palace these days, the creature didn't have a reflection, so in the mirror Ruella's hair seemed to be moving around all by itself.

"Let's just worry about tonight, okay?"

"All right, all right. So what did you have in mind?"

"I want it all spikey on top, and then I want this bit here," she took hold of a large strand at the front, "to sort of come down over my forehead and cover one eye." She pulled the strand across. "Like this."

"Oh no no no! Look," the creature pulled Ruella's hair back, "you've got beautiful eyes and a high intelligent forehead – you don't want your hair hanging over your face. A nice upsweep, that's what you want."

"No it isn't!" Ruella snapped. "Stop trying to make me look like an old lady. Do what I tell you or I'll chop off your head!"

"Ooh, get her!" The creature placed its hands on its hips and rolled its one dangling eye. "That's your idea of a threat, is it? Well, let me tell you, Missy, I've been beheaded more times than you've had hot breakfasts! So you'll have to do better than that for a threat now, won't you?"

Ruella slumped down in her seat, pouting. "But it's my birthday!"

The creature pursed the fleshy side of its mouth. "Oh all right," it said, picking up a comb. "I can never stay mad at you for long, can I?"

There was another knock at the door, and another tall skeletal creature in black robes entered. It approached Ruella and leaned down, briefly pressing a fleshless mouth against her cheek. "Happy birthday," it said in a rasping voice not unlike the sound of gravel crunching beneath a pair of heavy boots.

Ruella brushed away a few worms the rasping-voiced creature had left on her face.

"Sorry," said the rasping voice.

"No problem. So what's up?"

The creature reached inside its robes and produced a scroll, which it unrolled with a quick flick of its wrist. "Behold the guest list for tonight."

Ruella scanned the list. "I don't see the Lord of Darkness – hasn't he RSVP'd?"

"Well, the Lord of Darkness doesn't go to many sweet-sixteen parties."

"But this isn't just any sweet-sixteen party! This is *my* sweet-sixteen party!"

"I sent him an invitation. There's nothing more I can do."

"Don't worry, honey," said the one with the dangling eye, "he might still turn up." It turned towards the rasping voice, "You better put him on the list, just in case. You don't want him vaporizing the guards or anything, do you?"

"You've actually met him, haven't you?" Ruella asked the dangling-eyed one.

"Once or twice."

"What's he like?"

"All seeing, never sleeping . . ." the rasping voice broke in.

"No, I mean is he cute?"

"Cute?" said the rasping voice.

"Cute?" said the dangling eye. "Honey, he's absolutely horrible! He's the epitome of evil! Cold and cruel without a shred of human decency or feeling. Of course he's cute."

"You think he'd be the type to mind that I murdered my father in order to take over the kingdom, then murdered my first husband in order to take over *his* kingdom, and then forcibly married my stepson who was actually kind of cute but then committed suicide on our wedding night rather than consummate the marriage? I mean, if he and I were dating?"

"He'd probably take it as a recommendation," said the dangling eye. "Now hold still and be quiet; I'm almost finished."

"Why don't you put her hair up?" the rasping voice asked the hairdresser. "She'd look so pretty with her hair up."

The party was well under way long before Ruella came downstairs. The throne room was packed with sorcerers, wizards, lesser despots, and corpses in various states of decay, all bopping to the latest music. Dozens of Dwarves were stationed on high platforms around the room, waving their hands in front of wall-mounted torches to make a strobe effect. Outside, a queue of nearly two thousand people and creatures waited in vain – the guards were under strict instructions: "If your name's not on the list, you're not getting in." And in the unlikely event that any woman or girl might possibly be considered even *slightly* prettier than Ruella, she was to be sent away immediately, list or not.

Ruella made her grand entrance at moonrise. After much argument, she'd finally got the hairstyle she wanted: huge back-combed spikes that stood out in all directions. She'd circled her eyes with black ash and dusted her face with Dead Body Shop Crushed Bone Powder (not tested on Hobbits) to give her a super-chic pallor. She wore a gown of skin-tight black leather slit to the thigh, and carried a ten-foot-long bullwhip loosely coiled in one hand.

A hushed silence fell over the room; all activity ceased. Ruella leaned petulantly beneath a gilded archway, the hand with the bullwhip resting on her hip. She studiously curled her upper lip, giving the crowd the *oh-so-mature-and-jaded, seen it all and found it too dull for words* look she'd been practising in the mirror for the past two hours.

A rasping, gravelly voice rose from somewhere near the back and the entire throng joined in a rousing chorus of "Happy Birthday". Ruella dropped her jaded lip-curl and fell into a fit of giggling as a group of hooded figures lifted her above the crowd, bouncing her up and down sixteen times. They finally dropped her onto her throne, where she fell back, gasping for air.

"Speech! Speech!" the hooded figures shouted.

Ruella stood up and signalled for silence. "I've only got one thing to say: where the hell are my presents, you bastards!"

The hooded hordes rushed forward and swept her up again.

"I'm sorry I asked!" she shouted as they carried her across to the stage. At the approach of a throng of hooded corpses, the musicians stepped aside, leaving the stage to Ruella, who'd been dumped stage-centre. "Okay," she said, looking down at her empty hands, "who's got my whip?"

"I do!" shouted a hooded figure surrounded by a haze of buzzing flies.

"You're dead, buddy," Ruella said, pointing a threatening finger.

"I know *that*!"

The room exploded into hysteria.

"I'm the one who's having the birthday!" Ruella whined in mock despair. "How dare you get all the laughs!"

Ruella had to stay on the stage as the guests trooped forward with their gifts, and she had to look grateful, though it wasn't easy. She'd never seen such a collection of rubbish: lengths of silk and emerald tiaras – real old lady stuff. Did they really think she'd be caught dead in a tiara? And then somebody gave her a solid gold spinning wheel! A *spinning wheel*? Who did they think she was, somebody's *grandmother*? "Gee, thanks," she said when it was all piled up in front of her.

"Make way! Make way!" a rasping voice shouted from the doorway. "Behold the beloved Queen of Tanalor and Hala's birthday present from the members of her household, for which we all chipped in!"

A hooded figure made its way towards the stage, leading a night-black horse.

Oh no, Ruella thought, not another horse. She already had a stable full of the damn things, and all they did was eat. "It's a horse," she said, trying not to sound too disappointed.

"This is no ordinary horse, my Lady," the rasping voice replied as it reached her. "This is what is known in the trade as 'souped-up'."

"Souped-up? What do you mean?"

"Behold the horse in first gear. It looks like an ordinary animal, does it not? Ideal for shopping or occasional leisurely jaunts to the country. But when I do this . . ." The creature grabbed the horse's tail and turned it clockwise twice. The hooves split open, revealing a set of wheels. "That's only second gear," said the rasping voice, "wait 'til you see third!" It turned the animal's tail three more times. A pair of wing-shaped panels sprang out from the animal's sides; its nostrils belched smoke. "You control it here." The rasping creature picked up a section of the horse's mane. "This way's up, this way's down, the middle holds it steady."

Ruella clapped her hands and jumped up and down. "It's fabulous!"

Of course she had to try it out right away. She jumped on the horse's back and rode outside, where the unfortunate thousands were still queuing. They cheered when they saw her and then they gasped in unison; the horse had risen from the ground and was circling several feet above their heads. "My beloved people," Ruella shouted down at them, "thank you for coming out to celebrate my sweet sixteen. I'm sorry none of you will be allowed inside the palace tonight, but then you're peasants so you understand how it is. Now, if you'll excuse me," she said, turning the horse back towards the palace, "I've got some partying to do." The horse dropped something unpleasant on several members of the crowd. "Oops," said Ruella, stifling a giggle.

It was early morning, and from her bedroom window high atop the palace, Ruella watched the last of the revellers leaving. She stepped back into the shadows when she saw a wizard from Lithia step into the courtyard; he was looking straight up at her window. She'd been hiding from him for the last hour; she never should have gone behind the stables with him to smoke that Wizard's Weed – the guy seemed to think that meant they were going steady. She watched her guards usher him through the gate, and sighed with relief. She was tired, and all she wanted to do was sleep.

She was just taking off her make-up when there was a loud knock at her door. "Oh no," she moaned, thinking the Lithian had found his way back into the palace. "Who is it?" she asked sharply.

"It's me," replied a rasping voice.

"Come in." She waited until the hooded figure had closed the door behind itself. "What's up?"

"I've brought you your birthday present."

"What? The horse?"

"No. The horse was a gift from all of us. This is a gift from *me*." The creature reached into its robes and pulled out a small round piece of clear crystal.

"What is it?"

"Behold the latest in communications. No longer need you rely on messengers that may not bring a reply for days – with this you can speak face to face with anyone you want to, instantly. Anyone who has one of these, that is."

"Wow," said Ruella. "How does it work?"

"You just tell it who you want to contact; it does the rest through a bit of minor sorcery."

"And you can see them and hear them and everything?"

"Yes. Provided they're at home."

"Nifty! And does the . . . um . . ." Ruella's cheeks were burning; she lowered her head and stared at her feet. "Does the . . . ?"

If the rasping-voiced creature had eyebrows, it would have raised them. "Does the Lord of Darkness have one? Is that what you're trying to ask me?"

Ruella giggled.

"I believe he does. He has all the latest gadgets."

As soon as Ruella was alone, she combed her hair and put on a fresh coat of make-up. She tried on six different outfits before she changed back into the one she'd been wearing to begin with. She practised a new facial expression in the mirror – she wanted the casual, *just called up to say "hi"* look, which she achieved by baring her teeth in an open-mouth grin and opening her eyes a little wider than usual.

She took a deep breath, gathered up her courage, and approached the table where the creature had placed the crystal ball. "The Lord of Darkness, please," she said. "Calling the Lord of Darkness."

A woman's voice replied, "That ball is busy. Will you hold?"

"Uh . . . okay." Ruella rushed back to the mirror for a quick check. She couldn't go through with it; she couldn't possibly let the Lord of Darkness see her like this, she'd been up all night and she looked *terrible*.

"Putting you through now," said the crystal.

The crystal ball transformed itself into a giant red eye. "Hello?" boomed a harsh male voice. "Who's there?"

Ruella crept behind the table and threw a cloth over the crystal, breaking the connection. A moment later, she grinned to herself. At least she knew that he was home.

She called him three more times that day, just to make sure he hadn't gone out.

After a week of calling the Lord of Darkness and throwing the cloth over the crystal as soon as she heard his voice, Ruella got the brilliant idea that if she just happened to be riding past his Dark Tower – because she just happened to be in the neighbourhood – she just might run into the Lord of Darkness in person. First she made a quick call on the crystal ball, just to make sure he was home, then she got dressed.

With her new horse cruising in third at an altitude of about two hundred feet, it took her less than two hours to reach the Dark Land. It was everything she'd ever dreamed of, a stark land almost bare of vegetation, where sulphur mists rose beneath a blood-red sky. And it would all be hers, once she got over the minor problem of making the Lord of Darkness fall madly in love with her.

She brought the horse in for a landing about a mile away from the Dark Tower, and had it continue at a leisurely trot. As she approached the Dark Tower, she noticed a single red light burning in a window near the top. That had to be his chamber.

She rode past once, watching the window from the corner of one eye. Then she rode past again. Then once more, just in case.

Ruella was sound asleep when the round crystal began to make a ringing noise. "Wha'?" she said, opening her eyes.

"Hello, Ruella!" said a man's voice. "Remember me?"

It was that moron from Lithia! Ruella had to think quickly. "Ruella no here," she said, disguising her voice and hiding her face behind a blanket, "I yam de cleaner. Ruella go out, she no say when she come back."

"I see. Can you tell her I called, please?"

"Yeah, yeah. I give her message. You go now, I gotta clean." She threw her blanket on top of the crystal and sighed.

Sometimes, when Ruella rode past the Dark Tower, the red light moved from one window to another, but no one ever came outside. In fact, she never ran into anyone when she was in the Dark Land; if it wasn't for the moving light in the tower, she would have thought the whole place was deserted. She began to wonder if it was time to change tack.

"What does the Lord of Darkness like better than anything?" she asked the creature with the dangling eye.

"Desolation, I suppose. He's quite big on desolation."

"No, I mean like what do you think he'd like to receive as a gift? You can't give someone desolation, can you?"

"No," the dangling eye agreed, "but you can give them the *means* of desolation."

"Like what? I would have thought he's got all the means of desolation he needs."

"Yeah, but he likes to get gifts of soldiers. He gets through a lot of soldiers in a year – he can always use more."

"Soldiers," Ruella said. "I never thought of that."

The Lord of Darkness didn't even send a thank you card. Ruella was sulking in her room when there was a knock at the door. "Go away," she said.

"It's me," said a rasping voice.

"I don't care who it is. Go away."

The door opened and the hooded figure entered. "I have urgent news," it said.

"I don't care," Ruella said, sticking out her lower lip.

"You must listen," said the rasping voice, grabbing her by the shoulders. "The Lord of Darkness has been defeated."

"WHAT?"

"He has been driven from his tower."

"But that can't happen! He's all-powerful."

A sound like the scraping together of two boulders came from somewhere deep within the creatures's skeletal chest; it was crying. "The Lord of Darkness has lost his powers," it said between sobs, "and with his fall, our own are greatly lessened."

"What are we gonna do?"

"I don't know."

Just then, the crystal made an awful ringing sound, loud and insistent. "If it's that Lithian again . . ." Ruella said, gritting her teeth. She moved over to the table where the crystal sat. "Hello?"

The crystal became filled with a single glowing red eye. "Ruella?" said a harsh male voice.

"Yes. Who is this?"

The eye moved backwards, becoming smaller. Finally, Ruella was able to make out a bald-headed man with a single red eye, a long crooked nose, and dark blue lips. He was holding a heart-shaped box of candy and a dozen roses. "It's me, baby. The Lord of Darkness. But you can call me 'Malcolm' – all my friends do."

"What do you want?"

"I was thinking maybe I could drop by tonight. I've been meaning to call you for a long time, but I've been so busy with this 'n' that, you know how it is. But now I've got some time on my hands, I thought we could get to know each other, know what I mean?" He winked and ran a forked blue tongue suggestively around his cracked blue lips. "You are one foxy chick, Ruella."

"I'm sorry," Ruella said, "but I'm busy. I'm washing my hair tonight."

"Oh, I see. Well, sure if you're busy." The Lord of Darkness paused a moment, thinking. "I know! How about if I just come over anyway, and kinda hide out in your castle for a while? You see there's these guys that are kinda looking for me . . ."

"Beat it, loser," Ruella said, throwing a cloth over the crystal.

"Your Majesty!" a herald shouted, rushing into the room. "The Knights of Light and Honour, led by the barbarian champion Glorioso, are heading this way! They should be here within four hours!"

"We're doomed!" said the rasping voice. "We don't even have an army any more, because you thought they'd make a nice gift!"

"Shut up and let me think," Ruella snapped. "Okay," she said, turning to the herald, "I want everyone in the throne room in fifteen minutes. Got it?"

"Got it," said the herald, exiting quickly.

"Don't worry," Ruella told the rasping voice as she pulled down her Lord of Darkness poster and scrunched it into a ball.

Fifteen minutes later, Ruella addressed her household. "I'm sure you've all heard the news by now. The Lord of Darkness is fallen, and the Knights of Light and Honour are marching this way, led by a champion. The way I see it, we've got two options: the first one is to go down fighting, but I'm going for the second. Or as someone much wiser than myself once said, 'If you can't beat 'em, join 'em.' But I intend to go one better on that second option, and make 'em think we were on their side all along. So what we need to do is this: dwarves, give the place a thorough going-over, and burn anything that might tie us with the forces of Darkness. And if anyone asks you anything, you don't know a thing, you're just the cleaners. Guards and heralds, go out to the stables, cover yourselves in shit and start working the fields – the Knights of Light and Honour *never* harm humble peasants, so hide your weapons and chew straw until further notice."

She pointed at the undead hooded figures, "You lot, come with me."

In a cavern far below the castle, Ruella and the hooded figures discussed their plans. "So how much magic have we got left?" she asked.

"I still have one or two tricks left up my sleeve," said the one with the dangling eye. "Light the cauldron!"

While several of the hooded figures gathered around the cauldron, two of them ran back upstairs. Returning with several bolts of white cloth and a selection of needles and thread, they sat down in a corner and went to work.

Ruella watched in fascination as the creatures poured several brightly coloured substances into the cauldron, all the time chanting in a strange forgotten tongue. Suddenly, they stopped. "It's ready," said the dangling eye.

"What's it for?" Ruella asked.

"It completely transforms your appearance."

Ruella made a face. "Do I have to drink it?"

"No. Sit down."

Ruella sat down next to the cauldron, surrounded by all but two of the hooded figures; they were still busy sewing. The hooded figures took turns dipping a large wooden ladle into the cauldron and saturating Ruella's hair with its contents.

At the end of one hour, they dipped Ruella's head in water and handed her a mirror. She gasped in amazement; her appearance had been completely transformed. She was a blonde!

The two creatures who'd been sewing presented her with a flowing white dress; the rasping voice placed a selection of dainty little flowers in her hair, which had been twisted into golden ringlets. The dangling eye placed both hands on its hips. "If this kid ain't a picture of innocence, I don't know who is!"

"Those Knights of Light and Honour won't know what hit 'em," said the one surrounded by buzzing flies.

"Yeah, but all the Knights of Light and Honour have to do is take one look at you guys . . ."

"We'll be okay," said the rasping voice. "We haven't lost *all* our powers; we can still do rudimentary shape-changing."

"Shape-changing? You mean you guys don't have to look like that?"

"No, of course not," said one with live rats scurrying around its ribcage.

"So how come you all look like refugees from a cemetery?"

"Fashion," said the one with the buzzing flies.

Far below the castle, Ruella held a last-minute inspection. She walked up and down, examining row upon row of golden-haired maidens in white dresses. "You," she said, pointing at a maiden's chest, "what are you doing with those?"

"What do you think?" asked the maiden.

"They're bigger than mine. Get rid of them!"

"Ooh!"

"I said, get rid of them!"

The maiden scowled, but her breasts shrank to half the size.

"That's better," Ruella said. "Everybody got their rose petals?"

Each maiden held up a full pouch.

"Okay," said Ruella. "Let's do it."

The Knights of Light and Honour expected trouble when they crossed the border. They'd heard Tanalor was a dark and dangerous land, ruled by an evil teenage sorceress and her undead minions. They were pleasantly surprised to find themselves greeted by scores of golden-haired maidens, blowing kisses and throwing rose petals.

The champion Glorioso pointed to the one he thought the fairest. "Come here, my pretty," he said, winking.

"I think he likes me," said the maiden with the rasping voice.

BEEN A LONG, LONG TIME

R. A. Lafferty

We end as we began with one of those rare treasures of fantasy and science fiction, R.A. Lafferty (b. 1914). Interestingly, the entry on Lafferty in The Encyclopedia of Fantasy *likens his work to that of Avram Davidson. Lafferty has written some fairly straightforward sf and fantasy, such as* Past Master *(1968) and* Fourth Mansions *(1969), but they're the exceptions. The rest of his work has an eccentric quality that makes it both bewildering and compulsive. If you like the following story, which is probably about as typical as you can get (which isn't saying much), then try to find his collections* Nine Hundred Grandmothers *(1970),* Strange Doings *(1972),* Does Anyone Else Have Something Further to Add? *(1974) and* Lafferty in Orbit *(1991) as a selection of his best work. You might also try his novels* East of Laughter *(1988) and* Sindbad: the 13th Voyage *(1989).*

It doesn't end with one – it *Begins* with a whimper.

It was a sundering Dawn – Incandescence to which all later lights are less than candles – Heat to which the heat of all later

suns is but a burnt-out match – the Polarities that set up the
tension forever.

And in the middle was a whimper, just as was felt the first
jerk that indicated that time had begun.

The two Challenges stood taller than the radius of the space
that was being born; and one weak creature, Boshel, stood in
the middle, too craven to accept either challenge.

"Uh, how long you fellows going to be gone?" Boshel
snuffled.

The Creative Event was the Revolt rending the Void in two.
The two sides formed, opposing Nations of Lightning split above
the steep chasm. Two Champions had it out with a bitterness
that has never passed – Michael wrapped in white fire – and
Helel swollen with black and purple blaze. And their followers
with them. It has been put into allegory as Acceptance and
Rejection, and as Good and Evil; but in the Beginning there
was the Polarity by which the universes are sustained.

Between them, like a pigmy, stood Boshel alone in whimpering
hesitation.

"Get the primordial metal out of it if you're coming with
us," Helel growled like cracked thunder as he led his followers
off in a fury to form a new settlement.

"Uh, you guys going to be back before night?" Boshel
whimpered.

"Oh, get to Hell out of here," Michael roared.

"Keep the little oaf!" Helel snorted. "He hasn't enough
brimstone in him to set fire to an outhouse."

The two great hosts separated, and Boshel was left alone in
the void. He was still standing there when there was a second
little jerk and time began in earnest, bursting the pod into a
shower of sparks that traveled and grew. He was still standing
there when the sparks acquired form and spin; and he stood
there yet when life began to appear on the soot specks thrown
off from the sparks. He stood there quite a long, long time.

"What are we going to do with the little bugger?" an underling
asked Michael. "We can't have him fouling up the landscape
forever."

"I'll go ask," said Mike, and he did.

But Michael was told that the responsibility was his; that

Boshel would have to be punished for his hesitancy; and that it was up to Michael to select the suitable punishment and see that it was carried out.

"You know, he made time itself stutter at the start," Mike told the underling. "He set up a random that affected everything. It's got to be a punishment with something to do with time."

"You got any ideas?" the underling asked.

"I'll think of something," Michael said.

Quite a while after this, Michael was thumbing through a book one afternoon at a news-stand in Los Angeles.

"It says here," Michael intoned, "that if six monkeys were set down to six typewriters and typed for a long enough time, they would type all the words of Shakespeare exactly. Time is something we've got plenty of. Let's try it, Kitabel, and see how long it takes."

"What's a monkey, Michael?"

"I don't know."

"What's a typewriter?"

"I don't know."

"What's a Shakespeare, Mike?"

"Anybody can ask questions, Kitabel. Get the things together and let's get the project started."

"It sounds like a lengthy project. Who will oversee it?"

"Boshel. It's a natural for him. It will teach him patience and a sense of order, and impress on him the majesty of time. It's exactly the punishment I've been looking for."

They got the things together and turned them over to Boshel.

"As soon as the project is finished, Bosh, your period of waiting will be over. Then you can join the group and enjoy yourself with the rest of us."

"Well, it's better than standing here doing nothing," Boshel said. "It'd go faster if I could educate the monkeys and let them copy it."

"No, the typing has to be random, Bosh. It was you who introduced the random factor into the universe. So, suffer for it."

"Any particular edition the copy has to correspond to?"

"The 'Blackstone Readers' Edition, Thirty-Seven and a half

Volumes in One that I have here in my hand will do fine," Michael said. "I've had a talk with the monkeys, and they're willing to stick with it. It took me eighty thousand years just to get them where they could talk, but that's nothing when we're talking about time."

"Man, are we ever talking about Time!" Boshel moaned.

"I made a deal with the monkeys. They will be immune to fatigue and boredom. I cannot promise the same for you."

"Uh, Michael, since it may be quite a while, I wonder if I could have some sort of clock to keep track of how fast things are going."

So Michael made him a clock. It was a cube of dressed stone measuring a parsec on each edge.

"You don't have to wind it, you don't have to do a thing to it, Bosh," Michael explained. "A small bird will come every millennium and sharpen its beak on this stone. You can tell the passing of time by the diminishing of the stone. It's a good clock, and it has only one moving part, the bird. I will not guarantee that your project will be finished by the time the entire stone is worn away, but you will be able to tell that time has passed."

"It's better than nothing," Boshel said, "but it's going to be a drag. I think this concept of time is a little medieval, though."

"So am I," Michael said. "I tell you what I can do, though, Bosh. I can chain you to that stone and have another large bird dive-bomb you and gouge out hunks of your liver. That was in a story in another book on that news-stand."

"You slay me, Mike. That won't be necessary. I'll pass the time somehow."

Boshel set the monkeys to work. They were conditioned to punch the typewriters at random. Within a short period of time (as the Larger Creatures count time) the monkeys had produced whole Shakespearian words: 'Let' which is found in scene two of act one of *Richard III*; 'Go' which is in scene two of act two of *Julius Caesar*; and 'Be' which occurs in the very first scene and act of *The Tempest*. Boshel was greatly encouraged.

Some time after this, one of the monkeys produced two Shakespearian words in succession. By this time, the home world of Shakespeare (which was also the home world of the news-stand in Los Angeles where was born a great idea) was long out of business.

After another while, the monkeys had done whole phrases. By then, quite a bit of time had run out.

The trouble with that little bird is that its beak did not seem to need much sharpening when it did come once every thousand years. Boshel discovered that Michael had played a dirty seraphic trick on him and had been feeding the bird entirely on bland custard. The bird would take two or three light swipes at the stone, and then be off for another thousand years. Yet, after no more than a thousand visitations, there was an unmistakable scratch on the stone. It was a hopeful sign.

Boshel began to see that the thing could be done. A monkey – and not the most brilliant of them – finally produced a whole sentence: "What say'st thou, bully-rook?" And at that very moment another thing happened. It was surprising to Boshel, for it was the first time he had ever seen it. But he would see it milliards of times before it was finished.

A speck of cosmic dust, on the far outreaches of space, met another speck. This should not have been unusual; specks were always meeting specks. But this case was different. Each speck – in the opposite direction – had been the outmost in the whole cosmos. You can't get farther apart than that. The speck (a teeming conglomerate of peopled worlds) looked at the other speck with eyes and instruments, and saw its own eyes and instruments looking back at it. What the speck saw was itself. The cosmic tetra-dimensionate sphere had been completed. The first speck had met itself coming from the other direction, and space had been transversed.

Then it all collapsed.

The stars went out, one by one, and billion by billion. Nightmares of falling! All the darkened orbs and oblates fell down into the void that was all bottom. There was nothing left but one tight pod in the void, and a few out of context things like Michael and his associates, and Boshel and his monkeys.

Boshel had a moment of unease: he had become used to the appearance of the expanding universe. But he need not have been uneasy. It began all over again.

A few billion centuries ticked by silently. Once more, the pod burst into a shower of sparks that traveled and grew. They acquired form and spin, and life appeared again on the soot specks thrown off from those sparks.

This happened again and again. Each cycle seemed damnably long while it was happening; but in retrospect, the cycles were only like a light blinking on and off. And in the Longer Retrospect, they were like a high-frequency alternator, producing a dizzy number of such cycles every over-second, and continuing for tumbling ages. Yet Boshel was becoming bored. There was just no other word for it.

When only a few billion cosmic cycles had been completed, there was a gash in the clock-rock that you could hide a horse in. The little bird made very many journeys back to sharpen its beak. And Pithekos Pete, the most rapid of the monkeys, had now random-written *The Tempest*, complete and perfect. They shook hands all around, monkeys and angel. It was something of a moment.

The moment did not last. Pete, instead of pecking at furious random to produce the rest of the plays, wrote his own improved version of *The Tempest*. Boshel was furious.

"But it's better, Bosh," Pete protested. "And I have some ideas about stage-craft that will really set this thing up."

"Of course it's better! We don't want them better. We want them just the same. Can't you monkeys realize that we are working out a problem of random probabilities? Oh, you clunker-heads!"

"Let me have that damned book for a month, Bosh, and I'll copy the plagued things off and we'll be finished," Pithekos Pete suggested.

"Rules, you lunk-heads, rules!" Boshel grated out. "We have to abide by the rules. You know that isn't allowed, and besides it would be found out. I have reason to suspect, and it cuts me to say this, that one of my own monkeys and associates here present is an informer. We'd never get by with it."

After the brief misunderstanding, things went better. The monkeys stayed with their task. And after a number of cycles expressed by nine followed by zeros in pica type sufficient to stretch around the universe at a period just prior to its collapse (the radius and the circumference of the ultimate sphere are, of course, the same), the first complete version was ready.

It was faulty, of course, and it had to be rejected. But there were less than thirty thousand errors in it; it presaged great things to come, and ultimate triumph.

Later (People, was it ever later!) they had it quite close. By the time that the gash in the clock-rock would hold a medium-sized solar system, they had a version with only five errors.

"It will come," Boshel said. "It will come in time. And time is the one thing we have plenty of."

Later – much, much later – they seemed to have it perfect; and by this time, the bird had worn away nearly a fifth of the bulk of the great stone with its millennial visits.

Michael himself read the version and could find no error. This was not conclusive, of course, for Michael was an impatient and hurried reader. Three readings were required for verification, but never was hope so high.

It passed the second reading, by a much more careful angel, and was pronounced letter-perfect. But it was later at night when that reader had finished it, and he may have gotten a little careless at the end.

And it passed the third reading, through all the thirty-seven plays of it, and into the poems at the end. This was Kitabel, the scribing angel himself, who was appointed to that third reading. He was just about to sign the certification when he paused.

"There is something sticking in my mind," he said, and he shook his head to clear it. "There is something like an echo that is not quite right. I wouldn't want to make a mistake."

He had written "Kitab—", but he had not finished his signature.

"I won't be able to sleep tonight if I don't think of it," he complained. "It wasn't in the plays; I know that they were perfect. It was something in the poems – quite near the end – some dissonance. Either the bard wrote a remarkably malapropos line, or there was an error in the transcription that my eye overlooked but my ear remembered. I acknowledge that I was sleepy near the end."

"Oh, by all the worlds that were ever made, sign!" pleaded Boshel.

"You have waited this long, a moment more won't kill you, Bosh."

"Don't bet on it, Kit. I'm about to blow, I tell you."

But Kitabel went back and he found it – a verse in *The Phoenix and the Turtle*:

> "From this session interdic
> Every fowl of tyrant wing,
> Save the eagle, feather'd king:
> Keep the obsequy so strict."

That is what the book itself said. And what Pithekos Pete had written was nearly, but not quite, the same thing:

> "From this session interdic
> Every fowl of tyrant wingg,
> Save the eaggle, feather'd kingg:
> Dam machine the g is sticked."

And if you never saw an angel cry, words cannot describe to you the show that Boshel put on then.

They are still at it tonight, typing away at random, for that last sad near-victory was less than a million billion cycles ago. And only a moment ago – halfway back in the present cycle – one of the monkeys put together no less than nine Shakespearian words in a row.

There is still hope. And the bird has now worn the rock down to about half its bulk.